The Campaign of
FEAR

The Campaign of
FEAR

WAYNE PLETCHER

BASCOM HILL BOOKS
Minneapolis

Copyright © 2010 by Wayne Pletcher.

BASCOM
HILL BOOKS

Bascom Hill Books
212 3rd Avenue North, Suite 290
Minneapolis, MN 55401
612.455.2293
www.bascomhillpublishing.com

All rights reserved. No part of this publication may be reproduced, stored in a retrieval system, or transmitted, in any form or by any means, electronic, mechanical, photocopying, recording, or otherwise, without the prior written permission of the author.

ISBN - 978-1-934938-83-6
ISBN - 1-934938-83-1
LCCN - 2009911466

Cover Design by Alan Pranke
Typeset by Kristeen Wegner in Times New Roman

Printed in the United States of America

"Arm you, I pray you, to this speedy voyage,

for we will fetters put upon this fear,

which now goes too free-footed."

-Hamlet

Part I

We Are Losing

Chapter 1

Acoustics Technology

The Plan

Technology Investment Corporation was a relatively new company. No one was sure how big it was, what it did to make money, how it operated in the U.S. or anything else about it. They had first made a big splash about five years ago by announcing several "unrestricted research grants" to major universities. It was mentioned in the several announcements since then that work in the areas such as Micro Electro Mechanical Systems (MEMS), nanotechnology, sensors, data analysis, acoustics and Organic Light Emitting Diodes (OLEDS) technologies would be logical to fund because they were some of the key global technologies for the future. TIC could not officially specify or direct how the monies would be used but this was a common way to get around the legal requirements of the "unrestricted research grants." The universities were selected because of their research and reputation in certain technology areas. It was logical to assume the monies would be applied to their specialties. If you added up the dollars over the years, it was a lot …. maybe $50 million to $100 million in "unrestricted research grants."

TIC was headed by a Mr. Omar Kharif, President and CEO, according to their website, TIC.com. The website also indicated their charter and top ten global technologies:

Charter
- To make strategic investments in key global technologies through research grants at major universities and equity positions in selected companies.
- Know current and future key global technologies through investments, conferences, scientific publications, patents, and government contracts.
- Grow and know the experts working in key global technology areas.
- Become known as a "go to source" for key global technology information.

Top Ten Global Technologies
- Sensors
- Chemical Analysis
- Microelectromechanical Systems (MEMS)
- Organic Light Emitting Diodes (OLEDS)
- Nanotechnology
- Microelectronics
- Data Augmentation Software
- Acoustics
- Wireless
- Explosives

There wasn't much more on the website. The central office was in Washington, D.C., and there were two field offices with nondescript post office boxes addresses, one on the East Coast, Boston and one on the West Coast, San Francisco.

Omar was in discussion with a man known as "the Liberator." The TIC central office in D.C. was small with a desk, two chairs, laptop computer, and a copier, fax, printer, scanner all-in-one unit. It was dark and quiet with the shades drawn and the main door closed. The closed and locked door within the two-room suite was the entrance to the equipment room. It held some of the most elaborate and powerful computer and communication equipment in the world.

THE CAMPAIGN OF FEAR

The Liberator was saying, "Omar, we are winning. We are winning because we are constantly learning and adapting. Fear of the unknown and fear of death make the Americans and their allies weak. This is why our improvised explosive devices, explosively formed penetrants, and suicide and car bombers are so effective. We do not have these fears and because of that we are strong. In fact, they are getting weaker and we are getting stronger. Omar, you have been very instrumental in carrying out our strategy. Under our technology investment guise, we have access to almost every world-class technology and application, every technology expert, and future technology strategies at universities, as well as in industry and government. You did all of this in just five years and with only $100 million. The people that I represent are very pleased with you and your work. My time is limited today. Let me tell you something very important. Our people believe that acoustical technology will be critical to our continuing to build this 'Campaign of Fear' against our enemies."

"It is on our key technology list but only because we were told to put it there. I don't think it measures up to MEMS or sensors or......"

The Liberator stood up and screamed, "Acoustical technology will be the key! Watch for my next instructions. In the meantime, use your contacts and keep an eye on everything about acoustics technology advancements at industrial companies, research-oriented economic development organizations, universities, new companies/IPOs, government contracts - I mean everything! Our sources tell us that several things could happen in the next few weeks or months that could weaken our 'Campaign of Fear'... or stop it dead in its tracks! We are counting on you, Omar."

With that, the Liberator turned and walked out. Omar sat there in the dark room for several minutes thinking about what he had just been told. Acoustics Technology? I don't want to disappoint so I must find out what is going on before it is too late. From what the Liberator said, their vision about how the world should be depended on it.

Customized Materials Technology

Thomas Kramley, director of logistics and supply chain for CMT, was meeting with Omar Kharif after work. Mr. Kharif had called him to set up the meeting, indicating that as head of Technology Investment Corporation, he wanted to stop and visit with him. Mr. Kharif had mentioned that he was on his way to Berkeley to present a grant to the university and since he had found that Thomas was the CMT representative to Berkeley for scholarships, fellowships, and technology grants, he wanted to talk and compare notes before making the gift. Thomas had agreed and because of Mr. Kharif's schedule, the meeting was to be at a small pub on his way home.

Thomas, a loyal but troubled CMT employee, had been stopping at the Squealing Pig a lot on the way home from work recently. He was drinking more these days, getting to be overweight and running a bit scared. Things at home were not good with the illness of his son and his wife's need for help coping with the situation. Her psychological problems were now becoming more troubling by the day. He needed more money, a lot of it, to get the right care for both of them.

As Thomas drove to the Squealing Pig and parked, he looked at his watch…6:30 PM…right on time. He got out of the car, walked to the entrance and pulled the door open. The pig squealed as the door opened just as always but he heard it more this time for some reason. The first time this happened to him, he just about jumped out of his skin. Hmm, I wonder what Mr. Kharif will think or do when it happens to him.

Thomas located a small table in the corner and way in the back as always. It was happy hour and everybody was busy serving drinks so he seated himself. The waiter finally came and Thomas, frowning and obviously nervous, ordered his regular, a New Castle. He kept fidgeting with his shirt collar and sweating as he looked toward the entrance. Omar had told him that he would wear a baseball cap with the letters TIC on the front.

Someone came in but he could only see that he was wearing a ball cap. It was too far away and too dark to read the lettering. He walked forward and saw that the writing on the cap did say TIC.

"Mr. Kharif, hello, I am Thomas Kramley." They shook hands and Thomas said, "I have a table in the back for us."

Omar said, "That would be great. I'd like to get away from that squealing pig noise."

When they arrived at the table, Thomas and Omar exchanged business cards and noticed there were two New Castles at the table. Thomas said, "Oh, yes, happy hour, buy one, get one free! Do you like New Castle? If so, we are all set."

"New Castle is fine; I am a fanatic about dark beer." He sat down, picked up his glass and said, "To the Squealing Pig." The toast was probably the same one all newcomers make, but Thomas sensed that this one had a more complex intent to it.

Omar said, "Thanks for seeing me on such short notice. My company, TIC," pointing to his ball cap, "is making a large 'unrestricted research grant' to Berkeley tomorrow. When I found out how much CMT is doing at the university and that you were the key contact, I just had to talk to you. I know your company is involved in detonation technology products and have several government contracts. Could you tell me a little about your products and technology?"

"A lot is confidential but if I'm careful, I can tell you some. We use non-conventional detonation technology in many of our newer products. In those cases, we use sensors, microelectronics, nanotechnology, wireless, and other kinds of new technologies. Controlled detonation of pre-positioned explosives. We have many older products that rely on more conventional technology like impact, chemical reaction, heat and/or time to trigger the detonation. Those are for more traditional applications like mining and building deconstruction. There is a new area that has to do with detonation of explosives using special sound waves. That is about all I can say. You know, government regulations."

Omar recognized the significance of what he had just heard and said, "It is interesting - what one does with technology these days. I'm a businessman but I still think we have to continue the development of key technologies and use them for the benefit of the country and the economy. This is what my company believes and why we give all this money to universities like Berkeley. Thomas, do you know the person in charge of research grants at Berkeley?"

"Yes, I do, and several other people in key positions, too. I'm a graduate and I teach there now as adjunct professor in the area of logistics. It keeps me up-to-date and I can make a little extra money to pay some bills."

The waiter came and they ordered another New Castle. Omar picked up on the "pay some bills" part of what Thomas had said. He had done his research no matter what he had said earlier and had found that Thomas' family had some health problems and there were huge bills to pay.

Omar said, "Yes, paying bills is never fun, is it?" Thomas shared with him the reasons why he needed the extra money. It was a touching story and Omar was outwardly sympathetic.

"I have a suggestion, Thomas. TIC occasionally hires consultants in specialized areas. I am sure we could use your skills. There have been many times that shipping of technology prototypes to various countries got to be almost impossible. We don't know all the regulations, the required paperwork and approvals, the protected technologies list, the countries to watch ... everything. You could be very useful in helping us to chart the proper course and meet all of the legal requirements. What do you think, Thomas?"

"That would be wonderful, Omar. Shipping various experimental technology units to foreign countries isn't easy. It has to be done by an expert otherwise you can get into big trouble with the government. I would have to help you mostly outside of my work with CMT... sort of off-hours. Would that be alright?"

"Of course," said Omar. "Thomas, I have to go to another meeting tonight. Would you be so kind as to phone your colleague at Berkeley and introduce me? My meeting to present the gift is early afternoon tomorrow."

"I will call him tomorrow morning, Omar. They will be very anxious to see you."

"I will be in contact and look forward to working together. Your expertise will be very valuable to TIC. Take a look at our website, TIC.com, to see what we do and our Top Ten List of

Technologies. Thanks for meeting with me and introducing me to the Squealing Pig. Goodbye Thomas."

"Goodbye, Omar."

Dr. Bradford Tully

Brad was driving home deep in thought about work. The job was getting to him so he decided to stop at the gym and work off his frustrations. Keeping in shape was becoming more difficult all the time with the late night and weekend work. In fact, there was nothing but work. His routine included some weights and equipment but it was mostly calisthenics. Happily standing at an average height of about five-nine, he felt blessed with broad shoulders and a wrestler's body, mostly all muscle. During the third repitition of the bicycle, curls, situps and pushups, he recognized he was doing everything faster and longer. Almost exhausted, he gasped, "I don't like it but I'm going to have to ask for more help. My work is too important. I'll do it tomorrow. I'll swallow my pride and ask. If Knight says no, I may leave the fucking place."

Bradford Tully knew he was a brilliant technologist, perhaps a little short on the social skills, but everyone forgave him for that since he was so smart. He had worked on chemical sensing and software code in graduate school and got his PhD at Stanford University in record time. Also, in his spare time there, he had started developing a new technology called acoustical sensing. His first job was with General Petroleum Research, Inc. in Dallas, Texas. The non-profit company, funded by a tax on vehicle licenses, developed new technology to help find oil. Grants and government contracts further sponsored their work. It was intense work as fewer and fewer new oil fields were being discovered.

Brad was assigned to the New Technology Building Laboratory. He convinced his boss that he should work on developing this new field of acoustical sensing to help find oil. The research was so far ahead of current theory that Brad was forced to work mostly alone. He was OK with that, because he worked well that way but in about two years' time, he was able to build a case for a much bigger project and more resources. Some of his more recent breakthrough findings were as follows:

- Acoustical waves could be more focused and less dispersed by the environment than thought previously.
- High-resolution and non-damaging waves, even traveling at long distances, were possible.
- Bounce-back patterns could be used to set up standards for known solids, liquids, and gases.
- Distance detection and sensing of materials seemed doable.
- Wave generation technology and software code were keys to increasing distances and establishing material standards respectively.

Things looked really promising but Brad needed more help. It was time to go talk to his boss, Dr. Elija Knight, President, GPRI.

The door was open so Brad, ready for a fight, barged into Dr. Knight's office and exclaimed, "We need to invest more in the research I'm doing. More people, more money, more equipment, and more computer time. The results show that we have something of great promise but we need more resources to move faster."

Dr. Knight, a slight man with dark skin, piercing eyes, and a beard, stood up from his desk. He held up his hands as if to stop Brad and said, "Let's discuss this later. I'm in the midst of planning some changes for the organization."

Brad said, "What kind of changes? If it will affect my work, I need to know now."

Dr. Knight said, "I can't say yet but it looks like we will have to cut back on our longer range research. Our budget is being reduced and I'm being told to get results fast. I can tell you something .... The best outcome will be continuing the project as it is currently resourced."

Brad didn't take 'no' well and said, "That's my answer, I guess. It is just the wrong answer." He took another chance and hastily asked, "What if I leave GPRI and take this technology with me? I'll set up my own company."

Dr. Knight's piercing eyes locked on Brad's eyes; there was a long silence and Dr. Knight said, "Leaving GPRI will be no problem. I will have to think about whether you can take the technology. Can you come back tomorrow at about this same time?"

Walking out, Brad said, "I can, but it sounds like I'm leaving with or without the technology." He purposely slammed the door to punctuate his feelings.

Very quietly, Elija thought this could be the answer to his problem. The contact about this new work Brad was doing. It was a strange contact a few weeks ago by a Middle-Eastern-sounding man by the name of Omar Kharif. He asked if he could get the technical reports on the acoustical program, the background and contact information on Bradford Tully, how the project was funded, and who the sponsors were, and if the technology was protected in any of its intellectual property aspects. He asked if it was for sale. Even with the aggressive questioning, Dr. Knight decided not to give the caller any information at all. It was a very disconcerting telephone call. He had a bad feeling about this guy and, quite frankly, he had enough problems. Something like this had happened a long time ago when he was a senior researcher for the organization. What seemed to be a harmless request for information on his work had caused a major upheaval in the organization. He couldn't go through that again. Having Tully leave with the technology might be the answer. He wanted to think a lot more about the ramifications of this kind of decision before tomorrow's meeting. Just in case he wanted to do it, he made a quick call to the board chair to get approval of the technology transfer.

Arriving at the office the next day, his assistant interrupted him saying, "Dr. Knight ... you have a call on line two. It is that pushy guy, Omar, again."

Dr. Knight picked up the phone and pushed the button. "Dr. Knight speaking."

"Omar Kharif here, sir. You knew that I would call back. I need some answers about this acoustical project, please. I have found that the research is funded by our tax dollars and therefore should be public information. If you will not provide it, I plan to go to your board as well as to your government funders and demand that I acquire access to this information."

Elija gulped because this guy sounded dangerous! He was very concerned, almost afraid of the perceived aggressiveness in Mr. Kharif's voice. In his most diplomatic voice, Dr. Knight said, "I don't think that will be necessary. We have just decided that the researcher and the project will be leaving the organization. You can deal with Dr. Bradford Tully directly after certain announcements and preparations are made for the technology transfer. Thank you for your interest in GPRI." Then he hung up.

Dr. Tully Leaves GPRI

Bradford Tully walked into Elija Knight's office at precisely the time he had arrived there the day before. They looked at each other, maybe stared is a better word. Brad broke the ice. "Have technology, will travel, and I have my bags packed."

"Brad, I am not asking you to leave. You have done good work here. You raised the level of our research and how we are considered as a research organization. I also feel that the acoustics work has great potential but it will develop too slowly here. I'm going to grant your request to transfer the acoustics technology so you can set up your own company. Our statutes require that all the work to date will have to be made public. It doesn't have to be overly detailed but it has to include an official report attached to the transfer of technology announcement that I will write. You can prepare that report today. A bit of advice, if I may? Do not insert any speculation about how the technology will develop, the applications that might be possible, the timing, or anything about future work. Let's just meet the letter-of-the-law on this. Also, protect everything you do from here on out in this technology area. Use patents, trademarks, copyrights, and publishing, everything to tie up the technology for the new venture company. There may be a lot of people wanting to get their hands on it. Watch your back."

Brad was dumbfounded. He was processing what Elija

had said but he was not sure he could believe his ears. Quickly he said, "Alright, and thanks, Dr. Knight. I had hoped you would agree to transfer the technology. I'll have those reports for you very quickly. Thanks again." Brad, with his boyish smirk, turned and left the office very pleased with himself.

Elija was wondering if he did the right thing. Deadlines, convenience, and fear are not always the best parameters upon which to make decisions. He started to draft the announcement and by the time he finished, the two reports from Brad came in electronically. He read the two documents and thought, this guy is good.

The Announcement
According to statute 106.92.003...

Be it known to our constituents that the Bounce-Back Acoustical Wave Technology project will not be continued by GPRI. Its longer-range nature would require significant additional investment and years of development.

With full approval of the board and effective immediately, the BBAW technology will be transferred to its inventor, Senior Scientist, Dr. Bradford Tully. Dr. Tully will leave GPRI and seek investors in a private venture to develop the technology for several applications. We know he will be successful. Also, as required by statute, attached are up-to-date and full disclosure reports on the Bounce-Back Acoustical Wave Technology Project.

Dr. Elija Knight, President GPRI

Report I
Bounce-Back Acoustical Wave Technology (BBAWT)
And The Search for New Oil

Special Acoustical Wave Generation equipment and technology have been developed to provide tightly controlled bounce-back features. The returning wave front has captured chemical elements and compounds that can be analyzed and identified. These are compared with standards set up from known oil fields and probabilities of new oil field finds are produced.

Key advancements include: new acoustical wave generation equipment that can cover short and long distances, dampening and contracting the wave, capture techniques, and analytical techniques including computerized data augmentation and identification. Next work will be in the area of wave pattern elucidation.

Bradford Tully, Senior Scientist, GPRI

Report II
Bounce-Back Acoustical Wave Technology

In the constant search for new oil, special acoustical wave generation equipment and technology have been developed to provide tightly controlled bounce-back features. On impact, the focused wave penetrates the substrate surface to a managed degree and bounces back to a defined and specific wave pattern for each material. A catalog of these specific and unique wave patterns or standards for known materials at or near currently operating oil fields is being established.

The research program is in its early stages but appears very promising. Already BBAWT has proven faster and more reliable than visual comparison of oil drilling samples, wet chemical analysis, magnetic resonance x-ray, mass spectroscopy, or any other kind of comparative qualitative analysis known today. Much work is necessary still in the areas of focused acoustical wave generation, bounce-back control and capture, separation of the individual patterns and cataloguing standards for all of the materials.

Considerable investment dollars will be necessary to develop the Bounce-back Acoustical Wave Technology to the level required for commercialization.

Bradford Tully, Senior Scientist, GPRI

The First Project

Omar was calling. They had agreed that the work would take place mostly during off-hours. Thomas was more than a little annoyed. However, he knew that this contact could mean some additional money to pay his mounting medical bills.

Thomas said, "Hello, Mr. Kharif, how are things on the East Coast?"

The telecommunications technology used at CMT had allowed him to see the number, name, and location instantly. This included calls from landlines and cell phones. Additionally, some calls were digitally recorded, encrypted, and stored for future review if the need ever arose. CMT's continuing top-secret contracts with the government made these protective measures absolutely essential. No one really knew the extent to which they were being monitored and CMT personnel were not allowed to tell them.

Omar said, "Not bad but our weather this time of the year is very dreary. I am jealous of your location."

Thomas, cringing at the small talk, said, "Yes, it is great, but then we have the earthquake thing!"

"Say, I want to thank you for the introductions at Berkeley. You have some great contacts there and because of that, my visit to present the TIC gift was greatly facilitated."

"I was glad I could help."

"Thomas, do you remember our discussion a few weeks ago about doing special work with TIC?"

Thomas thought, finally we get down to some business. "Yes I do, and I would like to get started as soon as possible."

"Good, we are excited about the possibilities of working with you. You have had a chance to see our website and the technologies we think are of critical importance to our country and our economy."

"Your Top Ten List of Technologies really dovetailed with CMT's strategy."

"Thank you, Thomas. The work we have in mind utilizes at least four or five of those technologies in their most advanced states. I know that you are already using radio frequency identification

13

technology at CMT. With the kinds of products you take on, it is so important to be able to track shipments and the environments to which they are subjected. Our new RFID Tag and Reader System simply replaces the standard tags while incorporating advances in several areas including an expanded frequency range to account for possible interference problems, reader assisted location verification, and new sensor capability. We can now sense chemicals, pressures, vibrations, shock and radiation. Also available are enhanced durability and tamperproof features, and major size and cost reductions."

Omar continued, "This work has taken years of development and millions of dollars of investment, but it is ready for real world field testing. We know that many of your products go to international markets. If you could place, say, one hundred of these tags on product packages that would go through your distribution system, travel by truck, train, ocean freighter, or air for delivery at an Eastern European location, we would really appreciate it. The tags are guaranteed not to interfere with the package contents or your current RFID system. Just tell us when it will arrive at its final destination and one of our people will coordinate to remove the tags before the product goes to your customer. It is that simple. Your reward will be realized once the tags are recovered in Eastern Europe!"

"This is a bit different from a project that would allow me to work off-hours. I don't want to get in trouble with….."

"I know, but we didn't think this new RFID Tag and Reader System would be ready so soon. I hope you don't think that I am trying to pull a fast one on you. We look at this as an opportunity to beta test a key product and set of technologies that could be critically important to our country's industrial and military advancement. I want to stress that we need not know your production schedule, the product or products being shipped, or any customer information. It won't take much of your time."

"Okay, if that is the case, I guess there would be no harm helping with the beta test on your new RFID system." Always a stickler for detail, he thought for a moment and said, "There will probably have to be two shipments, if you want to cover travel by both ocean freighter and air transport. Would that be alright?"

"Certainly!"

Thomas said, "Okay, then I will do it. When can I expect the tags to arrive?"

"They are nearby at our offices in San Francisco so I will have them brought over today. Look for a small package marked confidential and to your attention. It will have attachment instructions for placing the tags on the packages. Once this is done, they are self-activated and the tags will do the rest."

"Great, I will look for the package this afternoon. If I recall our production schedule right, we can get the beta test started this week."

"Fantastic. Please let me know when and where I should have our people collect the tags. Thanks again and I look forward to talking with you soon."

"And thank you, too. I will be in touch soon. Goodbye, Omar."

"Goodbye, Thomas."

While still holding the phone, Omar's mind was racing. He wondered if their conversation was recorded. Oh, well, he was careful enough anyway. He thought he'd do some checking on what they used and be ready for the next call. This deal with Thomas Kramley is going to really work. Omar would gain his confidence and proceed to even more important projects. The money, the cost of doing business (fifty thousand dollars) was insignificant when viewed from the big picture scheme of things. Access to the acoustics technology was what was important. What should the next contract work for Mr. Kramley be?

The phone started to beep, beep, beep, beep and it jerked Omar back to consciousness. He hung up the phone and said, "Maybe a software project!"

The Paths of Two Old Friends Converge

Grant Adams vividly remembered that fundraiser, nearly a year ago now, for his old college friend Charles Abbott. He liked him, respected him, and wanted him to be president of the United States.

If giving money to the campaign and attending events like this could help or even slightly influence the outcome, he was all for that.

Grant had walked into the huge ballroom set up with at least a hundred tables. He was a little late so most people were seated but things had not yet started. White tablecloths, flowers, china, crystal, and wine on the tables, each for ten people.... This was a big deal, he thought. Probably a thousand people at a thousand dollars each equals $1 million dollars. How many of these events did a guy need to run a first-class presidential campaign?

As his mind wandered, Grant had started toward the front of the room by the stage and the podium. He saw the waiters were staging to begin serving, starting with the tables near the stage. Table #4, why was he so far forward? He arrived at the table and was seated just as candidate Charles Abbott entered the ballroom by the side door. The music started, clapping began, people stood, and cheers filled the room. These people were determined to get Charles Abbott elected.

The candidate moved toward the podium, waving, smiling, and saying thank you as he passed the first three tables, stopping at Grant's table. Charles shook Grant's hand and said, "Hello, old friend. I am very glad you are here tonight. Do you think this is real and that I can get elected?"

Grant said, "Yes, it is real and we are going to make sure you get elected."

Charles pulled Grant close and whispered in his ear, "If it happens, I want you in my administration. It would be a cabinet position in a new Department of Advanced Technology. Start to give it some thought, please!"

Charles stepped back and continued waving and greeting the crowd. He turned and walked up the four steps to the podium and the teleprompter. The cheering and clapping died down.

"Friends, thank you for this outpouring of support for our run at the Oval Office. As I measure the electricity in this room tonight, we cannot be denied." The crowd applauded loudly. "The people want change and they want it now! People everywhere are willing to step up and be counted and help make change possible."

"Is it time?" There was a loud "yes!" in response.

"Are you with me?" This time an even louder, "yes!"

"Can we do it?" A thundering, "yes!" and more syncopated clapping were the enthusiastic responses.

"For us, it is obvious that education, technology and the economy are the keys to our success as a nation. All of our challenges whether they are social security, health care, trade, or terror can be addressed if we pay attention to the simple basics of education, technology and the economy."

"At each table, would you work together and give me three of your best ideas for creating change? Let's work and eat at the same time. We'll collect your note cards after our working dinner. Thanks everybody." More applause followed.

Grant was thinking as Charles Abbott left the podium and took his seat. WOW! He really has turned into quite a leader. I wonder what this Department of Advanced Technology will actually do. Do I want the job?

Secretary Grant Adams and Dr. Sam Elson

The now secretary of the newly formed U.S. Department of Advanced Technology had been settling into his new responsibilities and getting to know people. The new president, Charles Abbott, had appointed him and Congress had confirmed him in record time. That was just a few weeks ago.

The charge from the White House was clear: "Identify the technologies we need, get them developed, and protect them at all cost. Coordinate with the other departments so that we are talking, planning, and implementing without redundancy."

Grant Adams was in deep thought as he sat at his desk; that is what the president said. It sounded so simple and almost easy at the time. Can I do this job? Yes, of course. The new DoAT was the brainchild of the President. With a bachelor's in Chemistry, an MBA and a law degree, he knows enough about technology, business and legal matters to be dangerous on most any intellectual front. He is probably the best-educated president ever and a very personable guy. Grant liked him - not just because of the appointment or the education and personality, but because he wanted to get things done and make a difference.

President Charles Abbott and Grant Adams had met a long time ago in undergraduate school and had kept in touch. They pursued much different things in their careers.... Grant held an advanced degree in science from the University of Minnesota and eventually became chief technical officer of one of the largest companies in the world. President Charles Abbott participated in only politics from a local, state, and national progression that was phenomenal considering the relatively short time it took to get to the number one job. And the accomplishments ... no one could believe that one person could do all of that in fewer than twenty years. At 46, he was one of the youngest Presidents ever. Grant wondered what Charles was thinking just now.

Grant tried to get back to work; this was his last high-level appointment in his department. It was his style not to have a lot of direct reports. There were to be only three directors as top aides and recent interdepartmental transfers covered *identify and develop*. *Protect* was what his next meeting was about. He knew he had the right guy in Sam Elson if only he would say yes. The brain trust of the new department would not be complete without a psychologist. Sam's IQ was off the charts and he loved challenges. He was all business and worked all the time. Because he was so independent and a bit sarcastic at times, he probably was still single. I wonder if the women are still after him?.

A knock on the office door... Grant's assistant, Alice, said, "Sam Elson is here."

"Show him in, please."

He met Sam at the door. "Sam, it has been too long. Thank you for coming to talk about the new department and what we are up to."

"Secretary Adams, it is great to see you again. I am very happy to stop by. What are you up to?"

Seeing him caused Grant to have a flashback. Sam Elson

was tall, thin, and wore glasses but his grey-green eyes could still stare you down. He was confident, well-respected in the scientific community, and a tenured professor at the University of Virginia. Sam was a computer scientist and behavioral psychologist ... great teacher, extensively published and had had several graduate students working in the field of augmented adaptive reasoning. It was a relatively new area that Sam had pioneered seven or eight years ago. Using computer technology, one could add any kind of new information and reconstitute the already held facts and figures into new scenarios and predict outcomes quite accurately. His methodology had earned him some Army contracts evaluating and optimizing troop deployments and in predicting locations and types of potential terrorist activities. His reputation was growing as one of the "go to" guys for scenarios about the near-term future. Our government, the Fortune 500 companies, universities, and the stock markets were using his work.

Grant was thinking all of this was more than enough to consider him for this position in DoAT. But there was the other reason, too! Sam had been in private practice before becoming a university professor. Dr. Elson had been his therapist when he needed help the most. Grant remembered several years ago when he was a new CTO of General Security Systems. He was young and had not really learned how to build a vision, mentor, delegate, prioritize, and lead. Things were not going well and he was smart enough to seek some professional help.

Sam Elson was the professional help. They clicked and Sam was beginning to work on what he called then, "a scenario building" approach to career planning. It was actually the start of the new field to be called AAR, "augmented adaptive reasoning." Anyway, Sam was able to be of great help to Grant's career. They were able to plug in some possible course corrections and see the best scenarios and outcomes. Most of the key corrections that they identified happened to be in the management style area, and Grant made the changes as quickly as he could. Grant knew that he owed keeping his first CTO job and every other job after that to Sam. They had kept in touch since that first time.

"Sam, I hope it is, 'what are WE up to'. You know me - I am not going to mince words. I need you to consider a director position in my new Department of Advanced Technology. We have a chance to make a difference and I need your help. The department is to be involved with advanced technologies ... what we need, how to get it developed, and how to protect it. The President wants this because he feels we are slowing down, getting behind in our critical technology advancements and what we do have is under attack to be stolen away from us. We are the world leader in advanced technology but not for long if we don't identify, develop, and protect ... MORE! In this position, you would be responsible for protecting current and developing critical U.S. technologies, knowing the key people and companies, watching the terrorist organizations and stopping bad things from happening....PROTECT. Sam, through your industry, government, and university contacts, you have gotten to know a lot of people. You have a worldwide reputation and respect for your work in AAR; your country needs you to do this. What do you think?"

"Grant, what a sales job! You could have told me why the hell I was coming in. I have to think about this more. You should know that I have been cutting back on graduate students and doing more consulting. It is important to see that my research gets applied to real-life problems. Most of my recent consulting has been with companies utilizing advanced technology programs, usually under government contract."

"What kind of companies, Sam?"

"Well, for example, uh, Advanced Technology Products and its CTO Mike Jackson . . . . .and Customized Materials Technology and its president, Joe Blackstone."

"Those are pretty good companies that are doing work in the very technologies I'm talking about. This job would allow you to continue your work, but at an even more sophisticated level, and with a huge national security impact."

Grant thought he saw Sam's interest building so he used the clincher. "I will match your current salary at the University of Virginia and the monies you make in your consulting business, give you authority to coordinate work done in several departments like

Defense, Energy, and Homeland Security as it relates to protecting advanced technology, give you control of a supercomputer for your analyses, and assign to you people and other resources like you have never seen before."

Sam said, interrupting.....ced"OK, OK, I said that I would think about it. Can you give me a couple of days?"

"Sure. Give me a call if you have questions. Remember that I need you - the country needs you - to do this. Thanks for coming in."

"You are welcome, Grant. I'll give you a call soon. It does sound like something I should consider very seriously. I can show myself out. Thanks."

Sam Takes the Job

A couple of days later, Sam called Secretary Grant Adams's office. He had thought deeply about the position of director in the newly formed Department of Advanced Technology. He did know the companies, organizations, universities, and key people in this business of advanced technology. His knowledge of the field of Augmented Adaptive Reasoning would be very useful not only in protection, but also in identification and development. He was mostly comfortable in and around government, but was he ready to be the next thing to a secret agent? He thought so - and maybe he could make a difference.

Alice picked up on the third ring and said, "Secretary Adams's office."

"Hello, this is Sam Elson."

"Yes, sir, I recognize your voice."

"Thank you. Please don't interrupt the secretary but just tell him when you get a moment that I will take the job."

"I will tell him, sir. The secretary will be very pleased. Thank you."

"Thank you, Alice." Sam hung up the phone and thought ...what have I done? I am making the circuit from private practice to the university to the government. I hope this is the right decision.

The Second Project

Thomas Kramley pondered as he sat at his desk, excited about his work with TIC and Omar Kharif. The first project had gone very well. The RFID tags were incorporated onto CMT's packaging, shipped by every means of transportation possible, and the two shipments arrived at a distribution location in Budapest on the Danube River. TIC people collected the tags and the product was sent on and received by the customer without a hitch. He had been watching closely and step by step to see that things went well - and they did. He thought, whew, not a bad way to earn fifty thousand dollars in about two weeks time! That calculates to be five hundred dollars per tag for the beta test. He hoped there would be a second project soon.

He was waiting for the prearranged phone call from Omar. When the phone rang he answered, "Kramley here."

There was a long pause and then, "Hi, Thomas, this is Omar. Say, congratulations on our first project together. Your help was greatly appreciated and you should know the B-test has given us great data. The features, advantages, and benefits of the RFID system were all demonstrated to be superior. I believe we can consider a commercialization strategy very soon. Would CMT like to be a pilot for the first key account sales?"

"Why not? The tags would really help to improve the tracking and knowledge of the environmental history of our products."

"Thank you. We can talk about how to make that happen a little later. I want you to know that as of an hour ago your reward was delivered to the location you identified earlier. Thanks very much."

"Yes, I know. Thank you for the opportunity to help with such an important product, Omar."

"You are welcome, Thomas. Is it too soon or can we talk about the next project right now?"

"Of course we can. The money from the first project has already been spent on the health care of my wife and ten-year-old son."

"Here is what I would like to propose. Software rules the

world and even though I will never understand writing code, I do admire and respect those who do. We have recently acquired some software technology that fits into the data augmentation category. We think it has application in the logistics and supply chain arenas. Would you be willing to test it for us?"

"Maybe so, particularly if it would help us better meet the needs of our customers."

"It will. It has been written to align the customers' needs with your production, inventory, and shipping processes. I am told it can take the smallest amount of factual information and project future requirements. I have an example where, let's say, ABC Company puts a significant time-limited price decrease into place at year-end. When this was communicated to customers, they doubled up on their orders immediately to take advantage of the lower price. This continued for the duration of the special discounted price. Now, marketing and sales know that things will balance out in time. The customer buys more now and less later. Hopefully there will be at least a small increase in orders year after year. In this example, however, no one tells production. So what happens? Manufacturing boosts production to the order levels based on the lower price. The factory begins to scale up and orders raw materials, adds workers, adds a shift, makes a lot of product, inventories swell and costs escalate. We get to about February and now there are fewer orders. People are let go; numbers of shifts decreases, and inventories are still too high. Something like this happens on a regular basis at the majority of our manufacturing companies across the U.S. The new and highly sophisticated software protects the customer and the company from over or under reacting when there are planned or unplanned events that lead to change. It would have determined that the larger orders were due to lower pricing and compensated for it. This data augmentation software is remarkable. That was just a pricing example, but it can handle almost any event that leads to change. This includes products out of specification, ocean liner delays because of bad weather, customer cancelled orders, fires at plants, union strikes, customer orders with address inaccuracies, and many others. It is simply an add-on to your current production planning and logistics software. Your IT guy can install it in five minutes and you are set to go. Why don't you come up with a problem to test it on, we'll get it installed and let it go to work."

Thomas, caught up with the possibilities, quickly said, "Since you mentioned customer addresses, I have an idea. Our software system today allows us to read every package address label and crosscheck it against a specific customer order and its printed address. It is a pretty good system. The problem is that we have found the order address to be incomplete or inaccurate many times. In our business, sending product to the wrong address is a disaster as you can imagine. We have had this happen too many times recently yet there seemed to be no fix out there."

"Your new software would have to learn the correct addresses of all of our customers from our corporate records. These are kept up-to-date religiously and required to be checked monthly by government regulation. Can the new software system take each customer's order address information and make a comparison with the learned corporate data? It would have to red-flag those addresses that do not match up and get the address corrections made, right?"

"Right, it sounds like a perfect application and test for it. May I check with our technology expert to make sure we can do this?"

Thomas thought, I wonder how long this will take and if they even have the needed software technology? Hesitantly, he said, "Sure."

Omar said, "Let me put you on hold for one minute." Thomas waited sort of impatiently but Omar was back in no time at all. "Thomas we can do this. I am told it is one of the simpler applications for the data augmentation software. I will have the software and installation instructions sent to you today from our San Francisco office."

"Thank you, Omar. We will get the data augmentation software installed and operating immediately. How about a full week of factory orders, production, and shipping for the test? That would be thousands of address labels and packages."

"Sounds perfect. I will call you next week to see how things went."

"Thank you and talk to you next week." He whispered, "I wonder if this project is worth fifty thousand dollars? God knows I can use the money."

Sam and Brad

Just after Sam accepted the job as Director, Advanced Technology Protection in DoAT, he read the announcement by GPRI. It concerned the agreement to transfer ownership of the Bounce-Back Acoustical Wave Technology to its inventor, Dr. Bradford Tully. Dr. Tully was to seek investors in his private venture to commercialize the technology for several applications. Sam thought the target of finding new oil was admirable and necessary. He decided to give Dr. Tully a call and see what he really planned to do. This could be a key technology and one the government should help protect. It will be a long time before this country moves from its dependence on oil and gas to something else.

Sam googled Dr. Bradford Tully and got hundreds of hits. He assembled the information into compartments: brilliant scientist and technologist; very special expertise in multiple disciplines including chemical sensing, acoustics, and advanced software code; independent; innovative and results-oriented; and dependable. Sam read several papers in which Dr. Tully had used his special software code and computer enhancements to treat collected minute amounts of key information and data. He was able to project new scenarios and predict outcomes very accurately. It worked for finding specific chemicals and oil like nothing else! Sam thought that Brad had been doing in science and technology what he was doing in behavioral psychology with augmented adaptive reasoning! He just hadn't labeled his approach. What a team they would make!

Sam called Dr. Tully at the number given in the GPRI announcement.

"Dr. Tully, this is Sam Elson with the Department of Advanced Technology in Washington, D.C. I read the GPRI announcement about your acoustic technology and thought we should talk. I am a director in the Department and in charge of

Advanced Technology Protection. After reading about you and the acoustic technology, I thought we should talk about how you plan to take this technology private."

"Should I call you Director Elson?"

"Yes, or Sam is okay, too."

In his straightforward, no nonsense way Brad said, "Never heard of the DoAT. Are you looking to invest?"

"We are new. President Abbott thinks that technology identification, development, and protection are critical for the country's future. Congress agrees with him, too, so here we are."

"Great idea, but you never answered my question about investing in my technology."

"I think you know the rules, Brad. We can't invest like a private investor but we can talk about contracts to help develop the technology and commercialize it."

Brad thought, now you are talking, and said, "I would be very interested in learning more about what might be possible in the government contract area. The timing is great. I am just starting my search to find a location for the new venture. Know anything about Minneapolis?"

"Not too much, but it is known as a great high tech area ... University of Minnesota and their Institute of Technology, IBM, medical device companies, some venture capital companies and the mighty Mississippi River."

"Yes, it is worth a look."

"I'd like to talk with you again soon, Brad. May I have my assistant call and arrange something?"

"Yes, of course. I will be in D.C. soon. I have been contacted by Technology Investment Corporation, a company interested in investing in the venture. TIC invited me to D.C. to discuss the business plan and a potential partnership. We are just firming up the details of the trip."

"TIC? I'll have to do a little research on them before we meet. Please let my assistant know when you will be in D.C. and she will schedule some time for us to talk further. I think we have a lot in common, including protecting our country's key technologies of the future."

Brad smiled, thinking I like this guy and said, "I'll look forward to seeing you in D.C. Until then, goodbye sir."

"Goodbye, Brad."

The Third Project

Thomas was amazed. In reviewing the data on testing the software from TIC, he found results that were unbelievable. When he installed the new software, he decided to run a parallel and dual test, with the current system and the new system side by side, both utilizing integrated data augmentation. The current system found two internal label printing errors, which was about the historical level of accuracy. The new system actually found three internal label printing errors, in other words, all of them and ten addresses that were incomplete or wrong and had to be corrected using corporate records information. Wow! There was no question about whether CMT should purchase the software. Can you imagine the work and customer grief that will not happen because the new software caught and corrected the additional eleven errors? We have to have it!

The phone rang with the prearranged call from Omar to learn about the test results, "Kramley here."

"Hang on a minute, please." The seconds rolled by and finally, "Hello, Thomas. How did the test go?"

"Omar, we got exceptional results. They were better than one could have hoped, especially since we thought we were already state-of-the-art. Thirteen hits with the new system; with our current system we had two. How much is this software?"

"We are not quite ready to commercialize at this time so we don't have pricing. Why don't you keep it running and we'll talk about the cost later. I am so glad that it did the job for you. Remember, this software can do even more complicated tasks involving almost any reaction to planned or unplanned events leading to change."

"By the way, Thomas, your reward for this work will be delivered today. You have been of great help to TIC."

"Thank you, Omar." He thought excitedly about another

fifty thousand dollars and said, "I believe we are on a roll, so we can talk about the next project sometime soon?"

"Of course, do you want to do it right now?"

"Yes, if you have time."

"I have a little time so I can sketch it out. However, I just learned that I need to be in San Francisco next week. Maybe we could meet at the Squealing Pig and talk more then."

"Okay, that would be great."

"For our next project, I would like to further test these new technologies. The RFID data we got from the first test was excellent from a location verification and environmental history perspective. Mach I is orders of magnitude better than any RFID product on the market. We have something even better now that we call Mach II. It will have GPS capability and be able to interface with the new data augmentation software. The satellite will allow you to track a package second by second, read the sensor data, and send it to your system for review and augmentation. If anything is amiss, the system will provide corrective actions. It is going to be a little more costly and probably should be used for only critical shipments at the start. Maybe like the new product you mentioned to me earlier that detonates explosives using special sound waves."

Thomas flinched a bit and thought, Omar remembered what I said at the Squealing Pig! He didn't say anything but he knew there was a production run of the new item coming soon. It was intended for a longtime government customer so everything had to go right.

Omar continued, "Before we were talking about an advanced RFID system to protect the product and the customer but the Mach II tag could also be a security device for the company to protect its new technology. I think I can get permission for you to test it."

"That would be very good because our technology is our lifeblood. Can you imagine what could happen if our new detonation technology got into the wrong hands?"

"I can, and we must never let that happen! I'll have an answer for you next week about testing Mach II."

"I hope you can get approval. We have a production run

of this new product coming up soon. I really like constant tracking of the packages and knowing their second-by-second locations and being able to monitor the sensor data and react to change would give us a capability no one else has."

"Yes, we have got to make it happen. I promise to bring good news when we meet at the Squealing Pig next week."

"I'll plan on it," said Thomas.

Chapter 2

The "Black" Acoustics Project on Explosives Detection

The Stolen Notes

ATP's Awards Banquet

The emcee introduced Dr. Chadly Bromcast, who would announce the winners of the technology awards. Chad approached the podium and the teleprompter and began. "Hello, my name is Chadly Bromcast, technology manager for Advanced Systems." Chad was a little nervous but he had done this before so he powered through the first parts. "I am honored to announce the winners of the four technology awards tonight. These people are all very special to me, experts in their fields, individuals making great contributions to our great company and our great country. Please hold your applause until I name all four winners. Our first award tonight goes to William Brewer for his innovative work in acoustics. The second award is made to Lyncoln Fuller for his futuristic work in data augmentation. Kan Deng Shin is our third recipient for her advanced work in nanotechnology and microelectromechanical systems. Our fourth and final award tonight is to Zenica Lang, who has been here only about a year, for her exceptional work in sensor technology."

There was loud applause as Chad handed each their bronze American eagle sculpture. The base of each sculpture was inscribed with the recipient's name and technology specialty along with the words: Advanced Technology Products, Technology Award 2009.

After shaking hands with each winner Chad continued. "These four scientists were chosen for their work in significantly advancing their fields of technology and applying those advancements to new products and processes. They were chosen from a staff of thousands of technical people as the best of the best. Let's give them all another hand!"

As the thunderous applause began, Chad thanked the audience. The applause continued. People were standing, smiling, clapping, and nodding their agreement about the selected winners.

Chad whispered to the four on stage....."Can I see all of you after dinner for a few moments? Let's meet in the office just off the hotel lobby by the escalator. Okay?" All four nodded and silently mouthed, "Okay." Chad turned to the crowd and said, "Thank you, and congratulations to the winners again." He looked at the crowd and at the four on stage with him and said to the winners again "I knew this would happen when I hired you! Thank you so much for your outstanding contributions."

They left the stage together and returned to their seats as the awards presentations continued.

Eventually, the rest of the non-technology award winners were named and seated at the front tables. The technology award winners were all together at one table. Zen finally asked the question that was on everyone's mind. "Why does Chad want to see us?"

Bill thought for a moment and then said, "It is probably just to say thanks and good work again. If it was anything about business, he would surely wait until tomorrow."

Lyncoln said, "I thought it was to talk about keeping our work confidential when we are interviewed by the press. These awards are pretty big deals, especially because our company lives or dies by our military applications of key technologies. Chad will probably just remind us to keep our cards close to the vest."

Kan D said, "It might be to set up the standard next-day meeting with the company CEO. I am looking forward to that."

Zen was thoughtful. It was a long time until she finally said, "Too obvious! I think there is something else here. Remember, Chad hired each one of us. It was no accident that he introduced us tonight, even though his responsibilities are in a different area of the company now. Maybe the technologies we represent fit together as a team. Chad does have a reputation as the best program manager in the company. Will we get a chance to work together on a special program?"

Bill summed up saying, "We all have our award-winning work to continue. Let's just wait and see what he has to say after dinner."

Chad was seated at the head table. During dinner he outlined the explosives detection and detonation project that he titled Close-In Explosives Detection, CIED. It was just a set of notes and a rough sketch or drawing but contained all the elements needed. He had put in an acoustical wave hitting suspected targets 100 feet away like IED's, EFP's, car bombs, suicide bombers and bouncing back but now containing all the key identifiers of the components of the target. The returning wave-front would be collected and chemically analyzed with the help of computer data augmentation and determined if it contained explosive or bomb ingredients. Once detected, it would be prematurely detonated and destroyed. The notes also had assignments for the four scientists to include: Bill on acoustical generation; Zen on collection and analysis; Lyncoln on data crunching or augmentation and Kan D on MEMS and nanotechnology. Chad whispered to himself, "And one more thing." He penciled in NEED DETONATION TECHNOLOGY!

Dessert was brought in; Chad looked around to see if anyone noticed what he was doing. His notes were on the back of the award program and big enough to be seen by three or four people at the table. He didn't think that was the case but he very quietly put the notes away in his coat pocket. He would use the notes when he met with the team in a few minutes.

Mike Jackson, his boss seated next to him, said, "That is it, a perfect description, just make sure that you keep those notes and this project confidential and within a 'need to know' limited number of people."

Chad said, "Sorry, I did not mean for my notes to be seen by anyone."

Mike said, "It's okay if only seen by you, me and the four

team leaders, the experts who will lead the R&D. We really have to be careful about this project. It will have the highest possible clearance rating assigned to it and be the most important project for the U.S. government and us. Can these 'hot shots' do this, Chad?"

"If they can't do it, no one can, Mike. I will be more careful about my notes. You should know that I am meeting with the hot shots in just a few minutes after the emcee thanks everyone for coming and closes the awards presentation Mike, what a great event and thank you for all the support you give the technical staff and me, in particular, as we accept this challenge from the U.S. government." Chad whispered, "If we can do this, just think of the lives it will save." Mike smiled and nodded.

They both listened as the emcee brought the dinner, the acknowledgments and the evening festivities to a close. Mike and Chad shook hands and Chad headed for the lobby and the meeting with his team.

Chad passed the local press on his way out. Before they started packing up all their gear, they took a couple pictures of him. With the microphones still on, he said, "Quite a team for the technical awards, right?" He thought, this will be in all the papers tomorrow and we don't really need the visibility right now. Oh well, there is nothing I can do about it now.

The Challenge

After the awards banquet, Chad opened the door of the lobby office by the escalator. As he expected, Bill, Kan D, Lyncoln, and Zen were already there waiting for him. The lights were low and there were not enough chairs. Bill and Lyncoln were sitting on the desk, Kan D and Zen in the chairs so that they appeared to be huddled together in some kind of joint and secret discussion. Chad thought, this is a good start for the program that I want them to lead. They not only have to use all of their technical skills but they also need to communicate constantly and trust each other completely.

"Hello, everybody. May I say again how proud I was to be able to introduce you as the winners of the technology awards tonight? It is just what I expected when you were hired. I'll get right to it so you can get home at a decent time tonight. We have a special request from the United States Government. It is because of our success, primarily through your work with government contracts and providing technology and products to the military, that they contacted us."

"They want us to develop a product that will take all of our expertise and skills if we are to be successful. It would save thousands of lives in the military and elsewhere and cripple the enemy's approach to spreading anxiety, with their so-called 'Campaign of Fear'. The company has agreed to do this work and assigned us to the program. It will be fully resourced, top priority, top secret, need-to-know, and *black*."

The four researchers were staring at him in disbelief. They all had the right clearances but only Zen had actually worked on a *black* program. Zen said, "Now I get all this secret meeting, dark room stuff. When do we find out what this assigned program is?"

Chad pulled out the awards event program. He said, "This is all I have right now; take a look at my notes." He placed the program on the desk. They all huddled over the notes, sizing up the sketch, how each would contribute and the obvious challenges that were presented. It was obvious the product needs to locate and destroy IED's, EFP's, and suicide and car bombers......fast!

Bill said, "A returning acoustical wave-front that is in effect a sophisticated giant air collector ...I guess that might be possible."

Chad took that to mean a high chance of success based on how Bill talked.

Zen said, "There must be billions of cm^3 of air to analyze. What are we looking for anyway?" Chad took that to be positive, too.

Kan D pointed out that the funny looking box with a wine glass sticking out didn't have any dimensions. She said, "I'm assuming that it has to be small, right?"

"You are right," Chad said but he couldn't or wouldn't give her any ballpark dimensions. Nor did he tell her that it had to be mobile and probably carried by a truck going at slow but reasonable speeds.

Lyncoln popped up and said, "Data crunching? No one says that anymore. Do you mean data augmentation? It is a science you know."

"Okay Lyncoln, sorry about that! I think you all get the picture about the program and its challenges." What Chad didn't tell them was just how fast this system had to produce answers to find roadside bombs and provide information so they could be destroyed. By his calculation, a truck traveling ~5 miles per hour would need this data collected, analyzed, confirmed, and pinpointed in less than five seconds. If that were possible, then detonation technology would do the rest. "Let's plan to meet next week and scope out the program and the resources you will need. Remember: don't talk to anyone about this, not a soul. Thanks for volunteering." Chad picked up the program, put it in his coat, and said good evening to everyone.

Chance Meeting At The Conference

The American Chemical Society Annual Conference on Chemical Sensing was in the Twin Cities of Minneapolis-St. Paul. The Convention Center in Minneapolis was packed with thousands of people. There were hundreds of exhibits by companies with all kinds of products for chemical sensing applications. Seminars, lectures, tutorials, workshops, and the like were also available to cover new products and technology. You could pick and choose whatever you needed to learn about.

Dr. Bradford Tully was attending the Chemical Sensing Conference for two reasons. Minneapolis-St. Paul might be a good location for his new business venture and he wanted to keep up on one of his passions and the subject of his PhD thesis. Quite frankly, the conference was very boring for someone of Brad's abilities. He knew nuclear magnetic resonance, magnetic resonance imaging, X-ray, infrared, mass spectrometry, and wet chemical analysis techniques backwards and forwards. All the exhibits were old hat to him. Even the new products and technologies areas were mostly line extensions and evolutionary advancements. He had hoped to see some revolutionary stuff but it was too much to ask for this time.

As he was about to leave the Convention Center, he noticed someone that he knew more than casually. It was Zenica Lang, who had been in his class at Stanford. She was still as beautiful as ever and what a body. They were in different research groups, under different advisors, but both worked on chemical sensing projects. It turned out that Brad finished his PhD in approximately three years, a record time at Stanford. This meant that he graduated at least a year before Ms. Lang. There always seemed to be a little friction between them. He was more of a loner and unskilled in knowing the ways of women, especially smart women. Zenica Lang, without a doubt, fit into that category. Maybe she made all men feel uncomfortable.

Brad yelled, "Hello Zen," and waved to her across the way.

Zen heard the voice and thought she recognized it. Then she saw the hand waving in the distance. She thought, Bradford Tully, I wonder what he is doing here? He thought he knew everything when he was at Stanford. You don't expect to see people like that at product and technology conferences. She smiled, took his hand and said, "Hello, Brad. Long time, no see."

"Yes, it has been at least a couple of years. I am here to check out Minneapolis-St. Paul as a location for my new technology venture."

"Wow, I heard that you were working for that General Petroleum Research Institute in Texas." Their eyes met briefly and she thought, He is even better looking than before. Then she said quickly, "What is the technology?"

"I can't tell you a lot except that it is in the area of acoustics. If you go to the our website you can get more information. It is nothing like what we did with chemical sensing at Stanford. GPRI thought that it was great technology but could take too long and cost too much to commercialize it. I asked if I could have it, and they said yes. It is my intent to set up shop someplace, maybe here, find investors, and develop the technology as fast as possible. Where are you now and what are you doing?"

"I am with Advanced Technology Products in Boston doing chemical sensor technology work. They are a large company, deep into the technology stuff we like, they have government contracts, and they produce both industrial and military products. It is so exciting. We just had our awards banquet, and I won one of the four technology awards! Right afterwards, I was assigned to a new project to be led by me and the other three technology award winners. One of them is an acoustics expert."

"Who is he? I probably know him."

"How do you know it is a he?" Zen asked before sighing. "His name is Bill Brewer from Harvard. Do you know him?"

Brad smiled and thought, same old Zen then responded, "I know of him but he hasn't published much recently. It must be because of those government contracts."

"Yes and because of those government contracts I probably have said too much already. I am meeting some friends, Brad, so I have to run. It was very good to see you again. Here is my card so that we can stay in touch."

As he walked away, Zen winked and said, "Maybe you should come to Boston to start your new company."

Brad watched her every step, mesmerized, as she walked to the exit doors. What a beautiful woman, he thought. As always, he couldn't figure out exactly what was meant in a conversation with Zen. Did she really mean she wanted to stay in touch and what about Boston?

One thing was certain. Zen was on a key project at Advanced Technology Products that included both chemical sensing and acoustical technologies. Further, it was being done under government contract and therefore was probably for military purposes. He would have to see her and talk with her more....for a lot of reasons. Soon.

Awards Announcement

Omar was in the Boston field office this week. He was constantly searching for information on acoustics technology. He had noticed a small announcement about an awards banquet in a Boston paper. It simply said:

Advanced Technology Products announces the individual

winners of their yearly technology awards. Out of thousands of technical workers, four people won this prestigious award. Bill Brewer, PhD Harvard – Acoustics; Lyncoln Fuller, BS MIT – Data Augmentation; Kan Deng Shin, PhD University of Michigan – MEMS, and Zenica Lang, PhD Stanford – Sensors. Their original hiring manager, Chadly Bromcast, PhD Berkeley, new technology manager for Advanced Systems, announced all awardees. Showing his pride after the ceremony, he said, "Quite a team, right?" Congratulations to the winners and to Dr. Bromcast.

Omar put the paper down and thought about the notice. There was mention of acoustics but how would he find out what Advanced Technology Products was really doing with it? Then it hit him. TIC had given unrestricted research grants to the alma maters of all of the winners and the announcing manager. That should be enough to get me in.

He googled Advanced Technology Products, found their website, and telephone number for information and customer service. Calling the number by cell phone might be safer so he dialed the number. The phone rang once, twice

"Advanced Technology Products Information, this is Tara. How may I help you?"

"This is Omar Kharif, president of the Technology Investment Corporation. We have offices in Boston and I read about the technology award winners in the local paper. Is it possible that you could transfer me to Dr. Chadly Bromcast, who was mentioned in the notice?"

"Sure, he is getting a lot of calls today, and it is still morning. I will ring his direct number for you."

"Thank you, Tara, could you give that number to me in case he is busy or out of the office?"

"Sure, it is 617-982-5734. I will ring now."

"Hello, Chadly Bromcast speaking."

"Hello, Dr. Bromcast, this is Omar Kharif from Technology Investment Corporation. You don't know me, but I want to offer my congratulations to the winners of your technology awards. I just read about it in the newspaper this morning. What an accomplishment for each of the individuals and for you as the one who hired all of them. My company has a real interest in these technologies."

"Thank you, sir."

Omar continued, "They are all important technologies for the future of our country. Dr. Bromcast, if I may, there are two additional things that I noticed in the paper. You all attended great schools: Berkley, Harvard, MIT, University of Michigan, and Stanford. Amazingly, in the past five years, my company has given significant unrestricted research grants to all of them. What a coincidence. Second, a suggestion -- they would make a powerful team if all were on the same project. Is it possible that I could make an appointment to come in and see you? I would like to talk about technology and the Technology Investment Corporation and let you know what we are doing. It might be helpful in the future."

Chad was so busy that he said, after pulling up his electronic calendar and schedule, "Sure, how about 9 AM tomorrow morning?"

"Perfect, I will see you tomorrow at 9 o'clock at your office. Thank you, sir."

The Liberator Calls

Omar did not think this visit with Dr. Chadly Bromcast would happen so quickly. He got busy and started to prepare for the meeting. He wanted to expand on TIC's charter of investing in key global technologies and in-depth knowledge of technologies and the practicing experts. He had not done any investing in established companies involved in these key technologies, let alone companies with a technology track record like Advanced Technology Products - a track record that included military/government contracts and much business success. They probably did not need him or TIC money. What angle could he use to make and keep the contact with Dr. Chadly Bromcast and ATP?

Omar's phone rang ... It was the Liberator. It is too soon for his next instruction to be coming. He must just be checking on me.

"Omar, I have just a minute; how are things going with the acoustical research and investigations?"

"There are some things happening on several fronts, sir. A recent discovery involves what is happening in acoustics research at Advanced Technology Products here in Boston. I found out about this in the Boston newspapers and have a meeting with a key manager, Dr. Chadly Bromcast, tomorrow. We are going to discuss how there might be some cooperation between TIC and ATP. I need some ideas. Advanced Technology Products is a major company in technology and military contracts. They don't really need us but I think something big might be going on there. We need to be involved somehow."

"Omar, I know the CTO there, Mike Jackson. The alias I used when I met him was Patek Kumat, and you may use that to get closer to Bromcast."

"What was the circumstance of your meeting Mr. Jackson?"

"It was at an annual meeting of the Industrial Research Institute. We happened to be seated alphabetically by last names and I was next to him. He and I talked a lot about military products and war. There were many topics that lead me to believe that he not so comfortable with the speed at which his company completes high priority programs. I built enough of a bond that he may remember my name and our discussions. We also talked about a possible joint venture of some kind if a situation existed where TIC controlled the technology that Advanced Technology Products needed. If you are right and something big is happening there, they may need some of our technology."

Omar thanked the Liberator and added, "This is exactly what I need for tomorrow's meeting."

"Good, I am glad to help and keep me up to date on developments.

"Of course, sir. Please send me an encrypted email with the time of your next call. I will update you then on three subjects -- the meeting at ATP, what I have learned about acoustical work at Customized Materials Technology, and new acoustical work done at

GPRI, soon to be commercialized through a new venture."

"Thank you, Omar; you have been busy these last few months. We will plan to talk more often."

The Notes

Omar arrived at Advanced Technology Products on the outskirts of Boston. It looked like a college campus with twenty or thirty buildings scattered on tens of acres. There were two security booths at the main entrance. He stopped and gave them his driver's license and his appointment information.

The guard gave him a map, pointed to building #220, and waved him on. As he drove through the main gate, he noticed that before one could get close to any building, you had to pass through specially constructed barricades. There were two circles of barricades around each building. As he got closer to the designated entry point for Dr. Bromcast's building, #220, the gate opened. He pulled through and the gate closed behind him, but the next circle of barricades stopped him. Actually, he was in a box-like structure that seemed to have all kinds of electronic scanning equipment in its sides, top, and bottom. The process of checking out Omar and the car took about five minutes with lights, vibrations, strange vacuum cleaner sounds, and odors involved. When it was over, the door opened on the inner circle barricade. A computer-generated voice said, "You are cleared for passage to building 220. Have a nice day." He drove on and parked in the visitor's area of the parking lot. Omar sat quickly thinking about what had just happened and what technology they were using to check him out ... especially the vibration, the vacuum, and that strange odorant.

Omar got out of his car and walked toward the entrance of Building 220. The guard at the door patted him down and explained the metal detector and x-ray security system to him. The guard said, "It is just like the airport except we also take photos, fingerprints, handwriting samples, and a voice recognition record. I hope you are okay with doing all of that."

Omar gulped and said, "Sure, as long as I get a copy of

everything you document."

"We get that request a lot; it will be ready after you finish your meeting with Dr. Bromcast."

Omar emptied his pockets into the plastic tray. He took off his watch, shoes, and glasses and placed them into a plastic tub. He pushed the tray and the tub through the X-ray machine. Then he walked through the metal detector in his stocking feet.

Once through, he got his stuff, and put his shoes on. The guard gave him a visitor's badge and asked him to follow him into the control room. The control room was packed with all kinds of electronic monitors and equipment. Omar was photographed, fingerprinted, and asked for a handwriting sample. He wrote, *My name is Omar Kharif. My visit to Advanced Technology Products and Dr. Chadly Bromcast is for the purpose of discussing the recent technology awards and Technology Investment Corporation's interest and investment in specific technologies.* Omar wrote the sentence with the intent of disguising his real handwriting. He used a different slant, more loops, placed letters closer together, and used a sloppy style. Little did he know that all of these had been tried many times before and that the computer software could accommodate his attempt to disguise his natural handwriting. It is almost impossible to trick the computer. Next, the guard asked him to read a statement that would be digitally recorded. The statement said, "*My name is Omar Kharif and I am president and CEO of Technology Investment Corporation. We are interested in knowing about key global technologies, the experts in those fields, and making selective investments where appropriate.*" Omar read the statement in his normal speaking voice as he was asked. He was then asked to re-read it two more times. This completed, the guard said, "Mr. Kharif, would you come with me to the office next door where you will wait until I come to get you?"

"Of course."

The guard took him to the office beside the control room and asked him to be seated at the table. "It will be about ten minutes. Is that okay?"

"Yes."

The guard closed the door and went back to the control room. The room was empty except for the table and chair. Omar sensed that he was being watched. He thought that this whole process was a bit much just to see a mid-level manager at Advanced Technology Products. However, they did have significant government contracts, produced military products, and were very protective of their technology. Omar smiled and thought,"If they only knew who I really am, why I am here, and what I intend to do for the cause. Would any of the information documented today damage his ability to function in the future?" He was fidgeting as the guard opened the office door and said, "You may take the elevator up to the fifth floor where someone will meet you and escort you to Dr. Bromcast's office. Your visitor's badge has GPS capability and your movements will be tracked. Go only to the fifth floor."

"Yes, sir."

Omar got off the elevator on the fifth floor and waiting for him was Dr. Bromcast's assistant, Melinda. "Hello Mr. Kharif, and welcome to Advanced Technology Products. Our records show that this is your first visit. We hope you were not intimidated too much by our security measures. Every visitor goes through the same process. In our business, we have to be very careful. I'm sure you understand."

"It was okay, just a little more extensive than I expected."

"Yes, most people say that. This way, please."

Omar followed Melinda past several offices to where he saw a gentlemen who must be Dr. Chadly Bromcast standing in the hallway.

"Hello Mr. Kharif and thank you for coming to see me."

"Thank you, Dr. Bromcast."

"You can call me Chad."

"Please call me Omar."

"Visitors really do have to want to come here and meet with Advanced Technology Products personnel. Your security and protective measures are quite extensive."

"Yes, and who knows if we have gone overboard or not. At this time, I believe it is needed for companies in our business. There is a lot at stake. Please step into my office so we can talk."

As Omar entered the office, he was struck by its spacious size, twenty feet long and twenty feet wide, but it had only one small window about two feet by six inches.

"Let's sit at the table, Omar."

As he sat, Omar noticed the stacks and stacks of books and some papers on the table. He noticed that one of the books on top was about acoustics. The pile of papers was about an inch thick and near the edge of the table, almost falling off.

Chad pushed the books and papers together and out of the way so that they could have room to talk. This is when Omar noticed the pamphlet-sized paper on the floor by the table. It had not fallen when Dr. Bromcast was organizing the table space for their discussion. So it had been there for some time. On the side facing upward was the handwritten word CIED along with a drawing of some kind and some other writing. What really caught his attention was the word *acoustical* written at least twice in the notes. Omar looked quickly from the floor to the table, hoping that Chad had not seen him looking at the floor.

Chad said, "So you saw the article about our awards program in the paper."

"Yes, it must have been a wonderful event. Your company is known globally for its technology development and new products."

"Thank you very much."

Omar continued, "I am president and CEO of Technology Investment Corporation, TIC for short. We hold equity positions in many sophisticated technology companies and therefore have access and control over many new technologies. Growth in these companies allows us to operate in several arenas. We do technology licensing, joint ventures, cooperative programs, acquisitions and the like. We fund technology building at major universities via unrestricted research grants. I mentioned that we have active grants at all the universities represented by you and your technology award winners. Check our website and you will see that I had been at Berkeley recently to provide additional unrestricted monies. TIC.com shows the technologies that we believe are key to the future. We are a "knowledge company" in that we not only know the technologies, we know the practicing experts in the various technology fields."

Omar continued, "Seeing your technology award winners and their fields was very interesting for us. Each of those technologies named is one we have identified within our 'Top Ten Global Technologies.' If you like, you can pull up our website on your computer and check it out."

"Okay, I will." Chad got up and went to his desk and googled TIC.com.

Omar took the opportunity to quickly and quietly reach down and pick up the pamphlet off the floor and put it into his inside coat pocket.

Chad said, "Here we are. You are right; those technologies are all on your list."

Omar added, "Those technologies are where we are making significant investments and major business decisions. I noticed that the paper not only congratulated the winners of the technology award but also quoted you saying, "Quite a team, right?" Do they have an inside scoop on a new project? I know you can't answer that but if something like that happened and you need help with these and related technologies, just let me know. We would be glad to help in any way we can."

Chad returned to his seat and said, "Thank you but you know how newspapers are. They sometimes use a little creative writing to enhance their story." Chad decided he better sidestep this a bit and added, "The four technology award winners are making such significant contributions to their individual projects that we could not afford to make any changes at this time."

"Of course, I understand, but the newspaper did for once put two and two together and arrive at an obvious conclusion."

"Yes, a team project could happen sometime in the future and they would be a great and powerful team. But for now, we need these people where they are."

"One more thing about the seriousness of my offer to help with your technology needs. A principal in my company, Mr. Patek Kumat, had an occasion to meet your chief technology officer, Mike

Jackson. It was at an Industrial Research Institute annual meeting and they had some time to talk. I believe they discussed a possible joint venture between TIC and Advanced Technology Products if the need arose. I am simply indicating that our bosses have already discussed a potential business arrangement. It should be easy sailing if you identify a need."

"Thank you. I will consider your standing offer very seriously. I appreciate you coming to see my company and me."

Omar stood, shook hands with Chad, and said, "Thank you for seeing me on such short notice. I enjoyed meeting and talking with you." Chad walked Omar to the door where Melinda was waiting to escort him to the elevator.

"Goodbye, Chad. 'Til next time."

"Goodbye, Omar."

Melinda took Omar to the waiting elevator and said, "Goodbye, Mr. Kharif."

"Goodbye, Melinda, and thanks for your help." He stepped into the elevator, pushed the button for the first floor, and the door closed. On reaching the first floor, he was met by the guard who asked for his visitor's badge and then presented him with a packet containing the documents he had requested. Omar peeked in quickly and saw photos, a disc, handwriting sample, and fingerprints. He said thank you and walked out the front door to the parking lot. He got into his car thinking, I did it. Could this be my lucky day? He patted his coat pocket to make sure the pamphlet was still there. It would be a while before it would be safe to look at it, but he already knew it was something very important.

CIED

Chad was preparing for the team meeting with the "hot shots." This was to be the first meeting to scope out the project, its milestones, timing, and resources. He was excited and frustrated at the same time. Chad said aloud to no one in the office, "Where are those goddamned notes? I know they are here some place." He checked on his desk by moving every piece of paper and folder. The table was next, where he moved the stacks of books and a stack of papers around. Nothing there. We'll be able to recreate the notes but that is not the issue. The issue is where have they gone and does someone else have them? I hope I haven't screwed up big time. Chad's face flushed and he felt a tinge of anxiety as he quickly checked the wastebaskets. Nothing there either.

"Oh, shit" was what came next from his mouth. He sat down in his desk chair and thought about the notes. After the award event and banquet, he had gone home, taken the notes out of his inside coat pocket and placed the program face up on his desk. He remembered because his wife, Marge, had asked, "How was the event?"

"It was great and my guys won the technology awards. Maybe next year the company will get off this confidentiality kick and open the award event to spouses and significant others."

"I hope so."

Chad's mind was racing now. He remembered the pamphlet was on his desk undisturbed all weekend. He had picked it up Monday morning from exactly the same place on the desk and put it into his coat pocket to take to work. As he arrived at the office, he took off his coat, removed the program, and tossed it onto his table. Chad thought deeply now. Yes, I put it on that stack of papers and I remember that the backside or notes side was up. It had caught his eye that it was next to the book on acoustics and thought how appropriate. I did not move it so it was there all day. I worked at the table a lot and things may have gotten pushed around, but it should still be here. The door was locked all last night until I arrived this morning. I don't remember seeing it this morning, but I wasn't looking for it either. Then it hit him! His nine o'clock appointment, Omar Kharif, was at the table nearest to where he remembered the NOTES were last. He checked the floor and chairs. No luck. It had to have been Mr. Kharif who took the notes. Who was this guy really and what was his offer to help us with our technology needs all about? And, Mr. Kumat greasing the skids with my boss, Mike Jackson, in order to hasten the establishment of a joint technology venture? I might have to contact Mr. Kharif and confront him directly about the lost NOTES.

Chad looked at his watch and said, "Good God, I'm ten minutes late for the meeting."

He grabbed his coat and raced for the conference room just down the hall. Everyone was there; in fact they were busily recreating the notes they had all seen in their first meeting at the hotel after the awards event. Chad decided not to say anything about the lost NOTES. As he walked closer to the table, they all said hi without raising their heads and continued working. The only parts they needed help on were the letters for the title CIED and that it meant close-in explosives detection and meanings for EFP's or explosively formed penetrants and IED's or improvised explosive devices. Everything was there, including the words *data crunching* changed to d*ata augmentation.*

Chad started by saying, "We have been contacted by the government to take on a special project in the area of Close-In Explosives Detection. A new federal government department has been formed recently called Department of Advanced Technology. The president appointed and Congress confirmed Secretary Grant Adams to head it up. They will consolidate all government and government sponsored work of identifying, developing, and protecting advanced technology for the future. Secretary Adams came to see us recently about this special project because of our record with government contracts and business success. He knew that we had to have people like you "hot shots" was his terminology and technology positions that are way ahead of anybody else. He made a special request to tackle a problem that we have and put our best people and best technologies on it. The problem he outlined was rather frightful but known to everybody. It is constant, never-ending, and actually taking the lifeblood of our people and our nation both physically and mentally. Secretary Adams said we have to solve the problem before more lives are lost and fear overcomes us as a people and a nation. We are a courageous people; we go to war for a reason, we fight, and we die for the cause and mostly we win. Today, we are in danger of losing that courage because the problem, as bad as it is on the battlefield, is evolving into other areas. We have to stop it before it grows and we are encased with fear. Stop it on the battlefield and before it gets to our cities and our civilian men, women, and children."

"The problem Secretary Adams was talking about that is creating this fear includes: suicide bombers, car bombers, EFPs, IEDs and the like. The government wants a way to detect these makeshift killing machines that promote fear and resignation. More so, it wants to be able to safely detonate the devices at short and long distances. Our first assignment is the short distance detection, which is why the project is called Close-In Explosives Detection."

Chad stopped a minute and asked, "Are there any questions up to this point?"

There were none so Chad continued. "This is a one-year project, top secret, everything classified and any resources you require. Why you? This new department, DoAT, has been evaluating all kinds of technology for the last several months. They believe we have most of what is needed and the keys are acoustical, microelectromechanical air collection, and chemical detection and data crunching, I mean data accumulation, interpretation and augmentation technologies. In spades, this is why you have been chosen for the project. They also have been watching what is to be a small start up led by Dr. Bradford Tully, who was previously with the non-profit, General Petroleum Research Institute. He took technology that was being developed there and was allowed to spin it off into an IPO of sorts. Bill, do you know him? He seems to be focused on acoustical wave generation with bounce-back features and generating standards for materials found in oil fields."

"Yes, I know of some of his work. He hasn't published much but I heard him give a couple of presentations. Seems to know his stuff but he's a little testy sometimes."

Chad thought, sounds just like you, Bill.

Zen raised her hand, "I know Dr. Tully from Stanford. We went to school together. I hate to admit it, but he is brilliant – maybe the most brilliant scientist and technologist I have ever known. He graduated in three years and that had never been done before at Stanford. I met him unexpectedly at the ACS conference on chemical sensing in Minneapolis yesterday. He is working in acoustical technology but could not or would not say much about it. He is also looking for a location for his new company in the Minneapolis-St. Paul area of Minnesota." She shifted a bit in her seat and said, "I told him to consider Boston and to stay in touch."

Chad continued, "Okay, all this may come in handy as we get into our project. In addition, they have been watching Customized Materials Technology run by Joe Blackstone. They have products and expertise in detonation technology and could also come in handy for our project. Anybody know anyone at Customized Materials Technology? Kan D raised her hand and said, " It has been a long time but I know one of their people, Thomas Kramley. He was their representative for company scholarships, fellowships, and technology grants to some major universities. I received a fellowship from CMT at Michigan several years ago."

Chad said, "Thomas Kramley, yes I know him too. He was CMT's contact at Berkeley, too. I'll have our business intelligence people start compiling all the information available on Bradford Tully's acoustical technology and his progress on an IPO or whatever he calls it, on CMT's detonation technology and products and on Thomas Kramley's recent activities at Michigan and Berkeley. The government will help us as much as they can. Secretary Adams said he had just appointed a new director, Sam Elson, who will be our key contact. He is a psychologist, with some special skills in augmented adaptive reasoning or AAR."

Lyncoln chimed in with "Hey, I know him! He is from the University of Virginia and has done some great work in Data Augmentation. This is going to be an interesting project."

Chad resumed with, "That is all the background and information that I have."

"What are we going to do first?" Kan D asked. "Let's sketch out the rough product or system definition and needs. That will help us see where the bottlenecks are."

Chad had ordered lunch and it arrived at noon. He left and went back to his office. The team worked through lunch and into the late afternoon, knowing this was probably the most important part of the project. What was the target?

Kan D went to get Chad to show him what they had come up with so far. Chad walked into the conference room with Kan D and saw the walls filled with flip chart pages, all in some order and leading to two final pages entitled: CIED-Definitions and Needs and CIED-Activities, Timing, Milestone, and Resources.

CIED-Definitions and Needs:

- *Close-in* means at or less than 100 feet.
- An *explosive* means all components of standard and new systems known today.
- *Detection* means rapid analysis and identification of all chemical components.
- Acoustical Wave Generation equipment - Bill's work is a start; reversal technology needs further development; decibel level needs optimization; miniaturization will be challenging.
- Wave front air collection and analysis - Zen's work is a start; high power vacuum cleaner needed; chemical standards on all explosive components needed; chemical sensor and identification technology mostly available; miniaturization will be challenging.
- MEMS and System Miniaturization- Kan D's work is a start; sound wave generation equipment and vacuum cleaner equipment miniaturization technology needs further development.
- Data Collection, Interpretation and Augmentation- Lyncoln's work is close to what is thought to be needed.
- Detonation Technology- We have none in-house. Will standard detonation technology be acceptable? If not, we need a cooperative program with Customized Materials Technology.

CIED
Activities/Timing Milestones and Resources

Month	Activity Completion	Staff (20)	Budget $5MM	Leaders
April	Chemical Standards	2		Zen/Lyncoln
May	Sensors/Data Augmentation	3	$1MM	Zen/Lyncoln
June	Analysis			All
July	AWG Decibels	2	$0.5MM	Bill
August	Analysis			All
September	AWG Reversal	3	$0.5MM	Bill
October	Analysis			All
November	Vacuum Cleaner	2	$1MM	Zen
December	Analysis			All
January	Miniaturization	4	$1MM	Kan D
February	Analysis			All
March	Field Test	All	$1MM	All

Chad smiled at his four protégés and said, "This looks really good! You start identifying the people you need and I'll get them transferred ASAP. The money is no problem. Start ordering equipment, software, and materials immediately. Let's get to work."

Bill, Zen, Lyncoln, and Kan D looked at each other, nodded, picked up their stuff and started to leave.

Chad said, "Another thing - You will all be in new office space and laboratories located in this building. The movers will be at your old locations by the time you get back. Just tell them what goes and what stays and they will work until the move is completed. Welcome to Building 220."

Chapter 3

The Theft of Acoustics Detonation Technology

Firm Up the Third Project

Thomas arrived at the Squealing Pig early. He asked for the same table as before and ordered his happy hour beers. Two bottles of New Castle arrived at about the same time he heard the sound of the pig squeal, then saw Omar walk through the door carrying his briefcase. Thomas saw him look at the back table where they had sat before and waved his hand.

Omar waved back and headed for the table. He was smiling when he arrived and said, "I will never get used to the sound of the squealing pig when the door opens."

Thomas said, "I know, nor will I. The beers just arrived so please be seated and we can talk."

"Thank you." Omar picked up the large glass and took a big drink. "Thomas, I bring good news! I was able to get permission for you to test Mach II."

Thomas took a drink and said, "I thought you would, so I have done some pre-work to get ready. We have a production run this week. It will be a short run of that new product for a special customer that I told you about. We will be able to track each package as it travels its path to the customer, then take corrective measures if something goes awry. That will be fantastic. Our people are very excited about this, too! They have shared with me that the packages will travel a very circuitous path to their final destination of Israel. It is a safety precaution. I will be given the route only at the last minute. Will that matter with our test?"

"No way, in fact it is even better. A complex route will be the best way to test Mach II. Remember, the GPS will be able to track the packages no matter how many stops or where they are. The software will alert us if the sensors pick up anything abnormal or if the packages need a course correction. This is perfect!"

Thomas finished his beer and signaled the waiter to bring two more. "Okay, then we can proceed if you can get the new tags to me with the instructions as to how they are synchronized with the software."

"I have everything you will need, Thomas, in my briefcase. Ten tags, software, upgrade instructions, and special codes."

"I think we will have up to fifteen packages, but it will be okay. They do not all have to be tagged to go as one shipment."

Omar opened his briefcase and took out a colorfully wrapped box. "This is a small gift for your son. I hope he will like some superhero comic books."

"He certainly will, because his illness makes him less mobile than a ten-year-old would like. He loves comic books and reading is more desirable than television from my perspective. Thank you very much for being so thoughtful, Omar."

"No problem." Omar reached into his briefcase again and this time brought out the package with the Mach II tags, software upgrade instructions, and codes. "Don't open it here; give me a call if you have any questions. Okay?"

"Good idea."

The beers arrived and as they drank, Omar said, "I don't think I gave you an update about my trip to Berkeley last month. It went well, of course, it always does when you are presenting a gift. Do you know that in the course of our meeting and discussion, a couple of other names came up?"

"What names?"

"One was Chadly Bromcast of Advanced Technology

Products. I actually had a chance to meet him recently when I visited the company. They had had a technology award event and I got his name from the newspaper article about the award winners."

"Yes, I know him. He is a graduate of Berkeley and also a peer in the business that is similar but non-competitive to ours. He has done well at ATP."

"Yes, I would say so. I also recall the name Kan Deng Shin came up in our discussion of nanotechnology and that Chad had hired her from Michigan. As was explained, you are also the CMT representative to the University of Michigan for scholarships, fellowships, and technology grants. You seemed to be the connecting point with Berkeley, Michigan, Dr. Bromcast and Dr. Shin. I bring this up because Dr. Shin was one of the Advanced Technology Products technology award winners. One of four, so she was in very select company."

"Yes, I know Kan D very well. Our clipping service found the article about her award. Customized Materials Technology was instrumental in funding some of her research at Michigan. She was one of their top students. For Chad and Kan D both to be at Advanced Technology Products is a real advantage for them. In fact, I may have heard that she is going to be working with Chad on a special project."

Omar thought, So the newspaper article on the awards event was right and Chad was lying to him.

"Interesting. It is probably time for me to return to the San Francisco office. Good that we could connect this way at the Squealing Pig and get our third test set up. We are 100% positive that you will be very pleased with what Mach II can do for you."

"I have things ready so you will find out starting this week. Thank you for getting permission for us to be involved in such an important and advanced technology."

"You are welcome, Thomas. Remember that this helps us immensely to validate the technology and gather data on its actual field performance. We are in this together. I'll be in touch in a week or so to check on results. In the meantime, if you need something, please call me immediately."

"Thank you, Omar, I will."

Both men got up and left together with the noise of the Squealing Pig echoing in the parking lot.

The Plan to Steal Detonation Technology

Omar arrived at the San Francisco office and immediately got in touch with the leader of his people in Israel. He covered the job, logistics, and timing in general and then got to the specifics. "There are only a few airports in Israel that can take large cargo planes. You will have to identify them and establish teams to be able to cover each one. I suggest four-man teams dressed as airport workers with the proper credentials for certain access to the cargo arrival areas. I would estimate that the trip, even with extraneous stops, would take two or three days. You will have to move fast to be ready. To be clear, this is of very high priority for our organization and our mission. We must try to acquire this new technology. The shipment will probably be bundled with Customized Materials Technology markings all over it. The bundle will have up to fifteen separate packages and ten of them will be tagged with the Mach II RFID tags with special sensors, GPS, and the data augmentation software capability. They are being tracked and monitored constantly, of course, by CMT. Do not tamper with or otherwise mishandle those ten packages with the Mach II tags. If you do, it will be detected by the sensors, interpreted by the data augmentation software and you will be caught, as they say, *red handed*. Simply remove the untagged packages, probably numbered 11 and higher, and re-tape the bundle. There are no tags, no software to worry about on these so just put them on a cart and take them to the plane that should be waiting in the area. I have arranged for a Damascus based G-5, silver in color, and a "squealing pig" painted on the tail for your use. The pilot you choose should have a manifest that shows his return destination is Damascus and be ready to go. Any questions?"

The leader said, "No tactical questions but what is your guidance on how much force we should use if something happens?"

"Very good question! The detonation technology is high

priority for our organization as I mentioned. We believe it is very sophisticated technology and a significant advance over the state-of-the-art. However, we also believe that it is untested and may need further development before it can be commercialized. We view this shipment as product for a field test and expect that they will find some performance areas that will have to be improved. It is going to what was called a *special customer* (probably government and military) in Israel so they must be close to the product performance they were targeting. For that reason, we believe that this attempt to acquire the product/technology is necessary. Our people can reverse engineer it and, if needed, make additional improvements. We must try our damnedest to be successful but do not use deadly force. There will be a second chance because of our partnership with CMT and our contact there."

"Okay, but I cannot guarantee we will not use deadly force because we must recognize the possibility of the capture of our people."

"I know, you must choose the people for the teams well. You know what I mean."

"I do. We will be ready. Praise be to Allah!"

"Thank you, Praise be to Allah. Goodbye."

Minneapolis It Is

Brad was tired of looking for the perfect location for his company. He decided it would be Minnesota and specifically, Minneapolis.

In his line of work, he was going to have to travel all over the U.S. and the rest of the world. Why not be in the Midwest, as Minnesotans call it? Besides, he really liked what he saw on his recent trip. The Twin Cities of Minneapolis and St. Paul have everything ... an international airport, Minneapolis Institute of Art, The Guthrie Theatre, The Walker Art Museum, the Vikings football team, the Twins baseball team, the Timberwolves basketball team, the University of Minnesota, etc. The water is clean, the air is smog-free, traffic is not too bad, and the people are nice. What more can you ask for these days?

Besides all of this, there were other pluses that made the choice easy. The state has a host of Fortune 500 companies (many more than you would expect for its population and location) and it is known for its high-tech businesses and its innovation. It has 10,000 lakes - but even better, it has the Mississippi River. It has the University of Minnesota with the number-one -rated chemical engineering department in the country.

Brad had talked with a couple of venture capital companies in Minneapolis-St. Paul and thought that by locating there while maintaining contacts on the West Coast and in Texas, he would have a good chance of becoming funded.

He made the call to the real estate broker and rented living, office, and laboratory space all in one building in the warehouse district not too far from where the new Twins stadium was about to open for its first season. It was a lot of money from his savings account all at one time, but the location was great. He would have a light rail line and great access to the city, airport, sports, and culture. And, the mighty Mississippi was only five minutes away.

It was time to move north and get going on this new venture. He thought everything from his office and apartment would fit into his SUV. He'd get packed, say his goodbyes on the weekend, and depart on Monday morning. He had asked GPRI to send his equipment after he got to Minneapolis. It was a daunting task! What does he know about starting a new company? Can he really get money from investors, make the necessary technical breakthroughs, and begin to sell technology or product and make money? Time would tell.

CMT's Special Product

Thomas reviewed the production schedule and details of the very first run of the special product. He noticed the circuitous path for its final destination, Israel. He also noticed that there would be fifteen packages, more than he had tags for. Okay, okay, he thought, ten tags, fifteen packages; it will be fine. I will see that they go as one intact shipment so we will be over-tracking anyway.

He could feel his face flush and he felt hot and tingly all at the same time. Thomas said out loud, "As long as they stay as one intact shipment, but what if they don't?" He thought fast, noting it would still be okay. We would not be tracking any of them were it not for my initiative and the help of Omar and TIC. Better to track some than none. Thomas gave the go ahead to start the production run. It was a short run and went flawlessly. He had decided to put tags on the packages numbered 1-10 and not packages numbered 11-15. His computer and the data augmentation software were working perfectly. The readouts on the ten tagged packages were all the same ... no activity on the sensors; the location was identified as the CMT plant in San Francisco.

Thomas looked again at the transportation route and memorized all the stops and the final destination, which was the Zefat airport near the Golan Heights. Once the product leaves the plant, it will take about two days to get there. This is going to be an interesting 48 hours. I will have to work some on the weekend.

The Shipment Goes to Israel

Thomas arrived at his office early Saturday morning, anxious to see how things were going with the special product shipment. He logged in on the computer and used the special code to activate the RFID and data augmentation software. Up popped a map of the world showing San Francisco as the starting point and the Zefat International Airport in Israel as its final destination. There, blinking on the screen were ten Customized Materials Technology logos headed for Anchorage, Alaska. From there, stops were indicated for London, Frankfort, and finally Zefat. With all the stops, starts, and time changes, Thomas saw that the new software was estimating that the product would arrive in Israel on Sunday night or Monday morning. The GPS and software were working fine. He pointed to the sensor's icon and clicked. The next screen showed all the sensors within the RFID system. The temperature and time data were as expected and the readings for chemicals, radiation, pressures, vibrations, shock, etc.

were all indicating normal for air cargo transport environment. Everything was fine.

Thomas thought further. This Mach II product is going to be perfect for us. Customized Materials Technology will have a big advantage over its competition if I can negotiate an exclusive arrangement at least for some limited timeframe. Then Thomas said aloud to himself, "I just have to come back later tonight to see how things are going as the cargo travels to its next stop. Joe would be very pleased."

He shut the system down and left the office. As he walked past the guard desk, the guard said, "Another special project Mr. Kramley?"

"Yes, and I'll be back again around dinner time."

"Good day, sir."

"See you later."

Thomas arrived at the plant about 7 PM. He swiped his pass through the scanner and greeted the guard.

The guard said, "Good evening, Mr. Kramley. There was a note left by my colleague that you would be back around dinner time."

"Yes, but I will be just a few minutes this time. Thanks."

Thomas walked to his office, turned the lights on, and immediately booted up the computer to get into the tracking system. He said quietly, "The transfer in Anchorage has been made and the plane is in the air to London. Looks like an hour or two out." Clicking on the sensor icon, he saw all systems saying, "normal for air cargo transport environment."

Thomas thought that things were going just like clockwork. Nothing can happen in the air so I think I can leave and come back tomorrow. He turned the computer off, turned the lights off, and walked out, closing the door behind himself.

As Thomas approached the guard desk, he said, "Please tell your replacement that I plan to come back in tomorrow, probably after church so around noon"

"Yes, sir, I will tell him."

"Good night."

"Good night, sir."

As Thomas approached the guard desk the next day, he was realizing that this was the third time he had been in that weekend. He hoped his boss appreciated how hard he had worked on this new technology project. Once again, he swiped his pass through the scanner and the new guard said, "Good afternoon, Mr. Kramley. You have been here a lot this weekend."

"Good afternoon. Hopefully, I will not be too long this time. Maybe a few hours."

"Yes, sir. Sir you should know that Mr. Blackstone just arrived five minutes ago."

"That's interesting," Thomas said as he headed toward his office.

The lights in the office were on and there was Joe Blackstone, president of Customized Materials Technology, sitting in a chair near Thomas's desk and computer.

"Mr. Blackstone, it is good to see you on a Sunday afternoon." They shook hands and Thomas said, "You are about the last person I would have expected to see here today."

"I know, Thomas, and sorry you weren't given any advance notice. Through our discussions and your reports, I have been following your work with Technology Investment Corporation and have been very impressed. The combined capability test that you are running this weekend, RFID/GPS and data augmentation, is so novel and so made to order for what we do. I wanted to come in and see how it is going."

Thomas sat down at the computer and said, "As of last night, everything was fine and our shipment was headed for London. Let's see if it has arrived in Frankfurt yet." Thomas got the computer going and brought up the GPS map showing the product location. Mr. Blackstone had pulled his chair in close so he could see. The path was outlined, San Francisco, Anchorage, London, Frankfurt, and there were the blinking Customized Materials Technology logos. All ten of them were there positioned in a tight circle just south of Frankfurt.

Mr. Blackstone said, "What a fantastic display. What else do we know?"

"We know the transfer in Frankfurt has already occurred and the shipment is headed to Zefat. Let's see if the sensors have picked up any abnormalities since I last checked."

Thomas clicked on the sensor icon and a second screen opened.

Mr. Blackstone said, "Wow! I did not know that we could test for all of these things."

"Yes, we can and in fact, as you know, any abnormality will be interpreted by the data augmentation algorithm and recommendations provided immediately for any necessary adjustment."

Thomas continued, "See here on the shock data, the readings all say '50 foot pounds, outside the normal range for an air cargo transport environment.' In addition, data augmentation indicates that since all the readings are exactly the same, the product bundle has been dropped. Its estimate is from a height of about ten feet."

"Look at this, Mr. Blackstone. Data augmentation has taken packaging, product design, safety parameters, etc. into account and has come up with a recommendation. Data augmentation's input is that there is a 99.99% likelihood that product is undamaged and therefore the system recommends no action."

"This is great," replied Blackstone. "Without this kind of monitoring, we would never know about the actual condition of the product until our customer receives it. If something had happened, by then it may be too late to salvage the relationship. Also, with data from all these sensors, we can tell immediately if someone is up to no good. That will help to protect our intellectual property."

"Yes, sir," Thomas agreed. "It would be a major competitive advantage for us if we could secure some kind of exclusive arrangement with TIC. Do you think that might be possible?"

"Maybe so, but let's get through the test first and then we will have time to talk about next steps a little later."

"Okay, you got a deal! Look, data augmentation is estimating the time of arrival at Zefat to be in about an hour. Do you want to hang around and see that things go well at Zefat?"

"Yes, I do," said Blackstone. "I will advise our people there when to expect the shipment to arrive. Our customer had stressed that if possible they want to meet the shipment and take possession of the product at the airport."

"I will call TIC and tell them that everything is going very well indeed. I need to call my wife, too, and tell her that I'll be a little later than I estimated."

Blackstone had the special satellite phone with him so he left the office to make his call. Thomas stayed in his office to make his calls.

"Hello, Omar, I want to share some very good news. The shipment of 15 boxes of special product will touch down in about an hour in Zefat, Israel. Everything has been working perfectly during the test. We even had a sensor that read a shock and interpreted it to be a dropped bundle. The recommendation was, "product is undamaged, no action necessary."

"This is very good news, Thomas."

Thomas continued, "I also had a surprise visit by the president of the company, Joe Blackstone. He has been observing and monitoring the shipment with me for the past hour or so. If he can, he is going to have both our people and the customer's people there to receive the shipment. This technology really impresses him. By addressing the quality of the product for the customer and security of intellectual property for the company, TIC has done something very significant for our business."

"Thank you. Can we talk more next week, Thomas? I want to get the whole story from beginning to end."

"Of course, maybe you can call on Tuesday or Wednesday."

"I will," said Omar. "Goodbye."

"Until next week. Goodbye."

Thomas called his wife next but got no answer. He left the message ... "Hi, Hon. I'll be home a little later than planned. It will probably be a couple more hours. The president of the company dropped by to see how the project is going. He is very impressed with the new technology and wants to stay a little longer. Love ya, bye."

Thomas went back to watching the screens and how Mach II was performing for them. The plane and special product shipment were about to arrive at the Zefat airport.

Omar Contacts 'Leader' and Zefat Team

Immediately upon finishing his call with Thomas, Omar called the organization's leader in Israel. "Leader, it is going to be Zefat - 15 boxes, just as we had thought. Get your team there ready to go. You probably have about an hour before the plane touches down. My contact at Customized Materials Technology in San Francisco just called and confirmed the timing. He also said that the president of CMT was there with him monitoring the flight of the product and that he was going to try to have CMT people and customer people there to receive the shipment. You'll have to work fast. Since your team is already in place, there may be a window of time before the others arrive. One more thing, the shipment had been dropped in route so there may be some slight damage."

"I had guessed Zefat! I am here so I will be part of the team. We will capture the product and get it to Damascus."

"Thank you, Leader. Remember, no deadly force, but try everything possible to get that product for us."

"Praise be to Allah!" shouted the leader.

The leader made the call to Damascus for the plane to come to Zefat and then assembled his team and briefed them on their mission again. He stressed to avoid using deadly force and if capture was imminent, take the suicide route. "We are the lucky ones, praise be to Allah!" They got into position and waited for the one cargo plane arriving from Frankfurt.

The plane arrived right on time. As the tires met the runway, there was the usual screech and puff of smoke from the burnt rubber. The plane taxied to the cargo arrival area.

The waiting men in their black airport worker coveralls and ID tags around their necks could see the G-5 with what looked like a pig logo on the tail. Their weapons were hidden with arm sheath knives and leg holster 9 mm pistols. They had done jobs like this before.

The plane arrived at the off-loading area, the engines powered down, and the cargo bay doors opened. It was at that point that the leader and his team headed for the plane. He knew there would be some confusion since the real off-loading team had also arrived to start unloading. He had had authentic looking documents drawn up that allowed opening the bundle and removing five of the fifteen boxes. The orders were that the five boxes would be taken by private plane (G-5, squealing pig on the tail) to a confidential location nearby. The orders looked real and official.

The leader and his men arrived at the dock. He announced, "There has been a glitch in the shipment of product by Customized Materials Technology in San Francisco. There were two shipments bundled together accidentally. I have orders from CMT and the airport to separate the boxes and get them to the right customers. The boxes look different in that ten of them have RFID tags and go to one customer; five do not have RFID tags and go to a different customer." He could actually see the CMT bundle or pallet, shrink-wrapped and standing just inside the cargo plane's open door. "Yes, that is it right there! I can see the CMT logo on the boxes through the clear wrapping. They also told me the pallet had been dropped somehow during its transfer to this plane at its last stop, Frankfurt, Germany." The leader shifted his position, looked carefully at the pallet and said, "Yes, see there. The edge has been broken off. It looks like the boxes are okay, though. Mind if we do our work and get out of your way?"

The real off-loading crew chief said, "Let me see your orders first." He looked at the papers closely and was satisfied. "Go ahead and be quick about it."

"Men, open the shrinkwrap and remove the boxes without tags, probably numbered 11-15." The three men jumped into the plane; one tore the shrink-wrap open just enough to get the boxes out. They were fortunate in that the five boxes were all on top. The pallet had been loaded starting with box #1, five boxes to a layer, and three layers high. What they wanted was the top layer of boxes.

The boxes were removed one by one and handed to the

leader who put them on a large warehouse cart that he had positioned nearby just for this purpose. "See here, no tags on these. They are the ones." Two men jumped out of the plane, took charge of the cart, and started toward the waiting G-5. The other man in the plane was given some tape by the leader to seal the shrink-wrap. With that done, the leader said to the others waiting, "Thank you very much. I'm sure this will please CMT and they will give our airport high praise for correcting their mistake." He paused a moment then continued, "I was told that the customer for the remainder of the product on the pallet will be here shortly to take delivery. I hope we haven't caused too much of a delay in off-loading the shipment. Thank you."

"No problem, it only took five minutes so we can get back on schedule easily. Thanks for telling us about CMT customer coming to get his product; that is not normal procedure either. It's a strange day."

The leader said, "Thanks, again," then he and the other man ran to catch up with the two men pushing the cart toward the G-5. They could see the pilot waving at them as they got closer. They were within less than one hundred feet when all hell broke loose.

There were sirens, flashing lights, cars and trucks coming from every direction converging on the G-5 and them. The leader could see that the mission had failed so he issued two hurried orders. He and his team would run for the get-away cars that they had stashed in case something like this would happen just beyond the runway where the G-5 was waiting. Second, as he caught the pilot's eye, he made a slashing motion with his right hand across his throat. The pilot nodded that he understood. The leader picked up one of the boxes and he and his men ran, leaving the rest of the product sitting on the runway. The leader looked back to see the pilot slumped down onto the control panel. He thought the capsules containing this new poison really acted fast. He was glad they didn't have to use their own. They reached the cars on the service road and took off, two in each car. There had been no shots fired at them and no pursuit. He thought that was strange, too, but that is the way of the infidels.

Director Sam Elson

From the time of his appointment as Director of Technology Protection in the DoAT, Sam Elson and his people had been watching several key technologies, companies, and experts. They were the movers and shakers in government contracts and military technology and products. Customized Materials Technology was one of those principal players.

Sam was reading the report of the attempted theft of their new detonation technology in Israel.....*Director, please note:*
All product safe at Zefat airport; Four-man team escaped to cars hidden on a service road; No shots fired and no pursuit taken; Pilot found dead in the cockpit of the G-5, poison suspected; Manifest read his destination was to be Damascus; Mossad will investigate and keep you informed; Good luck on your end.
Sam thought, we were extremely lucky on this one. I was watching but we did not have intelligence to indicate something was very wrong about this shipment of advanced technology product. Since the customer was the Mossad, they had been watching and listening, too. It was they who picked up on the call from the States indicating that product was to be stolen at the Zefat airport and taken to Damascus. They also have more information on the man called "Leader" in Israel. It is my job to find out who was on the other end of that call, and I need to do that fast. I also need to call Joe Blackstone at CMT and tell him he screwed up. We'll have to investigate this one, big time.

Director Elson Talks with Absek

"Hello, Absek, how are things in your country?"

"Fine, Sam, every new day is filled with new opportunities. What can I do for you today?"

"First, on behalf of government I want to thank you for stopping the theft of Customized Materials Technology's experimental product. Your team intercepted the call and acted very expeditiously. What a system of advanced technology you must have in place. Do you know anything about the call and caller?"

"Not a lot, Sam. We caught the call because the president of Customized Materials Technology advised us that the shipment was coming in. It was only then that our listening technology went into peak operating mode. We know the call came from the States, maybe Washington, D.C., and was made on a special satellite phone. We are working to identify the caller using our voice recognition technology. We need more time and I am fairly sure we'll be successful. The voice was only about 50% garbled to our receivers; that is good news."

"Yes, and thank goodness you got enough to intercept. Is there anything else you can tell me?"

"Of course, we were able to discern Zefat as the airport location, and that the special shipment was arriving in about an hour's time. That was all we needed to act. There were other words that were somewhat discernable and translatable, like 'Customized Materials Technology contact, president, leader and no deadly force'. They usually have aliases or code names of some kind but in all my years with the Mossad, I have never heard 'no deadly force.' A little strange. Oh, yes, one more thing. The pilot who committed suicide rather than be captured used a rather deadly poison. His blood work showed it took only a very minute amount and we are still trying to identify it. We may need your help on this; I will let you know. His name was Kharif, Emar Kharif, as identified from records we can access. Does that help? It is about all we have at this time."

"It does help, Absek, thank you very much. You should know that I will be starting an investigation at Customized Materials Technology."

And, I will be investigating who this 'Leader' is and, of course, the pilot. Let's keep talking, Sam. We have to stop these terrorists."

"Thank you, Absek. Talk with you later."

Call from the Liberator to Omar

Omar had been waiting for the prearranged phone call. He was back in D.C. after the Boston trip and was very anxious to tell the

Liberator his news. His cell phone rang just once and Omar answered immediately, "Omar speaking."

"Hello, Omar. I hope you had a good trip to Boston."

"I did, sir. It was very eventful and I'll tell you why."

"Omar, just spit it out."

"I have some secret or confidential notes about a special acoustical project at Advanced Technology Products that have just come into my possession."

"Please tell me, Omar, that you have brought no adverse attention to our work, our cause. Tell me that these lost notes will not cause a huge internal and external investigation and that the police will not be brought in."

In a very quiet voice, Omar responded, "I don't think so, sir. I made an appointment to visit ATP after reading a newspaper article about their technology awards. There were references to acoustical technology. The notes were on the floor of Dr. Chadly Bromcast's office at ATP. When I saw the word "acoustical" all over the page, I just reacted, picked them up, and put them into my coat pocket. Dr. Bromcast saw nothing and probably is still trying to figure out what happened to them. It has been a few days since the meeting and he has not called to see if I mistakenly picked them up from the table. I think that is what he would have done because there was so much stuff on the table where we sat and talked."

"Good. Maybe we will get lucky! What do the notes say about acoustical technology?"

"It was written on the back of a program for the technology awards event given by Advanced Technology Products recently. Everything was there. Some of the words written on the left side were *Acoustics, Air Collection/Chemical Detection, Data Crunching,* and *'MEMS' technology* and there were also the names of people assigned to each. In the middle was written *Acoustical beam* or *wave-front*. On the right side the words *targets, IEDs, EFPs, suicide bombers*, and *car bombers*. On top, were the letters *CIED* and on the bottom the words *need detonation technology*. I think it is a new weapon to be used against us, sir."

"My Omar, you may have stumbled onto something

THE CAMPAIGN OF FEAR

extremely important! Protect the sketch with your life and let's see if we can figure out how to further penetrate ATP's secret project."

"I will, sir. The timing may be just right because I believe the project is now starting to be developed and resourced. When I was talking to Dr. Bromcast, he denied that the new technology award winners would be teamed up on a special project, as his quote in the newspaper maybe implied, but I think he was lying. Based on this, we may even know who the team leader will be for the special project. The information might help us as we start the information gathering process. Dr. Bromcast and I covered what TIC does and how we do it. It was interesting for him that the key technologies represented by the award winners were all accounted for on our Top Ten Technology list. I told him this is where we are making major investments and business decisions. Therefore, we are quite connected to universities and industrial companies. He seemed very impressed that it was all on our website."

Omar continued, "He knows that we have technology and that we do joint ventures, licensing, cooperative programs, technology mergers, and acquisitions. I sensed that he knows he will need help in some of these technology areas and might seek us out. It could be how we penetrate the special project from an early stage. Note that I did bring up that a principal of our company, Patek Kumat, had met the Advanced Technology Products CTO, Mike Jackson. I mentioned they had talked about a potential joint venture or some other type of business arrangement about technology. The way I put it was that because of this meeting, if he and Dr. Bromcast identified a technology need, it would be easy sailing to make something happen."

"Thank you, Omar. You have made wonderful progress in just a few months."

"Thank you, sir. There are a couple other things that might relate to our cause, that I have uncovered. I made contact sometime ago with Customized Materials Technology, a detonation technology company of worldwide reputation. I discovered they are also doing new work in sound wave technology. It was just luck that I was going to Berkeley to present an unrestricted research grant and had found that Thomas Kramley is CMT's representative to the university for scholarships, fellowships, grants, and the like. We talked and for reasons I won't go into here, I recruited him to do contract work in logistics and supply chain management for TIC. In the last several months, he has done a great deal of work for us. Because he needs money, he is willing to take some risks. In fact, the last job was to see if we could get certain new products from CMT close to or into Syria. It was a test to see how far he would go and how good he was."

Omar continued, "The product got stopped by the U.S. and Israeli governments but I don't think there will be any repercussions." The Liberator grimaced as Omar said, "We might be able to use him further when the time comes."

Omar went on to say, "Second, I also made contact with GPRI recently and tried to get access to their acoustical technology work. They have had a project the last two years on bounce-back acoustical wave technology led by a Dr. Bradford Tully, who people say is a brilliant scientist and technologist. The information is supposed to be public information but I could not get access to it. I basically threatened the head of the organization to get the project reports but he would not budge. Then, a few days later, I found out that Dr. Tully is leaving the organization and taking the technology with him. I read the obligatory announcement and final reports. Although they refer to the search for new oil, I believe the technology could be used for other applications. I am watching Dr. Tully closely to discover where he will set up his private venture. He was in Minneapolis recently attending a conference on chemical sensing and checking out the Twin Cities as a location for Tully Research, Incorporated."

Omar continued, "Things seem to be converging on acoustical technology, just as you said. We have Customized Materials Technology, with its detonation technology products, now involved in acoustical technology projects; Dr. Tully and his GPRI work on bounce-back acoustical wave technology with a focus on creating a new private company and Advanced Technology Products with its special project that is sketched out in the acquired confidential information. My investigation indicates that none of these are connected at this time. Further, I don't believe ATP, Tully, or CMT know anything about the others' projects. They might know some of the project participants but just because they are the leaders in the field or have some other connection related to their alma mater or something."

"I think you are right, Omar."

"Sir, it is my recommendation that we stay focused on these three parts. From all the work I have done, they seem to be the most important pieces of the puzzle. We have a head start now at ATP with the sketch and names of the possible project leaders. I propose to get more information through them when they attend conferences, seminars, and so forth. Also, I'll keep the pressure on their CTO and project manager to consider some kind of technology partnership."

"I agree, Omar, with your proposal on Advanced Technology Products."

"Thank you, sir. With Dr. Tully, I propose that we follow his travels and determine where he is going to locate. My guess is that it could be Minneapolis-St. Paul, Minnesota. They are high-tech cities in a high-tech state having proportionally more Fortune 500 companies than any other in the USA. There are military products work and government contract work done by several of these companies, too. Once the location is determined, I also propose that we invest in his venture company. Minnesota is not known for providing a lot of venture capital money to new start-up companies, but with Tully's reputation that could change."

"I agree, Omar, with your proposal for Dr. Tully and his new company. Make the investment large enough that we have access to all his work without any questions. You know what I mean."

"Yes, sir, and thank you, sir. With CMT, I propose we stay in close contact with them to see if we were compromised in any way because of my testing our recruited mole. If not, I will begin the process of having him get us more information about their sound wave program as it relates to detonation technology and products."

"I agree, Omar, with your proposal about CMT."

"Omar, you might have identified the key parts of continuing to win in our Campaign of Fear. Congratulations and good work, but there is much left to do. We must find out exactly what is being done in these acoustical technology areas before the companies realize that their separate results could be combined in ways that would damage us forever. If we know, maybe we can slow or even stop the work with our extensive resources. We must be successful. Praise be to Allah!"

The Liberator continued, "Omar, besides the congratulations, I have a word of caution for you so listen carefully. In your accounting of the events of the recent past, I have noted several areas that give me concern. You initiated a failed program with a recruit at Customized Materials Technology that might result in a federal investigation. You threatened the head of GPRI to get information, and you stole the special project notes while visiting Advanced Technology Products."

The Liberator was raising his voice with each noted concern. He talked faster and with increasing urgency. Omar was glad this was a telephone call and not a personal visit. He would have been even more uncomfortable in a face-to-face conversation.

"Do not put us at further risk, Omar. If you do, someone will connect the dots and trace all of this back to you. If that happens, they might also be able to figure out why we are so interested in acoustical technology in the U.S. Then we are doomed to failure. Keep a low profile and do your job without increasing your visibility. As they say in America, cool it for a while."

"Thank you, sir. I will, sir. I am sorry if I have disappointed you or put us at risk. I will do the work we agreed to but with a different operational style."

"Omar, we still need the results, of course, so you figure out how to get them without drawing attention to us."

"Yes, sir. I will, sir."

The 'visitor' said, "Good luck, Omar" and hung up.

Omar whispered, "I was making great progress, he said so himself. He liked the results but not the way I got them? I didn't think it mattered so much in a situation when we are protecting our most precious asset, the Campaign of Fear. The Liberator commands great respect; I have to be very careful and honor his advice. Can there be a different Omar inside me? I'll try but I am not so hopeful."

Progress on the Project at ATP

The new laboratory space was a hotbed of activity. It had been completed and occupied for only a couple weeks, but by the look of things they were really pumping out results. Laboratory space is usually discreet and compartmentalized with separate rooms with walls and doors. This was all open, sort of like walking into a cafeteria. An entryway led to the center of a huge circular space where the desks of the four project team leaders were located. From the center and radiating outward, were the laboratories for Bill's acoustical work, Zen's chemical collection and detection work, Kan D's MEMS and miniaturization work, and Lyncoln's data augmentation work.

As Chad surveyed the space from the hub, he noticed a few things apart from all the activity. First, he made a mental note that there had to be twenty to twenty-five people working, so staff had already been pulled from other parts of the organization. He would have to check with his manager colleagues to see if any feathers were ruffled. There are lots of politics to worry about when you are in charge of the company's number one project.

Chad noticed that the place was full of equipment and the people who were busily running it. He said to himself, "I am not going to ask how this much equipment got moved here or how it happens to be up and running so fast."

None of his four team leaders was at their desk. He found each of them at a spot in their labs and noted that Zen and Lyncoln were next to each other, probably collaborating on chemical standards and data augmentation. Lyncoln was wearing his Boston Red Sox hat and seated close to a huge array of computers. They seemed to all be connected and had a standing-only-accessible keyboard that could move along the bank of computers. It wasn't Big Blue but I bet he had come pretty close to its capability. There were a couple of people sitting at small desks next to the computers wearing iPods. They were using monitors and keyboards. Chad's guess was that they were writing code.

As his eyes moved to Zen's slice of the pie, he noticed all kinds of analytical equipment: mass spectrometers, nmr's, X-rays, gas chromatographs, anything one could think of for chemical analysis. There were also some wet chemistry lab benches. The equipment seemed to be already linked to the computers. Zen was less senior than the other team leaders but she had flair. She had painted each of the instrument types a certain color: passion pink, purple, orange, etc., and each technician wore a t-shirt. Chad squinted his eyes to read the wording on the t-shirt: "Chemistry is the Answer."

Chad thought to himself, she is going to do fine. Besides collaborating with Lyncoln and the others, she will challenge them. This is what the project needs.

Chad looked for Kan D and spotted her. What a difference in lab space. He saw CAD-CAM's, electronic stuff including breadboards and all the electronic components, test equipment, high powered microscopes, layout tables, everything. Scattered around were bowls of candy that had become Kan D's trademark since she arrived at Advanced Technology Products. She was at a stand-up table with her specialty magnifying glasses positioned on top of her head. A couple of technicians were set up nearby, manning cameras that were projecting images onto monitors. No doubt this was one of the miniature prototypes being developed. Chad thought, Go get 'em, Kan D! We just have to be successful with miniaturization.

Chad heard the sound or maybe he just barely felt it in the soles and toes of his feet. He listened carefully. Yes, there was sort of a buzz but not much beyond that. Bill was hovering over some strange looking equipment that seemed to be the source of the sound and vibration. Chad was about to yell at Bill to see how things were going when both the buzz and the vibration stopped. He thought, Whew, if that were to continue, there would be a problem with getting the other work done.

The acoustic research space was different, too, in that it was mostly equipment. Chad assumed it was both wave generation and reversal and sound dampening equipment. There was an area of the triangle that seemed devoted to specialty materials like ceramics, fibers, papers, etc., in unique designs and shapes. Chad thought, This is what one might see in mufflers, orchestra halls, silencers, ear protectors, and the like. Suddenly, Chad saw Bill turn the dial on the strange looking equipment. The buzz and vibration came back but for only an instant. Then it stopped for a second and started again. Bill tried the cycle of start-stop-start over and over again and seemed to be pleased at the results.

Chad thought to himself, Short distance generation and reversal with very little sound. Wow!

One by one, Chad caught the eye of each team leader and waved them into the hub. They all arrived looking a little dubious. "I want to congratulate you. I had no idea that you would be this far along. This is impressive. I'll just take a few minutes and give you the information I promised from our business intelligence people. Dr. Tully is going to locate in Minneapolis, Minnesota. Zen and Bill, maybe you already know that?" They both shook their heads indicating the chosen location was news to them.

"Sam Elson and Dr. Tully talked some time ago, maybe just after he parted company with GPRI. They may have struck up a friendship and Customized Materials Technology is doing some testing with their advanced acoustics technology in the areas of RFID and data augmentation software. We believe Thomas Kramley has been coordinating the program with an outside vendor. Mr. Kramley does not seem to have had a presence at either Berkeley or Michigan recently. There are some kind of health issues with his family at this time. That is all I have right now."

The four leaders looked at each other as if to say, "Who should go first?"

Zen started, "We were in early contact with DoAT to get the identification of almost every explosive component known to man. We know how to detect, analyze, and identify 90% of them at the ppb level. There are a few that, even if we get only at the ppt levels, we believe Lyncoln's data augmentation methodology will allow us to conclusively identify. We'll know next week. Lyncoln has all the analytical equipment tied into the computers so our chemical data is interpreted mathematically. To date, the ppb level work has given us statistically repeatable identification at 99.999% accuracy. If we can do this at the ppt level we are good to go with standards. The vacuum cleaner collection equipment might be a little more challenging, though, and then there is the miniaturization, of course."

Chad said, "Good work, Zen and Lyncoln!"

Lyncoln turned his baseball cap around so that the bill of the cap was facing backwards and said, "I believe Zen has said it all for me. We are making good progress and rest assured that I will find a way so that we won't have to carry a mainframe computer in the truck."

Chad said, "Thank you again, Lyncoln."

Kan D popped up with, "Does this whole thing come down to my nanoscale work?" They all nodded their heads indicating the answer was yes. "Well, I have made some progress in nano approaches to equipment for generating sound waves and to collecting large volumes of air. There will be continuing adjustments as I receive new data and information from Zen and Bill."

Chad responded, "I know this is the tough part, Kan D. Just keep working with these guys as they get close to a final design and prototype. Thanks."

Bill was last and always a strong team member saying, "We believe we are close with both acoustic wave generation and bounce-back or reversal capability and acceptable or manageable sounds levels based on our in-lab testing. Our next plan is to conduct outside testing at the required distances to confirm this. I hope the buzzing and slight vibrations did not disturb your work too much. Thanks for your patience!"

Chad said, "Thank you, Bill." I know we have a long way to go on our project but with a start like this, we are way ahead of schedule. A couple of things … keep up your professional contacts at conferences and universities and keep an eye out for people trying to get project information. Zen, you need to contact Dr. Tully in

Minneapolis and see where he is in setting up his new company. If he is ready to start work, you must find a way to get Bill to meet with him. Lyncoln, would you contact Director Elson and see if one of the government's supercomputers is available to us? Kan D, you mentioned knowing Thomas Kramley from CMT. Get in touch and see what we can find out about all their testing of advanced technologies. Meanwhile, I will contact Joe Blackstone, the CMT president, to begin discussions about a cooperative program or partnership on CIED. Thanks for all the good work and keep it up." They all nodded and headed back to their work.

Chapter 4

Detonation Technology
The Investigation at
Customized Materials Technology

Sam Lectures Joe Blackstone

During a telephone call, Sam was hot under the collar. He was giving Joe Blackstone a lecture this time as Director of Technology Protection in the DoAT. "Joe, I have known you a long time. Your company has been built on the strength of government contracts. You do good work with your detonation technology and have hundreds of products to show for it. The nation has benefited as well with many of these products still being used by the military and other agencies."

"I know but....."

Before Blackstone could say another word, Sam said, "Don't interrupt me, I haven't finished. How could you have been so careless? How could your newest and most sophisticated DT product be a part of an attempted theft and about to be secreted off to Syria?"

Sam continued, "This family of detonation technologies is classified. It is on the nationally protected technology list. The Arms Export Control Act and International Traffic in Arms Regulations cover it. For God's sake, your work put it there. What else is there to say? Joe, we have seized the entire special product that was manufactured by CMT. Some of it was in the process of being diverted to Damascus. We got to the staging area in Zefat just in time to be able to stop it. If it had crossed the border, they would have been able to reverse engineer the product, identify the technology, and use it against us. I am calling for a complete investigation. There will be penalties and big ones, mark my words!"

"Sam, I know the trouble we are in. Already we are using our Six Sigma groundings to check our processes. Do you want to know what I think? Sam, this had to be an inside job, a mole. The problem is that most of our people have had background checks. They have secret and top secret clearances. They have been with us for years and are very trustworthy. Even so, if I had to guess, this is not a process problem. I promise you, we will get to the bottom of it."

"Joe, we are going to help with that. I have a team already identified to come in and help with the investigation. They will be there tomorrow. I want you to give them total access to everything. We have to get some answers fast."

"Have your team leader contact my director of logistics, Thomas Kramley, when they arrive tomorrow. Thomas will start to get things organized here for the investigation."

"Thanks, Joe, and good luck. Oh, yes, you better plan a trip to D.C. in about a week."

Joe was ready for more from Director Elson but all he heard was a click from the other end.

The Team

The team that Sam Elson put together for the CMT investigation was top notch. He knew some personally and some came highly recommended by his closest confidantes.

The team leader, Jack Borson, was a military technology expert from the DoAT. Aldora Klein was a new honors program attorney from the Justice Department, Criminal Division. A logistics expert from the DoT, Frank Bloomfield, and Mark Strong, a senior field agent from the DoD, Defense Security Services, rounded out the team. They were coming to meet with Sam before they left for San Francisco. The meeting was scheduled in about ten minutes.

Sam was at his desk thinking.....There are only a few companies in the U.S. that make classified materials and products for sale to the government. CMT is one of them; they had been on the watch list for DoD for a long time. Their record was excellent, actually impeccable, up until now. What is going on? I have to be very careful; this is a delicate time. Our enemies might think that, with the consolidation of several governmental units into a central DoAT, they may have a unique window of opportunity. An opportunity in which reorganization and restructuring creates confusion and loss of focus as we take our eye off the ball. One in which they believe greater risk-taking is acceptable. Nothing could be farther from the truth, you SOB's. That is why the President selected a psychologist for this job and one adept at AAR.

Sam's assistant knocked on his door and pushed it open at the same time. This brought him suddenly back to real time and the matter at hand.

"Director Elson, the team that is going to San Francisco to investigate Customized Materials Technology has arrived. You know Jack Borson from our Department and Mark Strong from DoD. Aldora Klein from Justice and Frank Bloomfield from DoT are also here."

"Good afternoon and thanks for taking this very important assignment on such short notice. I know you have to leave for the airport in a few hours so I'll make this very brief. Please join me at the table."

After all were seated, Sam continued, "Every day we are seeing more and more reasons why the president and Congress decided to consolidate the identification, development, and protection of our technology into one central agency, the DoAT. We still need the active participation and cooperation of our sister departments. This is especially true when there are field assignments and we need special expertise to handle the job. We have one such job right now that is a matter of national security."

Sam went on, "CMT, a manufacturer of very sophisticated and high technology explosive detonation products, is in hot water for having almost allowed classified product to get to Syria. They have had numerous DoD contracts over the years, have a good track record, and are well regarded in both the government and industrial communities. Their president, Joe Blackstone, thinks it was an inside job. Others feel it was a slip up in one of the manufacturing and logistics process steps. I want you to find out the truth and get it corrected. They are expecting you tomorrow. Your CMT contact is Thomas Kramley. He is their director of logistics, knows manufacturing and every other department in the business and most of the people involved. Meet with him to get the investigation organized. Thomas will help get you into the departments and meet the personnel as you investigate the processes needed to determine the problem."

"I want you, Jack, to lead the team but also carry the technology part of the investigation. Bone up on detonation technology on the flight. What makes it classified, who else has something similar, who wants it, what they will they do to get it and at what price. Aldora, you should cover government contracts, regulations, publications, presentations, confidential disclosure agreements, and communications (formal and casual) - everything like that. I want to believe that they know the rules and are following them!"

Turning now to Frank, Sam said, "If it is a faulty process step, find it. It would seem to me that customer service and order entry might be the place to start. You will have to follow this through the ordering of raw materials, filling orders in production, packaging, labeling, shipping directly to customers or using distribution centers, trucking companies, and other transportation options, e.g., rail, sea, and air. CMT has been in this business a long time and has sophisticated logistic processes. Joe Blackstone might be right; look at the people in charge of process upgrades and optimization."

"Mark, if it is a mole or someone is being paid to steal classified technology, find that person. Do some profiling with the help of HR. See if anyone is in financial trouble, angry with the company about pay or a missed promotion, thinks detonation products are wrong, or has psychological problems. Look at people with military backgrounds or sophisticated technical skills, especially."

Sam concluded by asking, "Any questions?"

The team was smiling and gulping at the same time. Finally, Jack said, "Thank you, Director Elson. Let us get ready for the trip and get organized on the flight to San Francisco. We'll meet with Thomas Kramley first thing tomorrow morning and get things started. I'll give you a call tomorrow evening. My guess is that we will be asking for some additional and very specific resources to help us."

Sam said, "Jack, I will wait for your call and thanks again for taking this assignment on such short notice. The country and I appreciate it very much."

Brad Heads to D.C.

Brad was seated on Delta-Northwest Airlines, flight 1702 for Washington, D.C.'s Reagan airport. I like it, he thought, the move was uneventful. He was able to rent furniture for his apartment and the office of Tully Research, Inc. It was a first floor office, second floor apartment, and the lab was in the basement. His equipment had arrived from GPRI safely and was already set up for starting his research. What was the address? He could not remember the number, but it didn't matter. It was on his business cards, of course. What he did think was confusing about his location were the street names like Second Street North and Fifth Avenue North. He knew that there were sets of streets and avenues designated "South" as well. He would have to investigate all of this when he got back. The Minneapolis-St. Paul airport was great and would meet his needs very well. He thought about how the cities had honored Charles Lindberg and Hubert Humphrey, two of their favorite sons, when they named the airports. Could he be as fortunate some day?

Tully Research Incorporated was official now with the attorney filing the paperwork and the State responding with its stamp and seal of approval in record time. Brad realized that the plane was at cruising altitude already. Gauging the two-hour flying time with an hour's time change, he would be in Washington well before lunchtime. The luncheon with Omar was at 11:30 AM and his appointment with Director Sam Elson was at 3 PM. He would ride the train, the Yellow Line at Reagan toward D.C., to Gallery Place in Chinatown, meet Mr. Kharif, and have lunch there in Chinatown. From there it was not far to where he had arranged to meet Sam Elson. The location was actually a satellite office of the main downtown Department of Justice building. Everyone was trying to make it convenient and easy for him. That probably was supposed to tell him something.

Brad's thoughts were headed toward money, investors, partners, and the like. How much would he ask for and how much was he willing to give up were the key questions on his mind. He was struggling with all this because he had not had time to do his research on Omar or his company, Technology Investment Corporation. He always wondered if there had been contact with GPRI and Dr. Knight before Omar had contacted him directly. It all happened so fast after the announcement and the reports were issued. He had looked at the website for TIC and they seemed to be on the up and up. Their charter, business plan, and Top Ten Technologies were identified as well as offices in D.C., Boston, and San Francisco. The Top Ten Technologies were in line with his thinking except for maybe one. Why was "explosives technology" on the list with the others like sensors, nano, acoustics, etc.? It seemed out of place.
He knew they had invested in research at Stanford and many other top schools. They must be okay.

He thought to himself, Let's say my technology is worth about $100 million. Receiving about $5 million the first year would get me going as I round up additional funding. I would probably need twice that much the second year. What will I give up for $15 million? Maybe a sizeable chunk of the company, a seat on the board, profits in proportion to the investment and a first right of refusal for an exclusive licensing deal.

Brad noticed they were getting close to the airport. He could see the Potomac, the Washington Monument, and the Jefferson Memorial. ... what a great city. He put his papers away and got ready to meet with Mr. Omar Kharif, head of Technology Investment Corporation.

Brad Meets With Omar

Brad was one of the first passengers off the plane. He followed the signs to the baggage claim and ground transportation area. The signs for the Metro started showing up as he approached the baggage claim area. He had carried his duffel bag on board the airplane so he just kept walking. Finally, there was the station entrance where he bought a $5 Metro ticket card. Omar had told him that should be enough to get him to Gallery Place and back to the airport. Through the turnstile and up the steps to the right side of the platform where he saw an electronic sign showing Yellow Line train in three minutes. It was on time. Brad hopped on and after several stops, taking about ten minutes, he arrived at Gallery Place in Chinatown.

Brad stepped off the train and onto the platform. There seemed to be scores of people getting on and off the train and making it quite crowded to walk and look for Omar at the same time. Then Brad saw him standing not far away wearing the TIC cap that they had agreed would identify him.

"Hello, Mr. Kharif, I am Brad Tully."

"Hello, Brad, Omar Kharif with TIC," as he pointed to the cap. "Let's head this way to exit the station and enter the center of Chinatown. How was your trip?"

"Very good, thank you. It was actually my first flight from Minneapolis, where I have recently located my business.

They went through the turnstile using their Metro cards, walked up the stairs and exited to a street in the middle of Chinatown. As Brad tagged along, soaking in all that Chinatown had to offer, Omar said, "I have a reservation at a place not far away."

The noodle-making displays in the restaurants were fantastic and the smells of lunchtime were equally wonderful. Brad noticed something else – there seemed to be someone following them. He thought to himself, maybe I'm getting paranoid, but there he was in a dark suit, white shirt with a tie, short haircut, and wearing sunglasses – just like in the movies. Brad was a couple steps behind Omar and was able to see him because he was looking around so much. Brad was sure Omar didn't see the man following them because he was so intent on getting to the restaurant. The 'suit' guy stayed with them all the way to a restaurant identified as H.F. Chan's, which also had a noodle-making demonstration in the front window. Brad and Omar stepped inside and the host immediately showed them to what seemed to be a prearranged table. The host definitely knew Mr. Kharif. After being seated, a waiter brought hot tea for Brad and Omar. Brad looked out the window and saw the 'suit' on the other side of the street, leaning against the building, reading a paper, and waiting.

Brad opened the conversation. "I brought summaries of my work at Stanford and GPRI and a sketch of the business plan for Tully Research, Inc."

"I know about your work at Stanford in chemical sensing. It was groundbreaking work and now is referenced in practically every article and textbook in the field."

"I just got lucky with the research and I had a great advisor."

"Three years to get your PhD. Lucky? I don't think so. I know a little about the work at GPRI from the report that was issued about the time of your departure. I had contacted Dr. Knight previously to find out more, but he was unwilling to provide any information. Do you think the bounce-back acoustical wave technology can really help find new oil fields?"

"I have staked my career and future, at least partially, on that belief. As you will see in my business plan, I am going to use BBAWT to enter several markets with specialty products. The initial work in the petroleum industry looks very promising and we have identified several other applications in other industrial and military markets as well. I am an expert in chemical sensing, acoustics, hardware, and software. There are only a few people in the world that can build new, sophisticated, scientific equipment and also write the advanced software code to run it and get the outcome wanted. I am one of them and that is why you are here, right?"

"Yes, of course, Brad. Please tell me what this acoustics

technology does."

"In simple terms, this is what we have," Brad responds, showing him the summary.

1) Equipment with special wave generating capability.
2) Wave characteristics include uniquely focused, high resolution, non-damaging, long distance, and bounce-back features.
3) Bounce-back waves are collected, the contents analyzed, and identified. This is what I am calling Phase I. Note that I believe bounce-back acoustical patterns may be used to set up standards to identify known solids, liquids, and gasses. This is Phase II and not part of the business plan right now.
4) Advanced code and software for correlation and identification.

"All this is very exciting, to be able to dial in a distance, generate a wave, bounced it back and identify anything and everything captured in the returning wave. We have the potential of finding not just oil but almost any element or compound at distances of hundreds of feet away. The trick is to collect the airwaves, analyze them with sophisticated instrumentation, and have the software identify what is contained within. This is Phase I of the business plan. Simply put, it is to develop and exploit the BBAW technology ASAP!"

Brad continued, "Phase I will generate all the revenue proposed and justify all the investments required. Phase II is longer out into the future. I want to develop our technology and expertise to the level at which the bounce-back wave patterns will be correlated with the chemical elements and compounds. We will dispense with the instrumental analysis and be able to acoustically identify everything captured in the returning wave front. Can you imagine the order of magnitude simplification of the search and discovery process? Phase II is further off as I said. Even further out, can you think about using the system as a direct search tool? There would be no instrumental analysis or wave pattern identification necessary. We would tell the wave what to look for using advanced software code and data augmentation as artificial intelligence. The wave would be the search tool."

While Brad had been talking, Omar had ordered the specialty noodles dish for both of them along with servings of chicken and pork egg rolls to share. All this arrived at the same time. The table was covered with all the documents Brad brought. Omar quickly picked up all the documents and put them into his briefcase.

Brad said, "Thank you for ordering for both of us. This is just what I wanted."

Omar winked, "I saw you looking at every noodle display on our walk to this restaurant. Eat up."

"Thanks. I hope my brief discussion of the technology and the business plan was of interest to you, Omar."

"It was, Brad. My company is very interested in making a substantial investment in Tully Research, Inc. We have talked about you and your potential a lot; our interest is actually investing in you. If we can do that through Tully Research, that is okay, too. You no doubt have looked at our website and know what we do and how this fits into our charter, mission, and strategy. How much do you anticipate needing to get started?"

"Good question. We have a lot to do in equipment design, software code, chemical capture and analysis, wave pattern analysis and correlation, data augmentation, etc. By getting in now, at the very beginning, you would also have the possibility of investing in what will come out of Phase II and beyond. I will not offer those until after we reach a certain level of funding and maturity. Give me a number, Omar, and I'll tell you if you are in the ballpark."

"How about $10 million dollars a year for five years, voting rights, dividends, and control as if I owned ten percent of the company, a non-exclusive right to license any of the technology at a negotiated fee of <25% of the revenue it generates and access, if not prohibited by law, to all technical reports on a quarterly basis?"

Brad almost choked on his noodles but was able to say, "Why not? Write it up and I'll have my attorney review it. I think we can do this."

Omar knew it was a good deal for Tully Research, Inc. – maybe even too good. He didn't care because his aim was to seal the relationship in its early stages. The price did not matter; it was about Dr. Bradford Tully and the technology. How much money had they essentially given away to universities? This would be a fraction of that with greater focus and high potential. The waiter came with the bill and shook him out of his daydreaming.

"Great, Brad, I'll get the papers drawn up for your review. The monies can be made available in a matter of days; what bank are you using?"

"Bremer in downtown Minneapolis. Don't quote me; I think it is located close to Third Avenue South and Sixth Street South."

"Brad, it was great to meet you and hear about your technology and the new company. Thanks for giving TIC an early chance to invest in you."

"You are welcome, Omar. It was good to do business with you." Brad looked at his watch and saw 12:30, then realized he had not changed his watch to reflect Eastern Standard Time. As he did this, they said their goodbyes and Omar left to return to his office.

Brad Meets with Sam

Brad was standing and looking out the front window of the restaurant. He couldn't believe it; the 'suit' was still there. Enough of this, Brad picked up his duffel bag, walked out the door, and crossed the street toward the 'suit.' He wasn't moving either, just looking right at him. Brad reached the sidewalk and said, "Who the hell are you?"

The man in the suit said, "Hello, Dr. Tully. Director Elson sent me to make sure you didn't get lost or mugged or sidetracked."

"What? I didn't think an escort was needed."

"The director mentioned to you that he would do some research on Technology Investment Corporation before you arrived. That research, although not complete, has brought up some questions about who they are and what they do. If it is okay, the director would like to see you right away. We are only five minutes away."

Sizing up the man in the suit, Brad said, "Before we go, could I see some identification please?" The man in the suit was a real live FBI agent. Brad thought, what have I gotten myself into now?

They headed off to the meeting with Director Sam Elson. Brad was just following the agent because he was in deep thought about what all this could mean to him. The FBI agent was on his cell phone to the director as they approached the building. They were early but Sam was at the door as they arrived.

"Hello, Dr. Tully."

"Call me Brad. Hello, Director Elson."

"Sorry about the cloak and dagger stuff; one can never be too careful in our business. I have learned a lot in the few months I have been with DoAT."

"It is okay, you must have good reason for taking steps like this," motioning to the FBI agent.

Sam dismissed the FBI agent, thanking him.

"Let's go to my office, Brad."

They took the stairs to the director's second floor office. His assistant greeted them and Brad was shown into the office. It was spacious with all the trappings of responsibility and power.

"Let's sit at the table, Brad. I have some things to show you, but let me hear about Tully Research first."

"Where should I start? I have done the paperwork, through my attorney, to file and receive approval at both the state and federal levels to do business as Tully Research. My business address is Minneapolis, Minnesota. My office and laboratories are at the same location for now. I have been starting to raise money and hire people. It is very simple. I'm raising money either from investors or by doing Government R&D contract work, which is why I'm in D.C. today. The cloak and dagger stuff has me more than a bit surprised. I'd like to know what you know, but I'm almost afraid to ask."

"You don't have to ask because I'm going to tell you everything I know. We don't want to alarm you because our investigation is not complete. Things with Technology Investment Corporation may not be totally as they appear. I'm going to speak confidentially and ask that you respect and treat the information as part of a 'need to know' discussion just between the two of us."

"Is it absolutely essential that I keep the information confidential?"

"I would like it to be just between the two of us as we talk about technology and technology protection at the federal level. The government needs, and I need, some technology-savvy people to work with in order to understand exactly what might be going on around us. We believe you are one of those people. You are a top-flight scientist in multiple fields including sensing, acoustics, and data augmentation. You are an action-oriented, let's-get-it-done type of person with a love for your country. Why else would you take a job with GPRI, at the salary they gave you, to look for oil? You don't need to answer that question; it was rhetorical. With your skills and potential, you might be one in a million or two million. I need you to help us. Let me go on to help you understand the situation, as we know it now."

"When I became Director in DoAT, I began an investigation into all universities and companies that were deep into technologies that could be used for military applications. Examples of these companies are Advanced Technology Products, Customized Materials Technology, TIC, and several others. TIC, by its outward appearance, is doing some wonderful things to build technologies. They have given approximately $100 million dollars to universities during the past five years…. your alma mater, Stanford, included. We are also discovering they have been very proactive in making contacts within the companies, the movers and shakers that do military or related technology R&D. We don't yet know to what extent, but this includes all the companies I just mentioned and now your company. As a way of showing you how serious this might be I'll tell you a story."

He hesitated a bit then said, "I mentioned that GPRI was on our watch list, not so much because of your work, but because of other work that was being done under government contract. Dr.

THE CAMPAIGN OF FEAR

Elija Knight and I talked a lot in the last three months. During that time, he was contacted by TIC about your work specifically and this Omar Kharif made some rather aggressive demands. So much so, that Dr. Knight contacted me to talk about what he should do. You should know that Dr. Knight has the utmost respect for you and your research. He could see that it has applications far beyond searching for oil. He told me about the plan to have you leave GPRI and take the technology with you. I agreed that if that happened, you would automatically go on our watch list. So here we are!"

Stunned, Brad said, "Am I under federal government protection or something?"

"No, not really, we are just trying to find out what is going on. By the way, I can't give you any details, but we know Omar Kharif has made some inroads into Advanced Technology Products. After their awards banquet, he tried to get confidential information about a new and very important government funded project they have in the acoustics area. I am the sponsor; I'll tell you about that project at the right time."

"I know someone at ATP who might be working on that project. Did it start right after the awards banquet?"

"Yes, it did and it is going full force as we speak. A school friend, Zenica Lang, may be working on this project from what she told me."

"Interestingly, there is a link from TIC to Advanced Technology Products that we believe is very suspicious. We have been tracking some activities at CMT that TIC seems to be using them to test new supply chain technology. CMT makes detonation technology products and one of the field tests of a new acoustics product, with TIC, went terribly wrong. I'll tell you more about this at the right time, too."

"This is beginning to sound worse and worse all the time. Now you know TIC has talked with me with an interest in Tully Research and my acoustics and related technology?"

"Yes. We don't know how the pieces fit together nor do we believe we have all the pieces. But we do have enough to make us very concerned. This is why I needed to talk to you more about

93

government contracts. What did he offer you, if I may ask?"

"Lots of money and what I believe is a deal awkwardly tilted in favor of my company, Tully Research. Now, I am beginning to wonder why he is really willing to do that."

"I wonder, too. Brad, I have worked as a practicing behavioral psychologist, industrial consultant, university professor, and now a federal appointee in the DoAT. My specialty was something I called augmented adaptive reasoning. With a little information, I could build future state scenarios and make some reasonably close predictions as to what actually happened. I wrote code, used supercomputers, analyzed data, then came up with conclusions and recommendations. This was all on the individual and team behavior side of things, but it must sound similar to what you do on the science and technology side of things. I believe if we can build scenarios that combine both the behavior and technology of the bad guys, we may be able to mount a defense to short-stop their plans and maybe even go on the offense in some cases. Would you be interested in joining with me on behalf of the government to try to stop the bad guys?"

Brad was silent for what seemed a long time. As a behavioral psychologist, Sam thought he could place people well in the range of 'responders' given a particular set of circumstances. This guy might be different. The second ticked off, no response. More seconds, no response.

Then Brad said, "A behavioral psychologist who can write code and run a supercomputer. How in the hell did you get into this business? I thought all you guys wore guns and were skilled in the martial arts."

"I do and I am. The real story is probably that I knew one person too many, including the present secretary of DoAT. He thought my set of skills would be important for what we need to do in the department. The concept of *identify, develop, and protect our technology* is simple but one I totally believe in... especially in these times. So I said yes to his offer to head up the technology protection part of DoAT. That was about three months ago."

"What would you want me to do?"

"No guns or martial arts, just play along. Take Kharif up on his deal and see if you can find out what he is trying to do. They seem to be focusing on acoustics and related technologies. If there is one person who can help us to put the pieces of the puzzle together, it is Brad Tully. Watch, listen, talk, question, and see if you can gain some insight. With behavioral and technology input, perhaps we can build a future state scenario that would allow to stop this guy if necessary."

"I will do it but it is going to cost you a government contract. It is the real reason I came today. If this guy, Omar, is who you think he is, he probably knows already. I have the proposal already written and ready for you." He pulled it out of his duffel bag and gave it to Director Elson. "You'll like it. Having it funded will make Tully Research even more enticing to TIC and Omar Kharif, if you are right in your suspicions."

"You got yourself a deal, Mr. Tully."

"Only if you call me Brad."

"Fine, I will and you call me Sam."

"Goodbye, Sam, come to see me in Minnesota sometime."

"Perhaps sooner than you think, Brad. Goodbye"

As Brad left the office, he said, "Let's see, Gallery Place and the Yellow Line to the airport, right?"

Sam said, "Yes, very good. The agent can go with you if you like."

"No thank you, I'll find my way. I have some serious thinking to do about spending a lot of a questionable organization's money. Not only that, but I have to get my head around the notion of such spending as fully sanctioned by the U.S. Government and the DoAT. Further, to apply the spending to work on a U.S. Government contract so we can catch the organization in some nefarious act. Maybe we have already gone on the offense."

Sam said, "Now you see why they wanted a psychologist around. Goodbye for now. I'll stay in touch."

Brad Returns Home

Brad arrived back home right on time. The trip to D.C. and discussions with Mr. Kharif and Director Elson were a bit unsettling. A lot of "what-ifs" kept popping up in his mind. As he walked from the gate toward the terminal thinking about all that had transpired in D.C., he saw the LRT signs.

"I need to take the train to downtown Minneapolis," he said to himself. He followed the signs to the lightrail station, bought his ticket, went to the end of the line, and hopped on. It was a quick trip to Fifth Street South and Hennepin Avenue. On exiting the train, he realized this was very close to his apartment, office, and lab; he decided to walk. He had been thinking on and off about Zenica Lang and felt for her business card in his pocket. Brad decided to call her.

The phone rang three times, and then a voice on the other end said, "Hello, this is Zen."

"Hi, Zen, this is Brad Tully."

"Hi, Brad, are you calling me from Minneapolis? I heard you located there but realized I didn't have any contact information for you. I am really glad you called."

"Do you have a pen? I'll give you my contact information now."

"Yes, I am ready."

"My cell phone number is 612-272-3874. The last seven digits are for BRADTRI. TRI stands for Tully Research, Inc. so it will be easy to remember. My email is btully@tri.com. How are you doing, Zen?"

"I am doing fine. I am a little disappointed that you didn't locate in Boston where you would be closer."

Brad thought, There it is again. Was that a little hint about getting together? He said, "Minneapolis-St. Paul seems to be a great location for what we have to do. It is very convenient to the East, West, and South. Minnesota has special economic development grants ... something they call JOBZ. It all came together nicely so here I am."

"Have you started your research yet, Brad?"

"I have everything set up and ready to go tomorrow. I am in negotiations for some private funding and a government contract. An employment agency is trying to find people for the office and the laboratory. Are you looking for a job?"

"Not right this moment, but who knows? I mentioned that I was recently assigned to a new project at Advanced Technology Products. We've just really got it going I can't talk about it much but it will involve both chemical sensing and acoustics. I'm the lead in the chemical sensing area and this guy I mentioned before, Bill Brewer from Harvard, is the lead in acoustics. Knowing just how good you are in these areas, may I suggest that the three of us meet sometime soon? I am authorized to tell you that this is a critical and top-secret project, funded by the DoAT and our sponsor is the director of technology protection, Dr. Sam Elson. He has given approval for me to talk with you about this."

"Wow, I met and talked with Director Elson today. He actually mentioned the project at Advanced Technology Products, but he didn't give any details. Everything was to be hush-hush."

"I know, all of this confidential stuff makes it difficult to communicate. Maybe there would be a way for us to engage officially with Tully Research to work on our project. We are the prime contractor and TRI would be a subcontractor. Could I propose this to our project manager, Chad Bromcast, and then arrange for Chad and me to meet with you and talk about some of the details? I would love to work with you again."

"Yes, that would be fantastic. This sounds like it could be fun. I would love to see you again soon so let me know about the meeting."

"Okay, Brad, I'll get back to you soon."

"Thanks, Zen, good to talk to you. Goodbye."

Brad thought, Have I gotten to be too popular? I am being pulled into this thing deeper and deeper. And there is nothing I can do about it.

The Investigation Starts

Thomas arrived very early the morning he was to meet the government team coming to investigate Customized Materials Technology. He knew the urgency since he had gotten a call from Joe Blackstone last evening. As Thomas walked toward security, his mind was racing. Some of the shipment of new detonation technology product sent to Israel had almost gotten stolen; five of the packages without Mach II were taken from the cargo plane and almost successfully secreted off to Syria on an awaiting corporate jet. A dead pilot, four escaped thieves, and the Mossad were all parts of the puzzle. This did not have anything to do with him; Joe just asked him to be the CMT contact and coordinator for the government investigation because he was director of logistics. Thomas commented on the last point out loud, "Whatever Joe wants, Joe gets!"

As he arrived at security, the guard said, "Sorry about the problems with the shipment, Mr. Kramley. It is good that nothing was stolen. There is a government team waiting for you at your office." Thomas nodded and smiled as he used his card and passed through. He thought, Does everyone know about this already or is it just that security has been informed first? Time would tell.

As Thomas walked toward his office, he saw the group of four people huddled in the corridor. Jack was the first to notice him coming and said, "Hello, Mr. Kramley, I am Jack Borson, military technologist with the DoAT. Everyone seemed to know we were coming and that you were the contact so the guard brought us here to wait for you."

"Hello, Jack, it is good to meet you. I don't think I know anybody from DoAT."

"No wonder, it's a new department just created by the new administration. Let me introduce the rest of the team. This is Aldora Klein, an attorney from the Department of Justice; Frank Bloomfield, logistics expert from DoT; and Mark Strong, a field agent from DoD, Defense Security Services."

Thomas introduced himself, "I am director of logistics for the company and our president asked me to coordinate with your investigative team. Are we in big trouble? I have been here a long time and don't recall a time when anything similar has happened."

Jack smiled, "President Abbott and DoAT Secretary Adams have instituted a new emphasis on advanced technology for our country. It includes identification, development, and protection of key technologies that are of high national interest. Director Sam Elson is in charge of technology protection where this incident, of the attempted theft of your new detonation technology products, fits. Your company has been a model for government contract work and the development and commercialization of military and industrial detonation products. Your record has been clean and your accomplishments in new technology have been outstanding. We were surprised by what happened. The technology is deemed so important that we just have to investigate. Our objective is to find the facts, analyze the data, and come to some conclusions and recommendations so it doesn't happen again. Will you help us, please?"

"Of course I will. Whoever was behind this must be stopped. Where would you like to start?"

Mark took the cue and said, "It is always best to start with the people. I would like you to get me into HR. I want to review the personnel files of everyone who would have touched any aspect of this product from order entry to loading the delivery truck and all steps in between. I suspect a lot of the files are electronic. Once I meet with HR and agree on the people to be reviewed, I just need some office space and a computer."

"That will be easy. I estimate you are talking about one hundred or so people involved in the shipment before it left the plant."

Mark nodded agreement and said, "We'll get whatever resources we need."

Aldora was next saying, "I want to get into your government R&D contract department. I need to look at this new DT contract work specifically: who writes reports and where they go, who gives presentations and to whom, who the partners and vendors are, how confidential and classified information is handled, and the extent of both internal and external communications as they relate to government R&D contract rules and regulations."

Thomas said, "Your legal training is showing. I'll introduce you to the manager and get you an office and computer. One thing, they interface a lot with the legal departments, both IP and general counsel, and are in close proximity so you'll be right at home there."

"Thanks, Thomas."

Jack chimed in with his request, "Mine is easy. I need to learn about detonation technology. Get me in contact with your Director of R&D. Tell him I want to focus on the newer detonation technologies and especially the one involving acoustics. I assume he will have competitor information so that we can do some analyses on who might want to get their hands on this technology/product. You might as well get me the name and number of the marketing director, too. The marketing and sales people are the 'feet on the street' and know best about who would maybe kill to get this technology."

"Done, Jack. You best talk to our president too. He is the brain behind most of our technology products."

Frank was last and said, "Thomas, it is you and me. We are the logistics nerds so I want to follow you around and learn all the process steps involved in getting product to customers. Let's break it up into pieces of pre-production, production, and post-production with some special focus on new vendors and the process of their qualification. We'll be looking for any weak links, partners or otherwise, that exist in the supply chain."

"You can office next to me, Frank."

"Thank you, sir."

Addressing all four investigators, Thomas said, "I'll have my people help you make these contacts and set up the offices so that you can work. How long do you think this will take?"

Jack offered, "At the least, several days of gathering information and conducting the analyses on what seems pertinent and of course more for the conclusions and recommendations. I think we are looking at a couple of weeks. One more thing Thomas. Would you contact your IT people and tell them that our investigative team in D.C. will need to access their intranet system? We will need usernames, codes, passwords created just as if we were CMT employees being given top level security clearances."

Thomas responded, "Will do. That will be no problem inasmuch as you already have existing federal security clearances."

"Thanks, Thomas."

A Lot Done the First Day

By early evening, the team had actually accomplished quite a lot. The offices were set up with Mark in the human resources department, Aldora located in the intellectual property legal department nearby government R&D contracts, Frank in a plant office just off the production floor, and Jack, the lucky one, got an office next to Joe Blackstone. No one knew how that happened but, on second thought, it might have been prearranged by Director Elson.

The computers were top of the line with all the accessories, just like you would expect at such a technology-rich company. No expense was spared to help them do their job. The team members each had a crash course on the company intranet and its capabilities.

As Jack made the rounds, he wanted to capture a mental picture of each phase of the work so that he could justify resources needed and be able to talk intelligently with Director Elson.

Mark's office had about 100 files out on the desk, table, chairs, floor, etc. They were somehow categorized into somewhat discernable looking but not very orderly stacks. He looked up at Jack and simply said, "I'll be ready to go soon. For your information, there is nothing electronic here. It is all going to be done the old fashioned way. What else would you expect about personnel files?"

Jack said, "I guess so. Get them divided the way you want them and we'll send all the files to D.C. for review."

"I will and we'll ship them tomorrow. I'm keeping the files of the executive team and a few others for myself."

"Good idea, see you in fifteen?" Jack said as he walked to the legal department. Aldora was at her desk in IP with the best-looking stacks ever … even labeled. He saw contracts, reports, government regulations, presentations and public disclosures, patent proposals, patents pending, patents filed, etc. The stacks were organized with file wrappers, three-ring binders, the whole works. Jack realized that as he passed the several IP counsel offices to get to Aldora's, they were all the same. Stacks and stacks, maybe by the individual cases, everybody had them.

Aldora said, "What's up?"

"We are going back to the hotel in about ten minutes. Are you coming along? I think this is enough for the first day."

"Yes, this is getting tiring but you know what ... they keep excellent records."

"Let me know tonight how much help you'll need to go through everything thoroughly."

"It will be relatively easy, Jack, everything is electronic."

"Thank God for that. I am going to get Frank; we'll meet you at the car."

"Okay, Jack."

Jack was walking back to the production area wondering if all honors program attorneys at the Justice Department are that good. She is still wet behind the ears and isn't even fazed by fieldwork. Jack peeked into Frank's office and saw that Thomas was with him.

"Had enough for today?"

Frank said, "Just about. With Thomas's help, I have gotten off to a running start. The Six Sigma black belts have diagrammed everything. They have optimized and re-optimized every process. This place is running like a Swiss watch. Tomorrow we will look at vendors and weak links in the supply chain. Thanks to Thomas, this part has gone quickly. I'm ready; see you tomorrow, Thomas."

Smiling, Thomas said, "Good evening, Frank and Jack. See you all tomorrow."

The team met at the car and headed for the hotel. On the way, Jack called Director Elson. "Hello, Director Elson, we have had a busy day at Customized Materials Technology."

"Hello, Jack, is your team with you and listening on the speaker?"

"Yes, Director, and we are all exhausted."

THE CAMPAIGN OF FEAR

"Just give me the short version of your findings so far. I knew this would be a big job, but we have to find out who and what we are dealing with."

Jack was formulating the short version and said, "Here goes. We are getting great cooperation from all departments at CMT and, of course, Thomas Kramley and President Blackstone. Our offices are set up and operational; people in the various offices are actively helping us. We'll need several people in the D.C. offices to review personnel files, which Mark will send tomorrow with instructions on what to look for. Aldora will need help going over reports, IP files, presentations, and the like to see if we can identify anything abnormal. It's all on their intranet so we will get this part to D.C. electronically. Frank says the standard logistics and supply chain processes are well-documented and sophisticated as you might expect for this kind of business. Starting tomorrow, he will verify that they really follow them. That will be fairly easy and then the focus will switch to new products, systems, and processes. We know, of course, that someone outside of CMT knew all about the shipment to Israel and was able to communicate enough about the contents, method of transportation, schedule, and location to prepare and execute an intercept plan."

Sam said, "This is the key part, Jack. I want you to grill Mr. Blackstone about the new products. He has had a leadership role in practically every new product they have developed. Additionally, he is a very hands-on manager so he should know what is going on every step of the way. I have worked with him some and I trust him, but something bad is going on there. Find out what it is!"

"We will, Director. Our focus in all the work I talked about is to find out how CMT's confidential information got outside the company and who was involved in the process. Mark, Aldora, Frank, any comments or questions as we wrap up?"

Everyone was nodding 'no' as they arrived at the hotel. Then Aldora spoke up, "Sir, you must have been here before. Where is a good place to get a sandwich and a beer?"

"I seem to remember a pub close by called the Screaming Pig or something like that. They have great pork barbeque sandwiches. Nice work, guys. Keep me posted on progress and where the investigation is leading us. Thank you."

"Thank you, Director," they all said at one.

Jack pushed 'end' on his secure phone and said as he parked, "Meet you in the lobby in thirty minutes. We'll see if we can find the Screaming Pig pub."

Dinner at the Squealing Pig

The investigative team of Jack, Mark, Aldora, and Frank got directions to the restaurant from the front desk of the hotel. It turns out that the Customized Materials Technology site, the hotel, and the pub formed an equilateral triangle so exact that one would have thought there must be a connection with the three.

Jack said, "I see the flashing lights and the pig. . . it's the Squealing Pig, not the Screaming Pig." He turned in and parked fairly close to the door. They all got out of the car and approached the entry to the restaurant. Upon opening the door, the sound of a squealing pig greeted them. Everyone jumped at the loud sound and thought how annoying. Jack grimaced and said, "I guess if we are hungry enough, we'll just have to put up with it. Let's ask for a table at the back and as far away from the door as possible."

Aldora said, "Great idea." Frank and Mark nodded their agreement.

The host showed them to the back table. Once they were seated and had looked at the menu, they all agreed to order the same thing...the squealing pig barbeque pork sandwich with French fries and New Castle on tap. The waiter took their orders and brought the beers almost immediately.

Jack made a toast. "To our first investigation together as a team."

They all said, "Here, here" and drank up.

Jack opened the conversation just as the meals arrived saying, "We can't talk much here about what we found today, but are there any first impressions?"

Mark answered first, "The personnel files seem to be up

THE CAMPAIGN OF FEAR

to date, complete, and well- organized. The people in HR are very committed and do their jobs well. I haven't looked very closely but I was surprised that my random check showed long-term employees and secret or top secret clearances for almost all of them. Not the kind of people who steal military secrets. We'll have our work cut out for us with about one hundred files to review. Don't hold me to this; my guess is that if there is something nefarious going on, it is within the executive team. We'll see."

Aldora said, "Their internal contracts, IP, etc. records are well kept with just what you would expect for this kind of business. I didn't see any abnormal number or types of violations or even inquiries pertinent to their government contracts. The process used to get outside approvals seem good. We need to do a lot more, but first impressions are good. Do you know if they record every call in and out of there? I think they must, but I'll confirm it tomorrow. If they do, there could be something on the tapes."

Jack chimed in, "I believe I heard they do. Let me know what you find out. We may need some listening help for what was recorded over a couple of months or more of time."

"Logistics processes are in good shape," added Frank. "If they follow them, they are leaders in the field. One thing I have learned in the past is to look for how vendors interact with the company. This includes current, new, and potential vendors. My impression is that, if there is anything, it will be something outside of the normal processes. For example, Mr. Kramley makes a lot of decisions about supply chain himself...especially the new stuff. I'll check it out."

Jack said, "Good enough. I have my work cut out for me with Blackstone. He makes a lot of new product decisions himself, too... pretty hands on. I wonder if Mr. Blackstone and Mr. Kramley each know what the other is doing. Let's see if we can find out."

The sandwiches and beers were great. The team was ready for bed. Jack paid the bill and as they were leaving, he said, "The squealing pig sounds await us." They walked through the door with grimaces, plugging their ears with their fingers as they rushed to the car.

As they were driving to the hotel, Jack said, "Let's go hit this again tomorrow and get more answers. Frank, you and I will plan to spend time separately focusing on specific activities of the director of logistics and the president of the company. Could we meet for coffee tomorrow morning to get our questions formulated and coordinate our approach?"

"Sure, see you about 7 AM?"

Jack and Frank Meet for Breakfast

"That was a short night, Jack," commented Frank as he walked closer to the dining room table. It was 7 AM exactly.

"It sure was, have a seat. I ordered a full pot of coffee if you would like some."

"Thanks, Jack, just what I need.' As he poured his coffee, Frank said, "Do you think Mark is right about his guess?"

"What's that, Frank?"

"Mark's guess. If something is going on, it is within the executive team."

"Could be and actually our decision to focus on Kramley and Blackstone today was a good one. I talked with Director Elson again last night and updated him more on our first day's work and where we need help. He approved everything and said to simply mention his name, top priority, and charge it to DoAT. Here is the interesting part. He had talked with his colleague in Israel about the telephone call that was intercepted, the one that allowed the Mossad to stop the theft. He said the call mentioned a CMT contact and its president. The contact just might be Kramley. I know how independent and hands-on they are. We have to find out how each of them was connected to the shipment."

"Yes, separate activities and joint activities."

"Right, do you think there was a joint involvement on the shipment?"

"I don't know but this Kramley seems like a good guy. He probably kept his boss informed. If Blackstone is as interested in new technology as everyone says he is, I suspect they got together

THE CAMPAIGN OF FEAR

on this one."

"So what are the questions for Kramley?"

Just at that point, Frank pulled out his list and said, "I have a few so see what you think:

- Who decides on the method of shipment and the route used for experimental top-secret product?
- How is the product tracked in route?
- Were there any new or unusual things about this shipment like packaging, tracking, carriers, etc.?
- Any new vendors or suppliers used in production of the product or its shipment?
- Did you and President Blackstone get jointly involved with this new product?"

"Those are great, Frank! I was copying as you read so I have them all. Here goes my list for Blackstone:

- What does this new product do and what technology does it use?
- Who decides when it is ready for prototype testing?
- How was the production date of the prototype product decided and who knew about it?
- How was the customer selected and who knew their identity?
- Who decides how much experimental product o manufacture?
- At what stages do you personally get involved with new product development, testing and design finalization?
- Did you and the Logistics Director, Kramley, work together on this shipment specifically?"

Frank was writing feverishly and finally stopped and said, "Got 'em! If we put all the questions together and take out the overlaps, we'll have about ten questions for each."

"Good idea, I think we are all set. Thanks, Frank. I see Aldora and Mark heading this way. It must be time to get to work."

Chad's Confession

Chad was thinking about his regular calls to Director Sam Elson to update him on the project. The last call was very upbeat because of all the progress the team had made. Director Elson even offered the use of the supercomputer before Lyncoln could ask for it. Every resource was being made available. Chad was worried, however, and felt that he may not be holding up his end of the bargain. He had to call again, a special call, to let him know about the lost or stolen notes. He had mentioned the strange visit by Omar Kharif, head of the TIC. He had failed to mention the lost notes because he was embarrassed by his lack of responsibility. How could he have been so stupid with something so important and confidential? He dialed the number on his special cell phone.

"Hello, Chad, I wasn't expecting you to call for a couple of days. Anything wrong?"

"Hello, Sam. Nothing is wrong with the project. I want you to know about some things that could be related."

"Fire away, Chad. I'm in the car headed to my building so it is a good time to talk."

"Do you remember when I told you about a strange visit by the head of TIC, Mr. Omar Kharif? It was right after our awards banquet."

"Yes, I do. He had seen the event covered in the newspaper and came to offer his company's technology help to you. Maybe do a joint project of some kind."

"Yes, that is it. You have a great memory!"

"Thank you. In every job I have had, it has always been abundantly clear that the details matter. Whoever said, 'don't sweat the small stuff' didn't know what they were talking about."

"There is a detail that I did not tell you that may be critically important. I am sorry that I didn't bring it up earlier. My hope was that it would have been resolved by now. It hasn't been resolved and you need to know."

"Chad, I can't help until I know what happened."

"I know, here goes. At the awards banquet, during dinner, I made some notes and sketched our project out on the back of the

THE CAMPAIGN OF FEAR

program. I had set up a meeting with the future team leaders right after the event and was going to use the sketch to explain the new project. My boss, Mike Jackson, saw it at the table and liked it. I used it in the post event meeting with Bill, Zen, Kan D, and Lyncoln. They liked it. I found out later when we discussed the project further at work the next week that they had pretty well memorized the sketch. I took the program sketch home over the weekend and brought it to work on Monday. I believe it was on my table in the office until after my meeting with Mr. Kharif on Tuesday. When he left, I looked for it to use at a team leader meeting for the project that day. It was gone – nowhere to be found. This sketch, Director Elson, had enough of what someone would need to understand our plan to develop a defensive weapon for explosives' detection. It had the project name, technology pieces, people, assignments, targets and needs. Thank God I didn't include anything about how it would be done. I think Kharif took it. It is the only explanation. I have looked everywhere and it is simply just gone!"

Director Elson said, "It would not surprise me since he and his company are on our watch list. They are involved with some suspicious activities on a number of fronts. We cannot make accusations without the facts, the proof. I do need to know these things, Chad. Remember what I said about the details. These kinds of things are important to piece the puzzle together. Has anything else happened?"

"Since you put it that way, yes, there are several things that could all be related. Our IT people have been inordinately busy with hackers trying to get into our intranet. Our firewalls have been effective. To date, we can't identify the hackers and certainly can't tie this to TIC. The number of attempts has increased dramatically. We are getting numerous Internet and phone inquiries about our technology. Maybe it is because of our awards banquet and press coverage but it seems to be way out of proportion to what was expected. It is almost as if someone is trying to request all of our technology information, hoping to catch something that is confidential, something that would get out by mistake. When our four team leaders are out, they find they are recognized and asked about their work more frequently, almost to the point of being harassed or interrogated. It is by people they do not know and it is not friendly. Last, we are getting an abnormal number of hits on searches being done on obscure journals where we have historically published unpatented technology in order to disclose or make it public so that someone else cannot patent it. This takes a lot of knowledge about our company to know where to look but goes beyond industrial espionage. We are beginning to believe there is some darker reason why this is happening."

"Director Elson, I have to reiterate that I have no facts that any of this, the notes, inquiries, people harassment, or journal searches, have anything to do with TIC or Kharif. Can you help us find out? We are all very concerned about what the next steps might be."

"I will, Chad. TIC is not only on our watch list, but also in our crosshairs. We are following suspicious activity by TIC at Customized Materials Technology and Tully Research, Incorporated as well. I'll keep you updated and you let me know if anything else happens. Okay?"

"All right, Director Elson. Thanks for listening. One last thing, our team has plans to be in contact with Dr. Bradford Tully at Tully Research and both Thomas Kramley and Joe Blackstone at Customized Materials Technology. We believe their technology advances might be essential to the success of our project. Should we still do that based on the suspicious activity by TIC at those companies?"

"Good question, Chad. I think you should continue to carry out your project plans just like nothing has happened. We don't want to give Mr. Kharif any idea that something is amiss or that he may be part of an investigation."

"Thanks, Director. I thought that would be your answer. We'll talk more soon."

ATP Needs a Partner

Chad and Kan D talked about how best to be in contact with Customized Materials Technology. They did not want their calls to appear unrelated and someone being upset about disjointed communications. It was decided that Kan D would contact Thomas Kramley first and brief him on the subjects. The two of them then would arrange for a four-way conference call to include them and their bosses.

Kan D tried to remember all she could about her fellowship from CMT at Michigan. They were leaders in MEMS and nanotechnology and used both to make detonation technology products. She thought at the time that this was not a business for her but she took their money. It paid the bills for a big part of graduate school. Now she was working for Advanced Technology Products, in a similar field, and thinking about a cooperative program with CMT. She thought maybe she should have worked for them from the beginning. They invested so much in her and got nothing back. Oh, well, she couldn't look back.

Kan D dialed the number on an old business card that Thomas Kramley had given her from the University of Michigan days. To her surprise, he answered, "This is Thomas Kramley."

"Hello, Mr. Kramley, this is Kan Deng Shin."

"Kan D, how are you and how is the job at Advanced Technology Products?"

"Things are fine with me and I am doing very well at ATP. In fact, I just won a prestigious technology award and received an assignment to lead part of the company's number one priority project. That is actually why I am calling. My boss, and the project leader, Dr. Chadly Bromcast and I need to talk to you and your boss. Is that Joe Blackstone?"

"Yes, it is and he is very close to our technology products."

"The project I referred to will require some new detonation technology. This is CMT's bailiwick, of course. ATP has no detonation technology at all; that is why we need to talk. We are thinking about all kinds of options like cooperative programs, joint ventures, subcontractor in our DoAT contract, etc., but are open to your ideas, too. Could you identify a couple of dates/times that are suitable, give me a call, and we'll make one of them happen?"

"I sure can, Kan D. There may be one issue that could affect our commitment to your project at this specific time."

"What is that, TK?" Thank goodness Kan D remembered what she used to call him when he came to campus. In fact, it was he who thought up the nickname for her that everybody used. The best she could come up with for him at the time was TK.

"Kan D, we are currently under an audit or investigation of our internal processes and our people. There was an attempt to steal one of our new products recently. The work was under government contract and they want to know how this could have happened. I'd like to tell you more, but that is all I am allowed to say at this time."

"That is okay, TK. Those things happen in the kind of work you are in. I'm sure everything will be fine."

"I think so; we run a pretty tight ship. Anyway, I'll talk to Joe about some dates and times and get back to you."

"Thanks, TK. I really appreciate this."

"You are welcome, Kan D. I look forward to working on this big project with you."

"Thanks again, talk to you later. 'Bye."

Teleconference Call

Kan D had covered with Chad the conversation with Thomas Kramley at Customized Materials Technology. Chad knew about the DoAT's investigation of an attempted theft of a new experimental product. He also knew that Kan D was not able to get any more information than just that. Kramley seemed to be interested but could not commit to anything. Was it because of the investigation or did Joe Blackstone make all of the decisions?

It was lunchtime in Boston when Kan D and Chad made the call.

Thomas picked up as arranged in Joe's office and said, "Thomas Kramley, Customized Materials Technology."

"Hello, Thomas, this is Kan D and I have my boss, Dr. Chad Bromcast with me."

"Hello, Thomas."

Thomas said, "I also have my boss, Dr. Joe Blackstone, President of Customized Materials Technology with me."

"Good to meet you, Kan D and Chad," said Joe. "I am glad you thought of us and made contact with Thomas about a cooperative program."

"You are the 'go to' company in your niche technology," said Chad. By the way, there are a few other connections between our companies. You know, of course, that Thomas and Kan D know each other from her days at Michigan in graduate school. Thomas, representing CMT, had presented her with a graduate fellowship that continued for several years. I know Thomas from my Berkeley connection, PhD 1991. You graduated before I arrived and became the CMT representative shortly before I graduated. Do you remember, Thomas?"

Thomas said, "Yes, I remember now, there was just a brief overlap. You were with a small group of students at one of my first 'Career Days' presentations. I must not have been very impressive since you decided on a career with Advanced Technology Products."

"No, Thomas, it was a much more complicated set of variables than that. It wasn't you; it was time for a change of scenery. I had been on the West Coast for a long time. When ATP in Boston made me a great offer, after taking everything into account, I took it. I have been here ever since. Another connection is our Project Sponsor, Dr. Sam Elson. I believe he knows you, Dr. Blackstone."

Chad and Kan D heard the familiar 'click- click-click-click' on the phone. Chad asked, "Are you taping our call?"

Joe responded immediately, "Yes, it is automatic since we are under government contract. It is an interesting system of preset key words. If the words are not heard in the first thirty seconds, the recorder shuts off. That was the sound you just heard. The thought is that the bad guys have very brief conversations and the key words come up very early. It seems that you are not bad guys."

Joe continued by saying, "Yes, we go back a ways. Sam is one sharp guy with some unique skills. I can understand why DoAT

Secretary Adams wanted him as one of his directors. Chad and Kan D, if I may, I want to be as up front with you as possible. Thomas mentioned to Kan D that we are under investigation by DoAT. It is true and one of the reasons that I have talked with Sam just recently. He and I agree that it was very serious to have someone try to steal some of our experimental product. It was a failed attempt, thank God, but nevertheless, it seems like the perpetrators had some kind of access to inside information. We have to discover how this happened and who is responsible. Our company is committed to that but it doesn't mean that everything else stops. How can we help?"

Chad thought, I like this guy. "We have a government contract to provide a family of special military products to help fight the war on terror. They are to be basically defensive products using acoustics, MEMS/nanotechnology, sensing, data augmentation, etc., technologies that will help us locate explosives before they do damage to people and equipment. When we are successful finding the explosives, we will need advanced detonation technology to destroy them."

"That has been the 'Holy Grail' of new warfare theorists. We can destroy the explosives once we know where they are but … can you guys really do this? Do you have a way to find them before they find their target? Really?"

Kan D said, "We have a good start and it will take some breakthroughs. We are encouraged that we will be successful."

Thomas jumped in and said, "Joe, can I tell them?"

"I think so, Thomas. We are among friends here."

"When there is a 'Holy Grail', everyone searches for it or at least wants to search for it. Even we, at Customized Materials Technology, as experts in detonation technology are constantly looking for ways our technology can be extended to other areas. Our new experimental DT product uses acoustical technology. You know, the one that somebody wanted to steal and why we are under investigation right now. It would be great if we could combine our knowledge with what you have and get closer to that 'Holy Grail.'"

Joe said, "I could get really excited about that. How would you like to proceed?"

Chad said, "We don't want to get in the way of the investigation with personal visits at this time. How about we send you, by 24-hour delivery, a confidential disclosure agreement and a subcontractor agreement written around detonation technology? You can review, sign, and return it to Kan D. We can start slowly but once the investigation winds down, we'll step it up a notch or two. I will tell you there may be other companies/people with special skills brought in, too. This is a project of the highest priority."

Joe said, "That will work for us. Please send the documents to Thomas and he will coordinate their review and return to Kan D. Thank you very much."

Chad said, "Thank you and we look forward to having you on the team."

Thomas said, "Kan D, let's stay in touch as you send the documents and I'll review and return them. I am looking forward to what we can do together."

"I am, too," said Kan D. "Thank you, Dr. Blackstone. Thank you, Thomas, for helping get this set up. Anything else, Chad?"

"I don't believe so. We have a good plan in place. Goodbye, Joe and Thomas."

"Good bye, Joe and Thomas," said Kan D.

"Goodbye, Chad and Kan D," said Joe.

"Goodbye, Chad and Kan D," said Thomas.

Cooperative Agreement

Kan D had called Thomas and left a message that the confidential disclosure and subcontractor agreements were in the mail and should arrive in twenty-four hours.

He found the package when the mail was delivered to his office the next day. It was a standard CDA. There was the usual boilerplate stuff but essentially a two-year time period, a limited number of people able to access the information, stuff on communication and documentation and ATP inventions belong to them, CMT inventions are our own and joint inventions share jointly. Okay, we can live with this, Thomas thought.

As he looked at the subcontractor agreement, Thomas again thought, pretty standard. It was all about being able to marry ATP's new Close-In-Explosive Detection Acoustics Technology with CMT's new Acoustics Detonation Technology. It gave the particulars about what and how they would be paid based on time, materials, and milestones. That all seemed okay because it was very close to what he and Kan D had discussed. The last page was new to him. The first part was about CMT indemnifying, or holding harmless, ATP on everything related to the current federal investigation. It was to be in effect from the date of agreement 'in perpetuity' and covered virtually all aspects of their new detonation product past, present, and future. Thomas thought that is a bit much to put into the agreement, but I guess they have to protect themselves. The scenarios he came up with involved a big fine or an actual termination of the subcontractor agreement. Either or both could theoretically impact ATP negatively.

The last part was about compensation or accommodation to ATP if the subcontractor agreement was terminated for any reason associated with the results of the investigation. He thought this was also a bit extreme, but maybe ATP could get left holding the bag if we can't continue the work. The terminology in the agreement about compensation or accommodation included return of the monies paid to CMT up to termination or an exclusive cost-free license of any CMT technology developed up to termination. The choice was ATP's of course.

Thomas thought about this a long time with respect to the investigation, his involvement in the matter, the impact on the company, and what he should do.

He finally said to himself, I am going to recommend to Joe that we sign the agreement. First, CMT needs to be working with ATP on this major antiterrorist program. Who else is there with detonation technology like ours? Second, the investigation about the attempted theft of our new product is just that. It is not about me accepting small gifts from a potential supplier. Third, even if they find out what I did, they might terminate me but certainly not the subcontractor agreement. Last, return of the monies for work done during the agreement up to termination or access to the developed technology via a cost-free, exclusive license agreement seemed reasonable to him. They either get their money back or they get the technology they paid for. Sounds like something I would write into an agreement under these circumstances.

Thomas put the two agreements together, with signature pages flagged on both. He took a large Post-It® and wrote: Mr. Blackstone, I have reviewed both the CDA and the subcontractor agreement, and recommend you sign both. It would be to our great benefit to work with ATP on this top priority project. I would hope that the current investigation of attempted stolen goods will be completed soon with a positive outcome and therefore not impact our work under the agreements. Please sign in duplicate where flagged for each document and return to me. I will see that they get back to ATP immediately. Thank you. Thomas.

Thomas tossed the clipped documents into his outbox. He sat back and thought about working on the project with Kan D. She had some unusual talent.

More Investigation

As they arrived at CMT, the investigative team separated and went directly to their area offices.

Mark met with the HR manager, who was helping him and said, "Please have all the files, except the six of the executive team, boxed up like I have them categorized and sent one-day delivery to D.C. at this address."

"Pardon me, all eighty-eight of them?"

"Yes, please. I want to personally review the executive team files. We might need to look at more but for now eighty-eight to D.C. and six stay here. Thank you."

"Yes, sir."

As the employee files were carried from his office, Mark busied himself with the executive team files. He saw by Title, President, R&D Director, Marketing and Sales Director, Manufacturing Director, Logistics Director, and Administrative

Director. The latter was the largest and it contained what looked like everything else not included in the other five areas of responsibility: human resources, legal, regulatory, planning and strategy, etc. Based on the discussion by Jack and Frank last night at the Squealing Pig, he thought he should focus on the president, Joe Blackstone, and the logistics director, Thomas Kramley. It did seem logical that either separately or together they had a good chance to impact the outcome of a new product shipment. It was a good place to start.

The files were exquisite looking and very well done. The order of the files was all the same: work history, performance reviews, compensation, benefits, education, and other. Investigators always look at the "other" segment of the file first. Mark did the same; he had been through these HR investigations many times. He looked at Joe's first. This man was an icon. He started the company, was the technology brains behind the products with 52 patents, had many letters of commendation from government officials, was director on several non-profit boards, city council, and on and on. His jaw dropped when in amongst the last pages was the letter about the Presidential Medal of Honor. Mark thought, Oh my God. I guess we can take this guy off the suspect list. He simply closed the file and pushed it to the other side of the table.

Next was the file for Thomas. He had a rather skinny "other" section. There were letters of thank you about his work at Berkeley and the University of Michigan. Then Mark saw it – a note from Joe Blackstone indicating that Thomas was having family health problems and had been capped out on the lifetime maximum on his health insurance. The note also showed that he had loaned Thomas a lot of money, one hundred thousand dollars, to pay medical bills after the insurance stopped. In addition, he was trying to acquire what he called sub-prime health insurance from various insurers of whom Mark had never heard. "Cost and reputation are two big factors there, I bet," Mark said softly. "Joe Blackstone is quite a guy. Thomas has a need for extra money to take care of the health problems of his family. It must really be serious to have capped out the lifetime maximum. What a bummer!" Could this be enough to cause him to do some questionable things related to the

THE CAMPAIGN OF FEAR

CMT investigation? It is a lead; a good lead. Mark looked through the other four files and found nothing unusual. He stacked the five files into one pile and kept Thomas's file separate to review more closely when convenient. Mark immediately picked up the phone and dialed Frank.

"Hello, this is Frank."

"Hi, Frank, this is Mark. I think I may have found something but I want both you and Jack to hear it at the same time. Let me put you on hold and dial Jack, okay?"

"Okay."

"Hello, this is Jack."

"Hi, Jack, this is Mark. I have Frank on hold ready to be patched into our conversation. I have found something in Thomas Kramley's file that may be important to our investigation. I want to talk to both of you at the same time.

"Okay, Mark."

Mark said, "Okay, here we go" and pushed the conference button. "Are you there, Frank?"

"Yes, I am, Mark."

"Are you still there, Jack?"

"Yes, I am, Mark. It seems that you have mastered conference calling already. Hi, Frank."

"Hello, Jack. Say, Mark, Thomas and I are just getting ready to go through the list of questions that Jack and I put together. Is this related to supply chain process in any way?"

"Not directly but it could be an influencing factor in how certain decisions were made. I'll just tell you both straight out and you can factor the information into your work. Thomas's file indicates that his family, wife and one son, has severe health issues to the extent of maxing out his health insurance. Blackstone loaned him a hundred thousand dollars and is trying to get new off-market health insurance for him as we speak. I think it could put him at risk or vulnerable if put into a 'special gift' or 'bribe' situation. I thought both of you would like to know as soon as possible as you begin to focus on Kramley and Blackstone. By the way, I found nothing as a red flag on Blackstone. Everything points to the fact that he is a great guy. Did you know that he won the Presidential Medal of Honor?"

Jack and Frank both said something like, "what" and "wow" at the same time.

Mark said, "That is all I have for now. There is nothing on the other executives and I am sending the other files to D.C. to be reviewed."

"Thanks, Mark, and great work," Jack said.

"Thanks, Mark. It's good to have the new information and it could not be timelier," said Frank.

Jack said, "Frank, be careful not to let him know that you know, okay?"

Mark said, "Good plan. I'll talk to you two later. Goodbye for now."

"Bye, Mark."

"Bye, Mark."

Aldora Checks In With Jack

Jack had just hung up from the call with Mike and Frank when the phone rang again.

"Hello, this is Jack."

"Hi, Jack, this is Aldora. Just checking in to let you now that there are several people in D.C. looking at electronic records on patent proposals, reports, presentations, everything. A couple of things: Joe Blackstone seems to be squeaky clean and everything he does is strictly by the book. Our Thomas Kramley appears to be okay, too, but I need to a look a little further. He had some trips to Berkeley and Michigan where he carried large amounts of grant and fellowship monies to the universities. Looks like pretty standard practice, and I'll check some details. I don't have anything on anybody else yet."

"Thanks, Aldora. Say, I just talked with Mark and Frank. Mark discovered some things about Kramley, too, such as serious health issues with both his wife and son. The costs have been so enormous that he can no longer get regular health insurance.

Something about going over the lifetime cap. Blackstone has given him a personal loan of a hundred thousand dollars. I don't know any more right now; he may be desperate for money to pay bills. Would you look really closely at both his business and personal financial dealings, please? Go just far enough to not attract attention. If we have to subpoena him and his bank and credit records, we'll do that later."

"Will do Jack, glad that I called you. I'll let Frank and Mark know that I am up to speed on Kramley and what I'm doing in the financial area.

"Thanks, Aldora. I'll talk to you again later."

"Bye, Jack."

The Liberator Calls Omar

The call came on the special phone in the equipment room adjacent to Omar's office. Of course, he knew immediately who it was and rushed to answer.

"Hello, Liberator. I did not expect another call from you so soon."

"I had hoped this call could be avoided or at least the news would not be so potentially detrimental to our cause. Omar, the technology work that you have done for us has been wonderful. The gifts to the universities, the partnerships, the investments, all of these have been right on target. It is your lack of finesse or risk management or future-state scenario planning or outcome based predictive capabilities that have gotten us into trouble."

"I am sorry, sir."

"Our contacts and sources tell us that the U.S. government may be looking into your recent activities. President Abbott and Congress, to identify, develop, and protect the United States' most important technologies, have formed a new department, the DoAT. Secretary Grant Adams was confirmed to lead the effort. His three lieutenants are really serious about what they have been assigned to do, especially Director Dr. Sam Elson who is in charge of 'protection.' Our sources tell us that he is a behavioral psychologist and an expert

121

in using the smallest amounts of information to get very accurate predictions of the future. His computer and software skills have allowed him to be successful at the individual, team, corporate, organizational, domestic, and international levels. In other words, he is extremely good at using a small number of facts and figures to produce very accurate scenarios of what could be happening on a larger scale and further, what the outcome might be. It is like getting to the big picture, the puzzle picture using the smallest number of pixels or pieces. Why is this important? Don't try to answer that, it was a rhetorical question. We believe that Dr. Elson is on your trail as we speak. We believe he knows, by this time, about your technology testing and fieldwork on new products at CMT. There is a big investigation going on because of the failed attempt to steal their new product. We believe he knows about your visit to ATP and the project notes that were lost at that time. We believe he knows about your contact with GPRI to get technology information and now your proposed investment in the spin off, Tully Research, Inc. If Dr. Elson and his people at DoAT can collect enough information and put it together in the right way, they will know what we are doing to protect our 'Campaign of Fear'. I will not allow them to beat us in this race. We have to find out very quickly exactly what they are planning to do with this acoustical technology."

Omar ventured a comment, at great risk of angering the caller even more saying, "Of the three leads that seem to be promising, I think our inroads at CMT might be our greatest advantage, even though there is a current investigation. I believe that our contact there has been protected from involvement in the attempted theft. I know that he is very interested in having CMT license our technology. Even though there is an ongoing investigation, is there an angle we could play with him?"

"There may be. However, I would rather try to penetrate ATP further since they have the government contract and seem to be the lead in this new project involving acoustics. My guess is that if anything happens with Tully Research, Incorporated or CMT, it will be to benefit the work that ATP is doing. What do you think?"

"You might be right, sir. We have been doing so much

with their intranet, company contacts, project people contacts, and journal searches that they may already believe they are being infiltrated. I was actually planning to slow down with them until a little later. They might believe that I stole the notes but they have no proof. The same is true with the contacts and the searches we have been making. They might suspect something but have absolutely no proof. If we try to penetrate further now, they may well start putting two and two together."

"That is good thinking, Omar; what would you suggest?"

"I have a confession to make first, sir. In my eagerness to set up our contact at CMT, Mr. Thomas Kramley, I might have made a mistake. What do they say in this country? Hindsight is 20:20? Anyway, I offered money and he accepted it to work with us on the so-called field tests. His family has some health issues."

"Oh, my, Omar. Was it a significant amount and can it be found in the DoAT investigation?"

"We paid him fifty thousand dollars each time to help us field test our experimental products. It went into a secret offshore bank account so finding it will be almost impossible unless he tells them."

Omar could tell he was in trouble when the caller said, "Fifty thousand dollars for each test?"

"Yes sir."

"You can hide the account but you can't hide the spending."

"Sir, Mr. Kramley did mention that the first fifty thousand had already been spent even before the second project."

"That is what the investigation will turn up. They will see large amounts spent on family health and inquire from where it came. And, our Mr. Kramley will eventually tell them. His not-so-logical reasoning was that it was a good deal for him and his company. He got money for paying health care bills and the company got a first crack at new technology to help them succeed. What didn't cross his mind were that TIC's motives beyond testing new technology and the ethics behind accepting money unbeknownst to the company for doing this. Personally, I don't give a damn about company or personal ethics, Omar. This is war and our 'Campaign of Fear' must continue."

Omar ventured another comment, "Praise be to Allah."

"Don't interrupt, Omar. My conclusion is that this man, Kramley, will talk and you, Omar, have put us at great risk again."

"I am sorry, sir, but it seemed appropriate at the time. My thinking was that it would not seem far-fetched to pay for field testing of our new technology products. What I did not consider was in what form the payment should be made. Perhaps it should have been something to benefit not just one person but the whole company instead. One consideration would have been a royalty-free license of the technology for a year or something like that."

"There were many options possible at the time you made the decision, Omar. I should have been consulted."

"I know sir. It was just that it was so easy to suck Kramley in with money that he needed for additional health care for his family."

"You acted too fast! I believe he would have done it for nothing because of the value our new technology and products brought to his company and their logistics operation."

"No doubt you are correct, sir."

"Omar, here's what I want you to do. Immediately get in touch with your Mr. Thomas Kramley and tell him to stop spending the money you have paid him. Get him to agree to keep you apprised of the investigation so we will know if the government is getting too close. Tell him in no uncertain terms that divulging the information about the money to the investigators would not be good for him or us. It must be kept a secret or else!"

"Yes, sir, I will do it immediately. I believe Mr. Kramley will be agreeable to those conditions."

"Good. Next, make a plan for the elimination of Kramley. I want to review and approve it, of course. If we see the DoAT investigation getting too close, we will implement it."

Without thinking, Omar said, "Are you sure, sir?"

"Omar, you will follow my orders explicitly from now on or you will be removed and replaced."

Omar gulped as he thought what that would mean to his reputation and future with the organization.

"Yes, sir, you have my word, sir."

"Now, let's both think about ATP and how to penetrate further without making them even more suspicious or worse yet, getting caught. The next time I contact you, please have both the elimination plan and the penetration plan ready for discussion.

"Yes, sir, I will." Omar heard the phone go silent so he also ended the call. He stood there shaking. He thought, I will have to work fast because who knows when he will call again. If I am removed, it will be a suicide bomber mission for me. Can I do this? If not, is my faith strong enough to give up my life? Maybe, maybe not.

The Ultimatum

Omar was still shaking as he dialed the number for Thomas Kramley and waited for him to answer.

"Thomas Kramley here."

There was the usual long pause when he called. Then "Hello, Thomas, this is Omar Kharif from TIC."

"Omar, thank God, did you hear what happened to our shipment of new technology product on which we used your Mach II system and data augmentation software?"

Omar was thinking fast, "No, Thomas, I have been out of town a few days and just got time to call and see how things went."

"I think the field test of your new product went very well indeed, but all hell broke loose once the shipment arrived at its destination in Israel."

"What happened?"

"Someone, actually an organized team of men, tried to steal some of the product. The Mossad, who was the actual customer, somehow found about the plan and were there to stop it." Thomas took a deep breath and continued, "The men all escaped except for the pilot of a second plane; he committed suicide. The second plane was there to transport the product from Zefat to some unknown destination."

"The experimental product must have been very valuable for them to go to such lengths."

"Yes, our technology is new and top secret so we suspect that many terrorist organizations would like to gain access to it. We have talked about that before."

"I know, Thomas. Is there any chance that TIC can get hurt by any of this? Our field test had nothing to do with what happened, of course. The terrorists were after your product and technology."

"I believe that is true, Omar. However, it is so serious that the federal government has sent an investigative team here to review our personnel and processes. Who knows what they will find!"

"Thomas, our work was for the good of CMT and TIC, as you know. You were provided access to some cutting edge technology that would improve your supply chain operations. We were getting our new product tested in the field under real-life conditions. No one can fault anyone for that. The one area that could be a bit sticky is the money we gave you. I know it was for a good cause and we were glad to pay it, but it might not pass the corporate ethics test."

"I know. I have been worried about the money ever since the investigation started. If they find out, it is going to be trouble for both of us."

"Thomas, TIC cannot afford that kind of visibility, ever. I have some conditions that you must meet. You must stop spending the money right now. You must agree to keep me posted on the investigation. You must not disclose that there was ever a financial arrangement between us. If you do not keep TIC out of this, there will be dire consequences to pay."

"Are you threatening me, Omar?"

"Thomas, we have been friends, colleagues, businessmen together but all that goes away if TIC gets caught up in a federal investigation. I'm afraid that my superiors will take very drastic action to protect our organization and its mission. Do you understand?"

"Not the part about the dire consequences. What the hell does that mean?"

"I think you know what it means. Both of us are in big trouble if this is discovered. Just play this smart and everything will be fine. We have protected ourselves with the offshore account. They will never find that. The only way they can learn about the money is for you to tell them. Just keep your mouth shut and we'll get through this. Remember, it is not just TIC that would be in trouble. You would be charged with accepting payoffs from potential suppliers and giving them special favors. Since your work is under government military contract, they would probably lock you up under some obscure article of the Patriot Act for a long, long time ... that is, if we don't get to you first."

"You are serious, aren't you?"

"Damn right! If we are both to survive this, stop spending the money, keep me updated on the investigation, and don't talk about our arrangement no matter what. Okay?"

Omar ended the call and wondered if his warning was enough. Still feeling the surge of adrenaline, he thought about an elimination plan for Thomas. *I have never done this before, but I can see it is necessary. The Liberator was right.*

Chapter 5

Brad's Acoustic Technology Breakthrough

The Breakthrough

After returning from D.C., Brad spent a lot of concentrated time on his research. He preferred that to rounding up investors, doing subcontract work for others, or being a secret agent man. He knew he was very close with his most recent work done at GPRI. No matter what was in those reports, the most important advancement would be the software code to separate each unique wave pattern. If he could do that, Phase II would be achievable. Maybe Phase I would even be very short-lived and eliminated.

Brad was up early that morning. From the breakfast table, where he was having a bagel and yogurt, he was able to look out the window and see the Mississippi River, the locks and dam, the Post Office, the light rail on Fifth Street, Mill City, and the Guthrie beyond. If he craned his neck even more, he could see the bigger part of downtown Minneapolis.

I like the place, Brad thought. When Zen comes, maybe we will do some exploring together. Can I hope that there would be something lasting between us this time? He let his mind wander to the last time. Brad smiled. The last time had been the first time. Some years back he had been writing his thesis and Zen had just passed her original research proposal defense. They were in the same department, the same research area of chemical sensing. Brad had told her once that he thought her work was pretty darn good and when she passed her proposal, he would buy her a beer. Secretly, he really liked her and hoped she would like him. The research proposals were always a little traumatic for graduate students. It was another hurdle on the road to the PhD where the student had to come up with an original research idea and defend it before the faculty. This was in addition to qualifiers, cumulatives, course work, thesis research and having a life, too. In the sequence of requirements for the PhD, the research proposal was a big step. By finishing it successfully, one was recognized as well on the way to finishing your PhD. Yes, you had to finish the thesis work but you were considered capable of novel and significant research ideas. Admittedly, this was important because whether in academia or industry, one would have to generate these new ideas for the rest of one's career.

Brad's reverie continued. The faculty sometimes really gave the students a hard time. This had happened to Zen, but not because of the quality of her proposal; it was excellent. She had shown it to me beforehand, I assumed because she liked and respected me, and being the great guy I am, I told her it was 'pretty good'. Why did he use that term with her? It was intended to be sort of a put down because, hey, I'm the lead dog here, right? Anyway, she went into her proposal defense with a little too much hesitancy and got hammered by a couple of faculty members. In the ordeal, she recovered well enough to pass because it was a great proposal and she did finally get most of her confidence back. I remember to this day, she left the conference room by my laboratory, stood outside while the faculty voted, and paced back and forth. She wouldn't look at me in the lab, even as I tried to give her a thumbs up, and carried a very serious and concerned look on her face. Her advisor came out of the conference room, found her pacing and, from my vantage point, by reading his lips made out that he said, "Zen, you passed!" She didn't need to hear anything else and started jumping up and down and yelling, "I passed, I passed." That was when Zen opened the door to my lab and said, "I passed" as if she was saying, "So there, lead dog." In her euphoria and in my charismatic style, I said, "Good. Guess I owe you a beer sometime." She said, "You sure as hell do; so let's go Mr. Bradford Tully."

I was so surprised that I immediately stopped writing, pushed away from the computer, and started to the door. She had moved away from the door a bit and her advisor caught up to her and finished talking about the defense. He congratulated her and held out his hand to shake. Zen just gave him a big hug and a kiss. The she came to collect me.

We drank more than one beer that evening. Zen had more than I did; it resulted in me offering to let her sleep at my apartment, which was really close by. We swung back to the lab, picked up her bicycle, and arrived at my place after midnight. One thing let to another and, well, it just happened. It was good. Then we zonked out quickly and the night went by fast. The next morning I could tell she was very quiet and preoccupied. She quickly gathered her things and as she opened the door to leave, said, "Thanks for the beer, see you at the lab." I didn't have the presence of mind to say anything, of course. That was the last time I had really seen her prior to the recent ACS conference.

Brad shook himself out of his thoughts of the past. I need to get to work, he said to himself. He made his way to the lab in order to review what he had done in the last couple of days. Based on the little he knew about the work being done by ATP, CMT, TIC and references by Director Elson, Brad had concluded a couple of things. He might have already technically passed beyond the acoustics and sensing work of Advanced Technology Products. It sounded like explosives, their location, and detonation was the name of the game. Based on those conclusions, he had made several trips to the local stores and purchased the components of every explosive he could find. Not all were available but surprisingly about 90% were. He was able to purchase them with few questions asked. They were brought back to the lab for testing. Brad thought at one point that if anybody found all this stuff in his lab, he would be arrested. Brad smiled. His one phone call would be to Director of DoAT, Dr. Sam Elson.

The box of explosive components with perhaps twenty

different items was located at the far end of the laboratory for several hours. The first experiment was to confirm that Phase I technology worked. That is, could he generate the wave, have it travel the distance of a couple hundred feet from wall to wall in the warehouse basement to the box of goodies, reverse the wave, collect it, and analyze it? The answer was yes. It would work for every component in the wave-front where he had created a standard using his new computer software. A way of thinking about this for the non-chemist is to take a component, say dynamite, TNT, or trinitrotoluene, which are all the same thing. Its chemical fingerprint is collected from the returning wave using unique vacuum techniques that he had developed and analyzed by special spectroscopy methods. The results of the analysis are fed into the software program, which uses its enormous database to search through and identify the $C_7H_5N_3O_6$ compounds to be dynamite. This is done instantaneously, continuously, automatically, and effortlessly. Each element, compound, and composition that has a vapor pressure gives off a telltale chemical marker, if you will, that can be collected and identified. Since there are only very small amounts of these materials to collect, we are talking advanced analytical techniques, computer augmentation, software enhancements, and best-case identification with the information available. The equipment is a little bulky and the methodology has a cumbersome number of steps, but it works. The box at the other end of the warehouse does contain TNT among other components. Thank God now you know it and can decide what to do about it, he thought.

Phase II was more elegant and sophisticated as a solution but required some of the most advanced software code known. Before leaving GPRI, Brad was able to identify and catalogue several of the unique wave patterns that belong to individual elements and compounds. There was much more work needed to separate the very complex compositions, but it was a start. The hard part was what he had done in the past few days. Almost nonstop, he had written the software code for the separation of the total wave front into its separate wave front components. How many individual wave patterns can be contained within a wave front? It depended on where the wave originated and its environment as it was generated and then reversed. He had proved that each component contained therein would have a unique wave pattern. In fact, he had a starter catalogue, but could he separate them? You might use this example for a better understanding, he thought. Suppose you had an audio recording that contained twenty different languages all saying something different at the same time. Could you separate them into the individual languages and be able to translate each one of them? An acoustical wave front with its twenty different signature component wave patterns isn't much different. Can you separate and identify them?

Brad thought that his software code was groundbreaking but he couldn't be sure until it had been tested. This was the morning for the test. He wanted to go slowly so he had decided there would be only a few different things in the box, a few things from oil fields, like oil shale, sulphur, crude oil, and some explosives like TNT and nitroglycerine. The computer had the data on the wave patterns for the oil-related components and he had just generated the acoustic patterns for TNT and nitroglycerine. Everything was ready. He loaded and activated the new separation software and synched it with the database, focused the wave generator, set the distance and the sensors, and pulled the trigger. The damper worked really well, again making hardly any sound. It was over in a second. The computer was chugging along, one second, two seconds and then began to spit out the data. It was organized into several columns titled *wave pattern #, % total, db match, degree of confidence with data augmentation* and *without data augmentation*, etc. The printout named five wave patterns, identified how much of each, matched the patterns to the components in the box, and gave the percent confidence as 80-85% without data augmentation and 100% with data augmentation. Brad was jumping up and down, hollering at the top of his voice, "It works, it works!!"

Suddenly his mind shifted to the time when Zen had passed her proposal defense. He was acting the same way she did. What did that mean? Shaking himself back to reality, Brad knew he needed to get the unique wave patterns of more components and complex compositions into the system and do a lot more testing to catch any bugs in the code, but this was a real breakthrough. Who should he tell? Investors? The government? Partners? Everyone? Or no one?

Zen Does the Advance Work

Zen had talked to Chad and he was very interested in having Brad and Tully Research as a partner on the CIED project. With Brad's background, Chad knew he could help on both acoustics and sensing. Furthermore, he had discussed it with Director Elson and had received his approval as well.

Even though Zen was the youngest and least senior of the project team, she knew how to get things done. She understood the advance planning needed to make a meeting go well. She knew how to get to yes and she understood the politics at play. For these reasons she had already talked with Bill. It was one thing to bring in an expert in your own area like sensing and be okay with that. It was something quite different to bring in an expert who would no doubt challenge one of your colleagues. This was the case with Bill Brewer and Brad Tully and acoustics.

Zen said, "Hi, Bill. In our recent impromptu meeting, Chad asked me to get us together with Brad Tully. He has located his new company, Tully Research, Inc., in Minneapolis, Minnesota, and is ready to do business. I know he can help me in sensing. Would you be interested in talking with him about acoustics?"

"Zen, I wondered if and how you were going to approach me before the telephone conference call actually happened. You are going to make a great manager one of these days soon. Yes, I would be interested in talking with Dr. Tully. His work, if I am right, might be the technology extension we need for our Generation II product. Right now, even though there is a lot to do, I am comfortable we will be able to generate the short-range wave-front, reverse it, collect, analyze, and identify even the minutest components captured. I believe his work might allow for longer distances and faster identification of the components. We will need both. He is no doubt searching for funding as we speak. A short-term, specific-task subcontract opportunity might look pretty good to him right now. There are always bills to pay."

"Bill, I hoped you would say that but sometimes you really surprise me."

"I know when I need help. With a project like this, it is not so much the acoustics technology as it is the software. He might be able to help Lyncoln as much as me."

"I'll set up the call as soon as possible. Thank you."

Conference Call

It was ungodly early when the call came in, but Brad had agreed to 7 AM CST. He picked up the phone on the third ring and said, "Hello from Minnesota."

Zen was leading the call from Boston and responded, "Hello from Boston. I have my boss, Chad Bromcast, and colleague, Bill Brewer, on the line with me."

Chad said, "Hello, Brad. Zen has told me so much about you; I am glad we can finally meet and talk."

"Likewise, Chad."

Bill chimed in, "Hello, Brad. I know of your work and I have been impressed by it. I assume you are still working in advanced acoustics."

"Hi, Bill. I know a few things about your work, too. It has been hard to keep up with you. Yes, I have finally been able to get back to my acoustics research. Starting my new company has not been easy, but I'm beginning to make some progress.

Chad spoke up, "Zen, if I may, I'll give Brad the fifteen-second summary of our project and how his expertise could help."

"Great, Chad. Brad, can you see that we are really organized here?"

"It appears that way. Good pre-planning and I'm glad someone else is doing the talking. Fire away, Chad."

"We'll get to the real confidential stuff later when we have a confidential disclosure agreement in place. For now, suffice it to say we have a huge government contract to provide products to our military to help in the war on terror. We plan to develop a family of defensive products that rely, in large part on acoustics technology but also will depend on sensing, MEMS, OLEDS, data augmentation, and nanotechnologies. Timing is short and we are moving very fast. Bill has his hands full on our Generation I product. Is that how you would say it, Bill?"

"Yes, it is true that Generation I will buy us some time but we do not know how much. Chad and all of the team leaders believe we should start on Generation II as soon as possible. Since we are all so busy, this is where you come in. There is no one else in the world who has your set of proven skills, Brad, in advanced acoustics, sensing, and software code technology. Simply put, we need your help. Chad, back to you."

"Thanks, Bill. Brad, there are a number of ways we can do this if you are interested."

Brad said, "Do you know Sam Elson?"

Chad spoke first, "Yes, we do, He is Director of DoAT and the sponsor of our contract. He knew that we would be talking to you."

"I thought so, you all sound alike. May I suggest something? Why don't you send Zen out here with a CDA and a proposal for a subcontractor relationship between Tully Research, Inc. and Advanced Technology Products? I'll sign the CDA and Zen can give me the details about the project and how I would fit in. Bill, I would appreciate some notes from you on what you think is needed in the acoustics area for Generation II. Your candid assessment will help me a lot. If it all hangs together and I think I can help, I'll sign the subcontractor agreement too. Zen, there is a great Cuban restaurant just a few blocks from my place. Their "Midnight Pie" is something special. How does that sound?"

Zen said, "Your business suggestion or the Midnight Pie? Either is alright with me, but Chad, what do you think?"

"It's a deal, Brad. I know Zen will be able to convince you to join us. Thanks for the opportunity to get you on our team. I think we can have things put together quickly and Zen can be there in a couple of days."

"Great. Good to talk with all of you. Zen, I will see you in a couple of days. Call me when your schedule is firm and remember you just take the train from the airport to the last stop in Minneapolis. I'll meet you at the time you tell me."

Zen thanked Brad by saying, "It's going to be great having you on the team. See you soon."

Bill said, "Thanks, Brad, good discussion. If you don't mind, I will send along a summary of the Generation I acoustics so you will more fully understand where we are. This will put my assessment on what is needed for Generation II more into perspective."

"I would not have expected anything less from you, Bill. Thanks very much."

Chad closed with, "Thank you, Brad. This was a very productive call. Sorry it was so early for you. We'll follow the plan we laid out and as we have all said, we need you and look forward to having you on the team?"

"Thanks, Chad, it sounds like we can make this work. See you soon, Zen. Goodbye."

Zen, Chad, and Bill all responded, "Goodbye, Brad."

They hung up the phone and Chad said, "I think we got him. The others, Zen and Bill, nodded their heads and smiled. They headed out of the office to get back to work. Zen was thinking that Midnight Pie sounded good.

Sam Talks With Brad

The phone was ringing as Brad ran from the basement to the first floor of his warehouse district lab, office and apartment unit. He picked it up on the fourth ring. "Hello, Tully Research, Brad Tully speaking."

"Hello, Brad, this is Sam Elson, how are you doing?"

"Good, Sam, actually better than good. Things are happening so fast, maybe too fast. You no doubt know that Advanced Technology Products has contacted me about helping with their big government contract project. In the next few days, Zenica Lang will bring a CDA and subcontractor agreement for me

THE CAMPAIGN OF FEAR

to review and sign. They were really pushing to peak my interest but I think it is right up my alley. Why not get paid to do work I was planning to do anyway? I talked to Chad Bromcast and Bill Brewer as well. Chad seems very competent and I know of Bill's work. He is a top-notch acoustics scientist and it was important that he thinks I can help and wants me to be part of the team. Based on what we talked about, Sam, do you think this is a good idea?"

"I do, Brad. In fact, it will make our work easier as we develop information about TIC. Do you need to know anymore about the project?"

"I probably have enough for now, Sam, and Zen will be here soon. I'll sign the CDA and then she can give me all the details."

"Sounds good."

Brad continued, "Speaking of TIC, the paperwork for their investment in Tully Research arrived recently."

"Yes, you mentioned they offered you lots of money. How much are they investing and under what terms?"

"$10 million per year for five years. They have some stuff in the agreement relating to a 10% ownership of the company, the ability to license the technology for a fee, and access to my technical reports. It all sounds okay on the surface. My attorney says it's a good deal and I should sign it."

"Maybe too good? I hope we are wrong about our suspicions concerning TIC, but until we find out, let's play along. Sign it and see if you get the first $10 million."

"Okay, partner, I will. Sam, I wanted to tell you about my research too. In just a few days of concentrated work writing code, I have had a scientific breakthrough that is almost unimaginable. We are on a secure line, right?"

"Yes, of course, I should have told you when we started talking. It will be standard practice with us from now on."

"Good. You write code so you will understand my excitement. My business plan involves a rather normal progression of acoustics technology development. Phase I is simply to generate

137

a wave that travels a certain distance, bounce it back and identify anything and everything captured in the returning wave. This is basically what I was doing early on at GPRI to help find new petroleum deposits. The kicker is that, although this technology can be used to identify almost anything that is chemically based, it is very cumbersome. I'm not sure; this might be the guts of the Advanced Technology Products project that you sponsor."

"Brad, you are closer than you might guess. I am so glad that you are on our side and we are working on this together."

"Thanks. Here is the exciting part. I believe my theory about the potential for acoustics was right. In analyzing the bounce-back waves, I have found they are indeed uniquely changed. It is not just a returning wave of the type generated but a combination of a number of smaller waves. Using a novel computer separation technique, I can isolate each separate and unique wave, which can be correlated with individual chemical elements and compounds. My new software code does everything: the separation, the correlation, and the identification. Can you believe it? We may have leapfrogged the best current technology that is still under development. This is not evolutionary but revolutionary stuff. Whoops, wrong word, but you know what I mean."

"I do, Brad. This will be a huge help for ATP's project. Did you mention your theory to TIC?"

"In sort of a sketchy way but I also mentioned that it was pretty far off and not really part of the business plan."

"Good, please keep this part about your recent research findings very quiet. Tell no one. I know there is a lot of work to do to realize its full potential, but this might be an advancement worth killing for. I don't want to scare you, but we have to be very careful. Your open strategy should be to stay laser focused on the technology outlined in the current published business plan. Do you understand?"

Brad could sense the tenseness in Sam's voice and said, "Yes, sir. I just had to tell someone and who better than my government agent partner? Can it be useful in those scenarios you were talking about?"

"Maybe, maybe so; I'll work on it. Thanks for all the information about ATP, TIC and your research. Let's talk again soon."

"I would like that, partner. Goodbye for now."

"Goodbye, Brad."

Jack Talks With Joe

Jack saw Joe Blackstone go into his office. It was the first time he had been around since the investigation started. He walked over, hoping to get some of his time. No, expecting to get some of his time.

"Hello, Mr. Blackstone. I am Jack Borson, team leader for the DoAT investigation here."

"Hi, Jack, it's Joe, Joe Blackstone. I know your boss, Sam Elson, from way back. Good guy, too! Sam reamed me a new one just before you arrived, but I am glad you are here. We have never had anything like this happen before. I want some answers, too. I am at your disposal for as long as you need me."

"Thank you, Joe. Director Elson said good things about you, too. It has been a busy few days since leaving D.C. so first I'll try to bring you up to date on the work of the team investigating the attempted theft of prototype, top secret, and detonation technology military products. As you know, it usually comes down to people and events in cases like this. The director said you think it must be an inside job. I assume you believe that the massive confidential information pool, security protection measures, and other safeguards would not allow an outsider to learn enough to do this."

"That's right, I do. Whoever it is had to have some help!" This company has done some great things for our country and most of our people are as committed to it as I am. Mark my words, something happened inside!"

"We are looking at all the angles right now and your people are giving us good support. Thanks for that."

"Listen, I want this resolved. Do you need anything?

Anything at all?"

"Not really, at least for the time being. Do you know much about Thomas Kramley?"

"Thomas? You are not thinking he had something to do with this, are you?"

"Everybody is on the list until we know enough to take them off."

"Fair enough, I hope you are looking at me the same way."

"You can be sure we are, sir."

"What about Thomas? He is part of the leadership team of the company. He has been here a long time and really knows his stuff. Logistics and supply chain has been a great niche for him. He has saved our butt many times with his knowledge of advanced technology in these areas. He keeps us on the leading edge of getting products to our customers. He represents us well at universities, primarily Berkeley and Michigan, when we make research grants or provide scholarships and fellowships. It is a big responsibility to know the professors and their research and the top undergraduate and graduate students to best direct our funding. Over the years, this has amounted to millions of dollars and the top schools and professors get the most money. Thomas has been able to bring needed technology to our programs, hire people into several different areas, and secure some community, state and national recognition for CMT."

Jack said, "Looks like he is one of the good ones. We saw mentioned some very severe health issues with his wife and son. Can you tell me about this, please?"

"Yes, I know some of the facts but not all of them. It has been very tough for him. The remarkable thing is that he still keeps contributing at about the same high level all the time. As I understand, his son has multiple sclerosis and his wife has not been able to cope. She has severe psychological problems and has become basically dysfunctional. The MS is a more rapidly advancing type and very debilitating. It started with what Thomas described as tingly feelings in the boy's fingers and progressed throughout his body. His son is less than ten years old and almost unable to do anything for himself. This has taken a lot of money and he was handling it until his wife started fantasizing about everything. She needs psychiatric care, hospitalization, and deep medication on an ongoing basis. Anyway, he maxed out his health insurance, they cancelled his policy, and I made a personal loan to him of one hundred thousand dollars. I suspect that it is mostly gone by now. There is a chance that some off-market health insurance is available, so I'm trying that route for him."

"What a sad story. Do you think he might have been compromised in his search for money to care for his family and put the company at risk?"

"Thomas? No way! I believe that even in the darkest of times, he would never do anything to endanger the company."

"That's good, Joe. We'll continue to look at him but your support gives me hope that there is nothing untoward happening here. May I ask you some questions about the shipment of product to Israel?"

"Yes, of course. That is why you are here, right?"

"Right. Just what does this top secret product do?"

"It uses a sophisticated acoustical wave to detonate various kinds of roadside bombs. You can guess where in the world the product could be useful."

"It sounds so simple. Does it work?"

"We think it does but it is being field tested now by the Mossad. Some characteristics can be improved. For example: sensitivity, it won't detonate all roadside bombs; distance, it only works at fairly short distances; the technology needs high energy to generate the wave front, etc. But ... it is the best we have at this time. A lot of lives will be saved by this product."

"Who decides when a product like this will be field tested?"

"I do, but I will tell you that the military, our government defense, and technology-related departments and the coalition countries have been clamoring for this product for six months. It may not be perfect, but it will definitely help."

"Did you decide on Israel?"

"Are you kidding me? The powers-that-be met and told me the test country. Only a few internal people knew about the location

.... strictly on a need to know basis."

"What about the production date and the amount to be manufactured?"

"Again, we had to agree, but basically we were told to manufacture within a small window of time. The amount was pretty typical for a prototype or experimental products run. I believe it was somewhat limited by the raw materials available, but fifteen units was a good number."

"Is this another one of your products, sir? I understand you have a hand in the technology of most of the new products. Maybe even the final design and testing? I mean that in only the most positive way, sir. Sorry if it sounded otherwise."

"It's okay, Jack. I get that all the time. The answers are yes, yes, and yes. It is my specialty but I had a lot of help. We have top-notch people here and they have great track records in successful product development."

"One last question. Did you work closely with Thomas Kramley on any aspect of this product and shipment?"

"Not really. I did meet with him in his office on the weekend of the shipment. He was testing some new RFID and software technology that would help track the product during its shipment to Israel. I just popped in; he didn't know I was coming. The new technology was from an outfit called TIC, I think. It was something special and allowed us to follow our product and check on its safety in a way we have never been able to do before. It uses new radio frequency tags with GPS and continuous special sensor information fed back here and analyzed by data augmentation software in our computers."

"Do you think it could have helped our thieves?" asked Jack.

"I don't think so. Only a few people knew the country and the final destination was not known until shortly before shipment was made. The route was very circuitous and the timing was not exact. Thomas and I together watched the tracking components in action as data on location and safety were constantly being monitored on the screen. There was nothing being hidden that I could tell; it was just Thomas doing his job. He was doing it well and on a weekend at that!"

"Thank you, sir. We'll be talking with Thomas soon and get more information on TIC and the tracking device and software. It does sound like they could really help a company in your kind of business. Thanks again."

"You are welcome. Let's plan to talk every few days so that I will know what's going on and if I can help."

"You got it. That is why I am located next door. Goodbye."

Frank Talks With Thomas

Frank was mulling over the information that Mike provided during the three-way conference call. He could not imagine family health issues so severe that no health care provider would touch you. Family is everything and it's not a stretch to think that one would do most anything to protect them. Job and career are always secondary to family under normal circumstances. In this case, the gap becomes much, much wider and the pressure could cause some erratic and risky behavior. I'll have to watch for the signs as I question him and we work together.

"Hey, Thomas, sorry I am a bit late. I had to take a telephone call from my boss. You know how that goes."

"It's okay and yes, I do know about chain of command. I hope your boss is as good as mine. I'm not sucking up; it is really true. The guy is a saint."

"I have been hearing some very impressive things about him. A Presidential Medal of Honor winner?"

"That is just for starters. Do you know he gave me a no-interest personal loan to help pay for family medical bills?"

Frank fibbed a bit and said, "No, I did not. It was great that he could do that for your family. I hope the health issues have been resolved."

"Not really, but we are getting by somehow, thank you. You had some questions for me about what happened with our special shipment to Israel."

"Yes, I do. Let's just plow through them. Don't take offense at any question. I am only trying to get all of the information related to the case. First, who decides on the method of shipment and the route the product takes?"

"Our company does not make the decision on government contracts and experimental products like this. It was a beta test, a field test essentially and the first one on this product. I'll just say the higher ups outside the company made the decision on both the method and route of the shipment. As we displayed on one of the charts, it was a circuitous route but not unusual for a top-secret project. I didn't give it much thought when I saw the plan."

"How do you follow products like this enroute?"

"Up to now, there has been no good way to do it. RFID is beginning to help, but it needs to be more sophisticated. Global positioning systems work but they are expensive and don't work well on small packages. Up to now, our people would physically check the product at various points along the route and report back. With the secrecy imposed on our shipments, this worked most of the time. It just takes one incident, however, to lose critical technology just like what almost happened with our new detonation technology product. Because of that chance, I have been charged with identifying any new and advanced technology that is out there. If appropriate, test it and get it approved for our use."

"That brings up the next question. Were any of these new technology tracking systems incorporated into this shipment?"

"Yes, it is fantastic new technology that I hope we can license soon." Thomas caught himself thinking about the call from Omar threatening him if he talked about the money he received for testing. "We have been testing the technology parts over a period of several weeks. Essentially, it involves an enhanced RFID system with new sensor capability to record various environments to which the product has been subjected. The technology has new and very sophisticated data augmentation software that allows us to react to planned or unplanned events that may impact the viability of the product. It provides, with just minute, factual information, the best possible reaction scenarios. It has a small low-cost GPS with everything connected to our central computer system. That is how we were tracking the shipment, or at least part of it.

"I'm not sure I understood all that but a couple of questions, if I may. You said 'we.' What or who does that mean?"

"Mostly me but Joe came in on the weekend of the shipment to observe. I had kept him up to date on all the testing that eventually led to what we called Mach II. He wanted to see it in operation. He was there on the Sunday before the attempted theft."

"You mentioned that only part of the shipment was being tracked."

"Yes, we only had enough tags for ten of the fifteen packages. TIC could only supply ten tags, but they really worked well. I have recommended that we license the technology from them if at all possible. You had to have been there, Frank. With everything tied into our computers, we could watch the shipment on the monitor travel from San Francisco to Anchorage, London, Frankfurt, and then to Zefat. The readings for all the sensors were displayed continuously to show the product was safe. We had one shock reading from Frankfurt, I think, that was outside the normal range. The data augmentation software took over, predicted the package had been dropped from a height of ten feet. Taking into account packaging, product design features, safety factors, etc. as parameter, the system came up with a scenario that there was 99.9% likelihood the product was undamaged and recommended no action. We have never been able to do anything like this. It is fantastic technology!"

"Who is this TIC that you mentioned?"

"Technology Investment Corporation, headed by Mr. Omar Kharif. I met him sometime ago when he was on his way to Berkeley to present unrestricted research grants to some of the faculty. Their grants to the top universities in the U.S. probably total in the several hundreds of millions of dollars by now. As I understand, they also buy into technology companies, particularly IPO's, and then license their technology to make money. Mr. Kharif found me because I was CMT's representative to Berkeley, my alma mater, for grants, scholarships, and fellowships. He wanted to check notes about Berkeley before he made his visit. I was glad to do it

145

if it would help Berkeley. We got talking about technology relating to supply chain, and he suggested we do some testing of some of their experimental products. I agreed and it turned out to be fantastic technology, especially for a business like ours. Before you ask, I will say there isn't any chance that any of what we did together is related to the attempted theft of our product."

"It does seem like a stretch, giving away money to do technology research on one hand and stealing technology on the other, but I have heard of stranger happenings. Any other new vendors or suppliers involved in the production of the product or the shipment?"

"No, I don't believe so."

"Sorry, this has taken so long. Last question for now... Was Joe involved in any other way with the shipment? I mean other than as an observer of the tracking system working in your office the Sunday just before the attempted theft."

"Not to my knowledge, Frank."

"Thanks, Thomas. That's enough for now. Now I can get to my review of the documentation about the production and shipment and tracking of this special product. Will you show me how to access all the information generated by the data augmentation software working in conjunction with Mach II?"

"Of course. The special code is M2DAS. That will take you to the special project screen. Click on the Mach II icon. The instructions to access any part of the past up to current information will be there. It is easy."

"Thank you, talk to you later."

"You are welcome and good luck with your search."

The Team Huddles

They were so tired, it seemed like individual room service was the best idea for this evening. No one was up to the Squealing Pig again and all of them needed some time by themselves. They wanted to catch up at home, of course, and those calls get lengthy. Also, they needed some time to put their new information together so it would be understandable and there could be good conclusions made using it.

Jack said, "Let's get our newest information together and meet for breakfast tomorrow morning at about 7 AM in the hotel dining room. See you then. Goodnight."

"Goodnight," they all chimed in.

Breakfast at 7 AM was still a little strange with the time difference between D.C. and San Francisco. They had almost adapted but not quite. Jack seemed most awake, then Aldora, Frank, and then Mark. Jack said, "Aldora, why don't you start, please."

"Sure, I have been up for a couple of hours reading my email and making a few calls to my team working on the case back home. First, did I tell you that I was able to confirm that some calls are recorded? It's a relatively new system that is still evolving, as I understand it. This is how it works. A call comes in and is screened for key words for approximately thirty seconds. If certain key words are identified in that time, the entire call is recorded and kept for a period of one year. If the keywords are not heard, the call is not recorded. As an attorney, I can tell you it is not the best system. They probably are trying to accommodate the terms of the privacy act, but at the same time are taking some risks. No one, without a top-secret security clearance, knows how it works or the words that are currently used for screening. However, if someone found out, the system would be easy to scheme."

Jack said, "You can see how it might have developed, though. Most questionable calls would be short and sweet, pass along or get information in the shortest time possible. What are some of the words?"

"That is the interesting part. Only a few people I interviewed knew about the time factor and each one thought it was different… from a few seconds to even several minutes were mentioned. No one knew the key words but several people thought they were perhaps computer generated based on current contracts or something like that. If this was ever covered with the employees, it must have been very general and qualitative. For example, they may have said, this is just another security measure instituted by the company and, as

147

you know, all companies with government contracts have to do things like this. Thank you very much!"

Frank said, "I wonder what is used back home within our departments."

No one knew, of course, but all were thinking, I'm going to find out ASAP and until then keep my personal calls to a minimum!

Aldora said, "I'll do some checking when we get back. In the meantime, I have collected the tapes from the period in question and have my team checking content. We should know something in a few days."

"We are trying not to attract too much attention to Thomas Kramley but at the same time get some information about his personal and business financial dealings. Let me say that our investigation is not complete. That is a disclaimer but we found two interesting things so far. There seems to be an increase in his personal bank account every time he makes a company trip to deliver research grant monies to either Berkeley or Michigan. It is not accounted for by his regular company compensation, bonuses, stock options, investment dividends, or interest payments. Over the last three years, the total appears to be in the range of one hundred fifty thousand dollars or about 10% of the amounts granted to the universities by Customized Materials Technology. If I didn't know better, I would say that Mr. Kramley deducted an administrative fee for his services as courier and company representative extraordinaire. Who am I to judge though and how would he have done it? Obviously, we have more checking to do. His cash flow, especially recently, just doesn't add up. We did a zero sum balance exercise to check income versus bill payments. Our math shows that his spending exceeds his income over the past year by about one hundred thousand dollars. Yes, we took into account the loan from Joe Blackstone! He has debt in medical/health areas but it is less than you would expect by about that one hundred thousand dollar amount. So where is the hundred thousand dollars coming from? He must have an unknown benefactor who wants to remain anonymous and is able to keep everything off the books. More checking is needed as well but in either case our

THE CAMPAIGN OF FEAR

work might begin to attract attention and Mr. Kramley will know his personal finances are being scrutinized. My recommendation is to be direct and broach the subject with him. Let's see what kind of answers we get. Maybe he has a perfectly valid explanation. If he doesn't and won't talk about it, then our next steps become very obvious."

Aldora continued, "So, in summary my team will review the tapes and make any relevant information available in a few days. In addition, we will do a little more checking on Kramley's finances and then I will schedule time for a special discussion with him. Jack, I think you and I and Blackstone should all be in that discussion with Kramley. Do you agree?"

"Yes, and great work, Aldora. Any comments, Mark or Frank?"

Mark said, "All of this seems consistent with my findings, too. Huge health issues with his family, no health insurance, loan is used up. It all adds up to create a very vulnerable situation. How far would he go to get the help his family needs? I like your direct approach, Aldora."

Frank said, "This guy seems so genuine. He answered every question we had for him. There is a great commitment to the company and the president. On the surface, it seems he is trying to do the right thing. He is a logistics director and represents the company at key universities, he tests new technology to better the company products and help their customers, works weekends, and is well respected inside and outside the company. Even when I asked him to study the capability of this new RFID/software product, M2DAS, from TIC, he gave me the identification code, password, etc., the whole nine yards without hesitation. He does not seem to be a man with anything to hide. I agree with the approach you outlined, Aldora, but let's be very careful that we give him a chance to explain. Let's use more of the 'benefit of the doubt' approach."

"I agree. I believe he has earned that because Blackstone stands by him 100% too."

"Joe said things like, 'He would never do anything to harm the company; he brings needed technology to the company, hires

149

great people from Berkeley and Michigan into different departments and gives our company community, state, and national recognition. Thomas does his job and does it well and works weekends, too.' He was serious and really meant what he was saying about our Mr. Thomas Kramley."

Aldora said, "Yes, Jack, and maybe there are some good explanations for these strange financial records. I agree that we use a kid glove approach and try to get some answers."

"Set up the discussion with the foursome, Aldora, and thanks again for the great work and input. I like the thoroughness, the intensity, and yes, the sensitivity of how we are conducting the investigation. We make a great team so let's get to work. Aldora, you have your list; Mark, keep searching the personnel files; Frank, really focus on this TIC product; and I will follow up with Joe Blackstone to let him know what's up. I will also brief Director Elson on our status. Thanks again."

Sam Talks With Absek About The Case

Sam was thinking as he dialed Absek in Israel, just what do we know that I should discuss with him? The phone was ringing once, twice … "Hello, Director Elson, this is Absek."

"Hello, Absek, how are you today?"

"I am fine. It is a wonderful afternoon here."

"As I was dialing you, Absek, I was mentally summarizing what we know about the case. Forgive me if I repeat some things, but may I recount some points?"

"Yes, please, and then I will comment too."

"Here goes. First, there is a company here that we have under close watch. It is called TIC or Technology Investment Corporation, headed up by a man named Omar Kharif. The company invests in specific technologies at key universities by giving unrestricted research grants. They also invest in small or start-up technology companies. TIC happened to be conducting a field test on new product-tracking technology with Customized Materials Technology at the time, and on this shipment specifically. It may be on the up and up, but because they have been found to be connected to some seemingly questionable dealings with other companies, we are watching closely. Do you know if the name Kharif is common and if there might be a connection between my Omar Kharif and your Emar Kharif? Omar may in fact be the caller whose message you intercepted. Just a guess right now."

"I believe the name is not so common; I will do some checking. The first names are so similar; too, there must be something there. It is a good lead. Can you get us a sample of Omar's voice?

"We believe the telephone calls at Customized Materials Technology are recorded. One way or another, I'll get it for you Absek."

"Thank you, sir."

"Second, our investigation at Customized Materials Technology is going well, with some angles beginning to show up. We are focusing on the executive team, primarily on Thomas Kramley, the logistics director. There seems to be motive or maybe he was just gullible. And, Kramley has the closest and maybe the only working relationship with TIC and Kharif. He might be the CMT contact that the caller mentioned. Anything you can do to firm up a connection between the two would help also."

"We'll let you know if something turns up about Kramley in our search on the Kharifs and their relationships and dealings with CMT. We have been investigating the use of titles, i.e., leader, instead of names and the strange directive of 'no deadly force.' Both are new to the terrorist organizations we know in our region. It is our conclusion that this is probably coming from the operative in the States. Maybe someone using extra precautions to protect one's self and colleagues until the time is right. We are not psychologists here, Director Elson; we'll leave the psychoanalyzing to people like you. What do you think about these new, more secretive descriptions and conservative approaches to terrorism?"

"It's a good question that I haven't done much thinking about up to now. I should do a scenario with my augmented adaptive reasoning software. Thanks for challenging me on this. My gut tells me it is someone willing to travel a little different path than the

151

average terrorist, maybe someone who questions if they are doing the right thing. Any luck identifying who 'leader' might be?"

"We know the leaders of all the terrorist organization in Israel. Our approach was to try to check on their individual activities just before and after the attempted theft. Our people watch them when we actually know where they are. The rest of the time, we are trying to find them. It is what you call the 'mouse and cat' game, no? There are about ten terrorist organizations active in the region so this is a huge amount of work. You know about al Qaeda, Hamas, Fatah, and Hezbollah but there are many others. One of the small groups working at the behest of al Qaeda is known as the Technolibertat or as you would translate 'liberty via technology.' A former university professor who decided it was time for a second career heads it. My people tell me that before the attempted theft, he visited all of the airports in Israel at least once. There were also times when he seemed to be recruiting people more than normal. We know he was in the Zefat airport area on or about the day of the attempted theft. The problem is that he has gone into hiding and nowhere to be found."

"What is his name?" Sam asked.

"We believe it to be Professor Patek Kumat, a physical scientist of some significant reputation and accomplishment in the academic world. He recruited most of his group while at the university but constantly recruits new people at his Technolibertat informational meetings."

"We'll do some searches on him immediately, Absek. Do you think he uses any other names?"

"It is not certain but perhaps 'Professor' might show up someplace, don't you think?"

"It is a good guess. Absek, what turns these guys from a life in education and scientific research to one in terrorism anyway?"

"To this day and with all this history behind us, we still do not know. As in your country, it is almost beyond any comprehension for us, too."

Sam said, "For us to be successful in fighting terror, we are going to need to answer that question."

"I know Sam, that is why we are so encouraged to work with you. As a psychologist, maybe you can help us get past blaming everything on religion and our tendency to react by striking back at terror. Maybe we can actually analyze the groups, their actions, their leaders, their people, and get at the root cause of the evil. It has to be a human, social, psychological, and behavioral issue, doesn't it?"

"I don't know, Absek, but what we are doing isn't working. There seems to be no end to the numbers of terrorists working to eliminate us from the face of the earth. Let's continue talking about the case and any new information. I will call again soon."

"Thank you, Sam; sorry I got off on a tangent."

"No problem, Absek, it was a good discussion. Until next time, goodbye."

"Goodbye, Sam"

Jack and Joe Talk Again

Jack saw Joe Blackstone walking back from where his board meeting was to be held. It was the main conference room down the hall from his office. He knew the meetings were usually high pressure, full-day sessions that required a lot of preparation. Rightly so, he thought, that's the price of being a CEO of a company in the detonation technology business. Today, however, the Board was to be there primarily to discuss the government investigation and its status. Jack believed that it was his job to make sure that Joe had the most up-to-date information.

Joe saw Jack standing by his office door and said, "Hi, Jack, is there anything new in the investigation since we last talked? I know I'm going to get grilled today."

"A few things are cooking but we need more information to talk about conclusively. Here are the newest findings: Thomas Kramley's financials do not add up as we have the numbers today. He seems to have more money than his sources of income would allow. We are checking to see if it might be somehow connected to his role as CMT representative to Berkeley and Michigan."

"You mean he might be taking part of the scholarship,

153

fellowship, and research grant monies that we gift to these universities?"

"That's the theory but we don't have any proof other than monies deposited into his account after each university trip. It turns out to be about 10% of the total, but we need to check further to be sure there isn't some logical explanation. We all felt that, with Thomas's record, he should be given the benefit of a doubt."

"I hope so; these are very damaging accusations if they are not correct. You will either have to get undeniable evidence or I will have to hear this from Thomas to believe it. I just cannot imagine him doing this, no matter what the circumstances."

"We know how you feel about him, Joe. In addition to what I have already told you, there seems to be a cash flow imbalance in his accounts. That is, even with this 'extra money', his spending is much higher than the income without his debt increasing. We have to find out how that can be. Last, we are still focusing on TIC, Omar Kharif, and their new products you were testing. We think we might get some clues by looking very closely at the Mach II Data Augmentation System that has been embedded into your intranet operating system. The best leads right now seem to be Thomas Kramley and TIC."

"Thanks, Jack, for how you are handling the investigation. It is very important for the board, the company, and me that you are very thorough in your work and have an airtight case before anything goes public."

"I promise you that, Joe. We want to set up a meeting with Thomas, Aldora, and you. Aldora is leading the financial investigation. We'll have more information at that time and want to give Thomas a chance to bring forward his explanation and his side of the story. Is that alright with you?"

"Good approach. It is probably time that we get some answers from Thomas. He has always been straightforward with me, even in tough times. You should know that I will be in his corner at that meeting."

"Fair enough, Joe. Good luck at the board meeting. Please take an offer from me to join them at one of their future meetings to discuss the ongoing investigation more thoroughly."

"Thanks, Jack. I know that will be one of the questions today. I'll see you later."

Jack nodded and watched the grim-faced president pick up his board packet and head off to the conference room. He thought, I hope we can get through this without too much damage to him or his company. I'd better call the boss and let him know what's happening. I don't want him to think that he is the last to know.

Jack Updates Director Elson

"Director Elson, is this a good time to update you on the case at Customized Materials Technology?"

"Of course, Jack, anytime is okay. This is the most important case we are working on today. First, how are you?"

"I am fine, sir, and thanks for asking. We did find that restaurant you mentioned."

"The Screaming Pig?"

"Yes, but it is called the Squealing Pig today."

"I probably had it wrong, the Squealing Pig seems more reasonable, of course."

"Yes, sir, but we knew what to expect when we arrived. They have the best barbeque pork sandwiches that I have ever tasted."

"Jack, before I forget, would you tell Joe that he needn't make a trip to D.C. to see me about the investigation just yet. Earlier, I suggested he come and make a special appearance in a few days. It was mostly to scare him into recognizing how serious this attempted theft was."

"I will, sir. I believe he got the message loud and clear. He continues to be very helpful and wants the case resolved so he can get back to business as usual. Today was his board meeting; I am sure he is going to get some very pointed questions. The board meets every month. I told Joe that we could meet with them sometime if they wanted. I hope you approve of that."

"Sure, Jack. In a few weeks or so we will be in a much

better position of understanding exactly what is going on. That is, unless you are going to tell me today that we have all the answers."

"No way, but we are looking at both Thomas Kramley here and Omar Kharif of TIC even more closely. We have to confirm this but Kramley's financial accounts seem to have at least two areas of question. There have been unidentified deposits that amount to one hundred fifty thousand dollars and ... even with this extra money, he is able to spend more without building debt. This amounts to about another one hundred thousand dollars. We have at least a quarter of a million dollar imbalance in his financial accounting. Aldora is handling this area and will be checking further. We may have to ask for subpoenas to get all the information we need. Is that okay?"

"You bet. Just let me know so that I can ease the way with a little pre-work."

"Will do. Note that we soon plan to confront Kramley, with Joe Blackstone present, about the information we have collected on his finances and simply ask if he has an explanation. We'll take sort of a soft but firm approach and see what he has to say."

"I like that; be direct and give him an opportunity to get everything out on the table. Just be aware that his natural reaction to what will be an accusation will be to clam up. That is my psychology background showing, but it might be useful for you to know that going into the meeting."

"Thank you, sir. One more thing on Aldora's work - she just called and told me that she has had her team reviewing the tape-recorded conversations between CMT personnel and outside callers. They covered the calls during the pertinent times before and after the shipment in question. Not a lot came up as interesting but there were two calls between Kharif and Kramley. One was about Kharif's upcoming visit to Berkeley. He wanted to meet with Kramley as CMT's representative to Berkeley. No red flags there. The second call was about setting up the field test for the new RFID tracking product that TIC has developed. It seems what one might expect for a supplier/customer relationship except for some strange wording in the middle of the conversation. It was something like Kharif saying, 'the reward will be recognized once the tags are recovered in Eastern Europe.' At this time, we don't know what that means. It could be one of the questions we ask Kramley."

"'The reward will be recognized'....I wonder if someone was purposely trying to hide something. By the way, Jack, when I talked to our colleague in Israel, he needed a sample of Kharif's voice to do some voice recognition comparisons. Can you get me a copy of that second tape so that I can send it to him, please?"

"Sure, I'll have Aldora get a copy for you right away. Director Elson, the other things taking our attention and time relate to the relationship between Omar and Thomas and the new product that is being tested called Mach II, Data Acquisition System. Frank will be going through it with a fine-tooth comb; it is still embedded within CMT's intranet operating system."

"Good. We need to know every nuance about the system and how it works. It could hold the key to what the terrorists were really trying to do. Please send me a copy of the DAS software. I have some experience in this area and might be able to lend a hand in the analysis."

"Of course, sir. I'll try to send the tape and the software to you electronically at the same time. That is about all we have. Mike and his team are still reviewing personnel files but aren't finding much. It looks like he made the right decision to focus first on the executive team."

"Good work, Jack. I mentioned our colleague in Israel. His team is working hard on this, too, of course. They have some very recent information about the possible organization involved with the attempted theft and its leader. They may have also found a connection between Kharif and the pilot who committed suicide. His name seems to have been Emar Kharif. Is it coincidence or is there a real connection? We just don't know at this time. That is about all I have right now. Call anytime, Jack, and tell your team that I am very impressed with their results and I appreciate their work very much."

"I will, sir, and thank you. It is very fortunate for us to have you as our sponsor. We are constantly aware of the importance of this investigation to the department and to the future of our country."

"Thank you, Jack, we'll talk again soon."

"Yes, sir, goodbye."

Chapter 6

The Elimination – Penetration Plan
Death and Subterfuge

The Elimination Plan

Omar was deep in thought. He was hesitant to put anything called an elimination plan on paper. He also had thoughts about Thomas's wife and son and who would take care of them afterwards. Why did he feel this way? It was a sign of weakness, a lack of loyalty to the organization, and some would say a lack of faith for a true believer. But he knew why.

Omar thought, That pilot in Israel where they tried to steal the new technology was my brother. Yes, just another soldier lost in the battle against the infidels. This time it was my older brother. He remembered the times growing up when they were close. We both wanted to same things: education, family, career, etc. We were recruited out of college, I studied business and my brother studied engineering. We signed up thinking … this is what our friends are doing. Why not?

The way the story was told, it seemed okay from a religious, political, and economic perspective. The infidels were threatening Islam and our way of life. Their intrusion into our part of the world was evident to everyone, and it was spreading methodically. I thought my brother and I could help protect the future. We were told it was the oil, all about the oil. We were told the U.S. and its partners had implemented a plan to forcibly take over the Middle East countries, change their forms of government, their politics, their economics, and their ways of life. Maybe it did look that way when looking from a distance with a scarcity of facts and figures. Superficial thinking, I guess.

Having lived in the U.S. for more than five years had given him more of those facts and figures, information that would lead one to perhaps a different conclusion, if taken seriously. Omar had taken a liking to these people. The universities were full of professors and students intent on teaching and learning and stretching the boundaries of knowledge and abilities. The companies were full of innovative, hard working people trying to make the business grow and at the same time create a better life for themselves. There were no plots against Islam or the Middle East at the university, company, or people level. In fact there were as many people against the U.S. involvement in the Middle East as there were for it, maybe more. The people against it probably feel that way because there are too many lives being lost and the U.S. has been there long enough. Maybe even that the majority of people in the Middle East didn't want us there in the first place and were able to handle their own affairs. The people who are for it are still good people basically. They believe help is needed to make things better. This includes democracy with self-rule and self-choice. Peace and freedom, doesn't sound all that bad.

Omar tried to shake himself out of his funk. Oh, dear brother, why have I lost you? Will I follow the same path? What can I do? What should I do?

He slammed his fist down on the table hard enough to scare himself into consciousness. The Liberator says I need a plan. Let's do the same thing to Kramley that was done to my brother. The poison used was very potent, deadly with less than a drop. To take it willingly is one thing, but unwillingly is another. How about in a drink, a New Castle on tap, at the Squealing Pig. I will ask the Liberator to get me a vial of poison and leave the rest up to me. If we see the government investigators getting too close, I can ask for a get together at the pub. Thomas would bring his update; we'll talk and figure out next steps. When he goes to the bathroom or is otherwise distracted, I can spice up the drink. It works fast, almost instantaneously; I have to be prepared to leave very quickly. That will be easy because it is so dark at our favorite table and the pub is noisy. Anybody who notices will just think he has had too much to drink. If no one else is at the table, the tendency will be to leave him alone for a while. He's just sleeping it off, why bother him? I think it will work. I wonder if the Liberator will feel the same way.

The Penetration Plan

Omar was pleased with the elimination plan, his first one. Now he was deep in thought about the penetration plan for Advanced Technology Products. He initially thought that a Customized Materials Technology approach would be higher priority but on reconsideration, he had to admit the Liberator was right. ATP has the contract and they are the lead. They must have the core technology capability. It could be that it is not advanced enough or they could need some smaller pieces to make the product workable. What do we know? We know about the notes with an outline of the project, elements, and people. We know about my visit to the company and the project leader, Chadly Bromcast. The company is like a fortress with all of its high technology security devices and measures. We know Chad has four top-notch people working on this project. They have contacts at Tully Research, Incorporated and CMT. One could presume there is a potential for cooperative programs.

The notes and sketch indicate a huge program. Timing must be important too, otherwise they wouldn't put their best people on it. The Liberator knows the CTO, Mike Jackson. He seems to be keen about licensing technology or doing a joint venture to increase the velocity at which his company introduces successful new products. It must be about his compensation package, the products or the higher the bonus. These executives will do most anything for money. Should it not be about the cause and the team, the larger good?

Omar spoke out loud, "Here is the penetration plan. I will ask the Liberator, also known as Mr. Patek Kumat, to contact Mr. Jackson and see if he wants to do a deal. We have any number of technologies in our arsenal that could theoretically speed up his so-called CIED project. I think he will bite. Why else would they be interested in such close association with people at TRI and CMT? Then there is the boost in Mr. Jackson's ego, the recognition and visibility for having contributed a key part to the success of the project. Of course, the money, it is always about the money! I'm ready for the Liberator's next call."

The Liberator Calls to Check on the Plans

The Liberator was calling. This time Omar was ready, answering the special telephone on the first ring.

"Yes, sir, this is Omar."

"Do you have the plans we talked about?"

"I do, sir. I talked to Kramley and basically threatened him against talking about the money. He knows that he could lose his job, go to jail or worse, if we get to him first."

"Good. If you have to, take it a step further a little later and threaten his wife and kid, too."

Omar grimaced when he heard that and wondered if he was really cut out for this. "If I need to, sir. One thing, sir, Kramley has no idea what we are doing; he only knows that we paid him money to test our new products."

"I know that, of course. What is your plan to terminate if necessary?"

"Poison, sir, like the pilot used in the failed theft attempt. Can you get a vial or some capsules? I thought the poison could be used at the pub where Thomas and I meet when I am in San Francisco. Seems that it would be easy enough to get it into his drink and exit before anyone really notices. I have an arrangement with him to keep me updated on the investigation. If there is pressure and he is wavering, I'll be able to tell."

"Excellent, Omar. Think about the wife and kid, too. He may have told her by now and she could be just as damaging to us. Are you strong enough to do this?"

Omar gulped, 'Yes, sir, if need be."

"I will send you enough poison for the whole family. It will arrive by special courier at your D.C. office tomorrow. Remember, these capsules are made to swallow. They can be carefully broken and poured into a drink like you planned, but remember if it touches your skin, you are dead, too."

Almost without thinking, Omar said, "I was afraid of that, I mean, yes, sir I will be very careful."

"Now, what about the penetration into Advanced Technology Products?"

Omar continued, "I believe ATP has a large need for additional technology for the CIED project. There have been contacts made at Tully Research, Incorporated and Customized Materials Technology. Why else would they do that? You know the CTO, Mike Jackson; I have it on good report that he is all about, what do they say, 'feathering his own nest', like successful projects, recognition, speed, compensation, visibility, money, etc. For all these reasons, I believe he is ripe to do a deal. Since you know him, I would like you to make contact with him and offer something that would be enticing. He'll probably grab at anything in advanced acoustics or detonation technology. What do you think?"

"I think it could work if we can find the right technology need."

"Remember, sir, in your first meeting, he was ready to license some technology and do a deal. When I met with Chad, he was more careful and hesitant about getting outsiders involved at this stage. The selling point could be that this is added insurance in case it is needed. Contingency plans are always looked upon favorably in government contract work. That way, you can meet the needs of both Dr. Jackson and Dr. Bromcast."

"Good points, Omar. I will take a look at our technologies and select something appropriate. We don't want to give them anything that will help too much. Then I'll contact Dr. Jackson and engage him in a deal he can't refuse. I'll be back in touch soon for the next update. We are at a critical time so stay close to all parties. Praise Allah!"

"Praise Allah. Goodbye, sir."

The Liberator Talks With Mike Jackson

"Hello, Dr. Jackson, this is Patek Kumat. Remember that we met at a conference sometime ago?"

"I do, Mr. Kumat. We talked about a lot of things that day, including technology licensing. It was interesting that the first letters of our last names allowed us to be seated next to each other and explore some common interests."

"Yes, I agree. Fate sometimes controls what happens more than we know. Are you still seeking to acquire technology for your big project?"

"Always. Our biggest need is in the area of acoustics. I can't tell you about the specifics of our project, but is there a way we could review what you control and see if anything would fit our needs?"

Kumat continued, "Of course, our business is to license our technology. We have briefs of our key technologies available electronically for interested companies like yours. I can send them to you right away to review."

"Thank you, Mr. Kumat. I appreciate that."

"Dr. Jackson, there is one other possibility that I believe will be available soon. We have recently made a substantial investment proposal on what has to be the most advanced acoustics research currently being done. I can tell you it comes from both academic and non-profit research combined into a new start-up company. Our investment proposal will no doubt be accepted and we will have access to the state-of-the-art advancement."

"Can't I just invest in the start-up company?"

"I don't think so. It has to do with the adverse competition that public companies might bring if several are involved. They seem to be looking for venture capital money and other non-competitive investors. As Technology Investment Corporation, here is where we have an advantage. You can ride on our coattails if you like. That is, once our proposal is accepted."

"Sure. I would just license any technology we need through you, right?"

"Yes. We will have access to all the technical information

that comes from the research and part ownership of the company. I'll keep the communication lines open with you and if you see something you like, I'll make sure you get it."

"That sounds great. I'll wait for your electronic briefs and stay in touch with you about the work being done by this new start-up company. Thanks for the opportunity to join you in this venture. May I tell my superiors about this?"

"Of course, but tell them it is contingent on our proposal being accepted. We should know about that soon."

"Thanks, again, Mr. Kumat. While I have you on the line, do you know anything about micronizing or miniaturizing chemical analytical instruments? We need technology that would allow us to make at least a ten-fold reduction in size. Even more is desired."

Smiling to himself, Kumat answered, "Yes, I do. NASA has done some fantastic work in that area with their space particle collection and identification system. I have a senior scientist contact there that would be able to discuss the subject with you and get you access to the technology. It's free, you know, you have already paid for it with your tax dollars. May I send the contact information to you electronically when I provide the technology briefs?"

"That would be great, Mr. Kumat. My team would be very appreciative. Thank you so much. You have been very helpful today. I will not forget that."

"My pleasure, Dr. Jackson, I will be in touch soon. Goodbye."

"Goodbye, Mr. Kumat."

The Liberator Calls Omar

The Liberator was calling again. Omar rushed to get the phone, "Hello, Professor, I mean Liberator."

"Omar, you are really testing my patience with the mistakes you are making. Don't ever call me that again. Anything we do outside of our plan will put us increasingly at risk. Your role is to follow orders, execute, and be at the top of your game at all times. I have to be able to trust you and your abilities."

"I am sorry, sir, it just slipped out. After all those years, can one really change so completely?"

"It is hard, Son, but you have to set the example for the others. My leadership is gaining ground in all the right places. Your success will help both of us. The sacrifice your brother made was unexpected and sad, but he did it without question. He did it for the cause and for me. I expect no less dedication and commitment from you. Can you do this?"

"Of course I can," Omar rushed to say without hesitation. It may not have been his true feelings but it would have to suffice at this moment. "How did the contact with Dr. Jackson go?"

"It went well. Three things happened. I offered him all of our electronic database information, including acoustics technology, for his review. "Send that to him please."

"Yes, sir, right away."

"I also offered, once our proposal is accepted, all the acoustics technology information that we get from TRI and the ability to license it through us. This may get a little complicated but the time was right to get him into our camp. He readily accepted!"

"Complicated? I guess! If this is the price we have to pay to find out what ATP is doing, it is well worth it. We will have to watch this company, Tully Research, closely because my sources tell me that ATP has been in contact with them. Dr. Jackson may not even know this. If they set up some kind of cooperative program, they may not need us."

"Let's play it out. We are simply making a good faith offer based on an investment proposal that we believe will be accepted. If we do the deal with TRI, we will have paid handsomely for the research results and they are ours to do with what we choose. It's still the best way I know to get into Advanced Technology Products and their special project without breaking federal and state laws. Later, if we find that it is necessary, we'll do that, too."

"I'll let you know if our proposal is accepted and when technical information becomes available."

Continuing with the three accomplishments, the Liberator said, "I was able to help Dr. Jackson on a request to get technology on miniaturization of equipment to do analysis of chemical compositions. For your information, it was our contact at NASA, where recent work was done on the space particle analyzers. You should factor this into your conclusions about ATP special project and where they are in reaching their goals described in the stolen sketch. I will be looking for additional recommendations beyond what we have in place at this time. Remember, we are the lead technology resource organization in what must now be the top program for our combined efforts. If we are not successful in stopping or sidetracking ATP from developing this CIED product, our 'Campaign of Fear' will have failed. And, life without the infidels will not exist. They will be in every country, city, and village in our region from now to the end of time. Do you see why the work that we do, that you do, is so important, Omar? I know you do, Son. Praise Allah!"

"Thank you, sir, until we talk again. I will then further the cause with good reports from TRI and CMT. Praise Allah! Goodbye, sir."

"Goodbye, Omar."

Agreement Is Signed

The special phone rang. Sam could see that it was Brad so he answered quickly.

"Hello, Brad, how are things in Minnesota?"

"Things are fine here, Sam. I thought I should let you know that the proposed agreement between Tully Research and Technology Investment Corporation was signed and returned as of yesterday. I'm just sitting back waiting for the money to start rolling in."

"This is good, Brad. Remember our agreement that you will tell no one about your most recent research results. I'm sure there will be a special time and place to announce those results. One that would be to our great advantage!"

"We have a deal, partner. I suspect that Mr. Kharif will personally deliver the money so I might begin to get some pressure from him right away. He probably will be asking for immediate access to all of my technical information, don't you think?"

"If we are right about him, yes. Just hold him off by telling him you have other potential investors that are under consideration. This will take some time because you are also drafting the company by-laws and operating procedures. Once the board is formed, then what you do and the process by which you do it will be decided officially."

"Sounds like a plan, thanks for the advice."

"Brad, can I take a couple of minutes to give you a little more information about the Advanced Technology Products project and Customized Materials Technology investigation?"

"Yes, of course, but remember Ms. Lang from ATP is coming to Minneapolis soon and I plan to sign the proposed subcontractor agreement. She will update me on their project at that time."

"I know, Brad. What I want to tell you is that we believe TIC, through a contact other than Omar, may be trying to penetrate ATP even further. I'm sure they believe the work at ATP is state-of-the-art and their biggest threat. Let me put things in perspective for you. If the ATP work on acoustics is considered first generation R&D, then your work is second generation R&D or beyond. You have already done the science and technology development that is currently underway at ATP. Only you and I know this and no one else must find out. When Ms. Lang visits, you cannot, under any circumstances, make reference to this new work you have done. Do you understand?"

"Yes, but I had no idea. I just assumed they were on the same path and working on more advanced technology. Sir, I do understand. It is probably a bit safer for me but do you know what you are asking of me? You are asking me to keep this new work from the scientific community, from my friends and colleagues in the field, and worse yet, from my company."

"Yes, that is correct. I believe it is best for you and all concerned including our country."

"But I'm not thrilled about this. What else do you have for me?"

"One more thing. In our investigation at CMT that I

mentioned before, we have reason to believe that Omar and TIC had some part in the attempted theft of top secret, new detonating products in Israel. Our friends there are helping us follow some leads."

"Oh, God, now you are going to tell me that the Mossad is involved in all of this."

"Yes, that is right, Brad. Sorry to get you involved in this international conspiracy but I didn't have any choice. The message is --be very careful in your dealings with Omar and TIC. The scenario building I have done thus far does not paint a very good picture about them and what they might be planning to do."

"I'm beginning to get the same picture. Is there anything I should be doing besides keeping my mouth shut and watching my back?"

"Yes, you have most of the information that I have on TIC now. Help me understand what their next technology moves might be given all we know about the interaction between Tully, ATP and CMT. I will continue to work on the personal, behavioral, cultural, and other aspects. Maybe together we can come up with something that makes sense."

"Okay, partner, let's stay close."

"Thanks, Brad. Goodbye for now."

Progress on the Project

Chad had the team together in the hub where they had gathered for the weekly update. Director Sam Elson was on the speakerphone, too.

Chad said, "Hello, Director, we all here. Thanks for taking the time to review the progress on our project."

"Hello, Chad, and a hello to Zen, Lyncoln, Kan D, and Bill. Say, this is the most important project in DoAT certainly and perhaps within the whole federal government. Don't thank me for being keenly interested and involved. It's my job and our country's future depends on the success of your project. You have a lot of responsibility so let me officially say thanks to all of you."

The team leaders were taken aback by the seriousness in the director's voice and his no-nonsense approach to this specific project and its importance. They were all looking at one another and facially exclaiming that they now understood more deeply the priority of the project as well as its significance. And, further, that their individual roles as team leaders were to make the project succeed. This obviously was not a best effort project. Much, much more was expected.

Chad looked around, nodded, and said, "Let's get started. Bill, you were last in our previous update. Would you go first this time, please?"

"Of course. Last time we covered the wave generation and reversal or bounce-back characteristics and sound dampening capability developed in the laboratory. We have not done outside testing to determine our optimum distances. Our results show that up to one hundred feet we are okay. That was our target for this particular contract and we are quite pleased about it. If, in the future, there is a need to go further, that will require us to plow some significantly new ground. I will need some help because of the tendency of the returning wave coming from longer distances to disperse or scatter more. We have been in contact with Dr. Bradford Tully at Tully Research to begin discussions with him on that very topic. Zen will be visiting him soon with a CDA and a draft subcontractor agreement."

"Good work, Bill. If you can do one hundred feet, we'll make that work to get started. Just so you all know, I have been in contact with Dr. Tully, too, about being a technology consultant to the department. Sounds like he will be part of the team in more ways than one."

Chad said, "Zen told us we would be impressed with him. We are only beginning to find out how much. Wish us luck with our subcontractor proposal."

"Good luck and make it happen, Bill and Zen. Thank you."

"Thank you, Director," they said in unison.

Since her part was logically next, Zen said, "Chad, do you want me to go next?"

"Yes."

"Director, we can take that returning wave front that Bill just talked about and identify everything contained therein. Our challenge was to identify all of the explosive components even if they were present in concentrations below the ppb level. Lyncoln will talk about the good news there in a second. My challenge was to create a high performance vacuum cleaner that would suck the returning wave front into the analytical equipment so we could identify what it contains. It's too big right now but it works pretty well. Let me explain it this way. In magnetism theory and practice, for example, like polarity materials attract and unlike polarity materials repel. Acoustic wave theory is just the same. Like resonances attract and unlike resonances repel. In practice, this is what helps us collect the wave front. We know the total resonance of the returning wave front. By building a vacuum wand or head that vibrates at approximately the same frequency as the returning wave, it acts as a magnet to gather up everything coming back. It is large right now but it really does work. We also have all the standards in place for every explosive component known to the U.S. Government. So from a vibrating vacuum cleaner to special spectroscopic analytical instrumentation to the computer array, we are making good progress. I'll turn it over to Lyncoln to talk about the identification of low concentration components using his data augmentation methodology. Lyncoln, your turn."

"Thank you, Zen. I love this vibrating vacuum cleaner. You better get that patented because it sounds like there may be a number of applications out there for it. Keep up the good work!"

Lyncoln started by saying, "Thanks for the access to and use of the DoAT supercomputer.'

"Don't mention it, Lyncoln, I'm glad we are able to make good use of it."

"I hope you don't mind that I have been experimenting with remote access via special techniques demonstrated by one of your experts. Having those satellites located where they are means we won't have to have an extra truck to haul around the supercomputer."

171

"Or even better, Kan D doesn't have to work on miniaturization of the supercomputer on this project," said Director Elson.

Kan D joined in by saying, "Yes, but you never can tell what we'll be asked to do on the next project, can you?"

Lyncoln continued, "We are good to go on computational capability. Next on the identification of components present in the wave at lower than the ppb level, we do have some good news as Zen said. With our new software, we are able to identify components at the ppt level. Director Elson, you know about data augmentation, of course, but for the others, I'll explain further. This is sort of like a very thin and unidentifiable coat of paint made thicker and identifiable by computer magnification. The computer can take in a very small amount of real information or data, like at the ppt level, and generate a very thin coat. By using our special software code it can then create virtual additional identical thin coats or layers until a level is reached where the paint can be identified using the standards we have developed. It works quite well. You should know that the program I wrote is a modification of your work on multiple personalities sir. In your case study, the person had one dominant personality and three strong to medium personalities that were all fairly easy to identify. The program you wrote in this case study allowed you to identify the fifth personality. There was only a hint that it was there, but by building the additional layers on top of a thin coat, you were able to identify it. Turned out that was the key to a successful resolution in the case as I remember."

"It was, Lyncoln. I always wondered if that work in psychology could be extended to other scientific areas. There is my answer. Nice work!"

"Thank you, so with the satellite access of the super computer and the ability to identify even ppt level components at 99.999% accuracy, we are in good shape." Adjusting his Red Sox baseball cap, Lyncoln said, "It is time to have our clean up hitter come up to bat. Kan D."

"Thanks, Lyncoln, and thanks, dear God, that I don't have to miniaturize the super computer. First, we had our telephone conference call with CMT about a detonation technology subcontract on our project. They seem very interested in joining us and sharing their technology even though they are currently under government investigation. Are you still okay with us partnering with them?"

"Yes, Kan D. I suspect the investigation will turn up some surprises but they are a great company with great technology and people. They will be able to help our project. Go for it!"

"I just wanted to be sure before we start signing papers." Kan D stopped for a second, looked at Zen, and said, "Zen, you don't know about this yet. In just the last few hours, I think I have discovered how to make the vacuum work off the Humvee engine. It is not miniaturization, but it is innovation. The Humvee engines are so powerful and usually use only a fraction of their horsepower. I found a way to draw off enough horsepower to both create the vacuum and the resonance or vibration needed for the collection system."

"I did notice the huge engine you brought in here a couple days ago. This is great news. We really just need to worry about the collection head; that will be a piece of cake!"

Kan D continued, "So what is nice about Lyncoln's and Zen's work on computer-aided chemical identification is that we only need one piece of analytical spectroscopy equipment. By feeding in just that data, we believe that the new data augmentation software will facilitate both virtual and actual identification of all components. Therefore, I just have to miniaturize the one piece of equipment that is most sensitive. With Zen's help, we have concluded that piece to be the chemical analyzer and here we are fortunate, too. NASA has already done a lot of work collecting and analyzing space particles as you know. Guess what -- they have done the basic work on nanoscale element and compound analyzers. It is all available for our project, free of charge. Director Elson, you have some powerful people willing to help on this project. We are very appreciative."

"Kan D, I said this was probably the top program in the federal government so don't expect anything less. If it is available and you need it, you'll get it. Just let me know if you have any trouble."

"Thank you, sir. For me, I think that leaves some work on Bill's wave generator. The intent would be to reduce it to the size of a carry-on suitcase. Could it be that the whole system could be contained in a case that size? Smaller than the object we are trying to find?"

"Great work - and innovative is right, Kan D. Where did you find out about the NASA work? I had forgotten about it."

"From our CTO, Mike Jackson. I believe he had been talking to a friend about technology needs and it came up. Mike was very discreet but the friend knew a contact in NASA. She gave the information to Mike; Mike gave it to Chad, and so on. It was a perfect match with what we needed."

Chad was noticing his watch and that the hour was up. He said, "Director Elson, that is our update for today. The team is doing groundbreaking work in all of these scientific areas, and on a pace that is unbelievable. I want to thank them personally with you on the line. We'll plan to review the project with you again soon."

"Thank you, Chad, Bill, Zen, Lyncoln, and Kan D. I want you all to know that the work you are doing is critical to our country and its future. I will make sure every resource is available, every door open, and every measure taken to ensure success. That is my promise to all of you. You should also know that I am keeping the secretary of DoAT and the president of the United States up to date on this project. They both said to thank you and wish you Godspeed. I'll talk to all of you again soon."

All five chimed in at the same time with "Goodbye, Director Elson and thank you."

Chad pushed the off button and they all sat there looking at each other with blank faces.

Part II

The Tide Turns In Our Favor

Chapter 7

"Hot"
The Relationship Builds

Zen jumped off the light rail train to find Brad waiting for her. It was about 8:30 PM.

"Hi Zen, you are looking good!"

"Hi Brad, you are looking good, too." She dropped her briefcase and duffel bag and they embraced and kissed. It was a long, warm, and intimate kiss. Zen whispered in Brad's ear, "Let's go back to your apartment before we do anything else."

Brad, still holding her close, feeling her warmth against him, looked into her eyes and said, "I had hoped that you would say that." He picked up her duffel bag, she took the briefcase and off they went hand-in-hand to Brad's apartment. There wasn't much talking, just considered determination and a fast pace.

As they arrived at the building, Brad unlocked the door and said, "The laboratory is in the basement, the office is here on the first floor and I live upstairs."

Zen took his hand again and started upstairs. The stairs were wide, wooden, beautifully finished oak steps in this old warehouse building. It still had the original supporting structure of partially squared-off oak logs. Everything was oak – the floors, the paneling, the ceiling, everything. None of this was noticed by Zen nor did Brad have time to point out any of the interesting features.

Brad fumbled for his apartment key, unlocked the door and ushered Zen inside. He said, "Welcome, this is home for me."

Zen grabbed her duffel bag from him and went toward the bathroom saying, "I will be just a minute. Do you have any wine, Brad?" She closed the bathroom door and Brad was left wondering if he should get the wine or check to see if the bedroom was okay. He decided to open and pour the wine first.

The wine rack was in the living room nearby, so he walked over thinking, I hope she likes red wine. He selected a Dancing Bull 2003 Cabernet Sauvignon and went to the kitchen. In no time, he had two glasses of wine poured and ready to go. He picked them up, turned and saw Zen coming from the bathroom. He was struck by how lovely she was.

Zen, wearing only a not very long t-shirt said, "Bring those and let's check out the bedroom." She met him about mid-room and took one of the glasses while bringing his hand to her breast. They stood looking at each other honestly and openly about how they felt about each other. Zen held his hand on her breast then slowly reached down and loosened Brad's belt. She massaged him slowly and gently as they stood just inches apart. It was easy for her to tell that he liked it. With only her eyes, she asked if it was okay to take the next step. Brad answered her silent question with his eyes and Zen unzipped the zipper, put her hand inside his boxer shorts and slid it down slowly until she was able to hold all of him. He was big and getting bigger. Brad was mesmerized, not moving, hoping this would never end.

Zen whispered quietly and with a quick smile, "Can you do this standing up with a glass of wine in one hand? I don't think I can!"

Brad smiled, held his pants up with his free hand and followed her to the bedroom. They put down their glasses and sat on one side of the bed. Zen proceeded to undress him. Shirt first. Then she got on the floor on her knees and took off his shoes and socks. She asked him to stand a little as she pulled his pants down and he stepped out of them somewhat embarrassed at his erection but not wanting it to stop. Zen pulled his shorts off the same way. She took him in her hands and caressed him gently. He was touching her breasts at the same time. They were full and firm with very defined nipples even through the t-shirt.

Zen started a slow back and forth movement with her hands. Brad was enjoying every moment as her movements were so deliberate and purposeful. She did this for some time looking up into his eyes. He was saying yes with his eyes so she increased the movement slightly still using two hands. Their eyes were still locked, he massaging her breasts and she was enjoying his pleasure. It felt like nothing he had ever experienced. It was ecstasy! Zen knew. She smiled and increased her movement more but not fast yet. Brad removed her t-shirt and caressed her breasts. He said to her, "Make me come, Zen." Zen responded quickly with faster, longer strokes watching expectantly. Brad came immediately. It was long and hard and seemed to last and last forever. Brad was holding her head as she continued to work to get every drop from his body and give him as much pleasure as possible. They still had their eyes locked when she released him. He pulled her close to him and hugged her. Her head was on his leg and she used one hand to hug him and the other to play with him, hoping this would continue.

Brad said, "Let's get into bed, Zen. I think I can do this again with your help."

"I hope so, Brad, it's my turn now." Zen positioned the pillows, pulled the covers all the way back and jumped into bed. She sat looking at him and said, "Top or bottom?"

With that smile and body being so enticing, Brad immediately said, "Top!" Zen stretched out, opened her legs and said, "Let's see what you have left, big guy."

With that challenge, Brad was on all fours over her and between her legs. Zen playfully took him in her hands and teased him by rubbing against her, putting him inside just barely then pulling back. Brad grew even bigger at each cycle and then at last she arched her back and pulled him inside some, then more, then all the way. She held him tight with her muscles as she put a pillow under her back but down low. Then she said, "Relax now and let me lead and do most of the work."

They sunk down into the mattress together, connected in so many ways, together in mind and body. They had one and only one purpose and each was thinking about it with no limitations, no barriers. Zen began to move, still holding him tight and encouraged Brad to raise himself a little. She was controlling the amount of movement, only a little at first then more. Brad could feel her warmth, her ease of movement, and her eagerness. He massaged her breasts; then he put his hands under her butt trying to help as much as he could. Zen removed the pillow and the movement became more exaggerated. A few inches, then several inches both up and down but with rotation, too. She finally began moving the full length of him. The thrust upward gave Brad full penetration really deep into her. When she pulled back, it was almost to the tip. He was afraid that he would come out sometimes. She continued to move full length faster and faster with stronger and stronger thrusts. Zen was watching his eyes because she was in control and could come when he was ready. Brad instinctively knew this and gave her a wink; he was ready. Just when he felt he could hold himself no longer, Zen moved back and was ready to make the final thrusts. The first time he met her hard and was even deeper than before. She gave out a cry and said, "Again." She thrust upward, Brad met her at the peak, he came and she cried out, "Again, again." Thrust and back, thrust and back with cries of joy and ecstasy and utter exhaustion. They both collapsed. She into the mattress and he on top of her. Brad gave her a kiss and started to roll off. She whispered, "Wait just a minute. I want to feel you inside me a little longer."

They lay there, as close as two people could be for the longest time. Finally, Zen gave Brad a kiss and a playful push telling him it was time to roll off. They both fell asleep in each other's arms in a matter of seconds.

The morning light was coming in the east window and Zen was trying to remember where she was so that she could get her bearings. She felt beside her and yes, Brad was still there sleeping. She got up, found her t-shirt and proceeded to the bathroom. In the mirror, she could see a woman that she wasn't sure she knew. She thought, did I really do that last night? I hope Brad doesn't think that it was too much, too soon. If the feelings are there, it cannot be too much or too soon, right? It is not my modus operandi to be subtle, so I hope he feels the same way. I'm not leaving this time until I know. That about summed it up and she headed to the kitchen.

In the fridge, she found bagels, orange juice, and yogurt. As the bagels toasted, she took the other things to the deck that faced mostly toward the Mississippi River. There was a comfortable table and chair and even several flowers in huge clay pots.

Zen thought it was a nice touch for a bachelor scientist. On her way back to the toaster, she peeked into the bedroom and saw Brad stirring. "Good morning, Dr. Tully. I am fixing breakfast on the deck when you are ready." He sat up with ruffled hair and a sleepy look. "Can you cook, too?"

"Ha, you could wish. Come on, up and at 'em. I am only here for the day. It's a good thing we got a lot done last night."

"I agree, a lot! I'll be there in a second."

Zen grabbed the bagels from the four-slice toaster, found some plates, knives, spoons, and napkins, and proceeded to the deck. She could hear noise in the bathroom. She sat things down thinking *cream cheese*, and went back toward the kitchen.

Brad was coming out of the bathroom, grabbed her arm, and pulled her close to him. He kissed her nose, mouth, ear, and whispered, "Wow! I am really glad we are getting to know each other better."

"Me, too. Do you have cream cheese?"

"Yes, can't live without it -- top shelf in the refrigerator."

"Meet you on the deck. I have the juice, bagels, and yogurt out there already."

"Do you want coffee, too? I have it ready to be made, just push the button."

"How did I forget about coffee? I can't live without it in the mornings. Of course I do. I'll get it started, Brad. Thanks."

Brad went to the deck. The sun was bright and warm and the sky was by far the darkest blue he had seen yet. There seemed to be a lot of blue-sky days in Minnesota. He felt comfortable here and thought it was definitely better when Zen came to visit.

Zen stepped back onto the deck with the cream cheese under one arm and two cups of coffee. "Here we go."

"Thanks, Zen, this is wonderful."

They ate pretty much in silence each occasionally touching the other's hand, arm, or hair. Just taking care of each other and communicating without words.

Finally Brad broke the silence and said smiling, "Can we do it again?"

Knowing that he was halfway kidding, Zen replied, "I think we need to get our work done. I'm on the clock you know." She stood up to get her briefcase. Brad pulled her over to him and put his hands under the t-shirt. She had not put on anything else, maybe just to entice him. Her body was smooth, soft, and tight at the same time and those breasts. He leaned forward, kissed one, then the other. Zen was holding his head as he played with her. She could hardly stop him since it felt so good to have him fondle, suck, lick, and even bite her breasts. However, her practical side told her she was in the middle of the warehouse district, on the second floor deck of a large apartment building, and stark naked with her t-shirt around her neck letting some guy have his way with her. Better get this energy redirected and soon - otherwise they will not get anything done today or worse yet, the neighbors will call the police. Still holding his head, Zen leaned down and said, "If you want, my body is just for you from now until you decide differently but in times and places we carefully choose. I can't do this in public, out where it seems like I'm on stage for all the world to see. I hope you understand."

"Good God, I do, Zen. What the hell am I thinking and doing?" He pulled her shirt down hard, stretching it down to well below her butt as if suddenly understanding that everything needed to be covered.

Zen smacked him in the head playfully and said, "We got that straightened out. I'll go get my stuff and we can work at the table. Can you keep your hands off me or do I need to put something else on under and over this?" She pulled the t-shirt down hard again to stretch it over her butt just like he had done.

"You ask a lot but to answer your questions, yes, I will try and no, please don't."

"You have a deal!" She turned and went to get the papers in her briefcase.

"Here are the reports from Bill and the subcontractor agreement to help us on the acoustics project. We can talk about these as much as you want or at least to the limit of my knowledge. First, my company, ATP, and the federal government require that you sign a confidential disclosure agreement. Here it is in its most standard and unexciting form."

"Yes, I know it well. Did you bring a pen?"

"Here you go."

Brad signed the two identical CDA documents and gave one to Zen and kept the other for himself. Both had been pre-signed by ATP and they were now official. "OK, Zen, now I am ready for all of this confidential information."

"Here are Bill's reports. We haven't been working on this project very long so don't expect a whole lot. Bill said you would get the gist very quickly. The bottom line is that I believe we need your help on both the current product and the next generation products. We may have implied that we have the current product well under control, but at this point it is still a hope and a dream. Take a look and you'll see where we are and where we need help."

Brad reviewed the summary reports very quickly. He could speed read even technical materials and there were only ten or twelve pages. "Okay, I understand all that and based on what I heard during our phone discussion, I had just about guessed the status of the project. I have done a lot of this so I know where the hard parts are."

"I thought so, Brad. Because of that, and with Bill's permission, I had the subcontractor agreement written to read on both current product and future products. I hope this meets with your approval."

"Let me take a quick look, Zen." He read quickly and said, "Yes, up to one hundred feet, new technology needed for longer distances and second generation product. This is fine. Oh, yes, here is the part about the money…..payment is based on milestones and gets to be quite significant when the new technology is ready to go. I can sign this."

He flipped past the boilerplate stuff and signed one original and then the next. He gave Zen one copy and kept the other for himself. "What's next?"

"You were going to show me Minneapolis, at least this side of town, and then visit the Cuban restaurant."

"Oh, yes, Café Havana. Let's get some shorts on and we'll do a walking tour of the east side of town, have some lunch, and get you to the train for the airport. Maybe we can talk a little business along the way so I can learn what you are doing."

"Great idea."

Brad had an intense urge to tell Zen about his exciting new research findings. But the director had said to tell no one. He decided it should wait for another day.

Hand in hand, Brad and Zen walked down the oak stairs to the first floor office area. Brad opened the door and said peeking in, "Just an office area. We use the Minneapolis wireless service and I am also connected to the University of Minnesota's supercomputer. Want to see the laboratory?"

"Yes, of course. You know me and technical stuff."

They went down the stairs, Brad turned the lights on and before them was a huge laboratory that took up the footprint of the whole building. Zen thought it looked similar to his lab at Stanford but much, much bigger and almost identical to but more sophisticated than Bill's lab at ATP.

Zen said, "How did you get all this here and up and running so quickly?"

"I just kept working at it. There wasn't much else to do." They walked further into the laboratory and Brad said, "Here is the wave generator, over there the collector, there are the analytical instruments and of course the computer array. I have contracted with the University's Institute of Technology Department to help with the computations and analyses. There are some very talented faculty and graduate students there so the university connection has been

THE CAMPAIGN OF FEAR

great. It is one of the reasons I decided to locate here. I'll show you some of the other reasons along our tour."

"How is the work going, Brad?"

Not looking at her, he responded, "Not too bad. It is hard to relocate a laboratory like this and get everything set up and running again. I'm doing okay. Just between us, I think I am a little ahead of your team on your CIED project. Maybe I can help on the first generation product very soon."

"I guessed that from talking with you and now seeing the level of sophistication you have achieved, I'm sure of it. Can you tell me about the collector sometime? It is so small compared to what we are using."

"I would be happy to do that but today is our fun day. Okay?"

"Just one more question, please. This is all so exciting! The building or laboratory is long; I can't even see the end clearly. It's well over one hundred feet long and I do see targets set up even beyond that distance. Does your system work beyond one hundred feet?"

"I'm getting there," is all Brad could say. "I'll tell you all about it at the right time, Zen."

"I know you will, Brad. She took his hand and said, "Let's go on our walk."

They went up the steps and exited the building. "Right down that way is where the new Twins' stadium is under construction for opening in 2010. They finally got the land squabble settled and were able to start building last year. I like the design but it seems to be sized a bit small for a major league baseball stadium. We'll see. Target Center is right there; can you see it? That is where the Timberwolves play... so baseball and basketball to the north of us. To the east is the river, the mighty Mississippi. Let's walk this way toward Hennepin Avenue and what is called Mill City."

"Okay, you lead the way; I'll be right at your side."

Brad pointed out the Post Office, the Hennepin Avenue Bridge, the Third Avenue Bridge, and the start of Mill City. "This is an historic site where a huge amount of flour milling was done over a hundred years ago. They had the river access, the train station (now a hotel), buildings that used to be for barrel manufacturing, and of course the old grain storage towers. It was a major hub of agricultural activity. There is the Mill City Museum, the McKnight Foundation is here, and of course lots of apartments and condominiums. If you look down a little further, you can see a big blue structure."

"Yes, with part of it jutting out toward the river."

"Great architecture! It is the new Guthrie Theater that opened at that location in 2007, I think. I haven't been there yet but I hear it is wonderful. Two main stages for regular season productions and a third stage for experimental plays. Let's walk down to see it and the park next to it. Then we'll go see the Mississippi up close."

"Okay, so if I am oriented correctly, the city is to our right, sort of west. I can see the tall buildings but not as many as in Boston."

"Right. It is not a huge city. Its size is a little deceiving because it is spread out with a lot of close-in suburbs."

"The Guthrie is huge, can we walk through?"

"I don't know, let's try."

The doors were open so they walked in, past the gift shop, and took the escalator to the fourth floor and the main stages. Zen was most interested in taking the observation ramp out to see the Mississippi River. They got to the end of the ramp and luckily the doors to the viewing area were open, too. They stepped outside to a wonderful view of the river. To the left, St. Anthony Falls, a couple of locks and dams, the Stone Arch Bridge, an old railroad bridge, now for pedestrians and bicyclists. The power plant across the river and to the right the new 35W bridge that replaced the old one that collapsed in 2007.

Zen said, "Absolutely breathtaking! Am I right that the Mississippi starts in Minnesota?"

"Yes, a place called Itasca, I think. It's pretty far north and wasn't found for a long time. I hear it still isn't so obvious or easy to find for people who go to see the headwaters."

"I could sit here forever, Brad."

"I know; it's a great location. I bet the architect had a lot of fun with the design. Let's go see the park next door, Gold Medal Park. The story is that this park will indirectly help keep the Pillsbury name alive since the company was acquired by General Mills several years ago."

They walked back through the doors, down the incline and escalator and out the front doors. The park was a large area of green grass, lots of fairly mature trees, with a hill in the middle. There was a spiral path leading to the top.

Zen said, "Let's go sit in the grass on the hill." The spot they found allowed them to see the Guthrie, part of the city, and the river. It was perfect. Zen got a serious look on her face and said, "Brad, do you worry about terrorists?"

"Not in terms of my personal safety but in general I do. Mostly about the fear they were able to generate with the events of September 11 and threats of repeat attacks and with their explosive devices and suicide bombers in Afghanistan and Iraq and throughout the world. We are a courageous people but we cannot and will not be able to function with fear hanging over our heads. That is why the work that you and I are doing is so important. We have had thousands of people killed or injured because of IED's alone. Think about the fear being cultivated by the terrorists. We cannot fight this kind of action with more heavily armored Humvees and other combat vehicles. We have to be able to find the explosive and safely detonate it before it goes off under one of our trucks. There are several research teams working on different approaches like IED signal jammers, microwave based IED detonation systems and robotic systems. My opinion is that most of them are inadequate or a long way off and just plain too late in coming. The deaths and injuries and this 'campaign of fear' have to be stopped. Without the fear, the terrorists lose."

"I sort of feel the same way but is our project the answer? We are a ways off; it is complicated technology and might not be so adaptable to the battlefield, wherever that is these days."

"I know what you mean. With our best scientists working on this, we have to come up with something. A lot of people are depending on us, and I suspect a lot of people are hoping we fail. For the latter group, screw them. I'm not going to give them the satisfaction. I know you feel the same way."

"Of course I do. It's just that, in working for a military products' company, I have to always check my thinking and make sure I'm in balance with all the facts and figures. I do worry about terrorists and the fear they cause, but I want to do something about it -- something that will eliminate both and in the shortest possible time. I believe technology is our best approach."

"Spoken as a true scientist, Zen. How is your part of the project going?"

"My work is going fine. We have made good progress on identifying all types of explosive components with our new analytical equipment hooked into the computer array. Lyncoln has gotten us down to the ppt level with his data augmentation software. My main challenge now is to further perfect and then work with Kan D to miniaturize what we call the vibrating vacuum cleaner."

"I have a vibrating vacuum cleaner at my apartment. It's about six years old now and every year seems to vibrate even more. Don't they all do that?"

"Not that way. Maybe *tuned* is better terminology. I have a vacuum cleaned tuned to the frequency of the returning wave front. It acts like a magnet in collecting the wave and works quite well. I have to test it under non-lab conditions and, of course, it is too damn big."

All Brad could say was, "Hey, that is a very novel approach. Do you think it can work in the field?"

"No reason why it shouldn't. Maybe you can help me with the science and the application of the technology."

"Sure, it sounds like it would be fun. Want to walk along the Mississippi and see a ship go through the lock and dam?"

"I do. It's just past noon now so let's keep track of the time so I can make my 5 PM flight."

Brad nodded, took her hand, and helped her up. They walked toward the river and the Stone Arch Bridge. There was a ship coming downriver and if they timed it right, they could watch it go through the locks from there. They ran hand in hand like kids and got there just in time. The ship was in; the lock was closing, closing, fully closed. They could hear the powerful diesel engines begin pumping the water out and the ship was being lowered. It took only about ten minutes to get to the level required. The gates opened and the ship motored out on its way to the next lock and dam and on down the Mississippi.

"What a sight."

Zen was still watching in awe and replied, "It wasn't easy taming this river. I can see and feel its power. Wow!"

"You are beginning to like Minneapolis too, aren't you?"

Zen smiled, squeezed his hand and said, "Yes, I am."

"Let's go get a bite to eat at Café Havana. Are you hungry?"

"I'm starved. Do they serve Midnight Pie for a late lunch?"

"I don't know; we'll ask. Let's see, I think it is on North Fourth Street, just past Hennepin Avenue."

They walked quietly together for a while, mostly west and north. Zen said, "Yes, I see it just beside that building with the sign that says Sex City. What part of town have you taken me to, Dr. Tully?"

"I wondered about that, too, when I first ate there, but it's okay. I think it is safe enough, especially at one in the afternoon."

They went inside Café Havana. The hostess seated them at a corner table. Once seated, the waitress arrived to take their order. Zen asked, "Do you serve Midnight Pie for lunch?"

"Yes, it is our specialty and we serve it at every meal."

"I'll have that and a Diet Coke, please."

"Make that two, please."

The waitress took their orders, turned, and hurried to the kitchen. In no time, she returned with two huge pieces of Midnight Pie and their Cokes. Midnight Pie was usually served cold, like most pies. It had vegetables, meats, and cheeses in a thick crust. At most, it was like a potpie but with a thicker consistency. They took their first bites at the same time. As she savored every taste contained in that first bite, Zen said, "I'll come back, just to have this again."

"This is great but I think it would be even better served warm. When you come again, we'll try it that way."

"Is that an invitation, Dr. Tully?"

"Yes, it is Dr. Lang; I need to see a lot more of you." Brad amazed himself that he was actually able to tell her that, but that was how he felt. They were very quiet, just comfortable with Brad's hand on hers as they finished lunch.

After lunch, they hurried to the apartment because it was getting close to the time when Zen had to leave for the airport.

Zen was packing her suitcase and briefcase and said, "I'll take the agreements back and we'll propose a schedule to share our data. Maybe a couple of trips, you to Boston first and then people from the team to Minnesota to get started."

"That sounds good to me for the business part. What about us and the non-business part?"

"I liked what you said at the restaurant, Brad. I need to see a lot more of you, too. This was a wonderful trip but the time went by way too fast. Let's think about how to spend some more time together and get to know each other even better."

"I'll have some ideas when we talk next and you do the same."

"I already have some ideas so I won't have to think about it very hard." She pulled him to her with one hand grasping his and putting it on her breast. Their free hands were constantly exploring each other's body with light touches. They stood this way kissing, as if it were their last, while becoming even more familiar with all parts of their togetherness.

Zen pulled away slightly and said, "Time to get to the airport." She gave him another kiss and whispered in his ear, "Think about all this as we plan our next time together."

"How could I not? You are wonderful!"

"You are going to walk with me to the light rail, aren't you?"

"I sure am." Brad picked up her bag. "Are you ready?"

'Yes," Zen said, as she picked up her briefcase.

They walked hand in hand to the train station without saying another word. It was almost 3:30 and the train was getting ready to leave the station. Brad and Zen looked into each other's eyes. With body and soul, both were silently saying, "I can't wait until next time."

They kissed and Zen took the bag he was carrying and stepped onto the train. In seconds, the doors closed and the train was off leaving the two waving goodbye to each other. Brad headed back to the apartment to think about all that had just happened.

Chapter 8

Deeper and Deeper in Trouble

Aldora and the Tapes

Aldora had talked to her team that was checking the phone tapes. There were a lot of tapes to check, but only two included conversations between Kramley and Kharif. Both were from early in the relationship and in the January – February timeframe. Based on the content, there seemed to be only two calls between the two people. How could that be? Everyone knew they had to have talked by phone more than twice over the past several months. Aldora's mind went back to the parameters of the recordings. Thirty seconds and matching computer-generated key words. The team still had not figured out what the keywords were or how they were actually generated. What a crock! Is it that no one knows or is it that no one is talking?

She started looking at the briefs of the two phone calls. The first was a request by Kharif to meet with Kramley. Kharif had learned Kramley was the representative from Customized Materials Technology to the University of California, Berkeley. TIC was making an unrestricted research grant to Berkeley and Kharif wanted to check notes with Kramley before he visited the university to present the grant. Kramley had agreed to meet Kharif after work at a nearby pub, the Squealing Pig.

Aldora thought – nothing here, damn. Besides being one of the brightest attorneys to go through the Justice Department's honors program, she also had an edge to her modus operandi. When she got her teeth into something, it was nearly impossible for her to let loose. A great attribute for an attorney, usually.

She grabbed the second brief and started reading. There were some pleasantries about the weather in D.C. versus San Francisco, but San Francisco had earthquakes, etc. That part of the discussion seemed a bit contrived. Finally, Kharif got down to business by asking Kramley and CMT to do field testing of a new RFID product TIC had developed. It had an expanded frequency range, new sensors, enhanced durability and security; it featured size and cost reductions.

Aldora thought, this is motherhood and apple pie stuff. Kharif wanted a real world test for about one hundred tags that would be subject to all means of transportation, all environments, and arrive at an Eastern European location. Collection of the tags would take place there before transporting the product to the customer. Kramley agreed and Kharif was to have the tags delivered for incorporation into the scheduled production.

Sounds pretty straightforward as a supplier testing a new product with a potential customer, right? In fact, Aldora thought based on what they learned later…that the tags worked really well and that Kramley wanted to buy the product and do even more field-testing with TIC. Then Aldora saw a short note on the brief. It read,

"There is a sentence about midway in the conversation after Kharif had explained how the test would work and I quote, …'our people will coordinate to remove the tags before the product goes to your customer.' It is that simple. Your reward will be realized once the tags are recovered in Eastern Europe.'" We are not sure what this means. It seems to mean, it would be a successful test once the tags are collected. It could mean something totally different or nothing at all.

Aldora thought it was strange wording too and would ask Thomas about it when they met. In the meantime, she asked for copies of the recording tapes for Director Elson. She scanned the other fifty briefs in the next hour and saw nothing of interest and certainly no red flags. Aldora packed it all in her briefcase, made a note to tell Jack about the tapes, and went to work on the financials.

Aldora Pursues Thomas's Financial Records

Aldora decided that of the two areas, monies that seemed to come into his account each time he delivered grants to Michigan or Berkeley and his ability to even pay more bills with extra money from someplace without increasing debt, the first might be easier to nail down.

Her law degree was from Michigan so she knew a little about the school. The departments that Customized Materials Technology would have been interested in were all located in Literature, Science, and the Arts, LS&A. Advanced degree programs were all coordinated through the Rackham Graduate School. The approach was to contact LS&A and simply ask how much money they received from CMT. She had gone back into the records at CMT and knew the exact amounts given to both Michigan and Berkeley. It was very simple. The amounts were virtually identical as noted in the company documents. Over the pertinent timeframe, each school was to have received exactly $750 thousand.

Aldora had called the Dean's office the day before and set up today's call with his assistant. She punched in the numbers on her phone, pushed send, and immediately heard, "University of Michigan, LS&A Dean's office."

"Hello, this is Aldora Klein from the U.S. Department of Justice. I called yesterday to arrange a phone conversation with the dean."

"Yes, he is ready for your call. Hang on just a second while I transfer you."

"Thank you."

"Hello, Aldora," the dean said. "The Department of Justice? We aren't in any trouble, are we?"

"No, sir, I am just trying to gather information for an investigation. Sorry to bother you with what may seem to be a small issue from an accounting or financial standpoint."

"I understand there is no such thing as 'small' if the Department of Justice is asking about it. Let me say that we will cooperate in any way we can to help your case. That being said, I must stress that the relationship we have with CMT and Thomas Kramley is outstanding. The company has been one of our larger and more consistent donors over the years. To tell you the truth, I'm not sure from where the loyalty comes, but I certainly promote and appreciate it."

"Yes, sir, I understand."

"I would not violate any trust we have with CMT, of course, but in this case, you are asking for public information. It is not only public information, but information that the donor usually wants to see made visible. For that reason, it appears in any number of reports that we have available. If you need the actual documentation later, just go to the University's website and click on 'Gifting' and then on 'LS&A.' In the time frame you mentioned, we have received six hundred seventy-five thousand dollars from CMT, all of it delivered personally by Thomas Kramley."

"Six hundred seventy-five thousand, is that correct?"

"Yes, and most of it targeted for the science part of LS&A, such as chemistry and engineering. By the way, everyone loves their company representative, Thomas Kramley. He helps CMT make use of the science and technology advancements made under the grants, scholarships, and fellowships provided to our departments. Based on his representation, we have a fair number of our students going to CMT, where they are exhibiting great career potential. I believe he also must be a strong advocate for continuing to build the relationship between CMT and the University of Michigan. We like him here."

"Thank you, Dean, just a couple more questions today. How does this work at your university? Do you, LS&A, take out an amount or percentage to help manage the money and the paperwork involved?"

"Yes, we do. We normally receive one check from a company for the amount gifted. Our administrative fee is usually

10%, unless there are special circumstances. Most often, the company will pay the administrative fee separately so that the gift remains whole. In the case of CMT, our records show that we always received one check and the administrative fees were subtracted. We are very fortunate to get the money in the first place so however companies elect to do it is fine by us."

"Yes, sir. You know that our conversation is confidential, correct? We have reason to believe that more money was to have come to your university from CMT. Somehow, it seems that 10% has regularly been skimmed off even before it reaches the university. We don't know how it is done yet but we'll find out. May I ask your assistant to get your administrator's name and contact information for CMT? I need to ask that person a few questions. Who would endorse the check for the university?"

"The administrator for the specific company. They are usually assigned according to company or geographic area. The administrator for CMT has been with us for years, but we'll get her information for you."

"Thanks, Dean. I really appreciate your time to discuss this matter. Please keep everything about our discussion confidential. Thanks again. Please connect me with your assistant now."

"You are welcome. I'm sure you will confirm that the University of Michigan is not involved with this skimming. Let us know if we can be of further help. I'll transfer you to my assistant. Goodbye for now."

"Goodbye, sir, and thank you very much."

The assistant answered the line and said, "I am getting the contact information you requested. Hang on just a minute, please. The contact's name is Diane Bateson ; you can reach her at 734/692-4357. You can call anytime, of course, but she happens to be at her desk right now, Aldora."

"Can you transfer me, please?"

"Of course, it was nice to talk with you again today."

"Thank you very much. You have been very helpful." The phone was ringing, 'University of Michigan, Gifting, LS&A, Diane speaking."

"Hello, Diane, I am Aldora Klein with the Department of Justice. I have just spoken to the dean of LS&A; he referred me to you. May I ask you a couple of questions about one of your companies, CMT?"

"Yes, I know them well. You said you are with the Department of Justice. Is anything wrong?"

"No, I am gathering information on CMT and its representative to Michigan, Thomas Kramley. Do you know him very well?"

"Yes, I have known him for several years. He is a great guy who really believes in his company's support of our university. Why?"

"You can cover details of the case with the dean later, if that is okay. Today I just need to know if your dealings with Mr. Kramley have been on the up and up. I know that sounds harsh, but I need to know if he has ever asked you to do anything out of the ordinary with the checks he brings to the university."

"No, not that I remember."

"Has anything unusual happened in the past two or three years?"

"The only thing I can remember is this. Two or three years ago, the amounts of the checks changed a little. Instead of $250 thousand, they became $225 thousand. I asked Thomas about the change. He said the company was cutting back a bit on everything including gifting. It wasn't anything about being displeased with our university, just a company cost-cutting program. At the same time, I remember him asking a lot of questions about how the checks were cashed, who signed for the university, how letters of thanks were sent, etc. I told him that I handle all of that for his company. I remember this. He specifically asked if the amount of the gift is ever included in the thank you letter. I told him it was our policy not to do that in the letter. Rather, we refer companies to the gifting area of our website or publications where all donated amounts are documented."

Diane continued, "The other thing that was a little strange was that he asked me to write the thank you letter for CMT's gift right away. He wanted to hand carry it to his company. I did it for him that one time but he hasn't asked for that since. Does any of this help?"

"It does, Diane. You have been a big help. Please keep all of this confidential. It is part of a case we are working that may be bigger than even CMT and Thomas Kramley."

"Okay, I will. Let me know if you need any more information."

"Thank you, Diane. I may be in touch gain. Until then, goodbye."

"Goodbye."

The Mach II System

Frank used the information Thomas had given him to get into the Mach II, Data Augmentation System (M2DAS). It was fully integrated into CMT's intranet technology and still there, functional and waiting for its next project.

He was able to regenerate the software test done at the plant on customer addresses. It was labeled, Field Test #2 with TIC product. The results were surprisingly good, as Thomas had described, not unlike what one might expect from advance artificial intelligence. The software, disturbingly, seemed not only to have accessed and used corporate information that related to customer locations and addresses; it actually seemed to have learned the information and acquired it permanently. Frank thought M2DAS might have gone even further than customer information. It might have learned and acquired all of the corporate records. Could it absorb any information that it was linked to either directly or indirectly? It almost seemed like it had become a parallel system to CMT's intranet. Yes, the mini-search engine may have become the body of knowledge itself. He made a note to remind himself to do a full-scale test on this aspect of M2DAS. Frank wondered if someone could use this software capability to bypass CMT's firewalls and access their confidential corporate records. It was obvious that he needed more help. He was a logistics specialist, not an IT expert.

THE CAMPAIGN OF FEAR

He went on to Field Test #3, which had resulted in the attempted theft of a secret CMT product. In this case, the software was upgraded to be able to interface with the new RFID tags and sensors and have GPS capability. Frank reconstituted the path of the packages with time, U.S. to Europe to Israel. He read about the circuitous route, dropped packages, assessment of no damage, and arrival at Zefat. Fifteen packages and ten tags. Apparently they were only able to get ten tags for the field test. It seemed reasonable. Checking further, he found that the RFID tags and sensors had a lot of advanced features. They could sense for chemicals, pressures, vibrations, shocks, radiation, etc. There was the report and recommendation of no action when the pallet was dropped. All of this information was nicely recorded and filed away by the M2DAS software – very thorough. Frank was about to take a break when he noticed a little camera icon next to all the other sensor icons. The RFID tags also had cameras and each one recorded the travel of its package! As he scanned through the video streams, there were lots of extraneous pictures. His thoughts were racing as he hurried to the end of the recordings hoping to find something pertinent to what happened at Zefat. There were ten recordings and he had found nothing of use in the first five except in two recordings he could see what looked like the lower halves of the bodies of three or four people. He stopped for a moment and thought about how Thomas had described the loaded pallet. Five packages to a layer, three layers. Packages 1-5 were loaded first, then 6-10, and finally the packages numbered 11-15, the ones with no RFID tags.

The pallet was on the plane when all of this happened, of course. The top five packages were the ones that were targeted to be stolen, numbers 11-15. Cameras in the second layer, number 6-10 might have been at the right height to get the faces of the thieves. Now he was really excited! Package 6 showed nothing; 7, nothing; 8, yes. There were very dark, blurry, and jumpy pictures of four people and then primarily one person all in dark clothes. Frank jumped to the recording for package 9. Nothing there. On to package 10. Yes, the recording was the same as number 8 with dark, blurry pictures. There were definitely four people for only a

199

short time and then pictures of just one person. Both recordings on numbers 8 and 10 were basically the same. He reasoned it must be how the pallet was arranged. As he reviewed the two recordings, he could see the elderly man's face. The elderly man handled the five boxes, which he put on a cart. He handed something toward the pallet and two more men entered the picture. They took the cart away. Then a fourth man joined him and they ran toward the cart being pushed away by the first two men. Frank jumped up from the screen and said aloud, "We have the whole thing on video. The team of four stole the five packages and took them to the waiting airplane, no doubt. When the Mossad caught up with them, they took off like bats out of hell, and the pilot committed suicide. The distance and the angle from the pallet did not allow recording of the exciting parts. However, we may have enough of a recording to identify at least one man. He seemed to be the one coordinating or leading the team." Frank thought, I have to tell someone but I have to be careful. Thomas cannot know about this. In fact, no one at CMT should know at this time. This could be the key to breaking the case. I have to find Jack right away!

Thomas's Finances

Omar saw the call come in from Thomas so he transferred it to the adjacent room and the special equipment.

"Hello, Thomas, how are you and how is the investigation going? We are on a secure line so don't worry about what you say. I need to know everything."

"The investigation is why I called, Omar. I am worried. There is a four-way meeting set up to talk with me and Mr. Blackstone and two members from the investigating team. I don't know the subject but it might be something to do with my finances. There are hints that they have been snooping around."

"There is no possible way to trace our payments to your offshore account. Have you stopped spending the money?"

"Yes, but before we talked I had already spent about $100 thousand."

THE CAMPAIGN OF FEAR

"Just keep quiet and they will learn nothing and be able to do nothing. I hope you haven't done anything else with your finances that would arouse their suspicions."

"Well, there is one other thing. Before I met you, I had mounting medical bills, no health insurance, and was in a very desperate situation. It was also before President Blackstone gave me a personal loan of $100 thousand. As the company representative for grants to Berkeley and Michigan, I was taking huge checks to them every year. With the help of my banker, who had no part in the misdeed, I converted each individual grant check into two checks. One was for the grant; the other was for the administrative costs. I knew the administrators and with samples of their handwriting, I forged their names to cash the checks. It was very easy and no one ever noticed what was happening. The university researchers and students were happy to get their grants, whatever the amount, and the administrators didn't know they were to receive a separate check. The company trusted me and never noticed either. The money helped me pay a lot of medical bills over the past few years. I know it was wrong but my family needed the money worse than the universities did."

"My God, Thomas! The investigators will be able to track down exactly what you were doing if they have any indication that something was amiss. If they start to do that then our situation, the TIC situation, becomes more tenuous. I said we are safe with the offshore account but with subpoenas and whatever else, they might be able to somehow connect TIC to the payments to you."

"I certainly do not want to get TIC into trouble. Maybe it would be best for me to admit skimming from the grant money and say nothing about anything else. That would put it all on me and protect you and TIC, I believe."

"We are in a difficult situation, Thomas. You can try that but I suspect that we are still at risk. The problem is that I don't know anything else better to do. If it comes to that in a meeting, go with your plan and hope that the investigation is stopped. Thank you for making the sacrifice to keep TIC out of this."

"I hope it works and maybe the company will forgive me,

based on my difficult circumstances."

"I'm sure they will. Please contact me right after the meeting so we can do more planning if needed.

"Goodbye for now, Omar."

"Goodbye, Thomas."

Confronting Thomas

The four-way meeting was set up in Blackstone's office. Joe, Aldora, and Jack were there a little early to make sure Joe knew most of the facts uncovered so far in the investigation. They agreed in advance to have Aldora lead the discussion with Thomas. Joe and Jack would be there mostly as observers. At that moment, Thomas walked in.

"Hello everybody," Thomas said.

"Hello, Thomas," everyone answered.

Joe motioned to a chair and said, "Please have a seat, Thomas. There are some questions that Aldora would like to ask about things that are coming up in the investigation. Are you okay with that?"

"Yes, sir, of course. I want the case solved as much as anyone. What are the questions?"

Joe said, "Thanks, Thomas. Aldora?"

"Thank you, sir. Thomas, we would like to discuss your finances with you. I want to be very direct and upfront about our findings and some questions that have come up."

Jack could see Thomas shifting a bit in his chair, sort of acting uncomfortable. What he could notice even more was the change in Aldora's expression, intensity, tone, and cadence. She had her lawyer's face and voice working.

Aldora continued, "We know about your family's health issues and sympathize with your situation. The company had helped by continuing your insurance for as long as possible. Mr. Blackstone has given you a special loan and is trying to get special off-market health insurance for you as we speak. The bills just keep coming in, don't they?"

"Yes, they do and you know what is even worse? My wife

THE CAMPAIGN OF FEAR

and son do not seem to be getting any better. No matter how many doctors, how many treatments, how many hopes, things don't seem to change much."

"That is too bad, Thomas. We are all very sorry."

"I know and I also know how much everybody has tried to help. We are very appreciative. It has been difficult for us to go from being a very independent family with few worries in the world to being almost totally dependent, with so many worries that it is impossible to function normally. People tend to do desperate things in these situations."

"We want to talk about the monies that are gifted by CMT to the University of Michigan and University of California, Berkeley in research grants, scholarships, and fellowships. You are the company representative to these universities. You have the responsibility to build relationships, identify high potential faculty and students, as well as to make recommendations for funding. You have obviously done this very well. Your company appreciates the job you have done, and the universities believe you are one of the best. No one questions that part, Thomas. What we do question is …."

Thomas interrupted and said, "It is time that I admit to what I have been doing. I knew it wasn't right, but I had run out of choices. You have no doubt pieced together the scheme that I have been using for some time. I admit it. I admit that I have taken about $150 thousand from the monies that were to have gone to the universities."

Aldora said in her lawyer voice, "Let us make sure we understand. We found that for the last three years, you changed the gift amount each year from $250 thousand to $225 thousand. You suggested to both universities that this was a cost cutting decision by the company because of the economy and other factors."

"Yes, I did. Furthermore I asked the bank to make the gifting process more efficient by taking one check from the company and creating two new ones … one for the grant, the other for the administrative fees. I took the smaller one, about 10% of the total and, with some practice, endorsed it with the name of the administrator from Michigan or Berkeley and cashed it. Instant money for me and I used every penny to pay medical bills."

"We know, Thomas. It doesn't make it right but yes, we know what you did with the money."

"It was an easy decision for me. It was my family's health or extra money for the universities. I take the full responsibility for my actions."

"Are you telling us that no one else was involved with any part of the scheme?"

"That is correct."

"Did anyone else receive any of the monies that were skimmed off?"

"No, they did not."

"Company people, bankers, university administrators, anybody else?"

"No, no one else, only me."

"So that accounts for about $150 thousand over the three-year period. Were there any other monies obtained in other illegal schemes?"

"No, this was my one and only venture to try to make ends meet."

"What if I were to tell you that our investigation shows that you seem to be able to pay off more bills than what $150 thousand would be able to explain? Do you have another scheme of a similar magnitude to the one at the universities?"

"No, I do not."

"How do you explain this debt decreasing without any additional income? We estimate you have received an extra $100 thousand and applied it toward outstanding bills. Can you tell us where you got that money?"

"I can't tell you because I didn't get any extra money. Maybe you just didn't put the right numbers together or something was confused with the dates of the billings or bills for my wife's or my son's treatments. I don't know, I just don't know."

Thomas was almost in tears so Joe suggested they take a little break, have some water, and get collected. After a short break, Aldora went back to the questioning.

"So you don't know where this extra money would have come from? Investments, inheritance, gifts, insurance, anything like that?"

"No, I had no other income, period."

"Thomas, I don't want to scare you any more, but I believe you know more than you are telling us. The next step is for us to get a subpoena and really get into every aspect of your financial and personal records. Do you really want us to do that?"

"No, I don't but I cannot tell you what I don't know. I'm sorry."

"Then I will tell you that we are authorized to start the subpoena process. It will take about 24 hours and then we'll begin the process of reconstructing how you were able to pay these bills. Before we close today, I have a few more questions. They are in the area of tapes of phone conversations with outside callers made and kept by the company. Our investigation shows you received two recorded outside calls from the head of TIC, Omar Kharif."

"Yes, I did but there were probably more than two calls."

"We wondered about that, too, said Aldora aggressively. "Why do you think the other calls were not recorded?

"I don't know. What about the calls?"

"Did you tell Mr. Kharif how to bypass the criteria for recording? For example, wait 30 seconds and don't use certain key words, etc.?"

"No, I didn't. Why would I? I simply wanted to test his RFID and software products. That is all we talked about."

"You never talked about payment or rewards for testing product?"

"No, we did not."

"Listen to this recorded conversation and tell us what it means, please." Aldora pushed the button on the recorder. Kharif's voice was the first heard saying, 'It's that simple! Your reward will be realized once the tags are recovered in Eastern Europe.'

"I'm not sure." Thinking fast, Thomas said, "He probably meant something about the conclusion of a successful field test. The test of his new product was important to both our companies."

"Do you know how the key words are selected for the phone security system?"

"No, I might have known at one time, but it was a long time ago."

"And you didn't tell Mr. Kharif about the 30-second requirement?"

"No, I'm not sure that I remembered that it was 30 seconds."

"Were there sometimes long gaps before you two started talking?"

"There might have been but I don't remember them specifically."

"Do you know that there may be a way to reconstruct the calls even though they were not recorded on the company tapes?"

"I don't care. There is nothing that would negatively impact my dealings with TIC or me. What are you suggesting?"

"What about off-the-books payments by TIC?"

"No way, I cannot believe these questions."

"Our subpoena will cover this area, too. We'll find out about all the phone conversations, not just the first two. I'd like to give you one more chance to come clean before we take the subpoena approach. Is there anything more you would like to tell us about your finances and the tapes?"

Thomas sat there for the longest time considering all of his options and finally said, "Everything I have done was to protect my family. Yes, some things weren't quite right or legal but I didn't have many choices. I'm not sure I would have or could have done anything differently. If you have to get a subpoena to search my records even more, then go right ahead."

"Thank you, Thomas. I am sorry we could not come to an agreement or arrangement without the subpoena. If we find something, there could be even more severe repercussions than if you had been candid with us."

"I'll just have to take my chances, I guess."

Joe said, "Thomas, all of this is very disturbing to me, especially when you admitted stealing the company-gifted university money. It is almost too much to fathom."

Aldora excused Thomas by telling him, "You are to stay on the job but will be closely supervised during the rest of the investigation."

Thomas said "Thank you," and left the office.

The three huddled for a few minutes to check notes and their next action. Jack said, "Subpoena it is, with close supervision of Thomas by Joe and Frank. Aldora, please send me an electronic version of the second tape for the director. The Mossad want to do some voice recognition comparisons to see if Omar was the one who called about the arrival of the shipment at Zefat."

"I'll do that right away, Jack."

"Thanks, Aldora, and great work on the investigation of Thomas's financials and the tape recordings. You are one tough attorney when it comes to getting the facts and asking the questions. I will tell the director about the subpoena so he can help pave the way."

"Thanks, Jack; I'll get the paperwork started immediately. Joe, I am sorry about Thomas, but I still believe there is more to the story than we got today. Thanks for your support as we dig deeper and deeper."

"Thank you, Aldora and Jack. You know that I want to get this resolved, even if a friend is involved. I'll continue to help in any way I can."

"Thanks, Joe," Jack said as Aldora and he left Joe's office. "Let's get back to work."

Pictures of the Attempted Theft

Jack had barely finished his meeting with Aldora, Joe, and Thomas when he saw Frank running up the hall and yelling, "Jack, Jack, Jack!"

"Hi, Frank. I don't think I have ever seen you so excited. What did you find on the M2DAS?"

"You won't believe it. Each of those RFID tags had a mini-camera embedded in it. There were lots of video data produced, varying by where the tags were placed on the boxes and how the boxes were oriented. All this data was uploaded by the satellite and fed back via the software to CMT's intranet technology system."

"Great, Frank. Before I forget, the director needs a copy of the M2DAS software. You know him; he wants to play with it a bit to see if he can learn everything it does. He may believe that it is more than a data augmentation system. Could you send a copy to me electronically so I can send it and the tape recorded phone conversation to him ASAP, please?"

"Of course I can. I have some of the same questions about M2DAS. I am planning a full-scale test on it once I get some additional IT help from our buddies in D.C. But the news that I came to tell you about may be even more important. I believe one of the cameras captured video data of the man who was coordinating the attempted product theft in Zefat. We have a significant amount of footage of his face and upper body. It may be enough to identify him and give us a lead as to whom we are dealing with in this terrorist plot."

"You have the team leader of the Zefat operation on video?"

"Yes, clear as day. Do you think our colleagues in Israel might be able to identify him?"

"With their extensive computer data files, I would bet they could. This is fantastic. Would you send me the video at the same time you send the software?" I'll include these and the tape of the Omar-Thomas discussion about the field test in the note I am sending to the director. He is in frequent contact with the Mossad and the people who can help."

"You got it," Frank said.

Jack pondered, "If we can confirm that Omar made the call about the shipment and also identify the team leader of the terrorist organization, it will really help our investigation."

"I know, I know." Frank headed back to his office.

Jack was just standing there smiling as he said very quietly to himself, "You sons of bitches are not quite as smart as you think you are."

Jack went back to his office and immediately saw the emails from both Aldora (with an attachment that was the voice tape recording) and Frank (with an attachment that was the M2DAS software and the Zefat video). He quickly consolidated the attachments into his note to the Director. It read:

> *Director Elson, herein are attachments on both the Omar-Thomas discussion (for voice comparison) and the M2DAS software that you requested. You should know that today Thomas Kramley admitted to stealing money from the gifts that CMT made to both Berkeley and the University of Michigan. He would not admit to any other financial wrongdoing but we still suspect that we will find more. We will be submitting the paperwork to receive a subpoena to dig deeper into his finances. Any advance work you can do to facilitate the subpoena process would be appreciated. In addition, there has been breaking news in our investigation. The RFID tags contained tiny cameras and some of them shot footage of the attempted theft by the terrorist team in Zefat. The third attachment shows this and specifically the face and upper body of the man we believe to be the ringleader. It might be enough to identify him.*
>
> *I'll be in touch as the case continues to unfold. Thanks for your help on the subpoena.*
>
> *Regards, Jack*

Jack sent the email and eased back into his chair thinking, we may have them on the run. I wonder what the next revelation will be.

The Voice and Video Recordings

Sam received the attachments from Jack. He separated the voice recording and the video footage and got them ready to send to Absek as they talked. The videos were an added bonus that he had not expected.

Sam punched in the numbers. After a few moments, he heard, "Hello, Director Elson, how are things in D.C.?"

"Hello, Absek, sorry it got to be so late for our call."

"No worry, sir, we work all hours here just like you do."

"Any progress on the case?"

"Some, Sam. Data in our files leads us to believe that Omar and Emar were actually blood brothers and Mr. Patek Kumat is somehow related to them. We are not sure how yet or if it will mean anything to the case."

"Interesting, Absek! We did not find a lot on our search on Patek Kumat here either. It is thought that he had two sons, about 2 or 3 years apart in age. They may have gone to the same college, one in business, and one in engineering. You don't suppose these three are father and sons?"

"It does seem to fit. The use of titles may fit, too, in that sons never call their fathers by their given name, right? Using a title to show respect or for some organizational reason might be expected."

"Absek, I am going to send this email to you right now. It contains two attachments that might help us get to the bottom of this. One attachment is the voice recording you requested of Omar's discussion with the director of logistics at CMT, Mr. Thomas Kramley. It came from the company's repository of recorded outside calls and is quite lengthy. I hope you can make voice comparisons and determine if the caller telling the "leader" about the shipment was Omar. In addition, we have some exciting video footage of the key man on the team that attempted the theft of the top secret product at the Zefat airport."

"What? You have video of the theft as it was unfolding? Your satellites aren't that good; how did you do that? I can't believe it."

"The terrorists might have fooled themselves, Absek. The RFID tags had video capability. If the packages were oriented properly, the cameras were recording everything. Pretty dumb I would say."

"Sam, I just received your email. I want to get these attachments to our laboratories right away. Will you excuse me, please? I promise to call you back as soon as have any new information based on these audio and video recordings."

"Of course, Absek. I knew you would want to run with this. Before I let you go, you should know a couple of other things. The company we are talking about, whether it is Technology

Investment Corporation or Technolibertat, is also involved with two other companies in addition to CMT. They are Tully Research, Inc., where they have invested a considerable amount of money recently in acoustics R&D, and Advanced Technology Products, which has a big federal government project on explosives detection using acoustics technology. Please keep these names in mind as you run your investigation. We are trying to find out just what this terrorist organization is up to. We need all the help we can get to connect the dots."

"I will, Sam, thanks for the extra information. No doubt the case is bigger than what we see here in Israel. Whatever it is, we have to stop them!"

"You are so right. Thanks, Absek, and goodbye for now."

"Goodbye, Sam, and good hunting."

Patek Kumat Contacts Mike Jackson

"Hello, Dr. Jackson, this is Patek Kumat calling."

"Hello, Mr. Kumat, how are you?"

"I am fine and have good news for you. Our investment proposal in the area of advanced acoustics research has been accepted just recently. I wanted you to be the first to know."

"This is good news. You should know that the NASA contact you provided was very helpful to us in some of our nanoscale R&D. Thank you very much."

"I am pleased to be of help. What about the technical briefs on our current licensable technology? Did you see anything that could help you in your priority projects?"

"My staff is currently reviewing the information you provided. My quick personal review showed a couple technologies that I would identify as promising. Our experts are looking at the entire list of technologies being offered. I'm sure they will find some that are interesting and that we should explore licensing."

"Good, I hope so. TIC would enjoy a significant and longstanding relationship with Advanced Technology Products. Would it be beneficial if we were in contact with any of your project team members directly? It would seem that once we have access to the advanced acoustics work that would be important. You know - better communication, more effective technology transfer, and increased speed or velocity, as they say today."

"I think so, Mr. Kumat, but you or your delegate will have to talk with our team leader, Dr. Chadly Bromcast, and make the arrangements through him. He has a lot of pieces of the puzzle to manage and needs to factor in the potential of several technology resources. Our approach has been that there are no sacred cows. That is, internal technology will take a backseat to outside technology if it is shown to be better. Dr. Bromcast and his team are masters at identifying or developing the best technology. I promise that you will get a fair shake on this."

"I trust we will, Dr. Jackson. May I have our Mr. Omar Kharif contact Dr. Bromcast and begin the discussions? It seems that the importance of the project would merit that."

"Yes, you may. I know these two have talked in the past. It was perhaps in April and it didn't go well. Things will probably go better if you tell Mr. Kharif to be a little less aggressive in his interactions with Dr. Bromcast."

"That is good feedback. Omar sometimes wants to close the deal too fast. Truly though, he is very good at managing our technology investments and licensing in the U.S. I will talk with him."

"Thanks, Mr. Kumat. There is one other thing, too. In that previous meeting, Dr. Bromcast believes that Omar may have mistakenly picked up a document that belongs to our company. Please ask him to search his file from the meeting to see if he has any documents belonging to us. It is not a critical document per se, but it would help clear the air as we start our serious discussions on working together. If he unknowingly has it, the document should be returned immediately, of course. If he doesn't have it, then that should be made very clear as well. We are business people, Mr. Kumat. I do not wish to frighten you but in this case, the project sponsor is the federal government. The seriousness of the matter raises tenfold or more once the U.S. defense establishment gets involved. Please be assured that there are no accusations, just friends talking and planning to get a matter resolved."

"I understand, Dr. Jackson. The matter will be addressed immediately. I will handle it personally with Mr. Kharif and get back to you. It is the only way we can hope to work effectively with Advanced Technology Products."

"Thank you, Mr. Kumat. I hoped you would understand and take charge to clear the air."

"Yes sir, I will. Goodbye, Dr. Jackson."

"Goodbye, Mr. Kumat."

As he hung up the phone, Kumat screamed and pounded the desk but he resisted calling Omar immediately. He needed to think about what to do. Without ATP as a partner, they would be in a desperate situation. Omar's mistakes were very serious and their consequences were mounting. He needed a corrective action plan.

The ATP Team Talks with Sam

Mike Jackson had called Chad to tell him to arrange for the next update telephone conference call meeting with Director Elson as soon as possible. He wanted to attend.

They were all huddled in Chad's office - Mike, Bill, Kan D, Lyncoln, and Zen, as Chad placed the call. The phone rang. Once, twice, three times and then . . . . .

"Hello, this is Sam Elson."

"Hello, Director. The whole project team is with me: Bill, Kan D, Lyncoln, Zen, and our boss, Mike Jackson."

"Thanks for quickly getting together for this call. I had suggested this to Mike when we talked earlier today. There are several things happening that all of you need to know. Many relate to the Technology Investment Corporation (TIC) and your top priority project. I'll try to be brief because I have an important international call in a few minutes. Here is the most highly probable information we currently have:

TIC has penetrated CMT and established a mole of sorts to steal top-secret acoustics technology.

TIC has become the largest investor in Tully Research Inc., a start-up company that focues on advanced acoustics research and development.

TIC is in the process of trying to penetrate Advanced Technology Products. Both Mike and Chad have had contact with TIC principals under the guise of licensing technology.

TIC is not the company they purport to be.

There are some details that I won't go into right now but I want you all to be on your guard. If either Omar Kharif or Patek Kumat contacts you, refer them to Chad or Mike. They are going to be the front men until we figure out exactly what is going on."

Chad said, "Thank you, Director. We appreciate your thoroughness and concern. There are not many new developments since we talked last. Kan D, you have a brief update on our proposed cooperative program with Customized Materials Technology."

"Yes. Director, we have been in contact with Thomas Kramley, whom I know from my Michigan days. He was favorable to the subcontractor agreement on detonation technology that we sent him. I believe he will recommend to Mr. Blackstone that it be signed. Mr. Kramley is concerned about the federal government investigation at CMT. He is hoping for a quick resolution so it will not affect our working together on this project. Thank you, sir."

"Thanks, Kan D."

"Zen, you visited Tully Research recently."

"Yes, Chad. Director, recall that I know Brad Tully from graduate school at Stanford. We believe he and his new company, Tully Research, Inc., represent the most advanced and sophisticated acoustics research in the world today. We proposed a blanket confidential disclosure agreement and a subcontractor agreement that would focus on both our first and second-generation products. He signed both agreements. I tried to get close to him, I mean I tried to get more information but he didn't seem to want to talk too much about his research on this trip. After seeing his laboratory, my sense is that he may be close to some breakthroughs and could be far ahead of us from a technology standpoint. We agreed to two more meetings to be scheduled soon. He will come here for the first

THE CAMPAIGN OF FEAR

meeting and we will go there for the second meeting. Director, may I be candid, please?"

"Of course, Zen."

"Thank you. Regarding your points number two and four about TIC being the largest investor in Tully Research and that they may not be who them seem to be. Could Brad, Mr. Tully, be in any danger?"

"We don't think so, Zen, but we have agents watching him just in case. I think things will be fine."

"Thank you, sir; we need him and his technology." She thought about the agents watching and wondered if they saw what happened in the bedroom or on the deck. My God! Zen cleared her throat and said, "That is my update for today, sir. Thank you."

"Thank you, Zen. I have to leave in a minute. Thank you for your updates and please stay on guard with TIC. May I talk to Chad and Mike alone for just a second, please? Thanks again."

The four team leaders walked out of Chad's office, each with their own set of thoughts but more determined than ever to do their jobs, even if it meant some danger.

Chad closed and door and said, "Director, only Mike and I are on the phone with you now."

"Good. I want to get into a few of the details that I did not want to discuss with the whole team. We are putting TIC under a lot of pressure with our findings at CMT. There are voice recordings and video footage that may link TIC to a Mideast terrorist organization. Israel and their Mossad are helping us with the case. I am interested in seeing how TIC reacts to the pressure and finding out exactly what they are trying to do. Like it or not, ATP is caught up in this."

Mike said, "Director Elson, as you suggested, I have talked to Mr. Kumat about the lost sketch and notes on our project that Omar may have 'mistakenly' taken from Chad's office. I told him the federal government is the sponsor for our project and implied that if our lost sketch is not found, things could get very uncomfortable for them. He seemed very concerned because he promised to address it personally with Omar and get back to me ASAP."

"That's good, Mike. Chad, do you still think Omar is the culprit?"

"I do, sir. I like the direction of the pressure to get it resolved. Do you feel that the pressure on Omar might be too much for him?"

"It might be but only because his own organization will magnify the issues even more. Omar is at risk, yes, but he isn't the real concern. He has put his organization at risk. The terrorist organizations will go to any length to save themselves, as you know. Thanks for everything, Mike and Chad. Let's keep in touch as these things play out and watch for signs of the pressure building.

"Okay, Director, thank you," said Chad.

"Thanks, Director," said Mike.

Omar and Thomas Talk

Omar had just received the investment agreement paperwork from Dr. Bradford Tully and Tully Research, Incorporated. Omar said out loud, "He accepted it just as it was written, no modifications or changes of any kind. We are now partners, TIC and TRI." Omar was about to pick up the special phone to tell the Liberator the news when the other phone rang. He transferred the call to the special phone and said, "Hello, this is Omar."

"Hello, Omar, this is Thomas."

"Thomas, how are you doing?"

"Not too well. We just finished the meeting with Blackstone and two investigators. I followed our plan and admitted to stealing money from the company or the universities over a three-year period. It helped some that I did this before they actually accused me, but they had all the information about how and what I had done anyway. Things got worse when the attorney investigator asked if I had been involved in any other wrongdoing. She asked the question several different times. My firm answer was always, no, I have not been involved in any other wrongdoing. They did not have specifics but knew that I had other income because my medical debt had been reduced below what the university monies would account for totally. Then they threatened me with a subpoena and said that things would not go well for me if they found things. My answer was always the same: I have not been involved in any other wrongdoing."

"Did they accuse you of accepting money from TIC?"

"Well, yes, not in those exact words, but they strongly suggested it."

"What do you mean?"

"Omar, I believe you knew that our conversations might be recorded when you called me at my office."

"I did figure it out but it took some time."

"They have at least one recording of an early conversation about our first field test when you mentioned something like 'your reward will be realized once the tags are collected in Eastern Europe.' The words, *your reward,* are what they grabbed onto. I would not admit anything but my guess is that they do not believe me. I suspect they think this is where the other money to pay medical bills came from. Because of this, they are requesting a subpoena to dig very deep into my finances and maybe even into the other tapes of our conversations."

"What else do you think they can learn from the tapes, Thomas?"

"I don't know exactly but they have two tapes already. These are probably from our first discussions about Berkeley and field testing. They don't need a subpoena for those two tapes. The attorney implied that it might be possible to get the other taped conversations as well."

"How the hell could they do that if they aren't recorded?"

"I do seem to remember that our deal with the phone company included a year's backup of all incoming calls, just in case. It was to constantly test whether the software's continuing keyword changes were working properly. It was also a safeguard against someone finding out that to get around the system all they had to do was wait thirty seconds. The whole security system with the phone depended on our people not disclosing the recording guidelines."

"Then they might have us, Thomas!"

"I am afraid they might, Omar. I am so sorry that we are in this mess and that you and TIC might get into trouble because of it."

"Still, as I think about this, they have to prove that money actually changed hands for there to be a conviction. Their digging, even with a subpoena, will have to be very advanced and sophisticated for them to find out about the offshore account. Hang tough, Thomas, don't admit to anything more than you have. We may still be alright."

"I will, Omar. Is there anything else I can do to help?"

"Yes, there is. I will be in San Francisco again next week, Monday actually. Can we meet at our favorite place and discuss our strategy a little more? Maybe about 6 PM after work?"

"That would be fine, Omar. The investigative team has been going there for dinner, too; so let me check that we would not be bumping into them. I'll call you back if it is a problem. If you don't hear from me, I'll see you there on Monday evening.

"Okay, thanks, Thomas. Don't worry, we'll find a way out of this. How did your boy like those comic books?"

"He thought they were great and I believe has read them all about ten times each. Thank you so much for thinking of him."

"You are welcome, Thomas. See you next Monday."

"Thanks again, Omar, and goodbye until Monday."

"Goodbye, Thomas."

The Liberator Calls Omar

Omar was shaking as he took the call, "Hello, Liberator."

"Hello, Omar, what do you have for me today?"

"I have good news about our proposed investment in Tully Research, Inc. Dr. Tully has signed and returned the agreement with no changes. With your permission, I will make the first year's payment of $10 million."

"I am pleased, Omar. Yes, make the payment and then see what you can get from him in the way of technical reports and data on acoustics. Then we can see if we have anything for Dr. Jackson at Advanced Technology Products."

"Yes, sir, our plan is working. I will be in contact with TRI and Dr. Tully immediately. With this amount of money, I'm sure he will be very cooperative."

"I hope you are right, Omar. What about Thomas Kramley?"

"Yes, sir. He had the meeting with the president of the company and the two investigators. According to our plan, he admitted to stealing money from the company. It was actually money that was being gifted by the company to the University of Michigan and the University of California, Berkeley. He set up a neat little scheme to skim about 10% off the top before the money ever got to the universities. They didn't know what was going on and the company didn't check on Thomas's delivery of the gifts. He did this for three years before the current investigation started. They found out he had extra money to pay medical bills and the bank deposits always happened at the same time as the university gifts. They had enough evidence to lay it out and accuse him, but he admitted it before they had to do that. He was trying to draw attention away from us. That was our plan anyway."

"I'm afraid to ask if it worked. You are telling me that it worked, aren't you?"

"Yes and no. The investigators had also checked on cash flow and spending versus income and discovered there must be more money coming in beyond what was being skimmed from the university money. Thomas was able to pay more medical bills than could be accounted for with that money. They asked him about other sources of additional money. He would not admit to anything other than stealing the university money."

"I hope it ended there."

"Not quite, sir. The investigators found recorded tapes of conversations between Thomas and me."

"I told you about tape recordings. In most systems, all you have to do is wait no more than thirty seconds before speaking. The system won't record anything because the pause confuses the system."

"I know. I must not have waited long enough. They have a recording on which I used words like *your reward will be realized when we collect the tags from Eastern Europe."*

"Omar!"

"Thomas tried to explain that away and wouldn't say anything else. They threatened him with a subpoena and he still would not talk. The four-way meeting ended with Thomas being told that he would be under close supervision and that a subpoena would be requested immediately."

"This is trouble, Omar."

'I know but I don't believe they can tie it to us unless they can prove that money actually changed hands. It will be difficult to do that. Maybe impossible. I've told Thomas to stick to his story and to not admit to anything else. What do you think?"

"I know you are trying to resolve this, Omar, but I believe it is time to implement our elimination plan."

"Can we wait?"

"I don't believe so. The investigative team is too close to the truth. Be strong and implement your plan."

"I will, sir. Thomas and I have a meeting next Monday in San Francisco. I'll have a plan in place by that time."

"Will it be only Thomas or Thomas and his family?"

"What is your advice, sir?"

"It has to be his whole family. There are too many risks for us if he told his wife or son about what he was doing. We have to remove the entire threat."

"Sir, I do not find it easy to take the lives of women and children. It seems that our cause gets diluted when we do things like that. Do you ever feel that way?"

"No, Son, our cause is too important to worry about the lives of three people. We and only we are in the right. These people are of no consequence. We must be successful."

"Yes, sir, I will do as you say. The poison you sent arrived safely at my office. There may be a way to do this without drawing any further attention to our organization. I hope that it will result in a dead-end for the investigators in the CMT case. Wish me luck. Praise Allah!"

"Praise Allah, Son."

The Subpoena and More Revelations

The subpoena arrived very quickly. Aldora thought maybe the director was right when he said, "This was probably the top priority project for the federal government." Only the most powerful people or those working on a top program could get a subpoena approved so quickly. I have to be very careful that I don't abuse the powers that have been delegated to me, Aldora thought to herself. The first thing I will do is to contact all the World Banking System sector heads.

The World Banking System has twelve sectors, each responsible for ten to twenty banks and their subsidiaries, depending on the specific geography of their sector of the globe. Before the September 11 attack on the World Trade Centers, it was not well-organized and lots of things slipped through the cracks either accidentally or intentionally. After September 11, with the terrorist threat, new processes and people were put in place, checks and balances built and power given to make it work. The upshot was that all significant global or world money transactions had to go through the appropriate banking sector. If the transaction (deposit or withdrawal) was ten thousand dollars or short-term multiples making up ten thousand dollars, it had to be reviewed by the World Banking System, approved and documented. There were no exceptions and it meant there were no secret offshore accounts any longer. The average person did not know this because they had not been told about the changes in the World Banking System. Nor did they care because they did not have offshore accounts.

The Justice Department had created an electronic form to contact the WBS sector heads to give them the vital information. Aldora completed the form, attached the subpoena, and pushed the send button. It automatically went to the twelve sector heads and they were required to respond within twenty-four hours.

Speed of gathering facts was of utmost importance in terrorist cases. The WBS knew this and usually communicated the information they had in a few hours. The responses started arriving immediately. Within an hour, Aldora had ten responses of 'no information on the subpoena.' Another two responded shortly thereafter with 'Information on Subpoena S-2009-AKDOJ-TKCA-T available. We are compiling and confirming accuracy. You will have the information within the hour.' Aldora thought, fantastic! This is important enough that I am just going to wait right here. One response arrived within ten minutes. It was the Mideast WBS sector indicating three 50 thousand dollar wire transfers from a partner bank's subsidiaries in Lebanon, Jordan, and Syria. The partner bank's headquarters was in Syria with assets greater than one hundred billion U.S. dollars. The money transfers were from an account listed as Technolibertat/TIC and delivered to an account listed as Mr. Thomas Kramley, Cancun, Mexico. The other response arrived as Aldora was reading ... Cancun Mexico. It was from the Western WBS sector indicating receipt of three 50 thousand dollar deposits into the Thomas Kramley account in Cancun, Mexico. One hundred thousand dollars had been withdrawn and fifty thousand dollars remains in the account. The bank has its headquarters in the U.S. with assets of one hundred seventy-five billion U.S. dollars and subsidiaries in the U.S. Mexico, Canada, and South America.

Aldora wondered why they have to give their assets and the location of subsidiaries. She decided it didn't matter. We got Thomas Kramley, she thought, smiling. Money changed hands from Technolibertat/TIC to him for something. With this information, I think he will talk now. We'll have both Kramley and Kharif of TIC.

She copied the electronic messages from the two WBS sector heads and started walking down the hall toward Jack's office. She was thinking: The one hundred thousand dollars just about exactly matched the income-spending imbalance she found in Thomas's financials. She was walking fast not looking where she was going or who was approaching her in the hall.

Thomas said, "Hello Ms. Klein."

Aldora stopped, looked up, gulped, and said, "Hello, Thomas." She folded her papers quickly, smiled and said, "I'm on my way to a meeting; you'll have to excuse me."

"Did you get your subpoena?"

"Yes, we did and we have found your offshore bank account in Cancun, Mexico. We'll be getting together again soon so you better think hard about coming clean on the whole mess."

Thomas was bone white and in shock. All he could muster was, "I'll be gone on Monday so it will have to be after that. May I have my attorney with me when we meet?"

"I don't see why not, Thomas. This is a very serious matter involving a supposed terrorist organization. You should be with counsel."

"Thank you, Ms. Klein. See you later."

Brad and Director Elson Talk

Brad said, "Hello, Director."

"Hello, Brad. I am glad you called because I just completed some scenario building on Omar and TIC."

"Do you have agents watching me?"

"Yes, and I am sorry I did not tell you. Are they that obvious?"

"They? I have just caught a glimpse of one of them. It was the one assigned to me earlier in Chinatown, D.C. You mean there are others?"

"Yes, but I won't tell you how many or give you any other information. It's for your own safety."

"I know. Thank you very much." Brad was thinking back to the time he spent with Zen and wondering how much these guys saw. "When did they start, Director?"

"You don't need that information, Brad. Let's just say they have been there for a while."

"That's fine." Brad was really thinking about the morning on the balcony-deck with Zen wearing that long t-shirt and nothing else. And what was under that t-shirt for his exploration and how he felt as his hands moved under and up. The t-shirt was incidental as he reached for her breasts, touching the nipples first, then one breast in each hand massaging softly ...

"Brad, are you still there?"

"Yes, sorry. I was thinking about how in the hell I could have gotten myself into this mess."

"You'll be okay, just mind your P's and Q's. May I give you some of my scenario thinking on Omar and TIC?"

"Yes. I have done some work on the technology side using an adaptation of my data augmentation software."

"Great. Here goes. I have included the most recent information we have on Omar and the activities of TIC. New bits and pieces are coming in all the time so we'll have to augment the scenario constantly. Here are some pieces that have gone into the work. Omar does not have a technical background yet he is running Technology Investment Corporation. Omar works with universities well but seems to have bungled almost every interaction with companies. Specifically, stealing the notes and sketch from Chad's office on Advanced Technology Products' planned special project to develop a defensive weapon to detect explosives like IED's and bribing the logistics director at Customized Materials Technology so that, under the guise of new product testing, he can penetrate their detonation technology. Omar was so anxious to get access to your technology that he was willing to overpay to invest in your company. Then there were the audiotapes of his phone calls, video recordings at Zefat, and financial records in the Middle East and Mexico which all show a propensity to make major mistakes again and again."

"Omar might have relatives in the organization, a brother, the pilot who committed suicide at Zefat and a father who is perhaps the head of the terrorist organization."

"We believe Omar is getting help from a more senior member of the organization. Patek Kumat is helping at ATP. Another person known only by the title 'leader' is helping with CMT, and there is probably someone helping with you and TRI."

"The company, Technology Investment Corporation, has made large investments in key technologies at major universities. TIC has built its reputation by gifting $50 million to $100 million dollars over five years for unrestricted research grants to key professors and students. TIC seems to be focusing on acoustics technology recently with activities at all three companies."

"The TIC website has *explosives technology* listed as a key technology. TIC's focus on acoustics and explosives technology may indicate knowledge of the government's top priority project. TIC may be the U.S. subsidiary of a larger terrorist organization called Technolibertat. Technolibertat is separate but loyal to al Qaeda and might be working today at their behest. Technolibertat is most likely the organization that attempted the theft of top secret CMT's detonation technology at Zefat."

"So they know approximately what we are up to and may be doing everything possible to get tight with the key companies and people involved to access all information needed to learn about and counteract our plan."

"I couldn't have said it better, Brad. My scenario is dynamic and changes as we get new information, of course, but let me give you the augmented psychological profile on Omar. It is a disturbing picture because it paints an unpredictability aspect to his future actions. This man is unskilled at his job, not just in technology investment but also as a supposed terrorist. He is weak for our typical terrorist because we see his sympathetic nature in interacting with Thomas Kramley by helping to pay for medical bills. He is pulled between family and organization and feelings of right and wrong. He wants to please, prove himself and may function in ways that are extreme or unreal to his actual character. He may be suicidal or murderous and he may be influenced to turn from the dark side on which he has found himself."

"What a nutcase, Director. This is what we are going up against with logic, facts, and figures? How can we ever win?"

"Our philosophy in D.C. is that we have to bring to bear every asset we have to fight terrorism. Going on the offense has always been a hard decision for us as a country. We usually get involved that way because there was no other choice. For example: the attack on Pearl Harbor or the September 11 attack in New York City. Even when we go on the offensive, we have a tendency to slide back too soon and assume a more defensive posture. This has happened in both Afghanistan and Iraq over the last several years. The Abbott administration wants to fight fire with fire not with thicker Kevlar vests or more vehicle armor or more medics, evacuation units and hospitals. Fire with fire! There are so many lives now and in the future that depend on it."

"I know, sir, and I'm sorry for sounding hesitant. I'm in this with you all the way."

"I know, Brad. What have you done with your analysis of the technology situation? Your software and Big Blue must be having fun getting to the most reasonable projections."

"I'm afraid I haven't made as much progress as you sir. First, I need to tell you that Omar has come back asking for access to technology that he and TIC can license. The implication is that they need to start getting some of their investment back. I have stalled him a bit, with the story about policies and procedures, for maybe as much as several weeks. He seemed most interested in the first generation wave generator so when I get to it, I'll start feeding him information on that. It's basically what I did a long time ago at GPRI."

"Good approach, Brad. We have to make them think they have access to the most current and sophisticated acoustics technology."

"That's where my scenario building leads me, too, Director. Listen, if they have a sketch of the government project, they know what is being planned. The most successful tactic they have used over the last decade to create fear would be threatened if we are successful. They have to learn about the pieces of the project so they can somehow counteract whatever we come up with to find and destroy the IEDs, EFPs and the like. How do they get on top of things? They try to penetrate ATP to get more information about the project. Thus use an investment in my company to gain access to ATP by getting all of the state-of-the-art acoustics technology now and any further advances that may come along. They penetrate CMT to learn about detonation technology. Theoretically, they would have everything they need. Some $50 million to $100 million dollars of university research in sensors, chemical analyses, MEMS, OLEDS, nano, microelectronics, DAS, acoustics, wireless and explosives technology standing ready to use. The Berkeley's, Stanford's, MIT's, and Michigan's all love them. Put all of that with what they could learn from people, technical reports and prototypes at ATP, TRI, and CMT, they could theoretically copy or build most any kind of weapon imaginable. Maybe this is where Technolibertat got its name and what the founders were thinking originally. The computer, however, has a slightly different spin based on the information we have been able to provide. There was a flaw in the al Qaeda thinking and planning process. The flaw was about people; they don't have the technically trained people. Even though they had access to most of the key technologies, they didn't have the people to understand them and innovate and create the products. They saw the new initiative by our government and decided the best they could do was not to create a new weapon to preserve their 'Campaign of Fear' but something more modest. It was to reverse engineer what we had and find a way to stop it. The scenario has a high correlation factor but still makes the point that this approach is also naive. It is almost as difficult to reverse engineer a highly technical product as it is to develop it in the first place."

"I believe the computer scenario is accurate and this is very likely what they are trying to do. I wanted to get your expert opinion because I wasn't sure my program was giving me the correct result. You got the same answer I got a completely different way. Brad, you are a genius."

"Well, now I understand why you wanted my new research advancements in acoustics kept secret. It was to have TIC or Technolibertat use all their resources to address our first generation product while we focus on the second or third generation. They will be the ones introduced and we will skip the first generation completely."

"You got it. We'll have to continue the program at ATP but start a new program in parallel with your new research findings. Omar and his organization have to believe there is only one program and it is based on first generation technology. They also need to believe they are getting the most up to date technology from you and licensing it to ATP. We'll have to get CMT involved in a similar way with second generation detonation technology, don't you think?"

"I do. Finding the IEDs and EFPs is only part of the job.

We have to destroy them, too. Is CMT up to this?"

"Yes, I believe they are once we get through the investigation out there and learn about all the involved parties."

"Was the entire detonation technology product delivered safely even though there was an attempted theft?"

Sam hesitated a bit then said, "That is an excellent question. I believe it was but you know that is something I should check. They loaded a cart with the product and were running to an escape airplane. The Mossad was chasing them; the cart and product were left on the runway as the men ran to cars hidden a short distance away. I never knew the number of boxes sent. We may have just assumed none of it was taken. Good God, I hope we are right about that."

"I hope so, too, Director. Otherwise, if we are wrong, they are busy trying to reverse engineer the most sophisticated detonation technology available in the world."

'We make a good team, Brad. Let me know when you plan to go to Boston to visit ATP. I will go too and we'll get them up to speed on exactly what is happening and how we are going to run a parallel program on your new technology."

"I will have some dates for you very soon. It has been really good talking with you. I think we make a good team, too, sir."

"Thanks, Brad, see you in Boston soon."

"Yes, sir, thank you."

Chapter 9

The Elimination Plan

The Comic Books

Omar was scared to death as he pulled on the protective polyethylene coveralls. They were similar to those doctors wore at the hospital. Interestingly, they were available at the drugstore along with thick rubber gloves, a respirator that covered his whole face, and booties for the shoes he wore. He had no idea that things like these would be stocked in the local pharmacy. It was as if people were ready for chemical or biological terrorist attacks. He made a mental note to send word that the Americans were more prepared than his people had expected. He thought to himself as he continued to dress. We know about air, land, and sea travel security; the electrical grid and power station security; water and food security; sports and entertainment event security; politicians and political event security, etc. And now individuals can plan for their own safety and security in case something were to happen. These Americans are industrious, resourceful, and brave; they continue to resist our 'Campaign of Fear'. I wonder if we can win against a people so relentlessly courageous? Iraq and Afghanistan are unique with our IEDs, EFPs, suicide bombers, car bombs, and the like, exacting a costly toll day by day. Bringing those same tactics here and have them work similarly may not be possible. I'm not sure I believe in the 'Campaign of Fear'.

With that thought, Omar shook himself out of his daydream and continued to get dressed. He looked like a spaceman but was now ready to take the vial of poison capsules, large safety pin, two small bowls, an artist's brush, forceps, and two plastic Ziplock bags to the bathroom. He had already placed two comic books in the tub. The comic books were open with front and back covers facing him. He was hot, really hot, but concluded it wasn't just from the protective clothing. It was what he was doing, preparing to eliminate three people from the face of the earth. How could he be so different from his friends, his brother, and his father?

Again, he shook himself back to reality. Omar knelt alongside the tub, placed the tools alongside the open comic books and began his work. With gloved hands, he uncapped the vial, put the cap down and carefully poured three capsules into the first of the two small bowls while holding it steady. He recapped the vial and set it aside. There must have been five or six more capsules in the closed vial sitting there staring back wondering why it wasn't their turn and who their victims would be. Omar selected one of the capsules and held it between thumb and forefinger of his left hand. With his right hand, he picked up an open safety pin and carefully punctured the end of the capsule. Omar squeezed the contents of the capsule into the second small bowl while still holding the safety pin. There were only a few drops of the clear colorless liquid. It looked harmless but he knew better. He had to stay sharp and focused on what he was doing. Placing the empty capsule back into the first bowl, he picked up the next capsule and repeated the process a second and a third time. The drops added up to quite a bit of liquid in the small bowl. All of the empty capsules and the open safety pin were now in the first bowl. So far, so good.

Omar eased back from the tub and sat on his haunches, with his wrists resting on the side of the tub for several minutes. He thought of his next steps in the process including getting rid of his tools and protective clothing.

Omar got back up on his knees and picked up the artist's brush with his right hand. While holding the bowl, containing the menacing liquid with his left hand, he wetted the brush thoroughly. Then he painted several stripes on the front and back covers of the first comic book. Another brushful went to paint the second comic book. There was still more liquid so he repeated the process for each comic book. Now the liquid was gone. The comic books were not completely painted the second time but almost. There was slightly more on the edges of the front covers where he thought they might be touched more. Omar was amazed that after the poison dried or soaked in, the pictures were not smeared and the covers were not wrinkled. The comic books looked completely normal.

Now it was time for the disposal steps. He picked up the larger Ziplock bag and placed the brush inside along with the bowls, empty capsules, and safety pin now carefully closed. He set the bag aside in the tub for a moment. Then he picked up the smaller Ziplock bag, which was to be the bag for the comic books. With the bag in his left hand, Omar picked up the forceps with his right. He carefully picked up the first comic book by its spine, closing it in the process, and placed it into the Ziplock bag. He congratulated himself for not touching the outside of the bag at all. Thank God! Holding the bag with one comic book safely inside, he used the forceps in the same fashion to pick up the second comic book, allowing it to close, and then delicately placed it into the bag on top of the first comic book. No touching the outside of the bag again. Praise Allah.

He set the bag with the comic books aside while he picked up the first bag and put the forceps in reaching all the way to the bottom before he released the handles. He placed the bag aside while he zipped the comic book bag closed. It is ready, he thought. Now to get this outfit off according to my plan, he thought.

First the booties, left and into the bag and then right and into the bag. Next he removed the full-face respirator and placed it into the bag. Next, the left glove. He wrestled his left hand and arm somewhat out of the coveralls. With his left hand still inside the left sleeve of the coveralls, he removed the right glove and put it into the bag. Keeping his left hand inside the sleeve, he pulled the right sleeve down then the left and right legs, bunched it all up and put it into the bag. Nothing had touched his protective wear so it was okay to zip the bags with his unprotected hands. He did it quickly without thinking about it too much. It was done, he thought as he surveyed at the items in the tub.

All things accounted for: the capped vial with the extra poison capsules, the small closed Ziplock bag with the comic books and the large closed Ziplock bag with the tools and protective gear. Best of all, he was still breathing and alive.

Omar took the vial and comic books back to his desk for safekeeping until his trip to San Francisco. He took the cardboard box and tape to the bathroom. He put the large Ziplock bag into the box, closed the box and taped it shut. He carried it immediately to the dumpster behind his building. Returning to the office, he slumped into his chair and sat there as the clock hands slowly turned and turned. He sat hours and hours in the chair thinking and thinking. Omar got up and said aloud, "Yes, I am ready to go but am I really going to do this? I just don't know."

Omar's Trip

Omar was on his way to San Francisco via Minneapolis, Minnesota. He was very nervous as he reached Reagan National airport. The cab driver seemed to be watching him during the whole trip, not saying anything, just looking at him via the rear-view mirror. Not wanting to make eye contact, Omar couldn't figure out if the cabbie had been looking at him or his briefcase on the seat next to him. Anyway, it was very disturbing. He wondered, Am I just being paranoid because of what is in the briefcase? How many people carry around a cashier's check for $10 million and enough poison in different forms to kill at least ten people?

Omar paid the driver with a twenty-dollar bill and said, "Thank you, no change." It was the first time the driver had smiled. Omar picked up the briefcase, opened the door, and exited the cab. He was at Terminal 1. He walked across traffic to the sidewalk and approached the revolving doors at the entrance. He entered and walked directly to the Northwest counter area. Omar checked in electronically and got his boarding pass. There were no bags to check so he was ready to go through security. As he headed that way, there was a crazy American saying going through is head, 'killing two birds with one stone' and it wouldn't stop. He knew it was because of planning to do business in two major cities on one trip. Right? Or was it for another reason? And, maybe the saying was really 'killing three birds with one stone?'

Omar suddenly heard a strong voice say, 'Sir, may I see your boarding pass and picture ID please?" Shaken out of his funk, Omar pulled both out of his pants pocket and handed them to the security guard. The guard checked him through to the roller conveyor belt and scanners. He knew the drill. He very carefully placed his briefcase on the conveyor belt trying to avoid drawing any attention to it or to himself. Then, he put his shoes or really sandals, money clip, glasses, belt, and cell phone into the plastic tub on the rollers and watched as the briefcase went into the scanner for visual inspection. It passed through successfully so he pushed the tub onto the moving conveyor belt and walked to the personal scanner holding his boarding pass. The guard motioned him through, checked his boarding pass, and returned it to him. No alarm sounded and the briefcase and plastic tub were waiting for him as he walked to the end of the belt. Whew! Omar did not know what he would have done had there been questions, but just to be sure he had kept one of the capsules tucked away in his shirt pocket. He wondered if he could actually take it should the time come or would he be too frightened? He was in a fog as he headed for the Delta-Northwest gates all arranged in a neatly organized semicircle. Gate 1 was to his right; the plane was there and on time. Great, he thought, he would be in Minneapolis just before noon, have lunch with Dr. Tully at the airport as planned, and present him with the money. The flight to San Francisco would get him there in plenty of time for his meeting with Thomas at the Squealing Pig. He was deep in thought as he took a seat to wait for boarding. What if the capsule in my shirt pocket would rupture accidentally? Oh my God, I had better put it back into the vial. But, maybe not. I haven't decided if I'm after Thomas or Thomas and his family. You crazy shit! That means keeping the capsule in the shirt pocket for about ten hours. No matter what I decide, I shouldn't do that. It is too dangerous.

Omar opened his briefcase on the seat beside him, grabbed the vial, removed the cap quickly and set it aside. He wrestled the capsule out of his shirt pocket, put it into the vial, replaced the cap immediately, and positioned the vial safely in the briefcase. As he was breathing a sigh of relief, a small boy of 8 or 10 was walking by with his dad. He saw the comic books in the Ziplock bag and just about went nuts. Jumping up and down and yelling at the top of his lungs something about 'Super Heroes' this and 'Super Heroes' that. Omar slammed his briefcase shut; looked at the kid and the dad and gestured to indicate there was no way the comic book was going to be removed from the briefcase. Don't even think about it!

The boy's dad said, "I am sorry for my son's behavior of yelling and making quite a scene. Maybe you could let him take a quick look before we board. These are the new ones just published that he has not seen yet."

"I'm afraid not, sir. This is a gift and I don't want the comic books looking like they are used. I hope you understand."

"I do, totally." The son was still making quite a racket and very unhappy. It was obvious that he wasn't going to stop. The father said, "Maybe he could just hold them in the bag for a minute. I'm sure that will be enough to quiet him and I would appreciate it very much."

Omar looked at the guy as if to say, what the hell do you expect from me, buddy? Then he opened the briefcase slowly and said, "Only if you promise that he will not open the Ziplock bag."

"Yes, of course."

Omar, holding his breath, gave the bag to the father and the father handed it to his son saying, "You can only look. You cannot open the bag. If you do, there will never be another Super Hero comic book for you."

Omar thought, In more ways than one, you little bastard.

It was enough; the boy was content to look at the two front covers. Thank God, the books were back to back so he could see both. As he pondered the contents of the bag, Omar thought he could see the boy weighing his choices in his mind. Leave the bag closed and be satisfied or open the bag and take his chances. As the boy's hands were getting closer and closer to the top of the bag, Omar knew that something was going to happen. He didn't know what to do but he had to do something. Omar stood up, reached out, and at that very moment a voice over the P.A. system announced boarding for their flight. Omar said, "I'll put that back in my briefcase now. It's time for me to go."

The son instantly reacted by simply handing the bag back to him saying, "Thank you very much, sir."

The father nodded and said, "Thank you very much."

Omar quickly wiped the sticky fingerprints from the bag, put it into his briefcase, smiled and said, "You are welcome. I can tell it will be a great gift for my friend's son."

Omar got up to board the plane in first class thinking what almost happened was inexcusable and that he must be more careful. Perhaps he really was not cut out for this business.

Leg One, Minneapolis

The approximately two-hour flight time from D.C. to Minneapolis gave Omar time to think. The Liberator was acting differently. The change seemed to start right about the time Emar committed suicide during the Zefat airport mission. He had become more extreme in his tactics. Admittedly, killing or dying is not as big a thing to us as it is to those in the Western world. Yes, it had to be for a good reason and at the right time, of course. If so, Allah would take care of things. He thought and thought about what could have caused the change, especially in the Liberator's attitude toward him. The only conclusion that seemed to make sense was that the 'professor' blamed him for the death of his son, my brother. Omar thought, Oh, Father, could it be that I am to blame?

Had Omar not bumped into someone, who knows where he would have ended up? He had deplaned and was walking from the G gate toward the first floor exits. He and Brad had arranged to meet at the Northwest counters. There he was just as planned.

"Hello, Brad, how are you?"

"I am great," and reached out to shake hands with Omar. "Let's go quickly to my car before they tow it away. I know a small restaurant a couple miles away."

"Good, Brad, I have about three hours before my flight to San Francisco. This will be perfect."

Arriving at Champps in Sibley Plaza, they were seated and ordered almost immediately at Brad's insistence. The waitress seemed to understand that timing was very important in order to catch a connecting flight in a couple of hours. Maybe it was more the potential for a big tip.

Brad said, "I'm glad you could kill two birds with one stone."

"I am, too, Brad, but you should know that I would have made a special trip just to deliver the check." Omar opened his briefcase and pulled out the brown envelope containing the check and a copy of the TIC/TRI agreement. He opened the envelope and pulled out the check, attached to the agreement by paper clip, and handed both to Brad. He said, "This is our investment in Tully Research, Inc., for the first year of our five-year agreement. We are so proud to be a partner with someone having such enormous talent. May I propose a toast?"

They picked up their water glasses and Omar said, "To your future significant scientific and technological discoveries in acoustics research and development."

They clinked glasses, took a sip, and put the glasses down. Brad could hardly believe his eyes. "Thank you, Omar, for this great vote of confidence in me and Tully Research. I have never seen, felt, or held a check with so many zeros. Ten million dollars!"

"You are welcome. It is a great thrill for me to deliver it in person on behalf of Technology Investment Corporation. We know there are big things coming."

"I'm glad you are talking future because I certainly don't have anything worth $10 million dollars today." Brad reached into his vest pocket and found the folded ten-page report he had copied for Omar. Brad said, "I have information which includes some state-of-the-art work on acoustics for oil discovery. You can imagine where else it could be used and perhaps even the most obvious areas for significant enhancements. There are a few researchers who might be close but no one as far along as I am. And, there are more advancements where those came from."

Lunch arrived and they carefully put their papers away, especially Brad with his $10 million dollar check. Brad said, "We have been talking a lot so let's eat quickly and I'll get you back to the airport."

"Good idea. I have accomplished my mission with you and I must make that connecting flight to San Francisco."

As they finished, Brad signaled the waitress who had their bill waiting. He handed her his credit card and in no time she was back for his signature.

They were walking out when Brad said, "Thank you, Omar. I will always remember this as the $10 million dollar lunch."

Omar smiled and said, "Yes, and the start of a new partnership."

Leg Two, San Francisco

Omar was on the plane to San Francisco thinking about what he was going to do next. He needed to make a decision soon. He thought, what are my options? Mentally, he ran through several: Do nothing; just let things slowly play out with the federal government investigation. What could happen but maybe a fine to TIC for paying money to an employee of CMT for preferentially testing its new products? Thomas might lose his job. But those weren't the only things that might happen. What if they connect him to his father and the organization? What if the organization could not fulfill its mission to learn what weapon the infidels are developing to stop the 'Campaign of Fear'? Even worse, not be able to reverse engineer it and develop a weapon to counteract it. My father and our organization, the Technolibertat, were chosen for this mission because the al Qaeda Council had determined that when the chips were down, the U.S. always turned to technology answers for their most important decisions. They really weren't very good at political arrangements, negotiations, cooperative programs, or even superpower threats. It was only when they flexed their muscles with technology advancements that people, organizations, and governments took notice. Well, the chips are down and the new administration ran on a platform that had technology as one of its key pillars.

Omar knew where his thinking was leading him - that the current U.S. government's leadership was planning on technology, in large part, to win the battle. That is exactly the foundation, the philosophy, and the operating mandate of Technolibertat. He didn't have a problem with the two having both concluded that technology held the answers for the future. The issue of a significant difference in methodology, how things were done, was what bothered him. He could not justify the extremism, the suicides, and the loss of their own women, children, and families, not to mention the deaths of the enemies. Would taking the lives of the Kramley family help with any of this? It was very confusing.

What is another option? Admit to everything. He and Thomas could own up or confess to the illegal payments. The federal investigators would get to the bottom of things much faster but the conclusion would probably be the same. A fine given to TIC, Thomas loses his job, and the same potential to identify his organization and its leadership. Should the continuing viability of our organization depend on the timing at which Thomas spills the beans? He knew what the his father would say or more appropriately, has said.

So what about the other options? Eliminate the problem – get rid of Thomas or get rid of Thomas and his whole family. Omar thought about this option. Thomas is the problem and his father is right; Thomas probably talked to his wife about everything. She may not know all the details or even understand the illegalities, but she probably knows enough that it would be bad for TIC. People in situations like hers can easily think that helping the company and getting a little extra money for the special effort is a good thing. By the way, the extra money is being used for the best of all purposes. So what's wrong with that?

Omar realized that his father was right. There were no

options but just one thing that needed to be done. A voice over the P.A. system announced they would be arriving in San Francisco in about thirty minutes. He was shocked when he realized he had been doodling and saw that he had written *1.Don't Talk 2. Talk 3. Kill one 4. Kill them all* and drawn a big circle drawn around the last one. He crumpled the paper and put it into his pocket wondering if anybody had seen what he had written.

Leaning back, he thought, again, that his father was right. There is only one safe way to do this. I should stop this nonsense of personalizing everything. Think more about the good of the organization and do what I am told to do. I will do it and see how it feels. This will be a first and I must do it for the greater cause and mission. My brother died for that mission so the least I can do is to kill for it.

Omar was pumped up by the time the plane landed. At the gate he quickly opened his briefcase and saw the Ziploc bag with the treated comic books and the vial of capsules quietly resting and waiting to do their dirty work. Ready to deplane, he closed the briefcase, got up and walked down the jet way to ground transportation. A cab was his best bet to make the 6 PM appointment with Thomas at the Squealing Pig.

Omar walked through the door to the sound of the squealing pig. He thought it sounded louder tonight. His eyes had to adjust a bit but at last he saw Thomas at their favorite table. He waved and starting walking toward Thomas, thinking about the New Castle waiting for him. Such an irony that I could be thinking about beer at a time like this. Maybe I am made for this after all.

"Hello, Thomas, I got here as soon as I could." Omar looked at his watch and noticed that it was just past 6:30. Happy hour was over; there were four bottled beers on the table, but no glasses.

Sounding rather tired, Thomas said, "Hello, Omar, they let me preorder since I'm such a good customer. They do have some crazy rules though for last orders of happy hour. Like, no pitchers, only bottles. If you are alone, only one glass per table, and the transaction is cash only. Welcome!"

"Thank you. I am so ready for a beer or two after traveling

all the way across the country. You know what; I don't mind drinking out of a bottle."

"Are you interested in our usual barbecued pork sandwiches? I ordered those to be brought to our table when you arrived."

"Of course I am. They don't give you much food on airplanes anymore, even when you are flying first class." The waitress arrived just at that time with the sandwiches. Omar said, "Let's toast, Thomas. To the best company partner that a supplier could ever have."

They both drank their New Castle beer. Omar thought, he must not suspect anything. "Now, how are you doing with all this turmoil?"

"I'm alright, but I'm afraid we are in trouble, Omar. The investigative team got the subpoena and has found the offshore account. The attorney investigator has suggested to me that I should come clean on this messy situation. I was told there would be a meeting soon and when I inquired about bringing an attorney with me, she agreed it would be in my best interest. What do you think we should do, Omar?"

"Let's eat our sandwiches before they get cold. We can talk while we eat."

"You don't seem as concerned as I think you should be."

"Maybe I don't show it, but I am. I have thought of nothing else on the whole trip here. May I propose something that will involve both of us?"

"Of course. I want to get this resolved, even if it means losing my job."

"Hopefully it won't go that far. My proposal is to have both of us tell them what they need to know. Everything. Maybe they will go easier on us and especially you."

"What about the trouble this will bring to TIC?"

"Don't worry about that. As President and CEO of TIC, I can weather this storm personally and help deflect any negative aspects about what was done so the company doesn't suffer any long-term effects."

"Are you sure, Omar?"

"I am, Thomas," Omar answered, his mind racing. He was thinking about the strangest thing, the poison capsules, for some reason. How would he have ever opened a capsule and gotten the contents into a bottle? Or even in a glass if there had been one? He probably would have killed myself in the process. Breaking that train of thought, finally Omar said, "Listen to me, Thomas. What we did is really small peanuts for these guys. You found technology that your company needed to maintain its leadership in supply chain management and logistics. I had the new technology but needed to have it tested in the field under a variety of transportation conditions. It was a match. We often pay for an independent testing company to do field testing for us. When I heard about your family's health and medical problems, it wasn't a difficult jump to suggest that CMT do the testing and that we pay you. It seemed like a great solution. I get my testing, CMT helps validate that the products work and consist of advanced technology, and you get money to pay medical bills. All of us are winners, right?"

"Right Omar, it sounds viable when you talk about it that way. All this stuff about taped telephone calls, plots to steal the top-secret detonation technology, and terrorist organizations are pure fiction anyway. If there is a misdeed, it was my accepting your goodwill without discussing it with the company. I knew if I did that, they would not accept the money nor would they allow me to. So I called it a questionable decision on my part but for the best of reasons. I am willing to be held accountable for that and that alone."

"Then we agree. At the meeting you were told would be held soon, tell the truth and tell them everything. Also, carry a message from me that I will meet with them any place, anytime separately or together with you to further clarify the TIC involvement in our field testing arrangement. Will you do that, Thomas?"

"Yes. I think this will satisfy them and remove the mistrust they have about us as well. Thank you so much, Omar, and I hope you will forgive me for getting you into this mess."

"Listen, Thomas, it takes two to tango. Isn't that what they say? I made a conscious decision to pay you the money because it was for such a good reason. No hard feelings about me threatening you, are there?"

"None, Omar, thanks again. I'll let you know how the meeting goes and what they decide about talking with you."

"Thanks. Before I return to my office, I have a little gift for your son." He opened the briefcase, pulled out the Ziploc bag with the comic books, and said, "Here are a couple of the very newest ones. You have to promise to immediately put them in your briefcase and not take them out until you and your wife are ready to give them to your son. I was nearly accosted at the airport when someone noticed I had them. Do you promise?"

"I promise." He quickly put the plastic bag into his briefcase. Thomas thought it was like a drug dealer and customer exchanging drugs and money.

"Do you both read to him?"

"Yes, we read almost every night."

"Good. These are so special that you both need to be involved in reading tonight."

"We will. It is easy to be a good parent with friends like you."

"Thanks, Thomas, let's proceed as we discussed and agreed. Remember, I will make myself available at anytime to help get this resolved. I'll talk with you later."

"Goodbye, Omar, and thanks again."

"Goodbye." Omar walked toward the front door, dreading the noise of the squealing pig. That was the minor feeling, however. He was almost overcome with a feeling of fear. He had just implemented his first elimination plan with no idea how many people would be killed. One thing about this poison, it becomes inactive and almost undetectable in about 48 hours if left open to the air. That might save the people who find the Kramley family later. It usually takes a couple of days before people get suspicious and start checking. He hailed a cab and started the trip to the office. It was to be a short visit because he was on the red-eye flight to D.C. later that night. He thought it best not to be in town when all this went down. Turning back, he said, "I hope this was the last time I ever go into the Squealing Pig."

Thomas after Meeting with Omar

Thomas was glad that he and Omar were going to tell the whole story. He felt that what he did was wrong but it wasn't a federal crime for God's sake. The idea of an attorney was becoming more important all the time. Thomas decided that he would take another day off and get that put in place. The meeting that Ms. Klein was suggesting would be set up soon.

As he continued home, he pulled out his cell phone and called his assistant at the office. After several rings, her voice mail picked up. "Hi there," said Thomas, "I want you to know that I will not be in tomorrow. Sorry for the late notice. Please mark it as an extra day of vacation. I need to attend to some personal business that I wasn't able to finish today. Thanks. See you on Wednesday."

Thomas said to himself, "Okay TK, let's set up the attorney call and discussion tomorrow." That done, he said, "Tonight I am going to spend time with my family. Things are going to be alright."

Thomas pulled into the driveway, put the car into the garage, picked up his briefcase, and went in the front door. He was excited about the present for TK, Jr. that Omar had given him. The suggestions that he had to keep the special comic books in his briefcase until the last minute and that all three should be involved in reading them together were great. He smiled when there was no one there to greet him, knowing full well where they were. The bedroom. If he wanted to find them, it was usually in the bedroom. It was about 8 PM and Jr.'s bedtime. Thomas walked toward the bedroom still carrying his briefcase. He could see light in the bedroom through the partially open door. Pushing the door open quietly, he was taken aback by what he saw.

Sue and TK, Jr. were both sprawled out on the big bed, dead to the world. They did not move as he tiptoed toward the bed. He wondered if something was wrong because Sue was usually a light sleeper. She should have been awake by now. He was instantly afraid with thoughts bouncing around in his head about her depression and the toll it was taking. Could she have committed suicide, taken an overdose of that medication with all the bad side effects? And given some to Jr., too? Oh my god! He quickly looked round for the pills and saw the bottle on the dresser. He dropped his briefcase and picked up the bottle, shaking it a bit. The cap came off easily as he twisted it. At that moment, Sue rose up on her elbow and said, "Hi, Hon, what are you doing with my pills?" Thomas was so shaken when he heard her voice that he spun around, scattering the pills in every direction. It was almost a full bottle so the pills covered the floor from dresser to bed. The little clear capsules actually blended well with the carpet and they were hard to see with just the lamp light in the room. Thomas rushed over, cap in one hand, empty bottle in the other, sat on the edge of the bed, and pulled his wife to him. He hugged her as tightly as he could. All he could say was, "Hon, I thought … I thought…"

"You thought what? Stop squeezing me so hard; you are going to break a rib."

Thomas let her go. He sat there looking at her and then at the cap and bottle in his hand. He said, "How could I ever think that?"

Sue was sitting up fully now and fighting to get awake. "We were tired and fell asleep."

Jr. was awake now. He said, "Hi, Dad, did you bring any presents for me?"

Thank God he had not seen what had just happened. "As a matter of fact, I did, kiddo. Give me just a second." He looked at Sue and then leaned down. With the cap and bottle in one hand he used his other hand to pick up the pills that were strewn around the bed and in his direct path toward the dresser. The quick calculation was that he got about half of them. The other half could wait until tomorrow.

Thomas picked up his briefcase, went back to the bed, tracing his path carefully to avoid stepping on the unretrieved capsules. He sat on the bed and opened his briefcase. By this time, both Jr. and Sue were learning over, stretching to see what was inside. Jr. said it first, "Comic books!"

Sue said, "Thomas, did Omar give you more?"

"Yes, he did. He is such a great guy. One thing he said

THE CAMPAIGN OF FEAR

about these was that they were hard to get and that we should all enjoy them together."

Thomas picked up the Ziploc bag, closed the briefcase, and showed the front cover of the comic books to both of them. Jr. was so excited that both Thomas and Sue became excited, too, all of them sort of bouncing on the bed.

Jr. said, "Dad, open it and let's get started."

"There are two comic books. Can we do both tonight?" He looked at Sue to be sure it was all right.

She nodded and said, "I don't see why not. What do you think, Jr.?"

"Yes, please."

"Then let's do it."

Sue and Jr. scooted closer to each other and made room for Dad… all three sitting next to each other. Thomas opened the Ziploc bag, took out the two comic books, put the bag on the floor and tried to see which was published first. Holding one in each hand, he could see they were published a week apart. He handed the earliest one to his wife who immediately shared looking at it with Jr.

They were fingering the front cover with its action figures and the multitude of very bright colors. Thomas was doing the same with the second comic book. He was looking at the back cover trying to figure out who actually published the comics and was making all the money!

Sue said, "Here Jr., take this one and get started. Thomas, let me see yours."

Jr. was busy running his fingers over the front cover savoring every moment with his new possession. Sue playfully grabbed at Thomas' book, but he didn't let go. They each held a part of it with both hands, pulling but careful not to tear it.

They noticed something was happening to Jr. His face was very red and his arms were beginning to shake.

"Mom, I don't feel very good. Maybe I should lie down a little…." His voice got quieter and he slumped down against her, not moving.

"Thomas, something is wrong with him; call 911."

Immediately she could see that Thomas' face was red, too, and his arms were shaking. She felt like her face was hot, too. She was touching her cheeks and pushing Thomas up off the bed trying to get up. "Thomas, what is wrong with us? You have to do something."

They both were standing, looking at Jr. lying motionless in the bed. They looked at each other. They thought, red faces, arms shaking, we are dying.

Sue said it first, "It must have been something on the comic books, Thomas." Her words were all spoken but trailing off to almost no sound, just her mouth moving as she dropped the comic book on the floor.

Thomas was trying to think what to do but everything seemed to be in slow motion. As Sue was reaching for the telephone, he said, "The comic books? Oh, Omar, what have you done? The threat you made was real, wasn't it. You son of a bitch."

As Sue collapsed to her knees, Thomas said, "I am so sorry, Hon, it was my fault." He took her into his arms as her eyes rolled back and she slumped into him. He fell to his knees still holding her as best he could, knowing that the same fate awaited him. His arms were shaking almost violently now as he laid Sue carefully on the floor. He could feel life slipping away as he got close to her on the floor, lying side by side, together in life and in death. Thomas hung on a while longer, unable to move but thinking his last thoughts. Whoever finds us will think we committed suicide by overdosing. Oh, God, I must help them catch that bastard.

The letter to the attorney drafted just before meeting Omar at the Squealing Pig, where I documented everything exactly as it happened just in case, will they find it? He looked at his briefcase but he could hardly move any part of his body. Thomas's last look was at the comic book on the floor. He used all of his strength, throwing his arm toward the book. His hand landed on top. He pressed down as hard as he could, making a fist and crumpling the front cover and all those action figures in his closed hand. He took his last breath, mouthing the words, "I hope this helps them catch you, Omar." Then he was gone.

The Subpoena Information

Aldora finally found Jack to tell him about the information obtained with the subpoena.

"Jack, look at these emails showing three $50 thousand electronic transfers from banks in the Middle East. The accounts were all identified as 'Technolibertat/TIC' and the money went to Thomas Kramley in Cancun, Mexico. His account there shows receipt of the money, $150 thousand, and withdrawals of $100 thousand shortly thereafter. We have money changing hands, Jack. We have TIC named and Thomas named. I wonder what 'Technolibertat' is?"

"I don't know but we should call the director right away. He may need that name when he talks with our colleagues in Israel. Great work, Aldora!"

As Jack punched in the secure number, he said, "I'll let you explain what you found and the process you used, Aldora." Aldora nodded in response.

"Hello, Jack, I was about to leave the office. I'm glad you caught me before I left. Anybody else with you?"

"Yes, Aldora is here with new information we thought you should have. Aldora?"

"Hello, sir."

"I hope you are enjoying this assignment, Aldora. It's not the usual lawyer stuff, is it?"

"No, far from it. I really like it and we have an excellent team." She winked at Jack.

"I know. What do you have for me?"

"First thanks for the subpoena. I received it in record time."

"You are welcome. It is good to be able to pull some strings once in a while when the need is there."

"We have found documentation within the World Banking System that three banks located in the Middle East, Syria, Jordan, and Lebanon, transferred $50 thousand each to Thomas Kramley's account in Cancun, Mexico."

"Who transferred the money, Aldora?"

"That is one of the reasons we called. There are dual names

on the account. One is TIC, which we believe to be Technology Investment Corporation and the other is Technolibertat. That name is new to us, sir, and we thought you should know about it when you talk to our colleagues in Israel."

"Technolibertat? The name already has come up. They are a small terrorist organization under the influence of al Qaeda. Absek believes that they might be the ones who attempted the theft of the new detonation technology products. He also believes that Omar Kharif of TIC might be related to certain members of the organization. By the way, Absek was really excited about the voice and videotapes we sent recently. He almost hung up on me so he could go listen and look. Good work on this. I'm sure this will help Absek in his investigation. Please send the WBS information directly to him."

"Aldora, did you say Thomas used some of the money?"

"The Cancun bank shows withdrawal of $100 thousand shortly after the deposits were made. We believe that is the money he used to pay his medical bills."

"It's a sad state of affairs when you have to take money under the table to pay medical bills, isn't it? Do we think he knew what really was going on with Omar and TIC?"

"We'll hold on answering that for a couple of days, sir. Aldora is arranging a meeting with him and his attorney to discuss the new information soon. We'll see if he comes clean."

"Thanks, Aldora and Jack. Keep pushing hard. We need to know if this was a conspiracy with Thomas involved or whether it was all TIC. Good work and thanks again."

Aldora and Jack responded, "Thank you sir, goodbye sir."

The Liberator Calls Omar

The Liberator was calling back sooner than expected. Omar said to himself, I wonder what I have done now.

"Hello, Liberator."

"Hello, Omar. You told me, some time ago that when visiting with Dr. Bromcast at Advanced Technology Products you had stolen notes with a sketch from his office. We both hoped that nothing would come of it and there wouldn't be any connection to you. I just learned that hope is gone. In my recent discussion with Mike Jackson about our investment proposal in TRI being accepted, the matter came up. His words were that you might have mistakenly picked up the sketch. They want it back and are suggesting you check your files immediately and let him know. There was a hinted threat that the federal government, as the project's sponsor, might have to get involved if the matter isn't resolved immediately. What do you think we should do?"

"Oh my God. I feel like I have become a bumbling idiot."

"Omar, this is a case where commitment to the organization and skill has to match up. You seem to have some of both but maybe not enough of either. These are serious deficiencies and they will have to be addressed soon. I also see that you are both impulsive and weak. Your impulsiveness led to stealing the sketch and paying money to Mr. Kramley when it wasn't necessary. Both have gotten us into big trouble. The weakness is something I don't understand, but it is there. Essentially giving money to Mr. Kramley to help pay his medical bills – that was a sign of weakness. Telling me to not use deadly force is a sign of weakness. Questioning the elimination of the whole Kramley family is a weakness. I could go on, you know, but this must be enough for you to understand why I'm concerned. I have a theory, son. The lack of total commitment to our organization and its mission is making you weak and your impulsiveness is greatly affecting your decision-making and your business and technology skills. And to the extent that you may not be repairable."

"Father, I am repairable; I am doing better."

"Why can't you be like your brother who had total commitment, great skills, and gave everything for the cause? He's gone, Omar; he's gone."

"I know, Father, I loved him, too. I am not Emar; I am Omar and I can only be Omar. You have to accept me for who I am."

Omar's father hesitated to answer, finally saying, "We'll get back to this subject soon but for now what about the notes and sketch?"

"The choices we have are such that it is easy to decide. If we give it back, it means that we either took it mistakenly or intentionally. They would conclude the latter, of course. Either way, they know that we know about the special project. Since the project must utilize the most sophisticated technology available, they cannot really change the course of their project. We would always be under their watch, probably even moreso than we are today. On the other hand, if we say we don't have it, then they have to either accept that or somehow prove that we do. They may not like accepting it but they have no reason to come after us to prove anything. Until they can prove something, we can go on with business as usual. They will continue to function as if the sketch is lost, just like they are doing today. Our ability to work with any other organization or company is not diminished. I believe we can continue to work with Advanced Technology Products specifically. They know we have the most direct access to the next generation technology through our Tully Research investment. Challenging our position that we do not have the sketch nor do we know what they are talking about would put them at risk of losing that access. If they don't believe us, they can just kiss my ass."

Omar was hoping his thought process was reasonable and at the same time not demonstrating any of the litanies of deficiencies mentioned by his father. It was a bit rambling but he thought he arrived at the right choice. Omar was holding his breath as his father spoke again.

"Omar, I have arrived at the same conclusion. I will tell Dr. Jackson that we do not have the missing notes. If he pushes the issue, I will tell him that we have searched our files and are certain that it was not picked up accidentally. In fact, we are a little miffed at the implication that the federal government would get involved if it were not returned."

"Excellent, Father."

"Omar, I want to keep Dr. Jackson as a friend if possible. What do you have for me from TRI?"

"I have a ten-page report on the most sophisticated acoustics system that is available today. 'Available' is a generous term in that it only exists in pieces in Dr. Tully's basement research laboratory. He says it works and I believe him. What is interesting is that it contains all the parts of the infamous sketch, almost exactly, except he was using it to find oil and ATP wants to find our IEDs and EFPs. I believe all the technology parts are available to us for licensing."

"Get me a copy of that report and indicate the parts I should use with Dr. Jackson to build the relationship with ATP."

"If I judge this correctly, the most difficult areas are the wave generation and bounce-back feature, the air-collection technology, and data augmentation software."

"Let's give them something really important so they take us back into their confidence. Also, if they can build it, we can somehow access it and begin to reverse engineer it. Think about it and let me know."

"Yes, sir."

"One other thing, how did the job with the Kramley family go?"

Omar knew that question would eventually be asked and he was ready. He simply said, "The plan was carried out just last evening. I left on the red-eye flight later that night. I have not heard anything but do not expect the bodies to be found for a couple of days. Would you like to know how I did it?"

"Yes, but not all of the details at this time, just the key parts. How did you administer the poison and how did you confirm that all three are dead?"

Omar felt dryness in his throat but knew he had to be strong. Clearing his throat, he said, "I coated the poison onto the covers of two comic books, put them into a sealed Ziploc bag, and gave them to Thomas as a gift for his son. Thomas and his wife were going to read them to the boy together like they usually do. I assumed that by all of them handling the comic books, the poison would transfer to their fingers and be absorbed into their bodies. That would take care of all three at the same time."

"Does that mean you did not confirm the deaths?"

"I'm afraid not, sir. I'm sure it will be okay. The poison you provided seemed to be very potent."

251

"Yes, if taken as a capsule but we have no experience on its skin-absorption properties. Are you sure you used enough?"

"I think so, sir. I used three capsules for two comic books."

"The paper is porous in comic books; I hope enough of it stayed on the surface."

"The front and back covers are thicker with a shiny surface and must be less porous than the inside pages. I think we are okay."

"I hope so. To be sure, try to make contact with Kramley. If the call is detected, people will automatically think that you could not be involved. Why would you try to contact a dead person?"

"Good idea, sir. I'll do that."

"In the meantime, I will contact Dr. Jackson and give him our response about the sketch. Also, unless you tell me differently, I'll try to whet his appetite with the TRI wave generation equipment."

"I believe that is the best technology to entice them, sir. In fact, I was going to tell you that I didn't even have to think about it. It is obvious to choose that one."

"Omar, I want you to assume that the discussion with Dr. Jackson will go well. Please get additional information on the wave generation equipment from Dr. Tully and prepare to discuss a business deal with Dr. Bromcast. And, let me know about San Francisco ASAP."

"I will, sir."

"Thank you, Omar. We have a lot more to talk about but it will have to wait. Goodbye for now."

"Goodbye, Father."

The Missing Sketch

"Dr. Jackson, this is Patek Kumat from Technology Investment Corporation. I wanted to get back to you about the missing document you thought may have been taken mistakenly by Omar Kharif. We have searched our files, folders, papers, and everything several times to see if we could find this document. I can say with certainty that we do not have it nor did we ever have it. We are happy to be part of the search to help try to find it but I'm afraid we have done all we can. Good luck in finding this important document, wherever else you are searching, Mike."

Jackson could hear that Kumat was weighing and measuring every word carefully. He sounded strong in his response and ended up calling him by his first name. He took this as an unspoken request from Mr. Kumat to trust him and have his word accepted as a colleague and friend. He thought, I don't believe him but I have to accept what he says; there is really no choice. If I say that I don't believe him, what moves do I have open to me? He would demand that we provide proof and we have nothing. That would lead to a lot of ill will and nix any possible cooperative technology venture. Worse yet, it could result in a suit and litigation between ATP and TIC.

Thinking fast, Mike Jackson said, "Thank you, Mr. Kumat, that's good enough for me. You know I had to take a tough stance on this because our project is government-sponsored and important to our national security." He lied a bit and said, "It wasn't meant to be personal, and if it's any consolation, I treated everybody in the search in the same way."

"Thank you. Does that mean we have cleared the air and can get back to working together?"

"Yes, it does as far as I'm concerned. Are you in agreement?"

"Yes, but excuse me if I seem a little more cautious than before. I was quite taken aback at the implied accusation and veiled threat made during our previous discussion. Coming from a major company backed by the U.S. Government made it doubly disturbing."

"I didn't think it was quite that bad, but if that was your perspective, I am sorry."

"No apologies necessary. I just needed to put into words my feelings and thoughts on this matter. Thank you for listening."

"You are welcome, Mr. Kumat."

"I have talked with Omar about a softer approach with Dr. Bromcast. He will try his best to be the ultimate professional in future discussion with him. Omar sends an apology and hopes you understand that he knows he was pushing a little too hard."

"I will tell Chad. Thank you."

"Now for the exciting news. We have received our first report on the technology available by virtue of our Tully Research investment. There are some really advanced discoveries on acoustic wave generation and management available. May I have Omar get in touch with Dr. Bromcast as soon as he gets a few more details on the technology?"

"Of course. Dr. Bromcast and his team will judge the value of the technology and determine if we would be interested in licensing. I'm sure he will be very excited to evaluate almost any advanced technology in this area."

"I will have Omar contact him right away and make the arrangements. Thank you."

"You are welcome. Mr. Kumat, you should know that we have signed Tully Research to a subcontractor agreement recently. I don't know how this will work from a legal standpoint. Maybe it is as simple as our paying you to license the already-developed Tully technology and then paying Tully to help us implement it in our specific products. We'll have our attorneys take a look at it. Are you okay with that?"

"I think so. I'm glad you told us because our investment in Tully is quite large and we have to protect our ownership rights. I'm sure we can find a way around any perceived complications. It sounds as if both TIC and Tully want to help ATP succeed with this special project."

"Yes, and others, too. Thank you for being so understanding."

"You are welcome. Let's talk again after we both do some checking and Omar and Dr. Bromcast have a chance to discuss the new technology."

"Great and thanks again. Goodbye, Mr. Kumat."

"Goodbye, Mr. Jackson."

Chapter 10

Suicide or Murder?

Thomas and His Family

Aldora learned from Thomas's assistant that he would be on vacation another day and return to work on Wednesday.

"What exactly did he say, please?"

The assistant replied, "It was a voicemail message that he had to attend to some personal business he wasn't able to finish that day."

"Would you schedule a meeting for him at 9 AM. Wednesday morning with Joe, Jack, and me? Just mark the subject as "Subpoena Information."

"Done, on both his paper and electronic calendars. He'll see it when he turns on his computer first thing tomorrow morning."

"Thanks. Do you happen to have his home phone number?"

"Yes, Ms. Klein." She handed the number written on a Post-it® to Aldora.

Aldora walked away thinking, I hope this doesn't mean that he is running. I would not doubt it though. I'm going to call him at home.

She ran back to her office for some privacy and called the number on the Post-It®. One ring, two, three, four, no answer, just

"Kramley's residence. Please leave a message."

Aldora called several times during the day and always reached the answering machine. It was probably nothing; she was being paranoid. She called Jack anyway.

"Jack, I found out that Thomas decided to take today off, too. He took another day of vacation to attend to some personal business. I have called his home several times and no one answers. Do you think he would run?"

"I do! Would you mind making a trip to his house? It seems at least his wife and son should have been home sometime during the day to take your call."

"Yes, it is my understanding that they are pretty much housebound. We should act quickly, Jack. His call about extra vacation was Monday night about 8 PM. It is getting close to 24 hours since anyone has heard from him so we can't wait much longer."

"I know. I'll go with you but use your legal and Department of Justice connections to get a search warrant first."

"That will take about five minutes."

"I'll use that time to get a security guard from the company to go with us. If we find something amiss, we'll get local law enforcement involved, too. Meet you by the front door."

Jack left his office quickly, turned to go to the security station, and noticed that Joe was in. "I never got to ask you about the board meeting. How did things go?"

"Not too well, in fact. They had so many questions that I could not answer. No one could really. I gave your team high marks for what you have done in such a short time."

"Thanks, Joe."

"Oh, they might want you to attend one of the next meetings and give a full status report on your investigation."

I'll plan for that but now I have to run. Is it okay if Aldora and I take one of your security guards with us to check on Thomas at his home?"

"Sure, what's up?"

"He took an unexpected extra day of vacation and no one

has heard from him or his family for about 24 hours. Aldora and I believe that he might be on the run. That would be a typical reaction for someone in his predicament. We'll have a search warrant, too."

"Okay, go. Let me know what you find immediately, Jack. This is not like Thomas, and I fear that the worst has happened. Helping terrorists steal company secrets and now running from the law. Unbelievable!"

Jack said, "I'll call you soon." Taking the stairs to security, Jack saw the head of security that he had met earlier. "Captain, may I have one of your men to accompany us to check on an employee at his home?"

"I'm sorry, but we are understaffed today and everyone is assigned right now. Can it wait until shift change?"

"No way, we need someone now. I spoke to Joe Blackstone and he gave his approval. Does that make a difference?"

"It sure does. I will go with you right now."

"Thanks, Captain." Jack was checking to see that besides the uniform and all that stuff ... keys, radio, flashlight ... he was actually wearing a gun on his belt. "I see Ms. Klein coming now; she is with the Department of Justice and I am with the Department of Advanced Technology. We have a search warrant so we can enter the home if necessary. I'll catch you up on the case in the car; let's go."

"Hi, Aldora, this is the captain of security for CMT. He is going to accompany us to the Thomas Kramley residence."

"Hi, Captain, Aldora Klein, DoJ."

"Pleasure to meet you, Ms. Klein."

"Jack, I have the search warrant so we are ready to go. I hope we are not too late."

They arrived at the Kramley residence in about 30 minutes. It was a typical middle class neighborhood where all the houses were reasonably modest, one-story, three bedrooms, with an attached two-car garage. It was nearing 6 PM so they saw cars arriving from work, but all in all it was a pretty quiet area.

Aldora was first out of the car and peeked into the garage. "Two cars in the garage. They are both empty as far as I can tell, and

I don't see anything abnormal in the garage."

By the time she walked to the front door, Jack, with the captain standing by his side, was ringing the doorbell. Once, twice, three times, but no answer. Then both looked at each other and started pounding on the door at the same time. They pounded three or four times, waited, and pounded again. They looked at Aldora, who was grimacing, and returned very different looks. Jack's look said that he knew the next step. The captain's look said that he wondered what to do next.

Aldora waved the search warrant a couple of times. Jack asked the captain to hold the outside door open and with one strong right-legged kick, the bottom of his shoe met the front door surface, hard. With a resounding bang and some splintered wood, the door gave and flew open. Jack caught it on the rebound, looked at Aldora and the captain as if this was something he did every day and of course got the expected result. He told the incredulous looking officer, "Draw your gun and enter the house right behind me." Jack entered stooping low with the captain standing full height with gun drawn.

The captain was getting into this now and said, "You wait here. I'll clear the living room, dining room, and kitchen ahead and to the left."

Aldora was in the foyer saying, "I'm glad we brought him. It's not quite like when my FBI friends do this but he looks like he knows what he is doing."

They watched him as he proceeded through the living room and on to the dining room. They heard him say, "Living room and dining room, clear!" He disappeared for an instant as he entered the kitchen, seconds passed, and then, "Kitchen, clear! I will check the garage so stay right where you are, please." There was the sound of the door into the garage opening, more seconds passed, then "Garage clear!" They heard the sound of the door closing, footsteps, and the captain appeared retracing his steps – this time with gun pointed barrel up.

The captain said, "Nothing on the left or in the garage. Let me lead the way to the right and the bedrooms." He leveled his gun to a shooting position and started to the right. Past the bathroom with an open door, nothing there, and on to the first bedroom. The officer opened the door quietly, slowly stooping down, gun at eye level, and stepped in. With his free hand, he turned on the lights, swept the room, still stooping, with that menacing looking gun. He stood up and said, "First bedroom, clear!"

Aldora looked at Jack. They had the same thought at the same time. What would someone do if they were in one of the other bedrooms and heard us coming? The captain closed the first bedroom door very carefully and was proceeding to the second bedroom. Aldora and Jack were hanging back a bit as the level of tension and danger was increasing exponentially. The captain opened the second bedroom door even more carefully and quietly. He didn't exactly open it all the way but more like used it for protection as he peeked into the room. He felt for the light switch. The lights came on, he jumped back a bit, refocused his eyes, and swept the room with the gun held forward more so than last time. Still stooping, he backed out into the hallway mouthing the words, "Second bedroom clear. Bed covers pulled back and night light on." He closed the door.

Aldora understood everything he was mouthing to them. She also saw that Jack had a quizzical look on his face. She nodded her head and put her forefinger to her mouth indicating that he should be very quiet. Jack nodded his understanding.

They were ready for the master bedroom, the last place for someone to hide, the last place to find the Kramleys. Aldora's mind was racing. What if they are just in bed together, asleep? We'll scare them to death. What if no one is in there and we find they were just out of town for the day? What if the wife and son are in there and Thomas is on the run? She bit her tongue, grimaced even more, and convinced herself this had to be done. She caught up with the captain and Jack by taking a couple of quick steps. Watching the captain as he opened the last door, she pushed up against Jack and held on to him from the back. She was squeezing his arms tightly, holding her body rigid, while trying to be in a position to get a view of inside the room. Stooping, gun leveled, and opening the door slowly, the captain stepped forward one

259

small step, gasped, fell to his knees. He dropped his gun hand to the floor. He was slumped on his knees staring at the unbelievable sight. Seconds passed with Jack and Aldora frozen by the sight of him but still trying to peek in to see what it could possibly be.

Jack took the first steps around the captain and saw the horrific sight. "Oh my God, oh my God."

Aldora pushed him in a step so she could see. Gasping she said, "Why, Thomas, why?"

They were all professionals but badly affected by what appeared to be a family suicide or outright murder. Jack said it first, "This is a crime scene. We have to make sure we don't compromise it by our presence."

Aldora said, "You are right so let's all step back and leave things as they are. I'm going to capture this with my cell phone camera. As she scanned the horrific scene, she was verbally documenting the scene. "About 6:30 PM Tuesday, master bedroom lights on, boy on the bed sort of sitting up but slouched over, parents on the floor close together side by side, rigor mortis has set in, they have been dead longer than 6-8 hours. A briefcase is on the floor near the foot of the bed, a plastic Ziploc bag on the floor, one comic book on the bed and one of the floor – front cover squashed in Thomas's hand, pills strewn all over the floor, mostly near the dresser."

Aldora stepped back and could hear that the captain was talking to the local law enforcement people. "That's right, three people dead. Yes, we will stay until you get here. Thank you."

Jack was on his cell phone, too. "Yes, Joe, we found them all dead. From the looks of things, it was probably last night. Yes, local law enforcement has been notified and are on their way, right officer?"

"Yes. If that is Mr. Blackstone, please tell him that I will return as soon as possible and give him a report in his office."

"Did you hear that, Joe?"

"Yes. Jack, will you stay with the local officers until they are finished and then see me first thing tomorrow morning? There are lots of things to plan for depending on the circumstances, not the least of which is how to communicate this to the rest of the company."

"I will, Joe. Note that my directions to local law enforcement will be to delay any announcements until we decide what to do. The case just got orders of magnitude larger and more complex. We, the federal government, are in charge and will call the shots. If it was a triple suicide, that's one thing. If it was a triple murder, that is quite another. I will inform the director about what we found and have a federal team here tomorrow to help the local law enforcement figure this out. What they find will help us decide the course of action."

"Agreed, Jack, see you tomorrow morning."

"Goodbye, Joe."

"Aldora, you should go home and get some rest. We'll pick this up again tomorrow. I know you are very upset, but this is part of our job. Don't talk to anyone. Plan to join me at the meeting with Joe tomorrow morning."

"Okay, Jack, I am a bit shaken. Thank you."

"Remember, none of this is your fault. Just get some rest and we'll begin again tomorrow."

Absek's Investigation

The call came from Absek as Sam was having dinner at his desk. He was still amazed at the electronic capability of the federal government and for that matter our partner governments. He constantly felt challenged by the technology side of his job but knew he didn't have to understand everything to be effective. Thank goodness.

"Hello Absek. I'm glad you called. We are all very interested in the results of your investigation."

"Hello, Director, and good afternoon. We have exciting news on both the audio and video recordings."

"I knew you would, Absek. Can I guess the results?"

"If you wish, sir."

"It was Omar Kharif on the phone to the key contact in Israel."

"You are correct. Our voice recognition and matching

technology is state-of-the-art. With the recording you sent us, we were able to match the pronunciation of over one hundred key words even though the transmission was a bit garbled. There is no doubt and our conclusion is irrefutable. It will stand up on court for any legal proceeding that is necessary. To put it in perspective, Director, our experience is that it is better than fingerprints and almost as good as DNA or direct video recordings. I'm sending you the original audio recordings converted to electronic signals. From these, we have extracted the exact and similar words or signals that are used in both recordings. You will be able to see the 99.999% match with the exact words and 98.950% match with similar words. If the case were to depend on only these audio matching confidence factors, you have your man, Director. That is how good this data is."

"Excellent work, Absek. There are many other pieces to the puzzle, but we need this one to fit with no questions about the techniques used or the results obtained."

"You got it, Director. No expert witness or other technical specialist could look at this data and come to any other conclusion. Omar is the one on the call to the 'leader' in Israel about the CMT shipment arriving at Zefat. He talks about his contact at CMT confirming this and further about a team there to get the product. Also, note that we hear some faint words from this 'leader,' too. He used a common voice distortion device that we were able to neutralize somewhat. We think he says, "I will be part of the team.""

"That is interesting, Absek, a leader who is also an operative in the field. Excellent work on the audio. What about the video?"

"The video is another success story. It is amazing what commercial miniature cameras can do. They have gone way beyond those that are in our cell phones. The footage was excellent and after we removed all the extraneous material, we could easily identify the so-called 'leader' of the team at the Zefat airport. I think it is the person I mentioned previously. You know, the former professor, now head of the Technolibertat. Does anyone know you have this video footage?"

"No one but DoAT and the Mossad."

"Good, keep it that way, please."

"Absek, what about this guy? Were you able to make any more connections between the time before he was a professor and now that he is heading a terrorist organization?"

"Not much, Director. It seems most of his past has been erased. We were able to confirm that Omar and Emar are brothers and that this guy also known as Patek Kumat is their father. It seems that he did a name change when he left the university where he was known as Eomar Kharif. As I said before, the Technolibertat organization that he formed is small and loyal to al Qaeda. We think it was formed sometime before his wife died. That is about all we have right now."

"Good work, Absek. Keeping digging as I would like to know what makes this guy tick."

"I will, sir, and of course we are still trying to locate him. If al Qaeda is helping him, it might take a while."

"Pull out all the stops, Absek. This is our government's highest priority area so I can get you additional resources if needed. Please let me know."

"I will. First let me see if we can reassign people here. No offense but our people can do the same amount of work in half the time."

"I know that but my offer still stands. Absek, we have new information here, too. Our team has been looking into the financial records of Thomas Kramley at CMT. He was Omar's contact and we thought he had accepted money to field test TIC's RFID product. We couldn't prove it until now. It took a subpoena but we found through the World Banking System records that the transfer of money did happen. Three banks from Lebanon, Jordan, and Syria separately sent money to Kramley's offshore account in Cancun, Mexico. The transfers were from three accounts all identified as Technolibertat/TIC. We believe that TIC is the Technology Investment Corporation and the U.S. operation of Technolibertat. Since Omar Kharif is head of TIC we have also established the people and organizational links between the two."

"Well, well. This is good that you can verify our own conclusions using completely different data sources. Ms. Klein has sent us all the bank account numbers and other financial information. I suspect that we can look at the accounts and find other connections to things happening here."

"I knew you would know what to do with the information, Absek. One more thing, I hope you can help me with some accounting work."

"Accounting work, sir?"

"Yes, Absek. Do you recall the number of boxes of top secret detonation technology product you recovered at the Zefat airport?"

"I think I have that in the file. Hold on just a second. Yes, there were ten boxes still on the pallet in the cargo bay of the plane. They were the ones with the RFID tags. There were four boxes without tags recovered from the cart on the runway at Zefat. A total of fourteen boxes brought back to our location for testing."

"Four boxes recovered from the cart and a total of fourteen boxes?"

"Yes, that is what our records show."

"I just found out there were fifteen boxes, Absek. Five without tags and ten with tags. Is there a way you can double check the number while I hold?"

"Of course, hold on a minute." Sam could hear Absek asking his assistant to hurry and check with the head of the lab about the boxes. He must have been close by because the next thing he heard was "fourteen, tell Absek the number is fourteen." A second later, Absek was back on the line saying, "Fourteen, Director, only fourteen."

"Oh my God, you know what that means, Absek?"

"Yes, the head of Technolibertat was able to escape with one of the boxes from the cart on the runway."

"And they are testing and reverse engineering it as we speak. Damn!"

There was silence as the two gathered their thoughts. Absek was first to speak, "Director, my lab manager just shared some very new information from our testing of the CMT product. It seems there

THE CAMPAIGN OF FEAR

is a fatal flaw in the design of the product using the new detonation technology. We need time to pinpoint whether it is the acoustics or the microelectronics or what but it doesn't work. Anybody who copies this prototype will have wasted a lot of time and money."

"Really, I can't believe it. Has anyone else been made aware of the design flaw?"

"I'm told that we just discovered the flaw late this afternoon. Our field testing has been cancelled until a correction has been made by CMT. Our plan was to be in contact with them tomorrow after we did a few more tests so they can get started making the corrections."

"Wow. What could have been a disaster for us might have just turned into a decided advantage. How did we get to be so lucky in this? These bastards have a defective product and may not be smart enough to know it."

"We'll still plan to work with CMT to get it fixed if that is okay. We need that advanced technology now! Who should we use as a contact now that Kramley is under such intense investigation?"

"I could not agree more, Absek. Let me talk with Joe Blackstone, the real technical expert, to see how he would like to proceed."

"Thanks, Director, I'll wait to hear from you. In the meantime, may I suggest, regardless of what you said before, that we scale down the search for this 'leader' and let them think they were successful. It might mean a diversion of their resources that will eventually help us all."

"Excellent suggestion, Absek. Let's do it. Thanks and we'll talk again soon. Goodbye."

"Goodbye, Director."

Jack Calls the Director

The Director was no more off the phone with Absek when the phone rang again. This time it was Jack.

"Hello, Jack, how is the investigation going?"

"Director, we just found the whole Kramley family dead

265

in their home. I'm still at the crime scene waiting for local law enforcement to arrive."

"My God, Jack, we should have known that as the evidence against Kramley kept building so did the potential for extreme action. The question is by whom? Can you tell if it was suicide or murder?"

"I can't tell. There are pills of some kind all over the floor. The first thing we thought was an overdose, but who knows."

"How did you get wind of it?"

"It was Aldora. Thomas had unexpectedly taken an extra day of vacation. Because of the circumstances, Aldora thought he might be running. She called his home several times and didn't get an answer. I heard the story and was convinced that we should check. When we checked the house, we found three dead bodies. I hope you don't mind but I have already asked for a federal CSI team to be here tomorrow to start working with local law enforcement."

"It was the right thing to do, Jack. Have you talked with Blackstone?"

"I have. Aldora and I plan to meet with him tomorrow morning. I have recommended keeping things very quiet until we decide what to do. I hope the locals agree with me and go along with that for a while."

"They will, Jack. Please call me tomorrow morning and I'll join you in the Blackstone meeting. I have new information from our colleagues in Israel but it can wait; you have enough on your plate for now."

"Thank you. We'll talk tomorrow. Goodbye."

"Goodbye, Jack, and take care."

The Meeting Next Morning

Jack and Aldora walked into Joe's office first thing the next morning. Joe said, "I didn't sleep a wink last night. How did you guys do?"

Jack said, "About the same."

Aldora said, "Me, too."

"How did it come to this? I didn't care about the money at

the schools or from TIC, you know. I just cared about Thomas and his family."

"We know, sir. It is a tragedy. I need to get the director on the line so he can join the discussion. Can you give me a minute to dial him in please?" asked Jack.

"Of course."

"Hello, Jack," said Director Elson, as Jack put him on speaker phone. "Is everyone assembled?"

"Yes, we are in Joe's office. Joe, Aldora, and I are all here after a rather sleepless night."

"I am very sorry about the turn of events, but I want you to know that none of this was your fault. It doesn't matter whether it was suicide or murder, this was an act of desperation and disproportional to the underlying reasons for the action. Jack and Aldora, can you fill me and Joe in on the facts, please?" What did you see in the bedroom?"

"I'll start, sir. Aldora, will you fill in where necessary?"

"Sure, Jack."

"The bedroom was neat and tidy, quite different from most crime scenes I have experienced. Boy on the bed, husband and wife side by side on the floor. No blood, no overturned furniture, no bullet holes in the walls, no struggle, no notes, no weapons – just three dead bodies. We both noticed two things that might be clues. There was a medicine bottle on the dresser and a lot of pills all over the floor, mainly around the dresser and nightstand. There did not seem to be any between the dresser and the bed. Aldora, did you do a rough count of the pills on the floor?"

"I did. Strangely enough, there were about 30 pills. My immediate thought was that's too many remaining pills if they were used by all three for the suicides. And, the bottle on the dresser was half full," Aldora added.

"I thought the same thing. I was actually visualizing how many it would take the fill the bottle. It looked like the number of pills on the floor would just about fill the medicine bottle on the dresser. The second potential clue was the comic books. Thomas had squashed the front cover of one in his fist. I noticed another comic book on the bed by the boy. It was intact and must have been held last by the boy."

Aldora continued, "The books were the Super Hero comic books that the kids are raving about. Thomas Jr. was about ten years old. One more thing, Thomas's briefcase was on the floor by the dresser. I recognized it from seeing it at work. He must have come home, briefcase in hand, and gone directly to the bedroom. That would have been Monday night. He was supposed to have been on vacation Monday. I don't know, it just doesn't seem to add up."

"That is about all we saw from the doorway in just a short time," Jack went on. "The local law enforcement officers arrived soon after I talked with both of you. I explained who we were, why we were involved, and gave a statement. They taped off the site and did a little looking around. They planned to return today to get their investigation going. The federal team will arrive this morning and will be able to work with the local team. We have their agreement to keep this out of the papers for a couple of days."

"That's good, Jack and Aldora. What about internal communication at CMT, Joe?"

"Jack has recommended that we keep it quiet here as well. Just keep Thomas on vacation a couple more days. I like the idea until we find out if it was suicide or murder."

"I do, too, Joe. Is there anything else hanging?" asked the director.

"One thing from me," Joe said. "Thomas sent me a subcontractor proposal to work with ATP. He had reviewed it and was recommending that I sign it. I happen to agree with him. Should I sign it and send it back?"

"Let's wait a few days to see what the crime scene investigators come up with. I don't want to put anyone else in harm's way should we find these deaths to be the work of a terrorist organization."

"Thanks, Director. I wanted you to know that we at CMT will work with you on that special project you are sponsoring at ATP."

"Thanks, Joe. I appreciate that and we will need you. Jack and Aldora, keep me posted on the crime scene investigation, please. Does the federal team coming today have a poison expert?"

"Yes. I requested that expertise specifically. I remembered that the pilot at the Zefat airport had committed suicide by poisoning.

That, plus all those pills on the floor of the bedroom made my decision easy."

"Good thinking, Jack, thank you. I know all of you have a lot to do so I'll let you go. Keep in touch with any news."

"Director, could I talk to you privately about a personal matter? It will take a just second."

"Of course, Joe. I'll talk to you later, Jack and Aldora."

Jack and Aldora caught each other's eye and immediately took their leave from Joe's office.

"Director, I have a confession to make. You know that I am as patriotic as they come. My company and I have been working on government contacts for many, many years. Not just because we are good at it and it is a profitable business but because we truly believe we are making a difference. You also know that I am highly involved in the technical aspects of our products. Probably 95% of them contain technological advancements that I personally contributed. I know almost everything about our current products and our new products, even those being field tested. Thomas shared with me his work with TIC right from the beginning. I approved each stage because I believed we had to be involved. The technology was so advanced, I was amazed. As we went from the RFID tags to the DAS to M2DAS, I became more and more amazed and more and more frightened. It wasn't that I feared competitors might get this and scoop us in our business. It was the power of the technology. The software uses data augmentation principles like you pioneered, but with a twist. It doesn't need to wait for someone to input new data and then generate new scenarios. This software is able to penetrate the site it inhabits, like our intranet, and capture new information at will. Can you imagine all of our corporate secrets being available to whoever controls the software?"

"That would be bad news for CMT, Joe."

"I don't know if Omar Kharif and TIC know what they have, but it's a little scary. Some key advancements in code and wireless technology would provide a very powerful tool or weapon depending for whoever controls it."

"Frank and I were going to do some in-depth studies on

M2DAS. Sounds like you have done a lot of it for us, Joe."

"We need to talk more about this, Director, after you and your team take a look at it. Just so you know, I have left it on our internal system for now, but I'm not comfortable with it being there too long."

"I'm glad it's still there, Joe. It might be a key to our finding the bad guys. I have a question, too, are you aware your new product being tested by the Mossad doesn't work?"

"What?"

"The Israelis have tested the new detonation technology product and it does not work. They are talking about a flawed design and have cancelled their field test. They are ready to contact CMT directly but didn't know who to call to get it fixed. I asked them to let me talk with you first and get Kramley replaced as the contact. At that time, it was because of the federal investigation, not because he was dead."

"I'm sorry, Director. I wondered how long it would take for them to find out. Not too bad, not too bad at all."

"What do you mean by that, Joe?"

"I have another confession to make. You'll have to forgive me."

"What do you mean?"

"You know that I was frightened by the potential of the so-called M2DAS software. With further development in the wrong hands, it could wreak havoc in corporations, governments, stock markets, etc. Because of that, I started wondering about Mr. Kharif and his Technology Investment Corporation. Could they be after more than field testing their system in a very challenging supply chain environment? I decided yes. This is the reason I was in the plant the weekend our top secret DT product was manufactured. I made a few technical changes to the fifteen prototype products before they were assembled and packaged to render them totally inoperative. No one knew about it but me so I take full responsibility. I just could not let this product get into the hands of people I did not trust. I didn't know what else to do."

"Even before the product was manufactured and shipped,

your gut was telling you that things weren't quite right with TIC?"

"Yes. I knew Thomas very well and he was acting a little squirrelly. He wanted to license their product even before we were finished field testing. The clincher was what we were not told what the software was really designed to do. So I took independent and immediate action. Have I gotten us into more trouble now?"

"No, but I can hardly believe this, Joe. There is additional new information that comes from our friends in Israel. One box is missing from the shipment. Only fourteen boxes were recovered for testing."

"Who has the other box?"

"We don't know, but are assuming that it was taken from the cart on the runway by one of the terrorists. Probably by the head of the team and the organization called Technolibertat, Mr. Patek Kumat."

"They took the product that I made totally unusable and don't know it."

"No doubt they are busily reverse engineering it."

"If they are, they will come to some very erroneous conclusions about the design."

"Wouldn't that be great!"

"Maybe we lucked out on this, sir."

"I hope so, Joe. Let's keep this very quiet and just among you, the Mossad, and me. Please contact Absek and tell him that you will send the changes he needs to make so the product is functional for testing. They really need to get going on this."

"Of course. Thanks, Director."

"Goodbye, Joe."

"Goodbye, Director."

Omar Contacts Brad

Brad answered the phone in the lab and saw that it was Omar. "Hello Omar, how are things in D.C.?"

"They are fine, Dr. Tully. I had a chance to read your technology report. Wow! We would like to get additional information on the wave generation equipment and try to license it."

Brad was thinking fast and remembered what Sam had said. *Tell no one about your new discoveries. Let everyone think that generation one is the most advanced technology.* Brad smiled, thinking it is, for everybody but me. "Okay, but it will take a little time, Omar. I will have to dig it out of my research notebooks."

"Don't you have a prototype on which you did your experimentation?"

"Yes, I do but it is off limits. It is not part of the investment agreement and it could be very dangerous if not understood and used by an acoustics expert. I'll provide enough written documentation and specifications that people skilled in the art will be able to build the generator from scratch. It will be even better than mine."

"That will be fine, Brad. How long do you think before I can get the technical information?"

Brad's mind was churning. He wanted to take it slow and make sure he was doing it right. "Omar, I have some other potential investors to sign up and we are currently putting in place the new company's policies and procedures so it probably will be several weeks based on how my schedule looks right now. Is that okay?"

"That is fine, Brad. I know you are busy. I don't want to be pushy on this but we believe a potential licensee could be ATP and their special project."

"They have good people there, Omar. It will be good to work with them. Before you find out from someone else, you should know that I have a subcontracting agreement with ATP. The work has not been identified yet but probably some aspects of technology implementation into their kind of products."

"So they get the basic technology from TIC and TRI, and you help them implement it into their special product products. ATP is going all out on this project, aren't they?"

"I guess so. It will be good for the three companies to work together. The government needs our help."

"Brad, do you think we are really making a difference by helping?"

"I do because I have heard this may be the government's top priority project. For us to be involved is quite an honor."

"Thank you, Dr. Tully. Please send me the technical information as soon as possible. Upon receipt, I plan to make contact with Dr. Chad Bromcast immediately and begin licensing discussions."

"Thank you, Omar, and good luck with the licensing discussions. If they want the best acoustics technology in the world, it will be a slam dunk. Goodbye."

"Goodbye, Brad."

Chapter 11

Long-Range Explosives Detection
The Plan for the New L-RED System

Big Meeting at ATP

It was a bigger meeting than she expected. Zen thought that she, Kan D, Bill, and Lyncoln were meeting with Brad to synchronize their R&D efforts. They were all told to be in the main conference room at 9 AM. Everybody was there including the director and Joe Blackstone from CMT.

Zen asked Chad, "Why are all these other people here? I thought this was a working meeting. CMT hasn't even signed a subcontractor agreement with us."

"The director invited them. He thought it best if he talked to the key people from all three companies at the same time," Chad whispered.

Kan D was on the other side of Chad and said, "I haven't heard a peep from Thomas at CMT. Do you know what's going on there?"

Chad said, "Nope."

They seemed to have assigned seats at the conference table. Chad and his team were on one side and Mike, Brad, Joe, and the director on the other. Sam was finishing a side discussion with Joe, nodded his head and said, "Good morning to all of you. It was quite an ordeal to get through security. Mike, your process of screening

THE CAMPAIGN OF FEAR

and admitting is very impressive, almost intimidating."

"Thank you, sir. It is necessary in our line of work."

"A special thanks, if I may, to the ATP team for the great work you have done on our special project so far. There is a need for us to plan together for the next phase of the project. The complexity has increased and the stakes have risen dramatically. Before we do that, I have new information to cover with you. It is also a key reason why I have asked Joe to be here today. By the way, he has a signed subcontractor agreement to present to ATP. He wants to be part of this project for the same reasons the rest of us are here."

Joe tossed an envelope with the signed agreement to Mike and said, "Sorry we were a bit late coming on board but there are a lot of extenuating circumstances involved. We are honored to be part of this specially selected team and project. Thank you."

"Thanks, Joe. The full team is here and representing the greatest amount of talent possible to assemble on explosives detection and detonation. The president of the United States and the secretary of the Department of Advanced Technology are watching and hoping and planning for our success. That success will break the backs of the terrorists and their 'Campaign of Fear'. With peace in the Middle East comes safety at home. Before we start the project discussions, I have a very serious issue to cover with you. Thomas Kramley of CMT and his family were found dead at their home recently. Federal and local investigative teams are …"

Kan D interrupted and said, "Thomas and his family are dead? No, no, that cannot be. I talked with him not too long ago and he seemed in good spirits. What happened?"

"We don't know yet, Kan D. I knew you were close to him from the University of Michigan days and I am sorry. The federal and local teams are looking at both suicide and murder but don't have the answer yet. We are preparing for the worst. Thomas had a lot of money problems because of family health issues. This resulted in his making some very bad personal and business decisions recently. None of us thought this would happen. Joe and CMT are assisting with the investigation. Also, we have found that the attempted heist of CMT's top secret, experimental detonation technology product

275

was at least partially successful."

Bill asked, "What does that mean?"

"I can't go into details but part of the shipment of Joe's advanced DT product was stolen at the Zefat airport in Israel and is now in the hands of terrorists. The group we believe responsible is called Technolibertat. Their U.S. operation is called, you guessed it, the Technology Investment Corporation. As you know, they are involved in attempting to penetrate all of the companies represented here and our special project. TIC has acquired some very sophisticated software able to do data augmentation system decision making. It is the most advanced DAS that I have seen, working almost at an artificial intelligence level. Once embedded into a corporate intranet system, it is a step away from being able to take it over. That is, it may acquire all corporate data, including intellectual capital and be able to control via external access much of the company's decision making. Joe was the first to understand its potential and I have confirmed it. Its power is almost frightening if put to bad use. This is a good place to stop and ask if there are comments or questions."

Bill said, "Can they duplicate your new detonation technology product, Mr. Blackstone?"

Joe looked at Sam and after a second said, "Probably."

Sam quickly said, "We'll talk more about that later, too. There is a key point that needs to be understood as we plan the program."

Lyncoln had been fidgeting with his Blackberry during the director's comments. His mind was so fast and it was not unusual for him to do multitasking. He put the Blackberry down and quietly asked, "Director, you presented these three issues as if they are connected. Do you believe they are and do you have proof?"

"That's a fair question, Lyncoln. We know that Thomas Kramley had an arrangement, a financial one, to test TIC product. It was illegal and amounted to bribery. Thomas knew that we had information on money transfers to his offshore bank account. There was going to be a day of reckoning soon. The software on data augmentation was provided as part of the so-called M2DAS field test for tracking product through the supply chain. It worked well, almost too well. They were able to get one sample of the top-secret product meant for the Mossad. With some help, they might be able to reverse engineer the product and devise a defense against it. What we don't know is, were the deaths murder or suicide? Either way we believe the deaths were connected to the other issues. Also, who supplied the DAS to them? Regardless of who it was, the connection is still there. On this latter issue, I believe we may be able to resolve it right here, today, and now!"

"How do you mean?" said Lyncoln.

"I have looked at the software closely myself, Lyncoln. You know it was my field before the federal appointment and I was pretty good."

"Yes, I learned a lot from your work, sir."

"I know, Lyncoln. Here is my point. There are only three people in the world who could have created the software M2DAS. It turns out that all three of them are in this room right now. Brad, you, and me. I know it wasn't me. I know it wasn't Brad because his first contact with Kharif and TIC came much later, when they proposed investing in his company. That leaves you, Lyncoln!"

"Me, why would I do something like that?"

"I would guess it was either for money or notoriety or both."

The jaws of Zen, Kan D, Chad, and Mike were dropping farther and farther.

Zen leaned over to Lyncoln and said, "So that's what you have been doing. You were programming M2DAS on that damned Blackberry all this time. I thought you were playing games. You asshole!"

Kan D said, "If you got Thomas and his family killed, there will be hell to pay, Lyncoln."

The director stepped in saying, "Lyncoln, let's take a break and discuss this separately with Mike and Chad."

They excused themselves and retired to the anteroom for the serious discussion.

As the door closed, Lyncoln said, "You were right, it was

for the money. It was a project I had outside of work and there was a willing buyer. So I did it."

Mike and Chad looked at each other and collapsed into chairs next to each other. Lyncoln and the director were still standing looking at each other when the Director broke the silence. "How did you write the program to search for new internal information and feed itself rather than depending on new external input?"

"It was what I call 'learning code' in a closed loop program. The software is able to perform certain independent functions that basically inform it of what it doesn't know. You know all about that, I learned it from you a long time ago when I was at MIT. What is different is that my system, being embedded in a corporate intranet, doesn't wait for new external information to produce new scenarios. It goes to its surrounding environment and searches, learns, and evolves new scenarios continuously. It learns and grows but I stopped short of taking over the intranet and controlling the information. Actually, it wouldn't be so difficult but it seemed a little too much like 'Big Brother' or that computer, what was its name, Hal?"

The director was the next to collapse into a big overstuffed chair saying, "Please sit down, Lyncoln."

"Yes, sir." As he settled in facing the three incredulous looking faces, he said, "I asked the question about the connections amongst the three issues, right?"

"Right. To the best of our knowledge TIC, or Technolibertat, has a rather unsavory connection to all of these things that have happened," the director said. "And now this, too!"

Lyncoln said, "Do you know that this organization visited the MIT campus when I was there? They made a point of talking with the top undergraduate students in all of the departments related to the core technology disciplines. I was one of them and met Omar at that time along with a leader of the Technolibertat organization. The guy was impressive, a lot like some of my professors at MIT. He talked about the importance of technology to our future and how people like us were needed to step up and lead the way. I never actually got his name but Mr. Kharif kept referring to him as the Liberator. I knew they were recruiting but it wasn't a hard sell. We didn't sign our names in blood or anything like that. Omar kept in contact with ten or twelve of us especially after the Technology Investment Corporation was formed. TIC seemed like the perfect organization to carry out the charter of Technolibertat in the U.S. and show that they meant business. They pay us handsomely for developing all kinds of technology. There were never any questions asked about where the money came from or what was done with the technology or who was contributing what. I think we were all very naïve and wearing philosophical blinders. Anyway, all I can say at this point is that I am sorry."

"You met someone called the Liberator?"

"Yes. It was just one time but I'll never forget him. He was so knowledgeable, convincing, and impressive."

"Do you think you could identify him?"

"Maybe."

The director immediately got on his laptop, found the video footage from the heist at the Zefat airport the team at CMT had forwarded and said, "Here it is. Do you recognize this guy?"

"Sure. That's him, the one Omar called the Liberator. Is this the actual footage from the theft of the CMT top secret DT product?"

"Yes. The Liberator is the leader of the terrorist team caught in the act by a small digital camera in the RFID tags."

"My God you do have the proof. I had no idea they were a terrorist organization. What I've told you is all that I know. How can I get things squared away with the government, ATP, and my colleagues?"

"Mike and Chad, do you believe him?"

Mike was first to answer saying, "I don't like that he has secret software work going on with an outside company but yes, I believe him."

"I do, too," said Chad. "Lyncoln has always been one of our top contributors and was selected for this project because of that. I know his colleagues respect him and his work. There will be some repair work needed on his relationships but I believe that will be possible."

"Good! I believe him, too. In fact, there may be a way that Lyncoln can rebuild those company and colleague bridges and help us catch the terrorists at the same time. Would you be up to that, Lyncoln?"

"Anything that can help the team and help me redeem myself."

"I think we are ready to go back and join the team." As they walked out, the director whispered to Lyncoln, "You'll also need to show me the code you wrote on the closed loop learning."

Lyncoln smiled, nodded and said, "Do you think this puts me ahead of Brad's software work, too?"

"What's this 'too' stuff? Brad's got new work going that you'll hear about later. Both of you still continue to impress and amaze me. You should look at it not as a competition but as teaming up to win together. Okay?"

"Yes, sir, I know."

The meeting restarted after everyone returned to the conference room. Everyone was staring at Lyncoln. The director said, "We are back from the woodshed. Lyncoln has explained exactly what happened and we, Chad, Mike, and I believe him. He made some bad decisions and got involved with the wrong people and organizations. There is an apology on the table and a request that he be allowed to redeem himself. First the apology, are we okay with that?"

Brad said, "I am. Anybody who did what he did with that software we need on our side."

Bill said, "I am, too, but I want constant assurance, Lyncoln, that you are working on only our project. If you need more challenges in your assignment, just let me know."

Zen was next. She simply said, "Same here. We all have more than we know how to do."

Kan D was last, glaring at Lyncoln. She said, "I need to know that Thomas and his family didn't die because of something you did. Look me in the eyes and tell me you are innocent."

Lyncoln leaned toward Kan D and said, "I had no part in the death of Thomas Kramley family and I am sorry for the loss of your friend." He leaned over to Kan D, hugged her and said, "I want to do everything I can to beat and catch these terrorists, too."

With that, the director said, "Thanks everybody. Let's cover the redemption part now. Joe is here because he is part of the team. He also was one of the first to suspect the TIC organization and what it might be up to. So much so that he took it upon himself to make sure that if something happened to the product that was shipped to Israel, it would not work. That was brilliant because, even though we thought the shipment was fully recovered, it was not. There was one prototype or experimental product taken. What they don't know is that it is a non-functioning unit that they are probably busily reverse engineering. The other thing they don't know is that we have uncovered the secrets within the M2DAS system and that they have some level of external access to CMT's database and decision making. They also do not know that the expert was only naively involved and not a successful recruit committed to their terrorist cause. We have a couple of options open to us. We could act as though we do not know they have access to and some control over CMT's intranet. We would let them pick up our communications and act on specially formulated but erroneous information. Something like … 'shipment recovered except for one unit but a design flaw has been identified'. We would provide a fix but not the real fix and let them believe they are okay and haven't been discovered yet. The other option is to remove the M2DAS from the intranet and make no communication about anything. They might assume that the system had been compromised and take some kind of action against Lyncoln or even further action against CMT. It could be that they would become suspicious about the experimental product and do nothing to reverse engineer it. What do you think?"

Mike said, "Joe, can you really provide what appears to be a fix but isn't?"

"Yes, I can, Mike. It was my suggestion to the director."

"Are you also okay, Joe, with this software embedded in your intranet a little while longer?"

"I am as long as Lyncoln helps me manage just how much access and control TIC has over the information."

"I can do that, Joe."

Brad spoke up and said, "I am warming to option one also. Let me ask another question of Joe. Do you consider this generation of DT product the best you can do?"

"No, Brad, of course not. I have another one in the design phase right now."

"Would the new one obsolete the old one?"

"Yes, it would."

"So if we were to look at a system of 'Explosive Detection and Explosive Detonation', the product most likely to be used with ATP's explosive detection part, would not be the product that was stolen but the product that is currently being designed?"

"That is correct, Brad. You have a very good point. It is. It doesn't matter that they have our experimental product or even a fix (real or otherwise) because this technology will be made obsolete by the next generation coming soon. But, they don't know that and would likely chew up a lot of their resources if option one is in play."

"Yes," the director said, "and further defocuses them from what we are doing on the rest of the project. Are there any other comments on the options?"

Kan D ventured, "Do you believe that option one will protect Lyncoln and all of us more than option two?"

"Yes, I do, but we are still somewhat at risk. These people are terrorists. We may find out that what happened to Thomas and his family was their handiwork."

"Why can't we just go arrest the son of a bitch, Director?" asked Zen.

"I know how you all feel, but we have to get the head of the organization and bring him down too. Getting Omar would not make that much of a difference."

They all were nodding their heads around the table.

"OK, we are making great progress here. Joe, I would like you and Lyncoln to draw up the plans to use M2DAS safely as our communication tool with the terrorists. Give them a fix or two for the DT product even if you have to use the real fix. Brad, with your software expertise, I want you to be available as an advisor to Lyncoln and Joe. Joe, keep working on Generation II of your detonation technology and make sure it is ready to go when the ED part is completed. I will contact our friends in Israel and let them know. They will have to be a part of the deception."

Chad interrupted, as it was almost exactly noon, to say, "Lunches will be here shortly so I suggest we get to the next area and work through lunch. Is that okay with everybody?"

Nobody said a thing as thoughts bounced around inside their heads. They had just heard that Thomas and family were dead, the revelation about Lyncoln, the stolen experimental DT product, and terrorists that could control company intranets. The collective question forming around the table was, "What could the next area be, for God's sake?"

The director broke the silence saying, "The next area is the project at ATP. We have an unusual opportunity to do something very special on explosive detection. Brad would you help explain please?"

"Yes sir. I believe all of you know that TIC has invested in Tully Research, Incorporated to the tune of $10 million per year for five years. You also know now that TIC is up to no good. They want technology badly and especially acoustical technology. We believe this is because of the project here at ATP. The terrorists are frightened to death that we have something coming that will put a stop to their 'Campaign of Fear'. As you have been hearing, they will stop at nothing to win. Mr. Kharif has been pushing me to get something back for their investment. I have to give them something soon or I might be next on their list. This is why I am here. My work in acoustics has progressed much faster than I could have ever imagined. Since moving to Minneapolis, there has been discovery after discovery. From discussions with the director and Zen and written reports from Bill, I believe I have a good understanding of where you are with research and development on CIED. I was in the same place about three years ago. Sorry, but in other words, I'm three years ahead of you guys. My data and research conclusions are the same ones you are finding in your work today. Wave generation, bounce-back and capture, chemical analysis, vacuum and other collection techniques, miniaturization and mobility are all areas of specialty for me. Add to that a little software and code development, like we discussed today, and you get the picture. Yes, it was primarily for the oil industry but has high potential for applicability in many other areas including finding all kinds of explosives."

Chad commented, "I'm glad we signed you as a subcontractor, Brad. Our work may have become a whole lot easier."

"It actually gets better, Chad. I have recently shown that I can identify chemical elements and compounds at a distance by separating the returning wave into its individual and unique components. Each wave component has a unique telltale pattern for the element or compound it represents. We have been able to generate the wave, bounce it back after contacting the chemicals in the air, and separate the modified returning wave into a specific number of component waves representing those chemicals. After separation of the component waves, we compare to standards set up for waves produced from known chemicals within explosive devices. In fractions of seconds, we can sample the air, identify the chemicals represented by the wave components and determine where an explosive device is located. We think this will work on a moving target as well as a stationary one, but have yet to test that theory."

Bill asked, "Are you serious?"

Zen said, "And no need for vacuums or chemical analyzers?"

"Nope!"

"But you still need some miniaturization I bet," Kan D interjected.

"Yes, of course."

Lyncoln said, "The code, how did you separate the modified returning wave?"

"It wasn't much different from your closed loop learning model, Lyncoln. Find one, subtract it; use the standard to find the next one, etc."

"Brad, does this mean you have made obsolete the work of our project team even before we have completed the R&D?" Chad asked.

"Yes, essentially, but there is still much work to do."

"Thanks, Brad."

Lunch arrived at that very moment and the director said, "Great timing. Let me do some more talking while you eat. Brad's work gives us a very significant advantage in technology that we need to discuss before we come to a consensus. I'll pose the question like this: Should we continue the work on Gen. I CIED as we had planned or switch our efforts and resources to Gen. II? Before we try to answer that question, I need to give you some additional information. TIC, with their investment in Tully Research, is trying to get the most up-to-date technology from Brad as he has mentioned. They have made a tentative offer to ATP through Mike and Chad, to license that technology once available. We believe that, however strange that sounds, it is their way to penetrate ATP and learn more about our special project. They, of course, know a little about Brad's acoustic work at the GPRI but nothing about his Gen. II technology. TIC wants Brad's Gen. I acoustics technology because they believe it is the best available and that it is what this project needs. They would contribute to the project and get closer to ATP at the same time."

Zen popped in a question while chewing, "You are trying to pull TIC in to help catch the bad guys, right?"

"Good question, Zen. I believe TIC is convinced that Tully Research will operate legally and under the terms and conditions of its formation. There are two pertinent points: First, the president of TRI can sign certain consulting or other work agreements, on his own accord if they will enhance the viability, reputation, and growth of the company. Second, TRI cannot sell, license or otherwise transfer technology to outside entities unless approved by its investors and board of directors. Of course, they are currently the largest investor and believe they have control over decisions like this. It's interesting that in this case legal terms and conditions are brought to bear when their basic operating principles as a terrorist organization are outside the rule of law. Muddled thinking? Yes, and this always means some level of unpredictability on their part."

Brad winked at Zen and said, "To answer your questions, I believe we should do both."

"You mean continue the work on Gen. I and start a new project on Gen. II? Both?"

"Yes," Brad said. He could see some questioning looks and uneasiness building. "Let's do the same thing as we just decided for Joe's detonation technology. That is, have them believe that nothing has changed. We are still working on the special project, as they know it. We need them and their access to technology through TRI and we want them closer to us. In parallel, we run our top secret Gen. II program with most of our resources and pull out all the stops. Gen. I gets only minimum attention, just enough to fool the unlearned or casual outsider. I think we could pull it off."

The director said, "Interesting, Brad, and great innovative thinking. Any comments on this or are there other ideas?"

"Brad, are you suggesting that both programs be run at the same location, here at ATP?" Mike asked.

"Yes, I think they would have to be. Otherwise TIC might suspect something."

Zen said with a big smile, "What about you, going back and forth between Minneapolis and Boston so much?"

"Just part of my consulting work with ATP while helping to transfer technology being licensed by TIC for the special project," answered Brad, returning the smile.

Joe said, "I think it can work. If we can do it for my detonation technology, we can do it for your explosive technology. Should we move my program to Boston, too?"

"I don't think that is necessary right now, Joe," said the director. "Keeping the programs in separate locations will provide more challenges for our adversary than for us."

"I think you are right, sir."

'What about the project team: Chad, Bill, Lyncoln, Kan D, and Zen? Are you okay running a sham program alongside the real program?"

Chad said, "We'll do whatever is necessary to get the job done, Director."

Bill picked up on that and said, "Chad's right of course and we'll all have to work on swallowing our pride. How could you be so far ahead of us, Brad?"

"I was just lucky and as I said before, this stuff still needs a lot of work."

"Lyncoln?"

"I'm in."

"Kan D?"

"We still need miniaturization, right? I'm in."

"Zen?"

"I'm in. Remember, I tried to get Dr. Tully to settle in Boston when he was in the process of relocating from Texas. I knew how valuable he was going to be to our project. Welcome to the team, Brad."

"I think we are all in agreement. Let's do some smaller group work for the rest of the time we have. Brad, would you brief the team on your Gen. II please?"

"Yes. Let's go to the laboratory for our get together."

"Chad and Mike, would you do some space, equipment, and people resource planning for the Gen. II work? Remember that only the people in this room should know what we are doing so plan for the appropriate security as well."

Chad said, "We were just chatting, sir. Our thoughts are that we will need a different building, redundant equipment, a completely different group of technicians, and black operations security all the way around."

Mike said, "Let's work in my office, Chad. See you guys later."

"Great. Joe, let's you and I stay here and work on the information we want the terrorists to get from your intranet."

"Okay, Sam. I think, besides the detonation technology product news and fix, we need to communicate the deaths of Thomas and his wife and son to our employees."

"I agree, Joe. Let's take Thomas and his family first. The CSI team working with the local authorities must approve what you use for internal communications. I'm thinking only confirming they are dead and there is a police investigation underway."

"Maybe we can put in some details about his wife, son, and Thomas's company responsibility, position, and years of service at CMT."

"Joe, contact Jack and tell him what we want to do. Make the email brief but use the facts and the personal information you would like to add. Ask him to help formulate it for use as a special intranet communication to employees. Remember, the terrorists will see exactly what you distribute. One more thing, if we discover later that it was murder, will you be comfortable using you intranet to help catch these guys?"

"Yes. Isn't that what we are going to do with the deceptive communication on the stolen experimental product?"

"Yes, it is. I'm glad you recognize the similarities. You are the technical guy Joe. What do you need to tell them to keep them unsuspecting?"

"I modified the test products in two ways, Sam. The activation code was re-sequenced to one unique for each box based on the order it was to be packed on the shipping pallet. It is stamped on the outside of the box. I also switched the chip sets in the generators with the ones in the modulators. They look identical from the outside so no one could tell. We could disclose either."

"Why don't we just indicate that for safety purposes the activation code for each unit of the experimental lot was changed to a unique two-digit number stamped on the box? You could put this into a confidential email to the CMT people in Israel who are working with the customer. Let them know they are to communicate this to their customer before testing begins. Thank them for their help in recovering the product, getting it released from security officials, and, although there were delays, getting the lot delivered in a very timely fashion."

Joe said, "Yes, I think that would work. TIC and Technolibertat will see the email and believe that nothing like this would be communicated if we knew they had access to our intranet. Additionally, the code information means nothing to them in their reverse engineering project. They also know that activating and firing the device would mask some of the electronic component design features needed to understand how the product works. It is a great plan. I'll get the email written and sent to Jack for approval ASAP. This way we can get it out to employees today or tomorrow."

"Good, Joe. I will contact Absek and let him know what we are doing and how to make his product work for the field test."

Just at that moment, Mike and Chad came back into the main conference room each holding a flip chart page. Mike said, "We have space identified in the building next door." He put the page on the wall showing the sketch, saying, "An entire floor where we used to have a cafeteria before we outsourced food services for the complex. It has water, gas, air pressure, vents, etc. and can be easily converted into laboratory space. We have sketched out how we could duplicate the space in this building. Fortunately, there is an overhead passageway connecting the two buildings. It will be easy to move between the two locations without significant additional security checks. We could also restrict movement between the two buildings to a selected few people, say the key team members who are meeting here today."

"That really sounds good. How about getting the lab outfitted with equipment and skilled personnel?"

Chad said, "We think it could be ready in about two weeks, depending mostly on how much Brad has to move from Minnesota and how long it will take to get here. It won't take long to duplicate the equipment we have in our current project."

"Sounds great. What are we going to call these two projects so we don't get ourselves confused?"

"Mike and I believe we should keep the original name for the current project, 'CIED', which was on the lost/stolen notes. The new project could be something like L-RED, Long-Range Explosive Detection. How does that sound?"

"Fine with me. What about personnel?"

Mike said, "This will take some work. When we staffed CIED, we brought in the cream of the crop technicians. Changing assignments would bring too much attention to the new project

L-RED. The reality is that the two projects will probably overlap by ~ 50%. We can staff L-RED with different top-flight technicians for the ~50% non-overlap part of the project. There are just enough high-performance technicians left for that. As we keep CIED going, we'll depend on those currently assigned technicians to continue their work even though only half of it will be usable. Chad and I agree this is the only way we can make the numbers of top technicians available and the output needed match up without reassigning people."

"It's a good plan, don't you think, Joe?"

"I think it will work fine, Director."

"The other group is due back any minute. Could you fill Chad and Mike in on our part of the planning? I want to make a call to Jack and let him know that you will be in touch with him on the communication. Okay?"

"I sure will, Director," said Joe.

The director stepped into the hallway to call Jack. Calls using normal cell phones were not possible within the buildings of the ATP complex. It was a security thing and much needed for their kind of business. His phone was different and amazing. He could get a signal regardless of where he was or the specific environment involved. Sam was wondering, as he scrolled to Jack's number and pushed send, what news he could expect about the investigation. He said to himself, "I fear we have more bad news."

"Hello, Director," Jack said in a voice that Sam knew he was right.

"Hello, Jack, do I hear more bad news in your voice?"

"Yes, you do, sir, you are very perceptive."

"What happened?"

"You won't believe it, the comic books, it was the comic books."

"The comic books, what do you mean?"

"Two of the local laboratory technicians, who had access to the evidence, saw the comic books when they came in. Superheroes I think. They had to take a look. Their colleagues found them a couple hours later on the floor, eyes rolled back, hardly breathing, and got them to the hospital."

"The doctors think there was something on the comic books? A poison?"

"Yes. That's the theory right now. The comic books were found out of the paper evidence bag and on the floor nearby the lab techs. They are beginning to test for any poisonous material on the covers and pages. It is going to take several days but the CSI poison expert is there to help."

"Why didn't the poison kill them, Jack?"

"I asked the same question, sir. The CSI guy said maybe we just found them soon enough."

"I'm coming out, Jack. I'll be there as soon as I can."

"Sir, I thought you might want to see things first hand. We have a room for you at the hotel. I'll bring you up to date on the rest of the information from the investigation then."

"Thanks, Jack. I almost forgot; Joe Blackstone will be in touch to get your help on a communication piece to go to CMT employees. Please get it approved by our CSI team leader and local law enforcement so that Joe can put it on his company intranet. Try to keep it out of the newspapers a while longer. Thanks again; I'll see you tomorrow."

"Yes, sir, see you tomorrow."

Sam hurried back to the conference room wondering how much of this to tell the team. He decided to wait. "Sorry about the long call."

Mike said, "It is okay, sir. Joe reviewed the planning that the two of you did on the special intranet communications about the Kramley family and the top-secret detonation technology product. Chad and I discussed where and how we would set up the parallel program to be called L-RED. We are now ready to get the working team's insight on how to scope the new project."

Bill started by saying, "Wow! I would never have thought it was possible. To articulate a returning acoustic wave into its component waves based on its impact with explosive-type materials is phenomenal. Some of these materials barely have a vapor pressure. Then to correlate each of the wave components with known standards set up in advance, it is brilliant. I cannot say

291

enough superlatives about the acoustics work or the code. There are several things that we have identified to get to a prototype that we can field test. They are all simple compared to the technology work already done. These include fine tuning the wave generator for distance, return characteristics, the probe for identifying the wave components, and the computer elucidation capability. Lyncoln will have to speak to that."

Lyncoln said, "The technology is truly game-changing. In fact, it will allow Zen to refocus her work on the newer explosives that use more sophisticated packaging or have materials with lower vapor pressure. The wave has to be disruptive enough to find the explosive and its components either stationary or on the move. Zen, am I getting into your area of expertise?"

"No problem, Lyncoln, I'm just glad it was the chemical collection and analyses technology that was obsolete and not me and my position."

"From a software standpoint, I think I know what we have to do to make L-RED work in almost nanosecond timeframes. As the distances get longer, to hundreds of feet, that gets to be more challenging. Our previous work with satellite pickup and downloading to a Big Blue type mainframe will be very useful. Getting the chemical elements or compounds correlated with a specific wave component is not too difficult. Sorry, Zen, I didn't mean that like it sounded."

"It's okay, Lyncoln, I happen to agree with you."

"What is difficult, from a code perspective, is separating the individual wave components from the total returning wave. Brad has a good start but there is a lot of code work to be done on masked or hidden waves, extraneous waves, and false positive waves. I think we can write the program to find most of what is contained in the returning wave-front. I will wait, but once we get going I want to talk to Brad about an idea I have for the third generation. Zen, your turn."

"Lyncoln and I will work closely on the chemistry, standards, and thorough identification of the potential targets. Kan D?"

"We still need miniaturization, right? I figure most of the work will be focused on the wave generator and probe/collector. Besides small, we still need instant mobility, ruggedness, and reduction of complexity. I like the new technology. Brad, I'm glad you are on our team."

The director stood up and said, "Thanks Kan D and thanks to everyone. We accomplished quite a lot today. Our decisions and plans for our new focus on L-RED will give us something the terrorists are not expecting. Let's all thank Brad for providing the great technology advantage." There was instant clapping, whistling, yelling by the team. "If we can keep TIC and Technolibertat believing they know what we are doing, developing CIED, they will spend all their resources trying to counter our actions there. This includes the detonation technology as well. Together they become the weapon that threatens their 'Campaign of Fear'. Our intelligence says they will do anything to penetrate our operations, learn more, and be able to develop a defense. We are going to see that they fail! Bill, Lyncoln, Zen, Kan D, Chad, and Mike, good luck with L-RED. Our future depends on your success. Joe, I hope it is okay, I have decided to go back to San Francisco with you tonight. I want the same kind of effort on DT-A2 as we have on L-RED. One more thing, and Joe doesn't know about this yet either, there have been some new developments in the investigation of the deaths of Thomas Kramley and his family. Certain evidence found recently indicates more strongly that it may have been murder."

Joe blurted out, "My God, was it Omar and TIC?"

"We don't know yet, but I need to be there with you and see if I can lend a hand. One thing for sure, if it was Omar, we are going to get the son-of-a-bitch."

Mike said, "Director, I know I speak for the whole team. We will all do our parts to help you get him and his organization. You can count on us!"

"Thank you very much. The most important thing right now is your work on L-RED. Stay in touch and let me know how things are going. Thanks everybody."

Apology and Redemption

At the end of the big meeting, Chad leaned over to Lyncoln and said, "We need to talk afterwards, please."

Lyncoln said, "Yes, sir," as Kan D and the others who heard this just smiled.

As the group dispersed, Chad said, "Lyncoln, the director and I talked about your closed loop learning program or what TIC called M2DAS. We believe, for a number of reasons, you will be contacted soon to write code for the control aspect. When that happens, we want you to respond positively."

"What? And give them access to something that could be used against American industry and our government?"

"I said, respond positively, not just do it and give it to them. Let's pull them into the net even more and provide false confidence that their plans are working. You can let them get you under contract and, by the way, charge some big bucks since this is almost Nobel prize-winning work. If we can put a strain on their cash flow, it might create a situation where the leaders of Technolibertat will be forced to surface to save the sinking ship. The director and his department will soon be trying some things that will directly impact their financial situation. Their income sources could almost come to a halt."

"Okay, but do you recall what happened to Thomas Kramley at CMT? He probably was murdered by Omar and his cohorts."

"Yes, I do. I agree that it is somewhat dangerous, of course. One way to minimize the danger is to have another person in the deal with you. Everything changes with two people talking, listening, watching, and helping each other."

"Have you signed up to be my partner in crime?"

"I tried to volunteer but it was decided by the director that Dr. Tully will be your partner. I guess it had to be Brad or the director, if you think about it. As a partner, the director probably wouldn't go over too well with TIC. You can sell it as two world-class programmers working together to solve the biggest software challenge in history. They have this huge investment in Tully Research and don't want anything to happen to him. Also, he has a consulting agreement with ATP and your special project so for him to consult on this with you might not be too far- fetched. The way to talk about this, if it even comes up with Omar, is that you know the work is off the books, but Dr. Tully does not. He is being told it is a sanctioned but very, very top-secret part of the special project that only a few unnamed people know about. He is, therefore, more than willing to help. Now Brad knows all about this proposed arrangement, of course, and has agreed to be your partner in crime, but we need you to agree as well. Be assured that federal agents will be watching continuously."

"I'll do it, Chad. I've always wanted to work with Brad Tully anyway and the plan you guys have cooked up sounds like it could work. Can Brad and I really work on 'control' together?"

"Yes, of course. We just need to make sure it never gets into the hands of Omar, TIC, or Technolibertat."

"Draining their bank accounts to pay for something they will never get. I love it, and I'm in."

"Great! You and Brad need to talk and work out how contact with Omar or others will be handled. Set up a way to keep in constant contact with Brad on your parts of the work and the progress being made. I'm sure Omar will want updates regularly with the amount of money you are going to charge him. Remember, he is technically unskilled so he'll have to pass the information along to others to assess and evaluate. Keep them thinking that progress is being made but never give them enough to use by themselves. If you have to give them something, embed a virus that chews up the demonstration program after a brief introduction. You'll know better than I do how to protect your work with Brad and not give away any secrets. Just be sure to make every decision together and become inseparable on this project. Mike and I and the director will be watching very closely."

"Okay, I'll count on it. Chad, one more thing, this wipes the slate clean on redemption, right?"

"You bet, Lyncoln, in fact I think the balance will be tilted back to 'we owe you on this one'."

"Thank you, sir."

Brad Stays in Boston Overnight

Zen said, as they were leaving the conference room, "Let's eat in tonight at my apartment. We don't have a lot of time before you leave tomorrow morning."

Brad smiled and said, "Great, but we have to be careful because the feds have me under watch at all times. Our special breakfasts cannot be on the balcony anymore like in Minneapolis."

"You think they saw us in Minneapolis?"

"I found out later that the watch started well before your trip to Minneapolis so I assume they did. I am sorry, Zen."

"It's okay, you didn't know about it. Let's just hope they will be discreet in matters not relating to the case. They have probably seen a lot more than that."

"Zen, I do love you."

"I know. Wait here while I drop off my project stuff in the office area. It will take just a second, and then we'll get a cab to my place."

"Okay," said Brad as he watched her walk away conjuring up thoughts about what the evening would bring. In fact, Zen had told him to think about all this as they planned their next get-together. He thought, I'm just doing what she told me.

As she returned suddenly, Zen said, "You look like you're in a daze. Anything wrong?"

Brad, jolted back to the present moment, said, "No, nothing is wrong. I was just thinking about the best time in my life."

Zen took his hand and pulled him toward the stairs and the door, whispering in his ear, "You haven't seen anything yet, buddy."

The cab ride was uneventful, both willing themselves to keep their hands off the other. Thankfully, the apartment was not far away from ATP so they didn't have to wait long. Zen said, "Here it is, Brad." Brad paid the taxi fare and they exited the cab.

The apartment building looked new to him and it wasn't as big a high rise as he expected. Boston must have some zoning restrictions on the heights of new commercial and residential buildings. Brad said, "It looks like you are right in the center of things, work, the city, and the universities."

"It is a great location and my apartment is on the third floor. Bill helped me find this place when I first came to interview at ATP and was told that a job offer was forthcoming. They were just finishing the construction at the time but the units had been for sale for a while. This was the only one left so I took it."

They entered the building and walked to the lobby elevators hand in hand. Zen pushed the UP button and the elevator arrived quickly. Once inside Zen pushed the button for the third floor while Brad was kissing the back of her neck. Arriving at the third floor, the doors opened and Zen pulled Brad to the left toward her apartment. A few more steps down the hall and then they saw him in the shadows, just beyond her apartment door.

Brad thought, dark suit and tie, white shirt – looks like the guy in D.C. who was watching me. He pulled Zen to a stop, watching and waiting to see what the guy was going to do. He saw him reach toward the inside pocket of his suit coat. Brad was squeezing Zen's hand really hard and was just about ready to tell her to run for the exit steps when the man in the suit said, "FBI, hello, Dr. Tully."

He pulled out his FBI badge and said, "You probably remember me from D.C. but here is my identification. The director mentioned you would be under watch for your protection, right? Well, I got the assignment again. How do you do, Dr. Lang?"

"Hello," said Zen. "How do you know my name?"

"We know all of the people on the special project at ATP, ma'am. It is our job to keep Dr. Tully, you, and the others involved safe, whether you are in San Francisco, Minneapolis, Boston, or D.C. until we can deal with the terrorists."

"I'm not sure I need to be safe if it means someone sitting outside my door all the time."

"I know what you mean, ma'am. But if it has to be, it is better for you to know who I am and that I'm here to help you if needed. If not, we'll be as discreet and invisible as possible. Okay?"

"Did you say we?"

"Yes. I am the lead agent, but we do have a few others around, too. Again, it is all for your safety."

"Thanks, agent," said Brad, "We appreciate what you are doing. Do you really think all of this is necessary?"

"Yes. With what happened at CMT, we have to be very careful. Both of you are key to the success of our special project. From what I hear, it would be almost impossible to replace you so it is my job to see that nothing happens to you. I'm sorry if it seems to be too intrusive."

Zen concluded that the watch would continue regardless of what she said or thought. "It's okay, agent, I know you are just doing your job."

"Thank you. We'll be around if you need us."

"Thank you," said Brad as Zen let them into her apartment. "Wow, it's beautiful and your decorating has a hint of the Far East. I love it."

"My mother was from India and we traveled a lot to China, Japan, and even the Middle Eastern countries when I was young. My name has an Eastern connection. I'm not a Buddhist but maybe I should be with the things going on around here."

"I thought your name came from the book, 'Zen and the Art of Motorcycle Maintenance,'" said Brad, smiling.

"Yea, right. Let's have a glass of wine and talk, Brad. I'm a little shook up with the FBI watching us."

"That's a good idea."

Zen picked out a Cabernet and walked to the kitchen. She saw that Brad was following, found the corkscrew, and handed both to him. "You open and I'll get the glasses."

"As you know, I'm not too good at this, especially if they use a real cork."

"You'll do fine, here are the glasses." Zen was behind Brad suddenly embracing him, her hands on his chest and her body close to his, very close. She hugged tight with her hot breath and wet tongue on his ear.

Brad was fumbling around but finally got the cork out and poured two glasses of wine. He picked them up and turned in her arms, not losing one millimeter of closeness. He gave her a glass and said, "Let's have a toast to safety."

Zen stepped back, they touched glasses, and she said, "To safety." She took his hand and they walked to the sofa in the living room and sat down. "Brad, I'm a nobody compared to you on this project. I am really afraid that your life could be in danger. Look, with the changes we have made in the L-RED program, everything depends on you and your technology now. I hear you will be helping CMT on their DT A-2 so we have the same situation there. If the terrorists find out, they might take a completely different approach to learning about our latest technologies and finding ways to defend against them. They may try to just get rid of the source of the technologies – you! I am also very worried that we can keep what we are doing with CIED and L-RED confidential. As we make progress, the dangers and risks increase dramatically. You will be on the East Coast, West Coast, and in the Midwest. As good as they are, I'm not sure the FBI team can keep you safe. Doesn't all this bother you?"

"Of course it does but I don't know what I can do about it. The country needs help, our military and the troops need help, and our people need help. I'm just trying to do the best I can. The terrorists aren't very smart, technically, so let's hope they will telegraph their next move. If that happens, we can be ready."

"We have to ask if this is important enough to risk your life. There aren't many things that fit into that category."

"The director talked with me about this and I agreed that stopping the 'Campaign of Fear' was necessary. I firmly believe we have a chance to do that with my technology and know-how. I had to say yes. I wanted to say yes! The problem that I have now is that, because of me, you are also at risk and I can't do anything about it."

"I know, Brad, but don't worry about me."

"But I do, Zen. I love you." He took her in his arms and they held each other tight. It wasn't long before Zen fell asleep, fast asleep. Brad just kept holding her. After an hour or so, he whispered quietly, "Let's get you into bed, Zen." Brad found the bedroom, helped her take off her blouse and skirt, and tucked her in for the night. As he was leaving, Zen said, "Get in with me, Brad, please." He didn't hesitate and in no time they were curled together and sleeping with no thoughts of the terrorists, impending dangers, or even the FBI.

Zen was awake first. She felt Brad against her, hard and ready. She had been thinking about having him inside her ever since she woke up. She quietly removed her bra and panties and began touching him. It was so hot under the covers that she threw the heavier blanket off first. Brad was not fully awake yet but was responding to her touch. The light sheet was next to go and there she was completely nude, reaching into his boxers to free him from the restrictions. Brad's eyes opened suddenly and he whispered, "Am I missing something?"

"Yes, but I'll get you caught up soon. With that she was on top, put him inside her and began to move. She said, " Don't worry. I'll do all the work and give you the best wake up ever."

Brad said, getting more awake now, "You got yourself a deal."

As Zen moved and oh, how she moved, he must have grown a foot, at least it felt that way. He said, "How do you do this so that you can manage when I come?"

Zen said, "I watch your eyes. I can bring you up to almost the peak, back off a little, and then do it again and again and again."

"My God, Zen, I might go crazy after about the fourth time – it feels so good."

"Good, here we go again, almost there, back off a little, slow the movement, and wait a little. Your eyes tell me."

"Do you get the same pleasure as I do, Zen?"

"Of course, if we are in sync, the same thing is happening for me." She was moving slowly, still only about half penetrated, up and down, up and down to almost the peak; then she would back off and wait a little. Brad was almost crazy by this time and Zen noticed. She said, "Are we in sync? Let's go to the peak this time." She pulled herself to him hard now, more fully penetrated and then moved up all the way to the tip, then a full downward thrust, up to the tip, the movement got faster and faster and deeper and deeper. Soon, when Zen saw he was ready, made the last moves and they

THE CAMPAIGN OF FEAR

came together. It was sweaty ecstasy. It was the best wake up ever.

Brad wouldn't let her roll off this time, as he tried to stay hard and inside her as long as possible. Finally, he came out and she rolled to his side and they embraced, not talking, just being close for the longest time.

Zen said, "It's time for you to get to the airport, Brad. I will call a cab and you can get showered and dressed."

He was ready to go in ten minutes. She handed him a bagel and a cup of coffee as he got into the cab. There was a last kiss and a whisper, "Zen, I don't know if I can wait until next time."

"Me either, Brad, I love you."

"I love you, too; bye for now."

Chapter 12

The Investigation Intensifies

The CSI Teams

Jack had arranged for Joe and the director to meet with him and the heads of the CSI teams later that day.

Jack said, "Hello, Director Elson and President Blackstone. We have a hell of a mess here. Sorry we couldn't keep things under control."

"It's okay, Jack," the director said. "Some things can't be helped. How are the lab technicians?"

"They are struggling and the doctors think it's 50/50 whether they will survive. I want you to meet the federal CSI team leader, Andrew, and the local CSI team leader, Mary. They can brief you on what they have found so far. I'm glad we were able to talk earlier but remember please, it hasn't been long since all of this happened."

Andrew asked Mary to begin because her team processed the Kramley crime scene first, before the federal team arrived.

Mary said, "Director Elson, President Blackstone, we have a case like none other I have known about in San Francisco. We arrived with the police at the scene, the Kramley residence, where Jack was waiting for us. My people processed as much as we could, then moved the bodies to the CSI laboratory and morgue. Jack told us there was a federal CSI unit coming in ASAP so we decided to wait on them before we did anything else."

Andrew took it from there saying, "And they did a great job in such a short time and very late at night. As we were meeting this morning, a second crime scene was discovered. It was right here, the San Francisco CSI Laboratory and Morgue, where two lab technicians were both found in a comatose state. Mary and I recognized the symptoms of poisoning. We took immediate precautions to protect the scene and the people and still got the technicians to the hospital as quickly as possible. Whether they will survive is not yet known. The chemists have identified several foreign substances in the bodies of the Kramley family members and in the blood of the two recently affected technicians. Pinpointing the active poison itself has been very difficult because of its decomposition in the body."

The director said, "We are working on another part of this case in a Middle East country. There was a poisoning there where the experts were able to do the examination, lab testing, and analyses after only an hour or two."

"Would that make a difference?"

Mary and Andrew looked at each other. Andrew said, "It sure would, sir. I need to talk to your contact to see what they found. It must be a new poison because our data banks could not identify it even knowing the decomposition products. We thought the comic books could be the key but found a series of complex chemical compounds, most of which we assume are air oxidation products. Our data banks could not identify the active ingredient that way either."

"I'll get the contact information for you. Knowing the poison might help us learn more about the people using it."

"Thank you, sir. Do you have time to hear about the other evidence?"

"That's why we are here. We have to catch these bad guys before more bodies begin to stack up."

"Mary, do you want to cover the pills and the bag?"

"Yes. For now we have left the Kramley crime scene as pure as possible. There were antidepressant pills/capsules all over the floor and a partially filled bottle on the dresser. We took the bottle with us for prints. In counting the pills in the bottle and on the floor, we came up with only four missing. Our conclusion was that it had nothing to do with the deaths but we don't know why a lot of pills were on the floor. There was also a plastic bag on the floor, one of those Ziploc kinds. We didn't find anything in the room that would have required a Ziploc bag. However, after the technicians were poisoned by the comic books, we reasoned they were probably carried in the bag. On testing the inside surface of the bag, our experts found the same series of compounds that we found on the comic books. One more thing, and this is an exciting finding. There were two sets of prints on the bag, Kramley's and someone elses. Our fingerprint database search has come up empty so far. Is there a suspect that we should know about?"

The director looked at Joe and said, "Yes, and there must be a sample of his prints someplace. We'll check on that. Great work."

"Which brings us to the briefcase," said Andrew. "The combined team really did good work here, too, sir. They reasoned that if the comic books were carried in the Ziploc bag, Mr. Kramley probably carried the package into the bedroom in his briefcase. We wipe tested the inside of the briefcase and were unable to pick up any trace of any of the compounds identified so far. But, who in their right mind would have had that package open in their briefcase anyway?"

"Was there anything of interest in the briefcase?" Joe asked. "Thomas was so fastidious in his record keeping and how he organized things, I thought maybe …."

Andrew interrupted and said, "And you thought right, sir. Thomas had obviously talked to an attorney because his name was in the briefcase. He must have also planned for and scheduled a meeting for later with that attorney. We know this because we found the draft of his 'Chronicle of Events' from the first meeting with a Mr. Omar Kharif to the last meeting with him, which appears to be the day before he and his family were found dead at their home. In my experience, someone does this as a precaution and only if the think they are in trouble."

The director asked, 'Does it have all the financial transactions detailed?"

"Yes, sir, and a few threats by Kharif along the way," said Andrew.

"Did it seem that Thomas was doing this for any reason other than money for medical bills?" asked Joe.

"It appears to be only that, sir. In fact, in the last entries it seems he is going to try to convince Omar to join with him in telling the truth. The attorney thing is a precaution in case something happens to him before that, I believe. I have copies of the 'Chronicle of Events' for each of you. That's about all we have to report at this time. Anything else, Mary?"

"That's it for now, but still a lot of work to be done. Let us know about the fingerprints and the poison work done elsewhere on the case. Thank you."

"Thanks to both of you. How could you possibly have done all this in the short time you have had to work? Joe and I are very appreciative. I am going to be here a while longer so keep us posted on any new information, please."

The Director and Absek Talk

"Hello, Absek. I am glad you were in the office. Forgive me for an unscheduled call?"

"Hello, Director. It is always good to talk to you. Did you determine who I should talk to about the defective product?"

"Yes, I did Absek. There are also several other things I need to bring you up to date on today. Your contact will be Joe Blackstone. First let me tell you about the investigation because it has taken a decided turn for the worse. Mr. Kramley, his wife, and son were found dead in their home a couple of days ago. There was a poison involved but because of its degradation in the bodies over 24 hours and air oxidation of the residue, we have not been able to identify the active ingredient. It could be the same poison used in the Zefat suicide. Do you have any information on what was used there?"

"Three people dead? That is too bad, sir, when women and children get caught up in the plot."

"I know, Absek, it makes us work even harder to get the bastards."

"Yes. It sounds like we had the advantage on this one. Our medical examination of the pilot, who committed suicide, was within two hours. Bodily decomposition of the poison was not such a factor as in your case. Our people identified it as a derivative of a natural product, Warfarin, first made the 1940's at the University of Wisconsin and used as a rat poison. Later, in a much more diluted form, it was used as a blood thinner in humans. We believe the poison in question to be an even more potent derivative that kills almost instantaneously. We put the word out on its chemical description, mode of action, as well as some information on small amounts of decomposition products and the like. We found several pharmaceutical companies that say they sell something that sounded like this as a prescription blood thinner. They all purchased it from one contract manufacturer, Pharmatek, located at the University of Damascus in Syria. This is the university where Professor Eomar Kharif taught before Technolibertat. Because of the significance of this finding, we have not done anything that would affect the manufacturing operation. The university does not know that we know, as we watch and wait."

"Good idea, Absek. The manufacturing operation could be a source of funds for the terrorist organization. Let's keep what we know under our hats until just the right time."

"Yes, sir. In the meantime, I will send you the contact information for our medical examiner and poison expert on our case. Your people can start a dialogue with them about the technical comparisons of the poisonings and begin to tie the cases together even more."

"Thank you, Absek."

"One more thing on this university connection. You mentioned it could be a source of funds for Technolibertat. Given the financial records Aldora sent us, we were able to track the flow of money from Pharmatek to the three banks she identified. It is a major source of income for the organization. There are millions of dollars coming in!"

"Continue to watch and wait, Absek. As we said last time, ease up on the search for Kharif or Kumat or whatever his name is. We want them to think they are safe for now. Also there are no doubt legitimate needs for the drug and a lot of innocent people involved in its manufacture. We have to be careful."

"Yes, and it is in Syria, of course. You can be sure we'll be careful."

"Absek, I talked to Mr. Blackstone about the new detonation product that doesn't work. Do you know him very well?"

"Only by name and reputation. Great technical mind and even as CEO he still runs most of the R&D operations. He has his hands in a lot of the direct management of the company and is as hard-working and honest as they come."

"Well, that's right and he had this gut feeling about Technology Investment Corporation and their involvement in the testing of his top-secret, acoustics detonation technology product. It was a bad feeling, one of those 'this stuff is almost too good to be true' feelings. Anyway, he decided to take things into his own hands to protect his product. If it got into the wrong hands, he was going to make sure it didn't work."

"What did he do to the product, Director?"

"Now you should know that I just found this out so don't blame me. As I understand it, he changed the activation codes so they are unique for each experimental product. The code is stamped on the outside of the box. In addition, he switched the chip sets in the generators with the ones in the modulators. The outside packaging makes them look identical but they are much different inside. In essence, you have to use a new activation code and switch the two chip sets, Absek. Does that make sense?"

"Perfectly, sir. Why weren't we told about this before? We have spent a lot of time trying to get these damn things to work."

"I know but remember he was just trying to do the right thing for the right reason. There is one more aspect to the case that you need to know, Absek. The RFID tags and special software that TIC used to help CMT track the product were embedded into their intranet. Its program design/code allows it to absorb and use almost all of the company information. We believe it is only a step away from being able to take control of the company. Its nasty stuff but the bottom line is that Mr. Kharif/Kumat, Omar Kharif and maybe others have full access to ATP's intranet. We have decided to leave the software embedded and use it to our advantage. The idea is to make them believe we don't know they have access first and then later provide information that will allow us to know their next moves. Maybe with that we can locate and capture them and bring down this organization."

"Director, I think the DoAT is getting as devious as the Mossad. This is real progress!"

"We are feeding them two pieces of information already so they will have confidence we don't know about their access. We are telling them via an employee announcement, that the Kramley family was found dead at their home and that there is currently an active police investigation of the matter. Also, we told them, through a Blackstone email to the head of his Israel operation, about the new activation codes for each of the experimental products. His email will read that CMT people are to contact you and let you know about the code changes. If you would, just thank them and accept the information without a lot of discussion, more or less as though you are glad you hadn't started testing yet and this will help save time."

"Yes, sir, I understand what you are trying to do. It is a great plan and we will do our best to help."

"Thank you, Absek. I knew I could count on you. One last thing, don't test the experimental product too diligently; there is a second generation product coming that will be much more advanced. You will be impressed with the improvements."

"I can't wait, sir, we need these DT products now. The lives of our troops and civilians depend on it."

"We know, Absek. Thank you, my friend, and goodbye for now."

"Goodbye, sir; always good to talk with you."

New Developments

"Hello, Jack."

"Hello, Director, I am sorry, but we have more bad news. One of the technicians died and we are not sure the other one is going to make it."

"What happened, Jack?"

"Same thing that happened to Thomas and his family. Massive bleeding in and around the brain. The doctors could not get it stopped. The doctors think the technicians were exposed to a lower dose of the poison, because of air oxidation on the comic books, but it was enough."

"Jack, the reason I called is to give you the contact information for the medical personnel in Israel. They have identified the poison and may be able to suggest some better ways to treat the bleeding. Please get with Mary and Andrew and make the call. It could mean the difference between life and death of the second technician. Do you have your Blackberry?"

"I do. Send the number right away and we'll call immediately."

"Good luck. Call me back after afterwards so we can talk about the fingerprints."

"Got it, sir. I'll call you after we finish talking with the Israeli medical personnel."

"Thanks Jack. Goodbye."

"Goodbye, sir."

It seemed like a long time but Jack was able to call the director back in about an hour saying, "I think they are going to be able to save the second technician. After the doctors learned the poison is a more potent derivative of Warfarin, a new treatment regimen was started. It is beginning to work already. Thank you for the contact information."

"Good news about the technician, Jack. It seems that the pieces of our case are fitting together more tightly all the time. Same organization, same people, same modus operandi. Please tell Aldora that Absek used the financial information she found to identify the flow of money from Pharmatek, who makes the poison/

pharmaceutical for several big drug companies, to the banks in Syria, Jordan, and Iran. He accounted for millions and millions of dollars and concluded this is how they fund Technolibertat. Tell her 'good work' from both Absek and me!"

"I will, sir. The evidence against TIC/Technolibertat is beginning to mount up. Did you find fingerprints for Mr. Kharif so we can check them with those found on the plastic bag? We have checked several more obscure fingerprint data bases and still came up with no match."

"I thought that might be the case. Omar is smart and obviously, he has never been arrested. Jack, is anybody at the Kramley house right now?"

"Yes, one federal and one local crime scene investigators. They are doing additional work, trying to find more evidence."

"Good. I just ran one of my data augmented adaptive reasoning software scenarios on the comic books. The computer is telling me that these were probably not the first gifts Omar gave Thomas for his son. Have the agents check the boy's room for something that looks like a recent gift. Maybe even books on sports, science fiction, or more Superhero comics. I'll hold on while you call the house and have them check. Jack, remember to tell them to be careful, not just because of the fingerprints but of course the poison potential."

"Hang on, sir."

After several moments, Jack said, "There were two more comic books in the boy's room. The federal agent has them in a plastic bag and is bringing them to the laboratory. How in the world did you come up with that idea?"

"It seems logical now that there would have been a prior gift."

"You used data augmented adaptive reasoning? What is that?"

"Yes, from my old days as a psychologist. It's a program where you can add new data and it will build some possible scenarios on both the past and the future."

"Is it similar to what TIC supplied CMT for its supply chain logistics and product tracking?"

"Actually not too dissimilar, Jack."

"Well, sir, as long as it is used for good purposes. If we can confirm these are Omar's fingerprints, it ties a pretty tight knot on the evidence package for our murder case."

"Yes, one more piece to the puzzle and it increases our ability to draw out the leader of this terrorist organization. Even with a fingerprint match, we have to foil their plot to continue their 'Campaign of Fear'."

"Yes, sir. I'll let you tell me about that when the time comes. Give us about an hour and we'll have an answer on the fingerprints."

"Thanks, Jack; you are one great investigative team leader. We'll talk soon. Goodbye."

"Thanks you sir, I appreciate that. Goodbye."

The Fingerprint Match

"Hello, Jack, that was fast."

"Director, your idea about the other comic books was right on. Even though the boy had smudged most of the other prints, we found two that were definite matches with the ones on the plastic Ziploc bag. And, thank God there was no poison on these comic books."

"I know what you mean, Jack. Please go back to Thomas's 'Chronicle of Events' and see if there is a mention of comic books as a gift. It seems from your description that Thomas was very thorough. If it's there, we have direct evidence the prints are Omar's."

"Hold on, sir. I have a copy of Thomas's event chronicle with me. Yes, a gift, two Superhero comic books for his son from Omar given to Thomas at the Squealing Pig restaurant. It was about the time they were making the final arrangements to start the third field test."

"Then we have him, Jack. That is direct evidence that he gave the comic books as gifts twice. The last comic books were laced with a poison that killed the Kramley family and a technician at the local CSI laboratory. By the way, any further word on the other technician?"

"Yes, sir, I wanted to know and I knew you would ask. He continues to make improvement. The hemorrhaging has stopped and he is somewhat alert. The doctors believe there will be no permanent damage and he will make a complete recovery."

"That is good news, Jack. Say, I want to review my copy of Thomas's 'Chronicle of Events'."

"Anything special you will be looking for?"

"Yes, these murders seem totally out of character for the profiles we have built on Omar. In fact, our profiles bring question to whether he believes in the charter of the organization or what he is being asked to do. He must be under extreme psychological pressure for him to go this far. Maybe I can read the 'Chronicle of Events' and see which personality Thomas was dealing with. And, if it changed, how and why it changed."

"Yes, sir, I think I'll leave the profiling to you and the other experts. The way I look at it is very simple. These motherfuckers have killed five people already, including one of their own, in order to carry out some devious plan to learn what we are dong to stop their 'Campaign of Fear'. They will stop at nothing to achieve their so-called success. Regardless of mismatches between the profile and actions or psychological pressures, I have no sympathy for the sons-of-bitches. When they start killing women, children, and innocent people, for whatever reason, I say, 'all gloves are off!' Sorry, sir, but that is how I feel. One more thing, doing it in a foreign country while we are at war is one thing but then callously bringing it here is a big mistake. We have to get the bastards no matter what their psychological make up."

"I agree wholeheartedly. I just want to use every possible tool to catch the bastards."

'Yes, sir, I know, sir. I wasn't questioning your intent."

"Keep working hard on pulling the evidence on the case together. Tell Aldora that if I have a say, she gets to litigate this one."

"Okay, sir, she'll be excited about that. I'll keep you posted on any news."

"Thank you, Jack, and take care."

"Goodbye, sir."

The Liberator and Omar Talk

The call coming in was from the Liberator. Omar was frightened because it had been several days and he had not seen or heard anything about San Francisco. He thought, that is going to be his first question and I don't have an answer. "Hello, Liberator."

"Hello, Omar. I see that you must have done good work in San Francisco."

"I think so sir, but …"

"Yes, it was on their intranet. I was scanning through the confidential company communications to all employees. It was there amongst the news about sales, profits, new products, etc. The note said simply.. *Thomas Kramley, his wife, and son were found dead in their home recently. There is an active police investigation to determine the cause of their deaths. Thomas, Director of Logistics and Supply Chain had been with the company for 25 years.* Son, I'm glad you realized what was best for our organization and our cause."

"Yes, sir. It was an elaborate plan that I thought would work but I still feel bad it had to involve his wife and son."

"The note said his wife and son had lengthy medical illnesses. They may suspect this was a family suicide."

"Yes, sir, but remember, a team of investigators is there. And, they may have asked for additional help by now too. How easy is it to detect the poison after exposure to air or in the body?"

"Not easy at all. It oxidizes in air and degrades or decomposes in the body over time. Even the best chemists will have difficulty identifying the active ingredient. If they can't do that, it is against both state and federal law to officially make a determination of death by poisoning. Use our contact there to see if we can get more information and keep checking the newspapers. For some reason it has not been in there yet."

"Yes, sir. My thinking is that even if they find the active ingredient and determine it to be poisoning, the investigation will take a long time. It would seem that connecting us to the poison would be very difficult."

"I worry that your thinking is flawed, Omar. Remember your brother died from this same poison. If the authorities working the Zefat case were doing their jobs, they may have gotten him to the hospital soon enough to identify the poison. If that happened, they are seeking out all sources of manufacture now."

"Do we manufacture it?"

"Yes, I set up a laboratory at the university to make it. It is a derivative of the old rat poison, Warfarin, which kills by blocking blood clotting. The anti-clotting properties of the new derivative are greater than 100 times more effective. Its oxidation and bodily degradation properties are very different. We sell most of the product to the drug companies as Warfarin D. The drug companies dilute it further and sell it as a blood thinner. We keep the rest stockpiled in vials or capsules for our own private use. The money from our business with the big pharmaceutical companies finances most of the cost of our operations for both Technolibertat and TIC. The problem is that there is only one manufacturer so they will probably find it fairly soon. When they do, they will start making connections to your brother, you, the organization, and me. There are increasing risks for us now and our source of income may have been marginalized. We must be very careful."

"I understand, sir. My plan is to stay away from CMT and San Francisco for a while and concentrate efforts on Tully Research and ATP."

"I agree. When you get the Tully information, be sure to get in touch with Dr. Bromcast right away. The ATP project may be floundering. I think this new technology may actually rescue it. At the same time, it could get us on the inside. Act quickly and stay focused but remember you'll be watched because of all that has happened at CMT. Also, expect to be brought in for questioning about the details of the Kramley deaths and details of the M2DAS system testing."

"I would dread that."

"I know. If it is just questioning, it only means they don't have anything concrete. Be pleasant but don't tell them anything."

"Yes, sir."

"Omar, there is good news in all that is happening. Your work getting the M2DAS system embedded into CMT's intranet and giving us access to their corporate information looks like it is going to be invaluable. Besides the information on the Kramley family death, I was able to find one other juicy piece of news."

"I thought they would remove the software because of my connection with Mr. Kramley. Obviously, it is still functioning and allowing us to monitor what is going on at the company. What else did you find?"

"I found an email from Blackstone to the head of their operation in Israel. It was marked confidential and said: *Each product in the experimental lot shipped to Zefat has a unique activation code that is stamped on the outside of its box. Please communicate this to our customer as they prepare for field-testing.*"

"Does that affect how we reverse engineer the unit you were able to steal from the runway?"

"No, thank goodness! However, this kind of open communication tells me something very important."

"What is that sir?"

"Don't you see, Omar? They don't know that M2DAS gives us external access to their intranet….all of their test data, processes, policies, contracts, customers, and emails … everything. They don't know we have an in to everything the company does or is thinking about doing. I'm sure there will be more on the Kramley case and who knows what else coming along soon. We can get it all!"

"I had sort of forgotten about that capability, sir. You are right; the software gives us access to the whole intranet after it's embedded. As I remember, it is also just a step away from being able to control the CMT intranet."

"Who developed this for us, Omar?"

"It was actually freelanced by a virtual software genius who is now at ATP, Lyncoln Fuller. You met him with me at MIT several years ago."

"I don't remember him but it sounds like you were able

315

to recruit him successfully. This data augmentation software is phenomenal. Do you think he could write the code for the control aspect we might need at the next company?"

"I think so. He implied as much when he delivered the DAS to me."

"Would you make contact with him again and get him started on the project?"

"I believe he is one of the team leaders on the special project at ATP."

"What? Have you tried to get information from him about the project?"

"No, not yet. You have to know Lyncoln, sir. He was not recruited in the true sense of the word. What he did for us was for money, not loyalty or belief in our mission or anything like that. No blind following by this guy. My thinking was that once we were licensing technology to ATP, I could get closer to him. We would be more like partners then. Don't you think that would work better?"

"Maybe so. I'll have to trust your judgment on this, Omar. Somehow, we have to get him working on the data augmentation and control software. Shall we call it DACS?"

"A good acronym, sir."

"Omar, I have to go now. Please focus your efforts on Tully and ATP. Get the wave generation equipment from TRI and make a deal with ATP through Bromcast. Convince this Lyncoln to work on DACS for us and give us additional information about the special project. I will keep an eye on the Kramley investigation and the detonation product development at CMT."

"I'll do my best, sir. Praise be to Allah."

"Praise be to Allah."

Omar finished the call and leaned back in his chair. He wondered how long before the feds would come knocking on his door. He asked himself, Should I be working to save the organization and al Qaeda or to save myself? What would happen to me if I said I wanted out? He remembered what his father has said, "You are weak, Omar! You are weak and unskilled!"

Chapter 13

Lyncoln Agrees to Develop DACS
And
L-RED and DT-A2 Programs Start

Omar Talks With Lyncoln about DACS

Omar called Lyncoln soon after talking with the Liberator "Hello, Lyncoln. I thought I would call and let you know your data augmentation software system is really working well in a recent test installation."

"Oh yeah, where are you testing it?"

"That is confidential information Lyncoln, but I can tell you something about the application."

"That would be great, Omar."

"It was combined with an advanced RFID tag to help track highly valuable product as it traveled an intricate supply chain from here to an international location. At one point, the pallet of product was accidentally dropped and DAS was able to take information from the RFID sensors and make a judgment on damage to the product. It worked perfectly! In fact, the user was so impressed they asked that it be left embedded a while longer until they make their decision on buying a license from us. Your technology is going to be worth a lot of money to us, Lyncoln."

"I'm glad it is working so well. I knew it would. Maybe I didn't charge you enough money."

"That could be, Lyncoln. Would you be interested in

another contract?"

"I'm pretty busy with the project at ATP, but I guess I have a little extra time. What is it you need this time, Omar?"

"We need the next and final step in the DAS system. The one you referred to as *control*. Would you take that on for us, Lyncoln?"

"You want the control piece? That's the 'Holy Grail' Omar, or whatever its counterpart would be in your religion. It is very, very difficult if not impossible to do."

"But you could probably do it?"

"Probably, maybe, I don't know. There are only two or three people in the world who could even think about taking this on."

"And you are one of them, of course."

"Yes, but …"

'We would be willing to pay handsomely for the work."

"That's a given. I have a friend; one of those two or three people in the world who could even think about taking this on, that might be interested in helping. He just started a new company, Tully Research, Inc. Do you know Dr. Bradford Tully?"

"Of course I do. We are the largest investor in TRI and have a great relationship with Dr. Tully. He is providing some technology to us that ATP may be interested in licensing."

"Yes, I have been hearing about the acoustics technology. Boy, do we need that for our special government project and soon. We have a consulting agreement with Dr. Tully already so maybe I could sort of unofficially fold the control work into his consulting agreement."

"Whatever works so that the two of you could work on this together. We are thinking about calling it DACS. Is that alright?"

"Sure, if you mean data augmentation and control software."

"Yes, that's it."

"Are you saying it would be fine with you to bring in Dr. Tully without divulging all of the details to him? With Tully we can cut the development time and boost the chance of success dramatically."

"Yes, do it, bring him in anyway you choose. Would you also give me an idea what this might cost?"

"Omar, please sit down, get on your computer and check out the cost of a mainframe computer in the class of IBM's Blue Gene. Multiply that by two and that's what it will cost to hire the two people in the world who can do this project. Just between us, that is a bargain, a real bargain." Lyncoln could hear Omar's computer working.

Finally, Omar said, "$200 million dollars? Is that how much we are talking?"

"Yes, sir, give or take a little."

"You have yourself a deal, Lyncoln. I'll get the money to you in the usual way. Let me know if you and Brad need any other help with the project. Thank you very much and it will be good doing business with you again."

"Same here, Omar, thank you."

The phone clicked dead and Lyncoln thought about the money. Two hundred million and it didn't even faze him! I hope the director is right about Technolibertat's finances.

$200 Million In Advance

Lyncoln went to see Chad right after his discussion with Omar about the so-called control project or now Data Augmentation and Control Software (DACS) project.

"Chad, he contacted me about the project already."

"Do you mean Omar?"

"Yes, Omar. He told me about the success of DAS and how the customer probably wants to license the technology. So much so that he has left the software embedded in their intranet for further testing."

"What did you tell him?"

"I told him that if I could bring Brad in to help, we would do it. There were lots of caveats, however. I told him only two or three people in the world are capable of taking this on. I am one and Brad is another. Compared to DAS a lower percentage chance of success would apply. The work needs to be off the books so Brad thought it would be part of his consulting contract but it really wasn't, and it would cost a lot of money, about $200 million."

"$200 million? Lyncoln, I want to get both Brad and the director on the line so they can hear this. Can you hang on a second?"

"Of course."

The director was first on, then Brad.

"Lyncoln is with me after having just talked with Omar about starting the control project as an extension of M2DAS."

Brad said, "For Christ sake, this guy doesn't know when to run for cover."

Lyncoln said, "I know and he didn't bring up anything about what is really going on at CMT."

The director said, "Good, because he and the rest of them think they are safe. Our deception is working very well. What price did you agree to do the work?"

"Good question, Director. I didn't know what to ask for so I did a seat of the pants calculation while I talked to him. Brad, you will like this, too, I told him it would be the price of two 50-rack main frame computers in the class of IBM's Blue Gene."

Brad said, "You told him $200 million?"

"Yep. And, in advance."

The director said, "Good God, what did he say?"

"He said, 'You've got yourself a deal, Lyncoln. I'll get the money to you in the usual way.' I'll tell you what that means sometime later. It's a little bank account I have offshore."

The director said, "He'll pay $200 million in advance? He must have had prior approval to spend almost anything to get this. I cannot believe it. This will drain their reserves to almost nothing and if I can stop production at Pharmatek, they will have no money at all for their operations."

"Omar has always paid promptly so I expect the money to be there within the day," said Lyncoln.

"Chad, I want to get busy and have the Pharmatek production and Technolibertat's cash flow shut down. Will you work with Lyncoln and Brad to help set up the program on DACS and a mechanism to communicate progress both internally and to TIC?"

"Yes, sir, I will."

"Also, Lyncoln and Brad, be very careful. We have talked about the potential danger. For now, you are keys to their success and part of a huge investment they have made to protect their 'Campaign of Fear'. I suspect things could change at any moment. My people will be on watch continuously but you should be alert to signs from Omar or even Patek if you are contacted by him."

Lyncoln said, "Yes, sir."

Brad said, "Is there anything we should do, specifically?"

"Yes, on the DACS project, always have it planned out to work together. Keep the results, the real results of your work known to only a few select people. I want you to make progress but at the same time make it look like it is an impossible challenge to TIC and Omar. Last, Lyncoln, let us help you take care of the money so there is no chance they could try to get it back."

"Yes, sir, would you please? I'll get the information about the account to your office immediately."

Chad said, "Thank you, sir, these are good suggestions. I'll plan to help Lyncoln and Brad implement them."

"Thank you, Chad. I'll talk to you guys a little later. Goodbye."

They responded in unison, 'Goodbye, Director."

The OffShore Account

The director called his friend in the Treasury Department about the money in Lyncoln's offshore account.

"Hi, Doug, how are things going with your new job?"

"Very well, Sam. I have learned that adding about twelve zeros to the numbers I was used to in regular business helps a lot."

"Is the investment banking experience you have allowing for a different perspective on government securities and how they are managed?"

"Some, Sam, but basically it's the same deal just more

conservative investments, lower risk levels, and of course lower returns."

"Safety in your investments is sometimes the most important aspect of a portfolio. There are a lot of crazy things happening in the world that can impact stocks, bonds, precious metals, and commodity markets. Don't you agree?"

"Most definitely and it's one of the main reasons I took this job. With my background in hedge funds, diverse investment vehicles, and managing risk, I might be able to maintain the safety level of our investments but raise the return considerably. Do you know what an extra 1% would do for our investors and the Treasury?"

"Not exactly, but I am rapidly adding the twelve zeros. I get the idea, Doug, but it will probably be slow going with the existing conservatism in the Department. I can just imagine the eyes glazing over when you start talking about collateralized debt packages, futures trading, option markets, and currency exchange rates."

"Yes, Sam, it happens but there are more and more of us here everyday able to think about things differently."

"If anyone can make some changes for the better, it is you, buddy. I admire you for taking on a huge challenge."

"Thanks Sam, I appreciate that. You called for a reason, but I have to ask you about your new job, too. How is it going with Advanced Technology and catching the bad guys?"

"We are too slow, Doug. I feel like we are in the wake just collecting dead bodies as we try to identify, locate, and apprehend the terrorists. I have a case in which five people have been killed already and there may be more. If we can somehow get ahead of the terrorists to protect ourselves first and then begin to work with the various country leadership teams to resolve real differences, we can make some progress. Today we are playing catch up and reacting to the terrorist's program to destroy our way of life - and us. We never get a chance to be with the real people."

"I bet the background in psychology and that AAR stuff will help to get ahead of the terrorists. Remember when you worked with me on alternative energy hedges and came up with the future importance of ethanol as a blend with gasoline? It was five years in the future, nobody believed you, including my colleagues, but I convinced our CEO to make significant strategic investments. You know the rest of the story. Ethanol took off, I became the next CEO, and the company made a fortune."

"AAR has helped already, but I need to train more people to use it in their work. I know you are busy, Doug, so can I get to the real reason for my call?"

"Of course, Sam."

"For confidential reasons, I'll use general descriptions of the situation. I have a team leader who is part of a large government contract at ATP. This scientist, at my direction, has taken on some side work to develop special software for a terrorist organization. He required payment up front because the work is so specialized and he is recognized as one of the few world experts in the field. The terms were met and an advance payment of $200 million has been deposited into his offshore account. We believe that the transfer of monies occurred without full approval within the terrorist organization. Can they do anything to reverse the transfer and get the money back?"

"So, the money is now in this ATP scientist's offshore account?"

"Yes and verified by electronic confirmation."

"Do you trust the scientist and is he safe from harm's way?"

"What do you mean?"

"All kinds of things could happen if the terrorists have access to him. They could strike another deal to take the money back and pay more but in installments based on performance milestones. Or, they could just resort to old-fashioned torture to get to his account. Any chance of those happening?"

"Yes, I am afraid so. What should we do?"

"First, install a second lock on the account. The scientist will have to agree. Have a second set of password and personal identification codes assigned immediately. You should know his password and code but he should not know yours. Second, put this scientist under constant watch to ensure his safety. With $200 million at stake, people tend to do strange things."

"Sounds good to me. Doug, thank you very much. I will get your recommendations implemented as soon as possible. Good luck with the 1% and the twelve zeros!"

"You are welcome, Sam, and thanks for the update on your work. Let's stay in touch. Goodbye."

"Goodbye, Doug."

Wave Generation Equipment Reports and Data

Brad was on the phone to Omar soon after returning from Boston. "Hello, Omar."

"Hello, Dr. Tully, I hope you have good news for me about the technology."

"I do, Omar. First, you know I have a consulting agreement with ATP to work on one of their top priority projects."

"Yes, I do. Mr. Patek Kumat and I have discussed this. We believe it is on the same project where they need this new technology and we are okay with that."

"That's good; that's excellent. I have just come back from a trip to ATP and your assessment is correct. They are pretty much at a standstill and really need this technology. I can't help them so much with what they have but I can help them implement Tully technology. It may be the only way the project will survive. TIC and you, as the major investor in TRI, will be able to license the technology to them and be lifesavers in the process."

"It sounds like we could be co-lifesavers, Dr. Tully. This is great. How soon can I get the technical information on acoustical wave generation and the prototype equipment?"

"Omar, I changed my mind from when we talked before. To speed things up, I've decided to send both the equipment and the manual to your D.C. address today. The other technical reports and data packages are ready to be sent electronically right now. I just wanted to ask if you need anything else before I push the button."

"Thank you. I appreciate the timeliness in getting this ready. I know you have been very busy. May I ask a question, please? Did you get to meet Dr. Chadly Bromcast and Dr. Mike Jackson at ATP?"

"Yes, I did. Chad runs the project and reports to Mike. They both say they need this new technology ... and now. I think it will be an easy sell and it helps that I will be there to get it implemented."

"Do you believe Dr. Bromcast is truly convinced?"

"There is no doubt in my mind."

"In that case, I don't believe there is anything else needed. Push the send button and let's get this rolling."

"Very good, Omar; it's on its way."

"Thank you, Dr. Tully. I'll be in touch after my meeting with Dr. Bromcast."

"Goodbye, Omar."

"Goodbye, Dr. Tully."

Licensing The Tully Technology

"Dr. Bromcast, this is Omar Kharif from Technology Investment Corporation."

"Hello, Mr. Kharif. I hoped you would be calling soon. Dr. Jackson, my boss, told me he had been in discussions with Mr. Kumat about the possible licensing of the Tully Acoustic Wave Generation Technology through TIC. And, of course we have a consulting agreement with Dr. Tully."

"Yes. I will have the prototype equipment shortly but in the meantime I thought you might like to have a sample of the technical reports and data packages."

"I would, Mr. Kharif. Thank you very much. We have heard a lot about the advanced, even breakthrough, characteristics of the technology, but only in general terms. It would be beneficial to see details so we can begin to compare it to our in-house acoustics technology and work to appraise it with respect to our special government project."

"Great. I will send the materials to you right away. You will see immediately that the Tully technology is the best acoustics technology in the world. Remember, this is only the wave generation part of an entire portfolio of licensable technology. There are many others that you might be interested in, including bounce-back, returning wave capture, wave analysis, miniaturization, and computer data analysis."

"You are correct; we may be interested in more than wave generation. It's a good place for us to start a relationship with you and have it build with time and our success with the technology."

"We look forward to building that relationship. I will send the technical materials today along with a license agreement between TIC and ATP. It will be a non-exclusive and you'll see the cost is very reasonable. There can either be an upfront payment for a five-year license with an option to renew or you can elect to pay a royalty fee based on a percentage of the sales volume of your product. I am sure you have seen many license agreements like this."

"Thank you, Mr. Kharif. I look forward to receiving the materials from you."

"Once you have signed the license agreement, I will send the rest of the technical information to you immediately along with the prototype equipment. With these and a little of Dr. Tully's help, you will be able to implement the technology rapidly. The special government project will benefit greatly."

"Thank you, Omar. I am glad there are companies like yours that are willing to help on government projects to ensure the safety of our country. I hope we can do business together."

"Thank you, Dr. Bromcast. Please give Mr. Jackson best regards from me and Mr. Kumat."

"I will. I'll be in touch after we review the materials and make our licensing decision. Goodbye for now."

"Goodbye, sir."

Chad hung up the phone and thought, I think we have pulled them into the net – hook, line, and sinker. The plan is working!

The Prototype Equipment Arrives

Omar was deep in thought. It had been more than a week since he had talked with Dr. Tully about the prototype acoustics wave generation equipment. It had arrived that next day in a box smaller

THE CAMPAIGN OF FEAR

than he expected. In short order, he had read all of the technical reports and data package materials available and was thoroughly confused by the technical mumbo jumbo. Just looking and handling the piece of equipment had not provided any further enlightenment either. It looked like an oversized ray gun; so much so that he had been almost afraid to pick it up. When he did, he found it to be heavier than he imagined, but very simple in design with controls only for distance, a small dial, and firing by a trigger. He had said at the time, here I am a businessman playing Flash Gordon. Then there was the recurring thought about his father saying, "Omar, you are weak and unskilled." Weak and unskilled? I had just killed three people in probably one of the most ingenious plans ever devised. They will never figure it out. And I have recently obtained the most sophisticated wave generation equipment available to help preserve our 'Campaign of Fear'.

A call shook him out of his deep thoughts. "Hello, Sci-1, how are the testing and reverse engineering jobs on the wave generation equipment going?"

"Hello, Mr. Kharif. I must say that I had some doubts about a team this size working together effectively but they did it. They really did it! The ten people you brought in are all top-notch scientists. We owe you and Technology Investment Corporation immensely for our scholarships and fellowships during school. That and the extra bonus for this work helped us focus on getting the job done."

"Are you really finished Sci-1?"

"Yes, sir, my report will indicate just what fantastic technology this is. The acoustics technology is way beyond anything any of us has ever seen. No one had thought about using it this way before but the theory is based on simple echo principles. As in echoes, the special sound is produced and bounced back but here one can control the wave dissipation so it returns as a uniquely identifiable wave that has been formed by the actual environment it has experienced. This holds for distances of maybe several hundred feet. We believe it would be possible to recover the wave contents and identify chemical materials using known standards. Who knows what else? I guess theoretically one could acoustically analyze the new unique wave and study its component wave makeup, too. Anyway, yes, we are finished. Our team could design and set up manufacturing for any number of units you would require. They are sure you will make a mint selling the product or licensing the technology."

"Very good, Sci-1. What about the additional project I asked you to handle alone?"

"Yes, how to defend against it? I don't know a way yet. An analogy might be in submarine warfare. To avoid being pinged, you throw out all kinds of debris in hopes the sound waves get deflected and cannot get through to the real target. But, once pinged, about all you can do is take evasive action. The ideas I am working on involve the concepts of somehow staying out of range so you can't get pinged and developing sensors to know when you have been pinged and to take evasive action."

"The sensors sound like a good idea, Sci-1. What kind of evasive action might one take?"

"Just because they find you doesn't mean they have a way to immediately detonate the EFPs or the suicide explosives prematurely. If we can't find a way to counteract the so-called CIED maybe we can find a way to crack the new detonation technology I've heard of, the type called DT-A1. Do you know about it?"

Omar smiled and said, "I guess one way or the other we'll find something. Keep working on it, Sci-1, and get more help if you need it."

"I will, sir. Our advantage is in knowing what they are doing and that only close-in explosives detection is possible. We'll have to change some things we do and evolve better ways to defend ourselves but in the end, these advancements may not materially affect our 'Campaign of Fear'."

"Sci-1, you are a real scientist and a loyal member of our organization. Do you believe in liberty through technology and the things we are doing?"

"Omar, you and I have been friends for a long time and your brother, Praise be to Allah, and I even longer. Sometimes I feel the costs are too high, like losing Emar. Sometimes I feel technology cannot be our sole provider of freedom and liberty. We are too far behind and it will be impossible to catch up. Time is not supposed to be a factor in our thinking but it constantly creeps into my mind. Our lives are short and I value every second I have with my wife and children. What happened one thousand years ago or will happen one thousand years from now does not get a lot of my attention when I consider my life here and now. I'm glad I can help when you ask me because of my special training, but you must know, I do not volunteer. I do it because we are friends and Emar was my friend. But I have many American friends, too, just as you do. It is all too obvious that my feelings about these people are different from my regard for those back home. Do you think we are doing the right things, Omar?"

"I just don't know. The things I have been asked to do are troubling me greatly too. It was okay to bribe workers, steal technology, or even eliminate some difficult people. However, when we start eliminating people indiscriminately because they are in our way or for no good reason at all, we may have crossed the line. I now have the blood of women and children on my hands."

"I am sorry, Omar. I, too, feel there is something wrong with our direction. There must be a better way."

"Pray for me, Sci-1. I will need it. In the meantime, let me know if you come up with any ideas to defend more directly against CIED. Work on those sensors, too, as they could be quite valuable. Thanks for your help and for being a friend. Goodbye."

"Goodbye, Omar. Remember, if you need someone to talk to, I'm here."

"Thank you. Goodbye."

The Technology Licensing Agreement

Chad was deep in thought. He had signed the license agreement with TIC for the Tully Technology some time ago. It was a lop-sided deal favoring TIC of course. Whoever heard of a 25% royalty on the sales of all products using the technology? Anyway, the reason for doing this was not a financial one to benefit ATP but a military and homeland security one to benefit our country. Cost didn't matter when it is part of the plan to catch and put the terrorists away forever. The technical reports, data packages, manual and prototype equipment had arrived shortly thereafter. His team had been reviewing all of the technical information and Bill, specifically, had been testing the prototype wave generation equipment. Chad knew how hard this was on his team and especially Bill. To know that work you believed to be a breakthrough accomplishment had already been done several years ago was almost devastating. It was like plagiarizing, but without the help of a technical notebook or a written report or even a colleague-to-colleague discussion to draw from. Bill's reluctant assessment had been simply, "It does everything that mine does and more. I cannot believe he was or is this far ahead of me. This work was several years ago and today Brad has Generation II almost ready to go."

Zen, Kan D and Lyncoln could tell from the technical reports that Brad had also preempted them. He had actually sketched out key parts of what would be wave capture equipment, analyzers, miniaturization approaches and software code requirements in the future section of each report. Chad thought those would be the subjects of additional lopsided license agreements with TIC and TRI. If they could all suck up their disappointments at being scooped and start working on the new parallel program, their plan would work.

Chad thought the team could get past the scientific defeats but would they really agree to and want to work on someone else's technology for Generation II? Bill, Zen and Lyncoln seemed okay with it but he wasn't sure about Kan D.

Kan D had known Thomas, that was a fact. She had said that he had been instrumental in her getting a CMT fellowship at Michigan. She may have known him for several years but getting her to talk about it was a different thing. Chad knew Thomas's death really affected Kan D, but why? Could he get her back on track as they started the Generation II, L-RED program? Chad concluded he had a very touchy situation with the team leaders.

Bill come out as number two - or a loser - in the acoustical research race and had to swallow his pride and move on. Lyncoln had done research and development on the side for money and for a questionable company and wanted to do something to redeem himself. Zen with her building relationship with Brad Tully and its impact on her work, and Kan D with perhaps some kind of previous involvement with now deceased Thomas Kramley of CMT - or at least deeply affected by his death.

He had to get them started on L-RED as soon as possible regardless of these issues. The new space was ready now so he decided to call the team leaders together for an official kickoff of the new program.

L-RED Starts

Brad's Generation II equipment had arrived for the new L-RED program and was already positioned into the new lab space at ATP.

Only one with a very observant eye would notice that it was different from the CIED space. It was almost identical in size with the same center community space for the team leaders and four pie-shaped pieces radiating outward to the curved wall and windows. The idea of moving between buildings into and out of almost identical laboratory space would help the researchers with their deception. After all, the needs of the Generation II program weren't all that different. The wave gun would have to shoot farther and bounce-back more accurately but it still looked like a big gun. Of course, the wave capture vacuum equipment and computerized chemical analysis instruments would be gone. They would be replaced with a sophisticated sonic probe connected to a computer array whose job is to refine the wave articulation and identify the various sources from its components. Miniaturization would still be required and of course there would be more computers with more capacity and power. Chad knew Lyncoln would love that. In fact, after what he learned Lyncoln had done with M2DAS, Chad didn't think this work would be much of a challenge for him.

Chad was sorry that it had to be a quiet celebration and kick off but that was to be expected in government programs. He had the security guards hang a couple of banners. They were red, all red, meant to be a play on the program name, L-RED. A cake and juice were sitting on a table in the middle and Rocky Balboa theme music was coming from the public address speakers. As if on cue, the team leaders walked in at 8 AM, exactly when the music started. Chad saw them head for the refreshment table with big grins on their faces. He had poured the juice and was cutting the cake and smiling, too.

Chad said, "This is for the best four team leaders in the world." He handed each of them a drink and a piece of cake and proposed a toast. "To success in L-RED and our deception. May what we do here save lives and bring terrorists to justice!"

The four said, "Here, here!"

Chad said, "This program requires that we become the closest team that ever worked together. We must listen more, see more, understand more, open up more, demand more, and team more. We must be less prejudiced, less self-centered, less negative, less outside-of-the-project focused, less complex, and less critical of others."

The Rocky music continued so it was hard to talk and be heard. As the music faded, Bill was the first to speak, "Chad, the four of us met for about an hour this morning already. We all felt that it was necessary to renew our commitment to the war on terror and fighting the terrorists' 'Campaign of Fear'. You can depend on us 110%!"

"Thanks to all of you. I knew I could count on you."

Zen said, "The consensus was that this new project is different from CIED in which we were doing both R&D at the same time. Brad's work on the research part has made this more of a development project and much easier. It is always an uphill battle when you must develop both the technology and the new product at the same time."

"This is true and you were selected for the awards and this project because of your abilities to do both. Brad's work is a starting place that will allow you to establish a fast track development effort. We may be able to complete the product work for L-RED almost as fast or faster than what we had planned for CIED."

Lyncoln said, "As long as we aren't pulled away for whatever reason to help with something else." The group nodded their acknowledgment. They knew he was referring to possible work relating to extending the M2DAS software to include host control features. Then he said, "You know, that's the old Lyncoln. The new Lyncoln says I will do whatever needs to be done to make our project successful, catch the terrorists, and close their operation."

The group responded by applauding Lyncoln. His face flushed and one could notice a slight tinge of embarrassment in his reaction.

Kan D was crying. Chad noticed first. "Kan D, what is the matter?"

"I'm sorry. I need to tell you a family secret. Thomas Kramley and his family were very special to me. Long before Thomas was able to provide a fellowship for me through CMT, he was my friend. We met my first year at Michigan when he came with grants and fellowship money from CMT. I could barely speak English and wasn't a candidate for fellowship monies, but he sat and listened to me. He didn't have to do that but he was a good man. I told him about my family in China, only an older sister, because the rest of my family had been killed during the Cultural Revolution as being too intellectual and innovative. My sister wanted to come to the U.S. but needed a sponsor. I showed him her pictures and we talked. Finally, you know me; I asked if he could help. He said he would look into it and asked for her picture, background information, education, address, and contact information. They shared letters back and forth. They fell in love even though a great distance apart and never meeting one another face to face. Thomas was able to find a position for her at CMT, as a physicist, and they sponsored her to come as a foreigner with critical skills needed by the company. They immediately married. That was more than ten years ago. Disappointingly, we grew far apart over the years but this Omar and TIC and gang of terrorists have killed my sister, brother-in-law, and nephew. They were the only relatives I had left in this world. It probably would have been safer to stay in China!"

"Kan D, we are all so sorry; we had no idea. We all know

how hard it was to tell us about this."

"If you thought I was hesitant about the project, erase that from your minds. I just want to get these fanatic barbarians," added Kan D.

Zen said, "Of course, I remember you said Thomas gave you the nickname, Kan D. What I couldn't figure out was why a grant coordinator would get so familiar. It makes sense now and I love his play on your name, Kan Deng."

"I do have a sweet tooth, you know."

Chad said, "You'll notice that we have two filled candy dishes just like in the other building."

"Thank you, Chad."

Chad looked at the four team leaders, beamed, and finally said, "This is what I meant about getting together and becoming the closest team to ever handle a top priority government project. Our future depends on it so let's kick some ass!"

Everybody came to hug Kan D and each other, too. The race was on and they knew who the winners were going to be already. No one could beat the L-RED team now.

Each of the team leaders went to their section of the laboratory to see that everything was ready. As they made the tour, Chad could see the look of satisfaction on their faces, the thumbs- up signs and the nods of expectations filled. He said, as they collected at the center point, "How do things look?" Kan D said it all. "Right down to the candy dishes, WOW! It's time to get to work."

With that, the small group of five people, closer than they had ever been, let out a yell of togetherness and comradeship and team spirit with high fives all around, "YEA!!!!!"

Lyncoln's Payment

Omar put the call through. "Hello, Liberator."

"Hello, Omar, how are things going?"

"Sir, I want to report that I have contracted with Lyncoln to do the software work on control, what we are calling DACS."

"That is good, Omar, but first, is anything happening on the

West Coast with CMT? I haven't seen much on their intranet since we last talked."

"I have stayed away, sir, purposely. There has been no announcement in the papers about the deaths of Kramley and his family. No one has contacted me either. I think we are okay. If they thought it was anything but suicide, I would have been questioned by now, don't you think?"

"Yes, unless they are gathering evidence in a concerted attempt to bring some kind of federal case against our organization. Maybe something like foreign espionage or a similar charge. Also, they may have an agreement with the locals to keep things very quiet and out of the papers for a while. See if you can stay tuned in through your university contacts but be very judicious about discussing the subject."

"I will, sir; maybe someone has heard something."

"Now, what about DACS?"

"I signed Lyncoln to a contract to do this work recently. He has devised a way to have Dr. Tully of Tully Research, Inc., join him in the work. He said they were two of the only three people in the world who could take this on and have a chance of being successful. Do you know the term 'Holy Grail'? He called this the 'Holy Grail' of software development projects."

"I know the term, yes. It has to do with the cup their Jesus drank from shortly before his death on the cross. It has never been found and thus the reference to its value and the never-ending but as yet unsuccessful effort to find it. Was he trying to get more money?"

"I don't think so. He did mention that DAS was worth a lot more than he was paid. Especially since it had performed so well in the CMT field test. With the two highest-powered programmers working on this together and the challenge of the project, he said it would cost the price of two supercomputers like the IBM 'Blue Gene'."

"That sounds like a lot of money. I assume you negotiated with him for something reasonable."

"Actually, since I knew how important this was to you, I

did not negotiate. You told me more than once to get the project going and I took that to mean at almost any cost. How could I negotiate with Lyncoln and Dr. Tully? They hold the upper hand and I had no leverage. If Lyncoln had been perturbed or said no, there was nowhere else to go."

"Omar, how much did you agree to pay them for the job?"

"When we were talking about the job, Lyncoln told me to google Blue Gene, get the cost and multiple by two. I did that on line and found that a 50-stack Blue Gene was $100 million. The agreement was then $200 million to be paid in advance to his offshore account. The money has already been transferred and they have started the project. I think they will be successful."

"You paid what? A payment of $200 million will take our reserves down to almost nothing. You emptied our account without discussing this with me? How could you be so stupid?"

"It was the Holy Grail, Liberator. We had only one chance at it and I took it. I thought you would be proud of me."

"There are hundreds of people and projects that we sponsor to do our work. We have operating expenses, technology investment obligations, special project payments, scholarships, fellowships, and research grants that all have to be paid from our account. The major source of income is from our pharmaceutical business, as you know. If something happens to that income, we would have to close down. I don't think we could survive. How could you pay someone - anyone - $200 million in advance? Where are your brains?"

"Most of what we do is payment in advance: scholarships, fellowships and research grants, evaluation of selected technologies, IPO's like Tully Research, and independent research assignments. This just happened to be the biggest project ever for us, sir."

"Omar, I think you have put us in a very, very risky situation. Al Qaeda selected us for this project to help prolong the 'Campaign of Fear'. If we are not successful, or seen as weak and ineffective, they will seek retribution. You may have doomed our mission, our organization, and us in one fell swoop. I cannot imagine there could ever have been a worse decision."

"Sir, should we try to get the money back? We know a lot of people who have skills in the ins and outs of international banking. Maybe they could help us."

"Anything we do now will only draw more attention to us. I suspect they know a lot about us and our finances from the Kramley investigation. Your idea to reverse the transfer has merit, however. Let me see if someone can help us. If not, our only hope is that our pharmaceutical money keeps rolling in. Even with that, it will take several years to build back our reserves."

"Even if we cannot find someone to help us, nothing will happen to our blood thinner business, sir. You will see. This will turn out to be our greatest investment ever. The Holy Grail!"

"Omar, I will be coming to the States soon to visit. You obviously need some help managing our operation there. I'll let you know when I will make the trip; it will be very soon."

"Father, I can handle things here."

"I don't think so, Son. In the meantime, this is an order, go underground and become invisible. Make no other decisions on projects, investments, or people. As of today, you are relieved of duties as CEO of the Technology Investment Corporation."

"Father, I ..."

"My decision is final. I will visit you and evaluate the situation personally. We must decide how best to continue with TIC. Regardless, it's time for a change in your assignment. Before I arrive, it would be good for you to consider your future in Technolibertat. Maybe it is time for you to do something completely different. Goodbye, Son."

"Goodbye, Father."

Omar was shaking by the time the call ended. He thought he knew what his father's words meant because he had heard them before. Those other times, it was about someone else, distant and not so real. The result, however, was that those people disappeared, never to be seen or heard from again. His suspicion was always that his father took care of these jobs himself. How else could one be sure the job was done right? Do it yourself! His father thought like that a lot. That's why he worked in the field so much, running the pharmaceutical business and coordinating the Zefat theft. Would he come for him like those others? Omar's silent answer to his own question made his head spin. He cried, "Yes, he would."

DT-A1 and Technolibertat's Cash Flow

Thinking back, it had been a few days since the CMT local country VP for Israel had called. The conversation and events afterwards went something: "Hello, Sir, I have a message about the new detonation product. The message comes directly from our CMT president. How are you today?"

"I am fine," Absek said. "We did finally receive the experimental DT product shipment. Thanks for your help but it still took a little time to get it released from the Zefat airport by the local authorities. Our laboratory people are nearly ready to start testing the product."

"That is why I am calling, sir. It seems that for safety reasons and at the last minute in production, Blackstone incorporated a unique two-digit activation code for each box of product. The code is stamped on the outside of each box and must be used to unlock the product for testing. Also, the two chip sets have to be switched! If these are not done, the product will appear to be defective. I am glad you had not started testing, sir."

Absek had smiled and said, "Thank you very much for the information. Please tell Blackstone that his protective measures were well-founded after what happened at the airport."

"I will, sir. Good luck with the new DT product testing. We think the advancements using the new acoustics technology are very significant. Please let me know your results as soon as possible. I know how important a better product is to your operation and the safety of our people."

Absek said, "Of course, you will be the first to know about our test results. I appreciate your words of commitment and country loyalty. Thank you."

"Thank you, sir. Goodbye for now."

"Goodbye."

With that contact, Absek had walked directly to the laboratory manager and said, "You are not going to like what I'm about to tell you."

"What do you mean, sir?"

"You know the CMT product that we think is defective?"

"Yes, sir, we tried everything to make it work."

"Well, they made some changes in production, for safety reasons they say, to protect against the product being stolen. Not a bad idea based on what happened at the airport."

"What kind of changes, sir?"

"The CMT president made a change in the activation code for each product. The new two-digit code is stamped on the outside of the containers. You have to enter the unique code to unlock the safety mechanism. In addition, they switched the chip sets in the generators and the modulators. The outer wrappings of those two chip sets look identical; no one would ever have known. However, together or separately the changes acted to render the new product useless."

"I know that better than anybody, sir. All that work for nothing?"

"I know how you feel but it was done for the right reasons. The product could have been stolen."

Absek decided not to disclose that one box had been, in fact, stolen by the terrorists and instead said, "Anyway, we have the fixes now so start the testing program again immediately."

The lab manager said, "I will, sir. Sorry if I sounded negative. The CMT president must be some kind of clairvoyant."

"That and a technical genius, too. Just do a fast screen on the product first. I hear there is a Generation II coming that will be even better."

"Yes, sir, I will."

"Thank you and good luck. We need products like this in our battle with the terrorists."

Still thinking about the events, it was late the next day but he was still in his office when the lab manager burst in with the protocol test results, charts, and graphs bundled in both hands. He said, "I don't know how he did it but the new acoustics detonation technology product will work on every kind of explosive we have tested so far. We have tested EFPs, IEDs, and suicide bombs. It seems that the acoustic wave that is generated somehow matches the electronics signature of these crude devices and the vibrations created detonate them. We still have to know where the explosive is, within some reasonable area, but that's OK, right?"

"Sure. What kind of distances will it handle?"

"That is the only drawback we have noticed, sir. It works consistently only if we are within several meters. We would still have to wear body armor or use armed vehicles but it works on everything, everything! One device for everything!"

"This is quite an advancement. I wonder if the Generation II product will do long-range detonation." No matter, while they work on Generation II, we can use this product right away."

"I agree, sir, it will help a lot. Consider what it would be like if we had something that could detect or find explosive devices and combine it with this detonation tool. What a system that would be."

"And, what a blow to the terrorists' 'Campaign of Fear'. Bring our field coordinators in and let's teach them how to use our new weapon."

"Yes, sir. I'll order more product from CMT."

"Thank you," said Absek.

A call came in and Absek picked up, "Hello, Absek, this is Director Elson."

"Hello, Director. Your calls are always very timely, sir."

"How do you mean, Absek?"

"I was just reviewing our testing results of the new DT product and the results were way beyond our expectations."

"Joe is pretty good at this stuff, isn't he?"

"Pretty good? He is a genius. This new product will detonate everything within a distance of a few meters. It doesn't matter if they are EFPs, IEDs, mobile explosives, or what."

The director said, "You still have to know where it is so you know where to target and of course when to evacuate the area for safety."

"Yes, sir, but this is such an improvement over what we have today."

"I know and the next generation is coming."

"Yes, sir, but we are not going to wait. I have approved ordering more units from CMT and training our people to use the device."

"Good idea, Absek. I think we bought some time with the chip set switch. Even if the terrorists can reverse engineer it, the device still won't work. That lack of understanding means they will not be able to develop technology to combat or neutralize how it works in the field. By the time they figure it out, we will have made it obsolete with our Generation II product."

"I hope so, sir."

"Absek, can we change subjects? It sounds like you have an excellent plan for DT, Generation I."

"Of course, sir, it is probably why you called."

"Yes, it is about Technolibertat and TIC being funded through the sale of the Warfarin derivative produced by Pharmatek. We need to shutdown the source of the cash flow supporting these terrorist organizations. Do you have any ideas how to stop production at Pharmatek without hurting the university or the pharmaceutical companies and their patients?"

"The Massod has many ways to do this, Director. The university in Syria is state operated so we have no real legal power or authority there. Our ways would be as you say, 'off the books,' which is how we always operate outside Israel."

"You are talking about force, my friend. I would like this to be less obvious if possible. By the way, one of the big pharmaceutical companies that buys this drug from Pharmatek is located in Israel. It is Israpharm."

"I have an idea, sir. Why don't we, with the help of Israpharm, create a story that something is wrong with the drug? It has killed or at least made ill several patients. This will cause the other big pharmaceutical company customers who buy the drug from Pharmatek to stop ordering. Pharmatek will be dead in its tracks. Wrong choice of words, sir, but with no orders, Pharmatek is shut down and its cash flow for supporting the terrorists is terminated."

"It could work, Absek. Do the two of us have enough power to be able to convince Israpharm to help us?"

"Yes sir, people here don't question the Massod."

"Of course. It was a crazy question. With the good work your people did identifying the active ingredient that killed the pilot, I will have a contract manufacturer set up in the States to act as an approved second source. Tell Israpharm that they will have a continuing supply of blood thinner for all of their needs. We will be in touch with the other pharmaceutical companies and make sure they know not to order from Pharmatek and give them the new source of supply in the U.S."

"Good. I'll get with our contacts at Israpharm and set this up. It will be best if they communicate the bad news directly to Pharmatek."

"Absek, I think stopping the orders is the best way to shut them down. If we in the USA or Israel try to use force or some kind of legal mechanism, it would look bad to other countries. Do you know if Syria has our equivalent of the Food and Drug Administration?"

"I don't know, sir. I doubt it."

"I'll do some checking and through government channels try to have an international review of Pharmatek and its plant done. The very serious problem with its drug should initiate some action, don't you think?"

"I would think so, sir. Do you think we should try to protect the university as we implement our plan?"

"What are you thinking, Absek?"

"If there is a friend of Israel and the world in Damascus and Syria, it is the University. Pharmatek is in a leased building on University property but in our investigation, it has no real connection to the academic institution itself."

"It's a good point, Absek. I'll make sure the international body doing the review knows that. As we say here, we don't want one or two rotten apples to spoil the whole barrel."

"Thank you, sir."

"One more thing. We believe that Omar Kharif has been on a spending spree recently. There are significant funds going to new projects in software development as well as acoustics. There is good reason to believe Technolibertat's bank accounts will be drawn down considerably. With no money coming in from the sale of the blood thinner, they may become very desperate. One of the results may be to flush out the leaders of the organization. Have your people watch for Eomar Kharif/Patek Kumat and the people with whom he is dealing. Another result might be extreme action either there or here to strike back at what or who they believe has injured them. One last thought, they are working for al Qaeda, of course. Al Qaeda might decide to take their own action against an organization that has put them at risk. If that were to happen, we might get a chance at an al Qaeda leader. Please be prepared for all of these possibilities, my friend."

"I really like the third possibility, Director. The Massod is always ready so we would welcome the opportunity. I almost forgot – do you remember that our timeline indicates the professor left the University before his wife died and formed Technolibertat with his sons? Our sources have found more about his wife and how she died. It was said that a rogue agent, thought to have been hired by the CIA, had killed her. She was some kind of relative of Osama bin Laden and got caught up in helping him hide a couple nights when he was on the run. Anyway, the story goes, someone put out a contract on her and she was assassinated. The professor and his sons were at a soccer match or something at the time and found her dead when they returned. He was devastated. Later, when he found out how she supposedly died, it was said he vowed to seek revenge using all of his academic and technical skills and abilities. It was then that Technolibertat seemed to start the transformation to become a terrorist organization. What a story, Director."

"My God, Absek! Did we help create this monster? It is all more understandable now, isn't it?"

"I believe so, sir. If it really happened that way, maybe he is able to justify in his own mind the killing of innocent people. It is a tragedy, sir, but he still has to be stopped."

"I know, Absek. The event changed him forever – for the worse and yes, we must stop him."

"Sir, I will get started on our plan with Israpharm and I'll be in touch soon."

"Thank you, my friend. Until later, goodbye."

"Goodbye, sir."

DT-A2

Joe had called a meeting of his senior technical staff to discuss the new project, DT-A2.

The team was sitting around the conference room table talking as Joe walked in. The clapping started immediately and lasted until he sat down. Joe raised one hand saying, "Thank you but you are the ones who did the work. I say thank you for what you did on DT-A1."

The team leader for the project spoke up and said, "Joe, we know your designs are responsible for maintaining this company's position as a leader in detonation technology. There is a rumor around that even though DT-A1 was just barely finished as the first of the acoustics series, it isn't enough. The government is asking for the next generation product right now. Is this correct?"

Joe said, "How do you guys always know exactly what the meetings are about before we have them?"

Everyone smiled but no one said a word. That secret was going to stay a secret.

Joe continued, "As scientists, we know that victories are always short-lived. They have to be because then there is the next challenge, and the next, and the next that must be addressed. You are correct; there is a need for the next product in the series, DT-A2, and the need is now. I can't go into all of the details of why but suffice it to say that our war on terror demands it. You deserve to know as much as I can tell you about what we are dealing with in this life and death matter. First, there is a move by our government to go more decidedly on the offense to fight the terrorists. As you know, our products have more recently been developed with that in mind – to help with the government offensive against the 'Campaign of Fear'. Our DT products have been used against EFPs, suicide bombs, and others for some time now. We are good at what we do and have become very successful. This is the basic reason that we now have become a target for the terrorists."

The team leader piped in, "A target?"

"Yes," Joe said. "The investigation of the deaths of Thomas and his family at this time points to murder, not suicide. All this stays in this room, right? You need to know that a certain unnamed terrorist organization was attempting to penetrate our company through Thomas and we believe was responsible for both the attempted theft of our experimental product in Israel and the murder of Thomas and his family. Because we don't know exactly how much confidential information they got on our technology, we have been asked to obsolete ourselves and come up with the next revolutionary acoustics product."

"Revolutionary products take a while, Joe," the team leader said. "Do you know what we have to do?"

"Mostly but not completely. I believe our challenge is to have the product operate at long distances – maybe several hundred feet. We all knew that only short distance capability was a limitation of A1, right?"

"Limitation isn't quite the right word," said the team leader. "It's the best DT product out there; I bet the Massod will confirm that in their testing."

"I can tell you they already have confirmed its quality and they want to start using the A1 product as soon as we can supply them. The problem is if the terrorists have enough information to understand the technology used, they just might be able to find a way to counteract it. DT-A2 must be orders of magnitude better and beyond their capability to create a defense against it."

"I see," said the team leader. "If we can develop new technology that can perform at both short and long range and know it is confidential and proprietary, then the terrorists cannot defend

345

against it."

"Yes, that's right," said Joe "I have some ideas how to do this and there is an acoustics expert from Tully Research, Inc. that is going to help us. We have been asked to join forces with TRI and ATP, who is developing a special acoustics explosives detector, to create a system that can find and destroy the EFPs and other similar devices. This will stop the 'Campaign of Fear' the terrorists have implemented."

"It will certainly help, Joe. I hope someone is working to determine exactly why these people feel this way about us. That is, wanting to wipe us off the face of the earth with no regard for human life - ours or theirs, for that matter."

"There are people working on all fronts - political, economic, religious, social, education, and philosophical, but they readily acknowledge that it might take generations to impact the behavior. We believe that even in countries such as Syria and Iran the moderates are in the majority and are actually making some headway. The minority, the extremists and religious fanatics, are the only ones we hear about because of their tendency toward radical violence against the heathens - as they call others - and us in democratic countries. The question is – when will reason, logic, and sound thinking prevail and what do we do until then?"

"We keep fighting back," said the team leader.

"Yes," Joe said. "We keep defending ourselves, using the most sophisticated technology available and even going on the offense when necessary. And, we hope that our discussions with the moderates will serve us well as they gain more and more power. Is it worth it? I don't think we have any choice but to help them bring their countries along to be contributing members of the world community. Our grandchildren and great grandchildren will thank us for that."

"We all agree with that, Joe. Where should we focus our work on A2?"

"I have been in touch with Dr. Tully about his work on non-dissipating acoustic wave generation. He has used a special columnar arrangement to concentrate the beam as it is generated and projected. It is able to maintain its integrity of frequency and impact over much longer distances. If we can produce a defined wave front that remains intact over hundreds of feet of space, it will enable us to detonate the explosive. The Tully work was for a different application but we may be able to adapt and modify it for our detonation purposes. Here are his sketches of the special columnar designs for both oil detection and explosive detection and some of my ideas for improvement. We can get started right away. Don't worry about intellectual property on new and improved inventions, company ownership, or even cost at this point in the program. We'll address all of those as they come up. Just get results!"

    The entire team was caught up in the content of the design sketches when the team leader looked up and said, "This could really work. How did he ever think of doing it this way? Is it fair to liken it to a rotational slingshot effect which gains power and intensity with each revolution before the shot?"

    "Something like that. I think Dr. Tully would say the physics considerations are a bit more rigorous than that, but you are on the right track. Get the circular columnar physics right and we'll have our DT-A2 product."

    "Let's get to work. Thank you, Joe. Do you mind if I am in contact with Dr. Tully as we get started and make progress?"

    "It's part of the deal," Joe said. "Just be aware that we have been issued special phones, email accounts, and communications codes and passwords for this project. Nothing is to go via our company intranet or telecommunication system – absolutely nothing."

    "Is this another *black* project, Joe?"

    "The blackest of black if there is such a thing. We must act as if all of our normal internal communication channels for government projects have been compromised. It is imperative that our work be treated as highly confidential, shared only on a 'need to know' basis and kept within our small group of specially selected team members. I am depending on you to manage this program like none other we have had. Like it is a matter of life and death if we make missteps. Can you do that for me?"

The entire team responded, "Yes, sir!"

"Let's get going then and please remember to report back to me frequently. Thanks very much."

Progress on the ATP Programs

Bill said, "Zen, how is Kan D doing? I don't see much happening with nanoscaling my wave guns and probes."

"Don't you mean Brad's wave guns and probes?"

Zen bit her tongue after she said that. She knew it was uncalled for but everybody was a bit on edge with all of the recent developments.

"Yes, of course. I just meant …"

"I'm sorry, Bill, I shouldn't have said that. To answer your question, Kan D is not doing too well. Considering she just lost her sister, nephew, and brother-in-law, it is probably reasonable to have some down time."

"I would think so, Zen."

"Bill, you have done a wonderful job building the new prototypes. The work has really gone fast."

"Due a lot to your help, of course."

"I can hardly believe we have already confirmed Brad's results and have built several prototypes. The articulation of the returning wave into its individual components and representing detected explosive chemicals is Noble Prize work. Lyncoln continues to say 'it's the code, Zen, it's the code'."

"Lyncoln has done great work, too. I believe he has improved on the software that Brad provided. Did you notice that the probe is more sensitive and the wave articulation and component identification is even faster? He must be working on something else because I see him fiddling with his Blackberry all the time."

"I thought so too but I assumed it was just me. No one else has said anything."

"It doesn't matter. He has done what our project needs and in a first-class way."

"I agree as long as it isn't another terrorist project. Damn, I shouldn't have said that either. Sorry."

"It's okay; I know you didn't mean it, Zen. We both trust Lyncoln to do the right things now."

'Yes. Would you mind if I taper off helping you and start spending time helping Kan D?"

"No, I was going to suggest it myself. If you think I can help on miniaturization, just let me know. Maybe if we all pitch in we can catch up. Would Kan D be okay with that?"

"I think so. Maybe it will help her get out of her doldrums. It must be terrible to lose the only family you have left. Especially murdered that way by a terrorist."

"It's unimaginable."

"Thanks for the offer of help, Bill."

DACS

Chad had talked with both Lyncoln and Brad about the DACS project. They were in agreement about the communication plan. It was simple – no communication internally except among the three of them and their boss, Mike Jackson. Externally, they planned to build the deception with TIC and Omar Kharif. Building the deception included using words like: huge challenge, so difficult, no progress yet. After all, it is like hunting for the Holy Grail.

Chad said, "Lyncoln, how is DACS going?"

"We have been making great progress. Brad's code work on wave component separation helped a lot from an overall strategy standpoint. If you can segment the control into discreet packets, unique enough to be individually identifiable then you can write code for each of them. The key is to divide into small enough pieces and provide a marker to flag it or call it into play when needed."

Chad, not understanding anything Lyncoln was talking about said, "Good work. Did you and the director get the offshore account stuff taken care of by now?"

"Sure did. He has incorporated a second password and code set that not even I know. Unless my password and code and his new set are used together, it will be impossible to get into the account."

"He knows yours but you don't know his?"

"Right."

'That is good, Lyncoln. It was probably the safest thing to do."

"Chad, they have put a tail on me, too. It is rather annoying because it's there all the time and I can't shake it. I've tried."

"Well, stop trying. It's there for your own good. You'll thank them later. By the way, are you getting your parts of the L-RED project done?"

"Of course. I think I made advancements on Brad's work but only time will tell. Sensitivity and speed is where I was focusing."

"Both would be great to have, Lyncoln. Thanks. If you have any trouble balancing the two projects, please talk with me and we'll work something out."

"Thanks, Chad."

"Thanks, Lyncoln."

Chapter 14

Plan to Shut Down Pharmatek

Sam and Abesk

It was time to talk to Absek again. Things needed to move quickly to slow or stop the flow of money to Technolibertat.

"Hi, Absek, you are working late again."

'Yes, sir, we have just completed training on the DT-A1. The field coordinators all think this will help immensely. They can hardly believe that CMT might be able to have it perform at even longer distances. This technology has injected a sense of excitement and hope within Mossad that I haven't seen for quite a while. Thank you, sir."

"I'll be sure to tell Joe about your comments, Absek. Thank you."

"Director, you will be pleased to know that Israpharm has prepared a letter to Pharmatek stating their Warfarin-D blood thinner pharmaceutical has made ten patients severely ill and they have stopped the use of the drug as of today. They would not speculate on the cause of the illnesses but rather recommend that Pharmatek shut down production immediately. They go on to recommend that the company should begin to check their raw materials, production processes, packaging, and everything to find the problem and get it fixed. Additionally, they should submit to an international drug quality review before production would be allowed to restart. Until then, there would be no further orders by Israpharm and they copy the letter to all the pharmaceutical companies known to use the drug."

"This is great, Absek, have them send the letter and see that both DoAT and FDA are copied. We owe them one!"

"Yes, sir, I'll do that."

"It wasn't difficult to find an FDA approved pharmaceutical contract company in the U.S. to start making the drug. Israpharm knows this but I will have our FDA contact all the involved companies and tell them there will be a continuing supply available to meet all their needs. Currently there has been enough manufactured for a one-month supply worldwide and the inventory is building fast."

"This is good, sir. Israpharm's first question was about an approved alternate supply and how fast can they get it. All the others will want to know, too."

"I also found out that the FDA has often had to coordinate an international review on drug quality. There is a standing committee that operates under the auspices of the United Nations and called to act on an as-needed basis. I don't believe they have ever had to review drug quality issues in Syria but they have the authority to go anywhere in the world. As soon as the letter is issued, our FDA will submit the request for the review and the standing committee will be notified. I told the FDA that although the operation is on the university campus in Damascus, it is independent from the academic institution. They will use all caution to show that the university is not involved in any way with terrorists. Our challenge is to use the processes available to us to achieve our goals. If we would ever reach the point where Pharmatek seems to be close to justifying resuming production, I'll find another reason to cause a delay. This operation must not be able to fund terrorists and supply poison for them to use on innocent people. Maybe if we stop the funding source and get the leader, we can close it down forever."

"I agree, sir, and we'll do everything we can to help."

"I know, Absek, you have been a great help all along. Thank you very much."

Psychological Profile On Omar

Sam Elson had received Thomas's 'Chronicle of Events' from his team in San Francisco. He told his assistant to hold his calls and reschedule his meetings for the next two hours. Sam thought back as he held the folder. What do we already know about this guy, Omar? I'll make a list to include:

1) His work at major universities where TIC provided significant monies for research grants, scholarships, and fellowships.
2) The aggressive contacts with GPRI, which eventually led to the over investment in Tully Research, Inc.
3) The stolen notes about the CIED program from Chad Bromcast at ATP.
4) The bribes paid to Thomas Kramley at CMT, which connected TIC to Technolibertat and its leader.
5) The plot to steal CMT experimental product in Israel and the death of his brother.
6) Killing, by devising a unique poisoning method, of the Kramley family and a CSI laboratory worker.
7) Payment of the enormous amount of money, $200 million to Lyncoln and Brad to develop the data augmentation and control software.

The director thought as a psychologist and concluded: the job doesn't match skills, wants to gain favor and friends, prone to bad decision-making, questions what he is doing, knows he is in trouble, wants out.

The 'Chronicle of Events' was written by Thomas Kramley to be given to his attorney. It was too late but Thomas was trying to protect himself and his family. He had grown to mistrust Omar for whatever reasons. The chronicle was just that, a page or two on every telephone contact and fact-to-face meeting he had with Omar. The major events were: Omar's first contact requesting Thomas's help regarding his Berkeley visit, the jointly advantageous agreement to test the RFID and DAS systems separately and together in three field tests, disclosure of the Kramley family health problems and

Omar's empathy, several meetings at the Squealing Pig, gifts for his son, threats on his life, and finally an agreement for Thomas and Omar to tell CMT the truth about the bribes.

What a tumultuous relationship over a relatively short period of time. He saw the signs however. Omar was a puppet and someone else, probably this "leader," who was likely Omar's father, was pulling his strings. The director thought about the father and his perspective about his son. Omar was responsible for an ongoing federal investigation, five deaths including his oldest son, and an empty bank account for Technolibertat. He had to take some action.

Sam input the last of the "Chronicle of Events" information into the computer and his AAR program. The computer went to work, a small window on the monitor showed the super computer was engaged, utilized time was being tracked and best case scenarios were being constructed. The clock said 362 seconds when the two scenarios popped up. They were labeled, Omar Kharif, TIC: 1. Most Probable Future State Scenario – subject will be terminated. 2. Possible Future State Scenario – subject will return to Syria.

Sam was always amazed that, with all that information input to the computer, it could come up with these brief four or five word scenarios. And, he had written the program!

The supercomputer disengaged and the screen indicated 362 seconds, $5,000 charge to DoAT. Sam thought, Could I have come up with these two scenarios in six minutes? Probably not.

Okay, he said to himself, let's take a critical look at what these scenarios really say. The 'Most Probable' simply says that Omar has made so many flawed decisions, put the organization and its mission at enormous risk, and become such a liability as to be expendable. The scenario doesn't say who would terminate Omar, he thought. We do know that Omar's father tends to lead by being a visible field operative. He did that for sure in Zefat where he coordinated the airport team and gave the orders for his older son to commit suicide. Could he sacrifice a second son by contracting someone to eliminate him or even come here to do it himself? How many times do father-son relationships end up this way? Is this what

Islamic militancy or extremism is all about?

Sam buzzed his assistant immediately and said, "Call the Justice Department and tell them to put a watch on Eomar Kharif or Patek Kumat attempting to enter the U.S. Send them all the information we have on this guy including the videos from the airport theft. They can extract a picture for their agents to use at the major airports. I suspect he will try to fly into or nearby to Washington, D.C. in order to contact his son, Omar Kharif at his D.C. address. Tell them the watch is to be put into effect immediately and this man is to be considered armed and dangerous. If he is found, take him into custody and charge him with conspiracy against the United States Have the special agent in charge contact me when they find him."

"Yes, sir, immediately, sir. Should I alert Secretary Adams so there will be no surprises between departments?"

"Good idea. Grant can help run interference if we need it. Thanks."

"Yes, sir."

As the door closed, Sam started to address the second scenario - Subject Will Return to Syria. The points given to this scenario made a very distant second to 'termination.' Was it a real possibility? Probably not. Omar probably doesn't know that his situation is as bad as it is. We haven't announced what we know about the bribes, the murders, the poison, and the money – any of those facts. We haven't asked him to come in for questioning. We actually promoted the TIC relationship with Tully and indirectly with ATP. Given all of this, he may go quiet or dark but it isn't likely he would try to leave the country. If we do something overt now to stop him returning to Syria, it might be completely unnecessary. Any action of that type would decrease our chances of catching the number one terrorist from Technolibertat. Sam was almost sure Omar's father was coming to do his own dirty work and eliminate his own son. It could be a race to see who could find Omar first. Sam had to decide what to do if Eomar was successful eluding the federal agents. How would he find him and what would he do to protect Omar long enough to catch the number one prize?

The director noticed the note on the screen relating to scenario number one that said, very simply: subject may be turnable. Sam jumped out of his chair and said out loud, "Of course, he is a reluctant terrorist. He is in this because he thinks he has to be – because of the family. He harbors only weakly held beliefs in the mission and sees himself as a businessman, not a technologist. Everything he does goes wrong, and he must want out. I wonder what he would do if he knew someone was coming to kill him. He may not only want out, he might be turnable."

Sam thought fast. He needed a plan to find Omar now, not just to protect him in order to catch the leader but to enlist him to help catch the leader. He had some leverage points that could be helpful. Maybe the best was Omar's relationship with Lyncoln. If Lyncoln and Brad could somehow have a breakthrough on DACS to communicate, he might surface. The project was, after all, the Holy Grail and the money he spent on it was the straw that broke the camel's back, so to speak. Even if he knew his life was in danger, he most likely would surface if there were significant developments. He would think it might be enough to save him.

Sam kept thinking. What could we offer Omar to turn? Safety? Maybe, but that won't be enough. Besides it probably would just be temporary. Freedom? Hardly, he killed four people and justice would have to run its course. Try to turn Omar's father? Wow, direct ties to al Qaeda and bin Laden. He could be very valuable. Omar might be interested in this regardless of how remote the possibilities are. It's worth a try.

Bring Omar In For Questioning
"Hello, Director, it's Jack."

"Hello, Jack, I thought you would be calling soon."

"Yes, sir. I was talking to Aldora recently and told her what you said about litigation."

"Was she excited?"

"To say the least, sir. We agreed the evidence in hand now is sufficient to bring Omar in for questioning. With the bribes, the audio and videotapes, the poison, the comic books, the fingerprint match, and the 'Chronicle of Events' we can nail him to the wall. The problem, sir, is that we have tried to contact him at the TIC, San Francisco offices and there is no response, no answer."

"We knew he might go quiet or even go underground for a while, Jack. I'm not surprised. If we put more pressure on him, he may go deeper underground or even disappear. Besides the CMT dealings, he had some sketchy things going at Tully Research and ATP. Let's see: murders, financial blunders, and operational miscues. What else will it take to do him in? I suspect his bosses are ready to bring him home or get rid of him. If it looks like we are after him too, he will run for sure."

"How would you like to handle it, sir?"

"Let's use the CMT intranet again, Jack. Have it say that the authorities believe the Kramley deaths were suicides because of the deteriorating health situations of the wife and son. There will be a series of informal interview with friends and acquaintances by the CSI team to wrap up the case."

"A great idea, sir. If it is a non-threatening situation he more than likely will come out of hiding."

"Yes, just leave a message at his San Francisco and D.C. offices about the Kramley case and the need to do informal interviews with friends and acquaintances. The note about the deaths being a suicide on the intranet will do the rest."

"I'll do this right way."

"Thanks, Jack. You should know that we expect the head of Technolibertat, this Patek Kumat/Eomar Kharif, to surface somewhere in the States soon. He will probably show up on the East Coast but it's not out of the question for him to be in the San Francisco area. We just don't know when or where right now. If our guess is correct, he will be here to figure out what to do with Omar."

"Maybe even termination, sir?"

"I believe so, even though Omar is his son."

"We'll keep watch here, sir."

"Thanks, Jack. Talk to you later."

"Goodbye, sir."

Progress On DT-A2

The team leader for the Black Project, DT-A2, walked into Joe's office and said, "This Dr. Tully is a genius. With his knowledge of acoustic wave generation and long-distance wave integrity combined with our knowledge of acoustic detonation, we really have something."

"How do the test results look?"

"We are up to several football fields of distance. How far do you want to go?"

"Is it effective with all types of terrorist explosives?"

"Everything we have seen so far, Joe. It gets the EFPs and IEDs, and even the suicide bombs that are activated by either mechanical or electronic means. Because the beam is, even at longer distances, so much stronger, we had to dial down the sensitivity of our frequency scanner. Even with these changes, we may still set off a few security system alarms and open some garage doors mistakenly."

"If it saves lives, who cares?"

"My thoughts exactly. With the new sensitivity levels, we can detonate everything up to 400-500 meters. Is that far enough?"

"I think so. Great work. Now to the second phase of the project."

"The second phase? I thought ..."

"I know, always one more request."

"It's okay, Joe. We know technical projects never end. In fact, the team was guessing what the next request might be. We know this technology is the most sophisticated ever but there is still a limitation, our age-old nemesis really. The location of the explosive, whether stationary or mobile, must be known before we can detonate. Getting to an answer on that one has been impossible to date. Does Phase II have anything to do with a remote explosives locater device?"

"The team is good! You are exactly right. I probably should have told you before but everything is so hush-hush on these projects."

"Told me what, Joe?"

"I'll probably get shot for doing this but you and the team need to know. Remember when we had our first meeting on DT-A2? I mentioned joining forces with TRI and ATP to develop a system to both detect and destroy terrorists' explosives and bombs. With Dr. Tully's help, ATP has been able to make the same great progress we have. They have working prototypes that can detect these explosives at 400-500 meters. They call their prototype, L-RED, for long range explosive detection. Current work is highly-focused on the incorporation of nanoscale technology and miniaturization methodology."

"I can keep a secret, Joe. This is great news. Is the purpose of Phase II to integrate their detector into our detonator to form L-REDD?"

"ATP probably would say it the other way around, integrate our detonator into their detector, but yes, you got it. That is Phase II. I would like you and the team to draft a proposal on how to do this. Not so much the technical stuff since you don't know about the detector details but location, people, communication, testing, etc. I'd like to have that when I talk next with Director Elson."

"We will, sir. It will be great to work with ATP on a project of this magnitude. I want to meet Dr. Tully in person, too. He'll no doubt have some ideas for integrating the two parts. It will be essentially his product when you think about all of his technology being used."

"You are right there. I'm glad he is on our side."

"Yes, sir. I'll get to work on the integration plan."

"Thanks."

Get The Money Back?

Legally, there was no way to get the money back. His expert in financial matters told him he had to get the account password and code. That was the only way. The Liberator was furious with Omar, whose actions just might bring down the entire organization. He thought that going to the U.S. was even more imperative now. He had to deal with Omar first and foremost. Then there was Lyncoln

Fuller and his offshore account with almost all of Technolibertat's money in it. And, if the government's special programs in acoustics depended on only one man, Bradford Tully, why not take care of that problem at the same time?

The Liberator's thinking process today seemed to be linear and sequential. First, what about Omar? He began to outline the options. Have Omar continue working for the organization but in a different capacity. Fieldwork? No, he is weak and unskilled. Recruiter? No, he would not be convincing enough about our mission. Trainer? No, weak and unskilled. Manage one of our other country operations like the U.K. or Germany? No weak and unskilled. Manage our major business, Pharmatek? Maybe; he does have a degree in business. Would he screw Pharmatek up, too?

The Liberator pondered a while longer on Pharmatek and finally said, "That seems to be the only other possible position within the organization for Omar."

A second option occurred to him – let him muster out of the organization. If he can escape prosecution for the murder of the Kramley family, have him stay in the States. But, he knows too much, it wouldn't be wise to leave him unfettered and out there as a potential and significant threat. It just would not work.

He thought deeply before whispering the last option – terminate him just like any other member who doesn't work out. But Omar is my only son now. How could a father do that to his only son?

The Liberator thought back to when all this started. The CIA, the Americans, the infidels, killed his wife because bin Laden demanded to stay at our house. She had no choice and yet the heartless infidels killed her. That was when he swore to get retribution. Yes, he should kill the infidels, not his son. But sometimes a person has no choice.

The tears were dripping down his cheeks. Large drops that held together and flowed into his mouth. He tasted the saltiness more and more just sitting there knowing that the way forward was clear. There was only one real option for Omar.

What about Lyncoln Fuller and the $200 million? The

visitor thought if he could get re-introduced to Lyncoln, there might be a chance to somehow gain access to his offshore account password and personal identification code. How would I do that? he asked himself. A better question might be, Why would he give the confidential information about his bank account to me? The Liberator could think of no reason other than under duress. Would he rather have the project done or his money back? It was obvious to him; the two were incompatible. The answer flashed to him; he wanted the money back. To hell with the Holy Grail! They were never able to find it anyway, right? Still deep in thought, the wheels turning, what kind of duress? He decided it would first have to be enough physical pain to get the information and then followed eventually by death. He cursed Omar for putting him into this position. But, he had done this before - to people who had turned against the organization. It wasn't new to him but he always had a reason. He needed a justification for his actions, something to calm his mind about the gravity of the deed. This guy, Lyncoln, has really done nothing but sign a contract at a price that he required and be paid in advance. He doesn't deserve this but there seems to be no other way. The life of the organization is at stake. So what or more appropriately, who is next on the list? Oh, yes, Dr. Bradford Tully. This one is very complex to even consider. The boy genius helping everyone – the government, ATP, CMT, and of course TIC. If he has all the technology, as Omar implied, was it really prudent for TRI to be a conduit to help our enemies build weapons to be used against us? I understand the concept that it was probably going to happen anyway. Why not be involved and hope to gain understanding so that we can defend ourselves? The plan is so convoluted. Would it not be better just to eliminate the source of the technology expertise? The Liberator thought the government must be protecting someone so valuable. He would not be surprised if he were under constant surveillance at home and when he travels. This one will be more difficult, but he must act.

    He leaned back in his chair, his mind racing to manage his real concern. How will he deal with the expectations of al Qaeda? First and foremost, he would have to take care of Omar. One story might be that defensive weapons against CIED and DT-A1 were thought to be very difficult, if not impossible, to develop and beyond the grasp of the company's technologists. It was decided that the best approach was to slow or stop the projects by eliminating the key technical experts. It would take a long time to develop the technology if the experts were dead. This would buy us a lot of time to protect the 'Campaign of Fear'. The Liberator asked himself, Would that work and, could he sell it to bin Laden? If not, he would be a dead man, too. He cursed Omar again for putting him in this situation. He'll figure out how to do this on the airplane. He wheeled around and began the process of booking his round trip to San Francisco, Minneapolis, and Boston on line.

Problems at Pharmatek

The letter from Israpharm arrived in the morning mail. The secretary put it on Patek's desk with the rest of the mail. It was on the very top of the pile.

Patek saw it immediately when he came into the office. The logo was unforgettable with the letters IP inside a five-point star. IP was one of their biggest customers so his reaction was one of concern.

Still standing and reaching slowly for the envelope he picked it up cautiously as if it might break and held it to the light. There was nothing to see, as is the case with most business envelopes because of the hiding power of the blue color inside. He picked up the letter opener, made a quick forward hand movement providing a razor smooth cut on the long edge of the envelope.

Patek was thinking about his three problems in the U.S. and how a stroke like this could come in handy. He had done it before. If you don't think about it too much, there isn't much difference. His philosophy was that the end justifies the means. Patek put the letter opener on the desk, pulled out the letter, and began to read. It was addressed to him as President and CEO. The first line read, *'Due to many recent serious illnesses caused by your Warfarin derivative drug, Warfarin-D, we are immediately terminating our purchase agreement with Pharmatek. It is our recommendation that the Pharmatek plant be closed and subjected to both internal process quality investigations and external International Pharmaceutical Review panel evaluations. Re-certification would occur only on implementation of improvements stipulated and governed by the IPRP. The seriousness of the situation has required us to contact the pharmaceutical, medical, hospital, and health care communities about these serious illnesses and to advise them to stop purchasing, distributing, or prescribing this drug immediately. A copy of this letter has been sent to them as well. We expect they will take the same actions we are taking and require quality improvements and a monitored international review process be put in place. Because there will be potential legal action taken against Pharmatek, please be advised of your obligation to communicate this situation to the university, local authorities, and the Syrian government.*

Patek slumped into his chair, feeling his world crumbling around him. He threw the letter on the desk, trying to make sense of all this. He wondered if the other companies would cancel their orders. Quickly, he picked up the phone and punched the numbers for his plant manager.

"Hello Eomar," said the plant manager who had known him when he was a university professor.

"Would you check to see if our customers are canceling orders for Warfarin-D?"

"Why would they do that? There has been nothing but increased volumes the last three years."

"Just check! It seems that Israpharm has found a problem with our drug and is recommending everyone to stop using it."

"What was the reason? Our product has not changed at all."

"Call me back as soon as you check on the orders."

"Yes, sir."

Patek hung up. In less than two minutes, the plant manager called back saying, "You are correct. In addition to Israpharm, four other major customers have cancelled their orders and purchase agreements. Damn, there are numbers five and six cancellations. Eomar, we are out of business."

Patek hung up. His face was getting redder; he was clenching his hands into fists, and pounding the desk. He asked himself, How could this happen? No cash reserves, thanks to Omar. No money coming from Warfarin-D and many financial obligations to meet. Technolibertat, Technology Investment Corporation, the entire operation, hundreds of people, our mission, and I are all in jeopardy. I have to get this problem fixed and get back into production very soon. Otherwise, we are out of business.

He called to his secretary, "Cancel my trip to the States immediately. It doesn't matter what the financial penalties are. I have more important things to do here right now."

Patek was thinking fast. He needed Emar, the engineer son who was instrumental setting up the manufacturing operation. Emar would have known who to bring in to check the raw materials, the process steps, the on-line testing procedures, and packaging, and the people. Emar, why have you left me?

Patek put the Israpharm letter into his desk, stood up, and walked out of his office. "I will be gone about an hour at the Chemical Engineering Department across campus," he yelled to his secretary. "They'll be able to do a process review in the plant."

"Yes, sir. I overheard what happened. Should I draft a letter to our customers telling them the steps we are taking to remedy our production issues with Warfarin-D?"

"Thank you. Tell them we are doing exactly what Israpharm is suggesting. Get the letter from my desk and use their words about process and quality studies and International Pharmaceutical Review Panel re-certification. I'm going to get an expert team from the university to do the process and quality study. Check into IPRP and see who they are and what it takes for re-certification. I'll review the draft letter and information on IPRP when I get back and we'll decide on next steps. Thanks."

Integration of L-RED and DT-A2

Joe heard the light knock on his door and said, "Come in, please. Hi, Ray. I just finished reading your integration plan. It is very good and just what I wanted to see."

"Thank you, sir. Are you okay with the team picking up

THE CAMPAIGN OF FEAR

and moving to Boston for a while?"

"Of course. With the investigation still on going, it might be best that you are away. Our intranet has been compromised, technology stolen, and people have been killed by assailants for reasons unknown to us. Plus, this new system requires that the entire team be together for the greatest efficiency and effectiveness. There will be better planning, communication, and more timely results. Go for it!"

"Yes, sir. I'm glad you like the plan. I have taken the initiative to contact Dr. Chadly Bromcast at ATP to see what he thinks. After all, I couldn't actually propose it if he would not support me. He is the one who has to come up with all the extra laboratory and testing space, to say nothing of the temporary living quarters for our people."

"I'm glad you did. What did he say?"

"He loved it and made only one recommendation, a stipulation that I should have had in the proposal in the first place."

"What was that?"

"That Dr. Tully should join us in Boston, too. Chad agreed to make that happen if you approved my proposal."

Joe wrote 'approved', signed his name, and dated the front page of the proposal. "When do you start?"

"We are packing right now, transferring files, and getting our personal stuff in order. We are planning for 3-4 weeks, if that's okay."

Joe was smiling because this guy was so far ahead of him he simply said, "Whatever you have planned is okay with me. I'll back you up 100%."

"Thank you, sir. Just so you know, I will be staying with Dr. Bromcast. We thought it would show the team the importance of working together right from the start."

"Good. I like that. We have five people on DT-A2. How many do they have on L-RED?"

"I guess it must be 30-50 people, depending on how you count for CIED and L-RED. The project and team leaders are the key people though. We got to meet them, Chad, Bill, Lyncoln, Zen,

365

and Kan D, by video conference call recently."

"I have met them, too, and they are impressive. It will be a good team. Good luck."

"Thank you, sir."

Pharmatek is Closed Down

Patek was back in exactly one hour. The secretary thought, He is so organized and efficient, how could something like this happen? "Hello, sir, you are right on time."

"Yes. Thank goodness my friend in the chemical engineering department was in. He was one of Emar's favorite professors so I got to know him very well. Take a note please for the plant manager saying, "Mr. Japer, there will be four engineers, two professors and two fourth- year graduate students from the University Chemical Engineering Department, arriving at the plant tomorrow to conduct a Six Sigma review on our manufacturing processes for Warfarin-D. They all have master black belts and will focus on raw material receipt and handling; derivatization, dilution, and purification; testing and quality control; and packaging materials and process. Please provide them our timely and complete cooperation. They have indicated we should expect 2-3 days before they will issue their recommendations. I will try to stop each day to see how things are going. If you have any insight into where contamination might be entering our processes, please provide the team this information immediately upon their arrival tomorrow. I don't have to remind you how important it is that we find the problems, fix them, and start to regain the confidence of our customers. Thanks, PK."

He pondered, "Do you think that is enough?"

"Yes, sir. Mr. Japer is an excellent plant manager and has had no problems with production for all these years. He'll appreciate the help to get to the bottom of this, I'm sure."

"We must find the problem fast. Our existence as a company, Pharmatek, and all of our jobs depends on it."

"I know, sir. Everyone is very worried, but they are confident you will be able to get us approved to restart production.

I have cancelled your trip to the U.S. There was no penalty because of the emergency nature of the reason. It helped that I assured them that it wasn't cancelled for good, just delayed."

"Thank you. I appreciate your handling of these matters so expeditiously."

"You are welcome, sir. I have also completed the draft letter to our major customers. You can read it, but it is simply an apology, our step-by-step plan to find the problem, resolve it, and states our commitment to receive international re-certification as an approved supplier of Warfarin-D in a timely fashion. We ask for their patience and understanding as they continue to believe in us as partners in the health care business. We close with a thank you for their business these last several years. Does that seem okay?"

Patek skimmed the draft, smiled, and signed it immediately. "I could not have said it better. Very good job."

"I will get this sent to our customers via special delivery today. They will be glad to know that we are thinking about them."

"Yes. Did you learn anything about this International Pharmaceutical Review Panel?"

"Before I could search very much, they contacted us. They operate under the auspices of the United Nations. It was set up sometime ago after terrorists started to use certain chemicals, liquids, solids, and gasses to kill people. One of their functions is to differentiate between accidental and intentional happenings with pharmaceuticals. The happenings can include multiple illnesses or deaths that have occurred in either controlled or uncontrolled environments. They try first to get to an immediate determination as to whether this was a terrorist activity or a mishap by the supplier or user of the pharmaceutical. I told him our product, Warfarin-D, is a blood thinner and there was nothing nefarious going on at the hospitals that Israpharm supplied. They will be working that angle in Israel. The man who called said he wants our entire Warfarin-D inventory put on hold immediately. They have required that we account for our total production for the last six months. As he put it - every last drop! I have informed Mr. Jasper of the two requests by the IPRP. He is in the process of complying with both requests right now. A two-man team will be here tomorrow to work in the plant and get the information they need. I agreed to that, but they were going to come no matter what I said."

"It's okay. You have done the right thing. We have to be very attentive to whatever they need. It's the only way we'll be able to be re-certified and get back into production."

"Yes, sir, it just seems to be a little, what do they call it, *overkill*?"

"Sounds like tomorrow is going to be a big day. The university Six Sigma team, the IPRP team, and our efforts to help search out what is going on. Thank you very much for your help. I appreciate it."

"You are welcome, sir. I will coordinate all the activities tomorrow so you can come and go as needed. Don't worry about anything."

"Thank you. I'll be in my office for a while if I'm needed."

Patek walked into his office, closed the door, sat down at his desk, and very quietly pondered the situation. Why do they want us to account for every last drop of Warfarin-D? Is there something else going on here? Do they know that we use the neat or concentrated form of Warfarin-D for our own private purposes? Did they somehow identify the poison used in my son's death and the Kramley's deaths and connect it to our operation here? Are they trying to shut me down and use the illnesses as a ruse? I must be getting paranoid, he thought.

A Note Is Caught On CMT Intranet

Omar was at least halfway in hiding. He had not been to the West Coast for sometime and wasn't taking many phone calls in the D.C. office. This call however was coming in on the special phone. It was from the Liberator.

"Hello, Liberator," said Omar cautiously.

"Hello, Omar. I have some good news and some bad news for you today. You can decide which is which. My trip to the States

THE CAMPAIGN OF FEAR

has been delayed. Something has happened to our Warfarin-D pharmaceutical and we have had to stop production for a while. I will be devoting all my attention to getting the manufacturing process restarted. Your payment to Dr. Fuller wiped out our reserves and I have found there is no way to reverse that transfer. With no income from Warfarin-D, we will be out of business soon if I can't get Warfarin-D back into production."

"I am so sorry, sir. I still believe our large investment in DACS will be our best investment ever. Can I help with the Warfarin-D situation?"

"It is not a business issue or problem based on what our customers are telling us. The drug is making patients severely ill. We must have some kind of impurity that is contaminating our manufacturing process. I need engineering help like Emar could have provided. Do you ever think about him, Omar?"

"Yes, Father, I do, everyday. I wonder what went wrong for this to have happened. How did we put ourselves into this situation in which people have to die? One that makes us kill?"

"Son, when you travel a certain path, sometimes there is no other choice. The decisions about the next steps are made for you. Sometimes you are able to continue, sometimes not. Anyway, for whatever reasons, we are at a great juncture... you, me, the organization, our mission ... everything we have been working for the last several years is in jeopardy. Saving us is up to me and only me."

"Yes, sir, I understand."

"Omar, I have been watching the CMT intranet constantly with the help of your embedded DAS system."

"Is there anything new on the investigation?"

"Yes, they report the authorities have concluded the Kramley deaths were suicides. The final thing being done is a series of informal interviews with friends and acquaintances."

"Suicide? This is great, sir. I told you my plan was too sophisticated for them to find out what really happened. This will explain the phone call messages I received in the San Francisco office and here from the CSI team. They must want to talk to me as

369

an acquaintance to help wrap up the case as suicide."

"I think so, too, Omar. Go ahead and return their calls and offer to be available for the informal interview. You will have to be very careful about what you say. They are trained to pick up on any kind of inconsistency that might develop from the conversation."

"It will be okay, sir. They have encouraged TIC and me, through our investment in Tully, to bring technology to ATP for their special government project. With the new development about the Kramley family, they may have even more confidence in me. Maybe I can even resurface soon in the San Francisco area."

"Let's see how things go with the interview, Omar. Will you get in touch with me immediately afterwards?"

"Of course, sir. Do you think it would be okay to tell them I will be traveling to San Francisco soon and the interview could be done there?"

"I believe so but the CSI team might not be in San Francisco much longer. They might be back in D.C. by the time they are ready to talk to you. Just don't look too anxious to get back to San Francisco. It might raise a red flag to them. Remember, there is still the issue of bribe money that was paid to Mr. Kramley. If their financial searches were complete, TIC and you might be implicated. This is small potatoes compared to murder charges, however. Still, expect some discussion and maybe even the payment of a small fine to make it go away."

"Good points, sir. I appreciate your input."

"I have to go, Omar, so good luck with the interview and congratulations on your success. Goodbye."

"Thank you and goodbye, sir."

The Set Up

Aldora was in Jack's office when the call came in. Jack said, "Let me get this, Aldora. It is a D.C. number. Hello, this is Jack Borson with the DoAT."

"Hello, Mr. Borson. This is Omar Kharif with Technology Investment Corporation. You left a couple of phone messages for me to contact you. Sorry about getting back to you a little late. My business has kept me out of the office the past several days."

"Hello, Mr. Kharif," Jack said as he nodded to Aldora. "Thank you for getting back. As part of an investigative team, we are in the process of interviewing several people connected to the Kramley case at CMT in San Francisco. You might recall that Mr. Kramley, his wife, and his son all were found dead in their home recently."

"Yes. It was a tragic accident. However, you must know that my only connection to CMT and Mr. Kramley was one of a potential vendor to an OEM. He was my CMT contact to field test our new logistics technology product based on RFID tracking of shipped goods."

"We do, Mr. Kharif. The cooperative testing program seemed to be of great interest to Mr. Kramley and CMT, and was very successful. There are questions we have about how well you knew Mr. Kramley and your perception of what could have been the next steps for the use of your products at CMT. We are trying to draw some conclusions about the deaths of the Kramley family and close the case."

"Why would you think that I know anything about that, sir? I was only working to become a supplier of our products to CMT."

"Yes, Mr. Kharif, we understand. Because of Mr. Kramley's untimely death, however, there are several gaps that we are trying to close in the story leading up to that dreadful day."

"I read that it was determined to be suicide. Is that correct?"

"Unless we find contradicting evidence, it seems the best scenario at this time. Mr. Kharif, were you aware that your DAS software is still embedded in the CMT intranet?"

"No, Mr. Borson. I just assumed that CMT had deactivated it after the tests and Mr. Kramley's death. Does CMT need technical assistance to help remove the program?"

"Probably. Are you going to be in San Francisco any time soon? We would like you to come in for an interview if possible. I'm sure it would help us fill the gaps in the Kramley case and you can take care of the DAS system at the same time."

"I can do that, Mr. Borson. Anything to help with the investigation and get to the facts in the case. When would you like to meet?"

"We are about midway in our plan to interview friends and acquaintances. Would the day after tomorrow work for you?"

"I can make it work. I have to get back to San Francisco soon anyway. This will be the impetus to get me there."

"Thank you, Mr. Kharif. How about noon at CMT? I'll have some different kinds of food to help with the time zone changes."

"That will be fine, Mr. Borson. Thank you very much."

"You are welcome, Mr. Kharif. You should know that we recently found a form of diary written by Mr. Kramley. It covers the last several weeks and seems to document mostly his relationship with you before, during, and after the field test programs on RFID/DAS."

"I wonder why he would have done that. The science and technology aspects of our program were being covered in the standard ways using CMT technical notebooks. You can check that yourself."

"We have and you are correct, Mr. Kharif. The diary seemed to be unusual. It did make reference to a couple areas that caught our attention. There was mention of both a gift for his son and multiple payments to him to help with medical bills. Would you come prepared to tell us what you know about these entries in the diary?" Jack smiled at Aldora.

Omar was silent. He was thinking about just what this diary really said. Finally, he said, "I will be as helpful as I can, but interpreting what someone writes in a diary is probably off limits for me. I did not know Thomas that well and of course knew nothing about his family, really."

"We understand, Mr. Kharif. We'll just expect you to do the best you can to fill the gaps. See you in a couple of days. I'll meet you in the lobby of CMT headquarters at noon."

"Yes, sir. See you there. Goodbye 'til then."

"Goodbye, Mr. Kharif."

Jack put down the phone and looked at Aldora. "What do you think about that conversation?"

"It was very interesting. I thought he was trying to be very careful and that he certainly knew a lot more than he was admitting. For example, he will have a lot of explaining to do about DAS and knowing about the communication on the family suicide. He really stepped into that one, didn't he."

"Yes, he did, Aldora. What about the gifts and the money? He was quiet a long time before he responded about those. I thought he came across as defensive, maybe even a bit scared. If we could only have seen his face."

"Do you think he'll show up for the interview?"

"I do and if it's okay, I want you to handle it."

"It's okay, Jack. I was hoping you would ask. We have enough evidence against him already that we could make an arrest and officially charge him for the murders."

"It's all about timing and bringing the organization and its leaders down. The big picture, Aldora."

"I agree. Let's use the meeting to see if we can get further information on the facts of the Kramley murders but also really focus on the organization and its mission and leadership. We should talk to the director and see if he has any ideas, too. I know there has been some mention of turning Mr. Kharif."

"Wouldn't that be something? My initial reaction to that was after killing four people what the hell! However, upon reflection, it might be the right thing to do. Big picture, right? I'll check it out with Director Elson and then we can firm up our interview strategy."

"Good, Jack. Better check to see if he wants to be here for the interview, too. We might need a good psychologist in the room when it gets down to family, religion, and country."

"That is so true, Aldora. Have you ever heard him talk about or seen him use the AAR approach? It is really powerful."

"Let me know what he says, Jack. Then we'll plan our Mr. Kharif interview strategy accordingly."

"Okay, see you later."

"Bye, Jack."

The Interview With Omar

The director had told Jack that he and Aldora should conduct the interview with Omar Kharif. However, at a key time in the interview, there was to be a dramatic phone call to the director to address the issue of turning Mr. Kharif.

Jack said as they entered the lobby, "Hello, Mr. Kharif, welcome back to San Francisco and CMT."

"Thank you, Mr. Borson."

"I would like you to meet Ms. Aldora Klein from the U.S. Department of Justice."

"Hello, Ms. Klein. The Justice Department? I hope this is all perfunctory and I can be on my way soon."

"We hope so, too, Mr. Kharif. If you would sign the visitors' book and we can proceed to the conference room."

"Of course. Let's see three o'clock Eastern or noon Pacific, right?"

Aldora said, "That's correct, right this way, please."

The conference room was just off the lobby and as they entered, Omar said, "You really did it, Mr. Borson."

"You mean the food? Well, we are from D.C., too, so I know what it's like to make a cross-country trip. Please get some food and have a seat."

Omar took breakfast food, an egg-ham-cheese bagel sandwich, with black coffee and sat down.

Aldora picked up a Caesar salad and bottled water and Jack chose the chili soup, a banana, and a Dr. Pepper. Both took seats opposite Omar with the conferencing telephone on the table between them.

Jack said, "Mr. Kharif, we are really pleased that you were able to make time to see us on this important case. Thank you very much."

"You are welcome. Anything I can do to help with a federal investigation. Can you tell me why it is a federal case?"

"Yes, of course. It is simply that CMT and Mr. Kramley were involved in a highly secret Department of Defense government contract. When prototype product from that contract

THE CAMPAIGN OF FEAR

was in route to the international customer, there was an attempted theft by terrorists. It was then that a federal investigative team was formed and tasked with the objectives of determining who was behind this attempted theft and to bring them to justice and to make specific recommendations for tightening our security measures in programs like these. The case took a turn shortly after we arrived in San Francisco with the deaths of the Kramley family and the laboratory technician. We are still trying to learn if the international incident and the domestic events are somehow related. That's where you come in, Mr. Kharif. We think you might be able to help us put the pieces of the puzzle together. If it is okay, I would like Ms. Klein to ask you some questions about your involvement with Mr. Kramley."

"Of course, anything I can do to help."

Aldora stated that the conversation would be recorded and started by asking a series of baseline questions. "Mr. Kharif, are you President and CEO of a company by the name of Technology Investment Corporation?"

"Yes, I am," said Omar, lying a little since it was only recently that he was relieved of those duties by his father. No one else knew that though.

"Do you have offices in D.C., Boston, and San Francisco?"

"Yes, we do."

"Your business involves acquiring technology in the hopes of licensing it to interested parties to make a profit. You also have a strong program of philanthropy that includes special research grants, fellowships, and scholarships to professors, graduate, and undergraduate students at several major universities across the United States."

"Yes and yes. We have given some $50 million to $100 million in the past five years to key university people working in selected technology areas."

"Do those technologies include explosives, Mr. Kharif?"

"Yes, but also MEMS, OLEDS, NANO, and the other technologies that you might expect to be important to the future of

375

our country."

"Are you or is your organization a part of any terrorist organization here or abroad, sir?"

"What? Are you kidding? Do you think we would have given these millions away to universities if we were a terrorist organization? In fact, my first contact with Mr. Kramley was to seek his help with contacts at Berkeley."

"We saw that in the diary, Mr. Kharif. Then you started interacting on the so-called RFID/DAS system, right?"

"Yes, we planned and conducted a series of three field tests that were very important to CMT's business. It was new and sophisticated technology but very successful from the perspective of the two companies. The attempted theft was an unfortunate incident but totally unrelated to the cooperative program between the two companies."

"Who developed the data augmented software system for you, Mr. Kharif?"

"As I recall, it was a very bright former MIT student that took on a contract with us to make extra money."

"Is he doing any further work on the project?"

"I don't believe so. This project is finished and he probably doesn't need money as much anymore."

"Talking about money, did you give money to Mr. Kramley so that he would test your products?"

"No, I didn't. To be honest, I gave him money because he needed it to pay the mounting medical bills for his wife and son."

"You felt sorry for him?"

"Yes, if you will, and my company could do it. We often pay to do field tests of various kinds so it wasn't much different from normal practice. Also, that kind of expense can all be included for the R&D Tax Credit. So, why not help? Before his death, we had sort of a gentlemen's agreement that I would come in and explain what had taken place. He told me about you discovering the money in his offshore account and all the consternation it was causing."

"You had planned to come in together and tell us your story?"

"Yes, that's right. We talked just before his death and agreed to it."

"Are you the compassionate one, Mr. Kharif, or is it your company?"

"I think it is both, Ms. Klein."

"What about the gifts to Mr. Kramley's son? I mentioned that we found notes to that effect in the diary. The comic books."

"Yes, again, his son's illness keeps him in … correction, kept him in the house much of the time. Thomas mentioned that he liked to read so I put two and two together and thought the gifts would be nice. Is there a problem with the gifts? It was just a small thing."

"Yes, there was a problem. The comic books were saturated with a poison that killed the family and later a CSI laboratory technician helping on the case."

"I am very sorry, but I do not know about any poison, only the comic books."

"Do you have any relatives in Syria, Mr. Kharif?"

"Yes, my father is still there. My brother died recently in a very unfortunate accident. I don't have all the details."

"Isn't it true he died of poisoning during the attempted theft of the secret ATP product, the same poison that saturated the comic books and killed the Kramley family?"

"I don't know about any of that, Ms. Klein. I only know that he died an accidental death."

"Who told you that, Mr. Kharif?"

"My father."

"Did he supply the poison that killed his son, your brother, and the Kramley family?"

"What do you mean? I don't know anything about a poison."

"Did you know your father was in on the attempted theft of the CMT secret DT product? Isn't he the head of a terrorist organization called Technolibertat?"

"No, I didn't. Technolibertat is an organization that believes technology will be a large part of our future and the key to freedom.

It is not a terrorist organization."

"Do you know how Technolibertat is funded?"

"Not really, it is my father's organization."

"He uses the profits of a small pharmaceutical company at the university in Damascus to run Technolibertat. Do you know anything about that?"

"A little, but I have been away for some time. Using money from Pharmatek to fund Technolibertat does not make it a terrorist organization."

"You are right. I guess there will be no repercussions if we shut it down. The terrorists will be okay with that?"

Jack had stepped out for just a second. When he came back into the room, the phone rang. He said, "It's our boss, we have to answer this. Sorry. Hello, Director Elson."

"Hello, Jack, Aldora, and Mr. Kharif. Omar, I knew your interview was taking place today. Thank you for coming in. There is breaking news that I thought you should have. My colleagues there do not have this information yet so you can all hear it at the same time. Our field agents have obtained reliable information that a leader by the name of Patek Kumat within the organization, Technolibertat, is on his way to the United States soon. His sole mission is to eliminate, repeat eliminate, someone connected to the organization that has effectively wiped out their entire bank account of tens of millions if not hundreds of millions of dollars. We think it was done in some kind of unapproved electronic transfer."

Omar looked like he had been kicked in the stomach but was able to say, "Why are you telling me this?"

Director Elson said, "I think you know why, Omar. We believe you are the one to be eliminated. You have made one too many mistakes and must pay the price."

"He wouldn't do that to me, not my own father."

"I think you have felt for some time that what you are being asked to do doesn't fit with your beliefs, Omar. With the loss of your brother and your own father out to kill you, it is time to break with this terrorist organization. If you will help us catch this Patek Kumat, your father, we will give you federal protection and a new life afterwards."

"What would happen to him if you catch him?"

"He would be put out of commission as head of Technolibertat and spend the rest of his years in federal prison. If you killed the Kramley family, as we believe you did, you would have to spend time in prison, too, maybe your whole life. It is possible we could arrange that the two of you could be together in a special high security facility."

"I would like that but I'm sure he would not agree. He believes rogue agents on the CIA payroll killed my mother. All of this is his way of getting back at the U.S."

"We heard that story and did some research to see if it was based on fact. What we found was quite striking. Your mother was actually killed by bin Laden's men after he stayed at your home that night. They may have been afraid she would talk and the secret of his whereabouts would be discovered. It didn't matter that she was a relative. They would have exterminated the whole village if that had been necessary, Omar."

"What are you saying? My own people did this to my mother? Why?"

"I'm afraid so, Omar. There is irrefutable evidence about what happened. Your father is acting on wrong information, a story fabricated by bin Laden to promote his own cause. I have the evidence if you care to see it, but I suspect you sensed all along that something was wrong with the story."

"I did, but my father would never listen. His mind was made up and he was a changed man forever. If we could convince him and I could get him back the remainder of his years, I would do this in an instant."

"I think we can, Omar, but first we must catch him before he kills you. Will you help?"

"Yes, I will but not just for me, for him too."

"Good. We'll put you under a protective watch and be ready. If you get information about when and where he will enter the U.S., please let us know. Until we get him in custody, your life is in danger. One more thing, Jack will accompany you as you leave

CMT today. We want to collect all of the remaining poison that you have in your possession. Thank you, Mr. Kharif, and I truly believe you have made the right decision today. Jack and Aldora, you can finish the interview and discuss the details of our protection plan with Mr. Kharif. I will talk with you later. Goodbye."

Jack said, "Yes, sir."

Aldora said, "Thank you, Director, goodbye."

Aldora looked at Jack and then at Omar and said, "Wow. Thank you, Mr. Kharif. I think you just made our day."

With the tape recorder still running, she said, "We have your comments on tape relating to several subjects including: Technology Investment Corporation, its mission and charter; the purpose of the RFID DAS field tests at CMT; the money to Mr. Kramley and the gifts to his son; the attempted theft of top secret CMT product; the poison and four deaths in San Francisco; your brother and father; and Pharmatek. Based on our discussion with Director Elson, do you wish to make any new or revised statements on those subjects?"

Omar hesitated several seconds as he pondered his next step. Finally he motioned to turn the tape recorder off. Aldora understood and shut it off. She said, "What is it, Omar?"

"I will turn over the drug that you call poison as an indication of my sincerity, but I will not revise my statements at this time." He nodded to turn the recorder back on. "I will leave the original statements stand until the next phase is completed to my satisfaction. I want to see that we are successful with our plan. Then I will make a revised statement. You can understand my situation; I hope that is satisfactory."

"It is, Mr. Kharif, but you should know that if you do not help us capture your father and succeed with our plan, we have enough evidence to arrest, indict, try, and convict you for crimes against the state, including multiple murders. I will personally handle the case in court and see that you face the death penalty. What we have offered is the only way to escape that fate. You help us, we help you, right?"

"I understand Ms. Klein and I appreciate what you are

doing for my father and me. On my mother's grave, I promise to do everything in my power to make the plan work."

"Thank you," said Aldora.

"Mr. Kharif, let's pick up that extra supply of poison you have stashed away and I will tell you about the protective watch under which you will be living starting today," said Jack. "It is not protective custody so it is not 100% foolproof. You have to stay in continuous communication with us and help us keep you safe. You will have a lead agent who will be your contact and your shadow. Other agents will be around at all times no matter where you are. Are we headed to your San Francisco office for the poison?"

"Yes, Mr. Borson, and thank you again for this chance for some redemption. I will do my best."

"Aldora, I will be back soon. Please start the process of setting up the protective watch for Mr. Kharif."

"I will, Jack. Goodbye, Mr. Kharif, and good luck."

"Thank you, Ms. Klein. It was good to meet and talk with you. Be assured that I never want to be on the other side of you in court. Goodbye."

Day One At The Plant

The plant manager, Mr. Japer, met Mr. Kumat as he walked into the plant the next day about noon.

"Hello, sir. The Six Sigma team from the university engineering department and the IPRP team from the United Nations both started first thing this morning. I have the engineers assigned to the four areas you identified, sir: RMs, DDP, T&QC, and Packaging. They drew straws on who would take which area and walked off, their arms loaded with pre-printed charts and whispering something about design, analyse, measure…..and control."

"Thank you, Mr. Japer. Have they found anything yet?"

"I don't think so, sir. They did ask for all of our data for the past six months on the tests we run for quality control. Oh, yes, and the RM specifications and process standards. That is what they are studying right now. The head professor mentioned that, after the data and document study, they will ask us to start a trial production run to observe firsthand the individual process steps. The target date for that is tomorrow."

"Study and evaluate the first day, trial runs to see how we operate versus standards the second day, and I bet address questions and issues and make recommendations the third day?"

"That's about how I have it figured, sir."

"How about the IPRP team?"

"We have put our entire inventory on hold at their request, of course. They have sampled every lot and begun gas chromatograph testing for contamination. We do this kind of testing, too, but it is right after the purification step. Their testing will take into account the packaging process and all the materials used or more appropriately how the hospital receives the product for its use."

"Good, Mr. Japer. I can't imagine they will find anything. This is a better than Class 100 operation. Better than a doctor's office, hospital room, or most any other pharmaceutical manufacturing plant."

"I think you are correct, sir. There is one thing that bothers me, however."

"The IPRP is also doing a mass balance study for the last six months. Their starting point is after derivatization and they want to answer the question, 'What is our yield and where does all of it go?' As you know, sir, your orders are to keep back 1% and hold under lock and key in case it would be needed in an emergency. Because the material is so poisonous at this stage before dilution, there are only two keys to this emergency supply, yours and mine. When I discovered they wanted us to account for every last drop, I checked the emergency supply. There is some missing, sir. It is not from the last six months; it is only a small amount from our first year of production, but definitely some is missing. I would not have noticed had I not been looking so closely. Do you know anything about that, sir?"

"Why would I, Mr. Japer? I have no need for poison. Isn't it so long ago and such a small amount that it will not be part of their investigation? Remember, they are interested primarily in the last six months of production."

"I think so, sir. From what I have seen, they are exceptionally thorough but really focused on their specific assignments. If you did not remove the material, sir, I wonder who did. It would be instant death for anyone who touched or tasted the undiluted material."

"Let's just keep quiet and see if they actually find there is some missing. In the meantime, would you do some discreet inquiries with the plant personnel to see if anyone knows where it might have gone? I can't imagine there would be any foul play here."

"Yes, sir. Maybe if it actually comes up as an issue, we can just say our production records could have been slightly off. We were just starting up."

"Maybe, but the most important thing right now is to get our inventories cleared and our production processes re-certified. I don't think the investigative teams will be so concerned about our not being able to locate a few milliliters of five-year old material that was never intended to be in the supply chain."

"I think you are right, sir. Let's stick with our priorities. Will you be in tomorrow for the trial run and process checks?"

"Yes, I will, Mr. Japer. We need to get back into production as soon as possible. Thank you for all the help and please give the investigative teams anything they need."

"I will, sir. See you tomorrow."

"See you tomorrow, Mr. Japer."

Day Two at The Plant

Day two of the Pharmatek plant investigation started very early. The university Six Sigma team was impressed with the process descriptions, standards, and data records - the whole documentation package for the production of Warfarin-D. Their study showed only a few areas where they would actually make recommendations for process improvements. These were rather insignificant regarding the matter at hand because they related more to cost reduction than quality. It was time to see if the plant personnel actually followed their own process descriptions and standards.

Everyone was at their station, including the Six Sigma team members. Even the two IPRP representatives were on the floor to watch the trial run. The head professor said, "Start it up, Mr. Japer."

The plant personnel knew it was just a trial but they wanted to make it a perfect run. Production of Warfarin-D took about seven hours from start to finish. They were really hyped-up for this and they intended to show they made only high quality product.

Mr. Kumat arrived a little past noon to greet Mr. Japer and watch some of the trial run.

"How are things going, Mr. Japer?"

"They seem to be satisfied so far, sir. All I see are checks on the forms on their clipboards, nods of their heads indicating standards are being met, and approvals to go to the next process step in production."

"Good. Maybe we'll get through this after all."

"The sooner the better, sir."

"Anything from the IPRP team?"

"Yes, they have tested several of the inventory lots, including the one in question for Israpharm, and found all of them to be good. They seemed quite surprised at the results."

"It could be that the multiple illnesses were a result of how the drug was handled at the hospitals, not something that happened here."

"IPRP said they are checking that angle with Israpharm, too, sir. Anyway, I think we look good so far."

"Have they mentioned anything about our emergency supply?"

"Some, especially to note that the last six months of production has been accounted for totally. They noted the small discrepancy between product manufactured and product shipped and inventory and appreciated me telling them about the 1% emergency supply. The head guy told me he did not understand the need for an emergency supply. In fact, he showed me it was marked as a hazardous material on his charts and noted there would be specific official recommendations on this for the future. He also said in a side comment, 'Why in the hell would you need an emergency supply with this much inventory? The product ages less in its diluted form and you have about a year's supply of inventory. If the wrong people got their hands on this, we could be looking at a disaster, thousands and thousands of deaths!' He was really worked up about it, sir."

"It sounds that way. Maybe they are right and it is not needed any longer."

Patek thought for a second then said, "Mr. Japer, as far as I am concerned, it doesn't matter as long as we can get back into production."

"One more thing, sir, they told me they will be accounting for our product produced, even beyond the six month time period. They want to account for the entire product since we started manufacturing. The existence of the emergency supply really has them worried. I told them to go ahead. Everything should be there since we started production five years ago."

Patek grimaced a bit when he heard that, but he recovered and said, "Let them do what they must to get us cleared."

"Yes, sir. I will, sir."

"Did your inquiries with the plant personnel turn up anything about the missing product?"

"No, sir. I asked several people but no one knew anything."

"Ok, Mr. Japer, I will be in tomorrow for the reports on our operation and recommendations for improvement leading to re-certification. Thank you for all your help."

"Thank you, sir. See you tomorrow."

Day Three at The Plant

The meeting was set up for mid-afternoon in the plant conference room. It was also the kitchen, break room, lunchroom, a multipurpose room with a large table and eight or ten molded plastic chairs. It was a little more high-tech looking today with the laptops, Six Sigma charts, trial run diagrams and test data, and product history records.

Dr. Kumat and Mr. Japer were walking toward the room

and noticed the two teams, all six people, huddled together talking outside the entrance. Patek could see the discussion was rather animated and somewhat loud. He said, "Hello, gentlemen, are we ready for the reviews and recommendations?"

The head professor from the Six Sigma team said, "Hello, Dr. Kumat and Mr. Japer, and good afternoon. Yes, we are ready and it has been suggested that the Six Sigma report would be first. Is that alright?"

As they entered the conference room, Patek was somewhat taken aback with all the wall charts and the laptop presentations ready to go. He said, "The order of the reports is up to you, so Six Sigma going first is fine. Before you begin, I want to thank the teams and the individuals for their work. Whatever the results, you should know that I appreciate the expertise, energy, and time invested in this plant process and re-certification review. When people are suspected of becoming ill by using our product, it is a very serious matter to all of us at Pharmatek. We believe we manufacture the highest quality pharmaceutical in the world but must always be open to opportunities for improvement. We welcome the results of your study and any recommendations you might have."

The professor from the university and head of the Six Sigma team said, "Thank you, Dr. Kumat. My report will be short with only one recommendation. For the record, we as a Six Sigma team focused on four areas: Raw Materials; Derivatization, Dilution, and Purification; Testing and Quality Control; and Packaging. In all areas, the standards and specifications are adhered to tenaciously and oversight is excellent. In five years time, the raw material specifications have tightened and the single source supplier has always been able to meet the requirements. The derivatization, dilution and purification process steps use common chemical methodology and best practices and the equipment is state-of-the-art. Yields have improved over the years and the use of clean room technology decreased the possibility of contamination to almost zero. Testing has been and is especially rigorous because of the application or use of the product in the health care industry. The data sets for each lot are recorded and documented for posterity. Data packages are sent, along with the

THE CAMPAIGN OF FEAR

product, to each customer. Packaging is within the higher part of the range of acceptable standards for health care products. The bottle positioning, filling, and capping processes, and individual boxing and case cartoning steps are all well planned. There are some cost reduction possibilities within the packaging materials and process area but it is first class in terms of expected quality. All in all, a very good report on the historical Pharmatek production of Warfarin-D. The trial run only verified what I have just discussed. It was like clockwork with exceptional processes and exceptional people. The output was the highest quality product that met and exceeded all of the testing and quality control guidelines required. I would have no hesitation allowing your plant, Mr. Kumat, to restart production immediately. Just keep doing what you have been doing."

"Thank you, professor. You said at the beginning you had one recommendation."

"Yes, I almost forgot. We were commissioned to focus on in-plant processes and possible contamination. My colleague handling the study of the packaging area recognized that you do not use tracking tags like RFID tags. Once product is ready for shipment, it is our recommendation that, because of the highly sensitive nature of the product it be tracked through the supply chain from Pharmatek to the customer, an RFID tag or similar technology would be a very beneficial add-on to your logistics planning."

Dr. Kumat thought for a second about all of the trouble Omar had caused as a result of his RFID/DAS technology. Emar was dead, four innocent people dead, bank account emptied, and more. Was it worth it? Is technology the answer? Can it be compatible with his faith? "Of course, professor. That is a great recommendation."

"Thank you, Dr. Kumat."

The head of the IPRP team started by saying, "My report will be equally short and with only one recommendation. I must stress this is only a partial report for the Pharmatek part. There are other studies being done by IPRP team members on shipping as well as at Israpharm and its customers reporting illnesses. The report will not be complete until all the parts of the study are finished."

"That said, we first tested every production lot you had

387

in inventory. It certainly included the lots in question, where the illnesses occurred, but several other lots as well. Our testing showed only the highest quality product, easily meeting test specifications with no contamination. It indicates that the plant produces very acceptable product and if some contamination happened, it probably occurred in shipping or at the Israpharm or customer locations. However, as I implied, the plant cannot be cleared for production until completion of the other parts of the study."

"How long do you think that might take, sir?" asked Dr. Kumat.

"These multiple site studies are more difficult and take more time. Remember, we are trying to gather facts and evidence to differentiate between accidental and intentional contamination. It is tough detective work. I would say two to three weeks, sir."

Dr. Kumat made a note and then heard the IPRP head say, "In the meantime, there is another very serious issue that could impact re-certification and start up. It turns out in International Pharmaceutical, Human and Animal Health Care and Industrial Businesses, all poisons must be accounted for down to the last drop. We were made aware of your storehouse of derivatized but undiluted material, concentrated Warfarin-D, that you call your emergency supply. It is officially categorized as a poison, one of the most potent at this stage and must be legally accounted for. Our investigation showed that by including this emergency supply, the last four years of product balanced between product manufactured and product shipped, used and in inventory. The problem is in the first year of production. There is an imbalance of about 50 milliliters, Dr. Kumat. We need to locate this missing material, this very, very potent poison, before we could ever even consider re-certification and start up."

"I have no idea where it could be," said Dr. Kumat. We had just started manufacturing; maybe our production records were a little off. We only save 1% so we can address any emergency where additional Warfarin-D would be needed in a crisis."

"I'm sorry, Dr. Kumat, this is not about convincing me; it is about international law. It gets worse, sir. There is an immediate confiscation of the so-called emergency supply and a $10 million fine regardless of whether the missing material is found. If the material is located in total and intact, you will need to appear before the IPRP and request reinstatement as a manufacturer of Warfarin-D. The fine sticks but reinstatement would be possible. I'm sure one condition of reinstatement would be your agreement to never keep an off-the-books storehouse of deadly poison."

"And what if the lost material is not found?" asked Dr. Kumat.

"That is a problem, sir. Our laboratories have been made aware of this poison being used in two separate incidents recently - one in Israel and one in the United States. The authorities might put two and two together and assume the lost material, your undiluted Warfarin-D, was used in those deaths. A total of five people were killed. For your sake, Dr. Kumat, I hope you find your lost material or know where someone else can find it. Otherwise, at the very least, you could be considered an accessory in the deaths. The penalties for being an accessory in international deaths are always severe."

Dr. Kumat looked at Mr. Japer and said, "Let's interview everyone to see if we can find out where this lost material is."

Gulping, Mr. Japer said, "Yes, sir."

"I said I had only one recommendation, sir. It is to pay the $10 million fine immediately and find the 50 ml of lost, undiluted Warfarin-D. Find it fast. My report will be in the hands of my superiors within the hour. Thank you."

There was a long silence. Finally Mr. Kumat said, "Thank you," got up and left the room deep in thought.

Somehow, automatically, he arrived at his office and collapsed in his desk chair. He thought ... $10 million? I have no money, Omar made sure of that. I can't return the lost material; some of it has already been used. I will be connected to the deaths in Israel and the U.S. if I'm not careful. Maybe I can put this on Omar. He stole the material and was responsible for the deaths. It just might work, he thought, but first things first. I have to get my money back so I can pay the fine. It was late so he left a note for his assistant to make the arrangements for the trip to the U.S. The note read, "*Please reschedule my trip to the U.S. immediately. Change the trip so that I am in Boston first, then Minneapolis-St. Paul, San Francisco, and then home. I will spend about one day in each location. Remember; book me as Professor Dr. Patek Kumat, CEO, Pharmatek. Thank you."*

The Integrated Team in Boston

It was a grand get together in Boston. The CMT team had arrived with all of their gear and within a couple of days was fully set up in nearby laboratory space just a floor away.

Chad and Brad had been watching the dynamics of this large team of ATP and CMT personnel for several days. The acoustics work had been refined on both the detection and detonation products. Code enhancements in the software were astounding considering the difficulties of wave articulation and identification of the explosive chemicals. Miniaturization was going well with much progress on the wave generators. Team meetings were being held but there was yet to be an integration of the two products into a system.

After about a week, Brad walked into Chad's office and said, "This isn't working, Chad."

Chad looked up from his computer, nodded, and said, "I know." He got up from his desk and motioned Brad to join him at the table. As he sat down, Brad said, "I'm not saying that the team hasn't made great progress. Good God, we have the most advanced, sophisticated, state of the art products ever for finding and detonating explosive devices. However, the efforts to integrate the technologies into a system have been timid and uneventful. Have you come to the same conclusion?"

"I have but it is still early. Maybe with a little more time they can learn to work together better."

"Maybe, but probably not. Chad, what's the most important management challenge in a project where two separate teams have to join and function as one team?"

"You are right, Brad – one leader. One team, one leader. We have four team leaders, they have one. My role is probably not so clear to CMT either. It is confusing and not obvious as to who is in charge."

"Yes and I walk around trying to help everyone but probably considered an outsider by both teams. You know, like consultants are."

"I do know and since it's your technology mostly, do the people listen to their team leaders or do they listen to you?"

"Chad, what is the other huge management challenge in a project like this one?"

"Besides leadership? For me it has always had to do with technology. If there were short timelines, there was always the need to get technology from the outside if it wasn't available internally. You cannot do technology development at the same time you are doing product development. Either from inside or outside, the technology has to be in hand."

"Right, and what we have here are outside technologies being imposed on the projects and the people. The NIH, 'not invented here' syndrome has always been real and it is showing up in our project. We have to address the two project management challenges soon in order to be successful. Otherwise, a month from now we will all be even more frustrated and no further ahead on a fully integrated system. Any ideas?"

"Yes, Brad. I believe you are the one to lead the combined project. As the designated team leader, your role would be more than an advisor or consultant. You are not from ATP or CMT and would not have potential biases favoring one company or the other. They respect you a lot now but if you are really on the team and the leader, they will respect you and follow you even more. What do you think about that?"

"I didn't sign up to be the team leader but what you say makes a lot of sense. I'll do it if you talk with your people and get some advance buy-in. I'll talk to the CMT team leader and see what he thinks."

"You got yourself a deal. What about the NIH syndrome?"

"Well, if I really do become team leader, I have an idea. In my observation, this team is one of great ability and high potential. They are actually getting very close to what I call the third generation in explosives detection and detonation. It does not require wave content analysis or wave articulation and correlation to chemical components as a second step. In the Generation III technology, a smart wave is programmed to find the chemical components of explosives in one step. In other words, it knows what it is looking for in advance. When it is found, the explosive can then be destroyed by simply turning the original searching wave into a detonating wave."

"It sounds like you have already done this."

"I have, but it needs to be developed further. If I can provide just a few more clues to the key people, they will believe it was their idea, something that belongs to them and the team. It could become the rallying point for the project."

"It is worth a try, a little risky to go after the next generation at this point, but why not? It would put us in such a superior position, but are you sure you have the technology that can pull this off?" Chad hesitated a second then said, "Cancel that question, please. Why would I even ask that after what I have seen you do so far, Brad. I'm sorry, let's go for it!"

"I appreciate your confidence, Chad. To ease your mind, I really do know how to do this. If you will have discussions with Bill, Lyncoln, Kan D, and Zen, I will do my part with CMT and create ownership for the project within the team."

"Great, you can consider it done."

"Let's go raise the bar another notch."

Patek's Contact with IPRP

The Liberator was still very troubled about Pharmatek and the missing, undiluted Warfarin-D. He knew he could come up with only about 50% of the "lost" material. With the capsules he had made and the vials used by Omar, that added up to about 25 ml. Would returning 25ml be enough to satisfy the IPRP? His scientific mind said no. Mr. Japer had gone through the process of interviewing everyone involved with the production of Warfarin-D. Of course no one knew anything about the missing material. He hoped the IPRP

THE CAMPAIGN OF FEAR

would recognize he was being very thorough in his search, even though it was only a delaying action, a cover-up to getting at the truth. His thinking process and consideration of various scenarios kept leading him to the same conclusion. Put it all on Omar and then get rid of him. Get the money back from Lyncoln Fuller so he can pay the fine and get Pharmatek back in operation so it can continue to fund Technolibertat. He would address the work for bin Laden later, after he personally determined the real status of the programs in the States. Besides being weak and unskilled, Omar could no longer be trusted. He thought back to his wife, Emar, and now Omar. He would be alone. The Liberator shook himself back to the reality of needing to report back to the IPRP. He picked up the phone, punched in the numbers, and heard the ring and the answer, "IPRP."

"This is Dr. Patek Kumat, CEO of Pharmatek. I would like to speak to …"

"The representative who lead the study at the Pharmatek plant recently?"

"Yes, please."

"He is right here, sir."

"Hello, Dr. Kumat. I thought you might be calling soon."

"I don't have much to report but I want you to know that we take this matter very seriously and are working hard on the resolution."

"You should, sir. The IPRP can shut you down, permanently, if you do not comply with the fine and finding the missing poison."

"I understand, sir, but this business is too important to our workers, community, and country to be shut down. Concerning the fine, it is difficult to come up with $10 million in 30 days. Can the IPRP be a little flexible and give us more time?"

"I'm sorry, sir, we are not talking about Syrian law or Middle East law. This is international law and there is no flexibility. There is only the expectation of compliance within the time allowed. Otherwise, you will be arrested. The same is the case for locating and returning the missing poison; 30 days or you will be arrested. Non-payment of the fine and an inability to return the poison would be treated as separate offenses and total 20-30 years prison time, depending on the circumstances."

"Twenty to thirty years? I cannot believe this is happening to me."

"I'm sorry, sir, but it is."

"You should know that Mr. Japer has held interviews with company personnel. They all have the same story. They know nothing about the missing material. We believe them, sir. On thinking about this further, the emergency supply is and has been handled very carefully. It was under lock and key. There are only two keys – Mr. Japer's and mine. Finding that the missing material was from our first year of production five years ago was interesting. Mr. Japer is single so no one would have had access to his key. My younger son, Omar, was around at that time. He was preparing to work in one of our subsidiary companies, Technology Investment Corporation, in the U.S. He might know something about this. He might have taken the missing material for some reason – I don't know. It's the only thing we can come up with as an explanation."

"As I mentioned sir, international law is different and to some a little strange. You had better do everything in your power to find the missing material in the 30-day timeframe. Why? Because, at that time, if the material is not returned, we will initiate an international search for the material and you will be arrested. By rule of international law, we cannot do anything until 30 days have passed. But after that, we will pursue every recourse."

"I understand, sir. It happens that I am traveling to the States very soon and will be meeting with my son. I hope there will be a timely resolution to the missing material issue and to our ability to pay the assessed fine."

"That is excellent, sir. Just remember, the clock is ticking and there are no borders for international law or search teams."

"I'll be in touch after returning from the States. Goodbye for now and thank you for the legal clarification."

"You are welcome, sir. Good luck. Goodbye."

Sci-1 Contacts Omar

"Omar, I have had second thoughts about my project."

"Hi, Sci-1. You mean additional thoughts about how to defend against CIED?"

"No, I mean second thoughts! I bought into the mission of Technolibertat because it seemed like it was time for scientists to do something to help the Muslim culture. I wanted to help use science and technology for economic and social development. Your assignment has me working to support the 'Campaign of Fear' with its use of EFPs, IEDs, car bombs, and suicide bombers. These cowardly tools and madmen are beginning to define our culture, religion, and our people. I will no longer be a part of this and I certainly will not use science and technology in such a perverse way. Please do not …"

"Wait a second, Sci-1. Confidentially, I just had an interesting discussion with a leader within Technolibertat. Quite frankly, I'm a little scared about what they might do but basically I feel the same way you do."

"I thought I might have to go it alone on this, Omar."

"No, but we have to be careful. The good thing is that we have done enough with CIED, RFID/DAS and DT-A1 that they might leave us alone."

"Don't be naïve, Omar. What do they say - once in, never out? I'm going to change my name, move away, and change careers. I'm going to become a different person. This is the last time you will hear from me. Don't try to find me."

"Goodbye, my friend, and good luck with your transformation."

The phone went dead and Omar felt a chill run all the way down his spine. His head felt tingly and he started to sweat. First his palms, then his armpits, forehead, and feet. His thoughts were racing. What if I cannot deliver, what if they decide I'm expendable, what if … He forced himself to stop that train of thought. He remembered he was already removed as head of TIC anyway and was probably to be terminated soon to boot. His deal with DoAT was the best choice for both him and his father. Please let it work. Praise be to Allah.

Omar Calls Brad

"Hello, Omar, how are you?"

"I am fine, Dr. Tully. This is just a quick call to see how our technology projects are going at TRI and ATP. It hasn't been too long since they licensed the wave generation technology but there will be a report due to my superiors soon."

Brad was thinking. Thank God for cell phones so he doesn't know where I am. Then he said, "Things are going well. I am functioning as an advisor to ATP already. We were right; they had come to a roadblock and needed this technology for their project."

Omar smiled but it was short-lived as he thought about Sci-1 leaving before he came up with a defense against the new technology. He said, "That is excellent, Dr. Tully. What about the other project with Dr. Fuller on DACS?"

Brad hesitated a second, then responded by saying, "You know this is a very, very tough project. We have had a couple of meetings and generated some ideas. Nothing concrete yet but some reasonably good approaches. Dr. Fuller is coming to Minnesota soon to work exclusively on this with me."

"Good. How are things going at TRI?"

"I haven't had time to do much with all this ATP and control stuff I'm doing."

"That is alright, Dr. Tully. The other two projects are the most important at this time. I wasn't trying to be pushy."

"It's okay, Omar. I know you have an investment to protect. Why don't you schedule some time and visit me in Minnesota?"

"I'd like that, Dr. Tully. My father will be visiting me soon so it would have to be after that."

"Any time is fine; just let me know a little in advance of your visit. Your father can visit, too, if you like."

Omar grimaced and said, "He is on a very tight schedule, but I'll check with him. Right now we think he is just going to visit San Francisco."

"The two of you are welcome any time, of course."

"Thanks, Dr. Tully, for both the update and the invitation. I appreciate it. Until later, goodbye."

"Goodbye, Omar."

Omar's Call To His Father

"Hello, Liberator. I am calling with good news after my interview with DoAT on the Kramley case."

"Hello, Omar. I'm glad you called. There are some things we need to discuss."

"Yes, sir. I want to report that the authorities believe the Kramley deaths to be suicides just as you had seen on the CMT intranet. They asked a lot of questions about TIC, the RFID/DAS field tests with CMT, the money and of course Thomas and his family. I justified our involvement with CMT and Mr. Kramley, explained away the money, and admitted to no wrongdoing. They seemed to be satisfied with my responses to all the questions and it did seem to be an informal interview to basically wrap up the case."

"I'm glad, Omar." The Liberator was thinking about whether all that made any difference in his plan for Omar. The unspoken answer that came booming from his brain was, NO! It was the naïve mishandling of the organization's finances that was most important. His decision on the fate of Omar still stands.

"Yes, sir. Will you be visiting the U.S. soon?"

"Yes, I plan to see you in a few days." He was careful to not divulge his travel plan and schedule just saying, "Pharmatek will be closed for some time so it is convenient for me to visit now. I hope you will have some ideas about your next assignment, Omar."

"I have a lot of ideas to share with you, father. It will be good to see you."

"Omar, do you have any of the poison left that I recently gave you?" The Liberator was still hoping if he could return most of the missing material, the IPRP might be sufficiently satisfied to allow him to restart production. "You must still have several vials."

Omar thought, I did but they are in the possession of DoAT now. What do I say?

"No, I used it all for the job I had, sir. Why do you need

more vials? You implied your supply is quite large."

The Liberator thought, damn, and then said, "It is, but I like to keep this material in my possession at all times until needed. As you know, it is very potent and dangerous if not handled properly. Are you sure you used it all?"

"Yes sir, I am quite sure." Switching the subject quickly, he said, "Say, since the authorities are looking at me a little differently now, I was able to check on the status of our projects. ATP has signed the licensing agreement on acoustic wave generation, Lyncoln and Brad are working on DACS, and TRI is working on other aspects of the CIED program. Our plans are being implemented just as we wanted, sir."

The Liberator thought, yes, everything except emptying our bank account. You still have to pay for that, Omar. He said, "That is good, Son. Be sure to get the phone message updates from your San Francisco office. I don't want to miss you when I visit."

"Yes, sir, I will be waiting here to see you. Call when you arrive at the airport."

"I will, Son. One last thing – have you been contacted by anyone from an organization called the IPRP, the International Pharmaceutical Review Panel run under the oversight of the United Nations?"

"No, sir. Should I expect to be? Would it be about Pharmatek?"

"Yes. I mentioned we are closed right now. This group has the responsibility for getting us re-certified."

"Why do we need to be re-certified? Did something happen at the plant?"

"It's a long and complex story. What I want to tell you is very simple. If they contact you about Pharmatek, tell them you are not very familiar with the operation. Just the basics, like the product is a blood thinner used by hospitals and that I kept a very small, emergency supply so that in unique circumstances if more were needed, we could have it available quickly. That is all you know, isn't it, Son?"

Omar thought, that's an interesting way to describe our very own personal, massive, deadly, poison supply. He finally said, "Of course, sir, that is all I know."

"Good, Omar. That will help us in our re-certification efforts. Anything else to discuss?"

"No, sir, see you in San Francisco."

"See you in San Francisco, Son."

Part III

Will Technology Prevail?

Chapter 15

The Liberator Plans to Travel to the U.S. to Take Care of Business

Al Qaeda Letter

Dr. Kumat was making his final plans for the trip to the States when the letter arrived. He thought it strange for it had no postage stamp, no return address, only his names, Professor Dr. Patek Kumat or Eomar Kharif, with no address. His assistant delivered it saying only, "It must have been hand delivered, sir. I found it on my desk. Who is Eomar Kharif, sir?"

"Someone I knew a long time ago but he is no longer around," said Patek as he walked into his office.

He opened the letter very carefully trying to keep everything intact. It was one page. As he unfolded it, he let out a gasp! Without reading the short paragraph what he saw at the bottom of the page was K, AQ. It was from one of bin Laden's closest lieutenants. He was terrified.

Patek threw the letter on his desk and walked away quickly as if it might ignite, explode, or something worse. He knew this K, this Krishna from before. 'K' was the one who told him about his wife's death and he was the one who approved the Technolibertat contract to help protect the 'Campaign of Fear'. His mind was racing with all kinds of thoughts: this letter is essentially from bin Laden; he found out about all the things that went wrong with

Technolibertat, TIC, and Pharmatek. Am I being put on notice or am I in even worse trouble? Patek stared at the letter from a distance and walked slowly towards his desk. He picked up the letter and read slowly, *Sir, we are aware of the ongoing United States federal investigation of your son and the Technology Investment Corporation in San Francisco and beyond. In addition we have learned about the International Pharmaceutical Review Panel investigation of you and the Pharmatek operation in Syria. These taken together pose a significant threat to the usefulness of Technolibertat and its ability to remain under contract to AQ. Please provide tangible and quantitative evidence that you have things under control. Until then, our relationship with you and Technolibertat remains in question. K, AQ*

Patek threw the letter back on the desk. He thought, . . . And this didn't mean in 30 days either! He was glad he had a plan and would be leaving tomorrow to implement it. If he were successful, it might be enough for him to return to Syria and survive. If not, he did not want to even think about that scenario. He put the letter into the envelope, jammed it into his suit pocket, and left the office white and shaken.

Omar Contacts Jack

Omar said, "Hello, Mr. Borson. I have some information about my father's visit."

"Hello, Omar, are you still in San Francisco?"

"Yes. I will be here for a while. I have just spoken to my father and he is coming here very soon. He never tells me exactly but I expect him within the next few days."

"He plans to meet with you in San Francisco?"

"Yes, he was very clear about that."

"That will make our watches a lot easier. We won't have to focus on the other cities. Remember, we have a protective watch on you as we discussed earlier and we also have a watch on your father entering the U.S. If he is coming directly to San Francisco, it will make our work a lot easier."

"Mr. Borson, I wasn't quite honest with you in the interview. I have been relieved of my duties as CEO of Technology Investment Corporation. My father believes that I am weak, unskilled, and he probably doesn't trust me either. Your director was right when he said Dr. Patek Kumat is coming here to kill me. He keeps talking about my next assignment, but I believe that to be a ruse. After the interview, I tried to talk to him about the original purpose of Technolibertat and how that has changed for the worse. He would hear none of it, none."

"I'm sorry, Omar. I believe the only way we have a chance is to convince him that we had nothing to do with the death of his wife, your mother. The evidence is available if we have the time and place to present it to him. Did anything else come up in your conversation with him?"

"Yes, he mentioned that Pharmatek was closed down and needed to be re-certified. Also, that I might be contacted by the IPRP, the organization responsible for certification. He was very worried; I could tell because he was coaching me on how I should answer their questions."

"Did you know that Pharmatek was being closed down?"

"No, I didn't. With his feelings about me, Pharmatek closed and having to be re-certified and whatever else, he seems to be under a lot of pressure. It might not be easy to convince him of anything let alone that al Qaeda killed my mother."

"We'll find a way, Omar. Trust me, it will work."

"Thank you, sir. I hope so. Goodbye."

"Goodbye Omar. Stay in touch."

The Feds' Watch Shifts to San Francisco

Jack called his FBI colleague immediately. "Hi, Dick, we have it on good authority that Mr. Patek Kumat or Eomar Kharif, whichever name he is using, will enter the U.S. at the San Francisco airport. Please focus your efforts there."

"We will, Jack. Where did you get the information?"

"It was from the man's son, who is helping us to take him

into custody and try to turn him. The son's name is Omar Kharif. His background is in the watch request we recently sent to you."

"Oh, yes, I recognize the name. San Francisco it is."

"Remember, it could be very soon. Today or tomorrow even. We need this guy, Dick. Thanks very much."

"Talk to you later, Jack. Maybe I'll see you soon. Goodbye."

"Great. Goodbye, Dick."

Dr. Kumat's arrival at Logan International was almost without incident. Professor Dr. Patek Kumat answered all of the questions at passport control acceptably. When the agent asked about Pharmatek and his business in the U.S., Dr. Kumat said, "It is a pharmaceutical company. We make only one product, a blood thinner used after surgery to prevent clots. I am here to visit some of our U.S. customers."

The agent said, "My mother needed a blood thinner after her recent heart surgery."

"I hope it was Warfarin-D, sir. It's the best blood thinner on the market."

"Maybe, I don't know for sure. Could you wait just a moment, please?" The agent had been checking the watch list every so often during the day and he was thinking that he recognized the name, Patek Kumat. He brought up the screen on his computer showing watches by international airports, clicked on Logan, and a list of about ten names appeared. He looked closely at the names several times. There was no Patek Kumat. He was almost sure he had seen it just hours ago.

"May I see your itinerary, Dr. Kumat?"

"Yes, sir. It is Boston, Minneapolis, and San Francisco in about four days. We have customers in all three cities."

"Thank you, sir. I see. Is this strictly a business trip?"

"Not exactly, I plan to see my son when I am in San Francisco. He has been in the U.S. for several years and works for a company called Technology Investment Corporation. Do you know it?"

"I don't believe so, sir. Do they have offices in Boston?"

"Yes, plus Washington, D.C. and San Francisco."

The agent was thinking, I must be wrong about seeing his name on the list. If he has a son in the States and he himself runs a pharmaceutical company, he must be okay. He hesitated a few seconds more then stamped the passport and said, "Dr. Kumat, have a good stay and visit with your son."

"Thank you, sir." Professor Dr. Patek Kumat walked to baggage claim thinking that was too close. The bag was already on the carousel. He picked it up and went immediately toward the exit. His bag was small and his papers were in order. No problems there. He thought, I made it and now to the work at hand.

Pharmatek and Cash Flow

"Hello, Director."

"Hello, Absek, I'm glad you called. I hear our plan with Pharmatek and Dr. Kumat is working."

"Yes. My sources tell me the orders for Warfarin-D have stopped, the plant is closed down, and there are sanctions against Dr. Kumat. A Six Sigma team from the university did a manufacturing process study focusing on contamination and gave Pharmatek a clean bill of health. Even a trial, start-up run was deemed to be very successful. No surprises there, my friend."

"That's correct Absek. We knew the operation was high quality but we had to get it shut down one way or another. Tell Israpharm that the U.S. Government is very grateful."

"I already have, sir. As you know, it was the study and following actions taken by the IPRP that really got Pharmatek and Dr. Kumat. We heard about a $10 million fine that is payable 30 days from the date issued and tens of years of jail time pending if it isn't paid and the lost, undiluted product is not found. Have you heard the same information?"

"Yes, I have, Absek. We fed the IPRP some information about the poison and gave them guidelines on fines, jail time, and timing. Based on our evidence about Pharmatek's profits funding the terrorist organization, Technolibertat, they were very willing to help. Have you heard anything about Dr. Kumat's reaction?"

"Not very much only that he is on his way to the U.S. or is there already. The word is that Boston is the entry point."

"Oh my God, our intelligence is that it would be San Francisco. We have removed him from the watch list at all other international airport cities."

"We are not sure our information is accurate, sir. I would, however, reinstate the watches for Boston and Washington, D.C. With the three cities covered, you should be okay."

"I'm doing that as we talk, Absek. I hope he hasn't gotten through our net. We'll know not to trust information from his son next time. Anything else, Absek?"

"One more item, sir. The sources also indicated there may have been contact made with Dr. Kumat by al Qaeda. It is sketchy, sir, so there is a big question mark behind this one. Anyway, the contact might have one of bin Laden's lieutenants by the name of Krishna. We only know the one name but he goes by K!"

"What was the nature of the contact, Absek?"

"Again, don't take this for fact, but it was said to put Dr. Kumat on notice about the viability of his organization, Technolibertat, and the continuing relationship with al Qaeda. Simply put, I guess his leadership was being questioned and he was to show proof that things were under control."

"Wow! Talking about reactions, first his bank account disappears, then Pharmatek and his cash flow gets shut down, and now al Qaeda is demanding proof of the viability of Technolibertat. As a psychologist, I would say this guy is ready to crack, Absek."

"Yes. I'm not a psychologist, but my experienced guess is that his objectives for the U.S. trip are to get his money back and to eliminate Omar and anybody else he has identified as problems. He is now in survival mode, not just saving the business or the organization. He wants to save his own life."

"I think you are right, Absek. I will put all of our people on alert. What is your experience about how al Qaeda works? Given the contact information is correct, would they be tracking him in the States already?"

"You can bet on it and how do you say, 'take the money to

the bank,' sir. It could be that this K, Krishna, would show up too under certain circumstances."

"What would those be, Absek?"

"The importance of technology to the future of the Muslim Nation is not shared by most of the followers of bin Laden's al Qaeda. They are the fundamentalists, the people who have a literal interpretation of Islam. In their thinking, there no place for technology in either their culture or their future. If Krishna is the one who approved the Technolibertat work for al Qaeda, he has taken a huge risk. It would not be out of the question that he would want to check on, take stock of, evaluate, and assess everything that has been done under the terms of the contract with Technolibertat and TIC. Remember the test for technology they set up was the ultimate test. It was to save their 'Campaign of Fear'. If it fails at that, there is good reason to believe the literalists will have won. They would say, 'I told you so, there is no place for technology.' 'K' would be eliminated for sure and technology squashed once again."

"Are you saying we should somehow let them think they have won?"

"My friend, their potential use of technology was distorted and for evil purposes. Cultures and futures aren't built on that. What I'm saying is that our original plan is the best one. Introducing technology to them but staying always one step ahead is best. We can't let technology take the hit for the failure and have it lose the potential for improving their cultural and human development."

"Absek, I really appreciate your insight on these complex cultural matters. You have given me much to think about but first I must find Dr. Kumat. Do you have a file on this 'K' or Krishna, bin Laden's lieutenant? I'll have to be on the lookout for him, too."

"Yes, we have a file but there is not much in the file, sir. I will send you what we have. Be careful, my friend, the Liberator could have you on his list of problems, too."

"I will, Absek, thanks again for all your help on the case. Let's talk again soon and let me know if you get any more information to locate 'K'. Okay?"

"I will, sir, until later, goodbye."

"Goodbye, Absek."

Chapter 16

The Attacks…..Who Lives And Who Dies?

The Liberator Tries To Get The Bank Codes

Lyncoln asked Brad, "Have you gotten used to all these people watching you?"

"Not really. It seems there are more recently. It isn't just because I'm in Boston with the team. I know some are watching me and some are watching you, but I sense something different. Just be careful."

"I will! Did I hear that you might not be here tonight because you are seeing Zen?"

"Yep. You'll have to get along without me tonight, roomie."

"She is a great gal; I just love working with her. Have you guys been together long?"

"Not really, but I'm hoping to catch up fast."

"She feels the same way?"

"I think so. I hope so! See you tomorrow sometime Lyncoln. I'm going to take off."

"Okay, see you tomorrow."

Brad left Lyncoln's apartment wondering how he had found out about his relationship with Zen. He was just a block from the bus stop. As he walked, he saw a man, hat pulled down over his eyes, watching. He had seen him before, just yesterday when he and Lyncoln came home together after working with the team at ATP. He didn't think much about it except that it was probably another FBI agent watching. He arrived at the bus stop just in time to board the bus and head off to see Zen.

Lyncoln was at his computer on the dining room table. There was a knock on the door. Lyncoln thought, I wonder who that could be.......anyway the FBI is watching, right? He cracked open the door with the safety lock on and peeked through. Suddenly, the man, an imposing figure, lunged at the door with his shoulder and all his weight busting the door open. The door hit Lyncoln hard on the head and neck and knocked him back. He staggered and fell, rapidly losing consciousness. The big guy was on top of him as things went black.

Lyncoln awoke feeling very strange, with his head throbbing. He was tied to a chair in front of his computer but couldn't move his arms or legs. He saw the intruder and tried to scream. What came out was barely discernable, "Who the fu…ck are you and wh…at the hell have you d…one to me?" He tried twisting his arms and turning his knees but nothing worked. His voice was affected but he tried again grunting, "What the sh…it do you wa…nt?"

The man smiled strangely and seemed satisfied. He put his knife down, nodded his head and said, "I want my money back. Omar paid too much for the DACS contract." He pulled a chair over and sat down beside Lyncoln. As he moved the mouse, the computer screen lit up. He went to bookmarks, clicked, scanned down to one labeled 'offshore account' and clicked again. A screen came up requesting an identification number and password. The man turned to Lyncoln, with one hand moving toward the knife, and said, "I need your ID number and password."

Lyncoln knew this guy was going to kill him. With all his mental strength, he reasoned the FBI didn't see him come into the building. They don't know what is going on. I'm on my own and besides I don't even know the second set of ID number and password. Lyncoln grunted, "No… I'm fu…cked any…way."

411

The intruder was furious slamming his fist so hard on the table the fruit bowl bounced up and banged back down. "Lyncoln, the drug I gave you was an over-dosage of a blood thinner. It causes immediate paralysis obviously." He picked up the knife menacingly and whispered, "And, with it in your system, if you are cut, you will bleed to death. If you give me the information, I'll transfer the money and let you go. Otherwise, ……."

Lyncoln grunted something unintelligible.

The man stood up, pointed a finger at Lyncoln and said, "I wonder if you have a little book of codes someplace?" He walked over to the desk, moved the papers around and saw the pocket calendar. Paging through, he could see it wasn't used as a calendar but in going all the way back to the address section, there they were, all by alphabet. He flipped to O and found OffShore Account-ID, 13467908; Password, Software. He walked back to the table, sat at the computer and entered the codes. Up came a new screen which read, "This account requires a second identification number and password for transfers and withdrawals." The intruder was dumbfounded and pissed. He knew he was beaten. He looked at Lyncoln, shook his head and said, "It didn't have to be this way. It was only money to you." He went back to the desk, searched through every page of the calendar…..nothing. Returning to the table, he looked at the screen, turned to Lyncoln as if to say, "One last chance."

Lyncoln said nothing and tried to close his eyes.

The intruder picked up the knife, reached over and grabbed Lyncoln's left hand and slashed it across the palm. It was a deep cut and he noticed Lyncoln's fingers moved ever so slightly as if he could feel the pain. Was the paralysis wearing off? It didn't matter, this wasn't going to take much longer. There was so much blood, his reaction was to grab towels from the bathroom to help catch it.

Lyncoln was watching in horror, silently accepting his fate.

The intruder picked up his knife and the black case with the drugs and put them in his pocket. He shut down the computer, straightened-up the desk and took a quick look at the kitchen and bathroom. Everything was in order.

Lyncoln was groaning and nodding a little as he moved in and out of consciousness.

The intruder took the ties off, put the towels and Lyncoln's arms on the table and pushed his head down on his arms. He thought, He's not going anywhere and the huge loss of blood means he will be dead soon. At least I'll have that satisfaction. It's time to leave.

Suddenly, the phone rang. One ring, two rings... the visitor stood silent as if the phone would hear the slightest noise. Three rings then the answering machine clicked on to say, "This is Lyncoln. I'm not available. Please leave a message."

"Lyncoln, this is Brad. I want you to know that Zen and I are going to make a quick weekend trip to Minnesota. If anyone at the party on Saturday asks, please tell them we'll be back for the Monday briefing. Have a good weekend, buddy."

The intruder said quietly, "What a coincidence. This could not have worked out better. Dr. Tully, you are next." He was able to lock the door behind him, went to the lobby, picked up his bag under the sofa where he had stashed it earlier, and proceeded to the back of the building to exit the same way he had come in. He thought, It was smart to come earlier today, after the FBI had escorted Lyncoln and Brad to work, enter through the front and unlock the back door. He opened the back door, carefully locked the lock, stepped outside and closed the door. Once outside, he quickly walked over, and peeked around the back corner of the building toward the front to see if the FBI agent was still there. He was, no more the wiser and still on watch alone. As he started to turn to make his get-away from the back of the building, he felt cold metal on his temple. His peripheral vision offered only a dark shadow with a long barrel gun. A voice from the shadow said, "Stay still, very still, brother. I bring a message from 'K' so listen well. The message is: "We are watching and waiting for a response to my letter. I trust you are doing the work of our leader. Praise Allah." Then he was gone, silently, quickly leaving nothing but those lasting words.

The intruder had not been able to breathe since K's emissary appeared and was finally able to let out a sigh and take in some air.

He said to himself, "I am in trouble if I am being watched

413

in the U.S. by 'K' and al Qaeda. If I can carry out my plan, however, I might be able to survive. There is one thing for sure. If there were too many questions or I had posed too much risk to al Qaeda, I would be dead already." He shook himself back into action, telling himself, I have to get to the airport for my flight to Minneapolis-St. Paul. It is getting late. I wonder what flight Dr. Tully and this Zen will be taking. The Liberator walked a block, flagged a cab, and was on his way to the airport. He put his gloves in the bag along with the small black case and knife so the bag could be checked and he would get through security with no problems. He sat thinking, planning, and trembling at what he had yet to do and what could be done to him. Time passed quickly and he arrived at the airport. He paid the cabbie and went inside to check the flight board. There were two flights to MSP; one leaving in about 30 minutes and his scheduled flight which would leave in about 90 minutes. As he reached the ticketing area, he checked in electronically and was issued his boarding pass and claim ticket for his bag. The agent was nice to him so he said, "I know you can't tell me if someone is on my flight, but can you tell me if Dr. Bradford Tully was scheduled to be on the earlier flight to MSP?" The agent looked at her records and said, "Yes, he is on the earlier flight.

"Thank you, madam. He is a friend of mine and we are to link up in Minneapolis. Thanks, again."

The Liberator felt a little more at ease now as he walked toward security. His breathing was better and he would have some time alone with his thoughts. It was a busy night ... too busy.

Later that evening:

The rest of Lyncoln's FBI watch team had come back to the apartment location. They were no longer needed to watch Brad because he had left safely with Zen for Minnesota. The agents checked in with the lone agent on duty who said, "Nothing going on here; I haven't seen anyone go in the front entrance all night and the back entrance is still locked." The senior agent positioned his men for the weekend duty. Lyncoln's lights were still on even though it was late, but that was normal for him. The senior agent said, "We'll make contact with him sometime tomorrow, I'm sure. We know he will be going to the team party about 3 PM. Stay sharp everyone."

The Liberator Leaves for Minneapolis-St. Paul

Getting through security took some time but there were no problems. Professor Dr. Patek Kumat did look the part of a professor so most people would not recognize his real reason for being here. He found a seat near his departure gate and started thinking and planning what to do about his next problem, Dr. Bradford Tully. What were his assets? First, there was a standing invitation to visit Tully Research, Inc. This had come through Omar and probably was just a courtesy. He thought he could use it to his advantage however. Second, in his checked bag, he had the knife and his black case containing more Warfarin-D blood thinner samples and several vials of poison. He wondered; could he risk using any of the precious poison? Probably not. They would know there would be a connection with the other deaths to him. What were his liabilities? First, the FBI is protecting Dr. Tully. He assumed this was around the clock but wasn't certain about that. There was nothing he could do about that. Second, Dr. Tully has a travel companion, Zenica Lang, who will be staying with him. He thought this would probably make getting to him more difficult. Third, Dr. Tully is on his home turf. I have to be careful so that this is not a bigger disadvantage than it should be. What else? The Liberator looked up from his notes to check on his flight. The plane was there and they were about 30 minutes from departure. Boarding was being announced for first-class passengers. That is when he saw him . . . . K's emissary. Was it really him? Was he following him to Minneapolis? This was serious and very troubling, if he was right. Or was it? A thought crossed his mind. What if the emissary would take care of his Dr. Tully problem? That's absurd, he thought, to even ask himself that. But, we are on the same side and it would help the cause. Could he risk broaching the subject? How would he do it? Professor Dr. Patek Kumat devised a plan. With the emissary sitting in first class, he decided to write a note and give it to him on his way through first class when he was boarding. On the envelope, he would simply write "K's Emissary." The note he penned quickly said only, "Need your expert assistance in Minneapolis. Must eliminate growing threat to AQ. Call me if available. Prof. Dr. Patek Kumat, Technolibertat." He sealed the envelope, got in line to board, and walked toward the agent. The scanner read his boarding pass IUPAC number, and he was cleared to board. As he got to the entrance and looked in, he could see the emissary in a window seat in row 3. Walking slowly, he handed the envelope toward seat 3D saying, "For K's emissary. Thank you." The man smiled briefly, took the envelope, read what was written on the outside and nodded before putting the envelope in his coat pocket. Dr. Kumat proceeded to his coach seat near the back and sat down. He was wondering when and how he would respond. He almost jumped out of his seat when his cell phone buzzed ... who could be contacting me here? It was a text message that read, 'If u mean BT, TRI, I wl handl'. Kumat wondered how he had gotten his cell phone number and how he knew about Dr. Tully. I must answer before the plane takes off and it is too late. He wrote, "Yes, thx. Try nxt am at apt, Minni Wrhus Dist. PK." and pushed send. The announcement came over the loud speaker that all electronic devices, including cell phones must be turned off. He thought the emissary would contact him later if he needed more information. He leaned back and closed his eyes to rest.

Three hours later, the stewardess awakened him telling him to prepare for landing in MSP. Could he have slept for three continuous hours? He looked around to see if anything had changed in his surroundings. As his head cleared, Dr. Kumat went into planning and reacting mode. First, he needed to call Dr. Tully to arrange a visit in the morning. He thought that he had his number in his address book. They were just landing and the all clear to use cell phones was given. He turned his on immediately and skipping through the list of names, found TRI, Tully Research, Inc. Calculating timing and thinking that Dr. Tully and Ms. Lang must be arriving at his apartment about now, he placed the call.

The phone rang several times. Finally someone said, "TRI,

Brad Tully speaking."

"Dr. Tully, this is Professor Kharif. I am Omar Kharif's father and chairman of the board of the Technology Investment Corporation. We have recently invested in your company."

"Yes. Hello, Professor Kharif. You caught me a little off guard because it is late and we have just returned from an out of town trip." He gave the apartment keys to Zen and motioned for her to go up to the apartment.

"I am sorry; my schedule has been hectic, too. It would have been better if I could have called earlier."

"It is okay, Professor Kharif. Omar, TIC, and you are very important to us. In fact, TIC is the largest investor in my company. We just transferred some acoustics technology to Omar so it could be licensed to ATP. It sounds like a great business deal for all the parties involved."

"Yes, it was. We would like to do even more as you know. Omar has told me about you and your technology. I was very impressed and quite frankly, it was you and your potential that made us decide on such a large investment in Tully Research, Inc."

"Thank you, sir, I appreciate that."

"Dr. Tully, I am in Minneapolis and have a little time tomorrow morning. Omar mentioned that you had given sort of an open invitation for us to visit sometime. I am alone on this trip but could you indulge me with a short visit and tour of your laboratory and offices about mid-morning tomorrow?"

By this time, Zen had walked down to the TRI office to see what was taking Brad so long. She called out, "Brad, what are you doing?" She saw him at the phone, one finger to his lips, and wincing.

"Mid-morning tomorrow? I think that would be fine, sir. I'll expect to see you about 10 AM. Thank you Professor Kharif. Goodbye."

"Thank you, Dr. Tully. See you tomorrow, goodbye."

Brad hung up and was staring at Zen trying to make some sense out of the phone call. Finally, he said, "That was Professor Kharif, Omar's father, you know from Technology Investment

Corporation."

"Yes, we licensed the acoustics technology from them and they invested in your company, right?"

"Right. He wants to make a short visit tomorrow morning to tour the facilities. Is that okay with you?"

"Sure, as long as we can sleep in some. Let's go to bed."

Brad was thinking fast. The director had briefed him on this guy, of course. He thought back. Let's see, head of a terrorist organization, involved in the theft of top secret DT product in Israel, possibly connected to the murders of the Kramley family... what else? Wasn't that enough? He wouldn't dare try anything with the FBI watching, right? I guess it's OK. Finally, Brad said, "Okay, Zen, but you have to be good tonight. I am dead tired."

Zen smiled and took his hand, walking up the steps, saying, "I'll try but I'm not promising anything." They were in bed in no time and Zen was asleep in about 30 seconds. Brad was actually okay with that because he needed time to think about tomorrow. Let's see, my FBI team must know all about this so that they are watching this guy's every move. That must be the only explanation about why they haven't picked him up yet, isn't it? They must want to see if he meets with other people, maybe a leader within al Qaeda. Would the director or someone have told me the plan? Probably not, they want the best chance possible to get one of bin Laden's lieutenants. They will certainly be watching so they can protect us. That is for sure! With that conclusion firmly established, Brad dozed off and was sound asleep, dead to the world.

The ringing doorbell and knocking on the door downstairs awakened them. Brad said, "Oh, my God, Zen, it is about 10 AM. How did we sleep so long? I bet that is Professor Kharif here for his tour. You can stay in bed and I'll take care of this."

Zen raised up on her elbow, said, "Good," and slumped down in bed again. She watched him get dressed and run to answer the door.

Brad opened the door quickly saying, "I'm sorry, we overslept a little. How are you, Professor Kharif?"

"I am very well, Dr. Tully. Thank you for letting me visit

on such short notice."

"It's fine, sir, come in and I'll show you around." Brad looked quickly around outside but did not see his FBI friend or anybody for that matter. He closed the door slowly, now a little more worried than last night. He thought it must be quite a job keeping up with him. Like traveling from Minneapolis to Boston and then unexpectedly back to Minneapolis. How do these guys keep up with the last minute changes to the schedule? A quick weekend back home and then return to Boston. Was that a good idea? They must be out there; I just can't see them.

Prof. Kharif was standing by the office door, smiling.

Brad said, "Yes, sir, these are the offices of TRI. We are still hiring but we have the basics like finance, legal, HR, government contracts, research, and development covered. I will be setting up a marketing and sales organization soon but we appreciate our partnership with your company. It is functioning somewhat like an outside contract resource in marketing and sales for us to work with ATP. We want to continue that approach while we establish our own department, too."

"Of course, Dr. Tully, I understand."

"May I show you the laboratory, sir? It's Saturday, so it will be pretty quiet in there."

"Yes, Dr. Tully. You know, it was on weekends that I used to get a lot of extra work done. It was my way of getting ahead of my professor colleagues. Their work habits changed when they got tenure, then weekends went by the wayside. I never understood that but ..."

"You are a man after my own heart, Professor Kharif. I, too, use weekends to stay ahead of my competitors." Brad opened the door, turned on the lights, and invited the professor in saying, "Here is the best acoustics laboratory in the world." As they walked the long aisle, Brad pointed out, "These are the wave generators, collectors, analytical equipment for instrumental analysis, computer arrays linked to a Blue Gene type computer at the University of Minnesota and targets of various kinds."

"Targets?"

"Yes, various combinations of chemicals similar to those I used at GPRI to find oil. Brad didn't want to go into that too much, so he added, "And what you don't see is the heart and soul of the laboratory, the software. It actually makes all of this work as a system."

"This is really very impressive, Dr. Tully. Speaking of software, I understand you and Dr. Lyncoln Fuller have a separate contract through TIC to develop special software. I think the project is called DACS."

"Yes, I don't know a lot about the project yet but I know it is based on some previous work Dr. Fuller did for CMT. He wants to enhance the data augmentation code to allow more control of the host site. It is an area that I am interested in and I said I would help."

"I think you are being too modest, Dr. Tully. My understanding is that you and Dr. Fuller might be the world's top experts in this field."

"Some people would say that but I will tell you there is one other expert who is probably better than either of us."

"Who is that?"

"Professor Dr. Sam Elson, psychologist by training, worked as a professor, worked in industry and is now in a key director position with the U.S. Government. I would say we three are the top experts in the field of data augmentation."

"That is interesting, Dr. Tully." Professor Kharif knew the answer but he asked anyway, "What part of government is he in today?"

"It is the Department of Advanced Technology. Do you know about it, sir?"

"Some. Omar talks about it from time to time. Our investment in the Fuller/Tully DACS project was huge. Can you help me understand why the cost is so high?"

"I'm just a helper on the project; I don't know the size of the contract, sir. Lyncoln talks about this as something like the Holy Grail. You know, whether it exists or not, something huge that everyone looks for but in the end never finds? This project is so difficult and challenging and if we are successful, it would be like finding the Holy Grail, buried treasure, or Mohammed's tomb."

"We know where Mohammed's tomb is, Dr. Tully."

"Of course. How foolish of me.. Anyway, if we can do DACS, it is worth any price tag one would want to attach. Do you understand?"

"Some, but is being able to control a host site really worth all that money?"

"All I can suggest is that you think about it in terms of the host site being a stock market, a high court, a government, a military, or a large industrial research center. What would some knowledge and control within those host sites be worth to you?"

"When you put it that way, I guess it would be a lot. Do you think you can do it?"

"We'll give it our best shot, Professor. It will take the two of us with two supercomputers working full time for quite a while. Well, that's the tour of TRI, sir. I hope you enjoyed seeing the facility and listening to me give you assurance that you have made a good investment."

"No doubt, Dr. Tully, in TRI, for sure, and hopefully none in your search for the Holy Grail. We all have to take some risks once in a while, don't we? Do you think I could get a cup of coffee before my next appointment, please?"

"Yes, sir, certainly. I would like some, too." As they headed to the apartment, Brad was wondering if Zen was up. No matter, he and Dr. Kharif were just going to have a quick cup of coffee and it would be time for him to go.

As they walked into the apartment, Zen said, "Hello, Professor Kharif. I am Dr. Zenica Lang, a friend and colleague of Dr. Tully. My company, ATP, has a cooperative project with Dr. Tully and TRI. I know of you because we have just leased some advanced acoustics technology from your company."

"Hello, Dr. Lang, I am very pleased to meet you."

Brad was watching all of this thinking, She was wearing one of his shirts, a baseball cap and very, very awake. How did she do that so fast? He said, "Do I smell coffee, Zen?"

421

"Yes, and I have a little brunch ready out on the balcony. I hope you have time to join us, Professor Kharif."

Brad was looking amazed at all this, as the professor said, "Of course I do." He looked at his watch; it was a little past 11 o'clock. "Thank you very much." Glancing at the balcony and brunch on the little table said, "How thoughtful of you."

Zen looked at Brad, winked and showed the way to the balcony. She seated Professor Kharif. Brad sat down facing him with his back to the street and Zen sat next to him. She said, "Please Professor Kharif, help yourself to the bagels, cheese, and fruit. I'll pour the coffee."

"Thank you, Dr. Lang. This looks so international. I feel very much at home."

"You are welcome, Professor Kharif."

Brad said, "Sir, you mentioned your next appointment. Is it in Minneapolis?"

"I actually am on my way to San Francisco to see my son. My flight is in a couple of hours. That is the appointment I meant." He caught sight, just a blur really, of some movement across the street. Could it be K's emissary? Then there was a reflection of sunlight off the scope. "May I use your bathroom, please?"

"Certainly, through the door and to the right."

As the professor left, Zen leaned over, put her arms around Brad's neck, pushed his head over a bit, and whispered in his ear, "As soon as he leaves, watch out, buddy! You are going to get to know me even bet ……. Ahhhhhhhh." There was no other sound, just Zen falling over into his lap. He had felt a sting in his arm at almost exactly the same time she yelled. Then he saw the blood, so much blood. He yelled, "She's been shot. My God, she's been shot!" Still holding Zen, he was able to grab his cell phone and call 911. "My friend has been shot. Fifth Street North and Third Avenue North, downtown Minneapolis. Please come quickly – I think she is dying."

Just at that moment, two FBI agents came crashing onto the balcony with their guns drawn. Seeing Zen in Brad's lap and the blood everywhere, one agent stepped over to try to help stop the bleeding. The other agent called for emergency medical help and went to start a search of the area. Brad recognized one FBI agent, his friend from D.C. Brad was crying as he held Zen, but managed to ask, "Where were you guys?"

"It was Professor Kharif and an accomplice. We got the shooter, Dr. Tully. He's dead but so is one of our agents."

"Oh, Zen, I am so sorry, please hang on. Where the hell is the ambulance?" Brad was holding her with one hand, the other on her neck from where blood was pouring. "Oh, God, why this, why this?"

Zen was losing so much blood but managed to say, "Brad, I love you," then she went very limp.

The sirens got louder and one agent ran down to guide them to the apartment. Meeting the ambulance, he yelled, "Second floor apartment on the balcony. She's been shot, a neck wound, losing a lot of blood and now in shock and unconscious."

The paramedic looked at his buddy and winced. They got up to the balcony, saw the mess, and immediately got Zen onto the stretcher. The lead paramedic said, "She is still alive but we must get her to the hospital immediately." Brad jumped up and said, "I'm coming with you." He was holding his arm as he followed them down the stairs to the ambulance. There was something wrong. Then he realized he had been shot, too. Was it one shot or two? We must get Zen to the hospital, he thought, I'll worry about myself later.

Boston Party

The party was just getting started. Chad had booked an upstairs room at a local pub not far from ATP. Chad asked Mike to make a couple of announcements. He said, "Could I have your attention for just a second. Then you can get back to some serious partying. Mike."

"Thank you, Chad. I know it's Saturday afternoon and you are ready for some fun time together. Before you really get going, I want to say 'thank you' and this comes from the management of both ATP and CMT. Joe and I talked earlier. He sends his best, his congratulations, and his thanks. We both believe what you are doing on this special project, L-REDD, is of utmost importance to our country and our people. It is the most important project within our government and military today. You were specially selected to be on the team and on the project. Your progress has been nothing short of outstanding so you are making all of us very proud, too. We certainly have the right team, don't you agree?" There was considerable hand clapping and 'yeas'. "Thank you isn't enough, but maybe the beer and pizza will help show our appreciation. Thank you all again and have fun!"

"Thanks, Mike. May I have a minute before you leave?"

"Of course, Chad. There is something I wanted to mention to you, too."

"You go first."

Mike pulled Chad to the side and said, "Joe and I talked about something else during our phone call. Do you see how ATP and CMT personnel are separated even here at the pub? We sense that even though tremendous progress is being made, we are still short of the system integration that is necessary. We need a way to unify this team and soon. Any ideas?"

"My subject was the same, Mike. In fact, Brad Tully came to my office recently and made the same observation you just explained. I won't bore you with the details, but we did agree on a recommendation. We need to have one Team Leader for L-REDD and it is my recommendation that it should be Dr. Bradford Tully."

Mike looked at him, not saying a word for the longest time, then, "I love it. Chad, you are a genius. Let's do it."

"I want to pass it by all the team leaders to get their input, but we'll implement this very soon. Thanks, Mike, I'm glad you are close enough to the project to recognize its needs. I appreciate your help."

"Sure thing. Anything else?"

"Yes, there are some technical changes that we are considering for the project, too. I'll come over and see you next week to discuss them."

"Good. Where is our new L-REDD team leader? I haven't seen him at the party yet."

"I noticed, too. He did mention possibly taking a quick trip to Minnesota for the weekend but said he would get word to us if that happened. Zen and Lyncoln aren't here either."

"Give him my congratulations when you see him."

"I will, Mike; see you next week."

"Thanks, Chad, and have a good weekend."

As Mike walked down the steps, Chad was wondering where Brad and Zen could be. He decided to call Lyncoln because he and Brad were staying together. No answer. He called Zen next. No answer again. He wondered what was going on, but went back to the party to join the fun.

The Boston Agents Find Lyncoln

By Saturday afternoon, the agents were concerned enough to take action. They had not seen Lyncoln since his return from work on Friday. The senior agent rang the doorbell. No answer. Again. No answer. Again. No answer. He stepped back, looked at the other agents and all drew their guns at the same time. With one huge kick, the locked door sprung open and banged against the wall. It ricocheted back; the agent grabbed it and entered the room slowly with the others close behind him. He saw Lyncoln immediately and walked quickly to the table. "Dr. Fuller! Dr. Fuller?" He shook Lyncoln by the shoulder lightly then harder. No response. The blood-soaked towels under his arms became obvious on closer inspection. The agent checked for a pulse. None! The other agents had checked the bedrooms and bathroom and cleared them. They were all huddled around the table but careful not to touch anything. The senior agent said, "I wonder what happened here......a note written in blood on a napkin saying, 'Defeat the Campaign of Fear for me, L', and a dead computer genius." A red light was blinking on the phone. The senior agent pushed the message button with the barrel of his gun to hear the message Brad had left yesterday.

"Make the call please." Immediately, one of the agents called the FBI CSI team to come and start the investigation. They holstered their weapons and left the apartment to wait for their arrival, two went to the back door and two to the front door. The senior agent called the director first, "Sir, I have very bad news. We just found Dr. Fuller dead in his apartment. There was a lot of blood. My opinion, it was not an accident sir. A CSI team is on their way and we'll have more information soon. I am sorry. Splitting our team to provide more coverage for Dr. Tully and his colleague, Dr. Lang, may have distracted us, sir. We might have screwed up."

"Agent, hold on please. I have been incommunicado for several hours and I see there was another urgent message for me."

"Yes, sir."

The director listened in shock as he heard the message. "Both Dr. Tully and his friend, Dr. Zenica Lang, were shot about noon on the balcony of his apartment. They are going to the hospital now. Dr. Tully suffered only a superficial arm wound, but it is touch and go with Dr. Lang. She suffered a neck wound and has lost a lot of blood. The assassin killed our agent on duty but we shot him as he tried to get away. He used what looked like a jointed, long barrel pistol with a scope. Professor Kharif was visiting with Dr. Tully and Ms. Lang at the time but he got away. As you may know, most of our team just got back from Boston last night. They were beat so I gave them some time off to rest. That was a mistake, sir, and I am very sorry. I'll keep you posted on the hospital situation and be assured that we will have the hospital locked down and other agents looking for the professor. I am also alerting San Francisco."

The director reconnected with the Boston call. "Agent, an assassin shot Dr. Tully and Dr. Lang. Both were taken to the hospital in Minneapolis. Tully sustained an arm wound and Lang is in serious condition with a neck wound. I am going to be very busy for a while. I want you to keep me posted on exactly what you find in Boston. If my assumptions are correct, there are multiple connections between what happened there and in Minneapolis. Let them know what has happened in Boston. Was there any indication that Dr. Patek Kumat a.k.a. Professor Eomar Kharif, had been at the crime scene?"

"No, sir, there was nothing obvious."

"Let CSI do their work and keep me posted. If I'm right,

I know where the next crime scene will be. Thank you, agent. Goodbye."

"Goodbye, sir."

Next the senior agent called Chad at the party. "Dr. Bromcast, I have very bad news. We just discovered Dr. Lyncoln Fuller dead in his apartment."

"What! Oh my God! How did that happen?"

"We are not sure, sir, but we suspect foul play. The CSI team is just arriving to start the investigation. I'm sorry, sir."

"What about Dr. Tully?" He was staying with Lyncoln. Is he okay?"

"I'm afraid there is more bad news, sir. We found a message on Dr. Fuller's answering machine from Dr. Tully on Friday evening. It said that he and Dr. Lang were taking a quick weekend trip to Minneapolis. The bad news is that when I called the director about Dr. Fuller, he told me about Dr. Tully and Dr. Lang."

"What bad news, agent?"

"Both were shot by an assassin earlier today. Dr. Tully is okay but Dr. Lang was wounded more seriously. They would be at the hospital by now. The agents there will let us know how she is doing."

"What in the hell is going on? Lyncoln dead, Brad and Zen shot, she critically wounded … should I get our people out of the pub?"

"I know how you feel, sir, but I would not. In my experience, if something were going to happen there, it would have happened already. These are most likely very selected personal attacks against individuals, not against groups of people."

"Why Zen? Maybe Lyncoln and Brad but why Zen?"

"I don't know, sir, she might have just gotten in the way. We'll find out. Let your people have some fun tonight and by Monday we'll have enough information to report on the events or crimes with confidence. We need to make a report that can withstand questioning by their colleagues. Without those answers, I think we'll just create group fear and who knows what might happen then."

"I think you are right, agent. Thank you for being so direct.

Please call me Sunday night or early Monday morning and we'll prepare to give them the sad news with all the possible facts and figures."

"I will, sir, thank you and goodbye."

"Goodbye, agent."

Chad stopped by the tables where Bill, Kan D and Ray, the CMT team leader, were talking. He said, "I am not feeling so well. I am going home. You guys have fun and I'll see you on Monday."

"Okay, Chad, hope you have a good weekend," said Bill. Kan D gave him a kiss and Ray said, "If it's okay, I'll stay a while and get a ride to your place after the party."

"Sure, that's fine. Good night all."

At the Hospital

The ride to the hospital was frantic. Brad heard the sirens, felt the swerves around traffic, sensed the high speeds, and watched the lights change when activated by the emergency van's traffic control system. Still, it was taking a long time. He asked the paramedic, holding the IV, "How much longer?"

"We'll be there soon; she's holding on."

Brad could tell because he and Zen were holding hands and there was a squeeze by Zen every time the van swerved or hit a bump. He said, "Zen, I'm here. We are almost at the hospital where they will take care of you. I love you very much."

Zen's eyes were closed, the oxygen mask was on so she couldn't talk, but she could hear and squeeze his hand. Brad was comforted by this, thinking, she's going to make it; I know it. She has, too.

The ambulance pulled up at the emergency entrance where people were waiting to take care of Zen and Brad. He was trying to stay out of the way so they could focus on her. With FBI agents already setting up a perimeter, he followed her into the emergency room lobby. The action was fast and furious with the paramedic saying, "You stay here, sir. We are taking her directly into the emergency room where doctors will get the bleeding stopped and decide on surgery. I'll be right back."

"Okay, I'll wait here for you." As he sat down in a chair nearby, he winced and held his arm. He realized, I have been shot, too. It could not have been the same bullet that hit Zen. She was on my left and I'm wounded in the right arm. There must have been two shots. Were they both meant for me? Did Zen just get in the way accidentally? The paramedic came back through the double doors, interrupting his thoughts but what a welcomed sight. "How is she?"

"We won't know for a while, and they will tell you as soon as they know. Trust me; I think we got her here in time."

Brad smiled, his head spinning and feeling faint said, "I have to lie down."

The paramedic helped him to the sofa and looked him over at the same time. There was so much blood on his pants and shirt that he had not noticed the arm wound. "You have been shot, too, sir. Let me take a look."

Brad was sitting on the sofa but lying down would have to wait. "Okay, but I think it just needs a bandage. What do you guys call it – a nick?"

"It is not a nick, sir, it is superficial though and you are very lucky. No bones hit, just a flesh wound. I'll get a doctor to give you a shot and bandage the wound." He motioned to one of the ER doctors to come over. "Could you take care of him, please? He has been shot in the arm."

As the doctor lead Brad from the waiting room to attend his wounds, the FBI agent friend came rushing in saying, "We have the area cordoned off and I need to talk to you right away."

"I'll have him back in a few minutes. Just come back here, please."

"What's wrong with him?" the FBI agent asked.

"He was shot, too, not seriously, just a superficial wound in the arm."

"Two shots?"

"Yes, sir," said the paramedic. "Someone wanted them dead. Could you tell him that I had to leave? Tell him I'm hoping

429

that he and the lady will be fine."

"I will."

"Good luck, FBI."

"Goodbye, thanks for the quick work."

The agent waited but it wasn't long. The ER doctors are something else. "Here he is, sir, he will be fine. Some loss of blood but nothing seriously damaged." Looking at Brad, he said, "Take the pain pills and you'll be okay. See your doctor in about three days to check the wound and put fresh dressing on it."

"Thanks Doctor," said Brad.

"Well, are you up to answering some questions, Dr. Tully?" asked his FBI agent friend.

"I think so. I'm not leaving the area until they tell me how Zen is doing."

"You mentioned Professor Kharif and an accomplice when we found you and Dr. Lang just after the shooting. Was the professor in the apartment?"

"Yes, he had come to tour the TRI facilities and then came up to the apartment. We were having a little brunch on the balcony."

"Where was he when the shooting happened? We did not see him anywhere."

"He had excused himself to go to the bathroom. It must have been a set up and he was getting out of the way, out of the apartment, and out of the building. I should have known. We all knew he wasn't to be trusted."

"Yes, I agree. We made some mistakes, too. So, there were two shots, Dr. Tully. One hit Dr. Lang in the neck and the other hit you in the arm. What were your positions when the shots were fired?"

"As I said, Professor Kharif had excused himself. Zen was seated next to me on my left, leaned over with both arms around my neck to whisper in my ear. That is when it happened, but we did not hear anything. Zen fell over in my lap and all this blood was coming from her neck. I felt a sting in my right arm at the same time."

"She was on your left and you were shot in the right arm.

So, the shots were maybe a foot apart?"

"Probably."

"Do you think the shooter was trying to kill both of you?"

"I can't imagine he knew anything about Zen. He was probably after me and just took two shots to make sure."

"Did you change position when she leaned over? Did she push you a little to your right maybe?"

"Maybe I tilted or moved my head a little. Do you think both shots were meant for me and for whatever reason he missed and hit Zen?"

"Do I remember Zen was wearing a man's shirt when she was shot?"

"Yes, one of my shirts and a baseball cap. I wonder ……"

"Do you suppose the shooter was unable to tell which one was you so he tried to eliminate both of you?"

"Oh, my God. I bet you are right. That son-of-a-bitch, I'm glad you got him."

"Yes, but he died instantly so we didn't get any intel from him. We need to find out who he is and if he was hired by the professor to kill you. Brad, I know a lot has happened in the last several hours but you need to know one more thing. Yesterday, in Boston after you left to visit with Zen at her place, something happened to Lyncoln."

"What happened to Lyncoln? Oh, God, no. Oh, God, no; it can't be."

"Yes, I learned that Lyncoln was found dead in his apartment. Probably foul play."

"No, no, noooo!"

"What about the professor, Dr. Tully? Can you tell us anything to help us find him?"

"He looked like a college professor you know and he knew about the TIC investment in my company. In fact, our technology transfer through TIC to ATP had just occurred and he was even up to date on that. The contract with Lyncoln on DACS, where I was to help, seemed to worry him. However, it was the money that he was concerned about. He kept asking if the investment was worth it. Oh, yes, damn. He did mention that he was to catch a flight in a couple of hours to see his son in San Francisco. He said that at about noon so the flight was probably scheduled around 2 or 3 PM"

"It's okay; we have had the San Francisco airport under watch for sometime. That's where we expected him to enter the U.S. The Boston and Minneapolis stops were the surprises. He may have left by now."

The agent stepped away to call San Francisco. "Yes sir, we believe he will arrive at about 3 or 4 PM your time. He looks just like the pictures we have of him. The best information we have at this moment is that he has been involved in a murder in Boston, two attempted murders in Minneapolis, and is on his way to meet with his son in San Francisco. As you know, the director believes that he wants Omar – the son - dead too."

"We haven't seen him yet of course, said the San Francisco agent. "It is just a little before one; we'll get him. I'll call you back when we have him in custody. Thanks for the update."

"You are welcome. Good luck."

"Goodbye, sir."

After learning what had happened in Minneapolis, the director called the Special Agent in Charge in San Francisco right away.

"Hello, this is Director Elson."

"Hello, Director. We got the word that things are heating up a bit, sir."

"Yes, Patek Kumat, a.k.a. Eomar Kharif, is probably on his way now to San Francisco. You must find him and arrest him. Maintain your watch on Omar and protect him from harm's way. We need them both alive."

"We'll do our best, sir. I'll report when there is new information. Are you on your way out?"

"Yes, I am. I'll see you soon."

"Thank you, sir. Goodbye."

"Goodbye."

The surgeon came into the waiting area, wearing his operating room garb to find Brad. "Dr. Tully please, Dr. Tully?"

"Yes, right here." Brad watched as he walked the doctor walked over, mask around his neck, blood on his sleeves, wearing disposable booties on his shoes. Mostly, Brad noticed the smile.

They shook hands and the doctor said, "She's going to be fine. Lost a lot of blood but once we fixed that, it was clear sailing. The bullet did some damage, but we have put her back together again. She will have a very sore and stiff neck for about a month. After that, she will be as good as new."

"Oh, thank God and thank you, Doctor. Can she come home today?"

"Let's keep her under observation tonight and if she is okay, she can go home tomorrow. Okay?"

"Yes, sir, may I see her?"

"Sure, she is a little groggy but I'm sure she would like to see you. We noticed that she is from Boston. When was she due to return?"

"Tomorrow evening."

"I think it will be okay."

"Thank you, sir."

"Sure thing, goodbye now."

Zen did not look so good when Brad walked in but she was awake. She said, "Someone doesn't like us very much, Brad. Are you okay?"

"I'm fine, Zen; how are you?"

"I have felt better. My neck hurts, I can't swallow very well, and we missed our afternoon rendezvous."

"The doctor says that if you behave yourself, you can get out of here tomorrow and maybe even travel to Boston in the evening. What do you think?"

"Great. I hope so. Brad, what the hell is going on? We knew doing this work was a little risky, but I didn't sign on to get killed."

"I know, Zen. Nor did I. They shot the shooter, so that is good. They are also tightening the net around the professor, who probably is on his way to San Francisco by now. They'll get him soon."

"Then we'll be safe?"

"Yes! Zen, there is some other bad news. I don't know if I should tell you now or wait until you are stronger."

"I want all the news now. If you hold something back, I'll never forgive you."

"I thought so. Here goes. They found Lyncoln dead in his apartment today. It looked like it might have been an accident but the FBI suspects foul play."

"Lyncoln dead? Are they trying to get all of us, Brad? I'm not sure I can do this anymore. Is it worth it?"

"The stakes are getting higher all the time. I expect a call from the director at any time. We'll get some answers from him."

"They better be damn good answers." The nurse came in and said, "It's time for her to get some rest. You can see her again tomorrow morning."

Brad leaned over to Zen's ear and whispered, "I love you. Get well and I'll see you tomorrow morning. We'll get you out of here and back to Boston. Good evening."

"Good evening, Brad. I love you."

Brad noticed her voice sort of trailed away and she was asleep. He said, "Take good care of her, nurse. I'll be back tomorrow morning."

"Good evening, sir."

After The Shooting

"Hello, Director. All hell has broken loose here, as you no doubt already know. Zen and I were shot while we were on the balcony of my apartment. I'm okay, but Zen was injured more seriously. The doctor thinks however that she will be released from the hospital tomorrow sometime. Now I hear that Lyncoln is dead, probably killed by the same people. The agents got the shooter here but the professor got away. Who is next on the list, sir? It was okay when I was the one taking the risk, but it isn't okay when it spreads to my friends, especially Zen. We are scared, Director."

"I know, Brad. I would be, too, but try to slow down a bit. Look, for a number of not so good reasons, we haven't done our job

THE CAMPAIGN OF FEAR

protecting you and your friends. We'll be doing better starting today, I assure you. I have talked with our people there and in Boston. They know we are going to operate differently. Schedules will have to be known in advance, changes will have to be approved, public appearances limited, and travel limited for the time being. We are not going to be reactionary any longer. Everything will be planned. If we can't ensure safety, the event won't happen."

"I guess we did throw things off by taking an unexpected weekend trip to Minnesota."

"Don't blame yourself, Brad; this wasn't your fault."

"If Zen is released from the hospital tomorrow, can you get us back to Boston safely?"

"Yes. I think that Boston is the best place for both of you right now. I'll have you taken back in a government chartered private plane. It sounds like Zen will be somewhat out of commission for a while. We will add a detail to watch her as she recovers and works from home. Would that work?"

"Yes, sir, thank you, sir."

"Brad, I have been talking with Chad and I know the two of you had a discussion about getting the project team more integrated and on a slightly different technical track. I'm 100% in agreement, by the way. When you get back to Boston, I want what happened to Zen, you, and Lyncoln to be the rallying point for the new project direction. I want you, as the project leader, to mobilize the people to work harder and smarter and finish the project successfully in record time. The window is open for us to deal a fatal blow to al Qaeda's 'Campaign of Fear'. They have no idea about our capabilities within L-REDD. Your work has given us this opportunity. You have to step up and lead the way, Brad. I know you are injured and scared but the country needs you now more than ever. Can you do it, Brad?"

"Director, get us back to Boston and convince me that Zen will be safe. Then I will be ready. Those bastards haven't seen anything yet."

"You've got a deal, Brad. I'm going to be busy with what's going on in and around San Francisco for a while, but I will be watching Boston. If you need anything, just let me know."

435

"I will, sir, and thank you. Goodbye."
"Goodbye, Brad, and good luck with L-REDD."

The Liberator in San Francisco

The Liberator was still shaking when he arrived at the airport. He had seen what happened on the balcony and to the emissary, but he had gotten away. Now, how do I get to the West Coast, he asked himself? They will be watching the airport in San Francisco, at least the commercial flights. It was hard to think, but he forced himself to go through the options: another flight, maybe a private plane, train, car, or bus. The options weren't so good. By train, car, or bus, he would never get there in time to do his business and catch his original flight back to Syria. A different commercial flight wouldn"t work either because they would be watching for that option too. He would have to charter a private plane. As he walked to that area of the terminal, he saw a group of people around the desk – maybe five or six professorial types like him. They all had CES/Berkeley buttons on their jackets. Then he saw him, a professor from the Berkeley Engineering Department that he had consulted with several years ago. "Professor Bagly, hello. Do you remember me, Professor Kharif from Damascus?"

"Of course, Eomar, how are you? What are you doing here?"

"It's a long story, but I'm trying to get to San Francisco to see my son. My flight seems to have been cancelled and I was just about to see if I could charter something. What are you doing here?"

"There was a two-day conference of the Chemical and Engineering Society in Minneapolis. My colleagues and I are just about to leave for the trip back home. Did you say you were going to charter something?"

"Yes, my schedule is tight so it seemed to be the only solution."

"Why don't you come with us? There are seven of us and we have a university-chartered G-6. I think there are 12 seats. We have extra seats and you are most welcome to join us."

"Are you sure it would be alright with your colleagues? I would be willing to pay, of course."

"Don't worry about it. The cost has already been handled so just come along and enjoy the ride. One more thing, they will ask for identification and because of your home country, will want to see your passport and visa. Are your papers in order?"

"Yes, they are. I actually entered in Boston a few days ago and traveled to Minneapolis yesterday. There were no difficulties at all."

"Great. Are you ready to go? We were told the bus would be here for us momentarily."

"I am. I travel very light for a number of reasons. Thank you very much, Professor Bagly."

The bus arrived and took them to the corporate jet arrival and departure area. Seated next to each other, Professor Bagly said, "The last I had heard, you left the university and started an organization called 'Freedom Through Technology' or something like that. How is it doing?"

"Yes, Professor. I called it Technolibertat. My objective is to show how science and technology can improve our human development. I hope Technolibertat can help be the start of our road back to modern civilization and the end of extremism."

"Professor Kharif, I admire you for doing this work, which I assume is at some considerable sacrifice and great risk to you. We in America do not understand the ones who advocate suicide bombings and death to all so-called 'infidels', and those who fail to recognize peoples of another country and have a general disrespect for human life. We do not know the first thing to do and there is much fear. How can we help you in this struggle?"

"I believe there is only one approach. It has two parts: selected technology transfer now by countries like yours to countries like mine with help in its adoption and utilization and help to start a new educational programs beginning in grade school on science and technology. It will take years and years but I believe there will be a continual evolution and growth of human development that

437

will result. Attitudes will change, alliances will be made in industry and government, culture will evolve, be understood and accepted, countries will be more compatible and peace will result. Do you agree?"

"It is certainly different than what we are doing today, which isn't working at all. As a scientist, I may be somewhat biased but I say, give it a try. How many billions have we spent supporting wars in Afghanistan, Iraq, Israel, Lebanon, and who knows where else? What if we had the same people and money resources involved in technology transfer and education efforts? I like it, Professor Kharif. You can count me as one of your members."

"Thank you, sir. I appreciate your kind words."

The G-6 traveled a bit faster and higher than the commercial planes. They arrived in San Francisco and were on approach to landing sooner than he expected. "What a way to travel, Professor Bagly. Thank you again for your hospitality and kindness. I will return the favor when you come to Damascus to see me."

"A trip to Syria, yes. It might be a while but I would love that."

"I will be seeing my son here and then returning to Damascus in a couple of days."

"Tell your son, it's Omar isn't it, hello from me. I have met him a couple of times when he came to the University to deliver research grants, scholarships, and fellowships. Technology Investment Corporation is making an impact here in the U.S. I wish you much success, my friend, with both Technolibertat and TIC."

"Thank you, sir. If I may, I will stay in touch. It always helps to have a professor from Berkeley on your side."

"Of course." They exchanged business cards. Professor Bagly noticed there was a different name on Eomar's card, a Professor Dr. Patek Kumat. "Have you changed your name, Eomar?"

"Yes, I have. You mentioned the risk I'm taking with Technolibertat. The risk is very real. In Syria, Professor Kharif works underground to further the cause of human development and Dr. Kumat is the publicly recognized leader of a small but very much respected pharmaceutical company, Pharmatek. I hope I'm not confusing you; it was necessary to survive in my country. Professor Eomar Kharif disappeared a long time ago; Dr. Kumat arrived to make his mark in the pharmaceutical business. What people don't know is that the one supports the other. Can you keep the secret?"

"Yes, Eomar or Patek, I can. I am forgetting my manners; why not stay at my home for the few days you will be here?"

"That would be wonderful, Professor Bagly. Are you sure it is okay and I won't be in the way?"

"It will be fine. My wife passed away a few years ago and I have a big empty house on the edge of campus. It would be good to have some company. Let's get a cab."

"Thank you very much, sir."

Chapter 17

Uncle/Brother "K"
Havoc in San Francisco

What About 'K'?

"Hello, Director; sorry about the weekend call. It will be brief."

"Hello, Absek, it's okay. Maybe you have something to help me piece the puzzle together. All hell has broken loose here. Patek Kumat somehow arrived in the States recently not via San Francisco but via Boston as you thought. We believe he was involved with a murder there and two attempted murders in Minneapolis already. I think Omar is next, so Kumat is probably traveling to or in San Francisco by now. Absek, there was an assassin that helped with the attempted murders in Minneapolis. Do you know anything about that?"

"We have some rumors flying around, Director. The most likely one says that a friend of 'K' was sent to the U.S. to watch Dr. Kharif. We don't know if it was to kill him or to help him. Did the assassin get away?"

"No, our agents put a bullet in his head as he attempted to escape the scene."

"Well, there is a second rumor, sir. It goes like this: something happened to 'K's friend in the U.S. 'K' is on his way to the States to find his friend or maybe even to take care of Dr. Kumat himself and anybody else who gets in the way."

"That's interesting. I got the file you sent on 'K.' Do you have anything else?"

"Yes, one more thing – a picture, sir. The Mossad paid a lot of money for it. We believe it to be fairly recent but who knows. I'm sending it now so take a look. With all the long hair and beard, I just hope it helps."

"Thank you, Absek. I'm sure it will."

"Be very careful, my friend. It sounds like this 'K' is out for vengeance. Remember, as a lieutenant of bin Laden, he will have a lot of resources at his disposal even in the U.S. It would be a real coup if you capture him alive, sir."

"If he is here, I intend to do exactly that, Absek."

"Good luck, sir. I will provide any further information on 'K' and his whereabouts as we get it."

"Thank you, Absek, goodbye."

"Goodbye, sir."

'K's Trip To The U.S.

The reports came in each morning via runners to his mountain hideout. As a lieutenant for bin Laden, 'K's responsibility was to plan and implement the smaller, more covert actions of al Qaeda in foreign countries like the U.S., U.K., Spain, France, and Germany, with the aim of enhancing its power and recognition. He read with interest the results of a train bomb attack in Spain, a subway bomb attack in England, training camps set up in France, and investment in technology in the U.S. He thought the last one could severely damage him personally and put the effectiveness and reputation of al Qaeda at risk. It was obvious that his nephew, Omar Kharif, was weak and unskilled. His brother reported as much earlier with the semi-botched theft of top-secret detonation technology, the federal government investigation, the murders to cover up things, and the enormous money transfer for a research project. Now it continues with Pharmatek being shut down and his aide, his emissary, being killed by FBI agents. He knew by killing Eomar's wife that night at their home, he could turn his brother to use technology, not for human development and cultural growth, but for the good of al Qaeda. He had convinced bin Laden to sign the contract with Technolibertat and TIC. It was a good idea; but because of Omar, it just wasn't working. Now his brother was becoming a problem. A

441

big problem. He must take care of this himself. Whoever creates the problem must fix it, right?

He summoned his aides, told them his plan, and made arrangements to travel to the U.S. - specifically to San Francisco. "Keep this to yourselves. I will return soon."

Brad Gets Zen From The Hospital And They Return To Boston

Brad heard the FBI driver say, "Sir, here we are." He hadn't remembered the trip from the hospital, the route that was taken, or the time it took to get to his apartment. He just got out of the car and said, "Thank you." Brad entered the building, went up the steps, and into his apartment. When he turned the lights on, he could see the yellow crime scene tape all around the balcony. Brad walked to the glass doors and saw the blood stains on the chair and on the balcony floor. He thought about the shots, Zen slumping into his arms, the blood, the paramedics, the rush trip to the hospital, the waiting, and finally learning that Zen was okay. He was so fatigued that he had to lie down on the sofa for a few minutes; he immediately fell asleep.

The automatic alarm had turned the radio on. Brad bolted upright, wondering where he was and what the sound was. The clocks all said 8 AM; he had slept over 12 hours on the sofa. As far as he knew, there was no movement, sound, smell, or anything significant enough to wake him during his sleep. Brad said to himself, "I really needed that sleep. It's almost time for me to get Zen and take her home." There was a knock on the door.

"Yes?"

"FBI, sir. It is nearly time to leave for the hospital. I'm your driver this morning, sir."

"Thank you, I'll be ready in about 10 minutes."

After a shower, a shave, change of clothes, Brad packed a few more things in his bag and grabbed Zen's bag. He opened the door and said, "I am ready."

"Yes sir, my orders are to take you to the hospital and then get you and Dr. Lang to the airport for the trip to Boston. Does that work for you, sir?"

"Yes, it does, thank you." Brad thought, "The director said

the watch detail was going to change. It has and I guess it is about time."

Arriving at the hospital, Brad almost ran to the information desk. "My friend, Dr. Zenica Lang, was in the emergency room area last evening. Can you tell me which room she is in this morning?"

The volunteer receptionist said, "Dr. Lang was just released. She should be down any second. You should wait right here."

Brad thought, I can't believe it. All that blood and she is okay to be released? He said, "Thank you."

The wheelchair arrived about a minute after he sat down in the waiting area. "Hi, Brad."

"Hi, Zen, are you okay?"

"Yes, I am; a little sore but still ready to go. The wheelchair is hospital policy. Once they deliver me to you, I'm your responsibility."

"I can handle that. Our FBI car and driver are waiting to take us to the airport. We are using a private jet to Boston to be sure that we are safe."

The attendant locked the wheelchair, Zen stood up, and stepped way. They embraced. "Oh, Zen, what would I have done if …"

"Don't even think about it, Brad. I'm back and will be good as new soon. Let's get out of here."

"Good idea," he said as he held her arm and headed for the exit and the waiting car.

"We are ready to go to the airport, agent."

"Yes, sir. Director Elson has asked that I greet you, Dr. Lang, on his behalf, and to tell you how glad he is that you are okay. He will see you after his work in San Francisco is finished. The other message is for you, Dr. Tully, and it was, 'I am counting on you, Project Leader. Good luck!'"

"Thank you, agent."

"That was nice of him but what did he mean when he said that he is counting on you, Project Leader, Brad?"

"There will be some changes announced at the project briefing on Monday, I believe. With all that has happened, it is probably going to be hard for people to focus on their work. I know a little bit how Kan D felt when she lost her only family recently."

'What changes, Brad?"

"They want me to lead both parts of Project L-REDD. We all agreed that good progress is being made but the parts are not integrated; we don't have a system. There is a need for an overall project leader and I was the one who drew the short straw."

"My God, Brad, that is great and it's just what we need. I agree that we had been cooperating well but not functioning as one team. Most of the technology is yours; it is reasonable that you lead the whole project."

"I guess."

"You mentioned changes, plural, what else, Brad?"

"You are almost back to normal and not missing a thing Zen. It's a secret but everyone will know on Monday. I have proposed that we go to Generation III in our explosive detection technology evolution immediately, to gain a revolutionary edge on the terrorists. They will never be able to catch up with the technical know-how they have today or can learn in the near future."

"What else is there beyond wave articulation?"

"It's a programmed smart wave that has been taught to know what to look for. There is no need for a second step of evaluation and identification to tell us we found the explosive. I found a way to write software code that teaches the wave to locate what we want to find. Once we find the explosive materials, we retune the search wave to detonate automatically. There is a little lag time electronically between finding and destroying, but it is almost instantaneous to the user."

"So the team will begin immediately on this new approach?"

"Yes, I believe everything will be announced tomorrow. Considering all that has happened at ATP, with Lyncoln, and with us, it is even more important than ever that we are successful and reach the goal faster. We hope it will be a rallying point for the team."

"It is for me, Brad. I want to stay on the project regardless of what has happened."

"Don't you think you should work from home for a while and recuperate?"

"Are you kidding me? I want to get the bastards as much as you do."

"Hey, here we are. Looks like the plane is waiting for us. Thank you, agent. Let's go, Zen."

"Project Leader, am I working with the L-REDD team at ATP starting Monday or not?"

Brad looked into those eyes, saw the determination and strength and said, "How can I say no? You must be the strongest woman I have ever known."

"Thank you, sir," said Zen smiling. They boarded the plane hand in hand.

More Information on 'K'

"Director, this is urgent. I have more information about 'K'."

"Hello, Absek. This is good; we are all focused on San Francisco right now. Somehow, Patek Kumat has to complete a planned intersection with his son, Omar, whom we have under a tight watch, and an unplanned intersection with 'K'. What do you have that will help us?"

"Remember, I told you we would get everything we could. Get this; our informants tell us that 'K' is really Krishna Kharif, brother of Eomar Kharif."

"What?"

"Yes, sir. Further, he might be the one who killed Eomar's wife after bin Laden stayed at their house that night."

"He killed his own sister-in-law?"

"We thought she was killed to keep her from talking about bin Laden. Our informants believe it was to get his brother to use technology to help al Qaeda and get back at the U.S. If we are right, Director, this guy, 'K', is a real threat to you and the U.S. Be very careful."

"I will, Absek. You know, this story makes more sense. Maybe we have a better chance of turning Dr. Kumat than I thought. If we can find him and convince him of the real story about his wife's death, he may realize what a fool he has been. What do you think?"

"I think so, sir. By the way, these same informants have confirmed that 'K' is coming to the States and may be there already. You should be aware that the long hair and the beard are both gone. Can you get your experts to take the picture we gave you and digitally present him as clean shaven with a crew haircut?"

"Good idea, Absek, and yes, we can. How old do you think he is?"

"Probably in his late forties, sir."

"Okay, with a new digital representation of his face and knowing his age we might be able to identify him. But you are saying we might have missed him at the airport."

"Yes, sir. Also, we are not sure about his formal training. This 'K' is talked about as being an electronics and explosives wizard. He might be behind the new communication system within al Qaeda and the more sophisticated explosive devices used in the recent car and roadside bomb attacks."

"A senior aide to bin Laden that is an actual practitioner of sophisticated technology? He would be a valuable catch! Anything else Absek?"

"No, sir, just wanted you to have the latest intelligence on K."

"Thank you, Absek."

"Goodbye, sir."

Poison

"The office for the Technology Investment Corporation is nothing more than a one-room rental property," said Jack as he walked into where Aldora was working. "It did have some sophisticated telecommunication equipment. I was able to tap into the system so we can listen to any calls coming in or going out."

"What about the poison?"

"I got it, a few vials. Not as much as I expected but considering its potency enough to do a lot of damage. I decided to take it to the San Francisco FBI office for safekeeping. How are you doing with setting up the watch?"

"It is in place, Jack. You know this guy, Omar, is as guilty as sin. With our investigation here winding down, do you mind if I stay and begin putting the case together? If we have to go to court, we'll need to move fast."

"Good idea. Do you need any help?"

"I think I can get by using an FBI agent every now and then and of course, resources from the home office here."

"If you agree, I think it is probably time for Frank, Mark,

and the federal CSI team to return to D.C."

"I agree."

"Aldora, with your legal background, do you know about an agency called IPRP, International Pharmaceutical Review Panel?"

"Didn't we hear the director was going to use some international group to go after the pharmaceutical plant that makes all the money for Technolibertat? I think the IPRP is a watchdog agency run out of the U.N. and has cross-country authority to investigate, to make recommendations, and to help implement actions in international pharmaceutical cases. Why do you ask?"

"I caught a bit of a one-way conversation on a call that came in just as we arrived at Omar's office. Omar mentioned IPRP and its name and then listened for a long time. His only response was, 'No, sir, I do not know anything about the production of Warfarin-D nor do I have any precursor products in my possession.' There was another time of listening then 'yes, he is my father but I do not know anything about poisons. It must be a mistake, sir.' Another silence then, 'thank you sir' and he hung up. Omar said, 'At the appropriate time, we should contact IPRP and tell them we have the poison that had been in his possession.' He didn't want to tell them anything until the plan had played out further for fear of somehow incriminating himself or his father."

"Let's give him a little more time to help us catch his father. Then I'll make the call to IPRP and give them the pertinent information that we have," advised Aldora.

"Sounds good. I am going to help with the watch on Omar. The SAC at the San Francisco FBI office filled me in on Omar's father. He is in the U.S. already but did not enter at San Francisco first. They think he has been in Boston where one of the ATP team members was found dead and foul play is suspected. The next stop was Minneapolis where Brad Tully from Tully Research and Zenica Lang from ATP were both shot at Brad's apartment. They are okay, but the shooter was killed and Omar's father got away. The SAC believes he is on his way to San Francisco or already here."

"My God, Jack, even if we catch this guy, is it going to be possible to turn him? It sounds like, besides his expertise at evading the authorities, he is prone to extreme and violent action. Maybe he has become a hardcore terrorist with only misplaced revenge and murder in mind."

"I don't know, Aldora. First we have to catch him and stop the carnage. The special agent in charge told me something else very interesting."

"What's that, Jack?"

"Omar has an uncle who goes by the name of 'K'. The FBI believes he is here to eliminate Omar's father, his brother."

"What is it with these people? Fathers killing sons, brothers killing brothers; I'll never understand it. When does it all stop?"

"It's a mystery to me, too, Aldora. Maybe we'll never understand it. With all that is going on in San Francisco, the director is coming, too. Stay on your toes. He'll be asking a lot of questions."

"I bet he is pissed that some of the people we are supposed to be protecting are getting killed or wounded and some of the perpetrators are still at large."

"Yes and not only that, they are putting the special government project at risk. The longer the 'Campaign of Fear' goes on, the bigger the snowball effect on our people. We have to get it stopped."

"I'll stay on my toes, but it is the field agents that have to protect Omar and catch the terrorist brothers. They'd better be on their toes, too."

"And that includes me now. See you later, Aldora."

"Bye, Jack. Stay safe."

The Director Arrives In San Francisco

The director arrived in San Francisco at a military base landing strip with no fanfare. He wanted it that way because he had to assess the real situation there. The latest augmented adaptive reasoning scenario the supercomputer had generated was frightening. It revealed an irony that he had not even remotely considered - that al Qaeda wanted its contract with Technolibertat to fail.

A nondescript car pulled out onto the runway where the plane was parked. The director exited the plane, walked over to the car, opened the passenger door and said, "Hello, Aldora; thanks for the ride."

"You are welcome, sir. We have been expecting you but I

didn't think I would be involved, sir. This is a field operation, isn't it?"

"Yes, it is Aldora. I believe it has become even more important to consider it a strategic operation. That's where you come in, with your legal training;I think you are by nature a logical thinker. I could tell that when we talked during the investigation. You knew, even though you are new and inexperienced with the Department, I was going to back you for 'attorney of record' when we went to trial. I need someone to listen to me now and push back if the logic isn't there."

"Okay, sir. Where would you like to go to talk?"

"Let's drive to the Berkeley campus. Maybe the environment will do us good and we'll be able to do some clear thinking."

There were benches near the main science buildings. They parked, walked over to a bench and sat down. Aldora said, "What a beautiful campus."

"Yes it is. Aldora, have you heard about the debate in the Muslim countries on 'Islam vs. Science'?"

"Some things, but I don't really know much."

"It goes like this, with science and technology comes human development. Science requires critical inquiry; the question is, are Muslim beliefs compatible with that requirement? The fundamentalists don't think so. They believe the word is to be interpreted literally without question or discussion. Therefore, since science requires critical inquiry, there is no place for science in Islam."

"Dr. Kharif is one of the more modern thinkers and as a scientist he didn't believe all this. The original concept for his organization, Technolibertat, was for trying to build a place for science and technology in Islam. He thought if he could acquire technology and put it to work for human development, it would win over some of the fundamentalist thinking. Are you with me so far, Aldora? Does this seem logical to you?"

"Yes. As I remember my ancient history from college, the Muslim countries had some of the best scientists in the world and some of the most advanced cultures. I don't remember what happened but it certainly isn't true today."

"You are correct. I believe Dr. Kharif was trying to help change that. When his wife was killed, al Qaeda told him it was by rogue CIA agents. That wasn't true, of course. We knew al Qaeda did it, but we thought it was to keep her quiet about the whereabouts of bin Laden. My recent work, however, indicates it was for a much different reason. They killed her to push him to get back at the U.S. How? By acquiring and using technology to prolong their 'Campaign of Fear'. Reasonable so far?"

"Yes. Are they smart enough to be that devious?"

"They are. However, here is where it gets a bit tricky. Remember that the followers of bin Laden are the fundamentalists. There is no place for science and technology because it requires critical inquiry. Why would they try to use science and technology through Dr. Kharif to help them? I couldn't figure it out. It just didn't make sense. So, I put all of this into my AAR program and the supercomputer spit out this unbelievable conclusion. Al Qaeda wanted Dr. Kharif to fail. They killed his wife, pushed him to distort the purpose of his organization to get back at the U.S., and hoped that he would fail. Why? His failure would mean a failure of science and technology. Are you still with me?"

"Yes, this is fascinating and very logical. The fundamentalists and the extremists would use the failure to prove they are right. Keep going."

"They have the best of both worlds. If the technology approach works for them, they'll take the gains and keep it as quiet as possible. If it doesn't, as they would prefer, they make it appear so negative that science and technology will never get another chance to blossom in a Muslim country."

"I agree. What does this mean for Omar and his father?" Aldora wanted to know.

"That is the question, isn't it? I believe even with the bumbling mistakes that Omar and his father were making, there was a sense that their work would be perceived as successful. Everything is relative, right, but here is a list of accomplishments which includes: faculty from top universities doing research for them; students, undergraduates and graduates recruited to the cause; technology licensed to industry; investments in research company IPO's'; possession of top-secret government technology; and invention by reverse engineering. The list goes on."

"So al Qaeda couldn't risk a technology success. The answer was to have father kill son and brother kill brother."

"Yes, their decision about the Kharifs was the same whether they were successful or unsuccessful ... death! Success would have meant an advantage on the battlefield but at the cost of millions of fundamentalist followers. They could not take the risk. Failure gives them the opportunity to show that the fundamentalists are right. Even giving science and technology a chance, it fails when they need it most. In both cases, the Kharifs have to go. Does it make sense, Aldora?"

"Perfect logic, Director. I can see why they were playing both ends against the middle, so to speak."

"Yes. If we can explain the real facts related to the death of the professor's wife and the scenario about success or failure of science and technology I think we can win the Kharifs over to our side."

"We know where the son is but we have to find the father fast, sir," Aldora warned.

Meeting with Omar

The meeting took place on the Berkeley Campus. Omar had been there many times but not under circumstances like this.

Omar said, "Do you know where my father is?"

"We don't know at this precise moment," answered Director Elson. "Our best guess is that he is in San Francisco but we don't know where. He escaped the scene of the shootings in Minneapolis and somehow eluded law enforcement officials watching public transportation, including airports and train and bus stations. There is a lead involving a private corporate jet that we believe requires further scrutiny. This is the major reason for meeting with you today, Omar. Do you have any idea where he might be and how he will contact you here?"

"I just don't know. Before all this stuff happened, he was just going to call me from the airport when he arrived. No doubt that is not going to happen now."

"Do you have any ideas what he might do now that he is on the run?"

"He doesn't know that I am being watched by the FBI so a safe phone contact is still possible at the TIC office. He would

451

not be anywhere nearby the office, however, because he knows that would be the first place to look for him. The other way is our pager code system on which he sends me a coded message to call him on a throwaway cell phone."

"Where would he go in the San Francisco area, Omar?"

"I don't know, but remember he was a professor in the Institute of Technology in Damascus so he has a lot of sentimental feelings for university campuses. There was a time when he collaborated with professors from all over the world. This is what made my work with TIC and the universities in the U.S. so easy. My father was known by some of the science faculty at most of the top schools here."

"Do you think he had friends like that at Berkeley?"

"I'm sure he did, but the names escape me."

The director nodded to Jack and the FBI special agent in charge and said, "We can check that out." Jack and the SAC excused themselves and went to get the team working on that angle. The director continued, "He might still call you and he might know someone here and even be close to or actually on campus at this time. Omar, has your father killed before?"

"Yes, I believe he has. I have no details but there were stories. Usually, they involved some kind of technology utilization, like the poison you know about, in situations he could justify in his own mind. There was never a simple shooting or knife attack."

"Did he ever get someone else to do his dirty work?"

"I don't know, but I assume so under certain circumstances."

"Omar, you should know that we found Dr. Fuller dead in his Boston apartment a few days ago. We believe your father was there and suspect foul play. Also, in Minneapolis, Dr. Tully and Dr. Lang were both shot recently. We know your father was there but this case involved a shooter that was killed trying to escape the scene. It is our assumption that your father was somehow responsible for these shootings, too. Could it be that he is on a rampage and is traveling from Boston to Minneapolis to San Francisco to take care of business?"

"Dr. Fuller dead? Dr. Tully shot? Is he okay?"

"Yes, both Dr. Tully and Dr. Lang are okay, thank God."

"I though he was coming to get me. There was never a

thought that others were in danger. I would have told you."

"I hope that is true, Omar, because the story gets worse. Do you know anybody that goes by the name of 'K'?"

"No, sir, I don't believe so. Wait a second – we all used to call my uncle that, Uncle Krishna or Uncle 'K'. He sort of dropped out of the family sometime before my mother was killed. There was some talk that he left to join al Qaeda, but we didn't know for sure. One day he was just gone and we never heard from him again. What about this 'K'?"

"We have it under reliable information that your uncle, Krishna Kharif, is coming here to kill your father. The director pulled out two pictures and said, "Do you recognize him from these pictures?"

"Oh, Uncle 'K', yes, this is Uncle 'K' pointing to the one that was digitally altered to have no beard and shorter hair. I don't recognize the man in the other picture."

"Both are the same man. One picture has been computer altered to remove the beard and long hair. The hairy one is a recent picture but we believe he might now be traveling with a clean cut look."

"My uncle is here to kill my father, his brother? I can hardly believe all this."

"You should start believing, Omar, and soon. 'K' is now a key lieutenant to bin Laden and currently responsible for the covert actions sponsored by al Qaeda in non-Muslim countries."

"Uncle K?"

"Yes, Uncle 'K' has changed a lot from when you knew him, I guess. We know he was the one to give the order to have your mother killed and create the story that it was done by rogue CIA agents. Our initial information was that it was to keep her quiet and to keep secret the whereabouts of bin Laden. Later we discovered it was done for another purpose, that of pushing your father to use his freedom via technology organization against the U.S. That is, to avenge the death of your mother."

"This is exactly when the direction of the Technolibertat organization changed. We went from technology for human development and freedom to technology for evil."

"We know that 'K' was the one who proposed the contract with Technolibertat and al Qaeda to help with the 'Campaign of

Fear' and got it approved through bin Laden. It was to access and use technology in any way possible to help the 'Campaign of Fear' and its IEDs, EFPs, suicide bombers, and car bombs. For TIC, it meant some cover-up activities with universities, like Berkeley, giving grants, scholarships, and fellowships. The important areas for them, however, were explosives technology and specifically acoustics technology used in any way to detect and detonate the explosives."

"It is becoming clearer to me with each part you explain. If my father only knew."

"There is a rather sinister twist to all of this, Omar. Our analysis shows that al Qaeda did not want you to succeed. The Technolibertat movement was to once again make technology more prominent in the Muslim culture and society. If it were successful, bin Laden and 'K' were fearful they would lose many of their most ardent followers, the literalists and fundamentalists. If that were to happen, it would be more serious than not helping to prolong the 'Campaign of Fear'. So, even though it seemed they wanted TIC to be avant-garde in the rebirth of the importance of technology, they really wanted you to fail. Do you understand?"

"Yes, I believe I do, sir. Do you think 'K', as you call him, had the perception that we were being too successful?"

"Somewhat. Even with all the blunders and the mistakes, you had actually done a good job, except for the deaths of the Kramley family. This goes for your father, too, up until his recent rampage in Boston and Minneapolis. It happened to be for the wrong reasons but technology was beginning to give you a reputation. 'K' concluded, however, the operation had the chance of becoming too visible because of the killings and that both you and your father must go. He is here to make sure that happens. The followers must not have any reason to begin to believe in science and technology."

Aldora had been listening intently, watching facial expressions and body language. She could tell that Omar was one scared individual. She said, "Omar, we know this is a lot to swallow all at one time. Your father is out to get you and your uncle is out to get your father - and you, too, if your father isn't successful. The bottom line is, we think we can help both you and your father …"

The special agent returned to the meeting and excitedly announced, "We found a Professor Bagley in his university office who says he knows Dr. Kharif and that he stayed at his home last night. Kharif is walking around campus right now."

At that very moment, a cell phone rang. The agent, Aldora, and Director all looked at Omar with only one thought - it's him.

Omar answered his cell phone saying, "Hello, Father, are you calling from the airport?" He put the phone on speaker.

"No, son, I am actually on campus right now."

The director was hurriedly writing a note. "Tell him you will meet him at the professor's house. Get an address and a time."

"I was able to stay nearby at an old friend's place last night. He is a professor at Berkeley."

The director placed the note in front of Omar.

"Father, I am fairly close to the campus right now. Maybe I could meet you at the professor's house and we could talk about my new assignment."

Dr. Kharif, thinking the professor was away for several hours at faculty meetings and his place would be a perfect location to take care of matters, said, "That would be fine. His house is at the corner of University and Central. How about in an hour?"

"Perfect. I will see you then. Goodbye, Father."

"Goodbye, Son."

"Good job, Omar," said the director. "Could you sense that he was anxious or nervous as one might expect for someone on the run?"

"No, sir, on the contrary. He sounded very much in control, always thinking and planning."

"I thought so, too," said the special agent, "but I haven't heard his voice before."

"Well, well, this is a most fortunate situation in which we find ourselves. Let's use the next half hour to plan how to capture him unharmed. Omar, are you up for this?"

"If this will protect him from 'K', yes, sir. Anything."

FBI Gives Chad The Lowdown

Chad was at the podium on Monday morning after a lengthy discussion with the FBI. He was thinking that this briefing was going to be a little different from the others. Are the people quieter than usual? Are they milling around less? Do they sense something? Lyncoln wasn't there but he often was late; they can't know about him. He saw Brad and Zen in the back. They looked pretty normal for what they had been through. Brad caught his eye and gave him a thumbs up. Thank God they are okay. The time passed slowly and finally the clock showed 8 AM; it was time to begin.

Chad said, "Good morning, everyone. I'd like to have your attention please. The briefing today will be different from before and focus more on commitment and success. We lost a team member this weekend. Dr. Lyncoln Fuller was found dead in his apartment on Saturday."

There were sighs and whispers, "Lyncoln?....oh God... what happened?...how?...when?" all coming from the group.

Chad said, "We don't know the full story yet but the FBI and the CSI team believe there was foul play. An autopsy, though not complete, has identified a foreign substance in his blood. It has the characteristics of a blood thinner and might have contributed to his death. Why was it there? How did it get in his bloodstream? The answers to those questions will come later. Lyncoln knew the importance of this program and the risk involved. He was okay with that and even as he was dying, he left a note for us. It was written in his own blood and said, 'Defeat the Campaign of Fear for me, L'." You could hear a pin drop, then finally the clapping started. First one person, then two, then three, and then the whole group. The people yelled and shook their fists at their terrorist adversaries. Chad said, "Yes, Lyncoln had commitment to defeat the terrorists even in the face of death, even while dying. Let's remember that commitment always when we are tested with project challenges and roadblocks. His last message for us was 'defeat the terrorists for me.' He was trying to tell all of us that we are doing the right thing and to be strong and successful." More clapping stopped him for a while, then he said, "Commitment is all around us and present in this room in another significant way this morning. In the back, I can see our friends, Dr. Bradford Tully and Dr. Zenica Lang. They are here as usual for the Monday briefing as key members of our team. You know that but what you do not know is that they were both shot by an assassin while they were in Minneapolis for the weekend. They are both okay, thank God, and thanks to some quick action by Dr. Tully and the FBI. The shooter was killed but is believed to be part of al Qaeda. Why were Brad and Zen targeted? We believe that they, like our friend Lyncoln, posed a threat with their knowledge of science and technology and its application to our project. Brad and Zen, thank you for all you do and thank you for being here this morning. Please take a bow."

The clapping started, then grew louder, louder, and louder. Several people nearby shook their hands and a chant that sounded like B-Z, B-Z, B-Z started….finally Chad said, "Now that is commitment. These two colleagues are still hurting from their injuries and scared because of what happened to them. By their presence here today, both are saying 'Let's defeat the terrorists'!" The group clapped and then yelled even louder.

"I have been talking with Dr. Jackson, the CTO of ATP, and Dr. Blackstone, president of CMT, about our project. They have agreed to a couple of changes we believe will ensure our success. Remember, I was going to talk about commitment and success. Well, success isn't just finishing the explosives detector and detonator parts of the project and sending them out the door for our customer to use. The change that we are announcing today is the immediate appointment of an overall project leader for L-REDD. This individual is one who speaks for both the detector and the detonator sides of the project, one who can bring technology and people together, integrate the parts, and develop a product that works as a system. We are confident this project leader will provide that overall guidance for maximum success. Effective today, our new L-REDD project leader is Dr. Bradford Tully. Let's give him a hand."

There was silence for a moment, then people turned to Brad and began clapping and yelling and as he raised his good arm up to acknowledge their acceptance, said, "Thank you, thank you all very much."

"Congratulations, Dr. Tully. The other change also has to do with Dr. Tully. Success for us, in the optimum sense, means that we remain ahead of the terrorists for decades to come. It's all about the technology. How much can they learn, how much can they copy, how much can they develop to defend against our technology? The safety margin we create is directly proportional to the sophistication of the technology used. The terrorists are technology poor and have only very few, if any, scientists who understand our most advance technology. This is how we defeat them. Dr. Tully has recently demonstrated and successfully tested another new explosives detector technology. It still uses acoustics technology, but is simpler and doesn't require wave content analysis or wave articulation correlation. Once the explosives are found, retuning the frequency of the original search wave can detonate them. Brad can tell you about this technology later but all of us agree that we must adopt this technology immediately and incorporate it into the L-REDD system. It will give us a magnitude higher level of success. The 'Campaign of Fear' will be dead in its tracks and our safety margin will be extended to an unimaginable level. Are you with us on this? Let's hear it for Brad and his technology."

The earlier clapping and yelling was comparatively mild because this time the building was shaking and it just didn't stop until Brad not only acknowledged their approval of him as project leader again but also their acceptance of the new technology approach by stepping to the podium and saying, "One of my best friends is dead, the blood of the woman I want to marry is on my clothes, she and I both have bullet wounds in our bodies, and we are scared. Have the terrorists achieved anything by doing this? Hell, yes. They have made us more committed, more determined, and more capable of dealing them a deathblow. I am proud to be the new project leader for L-REDD. I know you are proud to be on this team. Let's show the terrorists what we've got. Let's show them by our teamwork, our spirit, our results, and our rapid success. I'll talk to each of you about the new technology very soon. Chad and the whole L-REDD team, thank you all very much."

The noise of clapping and yelling was again shaking the building. Brad walked through the team shaking hands, doing high-fives and thanking people all the way to where Zen was waiting. She said, "Did you just propose to me?"

"I think so, but I didn't mean for it to be quite so public. I can wait for an answer later if you're not ready to commit."

"What? Commit? I have been waiting for this a long time but I didn't think it would happen this morning. The answer is yes, Brad, I love you and I want to marry you."

Chad came by and said, "It's your team, Brad, and they will follow you to the end. Congratulations on the project stuff and to the two of you."

"Thank you, Chad, for your confidence in me. Zen and I

really appreciate your friendship. We'll see you later; there is much work to do."

Hunting For The Professor

'K' left the San Francisco airport by cab heading for the TIC office. He was thinking that his passage through security seemed too easy. He was clean-shaven, had short hair, was wearing western clothes, wore glasses, and had a special passport created just for this trip. The passport stampings appeared as if he had traveled to San Francisco before. Krishna knew the U.S. passport control agents gave special treatment to foreigners who had visited before. They, on the other hand, were very wary of foreign travelers arriving in the U.S. for the first time. Anyway, he sailed right through.

The cabbie said, "Here you are, sir."

Krishna looked at the meter, made a calculation in his head, and paid cash saying, "thank you." He stepped out of the cab and looked around the area. The TIC office was dark and there were few other businesses in the area. No restaurants, commercial businesses, pubs, or anything else – just apartment buildings. He entered the TIC building knowing the office was street side and on the second floor. He proceeded up the steps quickly and tried the door to the office. It was locked. He opened his shoulder bag thinking, this lock will be easy to pick. With the right tool and a couple of twists, the door opened and the lights came on. 'K' surveyed the office, the desk, the computer, and the special telecommunications equipment. Nothing that would give him information as to the whereabouts of either the father or son was obvious. He decided to leave a message on Omar's phone in case he called to pick up his messages. The message said, "Hello, Omar, this is Uncle 'K'. I am in San Francisco a couple of days rather unexpectedly and thought we might get together for lunch or dinner. It would be good to see you. Give me a call on 707/646-8790. Thank you."

'K' left the office, locked the door, walked down the stairs, and left the building. He was thinking about Omar's message he had heard on the answering service. It said, 'I am out of the office, at the university today. Please leave a message and I will talk to you tomorrow.'

'K' said to himself, "If Omar is at the university, there is a good chance that Eomar is there, too. Maybe I can find them both!"

He headed down the street looking for a cab.

'K' Makes a Bomb

'K' had the cab driver stop at both a local hardware store and an electronics store on the way to campus. He thought that it was interesting what $182.15 will buy these days with respect to homemade bombs. I'll be able to build something crude but workable when I arrive on campus, he thought to himself, and have it available if I find Omar and Eomar conveniently together. The cab stopped in the center of campus near the chemistry and other science buildings. 'K' paid the fare and got out with his packages. He could see a mass exodus from the buildings was occurring so he sat on the bench and waited. It must have been the last class of the day since there were no new students arriving. He looked at his watch. It was 4 PM. He thought that was about right. Who would register for a 4-5 PM class anyway? He picked up the packages and headed for the chemistry building. There must be an empty chemistry laboratory that I can use undisturbed for about half an hour, he thought. As he walked on through the first floor, he found the administrative offices, lecture halls, and some faculty offices. The lecture halls and the faculty offices were completely empty. Then he saw the bulletin board notice announcing faculty meetings today after classes at the Union. Analytical, Physical, Organic, and Inorganic sections will meet in rooms A, B, C, and D respectively. Great. I'll do this in a professor's office. 'K' found a corner office, took his things inside, closed and locked the door, closed the blinds, and cleared the table that was located near the desk and computer. It's perfect. Out of the way, the smell of chemicals, everybody gone, no time pressure. He pulled the things out of the packages and arranged them on the table. First, the nitrate-rich fertilizers with their ammonium, sodium, and calcium nitrates; number two fuel oil, solvent-based aluminum paint, silica gel desiccant, antifreeze, guar gum, batteries, electrical wiring, a steel pipe with end caps, nails, and aluminum foil. Next the racing car with its electronic on/off switch and radio control device. All to be used, not for the intended applications, but for killing.

'K's mind flashed back to how much he had learned with al

Qaeda. IEDs and EFPs were his specialty before he became leader of covert operations in several key countries. He had made his name by advancing the art of the booby trap. Not as a scientist like his brother but as a terrorist. The technology was old and used in many countries and many previous wars. All that information was available and he had learned it because he was told it would be important. Three types: package, vehicle-borne, person-borne or suicide bomb, so simple. Basically, the IEDs share a common set of components: an initiation system or fuse, explosive fill, a detonator, a power supply, and a container. The explosives that can be made are almost endless from the organic pure explosives to the inorganic mixture explosives to combinations of both. The highly strained nitrogen and oxygen rich molecules like RDX, PETN, HMX, and even TNT and nitroglycerin were the best primary organic explosives. 'K' always marveled at the fact that most of these chemicals were first used as medication, dyes, and insecticides and not until later as explosives. PETN was in fact his own heart medication. He also learned they are all toxic and very dangerous and special precautions were always necessary. The inorganic mixtures of explosives were safer and had evolved from homemade formulas to commercial products by several international companies. He remembered DuPont for some reason. They had a product called Tovax, an explosive used for blasting for road construction, mining, quarries, seismic exploration, and tunneling. It was his proposal that brought these safer, less costly explosives, made with readily available materials, to al Qaeda and its war against the infidels. His work on firing devices, however, was what made it all so successful. The evolution from fuses, wires, and pressure release timers to electric FD's using distant command detonations took time. During that time, he developed both the wireless activation and voice communication systems for IED initiation. Triggering methods included garage door openers, radio-controlled toys, cell phones, and more recently handheld computers. The latter needed more work but was showing great promise. Their opponents were continually trying to implement counter measures including electronic jammers, radar, and x-rays. Examples are the recent Warlock Green and Red products. These devices send out RF signals to block the frequencies used by cell phones, satellite phones, and long-range cordless phones. Their challenge is to know the frequency of the trigger or initiator and that isn't easy.

He knew that other devices using microwaves and lasers were being developed to detect traces of explosives used for IEDs. Once found, premature detonation would be possible with pulses of high power electromagnetic energy or some other technology. The most promising technology was believed to be the new acoustic wave generation for both detection and detonation. He learned this after his brother had left the university to form Technolibertat. That is when the whole plan was developed to kill two birds with one stone. They had to learn more about what the great Satan, the United States, was doing to combat the IEDs and EFPs and most importantly to stop al Qaeda's 'Campaign of Fear'.

This meant learning about technology, making key contacts and becoming a player in the field, the goal being to use technology to defend themselves against whatever the U.S. was doing. The vehicle was Technolibertat and later TIC. The impetus to turn Eomar in this direction, rather than the insane freedom via technology route, was the planned killing of his wife. It was a great idea; we do it and blame it on the U.S. Eomar would use all of his abilities and resources for revenge.

If they were successful, the plan was to keep very quiet about the importance of science and technology in prolonging the 'Campaign of Fear'. If they were not successful, the plan was to make public the failure of technology and to once again demonstrate there was no place for science in Muslim beliefs. 'K' shook himself back to the here and now. All the planning, all of the effort, all of the time spent, all of the results brought him to this point. Here he was, in a chemistry professor's office on the campus of the University of California, Berkeley, getting ready to make a bomb to kill his brother and nephew. He wondered if this is where he wanted to be. His answer was, 'Yes'!

With that, he put the plastic sheet down and started mixing the chemicals in an empty paint can he had picked up in the hallway. He knew the amounts needed and the proportions of each component.

In no time all the ingredients had been combined and stirred together. The mixture was the consistency of a high-viscosity gel, like a fruit jelly that didn't have quite enough pectin, gray in color, and just barely able to be poured. Everything, including the nails went into the wide mouth length of pipe. Next, he dismantled the racing car, a black 911SC Porsche and used the on/off switch and other parts to wire the detonator and power supply. All of this fit into the outer cardboard box that the toy car came in. He would use the remote control that came with the car as the initiator. It was ready except the box needed a name on it. Using a black felt tip pen from the desk he wrote, Professor, Dr. Patek Kumat. He thought yes, this is a man I do not know. Eomar is gone forever. 'K' looked around and saw that he had a lot of stuff left over. Checking the bottom of the wastebasket, he found extra plastic bags. He put all the extra materials into the plastic bags with twist-ties and straightened up the office. He opened the blinds, unlocked the door, picked up everything, and left the office by carefully closing the door. He had seen a loading dock on the side of the building. There would be waste containers there for the left over materials. No one would be the wiser. With his small, carry-on bag now containing the remote control and the box, 'K' turned the corner to see a group of five people outside the chemistry building. Can it be? Yes, one of them is his nephew, Omar Kharif.

The Planning Session

The team of Aldora, Jack, Special Agent Hamilton and Director Elson knew they had limited time to come up with a workable plan to capture Dr. Kharif.

Director Elson said, "Let's go over what we know and don't know. We know his intent is to kill Omar; we don't know how but clearly his methods include poisons, blood thinners, and partner assassins."

While they were talking, Omar had called his office to pick up any messages. Suddenly he announced that "Uncle 'K' left a recent message on his phone."

Omar spoke up, "He said he was in San Francisco and wants to get together for lunch or dinner. I am to give him a call."

"We know that 'K' is in San Francisco; we know his target is Dr. Kharif. Any ideas?"

Aldora said, "Logically, our first step should be to get a watch team to the house where Dr. Kharif is to meet Omar right away. We don't know if 'K' knows where his brother is located or not."

"I think Aldora is right," said the director.

"I'm on it," said Special Agent Hamilton. "It will take a while."

"Next, let's get over to the house, too," the director said. "We can help until the watch team gets there. It might also be our chance to intercept and capture 'K.' Omar, give him a call and tell him you are planning to meet with your father soon at the Berkeley professor's house and he should go there. The three of you can go to dinner together. It will be like a family reunion."

Omar punched in the numbers and then send. One ring, two rings, three rings. Then 'leave a message, please.' At the beep, Omar said, "Uncle 'K', this is Omar. What a surprise to learn that you are in town. I am planning to meet my father in about an hour. He just arrived in San Francisco as well. The location is the corner of University and Central. Can you meet us there and we can go to dinner together?"

The team packed up and headed for the cars. It was decided that Omar would drive Aldora's car himself in case he was spotted by Dr. Kharif or Uncle 'K', to give the impression that he was alone. The director said, "We'll go first and you lag behind by about five minutes. Aldora will drive us nearby and park about a block away. After Jack, Special Agent Hamilton, and I determine it is safe, we will let her know. She will give you the high sign to drive to the house. We will be positioned around the house and be able to react at any time."

"What do I do when I meet him? I still think he wants to kill me."

"We know it is dangerous, Omar, and I believe he will want to hear you out about all the good things you have done and maybe even talk about new assignments back home. It would be too risky to do something at the professor's house, don't you think? He is due back almost anytime now."

"You are right; he is a planner and may not have had time to get ready. I'll just keep him talking until my Uncle 'K' arrives."

"Good. We had better leave. Remember, Omar, once the three of you are together, we will act quickly."

Aldora gave her keys to Omar and Special Agent Hamilton gave his keys to Aldora. Aldora drove off with Jack, Special Agent

Hamilton, and the director. She looked in the rearview mirror and saw Omar was waiting as told. She said, "Director, can we really protect him if his father decides to use the poison, a gun, or knife when they first meet? I don't think we can react fast enough."

"I know, Aldora, it is a risk we'll have to take. Our priorities are to capture 'K' and Dr. Kharif."

"And, Omar is the bait?"

"A key part of the plan is a better way to put it, I think."

It was only a short distance. Aldora parked and her three colleagues got out of the car. The director said, "That's the house up there; a one story with a garage in the front. I'll take the back. Jack, you take the left side and Special Agent Hamilton will take the right side."

As they started toward the house, Special Agent Hamilton received a text message. He said, "The watch team will be in place soon and able to focus heavily on the front of the house."

"Good. Let's go. We'll converge when the three of them are all together." Special Agent Hamilton let the watch team know and followed.

They took their positions around the house, moving quickly, quietly, and out of the line of sight from the windows. The director was first to see him. It looked like Dr. Kharif was dozing in a large armchair in the living room. Beside him on the end table were an open small black case and a cell phone. Jack and Special Agent Hamilton saw the same thing and came around to the back. "Jack, tell Aldora to tell Omar that he should just wait for our signal."

Jack said, "Right, sir," and made the call. They settled back to wait and watch for 'K'.

'K' Sees Omar

'K' had watched Omar with the group. He had elected not to answer the phone call just in case something was up. He decided after seeing the four strangers get into their car and leave and then Omar get into his, it was okay. It probably was one of Omar's meetings about Technology Investment. If he were being held, he couldn't make phone calls or drive his own car. 'K' stopped someone on the street and asked how to get to the address he had been given by Omar. He found that it was within walking distance and started off. The walk would do him good and he could plan how he was going to use the bomb. As he walked, he thought about some issues to arrive at his options. He said out loud, "Eomar is why I'm here. He is the brain of the organization. Overall, there have been technology gains that would benefit al Qaeda but he still could paint this operation as a failure. It was a failure that, if allowed to continue, would bring too much visibility to his participation and to bin Laden himself. Failure was okay; in fact they needed that to show their followers that technology was not for them. The experiment had worked but it was time for Eomar and his freedom via technology to go." Still talking to himself, he said, Omar, on the other hand is not so important. He would probably stay in the U.S. and without financial support have to close TIC. I don't think he is a threat the way his father is. So what are my options? He stopped dead in his tracks and thought, standing there for a long time. Then, he finally said to himself, "Shit, what the fuck am I thinking? I need to talk to Eomar before……" He slipped behind some bushes, grabbed his phone and punched in the long unused number in his contact list.

"Hello."

"Eomar, this is 'K'. I am close by."

"I was hoping you had come. I've been thinking about certain things."

"Me too."

The call was short but very enlightening. They talked about the death of Eomar's wife, K's predicament within al Qaeda, and Omar's ability to survive. There was a meeting of the minds on what had to be done. Hurriedly, a plan was put in place.

'K' started walking again, until he suddenly noticed he was only a short distance from the house. He thought, Omar should be there by now but there was no car yet. Maybe he stopped for something? Good. He kept walking. Reaching the door, 'K' knocked… no answer. The front door had opened a crack with the knocking. He pushed it open more. He was surprised but there was Eomar dozing in the armchair. "Dear brother, thank you for making this very easy."

'K' at The House

Jack, Special Agent Hamilton, and the director were all ready and on alert at the back door. They heard the knock and saw 'K' as he stepped into the house. They had cracked the door some and could see both men with a little effort, one man dozing in the armchair and one man standing in the front doorway waiting, listening, eyes scanning for movement. 'K' turned to look outside and then back to Eomar. He hadn't moved his feet, just rotated his upper body ~90° in each direction monitoring the area with his keen senses. They were holding their breath watching and waiting until 'K' got closer to Dr. Kharif.

The director thought - we can't split up. He would probably hear us and run out the front door. If only the watch team would arrive, we could take Dr. Kharif and they could take 'K'. It wasn't going to happen though. He caught the eyes of Jack and Special Agent Hamilton and mouthed the words, "Wait until he gets closer. When I move, you move." The two agents nodded indicating they understood. Guns ready, muscles tight, hardly breathing; they leaned against each other ready to spring. 'K' took another few steps into the room, put the box down, turned 180°, and ran out of the house at a sprint.

The director said, "Damn. Jack, arrest Dr. Kharif now. Hamilton, with me." Jack ran into the house and toward Dr. Kharif, gun ready. Hamilton and the director ran around the garage side of the house toward the street hoping to still see 'K' racing away. As they approached the street, they saw him at a distance. He stopped, turned toward the house, pulled something from his pocket, and pointed it at the house like you would a remote for the garage door. The director yelled at the top of his lungs, "Jack, the box, it's a bomb!"

Suddenly he heard and felt the explosion at the same time. The sound was so loud, concussion loud he thought. He felt himself being pummeled with debris, parts of boards, bricks, plastic, concrete blocks, and roofing while being lifted off his feet and thrown about ten feet away from the house. Dazed on the ground but still conscious, he looked around and saw Hamilton. His face was bloody, his clothes were torn, and he was not moving very much. The director forced himself up out of the rubble and started limping but running toward the middle of what used to be a house screaming,

"Jack! Jack!" He fought his way through what had been the garage pushing, shoving, straining to move enough of the tangled mess to get closer to the living room. He said aloud, "Thank God there were no cars in the garage." The roof had partially caved in on the middle part of the house so the entryway, kitchen, dining room, and living room were covered with pieces of the ceiling, rafters, roofing, and bricks.

When Aldora arrived, she saw what was left of the house first and then she saw Hamilton next. He had crawled toward the street and what used to be the front of the house. She called her emergency number, "Bomb explosion, agents down; need back-up and emergency vehicles at University and Central immediately. Perpetrator, believed to be 'K', is on foot fleeing the scene. Get help here fast." She threw down the phone, jumped out of the car, and ran to Hamilton. "Are you okay enough so that I can go and try to find the director and Jack?"

"Yes, my leg is broken but go help them. The director was with me but he's trying to find Jack and Dr. Kharif in the rubble. Watch out for secondary explosions."

Aldora could see the director. He was on his hands and knees digging and throwing the smoking debris out of the way in what she thought was probably once the living room. "Sam, Sam, are you okay?"

"Aldora? Yes, I am. Jack and Dr. Kharif are under here somewhere. Did you call emergency?"

"Yes, sir, and I found Special Agent Hamilton. He is okay but not mobile."

"Watch where you walk. Help me clear this area."

They pulled away a large section of plaster and roofing and there was Jack. They could see part of his back and legs but he wasn't moving. There was no sound, no pulse, nothing. Jack was dead. Then they heard the groan. The director looked at Aldora and said, "Dr. Kharif." They very carefully moved Jack's body by rolling him over into Aldora's lap to reveal Dr. Kharif. He had been completely covered by Jack, who took the full force of the explosion and the impact of the fallen debris.

Dr. Kharif was gasping for air, coughing up blood and holding his stomach. He slowly opened his eyes and tried to sit up but he couldn't. In a barely audible whisper, he asked, "I'm still alive?" Then he fainted. The director and Aldora sat in the rubble crying - with a friend who was dead and an enemy who was alive. They were both wondering how life and death could be so unfair.

Emergency sirens approached from a distance. The FBI watch team arrived along with back up help. Aldora said, "You are a bloody mess and need to go to the hospital. What would you like me to do?"

"I think I am okay. It probably looks worse than it is. I'll have them look me over here and then get back to work. In the meantime, take the FBI team and find out where Omar is. You have to protect him. Then go find this 'K' guy, capture, and arrest him. I'll catch up with you soon."

"Yes, sir." Aldora laid Jack down carefully, got up and said, "See you soon." She trudged through the rubble, signaled the watch team to join Special Agent Hamilton by the car. "Sir, Jack is dead! The director appears to be okay but he will stay here to be checked by the emergency team. Dr. Kharif is alive but unconscious and needs to go to the hospital immediately. Can you coordinate things here, sir?"

"Yes, Aldora, I'll take care of things and go to the hospital with Dr. Kharif. You think the director is okay?"

"Yes, he was very clear about my orders. I will lead the watch team to locate Omar and then proceed to find, capture, and arrest this son-of-a-bitch, 'K'."

"Aldora, I know the director will meet up with you shortly. Until then, stay in touch and I'll try to help you through the rough spots. Remember, these agents are trained in fieldwork; rely on them. Men, protect her with your lives; that's an order!"

Aldora took two agents in one car and the other two followed in another car racing to where Omar was last positioned. Aldora expected the worst because she could not reach him by phone anymore. They arrived and found nothing, no car, no Omar. Aldora said under her breath, "Shit, this is just not going well at all. Where the hell did he go?"

After The Explosion

'K' was running at top speed now. He noticed a car with a woman driver racing to the scene; he stopped behind some bushes. Once the car passed, he started running again in the direction from where the car had come. He thought it is always best to run in the opposite direction of the traffic. He slowed to a fast walk trying to notice everything around him. He soon heard the emergency sirens and saw other cars headed toward the explosion. Walking and thinking, he wondered where he should go now. Ahead, he saw the car parked with someone inside. Is this the car that Omar drove away from the University? Wouldn't this be great if it is Omar? As quietly as he could, he sneaked up on the driver's side and surprised Omar.

"Uncle 'K', we were supposed to meet at the house up ahead. What are you doing here?"

"What are you doing here, Omar?" 'K' got in on the passenger's side of the car and said, "I just got delayed a bit. Probably a good thing since I just witnessed a huge explosion at the house where we were to meet."

"I thought I heard something. It was you . . . . . Was my father there?"

"Yes, he was there. I don't think he felt much since he was asleep."

"Why, Uncle 'K', why?"

'K' knew this wasn't the right time so he said, "Because what you and your father were doing just wasn't good for al Qaeda in the long run. In the battle of Islam versus science, science must lose."

"But you gave us the contract to help al Qaeda."

"It was all for show. We wanted you to fail and then use it as an example so our followers would be even more entrenched in their literalist or fundamentalist beliefs. Now drive."

"Where do you want me to go?"

"Just drive, I want to think."

Omar headed back toward the office instinctively. He was thinking, too. He finally got enough courage to say, "Uncle 'K', do you know how my mother died?"

'K' looked at his nephew as if he were the enemy and said, "You are weak, Omar. You are not strong enough for the truth."

"You killed her, didn't you? You wanted to push my father to use his new organization and technology investments not for freedom for our people but against the Americans. You killed her and fabricated a story that it was done by the CIA so he would help prolong the 'Campaign of Fear'. When we started to make some progress, you got scared. A technology that could find IEDs could also find oil. A technology that could turn a poison into a lifesaving pharmaceutical. A technology that could track top-secret government products so we could steal them could also be a huge commercial success in the supply chain and logistics areas. You couldn't have that. What would your followers think? That there just might be a place for technology? Now you have killed my father, your own brother - and to what end?"

"I am sorry, Omar. I thought you, if anybody, would understand. You are not a scientist or technologist. You are a businessman. This was just business."

"It is never just business when you kill your own flesh and blood, Uncle 'K'."

"Listen, Omar, I am a technologist, not exactly a scientist or engineer like your father and brother. I was able to develop a much-needed specialty within al Qaeda. Yet I am still an oddball in the organization and even though I am a lieutenant, I am watched like a hawk. If I were not so valuable in our 'Campaign of Fear' and the covert operations in Europe and soon the U.S., my time would be limited."

"The people here would say you are living on borrowed time, Uncle 'K'. Our family has sacrificed too much for an organization that cares nothing about us. You have to see that soon. Why don't we just turn ourselves in? I am not a killer, yet I have killed three people just to protect our secrets and appease people. I can't do this anymore."

"Omar, I fear al Qaeda more than I fear the U.S. Government. There is no place to hide. They would find us sometime, someplace."

They arrived at the office building, parked the car, and went up to the office. Omar said, "They will be coming soon. We have to decide what we are going to do."

"Have you already talked to them? It sounds that way."

"I have only talked about me and my father. I believe if you help them, they will help you, too."

'K' said, "Could I really trust the infi…" Suddenly, clutching his heart, falling to his knees, grimacing, he grabbed at Omar's legs.

"My…… heart…… medication. Omar, in my ….." K collapsed on the floor, barely breathing.

Omar searched K's shirt pockets….nothing. Then his pants pockets….nothing. His mind was racing, where else could they be? He finally saw it, the bag K had brought with him. He unzipped the main part, reached in expecting to find bottle of pills….nothing. He emptied all the stuff out and shook the bag. He heard the pills rattling and realized, they were in the outside pocket. He unzipped, reached in and found the bottle labeled PETN with instructions to place one pill under the tongue for chest pain. He quickly removed the top, shook out one pill and placed it in K's mouth. Within seconds, his breathing was mostly regular and in a few minutes, he seemed to be okay. "Does this happen very often?"

"Yes, quite often unfortunately. That is why the doctor allows me to carry such a large supply. I'll take the bottle, please."

Omar handed 'K' the bottle. At that moment, there was a crash and Aldora and the watch team burst through the office door with guns drawn. "You are both under arrest. Cuff them, gentlemen."

The director finally caught up with Aldora and her team and with gun in hand, walked through the doorway making the observation, "It doesn't look like you need any help, Aldora. Good job."

The team was distracted just for an instant but long enough for the handcuffed 'K' to open his pill bottle, pour the entire contents in his mouth and swallow. It happened so fast and the reaction was immediate. He fell hard to the floor almost rigid and unable to move.

Omar said, "It's his heart medication, something called PETN. There must have been 25-30 pills in there."

The director said, "PETN? I know the name. It is a potent heart medication when used in small doses but is also used as an organic explosive. I believe it is more toxic than nitroglycerine. We have to get him to the hospital now. I want him alive."

Chapter 18

At the Hospital after the Bombing

At The Hospital

The hospital staff had heard about the house explosion from the ambulance driver who had called in saying, "I am also bringing in a federal agent with a broken leg and a Syrian national in federal custody with severe internal wounds. My colleague in the other emergency vehicle is still at the scene where another federal agent has suffered fatal wounds. Transport to the morgue will occur shortly."

If that weren't enough, the ER operator also received a call from Director Elson. "This is Sam Elson. I am a federal agent. My team is bringing in a terrorist who has taken an overdose of a heart medication called PETN. We need to do everything possible to save his life."

"Yes, sir, I will alert the ER."

"Thank you. I assume Special Agent Hamilton and Dr. Kharif have arrived by now. How are they?"

"Yes, sir, they have. Mr. Hamilton is fine with a leg cast and using a wheelchair. I can't say about the other guy. He is still in the operating room."

"Thank you. We'll be there in about 10 minutes."

"Yes, sir."

Two of the watch team put 'K' into their car and sped off with the siren blaring. The other two members and Omar took the director's car and followed closely. The director and Aldora stood on the sidewalk watching the cars race away. "Aldora, are you alright?"

"No, sir, I am not." She looked at him with cuts on his face and hands, torn clothes, blood on his pants leg, dust in his hair, and standing so as not to put much weight on his bad leg. Finally, with tears streaming down her cheeks, she asked, "Why Jack? Why Jack?"

The director took her into his arms. "Jack was my friend, too, Aldora. He knew all the risks that go with jobs like ours. Yet when it came right down to the critical time, there was no hesitation. Not a nanosecond. I am convinced that his last action was to save Dr. Kharif. He gave his own life to do that."

"Was it worth it, Sam? Someone will have to convince me that it was worth it."

"This kind of action defines who we are, Aldora. We value human life. Helping people and putting others first is part of our upbringing. Combine that with our training and Jack could have done nothing less. You and I would have done the same thing."

"I know, but it doesn't make it easy to accept that he is gone." Aldora pulled away slowly and said, "Thank you, sir. We had better get to the hospital."

"Can you drive, Aldora? I had some difficulty with the gas and brake pedals because of my leg." He limped toward the car as Aldora said, "Of course, sir," and got her keys ready.

On the way, she said, "Director, let's say both of these guys make it. What are you going to do with them?"

"I don't know exactly, Aldora. Both could be quite valuable. 'K' is probably the most important, short term. He is the top technologist within al Qaeda and could tell us a lot about the 'Campaign of Fear' in the Middle East and planned covert actions in some of the other major countries. If he could tell us how many people are being trained and where, who the key operatives are, where the explosives are made and kept, and how targets are identified and secrecy maintained, it would make a real difference."

"Do you think he actually came here believing he could kill his brother, maybe his nephew, escape the authorities, and get back home? How could any logical person think that?"

"I'm not sure using logic is part of the process, Aldora."

"Why didn't he blow himself up like the suicide bombers do, Director?"

"It could be that the job wasn't done yet. Maybe he still had to get Omar, I don't know."

"But he could have tried that before we caught up to him, and he didn't."

"You are correct. I have nothing to back this up. I am beginning to believe that he might have been compromised. He may not have wanted or been able to return home. After all the things that have gone wrong in the Technolibertat contract, they probably had him on a short leash and any misstep might have meant death."

"If he wanted to get out, why did he try to kill his brother and then try to commit suicide?"

"I believe it was more likely that he had to get out, not wanted to get out, Aldora. He still blamed his brother for his situation and wanted revenge."

"And the suicide attempt?"

"Again, maybe to be convincing for those watching back home. It would show them he was trying to be a loyal soldier and willing to die to keep the infidels from getting information from him."

"Director, you mentioned that 'K' was the most important in the short term. What about the long term?"

"Long term, I believe Dr. Kharif, with Omar, could be the most important, for different reasons, of course. If we could convince him of what really happened to his wife and why, he might decide to restart Technolibertat for the reasons it was originally formed. The question I have is, could he run it effectively from here?"

"You mean, have the U.S. Government support Technolibertat here to impact the thinking about science and technology in the Middle East?"

"Yes, and led by Dr. Kharif and, of course, Omar. They know hundreds of faculty and students, many of Middle Eastern descent, who would probably volunteer to help. Think of all the things they could do in the name of human development that would benefit their people and the entire Middle East."

"I see. We would fight the war on terror differently, one technological advancement at a time. It is not science versus Islam but science versus terrorism."

"Yes, win people over little by little by improving their lives using science and technology. The challenge would be to convert some of the fundamentalists to a more modern way of thinking. Anyway, it would be better than what we are doing today."

"Wow, people said you were different, sir. They were right. Here we are. Do you want to go in the emergency entrance?"

"Yes. Let's see if Dr. Kharif is out of surgery and if 'K' has had his stomach pumped."

"And you should have your leg examined, sir. You have lost a lot of blood by the looks of things."

"I will. Thanks, Aldora."

Emergency Procedures

The agents stood outside the two sectioned off parts of the emergency room. They knew that Dr. Kharif was involved in the death of one of their own in Minneapolis. They also knew that 'K' was responsible for the death of Jack here in San Francisco. The director looked at the agents and couldn't determine if they were guarding or plotting. Then he saw Special Agent Hamilton in the middle of the group, in his wheelchair, talking with them.

"Special Agent Hamilton, how are you and what is the status here?"

"I am fine, sir. One broken leg in a cast and they put me in this crazy wheelchair. It will probably slow me down a bit but not much, sir. Dr. Kharif is out of surgery and 'K' has had his stomach pumped. The surgeon told me privately that he didn't think Dr. Kharif is going to make it. He just couldn't get all the bleeding stopped. He has been taken to intensive care with 'watch and wait' orders."

"Will he regain consciousness and be able to talk?"

"The surgeon thought so. There won't be a lot of time, sir."

"I hope enough; we need some answers. What about K?"

"The pumping procedure went well. I think they got twenty-eight pills in some form or the other out of him. The doctor said PETN is very toxic if taken in large amounts. They gave him something like an antidote to counteract the poison. It will depend on how his body reacts. He is in intensive care also."

"What are his chances?"

"The doctor said maybe fifty/fifty. The doctor said something else, Sam. PETN is highly regulated in the States. It almost takes an act of Congress to get the drug in the first place. If you can get it, there is only about one chance in a trillion that a doctor would prescribe more than three to five pills of that strength."

"Things are different in Syria, Agent Hamilton. He may have carried enough to use it as an explosive for all I know. Do you have men in intensive care with them now?"

"Yes, sir, just in case."

"Have the men here secure the hospital immediately. I'm not so concerned about the patients doing something as I am about other people trying to get to the patients. Where is Omar?"

"My men took him up in case his father regains consciousness. He is under constant guard, too."

"Good. You get things organized here and meet Aldora and me in intensive care. Come on, Aldora; let's see if these guys are going to make it."

Upon reaching intensive care, the director noticed the FBI agents guarding rooms adjacent to each other. He thought, they are in rooms next to each other; how ironic. I wonder where Omar is.

Aldora showed her Justice Department badge to the agents and opened the first door. "He is in here with Dr. Kharif, sir."

They both entered the room and nodded to Omar. The director asked, "Omar, how is your father?"

There were tubes and life support machines all over the place. Omar said, "The doctors don't think he is going to make it, Director. He hasn't stirred since they brought him up here. I appreciate you and Agent Klein being here."

"Omar, it was a very strong explosion. The whole house came down on top of them. Agent Borson was killed and we got your father out as soon as possible."

"I know, sir, you were trying to save him. It was my uncle who did this. There is just no good motive for brother to kill brother."

Aldora noticed first. Dr. Kharif blinked once, twice, and opened his eyes. "Omar, Director, look."

Omar said, "Father, you are in the hospital. You have been injured in a bomb explosion. I am here with the people who helped save you."

Dr. Kharif did not move but was able to say just one word, "Letter." He exhaled and was gone.

Omar looked at his father, hugged him and kissed him saying, "I am so sorry. I am so sorry."

The nurse came in hurriedly because the monitors had gone off. She knew immediately he was gone, stepped closer, gently closed his eyes, removed all the IVs and other tubes and said, "I am sorry, sir. I will call a doctor to record the death of your father."

The doctor came in almost immediately. He wrote the time, date, and cause of death on a paper. "Omar, I am sorry, we did everything possible. His injuries were just too severe and we could not save him. I'm sorry." He pulled the sheet to cover Dr. Kharif's face and left the room. Omar was crying quietly and deep in thought. He said, "Director, my father mentioned a letter. What do you think he meant?"

The director went to the door and said, "Nurse, would you come in please?"

"Yes, sir?"

"Are Dr. Kharif's things here in the room?"

"Yes, sir. We have only his clothes, of course. I believe they are in a plastic bag in the closet. She went to the closet and said, "Yes, sir, here it is. Remember they are all torn and bloody."

Omar took the bag. With one hand he reached inside to feel around. He found his father's wallet in the coat pocket. It was wet with something and had a nail sticking through it. Omar removed the nail, opened the wallet and there it was, a folded paper with Omar's name on it. He put the nail and the wallet back into the bag and placed it on the floor. Slowly he unfolded the paper until it was a fully opened page, a letter.

Omar read, "Omar, if you are reading this letter it means that the plan your Uncle K and I put in place is working. He will explain more.

Uncle K's position with bin Laden had become tenuous and he wanted out. Also, he finally told me how your mother died. It was al Qaeda not the CIA. All this time, I have been on a misguided mission.

Our plan was to have K carry out his orders to kill me. He would be captured by the government and in a deal for his valuable information about IED placements, they would perhaps agree to announce his 'suicide' and later provide him a new identity.

I hope in time, they will allow you to restart Technolibertat supported by Pharmatek for its original purpose… 'liberty via technology'. Praise be to Allah. Eomar."

What Next?

Omar put his head down on his father's chest and embraced him in death. He looked up and said, "Will you help me?"

The director looked at Aldora then at Omar and said, "If he is right about your uncle - and that's a big if - I will do everything in my power to get the approvals necessary to help both of you."

The director put his hand on Omar's shoulder. "You stay here with your father. We need to go check on your uncle."

"Director, I may be able to help if ….."

"In time, Omar, in time."

The director and Aldora left the room together. As the door closed, Sam said, "What do you think, Aldora?"

"There are lots of hurdles to overcome, the least of which are the four murders in San Francisco. As a human being and a lawyer, I can't overlook those easily."

"There is a cost for most everything, Aldora. What if he could help us turn 'K', assuming he makes it? What if he could really make some headway in a new approach to fighting terrorism and religious fanatics? I'm not saying the four lives lost would have been worth it; rather that Thomas, his family, and the lab tech would not have died in vain. Anyway, I'll need your help to find the legal precedents to write our proposal and get it approved."

"I'll help with that, sir."

"Good. Now, let's go check on 'K'."

There was a doctor about to enter 'K''s room so the director stopped him saying, "Sir, I am Director Elson from DoAT and this is Agent Klein from the Justice Department. The man in there is a terrorist and in our custody. He has already killed two people today and, as you know, tried to commit suicide with a toxic heart medication. We believe he has some information valuable for the U.S. Government. If he lives, we must be able to protect him from himself first and foremost."

"Good God, man, he is in a coma, barely breathing, and fighting for his life. It does seem that the antidote is starting to work though. Are you suggesting we put him into a straight jacket sooner rather than later?"

"We want you and the rest of the staff to be safe. We don't know what he might try if and when he regains consciousness. May we go in with you?"

"Of course. You have to agree to let me handle his medical needs before doing anything else."

"I will, sir, but just in case …" The director opened his coat to show the doctor his holstered gun and then opened the door slowly and went in first. The agents on watch took heed of what was going on and were on high alert. Aldora followed the director and the doctor next. What they saw was shocking, mostly to the director and Aldora. The director grimaced, looked at Aldora and said, "It must be all that poison."

Aldora said, "Oh my God, he is dead!"

The doctor was finally able to squeeze through and seeing the patient said, "No, his vitals were okay just before we came in. His skin is yellow-green because of the PETN and the antidote. Most of these multi-nitro group compounds were first made as dyes. It was later that they were found to be effective as heart medication. They were very toxic but at the right concentration, they would work. Applications as explosives came several years after that. Anyway, this compound is a yellow-green dye as well as a poison and explosive. When the antidote works, it forces the dye to rise to the surface of the skin. That's what makes him look like a half-ripened banana. It also means he is going to make it. Let's leave him alone for a while longer. This is going to take several hours."

"I'll have the agents keep a close watch on him. The moment he awakens, they will notify me. Thank you, doctor; I didn't mean to scare you."

"No sir, I appreciate you telling me just how dangerous this guy is. We will take more precautions when we are in the room. Thank you."

"Let's let Omar know that his uncle is going to make it, Aldora. Then we have some work to do to get both Omar and 'K' to help us."

"Yes, sir. It looks like both the short and long term needs of our government can be met. This could get to be very interesting."

The director opened the door where Omar was still sitting with his lifeless father. "Omar, the doctor says that your uncle is going to make it."

Omar was still holding the letter and in deep thought. Looking up at the director and Aldora, he said, "If only I had not made so many mistakes and blunders. None of this would have had to happen. I am glad that Uncle 'K' will be alright."

"We are, too. When he has recovered, we'll start the process of debriefing him. With your help, I think he can be a great asset for us, but only if he wants to be."

"I'll do everything possible. Maybe he and I together can get things back on track. It is what my father wanted and what my people need."

"Thanks, Omar. I'll be back a little later when 'K' wakes up. Aldora, would you stay and talk with Omar about the next steps please? Oh yes, I haven't seen Special Agent Hamilton. Please bring him up to speed and also remind him to communicate with both Minneapolis and Boston. Thanks."

"Yes, sir, I will."

The Meeting With 'K'

The director and Aldora were told by the doctor that 'K' was awake and could talk now. They went into his room. "I am Director Elson and this is Agent Klein. We are from the United States government." Sam noticed 'K' was in some form of a straitjacket and said, "We know who you are and what you have done. The bomb you set off in the house near campus killed your brother. He died in the room next to you just minutes ago."

There was no reaction from 'K' except maybe a slight grimace that was gone in an instant. "What is more important, you also killed one of our agents in that explosion. There are friends of his here in the hospital that would like to have just a few seconds alone with you. We are trying to protect you from them and from yourself. If they knew that your man was also responsible for the death of the agent in Minneapolis, there would be no stopping them. Maybe your decision to commit suicide was the best idea. It made sense, except you failed."

'K' looked at Aldora and then the director. "It doesn't matter, I can't go back."

"We understand that. Our information was that your position, however important in al Qaeda, was tenuous."

"Yes, they wanted it both ways and it wasn't going to work."

"What do you mean?"

"Al Qaeda wanted the benefits that science and technology brought to the 'Campaign of Fear', but they couldn't let their followers know about it. There were always pockets of science and technology actively being pursued inside many of the Middle Eastern countries. They were always controlled and not allowed to blossom. More recently it has started again, more strongly, originating at the universities with professors and their students and beginning to spread ever so slowly. The stated intent was to use science and technology to improve human development and make a better life for our people. Even my brother and his sons got caught up in the movement. Eomar started Technolibertat and its subsidiary in the U.S., Technology Investment Corporation. He established a technology company, Pharmatek, to fund the organization. Al Qaeda believed this was the beginning of the end, this access to technology, its transfer to the Middle Eastern countries, and its use to improve our standard of living. With that would come the conversion of the fundamentalists, a few at first, then more. Bin Laden couldn't let that happen of course. That is why we developed the plan to show that technology would fail. I guess you know the rest."

"If you have doubts, why did you carry out your plan to kill your brother? Why not commit suicide or give up to the authorities. I don't understand."

"Eomar and I talked. It was the only way to have al Qaeda believe I had not turned against them. He thought his death and my attempted suicide would be enough to convince bin Laden that I had not been a traitor."

"You expected that we would be able to save you from the overdose of PETN?"

"Yes, sir. I am sorry about the death of the agent at the house; I did not know you would be there. I thought I could get in and get out before you caught up with me. As far as the other agent, Eomar was responsible for that. He knew later that he had gone too far with the murder in Boston and attempted murders in Minneapolis."

"What a turn of events if all this is true. Are you really willing to help us with all you know about al Qaeda?"

"I am, if you report me as having killed Professor Kharif and then committed suicide. In time, I will need a new identity and some help to disappear. By then you will have everything I know and I will be of no further use to you."

"We can handle that. Aldora, please make plans for the newspaper articles. As soon as he is able, get him back to D.C. and let's start using 'K' to help us."

"Yes, sir."

"Get Omar and let him get reacquainted with his uncle."

"Yes, sir."

"Thank you, 'K.'"

'K' smiled and nodded. The director and Aldora left the room.

"Aldora, I am going to leave as soon as possible for Boston," Sam announced. "I believe they will soon be testing the advanced L-REDD system. If we can couple our new detection and detonation system with information from 'K' about the planned targets for use of IEDs, EFPs, car bombs and suicide bombs, we might be able to make great headway in our fight against terror."

"Yes, sir. I'll bring both 'K' and Omar to D.C. as soon as possible. Just so you know, sir, I believe him, too. I don't like what happened to Jack and the other agent and to Lyncoln, Brad, and Zen. But in their own crazy ways, these men are trying to fix things as best they can."

"That's how I see it, too, Aldora. Well put and thanks. See you in D.C. soon."

"Yes sir."

Brad's Team on L-REDD

Brad asked, "Zen, how are Bill, Kan D, and Ray doing, from your perspective?"

"After you talked to them, they are doing fine. The unspoken question they all have is 'Can he do Lyncoln's job and be the project leader, too?'"

"I hope so, Zen. Lyncoln's code and software work was very similar to what I was doing. He had basically finished the wave articulation work and its correlation to known chemicals in IEDs and EFPs. His logical thinking brought him to the conclusion that one should be able to use this information not just to confirm the presence of an explosive but also as a search tool to find the explosive in the first place."

"I knew he was talented but not to that extent. Were you able to get into his system?"

"Finally, the hardest part was his password. I had written a program a long time ago to help identify passwords. It was for legitimate reasons because everybody has to have so many and they forget them. Anyway, it finally came up with ABEMIT. You know ABE, like Abraham Lincoln and MIT."

"Cute. Sounds like Lyncoln," said Zen.

"Yes; he was very talented. His code to use a chemically smart articulated wave as a search tool for explosives parallels mine exactly and therefore his work on the project was basically finished. He was beginning the foundation work on the so-called DACS, Data Augmentation Control System. Remember that I was to help him on that project. He didn't need my help. This guy was phenomenal. I miss him a lot, Zen."

"I do, too, Brad. Did you hear they traced that blood thinner to Syria and a company called Pharmatek? They are almost certain that it was their CEO, Dr. Kumat or Professor Kharif, who killed Lyncoln. Then the son of a bitch came to Minneapolis to get us."

"So, Zen, is Bill okay using my acoustics work?"

"Yes, now he is. It took a little time for him to accept the idea that someone could be so far ahead of him. He has a lot of pride, with his Harvard degrees and all. Bill also is taking Lyncoln's death very hard even though they were jousting about work all the time. Bill thought he knew code and software and Lyncoln thought he knew acoustics. They were always questioning each other's work in constructive ways. I think Bill has not only accepted the situation but has made some improvements on your technology. He talks about packetizing the several waves in a way so as to reduce flow friction. For me, as a chemist, he describes it as smoothing out a bumpy wave

... fewer bumps, more distance. Does that make sense to you?"

"Of course. If you have a number of waves with different frequencies, you can match them up to reduce interference. Has he found a way to better integrate or packetize the individual waves?"

"I guess so and it has extended our maximum distance by about twenty-five percent."

"Fantastic. A distance of ~ 400 meters is unbelievable. I must talk with him to see exactly how he did that."

"By the way, Bill and the others really appreciate the freedom you are giving them to do their work. Your management style is very much appreciated. Oh, there is more with Bill. This guy has found a way to almost eliminate the noise associated with continuous wave generation. Brad, it is almost the difference between those tornado sirens in Minnesota and the sound of an electric car engine. He said it was possible because of a new dampening material that he recently found. Anyway, it is quiet. My question is this: Is it really an acoustic wave if it doesn't make any sound?"

"Ha, ha, you are funny. Well, so I won't have to test our system only on Wednesdays at 1 PM. in Minneapolis. It sounds like Bill has things well under control. What about Kan D? How is she doing with recovering from the loss of her family?"

"Kan D is one tough woman, in case you didn't know. Her work is her way of getting even. You should see what she has done with Bill's wave generator and dampening system. We decided the sweep barrel should be hood-mounted on the Hummer with a control panel in the vehicle. The panel has the electronics and software to run the system, interpret the data, and find the explosive. No satellite wireless connection to a supercomputer somewhere or crunching data to the extent that we were doing it before. It is so simple and so small. As you know, the key component is the wave generator itself. We found some time ago that the Hummer engine could originate the wave. Generating a wave that would readily lend itself to separation into selected waves and also allow for reintegration was a bit tricky I'm told. Guess who figured that out."

"Bill, I suppose."

"No, it was Ray, the CMT team leader. Also, because the wave is coming from the Hummer, Kan D did not have to worry about miniaturization of the generator. She thinks her work is almost finished."

485

"That is great about Kan D. I know she is hurting but no one can focus more than she can. Terrific news, too, about Ray. I could see that he and Bill were working together a lot."

"They are, Brad, and it's good to see. He told me a little about their new detonation technology. Most of these explosives and bombs have controllers that are managed by someone in a remote location. The controllers use primarily radio waves like in garage door openers or a television remote. In places like Iraq and Afghanistan, radio waves are not government regulated. The terrorists can use any frequency they choose out of thousands possible. That is what makes it hard for us to find the right frequency and then use it to detonate. They have to manually scan the whole range of possible frequencies. It takes time and puts everything on hold until a match is found. The new system can digitally scan bundles or bands of frequencies all at the same time. Don't ask me how they do this. The net result is that detonation can occur very rapidly."

"But what about the integration with the long-range detector?"

"That's the beauty of it. As you know, Bill is already able to generate specific individual frequencies that correlate to identify chemicals. He then integrates and packages these in a special way to use in the search process. Think about detonation as a less fine cut of frequencies, maybe like flooding the target with all the frequencies of short-wave radio at one time. Then you do those of AM radio and then FM radio. There aren't very many other possibilities. Does this make any sense to you?"

"Sure. You may have just coined a new technical term for acoustics – wave flooding! The technique may open a few nearby garage doors or activate a child's toy car or turn on a TV but it sure as hell would also set off the explosive. It's perfect because detonation becomes the inverse of detection, a shotgun shot rather than a rifle shot. Retuning the detector wave to a few detonation bands should be like flipping a switch for Bill and Ray."

"Their first working prototype should be ready for testing today."

"I think I will have the software ready later today. Get everybody together about 4 PM tomorrow and let's try this thing out."

"They are chomping at the bit, Brad. Tomorrow at 4 PM

it is!"

"Zen, I know we are together every day and night but I probably don't bring up the subject of your health and recovery enough. Are you okay with how things are going?"

Zen leaned over and said, "Don't worry about me, buddy. Who cries uncle in bed?"

"You know I am trying to take it easy on you, don't you?"

Zen grabbed his hair and shook his head a bit, "Say what, buddy? We'll see tonight!"

"Seriously, I know you aren't working at the lab bench like before. It's no reflection on you or your skills. It is just that the project took a little different direction. The help you have been providing the others while coordinating the project for me has been invaluable. You know what? You are good at it and much better than I am. I want you to understand the significance of your contributions. This project wouldn't be where it is were it not for you. You are doing different things now. The project needs these new consulting and coordinating skills you have developed. I guess in my dumb way I am asking this - Are you happy Zen?"

Zen said, "It is not everyday you get shot and end up in the hospital fighting for your life. I have all these questions, Brad. Should I be doing this kind of work? Is it worth it? Am I going to lose you? Will someone attack us again? Is it healthy to be scared all the time? Will they catch the people behind this? If they do, will more come? Are more of my friends in danger? Who will protect us? So, to answer your question, no, I'm not very happy right now."

Brad nodded his head to show he understood then said, "What do you want me to do, Zen?"

"I know I have to be strong but that's different from being safe. Let's finish this project, get married, and get out of here. Go someplace far away and get our lives back to normal."

"How far away? I'm just kidding; I know what you mean. Hey, you got yourself a deal."

"Really? Are you okay with going away for a year or so?"

"Yes. Especially if they get Omar, his father, and whoever else wants us dead. I'm hoping for some good news from the West Coast."

"Oh, Brad, I do love you."

"I love you, too, Zen. Now let's get this project wrapped up so we can get married and get out of here."

"We could get married even sooner."

"Zen!"

"Okay, I'll have the team ready to test the prototype at 4 PM tomorrow. Will your software be ready an hour or so before?"

"Yes, I'll send it to you electronically and you can embed it into the existing control program."

"I am so excited, Brad."

"Don't let it show too much. We still have a lot of work to do."

"You watch me. We'll have this project done in no time. I know what comes next. Should I let the director's office know about the test?"

"Great idea! Thanks."

"See you later."

The Director and Absek Talk

"Hello, Director. We understand you have had a busy time in Boston, Minneapolis, and San Francisco."

"Yes, my friend. We lost two agents in the line of duty. The losses were the first on my watch, Absek; I am just sick over it. You have been at this a lot longer than I have. How do you handle the inevitable without losing it or, on the other hand, becoming so hard and calloused that it doesn't bother you?"

"It is a delicate balance, sir. First of all the agents know the line of work they have chosen and its potential dangers, including death. They don't do it for money as you know. For some, a minority, they do it because of the excitement and the danger. The others, a large majority, do it because they believe the country needs them and would benefit from their commitment. As leaders, we must make sure we choose the right people for the right reasons and then give them the most rigorous training possible. If we believe their expertise and physical and mental skills are the highest possible, we have done our jobs. Only assignments and experience will win out after that. There will always be losses, sir, no matter how good a job we do. That is the nature of the business. If you give orders that you know to be essential, orders you would carry out yourself, there will never be questions about the mission. There will be grief and sadness over loss of life but that is different from questions about the mission or training or specific assignments. Use your confidence that everything possible was done to ready your people, then plan to help the family of the deceased and the team members with whom he or she worked if that becomes necessary. I'll tell you, sir, it never gets easy and it shouldn't. The value of human life is what differentiates us, right?"

"Thanks, Absek. Your comments are much appreciated. Did your intelligence tell you that Patek Kumat, a.k.a. Eomar Kharif, was killed in San Francisco by a homemade bomb made by his brother?"

"Yes, we knew that but not a lot about the details of what happened after the blast. Did you capture 'K'?"

"We did. It was actually very weird how things happened. We captured 'K' at Omar's office in San Francisco. He had taken an overdose of a heart medication called PETN. Both Eomar and 'K' were in the hospital together. After surgery on Eomar and pumping 'K''s stomach, we knew the professor wasn't going to make it. 'K' stood a good chance. That is what happened, Absek."

"So, Eomar is dead and 'K' is alive and in custody?"

"Yes. Eomar regained consciousness just briefly and said one word to Omar, 'letter.' There was a letter in his billfold that he had written to Omar explaining that he and his brother had concocted both his death and the attempted death of his brother. 'K' confirmed all of this independently later. They had planned that we would be able to save 'K.' It is exactly what happened but he took quite a chance. Absek, the reason they said was so al Qaeda would believe 'K' had done his duty and they wouldn't come after him. We are to announce in the newspapers the deaths of both… 'K' having killed Eomar and then committing suicide."

"That is interesting, Director. Has he promised to help if you give him protection?"

"Yes. We think he could be very useful to us at least in the short term. He is the al Qaeda technology expert on IEDs, EFPS, and car/person suicide bombs. He trained the bomb builders, helped plan the locations and targets, the frequency and intensity. The information is available for almost a year out and it looks to be credible."

489

"Excellent, sir. What about Omar?"

"It seems the mantle has been passed from father to son, Absek. Before Eomar's death, 'K' told him that he had been the one behind his wife's death and the reason for it. It was this Islam versus science thing that they, al Qaeda, are trying to beat down before it begins to take hold."

"It is real, Director. The movement to reinvest in science and technology in their culture to help with human development is gaining ground."

"Al Qaeda saw this as an opportunity to show that science and technology would fail. Get Eomar to move to the dark side, give him a contract to help with the 'Campaign of Fear' and then hope for failure. When it happened, they were going to make it all very visible to the fundamentalists and further secure their support."

"My guess is that they were afraid it wasn't going to work that way."

"Yes, it wasn't a sure thing to fail and you are right, they got scared."

"Eomar and 'K' were going to come to the U.S. separately, one to kill his son, the other to kill his brother to fix things."

"Yes, but as we say, they got religion somewhere along the way. Somehow they talked, figured out what was going on and the net result was this plan they concocted. I have to hand it to them because they had us fooled. In fact, I am still having a hard time believing it."

"Yes, and Omar?"

"Omar is to restart Technolibertat, run it according to its original mission and get IPRP's approval to lift the closure of Pharmatek. He wants the U.S. Government to help him."

"It seems that it could work, Director. I am encouraged by the turn of events."

"I agree, Absek, and that is why I called. Could you help get the IPRP to call off any further investigation of what happened with Warfarin-D at Israpharm?"

"I think so, sir. How should we play it?"

"I learned that two things were identified at the plant in Damascus. Material, the poison, was siphoned off in pure form for 'emergency' purposes and some came up missing. There was a $10 million fine imposed and an imperative that lost material be returned. If not returned, there was to be significant jail time imposed on Dr. Patek Kumat. The second thing was that future shipments were to be RFID tagged so they could be tracked for safety purposes through the supply chain. I will handle the first corrective action. Because Dr. Kumat is dead, there can be no jail time, but the U.S. Government will pay the fine and return all the poison we were able to locate. I'm sure IPRP plans to destroy it officially just like they did with the supply at the plant. The second corrective action is where I need your help. A very talented Six Sigma team reviewed the entire manufacturing process of Warfarin-D and found that it was par-excellence. As I said, the only recommendation was to use RFID tags in the future. Can you set it up so the problem with Warfarin-D is found to be something that happened to it after it left the plant? That is, it had nothing to do with Pharmatek or their people, process steps, procedures, etc. It was something out of their control but could be fixed with the new RFID technology that TIC has available. Maybe you can keep Israpharm out of this and blame it on terrorists backed by al Qaeda."

"Perfect, Director, I know it will work. Israpharm will be relieved they don't have to take the blame for something they did to help the Israeli and U.S. Governments."

"Of course, Absek, and thank you. I do believe Pharmatek provides an excellent product for blood thinning. If we can get it up and running again it will continue to provide that product to its customers and funding for the real Technolibertat and Technology Investment Corporation. It would be good if you have your people, after Pharmatek is restarted, check on them from time to time. They don't have to know all the details except that you are watching and will help protect them if necessary."

"Yes, sir. I believe they will want to be part of the solution. Remember I said that if there is support in Syria for the fight against terrorism, it is at the university. Pharmatek, although independent, is still seen to be part of the university. I think they will be okay but we'll keep watch. By the way, Director, how much of the poison did you locate?"

"Not very much. Only a few vials that Omar had left after killing the Kramley family. Eomar's supply was destroyed in the bomb blast. We believe it was basically decomposed in the fire afterwards. Our people took special precautions but didn't detect

491

any of it at the scene."

"It is good to have it accounted for, or destroyed, and off the market for good."

"Thanks for all your help on this one, Absek. Remember we'll have the new explosives detection and detonation system ready soon. If we can get some up to date information from 'K', L-REDD will give us an even greater advantage. Wish us luck with our prototype testing. I'll plan to talk to you afterwards and we'll do some implementation planning."

"Thank you, sir. Good luck with the testing. I can hardly wait to hear about the results. Goodbye, sir."

"Goodbye, Absek."

Director Calls Joe Blackstone

"Hi, Joe, this is Sam Elson."

"Director Elson, how are you?"

"I'm fine. A lot of things have happened since we last talked and I need to bring you up to date. Are you headed to Boston for the L-REDD prototype testing?"

"Yes. I got a call from Brad and my detonation team leader telling me they were about ready and that I should be there."

"Do you want a ride? I'll be able to catch you up during the trip."

"Sure, how soon are you leaving?"

"The plane will be arriving at the military base landing strip in about three hours. Can you meet me there?"

"Three hours will be fine. See you at the base."

"Thanks, Joe, goodbye."

"Goodbye, sir."

Director Talks to Brad

"Hi, Brad."

"Hello, Director."

"I'm still in San Francisco, Brad, but will be leaving shortly for Boston. Can you hold the prototype testing until I get there? Joe Blackstone is coming with me."

"It is tentatively planned for 4 PM tomorrow. Are you taking the red-eye tonight?"

"Something like that. Four PM should be fine. I want you to know we got them all, Omar, his father, and 'K'."

"Yes, we heard from Special Agent Hamilton recently."

"Good. Dr. Kharif is dead, of course, but we believe Omar and his uncle are going to help us in our fight against terrorism."

"Are you sure we can trust them, Director?"

"Good question; we'll find out soon enough. They are being brought back to D.C. soon to start the process. I want you and Zen to know you don't have to be afraid any more. I'll fill you in on the details when I get there. Please let Chad and Mike know."

"I will, sir, and this is great news. Zen will be a lot more comfortable now."

"Is she doing alright?"

"Yes, sir, but this will help immensely. We have a great test planned for tomorrow. This thing, L-REDD, is about ready to go. I am finishing the code and the other parts are coming together. We might even have it Hummer mounted for the test. Want to drive?"

"Yes, I do. Brad, can you imagine what the possibilities are with this new defensive weapon? If we can get valuable information from K, we'll put some serious hurt on al Qaeda and their 'Campaign of Fear'."

"The sooner the better, sir."

"See you tomorrow, Brad. Goodbye."

"Goodbye, sir."

The Director Talks to IPRP

The director made the call to the IPRP. "May I speak to the lead investigator on the Pharmatek case in Syria?"

"Please hold, sir, may I ask who is calling?"

"Yes. Dr. Sam Elson, Director, DoAT, U.S. Federal Government."

"Thank you, sir, just a moment please."

"Hello, Dr. Elson. I am the lead in the Pharmatek investigation."

"Hello, sir. I am in charge of a multi-department U.S. federal government case on terrorism. Pharmatek's involvement might have been misconstrued, and I want to set the record straight."

"That would be helpful, sir. At this time, we have very serious charges pending against the CEO. He stockpiled a large quantity of a very, very potent poison at the plant without knowledge of the authorities. In addition, some of that material was taken and is unaccounted for currently. We, by law, have given him 30 days to pay a mandatory $10 million fine and to locate and return the lost material. The last I heard from him, he was to travel to the U.S. and take care of this matter and then return to Damascus."

"That is why I called, sir. Professor Dr. Patek Kumat has been killed by a bomb blast in San Francisco. It was an al Qaeda terrorist act carried out near the campus of the University of California, Berkeley, where he was visiting."

"My God, sir. I just met and talked with him a few days ago. He mentioned his son and that he might know where the lost material or poison might be."

"Yes, his son, Omar, is also part of our investigation and is in custody. The material he had is in our possession. Unfortunately, the material in Dr. Kumat's possession was destroyed in the bomb blast and ensuing fire."

"Do you believe this will account for all of the lost material, sir?"

"Yes, sir, and we are willing to return to IPRP the few vials that have been confiscated here so that they can be officially destroyed with the rest of the stockpile."

"That would take care of the charges on the lost poison. With Dr. Kumat dead and the remaining lost material returned, we would be satisfied that no further action is needed. There is the matter of the fine, however."

"We understand that, sir. The U.S. government has studied Pharmatek extensively, even before its shutdown because of the Warfarin-D scare in Israel. We believe the company makes a much-needed product for the hospital surgery business and that it is a very reputable company. The Six Sigma study at the plant showed that it operated as one of the elite pharmaceutical manufacturers. Also, I think you have recently learned that the product left the plant meeting and exceeding all quality standards. It was somehow contaminated in transport - most likely by al Qaeda terrorists."

"Yes, we have recently completed that part of the investigation and concluded there was no fault by either Pharmatek or Israpharm. Pharmatek is very willing to institute the use of RFID tags to ensure the safety of the product during shipment. This was a recommendation of the Six Sigma team as well."

"Yes, an excellent recommendation. Since the charges deal with a rogue CEO and not Pharmatek directly, we would suggest that the business be allowed to restart. The U.S. government will pay the $10 million fine to IPRP to ensure a continuing supply of Warfarin-D blood thinner to all the global pharmaceutical companies and their hospital customers. Would this settle all of the pending charges against Pharmatek and allow them to get back to running their business?"

"I believe so, sir. Who would be the new CEO?"

"The son, but only in name. Pharmatek will be restructured to be run by Mr. Japer and the employees as part owners. They are very excited to have the opportunity to run and to own the company."

"Mr. Japer was one of the best plant operations managers I have ever seen. I'm happy for him. As far as the IPRP is concerned, we will consider the case closed, sir. My report will indicate that."

"Thank you, sir, and good talking to you. May I say that we in the U.S. were very impressed at how efficiently and effectively your unit operated in an emergency situation?"

"Thank you, sir, we appreciate that. Goodbye."

Aldora Finds Precedents in Case Law

Aldora was always surprised at how all case law was now on-line. She had been asked by the director to find precedents to allow Omar and his uncle to work for the federal government even though they had committed major crimes. There were thousands of cases that applied in one way or the other and many involved murder. She looked at the Iran contra cases of the 80's, the mafia cases of the 90's and the Iraqi Saddam Hussein government crimes against the state cases of the recent past. She was struck by the mafia cases, especially those involving the Luchese family in New York and the pardon of one Anthony "Gaspipe" Casso for his role as an informant. She said quietly to herself, "They were able to justify a pardon for this guy, who was thought to have killed 36 people, for the information he had to bring down the mob. I think we can justify a couple of pardons to deal a potential crippling blow to the 'Campaign of Fear' and al Qaeda. If that doesn't work, we can delay indictments almost indefinitely while they help us in federal custody. In fact, that might be preferred because we can determine if these guys are trustworthy and have anything of value for us." She turned on the voice recorder, "This will be the essence of my proposal. Step 1: Federal custody and protection while we get the information from 'K' on the 'Campaign of Fear' and re-establish Technolibertat and TIC to be run in name by Omar, but strictly for human development in the Middle East. Step 2: If the first step proves valuable over the timeframe of six months to a year, then we can consider a formal legal effort to help 'K' and Omar as key players in our fight against terror. At that point, we can consider the very serious crimes they have committed and what to do about them."

She thought this was not exactly what the director asked for but probably a preferred route when considering the legal process and procedures. It would also cover their behinds by not acting too quickly and magnanimously without justification. And, for one, she thought – My career at the Department of Justice has just begun!

She wrote up the brief electronic proposal to the director and pushed 'send.' She said, "Now to get these guys back to D.C. and start the work." The laptop announced, 'you have one unread email'. Aldora said, "It's the director answering back."

"I am in route to Boston; I received your proposal on our legal approach with 'K' and Omar. It is excellent, Aldora, a logical, stepwise path where we act based on results, not on hope. Please get approval from your bosses and we'll go with it. I think you probably saved my butt on this one. Thanks. S"

To D.C.

The plane was coming tomorrow to get Aldora, Omar, and 'K" for the trip to D.C. She needed four FBI agents to guard and protect the men in custody.

"Special Agent Hamilton, may I speak with you, please?"

"Yes, Ms. Klein, of course."

"Can you spare four of your agents to help me get these guys to D.C.?"

"Sure. I like my men to go back to the home office periodically anyway. They need to get refreshed on what is being done in the FBI laboratory, get some time at the firing range, and to visit Quantico."

"Great. The plane is scheduled to be here before noon tomorrow. I will have 'K' released and checked out so he will be ready to transport. He might have to stay in a wheelchair so have them plan for that, please."

"Do you think there could be an attempt on their lives?"

"No, not since we announced the murder of Eomar and the successful suicide of his killer. I believe whoever is watching will consider Omar a non-entity and of no consequence to them. Don't you think so?"

"Yes, I do. One thing we might protect against is another suicide attempt. I know it is unlikely, but who knows with these guys."

"I agree. 'K' not only looks strange with his yellow-green skin coloration but he has been acting a little strange, too."

"How do you mean?"

"He is a little too nice, a little too cooperative, and a little too helpful. Do you know what I mean?"

"Yes, now that you say it. I just thought he was happy to have survived the poison and to be free of al Qaeda."

"Maybe I'm just being paranoid."

"What about Omar? Do you feel the same way about him?"

"No, I don't think so. He seems more normal but we don't have base lines for normalcy, do we? He did kill four people, you know."

"Yes, I do know. I'll get you four of my best agents to help tomorrow. We'll get these guys safely to D.C. and then someone else can worry about them."

"Thank you, Special Agent Hamilton."

Chapter 19

Long-Range Explosives Detection and Detonation Field Testing and Implementation of the L-REDD System

The Prototype Test At The Naval Air Base

The base had been built at least fifty years ago. It was part of the Strategic Air Command facilities and built during the early part of the Cold War. The design was old but functional with short, medium, and long take off and landing strips. Take off was possible to the west, north, and east respectively, all at the same time. The facility could accommodate any size airplane at that time and this still held true today. The terminal building was small and poorly designed by international airport standards. The adjacent control tower had the most sophisticated air traffic control and detection equipment in operation today. It had been maintained for many many years even though the base wasn't used much except by military brass and government officials. The problem was that the runway system needed to be replaced if the airport was to continue to function. The City of Boston had made the decision to take the U.S. government up on their offer. For the cost of $1.00, the City of Boston and the State of Massachusetts would take ownership of the naval air base from the federal government. Their only limiting obligation was to continue to make it available to military and government officials on an as needed basis. Boston city officials saw a chance to offload some of the increased corporate and private jet traffic from Logan International. It would be used almost exclusively for these purposes but also available for certain short-range local air traffic. Everybody was excited about the possibilities even though the renovation costs were estimated to be approximately $100 million. It was a steal, actually, with its location along the Charles River as prime real estate. To buy property and build a corporate and local airport would have cost $2 billion, easily. The City of Boston grabbed the deal within 24 hours of its offer even though there were military and government usage stipulations.

When Brad learned about this from Mike and Chad, who were up on local politics, he decided to try to invoke the stipulations even during renovation. It was perfect for the testing. He was able to get a copy of the purchase agreement from the online minutes of the city council meetings. He penned a note with the attachment to his attorney saying, "Please review and offer opinion whether DoAT, reporting directly to the president of the United States, can invoke clause 18 to take control of the soon to be (but currently under renovation) Boston Corporate and Local Airport, BCLA. DoAT wishes to use the facility for a period of 1-3 days for testing highly advanced and sophisticated defensive weapon systems. There will be no damage done to any of the structures and any ground damage will be returned to its original condition during this time period. I need your opinion today, please. Thank you. Brad."

The Legal Opinion

The return email read: "Brad, my legal opinion is that Clause 18 does allow takeover and control by the U.S. Government, in this case the DoAT, for selected usage. As written, the one to three day time frame seems very reasonable. We must make certain the construction company equipment is moved to the parking lots and its personnel are required to leave the airport area during the test period. I will contact one of our partners in Boston to have a court order drawn up, signed, and delivered to the construction company today. You will receive a copy. Good luck with the testing."

L-REDD Prototype Testing

The testing site and time were changed. Brad had made the decision based on the information that 'K' had been captured, survived his fake suicide attempt, and had agreed to help fight the 'Campaign of Fear'. Brad decided it should be the most realistic, strenuous, and full-scale test possible.

Brad said, "Director, on your authority, I have taken control of the naval air base that is under renovation near Boston. My people are busy planting IEDs and EFPs and preparing car and person bombs to be ready at the torn up airstrip. The test is at midnight."

"Well, I didn't know that taking over an old air base was within my authority, Brad, but I like your initiative. It is a great idea! I assume we'll use the old torn-up air strips as roads and some of the outlying buildings as points of potential attack."

"Yes, sir. We'll be able to test all types of explosives, at multiple distances, and under a variety of conditions. You have to realize we are pushing the schedule, the technology, and our people to get L-REDD ready as soon as possible. If 'K' really is the mastermind behind the 'Campaign of Fear' in Iraq, Afghanistan, and Pakistan, and the covert actions in other major countries like England, Spain, Italy, Germany, France, and Canada, we have a real opportunity. Our challenge will be to act on his information as rapidly as possible before it is old or they find out we know something."

"I agree, Brad. We'll have 'K' and Omar in D.C. soon and begin the process of information gathering. 'K' has indicated the schedule is already set for the next six months. They do their regular planning now to prepare continuously for month seven. After a month is past, the seventh month becomes the new sixth month and so on. The focus on the next six months is first on Iraq, north of Baghdad to locations where al Qaeda fled when the surge was implemented. Second they plan to hit the big four in Europe with attacks planned in London, Madrid, Rome, and Berlin. They are desperate, Brad. From what 'K' says, the talk is they are losing. This is a first. We can make a real difference if L-REDD works."

"It will work, sir. The bigger question will be about how we can get into production immediately."

"I have been thinking about that, too. You know that Joe came with me to see the demonstration."

"Yes, sir. I contacted him and made sure he knew he was invited and needed to be here."

"We had some time to talk on the airplane. He is willing to engage in a joint venture with ATP under a no-bid government contract to manufacture L-REDD starting immediately. There are meetings set up after the test to work out the details and sign the papers. I have asked them to keep the team leaders and their groups together for at least two months while we transition from R&D to manufacturing. Additionally, I'm having them write in you and TRI as general consultant for the joint venture. I hope that is alright."

"It's okay with me. Let's pick the right time to tell the team leaders. I know one of them that won't like your timeline so much."

"Let me guess; it is Zen, right?"

"Yes, she and I have some things planned after the project."

"It is only a couple of months. I'll make it worth your while to stay on and help."

"Thank you, sir. I'm sure she will try to understand."

"Is there anything I can do to help get ready for the test tonight?"

"Yes. Talk to Bill and Kan D. You have to practice driving the Hummer and learn how to operate the L-REDD system. The roads will be rough and dusty, and the system controls are a little underdeveloped. To keep it simple but make it work under all conditions was our intent. You'll get the hang of it quickly but some practice will help. If you can do it, anybody should be ... I didn't mean that, sir. I hope you know what I meant."

"Brad, it's okay. I know what you meant. I'll see you after my practice session."

"Thank you, sir."

The Test

Everyone had arrived at the old SAC naval air base early. The lights were on and the place looked like it was the expected landing site for an alien spaceship. Everything was staged on the tarmac. There were two Hummers appropriately outfitted with the wave generators, scanners, and control panels. Three cars marked X, Y, and Z with car bombs were positioned randomly off the runways to the north and east and controlled remotely at the command center in the tower. Two life-size robots marked A & B, one positioned near the hanger to the east and the other on the tarmac near the terminal with backpacks full of explosives and controlled remotely from the command center were set up and ready. There was a 'safe car' filled with video cameras to tape the whole event.

Zen had set it up so the key players were to run the show. Kan D would operate the robots. Bill operated the remotely controlled cars, Ray controlled one Hummer and the director controlled the second Hummer. Brad was in the safe car to be positioned at the intersection of the long east/west runway and the shorter north/south runway. He was an observer but also tasked with videotaping the test as it unfolded. Zen's laptop had the control panel with electronic locators for all of the explosives, IEDs, EFPs, car and person bombs, and she carried it everywhere she went. It was more for making sure everything was in place and ready to go. She did not intent to unlock any of the electronic switches for exploding the bombs.

The laptop was hooked up to the command center's new electronic map of the air base. All the components of the test, the explosives, the robots, remote cars, Hummers, the safe car were electronically tagged and depicted on the map. Any activity, explosion, robot, and vehicle movement would be tracked with lights and sounds on the e-map. There were eleven of these hidden roadside explosives alongside the runways, an almost equal number for each Hummer route. The half-hidden explosives were numbered one through eleven. The team had bomb experts make and place them using every kind of terrorist explosive known to have been used in the last two years in combat zones or non-military areas. This was a test but the explosives were the real thing. The rules were simple: the remote controlled cars could be stationary or moving and Bill would decide; the robots could be stationary or moving and Kan D would decide; and the Hummers had prearranged routes following the dug-up runways. Hummer #1 was to leave the tarmac, travel north to the runway intersection and turn east toward the river. Hummer #2 would leave the tarmac five minutes later, taking the same path north to the runway intersection, turn west, and then south back to the terminal. The communication system was set up so everyone could send and receive constantly. The goal was to detect and detonate all of the explosives and scientifically record the test.

The team was ready. Mike, Chad, and Joe arrived to officially represent ATP and CMT and document what they saw during the prototype testing. Zen thought it was best to have the people who would make future business decisions on hand to judge the success and lend their perspectives of the test. To eliminate any subtle bias, Mike was to focus on CMT's detonation technology, Joe was to focus on ATP's detection technology, and Chad was to observe 50% on each aspect. They were located in the command center with Bill, Kan D, and Zen. They were all huddled close to the Hummers where Ray and the director were making the last checks of their vehicles. Brad was getting the safe car video camera ready to go. His vehicle would be the first to move out, followed five minutes later by Hummer #1 and then five minutes later by Hummer #2.

Zen said, "Listen up, please. We are about ready for the official prototype testing on L-REDD. Before we start, both Brad and the director want to say a few words. Remember everyone, everything is being recorded – audio and video. Brad."

"Thanks, Zen. It wasn't so long ago the director asked me to help with the project. I said yes but had no idea what that really meant. You made the same commitment, of course. When our national security is threatened, people like us step up to help. I am amazed at what you were able to do with the L-REDD project in such a short time. When people look back ten years from now, I believe it will be clear that your work helped with the downfall of the 'Campaign of Fear' and al Qaeda in the Middle East. I am so proud of you and honored to be part of the team. Tonight let's each do our job and show just what this system can do. Quite literally, our country needs it now. Thank you. Director."

"Thank you, Brad. This project is priority one for those who directly impact national security. Brad is right. The quality of your technical work and the speed of execution have been outstanding. We expected that because you were specially selected for this project. Your commitment gave you a great opportunity to help your country but it also put you in harm's way. We saw direct examples of this with Lyncoln, Zen, and Brad and indirect examples for all of us. As we know, the price can be high, sometimes very high. I am truly sorry for that. What I can tell you tonight is that two terrorists are dead and two are in custody. Omar Kharif and his uncle, Krishna Kharif, have agreed to help us to further the science and technology approach to improve human development in the Middle East and to make sure the 'Campaign of Fear' is a failure. With

Kharif's inside information on targets and bomb locations and your L-REDD system, we will succeed in the war on terror even faster. Longer range, we'll show that science and technology can positively impact the cultural, societal, and personal growth of our friends in the Middle East. Converting the literalists and fundamentalists to a more liberal way of thinking will defeat all the extremists, al Qaeda, Hamas, Hezbollah, and the Taliban. You must understand that this project starts the ball rolling. You are the team that made the first major change to start the process. Once started, it cannot be stopped. Thank you for allowing me to be part of the team and this historical event. I say, let's give 'em hell tonight!"

"Thank you, Director. Let's all get to our stations and let the games begin. Hummer drivers, remember your controls are set to both detect and detonate automatically. If you want to test manual detonation, press the M button on the control panel. You'll be able to see when an explosive is found, a red light goes on. When detonation has occurred, a green light goes on. We provided for manual detonation basically for moving targets. Immediate detonation may not be preferred in some small number of cases. Proximity to buildings and groups of people may be factors so be very careful. The car bomber or suicide person bomber has only one thing in mind. That is to destroy a pre-arranged target and kill as many people as possible. There will be a detonation either by the bomber or by you. Waiting may actually make the situation worse. That is why the system is preset to automatic and defaults to automatic even after only one manual detonation."

Ray and the director looked at one another. The director said, "I'm going to leave mine on auto."

Ray said, "Me too, at least at the start."

"That's fine. Brad, time to move your safe car to the intersection."

Before he could move an inch, Zen took three quick steps over to him, put her hands on his shoulders, stood on her tiptoes, gave him a kiss, and whispered in his ear, "No heroics out there; stay in the car and do your job. Your reward will come a little later." With a lovely smile and a wink, she stepped back. "Remember Hummers, five minutes apart." With that, she left to catch up with the others headed for the control tower command center.

Brad said, "Let's plan to meet on the tarmac afterwards and

THE CAMPAIGN OF FEAR

compare notes. Good luck."

"Good idea," said the director.

"See you there," said Ray.

The director and Ray watched Brad get into his car and drive to the intersection, at least a couple hundred yards away. The two Hummer drivers shook hands and got into their vehicles. Ray turned his L-REDD system on and started in Hummer #1. In no time, the first explosive, #8, went off to his right. "Did you see that? I didn't have to do anything, just drive." Then he saw the second explosive, #6, go off to the left and beyond the intersection. Another explosive, #9 detonated beyond the intersection on the right. Before he made his turn east, toward the river, there was another explosion, #7 at the north end of the runway. Ray said, "Hummer #2, there may not be much left for you."

In the command center Zen said, "Hummer #1, please stay focused."

"Yes, ma'am." As he made the turn, Hummer #1 could see Hummer #2 start the assigned route. Just then a stationary car, Y, exploded with tremendous force. The driver in Hummer #1 said, "Well, it works on car bombs, too." Then explosive #10, the robot B running toward the hangars and IED #11 all exploded.

Hummer #2 had no hits up to the intersection but once it turned left, there was an explosion, #5, to the left up ahead. He saw the car, Z, moving toward the maintenance building just before it went up in flames. Then explosion #4 went off. He was about ready to make the left turn back to the terminal. Starting that way, explosives #3 then #2 to his left and #1 to his right all exploded. Robot A was running toward the terminal. The explosion took place before he got to the tarmac. The director was finally able to speak. "Reporting 7 hits; 5 roadside bombs, one car bomb, and one robot bomb."

Hummer #1 driver said, "Yes, 8 hits; 6 roadside bombs, one car bomb, and one robot bomb. I am at the end of the runway, turning, and switching to manual detonation. Then he saw the car racing toward the terminal out of the corner of his eye. He said, "There is X car racing toward the terminal. I am out of position …"

Hummer #2 had arrived at the tarmac and turned left toward the starting point. "I have him …" The explosion occurred immediately before the car got very close to the terminal. "Correction: 8 hits with two car bombs. Hummer #1, see you at the starting point. Same to you, Brad."

They jumped out of their vehicles and came together. "I know," said Brad, "A 180° sweep is not enough; it has to be 360°. We'll put it on top of the Hummers."

"That will fix the problems on turns or someone slipping in on the reverse sweep," said the director.

"What about automatic or manual? I'm afraid my reaction time was way too slow," said Ray.

Brad said, "Yes, it is probably best to have them all be automatic and very simple to operate. All you have to do is drive and let the L-REDD system do the work."

"Did you get all that on video, Brad?" asked the director. "It was like a war zone out there."

I got it all including the last car bomb and how close it got to the terminal. Remember that I promised the city there would be no damage to the buildings."

"Let's get everyone home for some rest." The director looked at his watch; it was almost 1 AM. In less than 45 minutes, we have taken care of 16 explosive devices."

The command center team came running out to the tarmac yelling, waving their arms, and jumping up and down.

Zen said, "We did it; we did it! You should have seen the electronic map."

Kan D said, "You killed my running robots."

Bill said, "You even got the last car bomb that almost sneaked through to the terminal."

Joe said, "We need some work on our scanner sweep angle but, except for that last car, it was perfect."

Mike said, "I agree with Joe; once detection occurred, detonation worked every time.

Chad said, "It was a great test. We could not have expected anything better. For my two cents, I would eliminate the manual option. It may use up a critical second or two in a do or die situation. Congratulations, everybody!"

Brad said, "Thank you, everybody. The director has given us an order to go home and get some rest! We'll review everything about this test at 1 PM tomorrow. Joe, Mike, and Chad, may we also have your initial thinking on the manufacturing plan at that time?"

Joe looked at Mike and Chad, nodded to see they agreed, and then said, "No need to wait on anything. L-REDD is ready to be scaled up and put into production. We'll be there tomorrow with a plan."

They all scanned the three runways and where the 16 bombs had been detected and detonated. Zen was thinking they had done it. The good guys won this time. She took Brad's arm and said, "Goodnight, everyone. See you tomorrow, but not before noon."

The Men In Custody

"Director, we will land at Andrews Air Force Base in about 30 minutes. Do you want us to bring the men in custody to your building?"

"No, I have made arrangements for them to stay at Andrews for the next few months, Aldora. I think they will be safe there from any outside attempts on their lives."

"Yes, sir. Are you coming over right away?"

"Yes, I am. It is even more important now to get the information from 'K'. We just completed our very sophisticated field trial of L-REDD. It really works, Aldora. We were able to detect and detonate every hidden and moving explosive target out there. I drove one of the Hummers with an installed unit. L-REDD did all the work; I just drove a predetermined route. If we can get general locations or targets of al Qaeda IEDs, EFPs, car or person bombs from 'K', we can find and destroy them immediately. I have assembled an interview team to help; I am going to lead the team. I also want the legal aspects covered closely all along the way. Will you join us on the I-team?"

"I would be honored, sir. By the way, the attorney general signed off on our proposal. There was a little handwritten note below the official DoJ stamp of approval and his signature. It said, 'Sam and Aldora – congratulations. I have passed the word that all DoJ proposals requesting reductions in sentencing be based on the value of information actually provided. I like your stepwise approach a lot and it will become the model. Thanks. AG"

"Congratulations, Aldora. I'll make sure he knows it was

your work. See you soon."

The jet landed at Andrews AFB with little fanfare except another four military police joined the four FBI agents to escort Omar and 'K' to a special part of the base designated for Department of Defense matters.

The director said, "Hello, Aldora, you are right on time, as he led her away from the prisoners. I'd like you to meet Colonel Smith, a military expert representing the offices of the president, DoD, and DoAT and Dr. Jones, special interrogator representing the CIA and NSA."

"Colonel Smith. Dr. Jones. Good to meet you. Are those your real names?"

Colonel Smith looked at Dr. Jones, smiled, and said, "Yes, madam, for most of our assignments."

"We have a van and car to take us to the DoD area," said the director. "Let's go."

It looked like a hangar and it was ... for two DoD, G-6 planes. The MPs led everyone to the large elevators. One of them pushed SB5 and down they went. The area was huge with more military police all around. The director, Aldora, Colonel Smith, and Dr. Jones were taken to the interview room. The prisoners were taken to their private rooms to use the facilities and see where they would be staying for a while.

Omar said, "Will we be next to each other?"

"Yes," said the MP Sergeant.

"Will we be able to talk to each other?"

"Yes."

'K' said, "After we finish here, where will we go?"

"Back to an interview room, together first, then you will be separated."

"Will we be tortured?" 'K' asked.

"No. It is not allowed under the Geneva Convention. These are your rooms. Please use the facilities to freshen up quickly. You will be under constant video surveillance."

The director said to Aldora, "The interview room has been fitted with computer capability using an enhanced version of my AAR software. I want to see if the information we get will help us build a better war on terror scenario. Every word spoken, every accent, inflection or emphasis used will be captured and evaluated.

Facial expressions, body positioning, physical habits are all characteristics that will add to the scenario. More complex areas like social skills, independency, reasoning power, inner strength will be probed to validate the information and build the credibility factor for the scenario. See the wall screens? They are capturing every word, every sound, every movement of the body and constantly evaluating, assessing, and interpreting the data. Every time information or data is added, the software adapts the scenario using its embedded artificial intelligence. The result is the most accurate picture of the future taking everything into account."

"Who asks the questions?"

"I have trained Dr. Jones; he is very good at this."

"And what does Colonel Smith do during the interview?"

"He has special knowledge of our own or coalition military planning, especially in the hot spot areas. It is essential to determine if we have been compromised. He will be the one to give the orders on the placement locations for the L-REDD system. You can bet he will be interested in the information 'K' has for us."

"What should I do, sir?"

"Two things, Aldora. One, make sure we are okay from a legal standpoint. There may never be a trial but if there is, I don't want a technicality to hurt us. Two, observe and use your logical mind and thinking to contribute. Make sure all the right questions get asked. I think Omar respects and trusts you a lot. You might be able to help him believe the U.S. government will really support him to restart Technolibertat under its original charter."

"And 'K'? What about him?"

"Yes, 'K'. Let's say he gives us the information about their plans for explosives of all kinds in all the different places for the next six months. Put that information with our new L-REDD capability and we have a gold mine. Probably enough to give him a full pardon?"

"Probably so, maybe."

"What we haven't been taking into account is that he is a bin Laden lieutenant. We believe there are only six lieutenants for God's sake. 'K' has been part of the closest inner circle of leadership within al Qaeda for several years. He no doubt knows bin Laden's schedule, hideouts, short- and long-term plans, allies, strengths and weakness, resources, terrorist deployment, financials, everything.

As the attorney general said, the model has become pay for play. I'll need you to help get all the intel from him outside of explosives. We'll pay him for it if we determine the value to be great enough. Will you think through how to manage that process if 'K' becomes the hottest al Qaeda property we've ever had?"

"I will. What a great opportunity to not just shorten but win the war on terror."

"Thank you, Aldora. Oh, yes, would you thank the FBI agents from San Francisco and tell them their assignment on this case is completed, please?"

"Yes, sir. I'll be right back."

The MPs brought the two men into the interview room together. "Sir, should we stay inside or outside the room?"

"Outside please. Thank you."

After the L-REDD Test

The director was excited when he called, "Absek, you should have seen the field test of L-REDD."

"From the sound of your voice, the results must have been very good."

"I would say excellent, Absek. We had two Hummers fitted with the L-REDD units to drive prearranged routes without knowing where the explosives were. They got them all."

"This is excellent news, sir. How soon will you be manufacturing and ready to supply units?"

"We can make several, probably tens of units, in the laboratory and we'll be doing that soon. Would you like to get some of the first pre-production units and test in real life field applications?"

"Yes, certainly. This is an advancement way beyond anything we have today. The sooner the better."

"Okay, Absek."

"Sir, have you been able to get information from 'K'?"

"We are working on it, Absek. We've started by asking 'K' to identify all of the planned explosive device targets for the next six months. If we can get those locations and get our manufacturing going, we'll know where those units should go. I have asked that he start with Israel."

"Thank you, sir. We can, however, use the L-REDD units even without the specific information 'K' has on explosive locations. Plan to send the lab units as soon as they are ready."

"We will, Absek. Expect them in about a week or ten days."

"Thank you, sir."

"Thanks, Absek, and 'til next time, goodbye."

"Goodbye, sir."

Andrews Air Force Base

Aldora said, "Do you believe the map of locations 'K' is preparing? Whatever you told him, it's working!"

"We'll see. I had him start with Israel and the Middle East to see if his information is accurate. Our expectations have to be tempered in that we should expect him to be only about 50% right. With the variables of locations, targets, dates, and types of explosives, he can be expected to remember only about half of what has been planned in the short term. As the time passes, his recollections will drop off even further. Our colleague, Absek, is ready to test the information as soon as he receives the L-REDD units."

"I think that is okay, sir. We had no information before about the location of explosive devices. Any information will be a real plus."

"That's the way I feel about it, too. If we expect more than he could possibly deliver, it will taint how we think about his help."

"Yes, and what we are prepared to do for him."

"Right. The part that struck me the most is the magnitude of the plan, Aldora. He says the al Qaeda 'Campaign of Fear' will be continuing and increasing in Iraq. Baghdad remains a target but at somewhat reduced levels. There are increases in other smaller cities where the surge has driven al Qaeda and the coalition forces still have a smaller presence. These include Ramadi, Fallujah, Mahmudiyah, Mandali, B'Qubah, Suwayra, and Karbala. This is a huge effort and represents some parts of each of the two strategies that I believe are in play."

511

"First, to remove any possibility of a Shiite religious sect exercising their majority rule in a Middle East country. If al Qaeda is successful in reestablishing Sunni rule in Iraq, there is then only one Shiite majority country left, Iran. With a bin Laden takeover, he would be able to exert a forced Sunni rule there as well, after expunging the Shiite population. A nuclear weapons capability will give him the staying power he needs. The second strategy is to defeat any movement toward democracy and independence. This has a religious bent to it as well since freedom and critical discussion of the issues do not lend themselves well to the beliefs of many of the Muslims who are Islamic literalists or fundamentalists. It is exactly the same argument that we have discussed about science and technology. They go together."

"You are right, sir. Egypt, Saudi Arabia, Yemen, Oman, the UAE, Syria, Turkey, Kuwait, and Qatar are all Sunni. Only Iraq and Iran have Shiite majorities. Is this why Saddam was so accepted in the region?"

"Yes, even though a Sunni, he was able to rule Iraq and their majority Shiites. All the other Sunni countries lined up behind him to provide support. It was strictly Sunni vs. Shiite. They even rooted for him or directly supported him during the Iraq/Iran war for that very reason."

"What about the democracy part, sir?"

"Well, here Israel is the example in the Middle East. Al Qaeda sees human and social development as pillars of democracy. Although they may need those things, it just doesn't make sense to the literalists. They think economic growth and societal advancement come at the expense of their religion and brand of government. And, that Israel is a pocket of infidels or disbelievers who have sold their souls for worldly things."

"And outside the Middle East, the disbelievers include almost everybody else like the U.S., Canada, Europe, and several South American countries along with many others."

"That is right, Aldora. By the way, did you notice the targets 'K' identified for Israel are mostly in and around Jerusalem?"

"Yes, but I didn't understand why."

"I think it is because Jerusalem is still said to be at the center of the world and Israel claims the city as its eternal capital. A loss of Jerusalem would be the beginning of the end for them. Al

Qaeda is attacking them at their heart. It might be just that simple or 'K' might be holding back on other locations."

"The Europe and U.S. plans seem to be scheduled later. I saw London, Berlin, Rome, Paris, and Madrid for Europe. Los Angeles, San Francisco, Chicago, Miami, New York City, and Washington, D.C. indicated for the U.S. How the hell can we stop all of these? The targets must add up to over 100 by now."

"We have to first get L-REDD units to these Middle East locations, find, and prematurely detonate the explosives. It will show them it isn't going to work and that we have a defensive weapon against their 'Campaign of Fear'. It will take about three months for them to realize they have failed. If we are successful in the Middle East, I don't think they will ever attempt what might be tentatively planned for Europe and the U.S. We are in a race, Aldora."

The Briefing

It was only a little past noon but everybody was already present in the briefing room. Brad and Zen walked to the front of the room. Brad said, "Good morning, everybody. Thanks for being early. I want to start by saying thank you and congratulations again. It wasn't a dream. We really did it! The whole room burst into clapping, yelling, and hugging each other. "Zen and I drove to the SAC Naval Air Base before coming to work. We wanted to see the results of our test in daylight. The deep holes from the IEDs and EFPs, the mangled and burned out cars and robots, and the untouched Hummers and safe car were all there. It looked like a battlefield scene for a movie, but we all know it was real. Thanks to you, the technology works and works very well." There was clapping, yelling, and hugging again. "There were some improvements already recommended last night, and I know you will have more. We need to factor these into our design plans as we prepare for manufacturing. Mike, Chad, and Joe will present a plan for production later today. First, let's get your input on what went well and what needs improving. Before we do that, Zen, are there some comments you would like to make as project coordinator?"

"Yes, thanks, Brad. First, we have some unnamed military experts who need to be thanked. These experts were responsible for making and positioning the explosive devices, setting up the communication and electronic systems, and the video coverage. Because of their great work, the L-REDD test went off as hoped and everything was thoroughly documented. Can we give them a hand even though they are not here?" There was clapping from the group. "I also think we need to thank our Hummer drivers and the safe car observer. The director had to get back to D.C. but Ray and Brad are here. A hand for all of them, please." There was clapping by the group. "The controllers for the cars and robots, Bill and Kan D." Clapping by the group. "And our system operation observers, Mike, Chad, and Joe." There was clapping by the group. "Thank you all very much. Now let's talk about the L-REDD system operation and results."

Brad said, "Right. But how about a hand for Zen in making the assignments, getting us trained and where we needed to be and coordinating the field test? Thanks, Zen."

Clapping, yelling, and whistling for Zen.

"Thank you. I hope I didn't come across as the prototypical master sergeant. You are a wonderful team, and I enjoy working with you. Now, what about your input?"

Ray was first to raise his hand saying, "Driving the Hummer was so exciting as I saw the system take over, find, and destroy the explosives. The distances must have been up to 400 meters so I didn't feel any danger at any time. I believe I messed up by turning the system to manual at the end of the runway. At that moment, a car bomb was moving toward the terminal. Having to turn the system back on meant a delay of a second or two. It was good that my partner, the director, in Hummer #2 had turned the right way and was able to destroy the car. I talked to him afterwards. We agreed on two changes. L-REDD should be designed to operate automatically. Only in special cases and under certain operating conditions would a switch to manual be possible. The L-REDD sweep should be changed from 180° hood-mounted to 360° roof-mounted. This would eliminate any possibility of missing something on a partial sweep. One more comment – our troops and civilians that are affected by these tools of the terrorists need L-REDD now. This product has been needed for years but no one knew how to do it. Brad, with your technology and the expertise of this team, we have a revolutionary product that can end the 'Campaign of Fear'. I am very proud to be

THE CAMPAIGN OF FEAR

part of the team."

"Thank you, Ray. Good input. I think we all agree that the changes you are recommending are much needed. Everybody knows we could not have done this project without you, Ray. Others?"

"Yes, Joe."

"I am thoroughly amazed. I have been in this business of explosives detonation for a long time as a scientist and business owner. When the government came to us suggesting that our new detonation technology could be part of a larger program involving detection, I was very skeptical. However, what really convinced us was the need to defeat what the government called the 'Campaign of Fear'. Even if the chances of success were small, we had to do this for the country. The terrorist-caused deaths by EFPs, IEDs, car and person bombs are reaching staggering and frightful numbers. London, Madrid, New York City, and others not to mention the everyday threat to our military and government officials throughout the world. For Iraq alone, more than 1500 dead and 5000 wounded by these cowardly explosive devices and methods. It has to stop and stop now! I am very proud to be part of the technology team to provide the product that will defeat the terrorist's strategy to kill enough military personnel and innocent civilians in this cowardly way and create enough fear for us to change our commitment to freedom and democracy and helping others. You said it last night, Zen, we did it; we really did it. I would like to recognize the one person who contributed a bit more and really made this happen, Dr. Brad Tully. Thank you, Brad, and thank you for this great acoustic technology you pioneered. I'm convinced that L-REDD will be the turning point in the war on terror. Let's all thank Brad." There was more clapping, yelling, whistling, and noise of all kinds.

Brad held his hand up for people to become quiet and said, "Thank you very much, Joe, and all of you. There is one of us unable to be here, Lyncoln Fuller. A free spirit but no one was sharper. His contributions to the project were very significant and he gave his life to help our cause. Let's give Lyncoln a proper thank you and a few moments of silence for the work he did and his commitment to freedom and democracy."

There were several minutes of silence to quietly honor his memory. Slow clapping became increasing to a level that told the world and the terrorists that Americans are not afraid and that we cannot be coerced into changing our beliefs. The whole building was vibrating and shaking.

"Thank you, I know Lyncoln heard that and is smiling back at us. You know I was in the safe car videoing as much of the test as possible. I've never been in a foxhole but that was what it felt like to me being positioned at the intersection of the runways. It was frightening!

The tapes being used had an audio track, which on review gave us some interesting information. The wave generation equipment operating off the Hummer engine produces an almost noiseless wave once it gets going, but there is a noticeable bang or crack when it is turned on. I don't know if it matters or not, but it is there. Bill, do you think we should do anything about it?"

"It is a good question as we plan for manufacturing the L-REDD units. The noise is like the crack of a whip, if you know what I mean. For me, it indicates for the driver that the equipment is on and operating correctly. The Hummers and even the Humvees are noisy vehicles. This start up sound might be useful. I'm not 100% certain how it happens, but it might be like a backfire from a car. You know, a little too much gasoline or a higher-than-ordinary gasoline/air mixture is injected and combusted in the pistons. When L-REDD is turned on, there is an instant when the engine is asked for more power, like stepping on the accelerator hard. The sound is the result. I decided not to change it, but what did the drivers think?"

"The director and I talked about a lot of things and this never came up," said Ray. I remember hearing it but it really was very insignificant with respect to operating the unit or the vehicle. Let's leave it alone for now would be my recommendation."

"Okay, good input," said Brad.

Zen said, "Any other input on performance and results?"

Chad was in the back of the room and raised his hand. "I want to bring this up with the whole team present. Our test results were fantastic and with the improvements suggested today, L-REDD will be even better. The system operates based on the best information we have today about the types of explosives used in all of these EFPs, IEDs, car and person bombs. There are two things we need to be concerned about: technology to make the currently used explosives and chemically new explosives to replace those currently used. Either of these two could effectively disable

THE CAMPAIGN OF FEAR

L-REDD. It is essential that our government and military provide constant intelligence on any attempts to develop and implement new explosives technology. If we have that, we can adapt very quickly."

Brad said, "Good point, Chad. We must not underestimate the terrorists even though there seems to be a paradox between technology and religion amongst the fundamentalists. Let's plan to bring this up with the director. We may want to put in place some additional special ways to collect information on explosives work and how they react to L-REDD."

Zen said, "Anything else before we talk about the manufacturing plan?" A couple of seconds passed. "Let's talk about the manufacturing plan. Joe, Mike, and Chad, come up and sketch out what you have. We know it has only been about 12 hours since the test; thanks for the quick and timely work."

Mike said, "As most of you know, the three companies involved, ATP, TRI, and CMT, have agreed on a joint venture arrangement to manufacture L-REDD. There are several elements, none of which is fully developed at this stage. Each of us will cover a few of the most important aspects. For my part, the laboratory operation will remain intact with the full complement of people and other resources we have today for at least a two-month time period. Specifically, we are asking Brad and our team leaders, Zen, Bill, Kan D and Ray, to continue their roles and lead the laboratory to manufacturing scale-up effort. There will be changes. First, to make the minor adjustments we covered today. Second, to make the transition from a laboratory project to a small scale manufacturing operation to make a couple of units a day. Third, we'll define, perfect, and implement the manufacturing processes to be used in large-scale manufacturing. The manufacturing plant will be here at the ATP location. The workers will be 65% ATP and 35% CMT personnel. Tully Research Incorporated will be the JV technology consultant/advisor and represented on the board. The JV manufacturing company will be led by Chad Bromcast as president, CEO, and chairman of the board. Chad."

"Thank you, Mike and Joe. As you might expect, the next two months will be the most important time for the future manufacturing operation. We need everybody's help to develop the best production processes and get them scaled up and transferred to manufacturing. I know some of you might be disappointed there is

517

no break, no time off. Please help make this work so we can get lab units made and tested in real life situations within a few days and concurrently develop the processes that will be used in production starting within a few weeks. I promise to have the manufacturing plant and personnel ready to accept the technology transfer, scale up and be ready to produce tens of units and more on a daily basis in 45-60 days. As has been implied, the project will have to continue and the director has confirmed this. At some point in time, the lab might also have to be part of the JV. We don't have to decide that right now. It has been discussed as part of the growth potential for the joint venture company. I'm excited about what we are embarking on and you should be, too. We have the best chance ever to end the terrorists' 'Campaign of Fear' and we can build a new business at the same time. Only this team can make that happen. Thanks. Joe?"

"Thanks, Chad and Mike. Mark this day on your calendar. Years from now we'll look back and say that this was the start of L-REDD's production and the demise of the 'Campaign of Fear'. The two events will be fully correlated. CMT is proud to be part of the L-REDD project and system development. We are also proud to be part of the joint venture and manufacture of the product. As indicated, CMT workers in the plant, representation on the board, and investment outlay will all be at the 35% level. We are very serious about our partnership with ATP. I have also talked to Ray and our present team. They will plan to stay at least the two months being requested. It is a little more difficult for us since we are from California, but there was no hesitation. Right, CMT personnel?" Cheers, yells, clapping by the CMT team. "Our two companies along with technology consulting from Brad and TRI have done great things and there is more to come. Thank you very much."

Zen said, "Thank you, Joe, Chad, Mike, and Brad. I think we have our marching orders. This is probably enough for today. Unless there are other questions or comments, I'm going to close the meeting." A few seconds passed. "Hearing none, I declare the meeting adjourned. Thanks, everybody."

Brad said, "Nice job, Zen. I'm sorry about the extra two months but it is the only way our plan will work. Don't you think it's okay to put off our personal plans for a little while?"

Zen was steaming and said, "Don't talk to me about this right now. I'm not very happy with you and the other powers that be.

I need some time to reprocess my thinking. Sorry."

Brad said, "I understand," as Zen walked away.

L-REDD Units for Absek

The first lab made L-REDD units, ten of them, were ready in a matter of days and sent as one shipment to Absek.

"Absek, how are you?"

"Very good, sir. I have been waiting to hear from you."

"The L-REDD units are on the way. They are being flown by military jet and will arrive tomorrow morning. I have just electronically sent you the best information we got from 'K' about targets in Israel. It is actually a map of Jerusalem with three marked targets. We don't know if it is accurate, Absek. 'K' seemed to be saying that al Qaeda is helping Hamas but who does what is unclear. Anyway, the three targets are the Church of the Holy Sepulcher, the Tower of David Museum, and the Cathedral of St. James. Does this make any sense to you?"

"Yes, they are all in Old City Jerusalem and in the Western quarters. You know, of course, that the Palestinians assert that East Jerusalem should be theirs."

"So this might be an attempt to convince Israel to give up additional land and control to stop the bombings?"

"It could be but they have never selected targets like this before, not in the old city. This would be so flagrant and extreme; it could have the reverse effect. The Jewish people and their government might become further solidified in their thinking about not giving up land to the Palestinians. Yes, it could backfire."

"Absek, the best 'K' could remember were the dates and types of explosives. There is nothing about times but your people might be able to get more information now that the targets are identified. Remember, we expect his intelligence to be no more than 50% accurate. Probably a lot less. As you said, the L-REDD units can be used even if we don't know the location of the bombs or explosives. That's the beauty of the technology of Long-Range Detection and Detonation."

"We'll use all the information you have given us, Director, and give the units a good test. You say these came from the laboratory. Are you getting the facility ready to start production on the timetable we discussed?"

"Yes, we are. It will be a joint venture between ATP and CMT with TRI heavily involved on the technology consulting side. The plan is to be up and running full bore in two months."

"Good. If the results are as good as described by you at the naval air base, we really have something. There is no need to wait on anything from our perspective."

"I agree, Absek. There is one area I haven't talked to anyone about. It won't slow us down but I do want to initiate some testing on the effects of the acoustic wave front on people. The unit is to be roof mounted and operate in a 360° mode continuously. We need to see if this specially dampened sound wave has any ill effects on humans or animals. It is just too new for us to be able to predict accurately."

"Are you doing this because of federal health regulatory requirements?"

"Not really, Absek. There are no specifically legislated statutes that apply. I'm doing it to be safe. When I put all of our data into my AAR program, something came out that was a little worrisome. AAR said that people have the potential of becoming physically and mentally impacted. The best I can tell you from the computer description is that it might be like a mild shock. One of those sensations during which you are not quite sure whether it feels good or bad."

"If that is all it is, it's probably worth it, Director. At least you are not blown to pieces and dead."

"Right, Absek. It is all theoretical right now until we get actual test data. Would you keep this confidential until then, Absek? No need to alarm anybody or unnecessarily slow down the program."

"I will, sir. Just remember there is always a cost versus benefit calculation that one must make in situations like this. If you actually find something, make sure it is significant enough before you do anything at all to impede the program."

"I agree, my friend. We finally have a technology to stop the 'Campaign of Fear' dead in its tracks. Let's not throw it away because it gives people tingling sensations."

"You got it, sir. We'll try to collect a little data on its effect on people when we use the new L-REDD units."

"Thanks, Absek, I appreciate that. Let's talk again after you have used the units at the target locations and other places. Good luck."

"Thank you, Director, I'll be in touch as soon as we have any information. Goodbye, sir."

"Goodbye, Absek."

The director was deep in thought ... should I tell people now or later? I'll have to set up testing soon and I don't necessarily want to be secretive about it. My sense is that I need to be upfront with the leadership team. My AAR program is a usually pretty accurate predicting outcome, he thought, but I hope this time it's wrong. Who can I get to do the testing and where do I get the subjects?

Effects On Humans

The unit was ready for testing. The subjects had all volunteered. They were patients of the local Veterans Administration Hospital and all had been wounded, some very seriously, by IEDs or EFPs. Those able to walk or in wheelchairs were stationed in the large back yard of the hospital. Some as small groups, as individuals and as two's and three's in a big circle but all averaging about 100 feet from the unit positioned in the center. The test was to run long enough for five revolutions or five impacts on each person by the wave front. It was close range, maybe beyond real life, but it would allow one to see very quickly if there were any negative effects.

The director said to his friend, "This is a Black Ops project as I mentioned. Nothing done here today nor any results of things done here today will ever be allowed to be discussed or disclosed. Do you understand?"

Dr. Samuels said, "I understand, Sam. All of the volunteers have signed their consent and waiver forms so we are ready to go."

"Thank you, Ben. I am going to participate in the test, too, so let me show you how to turn L-REDD on."

"No way, Sam. I know how important this is for our country. You would not have come to me with all this secrecy if it weren't. Trust me; it will be better for data interpretation to have two subjects without recent injuries. I'll be right there beside you."

Sam turned the unit on, heard the crack, and walked over to be with Ben. He said, "I owe you one, big time."

"I know. It is always good to hold markers on VIPs like you."

The director smiled as the first wave front passed through where they were standing. He said, "I wonder, can you feel sound?" He took out his notepad and pencil and wrote: slight sensory disturbances, vibrating nose hairs and inner ear parts; tingling in fingers. "Did you feel anything, Ben?"

"Maybe just a little breeze on my face and through my hair. I couldn't tell if it was the wind or the unit."

"Here it comes again." Sam was trying to absorb the full impact but still ready to record. He wrote: same feelings again but does not seem to be additive. No breeze on face or hair. "Did you feel the breeze again, Ben?"

"No, it must have been the wind last time. I do have some tingling in my fingers though and maybe my nose and ears feel a little different."

"Me, too, Ben. Let's see if it happens again."

The third, fourth, and fifth cycles were the same; he noted the same effect on the senses occurs as the waves passes through, dissipates, then recurs when the next wave arrives.

The director turned off the unit. He and Ben started interviewing the volunteers quickly in small groups and prearranged locations.

After about 30 minutes, Ben came over to Sam's location. The last volunteers were leaving. "I think it's okay, Sam. All I got were minor, for lack of a better term, sensory enhancements. Temporarily, it felt like my five senses were working better. What did you find?"

"Same thing, Ben. This is amazing and wonderful news. It looks like we are okay. Would you mind watching the patients for a few days to see whether there are any negative occurrences that might relate to our testing?"

"I sure will. Good to see you again, Sam. As always, good luck catching the bad guys."

"See you later, Ben, and thanks for your help."

"It was fun and the men enjoyed the break from the normal boring routine. Bye Sam."

L-REDD At Target Sites

"Hello, Director, your L-REDD system is amazing! We got three for three on the dates and at the locations provided by 'K'. No one was injured or killed except for the bombers. Thank you, sir."

"Excellent, Absek. What types of explosives were actually used?"

"A car bomb at the museum. Its route indicated that it was headed directly to the front entrance where a large group of people waited for it to open in the morning. We were stationed some 100 yards away from the museum on a little hill with the unit operating since daybreak. L-REDD picked up the car coming down the main entrance road and detonated it immediately about 300 yards from our location."

"Was there any collateral damage, Absek?"

"Yes, sir, some parked cars and trucks belonging to the people waiting to enter the museum. Nothing to worry about. If it had gotten through, there would have been a massacre of at least 100 people."

"L-REDD does have a manual operation mode, but at this time we made it difficult to use purposely. We might have to think more about how it should be activated and used to lessen the collateral damage that is bound to occur. There might be times that one has to make a conscious decision about the specific collateral damage they are willing to take. It could come down to sacrificing a few to save many. Other times, no considered decision will be possible because of the circumstances - just detonate the damn thing."

"For now, operating automatically is probably the best. This is new territory for us in that we have never had a choice before. All we could do was to react after the fact and clean up the carnage. I suspect our Humvee drivers with L-REDD will need a lot of training on making decisions involving life and death. Maybe like those your FBI agents go through at Quantico."

"I agree, Absek, it is an interesting dilemma and one good to have. As you said, before we had no choices. What about the churches?"

"Yes, they were individual suicide bombers at the churches. They had both timed their arrival to be after the church was full but had not yet started. Maybe the thinking was it would give them an advantage if several people were still milling around. Anyway,

L-REDD found them as they walked toward the church. I should not have been surprised; they were teenage girls with backpacks. Sam, teenage girls!"

"I know, Absek. I'll never be able to fathom this either. Will we ever get it stopped?"

"This is a start, sir. If we can show them this tactic is not going to work anymore, they'll have to conjure up something else. Hopefully it won't be as bad as teenage girls exploding suicide bombs in the middle of a church full of innocent men, women, and children."

"Anything else, Absek? Did the other units work as expected?"

"I almost forgot, Director. There was a fourth explosive, like an IED near the airport. One of our L-REDD vehicles found it as we swept the special access road near the VIP terminal. You mentioned the information from 'K' would have an al Qaeda connection to it and probably decreasing in accuracy as time passes. Our thinking is the museum and two churches were al Qaeda targets. They were emotional and historical landmarks at which killing a lot of innocent people would be easy. The 'Campaign of Fear' at work in full force. The fourth target might have been the brainchild of another terrorist group who was after a certain government official or dignitary who would have passed by who knows when. Anyway, the unit found it and made short work of it. It is clear that some advance information on location and date for the bombings is invaluable. However, the L-REDD will still be very effective even when we do not have that key information. With enough units, we can sweep all of our roads, plazas, squares, markets, sports fields, stadium parking lots, everywhere people are likely to congregate. I want more L-REDD units, Sam, so name your price."

"It will be a while, Absek. We plan to be in full production in about two months. In the meantime, we have needs in numerous other places. Try to make do with what you have while we address Iraq, Afghanistan, and a few other hot spots."

"Sir, I know we'll get them as soon as humanly possible. If you need any resources from us to help, just say so. The cost doesn't matter when the benefit is saving lives."

"Thanks, Absek. I appreciate the offer but I think we are okay for now. One more thing, it seems there are no ill effects from the acoustic wave's impact on people. I'll send you a report on the test we did. At least in the short term, the results indicate something quite the opposite. A non-medical term might be: temporary sensory enhancements. We'll have to do more testing and watch for longer-term effects but for now it's a go."

"That is good, very good news, sir. We were not able to collect much data ourselves. Qualitatively, we were aware that people did not seem to either notice or be concerned about what we were doing. Nobody stopped to look or listen at all. Just another patrol vehicle; they went about their business as usual."

"That's good, Absek. Unless we have missed something, we have a real winner here. Let's keep talking about your experience with the units. I'm sure it will help us as we provide L-REDD to other parts of the world."

"We definitely have a winner, sir. Thank you for letting us be the first to get the benefit of this magnificent technology. I'll keep you up to date on the performance in the field. Goodbye, Sir."

"Thank you, Absek. Goodbye for now."

The director hung up the secure phone thinking about this so-called moral issue. In crowded areas, there will always be collateral damage and death. It cannot be avoided but it is still hard. Who was it that said: to sacrifice the few to save the many was an easy decision? Not for me, but I know it will have to be done.

More L-REDD Lab Units

The next lot of lab units went to Iraq ... six to Baghdad and two each to Ramadi, Fallujah, Mahmudujah, Mandali, B'Qubah, Suwayra, and Karbala. L-REDD worked perfectly, pre-exploding mostly IEDs and EFPs and a couple of car bombs, in all of those locations identified by 'K'. Every military commander was clamoring to get as many units as were available. Israel and the U.S. were sharing their experiences in Jerusalem and Iraq as the next lab units were being shipped to Afghanistan. Success after success after success.

A conference call had been planned on the eve of starting full production with the Leadership Team, Brad, Chad, and the director.

The director said, "Well the product works perfectly and

we have created quite a demand throughout the Middle East."

"We are ready to start full production tomorrow, sir," said Chad. "We just need a priority list for who gets how many and when."

"We are still getting good information from 'K' on explosive locations and other strategies and tactics to be implemented by al Qaeda. You'll get the priority list for sending L-REDD units tomorrow, Chad. In the meantime, may I share a couple of things with you and the rest of the team?"

"Of course, sir."

"First, L-REDD is a resounding success in Israel, Iraq, and soon to be in Afghanistan. You would not believe the stories of pre-detonation and thousands of lives being saved, but it's true. What is so encouraging for me is that it destroys the known explosives no matter what type and it also finds and destroys explosives we didn't know existed. 'K's information was a real plus for us but our capability goes well beyond the help he is providing. In time, his information will be used up but L-REDD will continue detecting and detonating. This technology will be around a long time. It has only been two months but we think al Qaeda must be wondering what the hell is going on. There have been no deaths from IEDs, EFPs, suicide, or car bombs in the areas where we have L-REDD operating. None! Can you imagine what they will think as we begin to get production units in other locations. I believe their 'Campaign of Fear' is on the way to its demise."

"This is excellent news, sir," Brad said. Everybody agreed.

"Second, I did not tell you before doing this because I didn't want to disrupt our work. I had L-REDD tested for negative effects on humans."

Zen said, "Very interesting, sir. I wondered if we should do that. The practical application of the unique wave front is so new there is no information on any ill effects. Did you do an AAR scenario?"

"Yes, I did. The AAR computer description was the first thing that indicated a possible effect. Maybe something like a mild shock. I went further and tested on humans. It was on a group of volunteers at the V.A. Hospital serving patients from the

Iraq war. What we found were short term and temporary sensory enhancements for all of the patients. I joined the test and can say that I seemed to be able to smell and hear better, too. Good news here as well. There were no immediate negative effects of the wave front. The volunteers have agreed to follow-up testing in case something would develop later. It is just a precaution. We do not expect to find anything. I've sent reports to Israel, Iraq, and Afghanistan, and asked them to help us gather data so we'll be getting a lot more information on this subject."

"Sir, I know we have to do these things because it is part of who we are. My caution is that we not go overboard. I'm not an acoustics expert but remember this is just a high-energy sound wave that you can barely hear. Al Qaeda is killing thousands of innocent people a year and must be stopped. We can't let a few tingling fingers impede our progress," said Kan D.

"Well said, Kan D. I couldn't agree more. Let's all be very careful about this information so some advocacy group doesn't get hold of it and start questioning our results and motives."

"Yes, sir," said Kan D.

"Now, third and the part you didn't expect. I have arranged for government transportation, accommodations, and cash gifts for each of you and a spouse or friend to take a special two-week leave of absence. ATP and CMT have agreed with our plan and time away will not count against your personal vacation schedule. This is a thank you for the fantastic work you have done on the L-REDD project. This is for Bill, Kan D. and Ray. Brad and Zen, your time off is for a month. An extra couple of weeks for obvious reasons. What do you think?"

Zen said, "You got yourself a deal. We might decide to take even more time off but this will be a great start."

"Thank you, sir," said Brad.

"Chad, yours will have to come later since you have to manage the L-REDD production for now and until we get enough units to start to meet our demand."

"I understand, sir."

"That is all I have today except … I almost forgot. The Secretary of the DoAT and the President of the United States would like the pleasure of your company at a formal state dinner in your honor. It will be at the White House next week on Tuesday. Plan to be in a tux or evening gown because this is going to be really special. I'll be there, too, but the President and the Secretary want to thank you for all you have done for your country. Congratulations."

Chad said, "Wow and thank you, sir. We'll be ready."
"Goodbye for now."
"Goodbye, sir."

The Interrogation Results

After several days talking with Omar and 'K', the director and Aldora began to piece some things together. The director said, "Some of this information about al Qaeda and bin Laden is unbelievable. For example, their financial situations and resources are much better than we imagined. How did they accumulate so many assets and now in the billions of dollars?"

"I know, sir, and I tend to believe him. His information on bin Laden's hiding place was interesting, too. It does make sense that by being in Azerbaijan he had ready access to Iran, Turkey, Syria, and Iraq. Have we even looked for him there?"

"Not to my knowledge. Do you believe he has been successful in building allies among countries like Turkey and Saudi Arabia while we thought they were in partnership with the U.S.?"

"Yes, I do. Remember the religious component, sir. I breathed a sigh of relief when he talked about Europe and the U.S. No matter how we asked the question, he maintained that the 'Campaign of Fear' was not planned to expand in Europe and the U.S. until months later, if at all. As he said, al Qaeda has only limited technology resources and is using them predominantly to solidify their positions in the Middle East." Maybe it wasn't our new security measures that were saving us. We'll have to get into that more with him later. Aldora, I think the most surprising part for me was that 'K' has essentially indicated that bin Laden has a three-tier strategy targeted at the consolidation of the Middle East countries and their peoples under one leader. The major issues within the first tier include stopping America and its pro-democracy approach in Iraq and the already democratic Israel with a foothold right in the middle of the future empire. This is why the 'Campaign of Fear' supported the Sunnis in Iraq and the Hamas and Hezbollah against

Israel. The second tier of the strategy and maybe just as important as the first is the conversion of Iran from Shiite to Sunni by force if necessary. The tactic to make this happen is not so clear but the possibility he put forth involves the same thing that happened in Iraq. A takeover or coup occurs and a religious minority, a Sunni-led government run by a dictator is put in place. The large Shiite population would be systematically moved out or exterminated over time. The third tier of the strategy is the further expansion of the empire. Besides a consolidation of the first ring Sunni majority Middle East countries under bin Laden, there would be absorption of the second ring countries, Pakistan, Afghanistan, Turkmenistan; this would occur also by force. In all, the proposed United Countries of the Middle East would have a population of some 500 million people, Sunni dominated, with enough land mass and geographical integrity and importance to be a real world power. 'K' believes the motivations are religion, water/food, and oil in that order. It is thought that consolidation of the Sunni religion and control of the water, food, and oil would give the UCME the ability to chart its own destiny. Today, as we know, each country is trying to act independently and without enough power or regional foresight."

"I know. It blew me away but it is not totally unbelievable. If the 'Campaign of Fear' fails because of L-REDD what do you think they will do?"

"If we believe 'K', bin Laden might begin to focus his attention on Iran. Wouldn't that be ironic? He becomes our ally, of sorts, because we both view Iran as a threat but for hugely different reasons."

"Oh, my God, Director. That would never happen would it? Director, if this three-tier strategic plan is correct, all that has happened relating to L-REDD is worth it. We would not be able to put a value on 'K''s information. I'd give him anything he wants except bringing him back to life. He has to remain a martyr to al Qaeda. Do you think Omar has added much to our storehouse of information?"

"No, but I do believe he is serious about restarting Technolibertat. It might be an interesting experiment to run from here to see if he could make some inroads in this Islam vs. science confusion that exists."

"So he would stay in our custody and run it from a

distance abiding by its original charter using technology for human development?"

"Yes, and funded partially by Pharmatek under its new direction and leadership. A lot of people helped by TIC here and around the world might want to be involved in human and social development in the Muslim countries. I would like you to help Omar get the new Technolibertat up and running, Aldora, by following all the necessary legal guidelines. I believe it can develop a worldwide presence. If we are right about this, it could have fantastic results in building the standard of living in the Middle East. With that will come all kinds of changes in thinking, opportunities, and results."

"I will, sir. It will be a fun project now that it is to be reconstituted to do good things. At the same time, we have to remember that Omar did get off track and murdered four people in San Francisco."

"Yes, he will pay for that in a number of ways as you know. Make sure that his share of the Pharmatek profits gets used for the operation of Technolibertat. The sales or licensing of the technology should be more than enough to support the rest of the required infrastructure. I don't want any of the money getting funneled into an account for Omar."

"Of course, sir."

"Want to be on the board of directors?"

"Yes."

"Put Brad on it, too. You will be chair."

"Alright, sir."

"Thanks, Aldora. As you know, there is a special party at the White House for the L-REDD team tonight. Want to come and sit by me at the head table?"

"I would love that, sir."

"Remember, it is a black tie, evening gown kind of thing. Meet you there at 6 PM. Okay?"

"Yes, sir. See you at six."

Chapter 20

Success for L-REDD
The Party and the Awards

The Party

By the time of the party, there were even more successes: L-REDD had worked exceedingly well in Israel, Iraq, and Afghanistan; manufacturing planning was going full speed ahead; the information from 'K' had proven very useful so far and there were another four months of scheduled bombings identified. If accurate, the overall al Qaeda strategy would be identified and soon its 'Campaign of Fear' would be in ruins. Technolibertat would be restarted for the benefit of the people.

The honored guests were ushered, as a group, into one of the smaller dining rooms, given name badges and shown to the start of the receiving line. The President, Vice President, Speaker of the House, Majority Leader of the Senate, Secretary of DoD, Secretary of HS, Secretary of DoAT, Heads of the DoJ and FBI, Chief Justice of the Supreme Court, and Director Sam Elson were all there.

Brad said, "Jesus Christ, Zen, I had no idea."

Zen squeezed his hand, smiled, and said, "I did."

They all shook hands and exchanged pleasantries with the most powerful people in our country. Everyone knew something about them and L-REDD. There were sincere thank yous and congratulations. It took some time because everyone was there… Brad, Zen, Kan D, Bill, Chad, Mike, Joe, Ray, Aldora, Frank and Mark. Everyone, except Lyncoln and Jack.

The government officials were to be seated away from the podium at several small square tables and there was one large round table for the guests. Aldora noticed that she was seated next to the director and wondered if it meant anything. Then she saw it and said, "Here is a place setting for Jack!"

Chad was nearby looking at the seating arrangement, too. He said, "There is a place setting for Lyncoln, too."

The director came to the big table and said, "Please be seated and I'll be right back."

Sam went to the podium to welcome everybody saying, "This is a special evening for a special group seated at the head table. President Abbott and many other government luminaries here want to thank you for what you have done for our country. We know that two members of the team were fated to make the ultimate sacrifice. We have places for them at the head table, where I'm sure they have joined us in spirit. We know that others of you have been in harm's way at many times, lost family members, or have paid a heavy cost in other difficult circumstances to achieve our success. We know about L-REDD, what it has done so far, and the enormous potential it holds for the future. We know that our own war on terror and al Qaeda's 'Campaign of Fear' have been forever changed in our favor. We know you have uncovered the real long-term strategy of al Qaeda to consolidate the Middle East under the Sunni religious banner. We know all of this and are amazed that a team of thirteen scientists and technology experts representing three companies located in Boston, Minneapolis, and San Francisco did all this. Who said the number thirteen was unlucky?"

"This has been my first assignment in government; I didn't really know what to expect. I found that cooperative programs between the government and the private sector could be successful. They depend on good people, the right skills and abilities, and a desire to make a difference. This group meets all those requirements and more. Let's give them a hand!" Sam paused for thunderous clapping.

May I point out the project leader, Dr. Bradford Tully, CEO of Tully Research, Inc. and the originator of the new acoustics technology used in L-REDD."

He acknowledged the standing ovation. "And the Project Coordinator, Dr. Zenica Lang, chemical sensing expert and one tough lady. This group should know that Zen and Brad each took a sniper's bullet for the project and the team. They recovered quickly and remained committed to getting the job done with an even more greater intensity."

Brad and Zen looked at each other and smiling to the crowd, said "Thank you."

"Well deserved for both of them. There is one other person who needs some special recognition, Ms. Aldora Klein. She is largely responsible for breaking the San Francisco case, destabilizing the Technolibertat terrorist group financially, capturing 'K', and piecing together the real al Qaeda strategy."

Aldora gulped at the standing ovation and said "Thank you."

"Thank you, Aldora. May we give the whole team another round of applause? Thank you."

"Before our food gets too cold, I want to just mention that the agenda after dinner is to hear from Secretary Grant Adams and President Charles Abbott. We will then conclude with the award ceremony for the L-REDD team. The President wants to personally thank you for what you have done for your country. Waiters, you may serve dinner."

When dinner was finished, Grant went to the front and said, "When the president talked about his platform of education, technology, and the economy, I was struck that it included technology. Many of you in the room are scientists, as I am, and we could relate to that. We have a certain bias toward technical things and their importance in the future of our world. The president had no such bias toward technology but it become clear to him that technology should be one of the foundational pillars of our future. In many ways, it always has been. The building of our great industries and cities, the victory in World War II, going to the moon, transportation, the Internet and other communication systems, almost everything you can mention has its roots in technological advancements. Why not in government? Call it out and set the expectation to address social injustice, human development, religious differences, energy needs, and availability of food and water. Most of the conflict in this world is the result of these basic problems. Even terror is a crude reaction to perceived inequalities or differences that certain people have identified. Our president believed that technology could be a tool to help solve even the soft or qualitative issues. President

Abbott asked me to join the administration and head up the new Department of Advanced Technology. I agreed but I can tell you the best decision I made was bringing in Sam Elson to help lead the department. You know, it was Sam's idea to attack al Qaeda's 'Campaign of Fear' using technology. Bin Laden and other terrorists know how we feel about loss of life and injury to our troops and innocent men, women, and children. Their plan to use IEDs, EFPs, car bombs, suicide bombers was to strike at what we care about the most – human life. Random acts of violence to shake our beliefs and courage by creating fear. I can tell you, it was working!"

"Sam thought we needed a defensive weapon to detect and prematurely detonate these explosives and he found a way to put together this amazing team. A lot of credit goes to Mike and Chad of ATP and Joe of CMT and of course Brad of TRI to find the right people and expertise to successfully complete the project. As managers, they did a wonderful job. Also, I want to give special recognition to Dr. Tully. Yes, it was his technology, he was project leader and he took a bullet for us. All that is true, but did you know he was also acting as an unofficial special agent for our department? He and Sam made an unstoppable pair of special agents. And, to the whole L-REDD team, thank you very much. Your work is so significant with just the results we have today. It will only increase with time and mean thousands of lives saved and a new direction in the war on terror. Please enjoy your time off and return with the expectation that you may be called upon to serve your country again. Mr. President."

"Thank you, Grant. Thank you to the L-REDD team. I cannot emphasize how much this means to our country. In less than a year, you have done more to defeat the 'Campaign of Fear' and win the war on terror than anything done during the previous eight years. I had no reasonable expectation that anything like this could even be done, but why not try? Getting the right people in place and setting things in motion was key. Grant and I went to college together as many of you know. Because of our names, we sat up front and next to each other in most of our classes. He always scored higher than me on the tests, especially in the science classes. My approach has always been to get people smarter than me to help solve complex problems. Grant was clearly smarter and for that and other reasons, he was perfect for this assignment. "Thank you, Grant. Now to those at the round table, the government figures in this room know what I am going to share with you at this time. We have formed a team that will address the key strategic things that came out of the L-REDD program. Besides developing the best defensive weapon in the world you also provided the best information we have to date to move forward on the war on terror opposing those forces who hold the consolidation of all the Middle Eastern countries is the real objective. The banner is one of a powerful empire with a foundation built on a strict fundamentalist interpretation of Sunni, Islam. There are key questions that must be answered.

- Al Qaeda will have to change tactics around the world because of L-REDD. What might be coming and how do we react?
- We have relearned the importance of the question of Islam vs. science. Are Muslim beliefs compatible with critical inquiry? Technology can do much for their human and social development, if allowed by the fundamentalists. How do we create this promise?
- Al Qaeda has a much different focus on Iran. They are 65-70 million people and 90% of them Shiite. Al Qaeda views all Shiites as threats to their plan for Sunni dominance in the Middle East. What do we do about it?
- We knew about Afghanistan but we had not considered fully the importance of other near-by countries in their master plan. Now we do; so what do we do about it?
- We know that religion is important but also that water, food, and oil will be the drivers for all decisions and actions. How does this impact our planning?

These are the questions for which we seek answers. I have asked that each of you get a committee assignment to help us develop solutions. Are you willing to do that?"

There was a resounding, "Yes, sir" from guests at the round table.

"Great, we can use your help. Grant and Sam, please come up now and help me with the awards."

There were thirteen medals on the table that was brought in. Sam was stationed at the table to select the medal give it to Dr. Adams who in turn would give it to the president.

The president said, "Posthumously, to Lyncoln Fuller for contributions to our country in time of need, the Presidential Medal of Technology. Posthumously, to Jack Borson for contributions to our country in time of need, the Presidential Medal of Technology." He laid the two medals aside and after a moment of silence nodded he was ready to continue, saying "To Dr. Bradford Tully for contributions to our country in time of need, the Presidential Medal of Technology. One after the other, they went forward, shook hands with the President, received the medal, shook hands with Secretary Adams and Director Elson, and returned to their seats. You could have heard a pin drop during those eleven trips to the podium and back."

The director said, "Thank you, Mr. President, thank you, Mr. Secretary, and thank you L-REDD team." The ceremony attendees burst into clapping, yelling, whistling... it was thunderous.

"Mr. President, may I hold the two medals given posthumously to Lyncoln and Jack until they can be properly presented to their families?"

"Of course, Sam. He handed the medals to Sam and whispered, "Thank you, Sam, if you were not an appointed official, you would have gotten one, too."

Secretary Adams and Director Elson returned to their seats and the president said, "What a wonderful evening and what well-deserved recognition. Good night, everyone."

Sam leaned over to Zen and Brad and said, "Would you join me in the next room please? Aldora, would you come, too?"

They said goodbye to their friends and followed the director to the next room. It was a big surprise to Brad and for that matter to Aldora to enter the room and see the chief justice standing at the front of the room with the president and Secretary Adams on either side. Zen winked to Aldora and whispered, "Will you be my maid of honor?"

Aldora looked at Sam, who also winked, and said, "Yes, of course."

Sam looked at Brad and said, "I will be your best man."

Zen turned to Brad and said, "We are getting married

tonight. I hope you haven't gotten cold feet."

He looked at Zen, Aldora, the director, the secretary, the chief justice, and finally the president and said, "I bet this is a first, Zen. No one will believe us, but with the power in this room, I think it will be legal."

He picked up Zen, twirled her around and said, "I am so ready to be your husband." He kissed her, put her down, took her hand, and marched over to the chief justice.

The others took their positions and the chief justice said, "Bradford Tully, do you take Zenica Lang to be your lawfully wedded wife? If so, say I do."

"I do."

"Zenica Lang, do you take Bradford Tully to be you lawfully wedded husband? If so, say, I do."

"I do."

"I now pronounce you husband and wife."

Chapter 21

Iran
Assassinations and Takeover

The Restart of Technolibertat

Aldora called the director to say, "You will be interested to know that Omar has been hard at work helping to implement the new Technolibertat plan."

"Yes. I really liked his idea of focusing the technology held by the Technology Investment Corporation on the three major areas of water desalination, energy alternatives to oil, and plant genetics and agricultural mechanization."

"Work is going well with the projects. The first is to provide fresh water in Iraq. I didn't realize that Iraq is almost totally landlocked except for a small access to the Persian Gulf. Did you?"

"No, not really. How are they doing on the desalination plants?"

"Great! With the new technology Omar has and some rather mundane piping and pumping equipment, they'll be in business soon. The decreased threat of al Qaeda is making progress quite remarkable. Would you believe several tens of millions of gallons of fresh water will be in Baghdad and surrounding cities in less than a year? It will make quite a difference."

"Aldora, can we make sure that we, the U.S., get some credit for this?"

"Technolibertat is structured in such a way that as a private non-profit it reports only to the board of directors. That board is made up of U.S. citizens. Its funding comes from the sale of its intellectual capital through technology licenses and U.S. government and foundation support. We can take all the credit we want sir but I believe we would rather have advanced technology take the credit at this time. Remember, technology will bring human and social development and with that comes a change in thinking by the religious fundamentalists."

"Of course, forget I asked."

"The second project, sir, is on alternative energy in Syria. At first, I thought this was a crazy idea but as he explained, Syria's oil reserves are almost the lowest of any country in the Middle East. So wind turbine and solar panel farms are now being built. The projections are for up to one billion kilowatt hours per year to accommodate greater than 10% of the population."

"That is fantastic, Aldora. What about the food project in Iran?"

"This one will be a little slower, sir. We were finally given approval recently for several key U.S. agricultural scientists to travel to Iran and start working with their scientists on standard crop enhancement technology. Anyway, Iran is a very mountainous country with only about 25% tillable land. They need to enhance their crop productivity and soon. I think our food program will eventually win over a lot of people to be friends of technology and even the U.S. Remember, Iran has nearly 70 million people and with Turkey and Egypt is one of the three biggest countries in the Middle East. They will continue to be a factor in the region."

"I agree, Aldora. This is a good program for Iran. I have to run now, but thanks for the call. Keep up the good work."

"I will, sir. Good to talk to you. See you at the next board meeting."

"Goodbye, Aldora."

The Unforgettable Call

Sam was just off the line with Aldora when the call came from his boss.

Secretary Grant Adams said, "Sam, I have the president on the line with the heads of the CIA and NSA. I want you to hear first

539

hand what has happened in Iran."

President Charles Abbott said, "Hello, Sam."

"Hello, Mr. President."

"Sam, our people have just reported that the Ayatollah Khamenei has just been assassinated. We don't have a lot of information but it appears to have been done by al Qaeda and bin Laden."

"My God, sir, he is going after his largest threat in the region even sooner than we thought."

"Yes, Sam. Remember that the Ayatollah Khomeini set up the Islamic Republic of Iran after the ouster of the Shah almost 30 years ago. It is a theocracy dominated by Shiite clergy. What most people do not realize is that the majority of Shiite clerics never converted to Khomeinism and did not endorse the Islamic Republic. Also, Khomeini set up the Islamic Revolutionary Guard Corps after the revolution to serve both internal and external purposes. It is an organization that operates in parallel to Iran's regular military and answers only to the supreme leader of the Islamic Revolution. Their military has ground forces, navy, and air force at strength of about 125,000 men. But, the IRGC also is in a business conglomerate that controls over 500 companies in energy, finance, consumer, and industrial areas. It is the second largest business corporation in Iran only slightly smaller than the National Iranian Oil Company. The two commands within the IRGC with whom we are most familiar are the Quds Force of about 15,000 highly trained men and women who are charged with exporting the revolution. They are responsible for much of the havoc in Israel, Lebanon, Iraq, Afghanistan, and other countries but also finances and helps both the Hezbollah and Hamas organizations. All are martyrdom operations specializing in armed insurgency and terrorism. These are the people that L-REDD will help us stop. The other command within IRGC that is well known is the one that ensures internal repression. This is the command that Khamenei used to control the Iranians themselves and the one that now presumably is under the control of al Qaeda and bin Laden. Do you recognize the names of the so-called brigades: Karbala, Ashore, and Al Sahara?"

"Yes sir, I do."

"They are the ones charged with crushing popular revolt and the Iranians themselves see them as instruments of internal terror. Sam and Grant, this is a very serious situation. We need more information on what has happened, if anything, to President Ahmadinejad. He and the ayatollah were not always seeing eye to eye before anyway. The president was constantly losing power to the IRGC. Besides all of the above, it controlled the country's nuclear program, which was sucking up 10% of the annual national budget. It controlled the Basij Mustadafain, something called the 'mobilization of the dispossessed', a fanatical, voluntary force that could be built up to millions of fighters at a moment's notice. It controlled the recently formed Defense Planning Committee to better manage coordination of the IRGC and the regular military in case of a major war. I think it is clear that Khamenei was in control of everything but rhetoric. He left that to Ahmadinejad. It is also clear that if bin Laden has taken the ayatollah down, then he is in control now. What will he do with an infant nuclear capability and what will he do with sixty million Shiites? I don't know."

"My God, sir. I will assemble a team and start working with the other departments on scenarios and options. I do know that the majority of the Iranians saw the Khamenei regime as one that was increasingly repressive and unpopular. The new supreme leader, bin Laden, and his al Qaeda might be a welcome change for the moment. Longer term, I can't help but believe there are some very bad days ahead."

"Thanks, Sam. Grant, would you see that Sam gets what he needs, please?"

"Yes, sir. We'll be in constant touch as the situation develops. Timing will be critical."

"Thank you, Grant and Sam. I need something soon. Goodbye for now."

"Goodbye, sir," said Grant.

"Goodbye, sir," said Sam.

Grant held the line, "Sam, get me a position paper on this in 24 hours. Okay?"

"Yes, sir. I'll see you tomorrow. Goodbye."

"Goodbye, Sam."

The Director Makes Contact

"Aldora, I want you to meet me in my office in an hour, please."

"What is this about, sir?"

"I need your help with a situation in Iran. Come over as quickly as you can so we can develop some options for the President."

"I'm getting a text message from the attorney general right now that says . . . . 'coup in Iran, ayatollah assassinated.' Is that the situation you were referring to?"

"Yes, it is. Sorry for being so vague."

"Who did it, Director? Was it President Ahmadinejad and the military?"

"No, President Abbott and his advisors believe it was bin Laden and al Qaeda."

"Oh my God, sir. This is unbelievable. I am on my way, sir."

The Call to Absek

"Absek, I need some help from you, my friend."

"We just got the news, Director. This is very unsettling of course and we are trying to make sense of it, too."

"Does your intelligence say it was bin Laden who assassinated the Ayatollah Khamenei and took over the IRGC?"

"Yes, sir. It also says that even though President Ahmadinejad is a member of the IRGC, he will probably be gone within the month. We know that he and the ayatollah were not always in agreement on matters of strategy. Neither had the support of the people. There was intense hatred of the IRGC and most Iranians saw it as a monster protecting an evil regime. Something was bound to happen soon. We didn't think it would be from outside though."

"So the time was right. Absek, what will he do with this newfound nuclear capability?"

"I know, sir, plus bin Laden now has a way to consolidate the terrorist efforts of the likes of al Qaeda, Hamas, and Hezbollah in more than 20 different countries. He can operate safely out of Iran much more so than where he was in Azerbaijan. He will be protected like a savior come to free the people from repression and abuse.

Religion won't matter. He could be Hindu and the people would not care after what they have been through."

"I looked at the IRGC business conglomerate. It has sales of $12 billion and profits of about $2 billion. This could be an exponential jump in al Qaeda's financial strength and ability to support terrorist activities across the world."

"Yes, sir, I agree. Even with the potential nuclear capability, consolidation of the terrorist groups and the new wealth, there is one thing even more worrisome. It is those 60 million Shiites in Iran. What will become of them?"

"Are you saying this could be the beginning of the largest religious cleansing campaign ever?"

"That is a real fear. If that would happen, there would be no sizable population of Shiites anywhere in the world. In fact, there wouldn't be many Shiites left in the world, period."

"Absek, would you be willing to team up with Aldora Klein, Brad Tully, and me to figure out what to do about this new development?"

"I certainly would, sir. I'll have a military jet bring me to D.C. as soon as we finish. Is Andrews Air Force Base OK?"

"Thank you, Absek. Do you know if al Qaeda has done anything differently to combat our L-REDD systems in Israel, Iraq, or anywhere?"

"Not that we have identified. The explosive locations you are feeding us are very important. We are pre-detonating those explosives and others all the time. There are seemingly no new tactics being deployed to reduce the effectiveness of L-REDD. Now that we know about Iran, maybe it is logical that al Qaeda was just too busy. Maybe Iraq was just a distraction. It was Iran that was the most important target all along."

"That is what I was thinking, too. Thank you, my friend. Our team will get together here as soon as I can get Dr. Tully back in the country from his honeymoon. Goodbye for now."

"Goodbye, sir, and see you soon."

The Call To Brad

"Hello, Brad, this is Director Elson."

"I knew I should not have brought my Blackberry with

international VOIP capability on my honeymoon. How did you find me?"

"We have our ways, as you know. Contact information isn't so confidential when there is a worldwide emergency playing out."

"Zen and I have been purposely staying away from newspapers, TV, radio, e-news, and the like since we got here. What has happened?"

"There has been a coup d'état in Iran."

"How could that be? The ayatollah had that place locked down so tight nothing was possible internally. It must have been outsiders, right?"

"Yes, it was, Brad. It was …"

"Let me guess, Director. It would not have been Egypt; they are too far away. The only other country big enough is Turkey. It was Turkey, wasn't it? Sunni Islam, no oil reserves? This expands its border, solves its energy problems, harnesses the nuclear threat and consolidates Sunni power in every country but Iraq."

"I wish it had been Turkey, but this is very, very serious, Brad. The coup d'état was by bin Laden and al Qaeda."

"What? How could that be? He isn't strong enough."

"He assassinated the supreme leader, the Ayatollah Khamenei, and took over the IRGC. We also believe he will have the majority of the people behind him because the Iranians want a change, any change."

"Yes, but this could be even worse for them in the long run. My God, Director, I see why you called this a worldwide emergency. What about President Ahmadinejad?"

"We don't know yet but I don't see them sharing power in any way."

"I think you are right there."

"Brad, with Iran having even a limited nuclear weapons capability, I believe this to be our worst nightmare. Bin Laden and al Qaeda have the potential to take over the entire Middle East and hold the rest of the world hostage to their demands whether they are religious, political, or economical. I need you in D.C. immediately. You, Aldora, Absek, and I will form a team that has been charged by the president of the United States to come up with options for reacting to the coup d'état in Iran. I promised him something in 24 hours."

"Alright sir but it will take some time to get back home."

"A military jet is on the way to pick you and Zen up. Can you be at Heathrow in about two hours?"

"Yes. You know we are in London?"

"Our first team meeting will be as soon as you can get here. Get some sleep on the airplane."

"Yes, sir, I'll be ready."

"Thank you, Brad. Sorry for doing this to you on your honeymoon. Would you let Zen know that it just had to be done?"

"I will, sir. Goodbye, Director."

"Goodbye, Brad."

Readying for the Team Meeting

Sam and Aldora had gathered every piece of available intelligence on the coup d'état in Iran for the meeting. They had called in markers from all over the Middle East and elsewhere to get the most up-to-date information.

Sam was reading out loud as Aldora entered information into the database. "President Ahmadinejad and his ministers were executed. Al Qaeda units control the oil fields. Shiite clerics loyal to Khamenei have been executed. Sunni clerics and Shiite clerics who never converted to Khomeinism and did not endorse the Islamic Republic are working together to stabilize the situation. All aspects of the IRGC, including the business conglomerate are under the control of bin Laden. Practically every leader of a Middle East country had contacted the al Qaeda leader in order to offer acknowledgement of the takeover and gain some measure of his favor. The Iranian navy appears to be getting ready to blockade the Straits of Hormuz in the Persian Gulf, through which most of the oil from the region must pass."

"Aldora said, "This is going to get nasty, sir."

"I know, Aldora." The phone rang. "Yes, Secretary Adams?"

"Sam, there is one more piece of information for your team to consider."

"What is that, sir?"

"The president just received a call from bin Laden saying,

'Mr. President, no doubt you have heard about the situation in Iran. I want to let you know that the United States will no longer be able to purchase the same volume of oil from the Middle East and OPEC that you are buying today. Beyond that new quota, probably around 50%, there will be the opportunity to access more oil. We call it the Oil for Technology program. Let us know if you are interested. Praise be to Allah.' It was like a recording, Sam, with no chance to respond."

"A fifty percent reduction in oil will begin to dramatically hamstring our economy and our future, sir."

"I know, Sam."

"What technology does he want and at what cost? Looks to me like we are about to be held hostage sir."

"I know. Sam, get me some answers. Get me some damn answers fast."

About the Author

Having grown up in southeastern Ohio, Wayne Pletcher worked as a clerk in the Justice Department during the turbulent 1960s. After graduating college in Ohio, he went on to earn advanced MS and PhD degrees in chemistry at the University of Michigan. Much of his early research refuted popularly accepted standards and rules about common, synthetic organic chemistry reactions. He was hired by the 3M Company, initially working at the laboratory bench where he developed new and patented materials for industry, later becoming technical director of several of 3M's businesses. Some of his work there required a top secret clearance from the US Government. For several years following this time, he was CEO of Minnesota Technology, Inc. (now Enterprise Minnesota), a non-profit consulting firm.

Wayne became an adjunct professor at the U of Minnesota Institute of Technology and specifically within the Technological Leadership Institute.

In addition to a technical PhD dissertation, Wayne has written tens of articles and presentations for major scientific journals and audiences, a chapter for a book on adhesive technology, six US patents and their foreign counterparts, 20+ editorials for Minnesota Technology Magazine and course content for graduate level classes in the 'management of technology' and 'intellectual property management'.

Wayne and wife Carol, who holds a biochemistry PhD, started Pletcher, Inc., an innovation and business development consulting company, of which Ms. Pletcher is currently president. The Pletchers are parents to two sons and grandparents to young Alex Pletcher. This is Wayne's first novel.